THE WORLD OF
SHORT FICTION

THE WORLD OF SHORT FICTION

An International Collection

EDITED BY

Thomas A. Gullason
Associate Professor of English, University of Rhode Island

Leonard Casper
Professor of English, Boston College

HARPER & ROW, PUBLISHERS

NEW YORK, EVANSTON, AND LONDON

For Edward and Gretchen

Library of Congress catalog card number: 62–7145
C-1

Contents

PART TWO: Dialogues on Short Fiction

Introduction

THE WORLD OF FICTION IS A WORLD IN MOTION. The reader, through gradual refinement of his sensibility, advances toward mature understanding even when the central character of a story shows a decline in his powers of insight. Fiction involves us not in the logical arrangements common to exposition or to direct argument, but in life as a developing process. The reader experiences the passage of time and the evolution of meanings made visible through the fullness of human event. Reoriented by the action of the story, the reader moves toward a moral and social awareness of his own.

However abstract other modes for organizing thought may tend to be, narration is forced by its nature to reproduce or at least approximate some recognizable level of concrete reality. We must feel the truth of fiction on our fingertips. A story derives both clarity and persuasiveness from its capacity to make even the most subtle truth tangible through assembled human circumstance. It tests, in the flesh, every initial insight—and abolishes, verifies, or modifies. It searches for constants, but respects the unique.

The human figure—the character as our other self—is the center of fiction. All the rest is subordinate, though essential. Each full character is defined, as man is, by variables of time and of place (setting); by sequential action (plot); by the significant evolving design (theme) of events in which he participates, whether or not the focal character (point of view) is permitted an equal consciousness of that significance. It is this human presence, in action, which ultimately decides all questions of credibility and which distinguishes between the tale of entertainment (where there is no disbelief to suspend) and the truth of fiction (where it is impossible to withhold belief). It is this same human presence which allows the reader, to the degree determined by personal and cultural sensitivity, his entrance into that act of awakening or maturing which every story presents.

The movement of reader and character toward understanding, as the forms of fiction recognize, is usually minute, piecemeal, sidelong. The action of a short story has adequate duration, commonly, to define one stage only in this tremulous growth. Yet even when a story's occasion seems momentary, its implications can be momentous. The professional author makes no effort to compensate for brevity by melodramatic incident or violent climax. Instead, he deliberately chooses the restrictions imposed by the short story or novella to temper some small portion of the universe's rampant energy, to corner its meanings in some narrow, bright chamber of comprehension.

Consequently, the criteria of selection for *The World of Short Fiction* have been quality of insight and authentic intensity, rather than sensationalism or "historical interest" academically considered. A number of the authors included are seminal figures. Maupassant's well-plotted stories, rooted in the world of everyday reality, as well as Chekhov's "plotless" stories, dependent on characterization by suggestion, have become models for later writers everywhere. Yet *The World of Short Fiction* does not attempt to trace the chronological growth of a genre. Chekhov is presented first not because he was one of the earliest moderns, but because he still ranks among the most accomplished. His attention to telling detail, his delightful sense of immediacy prevent the foreign from appearing remote.

More importantly, however, *The World of Short Fiction* begins with Chekhov because his "stories of inexperience" in some ways resemble the uninitiated student's own feeling for exploration, with its attached frustrations and slight triumphs. Dostoevsky is offered next because one of the collection's principles of organization is to place side by side nationals of the same country or representatives of what can be considered the same culture in spite of intervening political boundaries. However, since the assumption is, in every case, that one writer complements another, each partner in a pair is represented by only two stories. Others—like Joyce—who are solitary spokesmen for a group or area are represented by three stories. In this way, some range in every author and in every geographical or ethnic unit is suggested. Variety of another sort will be evident in the alternation of novellas with shorter fiction.

In addition to such groupings according to author, the present arrangement tries to interlock the works themselves on the basis of related themes or techniques. For example, both Conrad and Crane use stories of action as a base of operations for the exploration of larger meanings, while Crane's imagery prepares for Porter's denser symbols; the private murmur of social accusation audible in Nadine Gordimer becomes a public reverberation throughout Lusin; Mann's study of his contemporary society's spiritual decay can be read as a stage in Kafka's more cosmic vision; and Maupassant's ironic reflections on the surface relations between men and women expands to more tense and complex psychological combat in Lawrence. At the same time the student might compare the stories in a number of equally valid ways: according to the degree of technical experimentation attempted, as the burden of expressing human subtlety compels deviation from straightforward narration; according to construction of several levels of meaning, through the use of impressionistic images, clusters of symbols, or the satirical concealment of fact behind façade; according to shifting emphases on psychological or mythological pattern; and the like.

One special category which emerges in this collection owes much, undoubtedly, to the fact that the short story is a relatively modern art form. Contemporary man's prolonged search for identity and self-assurance is manifest in the recurring theme of the alien abroad, brought to the moment of decision in the Mexico of Porter, Gordimer's South Africa, or Conrad's Micronesia. The sense of place in each of these stories (something far more intimate than the term "setting" can indicate) is presented not to satisfy some tourist curiosity about local color, though the reader's interest may have its origins there. However authentic the story's surface, it conveys not so much the place perceived as it does the perceiver's inner state. "Objective" description becomes a mode of insight into the onlooker. In strange situations even the best human motives take on such protective coloration that the whole truth of a character may be hidden from himself, and the delicate perspective of irony is required of the author to insinuate what is otherwise withheld. Commonly, too, the innocent character who expected to remain pure bystander becomes thoroughly involved, just as surely as the reader becomes entangled in what is supposedly "only a story," a "vicarious" experience. "Nothing human is alien to me," the writer says, confirming the classics.

The World of Short Fiction includes several stories in which authors describe not just home thoughts and the native scene but their wandering countrymen far abroad, suddenly shaken into self-consideration by unforeseen circumstances. Henry James explored this technique of observation in a number of stories about Americans in Europe and conveyed a double perspective into several societies simultaneously. Here, more engaging writers have been substituted for James. Consequently the collection is international in a second sense, inasmuch as it deals with the psychospiritual impact of traffic between cultures, whether by expatriate or holiday traveler. Such Outsiders, marked by a sense of displacement, clearly show a family resemblance to Kafka's cosmic exile or Maupassant's ostracized prostitute or Joyce's rejected adolescent, or others alienated from themselves or their surroundings.

The "international rub" is only a species of that resistance, that constant measurement of one man against others in actuality or in the imagination essential to all fiction as "conflict." It may not be coincidental that a modern art form such as the short story, in image and motif, so often reminds us of the moral consequences of man's mobility today and his global commitments. A prolonged tour abroad no longer is successful as flight but becomes, instead, appointment and confrontation, an opportunity for self-assessment. Everywhere man sees his own reflection, for better or for worse. Thus, the "international rub" recapitulates the reader's own unconscious involvement in fiction, as well as the changeover in his own motives as his experience ripens.

"International exchanges"—multiple insights—of a different sort appear at the end of the collection. Lawrence's incisive thoughts on Mann, Mann on Kafka, Conrad on Maupassant and Crane—here are conversations in which readers can participate. The views presented are considered opinions, without being definitive. They are as informative about the esthetic and personal philosophy of the writer-critic as about the criticized writer.

Throughout, the dual perspectives—the world of fiction and fiction of the world—collaborate in the same way that the editors themselves have collaborated, with their complementary interests in the art of writing and in comparative literature. While no attempt has been made to create a little "united nations of literature" at the expense of quality in fiction, major arcs have been selected in the great circle of Western readers' special interests.

The reasoned order of stories, the critical biographies, the excerpted commentaries of author on author—all are planned to bring reader, accomplished author, and potential writer together, with the aftermath of that meeting to depend on the infinite possibilities of student motives and classroom directives. A variety of opportunities have been provided to help the student stretch his imagination, refresh his attitudes, and move toward his own self-development.

We wish to thank Professor W. R. Keast, of Cornell University, for his very helpful suggestions and comments during the preparation of this volume.

THOMAS A. GULLASON

LEONARD CASPER

I

THE STORIES

Anton Chekhov

[1860—1904]

THOUGH HIGHLY GIFTED as a dramatist—Uncle Vanya (1897) and The Cherry Orchard (1903-1904) rank with the world's best—Anton Chekhov has won his greatest fame with nearly 800 short stories. By some he is called the "Russian Maupassant," and while there are points of similarity between the two, they are markedly different as storytellers. Chekhov's tales are rooted in the Russian character; yet he has a greater reputation in England and America than in his own native land, and for different reasons. To his countrymen he is known primarily as a writer of comic anecdotes, many of which have not been translated into English; to the English-speaking world he is regarded as a master of tragic-pathetic stories.

Born one year before the liberation of the serfs, Chekhov spent much of his brief life searching for freedom and dignity. His grandfather, born a serf, had earlier bought the family's freedom. But as a child in Taganrog, Chekhov was treated like a convict and beaten almost daily by a well-intentioned yet despotic father. This harsh treatment turned him into an uncommunicative recluse; years later he reflected sadly: "People must never be humiliated—that is the main thing." He found some solace from his kindly, sensitive mother. Once, he summed up the influence of his parents and recognized the effects of his father's love for music and art: "We owe our gifts to our father, our capacity for feeling to our mother."

3

His father had to flee to Moscow to escape creditors when his grocery business collapsed in 1876, and young Chekhov suddenly found himself independent. Left behind to finish his schooling at Taganrog, Chekhov became engrossed in the theater. He successfully organized an amateur production of Gogol's *The Government Inspector*. And though he preferred acting and directing plays, he had to find a way to support himself and his destitute family in Moscow, so, in 1877, he began sending anecdotes to his brother Alexander, who placed them in the humorous journal, *The Alarm-Clock*.

Medicine, however, finally became his profession. As early as 1876 when he suffered his first major illness—in 1884 it proved to be tuberculosis—he was attracted to science. His background as a medical student made him revere realism; later it was to make him highly critical of Zola and Tolstoy, because he felt they often wrote about things they did not know. When Chekhov started his medical practice, he had close contact with the common people and with provincial life; he widened his sympathetic understanding of human suffering; he became "doctor of the soul"—all important to his future success as a writer.

Chekhov could not support his family nor himself adequately enough as a doctor. He kept on writing comic sketches of about 100 lines for the humorous magazines. But in 1886 he became critical of his success: "I don't recall a single story upon which I have spent more than twenty-five hours. . . . I have composed my stories as reporters write their accounts of fires, mechanically, half unconsciously, with no concern either for the reader or myself." In 1887 he largely abandoned comic writing to write only serious stories. This was probably due to the tragedies he had witnessed among the common people and his discovery of Tolstoy's humanitarian philosophy and Turgenev's moving stories of peasant life. He did not abandon comedy altogether, for Gogol's satiric genius always remained with him. Chekhov improved his art of fiction by rewriting some of Tolstoy's and Turgenev's works.

Only after his journey to Sakhalin, Russia's Devil's Island, in 1890 did Chekhov move away from his imitative period. This journey resulted in an impressive book on prison reform; more important, it meant the end of Tolstoyan influence. Tolstoy's philosophy of nonresistance to evil seemed puerile, as did his controversial remarks on love and marriage. Chekhov wrote *The Duel* (1891) to mock Tolstoy's arguments in *The Kreutzer Sonata*, and *Ward No. 6* (1892) to renounce his philosophy of nonresistance to evil. Now independent as an artist, he wrote his best stories in the 1890s.

Though adept at many types of stories, Chekhov excels in those dealing with love. His many tempestuous affairs with women gave him mastery of his subject. Once he said: "I am finishing a story which is very boring, because woman and the element of love are quite lacking in it. I don't like that sort of story."

Like his famous plays, his stories are compact, understated, indirect-action mood dramas full of poetry and symbol. They are tales of delayed action, seemingly abrupt and incomplete. They are like life: trivial yet meaningful everyday experiences that are not solved, merely stated. One of his favorite themes is, as Prince Mirsky puts it, "the mutual lack of understanding between human beings, the impossibility for one person to feel in tune with another." He illuminates a soul's life with a psychology different from Dostoevsky's, which he considered "pretentious." His characters, not highly individualized, reflect Chekhov's pessimism; they are sad, pathetic people whose lives of quiet desperation bring "tears through laughter."

The Kiss

At EIGHT O'CLOCK on the evening of the twentieth of May all the six batteries of the N—— Reserve Artillery Brigade halted for the night in the village of Mestechki on their way to camp. At the height of the general commotion, while some officers were busily occupied around the guns, and others, gathered together in the square near the church enclosure, were receiving the reports of the quartermasters, a man in civilian dress, riding a queer horse, came into sight round the church. The little dun-colored horse with a fine neck and a short tail came, moving not straight forward, but as it were sideways, with a sort of dance step, as though it were being lashed about the legs. When he reached the officers the man on the horse took off his hat and said:

"His Excellency Lieutenant-General von Rabbeck, a local landowner, invites the officers to have tea with him this minute. . . ."

The horse bowed, danced, and retired sideways; the rider raised his hat once more and in an instant disappeared with his strange horse behind the church.

"What the devil does it mean?" grumbled some of the

The selection from Chekhov, *The Party and Other Stories*, trans. by Constance Garnett. Copyright 1917 by The Macmillan Company and used with their permission, and with the permission of Chatto and Windus Ltd.

6

officers, dispersing to their quarters. "One is sleepy, and here this von Rabbeck with his tea! We know what tea means."

The officers of all the six batteries remembered vividly an incident of the previous year, when during maneuvers they, together with the officers of a Cossack regiment, were in the same way invited to tea by a count who had an estate in the neighborhood and was a retired army officer; the hospitable and genial count made much of them, dined and wined them, refused to let them go to their quarters in the village, and made them stay the night. All that, of course, was very nice—nothing better could be desired, but the worst of.it was, the old army officer was so carried away by the pleasure of the young men's company that till sunrise he was telling the officers anecdotes of his glorious past, taking them over the house, showing them expensive pictures, old engravings, rare guns, reading them autograph letters from great people, while the weary and exhausted officers looked and listened, longing for their beds and yawning in their sleeves; when at last their host let them go, it was too late for sleep.

Might not this von Rabbeck be just such another? Whether he were or not, there was no help for it. The officers changed their uniforms, brushed themselves, and went all together in search of the gentleman's house. In the square by the church they were told they could get to his Excellency's by the lower road—going down behind the church to the river, walking along the bank to the garden, and there the alleys would take them to the house; or by the upper way—straight from the church by the road which, half a mile from the village, led right up to his Excellency's barns. The officers decided to go by the upper road.

"Which von Rabbeck is it?" they wondered on the way. "Surely not the one who was in command of the N—— cavalry division at Plevna?"

"No, that was not von Rabbeck, but simply Rabbe and no 'von.'"

"What lovely weather!"

At the first of the barns the road divided in two: one

branch went straight on and vanished in the evening darkness, the other led to the owner's house on the right. The
officers turned to the right and began to speak more softly.
. . . On both sides of the road stretched stone barns with
red roofs, heavy and sullen-looking, very much like barracks
in a district town. Ahead of them gleamed the windows of
the manor house.

"A good omen, gentlemen," said one of the officers. "Our
setter leads the way; no doubt he scents game ahead of
us! . . ."

Lieutenant Lobytko, who was walking in front, a tall and
stalwart fellow, though entirely without mustache (he was
over twenty-five, yet for some reason there was no sign of
hair on his round, well-fed face), renowned in the brigade
for his peculiar ability to divine the presence of women at a
distance, turned round and said:

"Yes, there must be women here; I feel that by instinct."

On the threshold the officers were met by von Rabbeck
himself, a comely looking man of sixty in civilian dress.
Shaking hands with his guests, he said that he was very glad
and happy to see them, but begged them earnestly for
God's sake to excuse him for not asking them to stay the
night; two sisters with their children, his brothers, and some
neighbors, had come on a visit to him, so that he had not
one spare room left.

The General shook hands with everyone, made his apolo-
gies, and smiled, but it was evident by his face that he was
by no means so delighted as last year's count, and that he
had invited the officers simply because, in his opinion, it
was a social obligation. And the officers themselves, as they
walked up the softly carpeted stairs, as they listened to him,
felt that they had been invited to this house simply because
it would have been awkward not to invite them; and at the
sight of the footmen, who hastened to light the lamps at
the entrance below and in the anteroom above, they began
to feel as though they had brought uneasiness and discomfort into the house with them. In a house in which two

sisters and their children, brothers, and neighbors were gathered together, probably on account of some family festivity or event, how could the presence of nineteen unknown officers possibly be welcome?

Upstairs at the entrance to the drawing room the officers were met by a tall, graceful old lady with black eyebrows and a long face, very much like the Empress Eugénie. Smiling graciously and majestically, she said she was glad and happy to see her guests, and apologized that her husband and she were on this occasion unable to invite *messieurs les officiers* to stay the night. From her beautiful majestic smile, which instantly vanished from her face every time she turned away from her guests, it was evident that she had seen numbers of officers in her day, that she was in no humor for them now, and if she invited them to her house and apologized for not doing more, it was only because her breeding and position in society required it of her.

When the officers went into the big dining-room, there were about a dozen people, men and ladies, young and old, sitting at tea at the end of a long table. A group of men wrapped in a haze of cigar smoke was dimly visible behind their chairs; in the midst of them stood a lanky young man with red whiskers, talking loudly in English, with a burr. Through a door beyond the group could be seen a light room with pale blue furniture.

"Gentlemen, there are so many of you that it is impossible to introduce you all!" said the General in a loud voice, trying to sound very gay. "Make each other's acquaintance, gentlemen, without any ceremony!"

The officers—some with very serious and even stern faces, others with forced smiles, and all feeling extremely awkward—somehow made their bows and sat down to tea.

The most ill at ease of them all was Ryabovich—a short, somewhat stooped officer in spectacles, with whiskers like a lynx's. While some of his comrades assumed a serious expression, while others wore forced smiles, his face, his lynx-like whiskers, and spectacles seemed to say, "I am the shyest, most modest, and most undistinguished officer in the whole brigade!" At first, on going into the room and later, sitting down at table, he could not fix his attention on any one face or object. The faces, the dresses, the cut-glass decanters of brandy, the steam from the glasses, the molded cornices—all blended in one general impression that inspired in Ryabovich alarm and a desire to hide his head. Like a lecturer making his first appearance before the public, he saw everything that was before his eyes, but apparently only had a dim understanding of it (among physiologists this condition, when the subject sees but does not understand, is called "mental blindness"). After a little while, growing accustomed to his surroundings, Ryabovich regained his sight and began to observe. As a shy man, unused to society, what struck him first was that in which he had always been deficient—namely, the extraordinary boldness of his new acquaintances. Von Rabbeck, his wife, two elderly ladies, a young lady in a lilac dress, and the young man with the red whiskers, who was, it appeared, a younger son of von Rabbeck, very cleverly, as though they had rehearsed it beforehand, took seats among the officers, and at once got up a heated discussion in which the visitors could not help taking part. The lilac young lady hotly asserted that the artillery had a much better time than the cavalry and the infantry, while von Rabbeck and the elderly ladies maintained the opposite. A brisk interchange followed. Ryabovich looked at the lilac young lady who argued so hotly about what was unfamiliar and utterly uninteresting to her, and watched artificial smiles come and go on her face.

Von Rabbeck and his family skillfully drew the officers into the discussion, and meanwhile kept a sharp eye on their glasses and mouths, to see whether all of them were drinking, whether all had enough sugar, why someone was not eating cakes or not drinking brandy. And the longer Ryabovich watched and listened, the more he was attracted by this insincere but splendidly disciplined family.

After tea the officers went into the drawing-room. Lieutenant Lobytko's instinct had not deceived him. There were a great many girls and young married ladies. The "setter" lieutenant was soon standing by a very young blonde in a black dress, and, bending over her jauntily, as though leaning on an unseen sword, smiled and twitched his shoulders coquettishly. He probably talked very interesting nonsense, for the blonde looked at his well-fed face condescendingly and asked indifferently, "Really?" And from that indifferent "Really?" the "setter," had he been intelligent, might have concluded that she would never call him to heel.

The piano struck up; the melancholy strains of a waltz floated out of the wide open windows, and everyone, for some reason, remembered that it was spring, a May evening. Everyone was conscious of the fragrance of roses, of lilac, and of the young leaves of the poplar. Ryabovich, who felt the brandy he had drunk, under the influence of the music stole a glance towards the window, smiled, and began watching the movements of the women, and it seemed to him that the smell of roses, of poplars, and lilac came not from the garden, but from the ladies' faces and dresses.

Von Rabbeck's son invited a scraggy-looking young lady to dance and waltzed round the room twice with her. Lobytko, gliding over the parquet floor, flew up to the lilac young lady and whirled her away. Dancing began. . . . Ryabovich stood near the door among those who were not dancing and looked on. He had never once danced in his whole life, and he had never once in his life put his arm round the waist of a respectable woman. He was highly delighted that a man should in the sight of all take a girl he did not know round the waist and offer her his shoulder to put her hand on, but he could not imagine himself in the position of such a man. There were times when he envied the boldness and swagger of his companions and was inwardly wretched; the knowledge that he was timid, round-shouldered, and uninteresting, that he had a long waist and lynx-like whiskers deeply mortified him, but with years he had grown used to this feeling, and now, looking at his comrades dancing or loudly talking, he no longer envied them, but only felt touched and mournful.

When the quadrille began, young von Rabbeck came up to those who were not dancing and invited two officers to have a game at billiards. The officers accepted and went with him out of the drawing-room. Ryabovich, having nothing to do and wishing to take at least some part in the general movement, slouched after them. From the big drawing-room they went into the little drawing-room, then into a narrow corridor with a glass roof, and thence into a room in which on their entrance three sleepy-looking footmen jumped up quickly from couches. At last, after passing through a long succession of rooms, young von Rabbeck and the officers came into a small room where there was a billiard table. They began to play.

Ryabovich, who had never played any game but cards, stood near the billiard table and looked indifferently at the players, while they in unbuttoned coats, with cues in their hands, stepped about, made puns, and kept shouting out unintelligible words.

The players took no notice of him, and only now and then one of them, shoving him with his elbow or accidentally touching him with his cue, would turn round and say "Pardon!" Before the first game was over he was weary of it, and began to feel that he was not wanted and in the way. . . . He felt disposed to return to the drawing-room and he went out.

On his way back he met with a little adventure. When he had gone half-way he noticed that he had taken a wrong turning. He distinctly remembered that he ought to meet three sleepy footmen on his way, but he had passed five or six rooms, and those sleepy figures seemed to have been swallowed up by the earth. Noticing his mistake, he walked back a little way and turned to the right; he found himself in a little room which was in semidarkness and which he had not seen on his way to the billiard room. After standing there a little while, he resolutely opened the first door that met his eyes and walked into an absolutely dark room. Straight ahead could be seen the crack in the doorway through which came a gleam of vivid light; from the other side of the door came the muffled sound of a melancholy mazurka. Here, too, as in the drawing-room, the windows were wide open and there was a smell of poplars, lilac, and roses. . . .

Ryabovich stood still in hesitation. . . . At that moment, to his surprise, he heard hurried footsteps and the rustling of a dress, a breathless feminine voice whispered "At last!" and two soft, fragrant, unmistakably feminine arms were clasped about his neck; a warm cheek was pressed against his, and simultaneously there was the sound of a kiss. But at once the bestower of the kiss uttered a faint shriek and sprang away from him, as it seemed to Ryabovich, with disgust. He, too, almost shrieked and rushed towards the gleam of light at the door. . . .

When he returned to the drawing-room his heart was palpitating and his hands were trembling so noticeably that he made haste to hide them behind his back. At first he was tormented by shame and dread that the whole drawing-room knew that he had just been kissed and embraced by a woman. He shrank into himself and looked uneasily about him, but as he became convinced that people were dancing and talking as calmly as ever, he gave himself up entirely to the new sensation which he had never experienced before in his life. Something strange was happening to him. . . . His neck, round which soft, fragrant arms had so lately been clasped, seemed to him to be anointed with oil; on his left cheek near his mustache where the unknown had kissed him there was a faint chilly tingling sensation as from peppermint drops, and the more he rubbed the place the more distinct was the chilly sensation; all of him, from head to foot, was full of a strange new feeling which grew stronger and stronger. . . . He wanted to dance, to talk, to run into the garden, to laugh aloud. . . . He quite forgot

that he was round-shouldered and uninteresting, that he
had lynx-like whiskers and an "undistinguished appearance"
(that was how his appearance had been described by some
ladies whose conversation he had accidentally overheard).
When von Rabbeck's wife happened to pass by him, he
gave her such a broad and friendly smile that she stood still
and looked at him inquiringly.

"I like your house immensely!" he said, setting his spectacles straight.

The General's wife smiled and said that the house had
belonged to her father; then she asked whether his parents
were living, whether he had long been in the army, why he
was so thin, and so on. . . . After receiving answers to her
questions, she went on, and after his conversation with her
his smiles were more friendly than ever, and he thought he
was surrounded by splendid people. . . .

At supper Ryabovich ate mechanically everything offered
him, drank, and without listening to anything, tried to understand what had just happened to him. . . . The adventure was of a mysterious and romantic character, but it was
not difficult to explain it. No doubt some girl or young married lady had arranged a tryst with some man in the dark
room; had waited a long time, and being nervous and excited had taken Ryabovich for her hero; this was the more
probable as Ryabovich had stood still hesitating in the dark
room, so that he, too, had looked like a person waiting for
something. . . . This was how Ryabovich explained to himself the kiss he had received.

"And who is she?" he wondered, looking round at the
women's faces. "She must be young, for elderly ladies don't
arrange rendezvous. That she was a lady, one could tell by
the rustle of her dress, her perfume, her voice. . . ."

His eyes rested on the lilac young lady, and he thought
her very attractive; she had beautiful shoulders and arms, a
clever face, and a delightful voice. Ryabovich, looking at
her, hoped that she and no one else was his unknown. . . .
But she laughed somehow artificially and wrinkled up her

long nose, which seemed to him to make her look old. Then
he turned his eyes upon the blonde in a black dress. She
was younger, simpler, and more genuine, had a charming
brow, and drank very daintily out of her wineglass. Ryabovich now hoped that it was she. But soon he began to think
her face flat, and fixed his eyes upon the one next her.

"It's difficult to guess," he thought, musing. "If one were
to take only the shoulders and arms of the lilac girl, add the
brow of the blonde and the eyes of the one on the left of
Lobytko, then . . ."

He made a combination of these things in his mind and
so formed the image of the girl who had kissed him, the
image that he desired but could not find at the table. . . .

After supper, replete and exhilarated, the officers began
to take leave and say thank you. Von Rabbeck and his wife
began again apologizing that they could not ask them to
stay the night.

"Very, very glad to have met you, gentlemen," said von
Rabbeck, and this time sincerely (probably because people
are far more sincere and good-humored at speeding their
parting guests than on meeting them). "Delighted. Come
again on your way back! Don't stand on ceremony! Where
are you going? Do you want to go by the upper way? No,
go across the garden; it's nearer by the lower road."

The officers went out into the garden. After the bright
light and the noise the garden seemed very dark and quiet.
They walked in silence all the way to the gate. They were
a little drunk, in good spirits, and contented, but the darkness and silence made them thoughtful for a minute. Probably the same idea occurred to each one of them as to Ryabovich: would there ever come a time for them when, like
von Rabbeck, they would have a large house, a family, a
garden—when they, too, would be able to welcome people,
even though insincerely, feed them, make them drunk and
contented?

Going out of the garden gate, they all began talking at
once and laughing loudly about nothing. They were walk-

ing now along the little path that led down to the river and then ran along the water's edge, winding round the bushes on the bank, the gulleys, and the willows that overhung the water. The bank and the path were scarcely visible, and the other bank was entirely plunged in darkness. Stars were reflected here and there in the dark water; they quivered and were broken up—and from that alone it could be seen that the river was flowing rapidly. It was still. Drowsy sandpipers cried plaintively on the farther bank, and in one of the bushes on the hither side a nightingale was trilling loudly, taking no notice of the crowd of officers. The officers stood round the bush, touched it, but the nightingale went on singing.

"What a fellow!" they exclaimed approvingly. "We stand beside him and he takes not a bit of notice! What a rascal!"

At the end of the way the path went uphill, and, skirting the church enclosure, led into the road. Here the officers, tired with walking uphill, sat down and lighted their cigarettes. On the farther bank of the river a murky red fire came into sight, and having nothing better to do, they spent a long time in discussing whether it was a camp fire or a light in a window, or something else. . . . Ryabovich, too, looked at the light, and he fancied that the light looked and winked at him, as though it knew about the kiss.

On reaching his quarters, Ryabovich undressed as quickly as possible and got into bed. Lobytko and Lieutenant Merzlyakov—a peaceable, silent fellow, who was considered in his own circle a highly educated officer, and was always, whenever it was possible, reading The Messenger of Europe, which he carried about with him everywhere—were quartered in the same cottage with Ryabovich. Lobytko undressed, walked up and down the room for a long while with the air of a man who has not been satisfied, and sent his orderly for beer. Merzlyakov got into bed, put a candle by his pillow, and plunged into The Messenger of Europe.

"Who was she?" Ryabovich wondered, looking at the sooty ceiling.

His neck still felt as though he had been anointed with oil, and there was still the chilly sensation near his mouth as though from peppermint drops. The shoulders and arms of the young lady in lilac, the brow and the candid eyes of the blonde in black, waists, dresses, and brooches, floated through his imagination. He tried to fix his attention on these images, but they danced about, broke up and flickered. When these images vanished altogether from the broad dark background which everyone sees when he closes his eyes, he began to hear hurried footsteps, the rustle of skirts, the sound of a kiss—and an intense baseless joy took possession of him. . . . Abandoning himself to this joy, he heard the orderly return and announce that there was no beer. Lobytko was terribly indignant, and began pacing up and down the room again.

"Well, isn't he an idiot?" he kept saying, stopping first before Ryabovich and then before Merzlyakov. "What a fool and a blockhead a man must be not to get hold of any beer! Eh? Isn't he a blackguard?"

"Of course you can't get beer here," said Merzlyakov, not removing his eyes from *The Messenger of Europe.*

"Oh! Is that your opinion?" Lobytko persisted. "Lord have mercy upon us, if you dropped me on the moon I'd find you beer and women directly! I'll go and find some at once. . . . You may call me a rascal if I don't!"

He spent a long time in dressing and pulling on his high boots, then finished smoking his cigarette in silence and went out.

"Rabbeck, Grabbeck, Labbeck," he muttered, stopping in the outer room. "I don't care to go alone, damn it all! Ryabovich, wouldn't you like to go for a walk? Eh?"

Receiving no answer, he returned, slowly undressed, and got into bed. Merzlyakov sighed, put *The Messenger of Europe* away, and extinguished the light.

"H'm! . . ." muttered Lobytko, lighting a cigarette in the dark.

Ryabovich pulled the bedclothes over his head, curled

himself up in bed, and tried to gather together the flashing images in his mind and to combine them into a whole. But nothing came of it. He soon fell asleep, and his last thought was that someone had caressed him and made him happy—that something extraordinary, foolish, but joyful and delightful, had come into his life. The thought did not leave him even in his sleep.

When he woke up the sensations of oil on his neck and the chill of peppermint about his lips had gone, but joy flooded his heart just as the day before. He looked enthusiastically at the window-frames, gilded by the light of the rising sun, and listened to the movement of the passers-by in the street. People were talking loudly close to the window. Lebedetzky, the commander of Ryabovich's battery, who had only just overtaken the brigade, was talking to his sergeant at the top of his voice, having lost the habit of speaking in ordinary tones.

"What else?" shouted the commander.

"When they were shoeing the horses yesterday, your Honor, they injured Pigeon's hoof with a nail. The vet put on clay and vinegar; they are leading him apart now. Also, your Honor, Artemyev got drunk yesterday, and the lieutenant ordered him to be put in the limber of a spare gun-carriage."

The sergeant reported that Karpov had forgotten the new cords for the trumpets and the pegs for the tents, and that their Honors the officers had spent the previous evening visiting General von Rabbeck. In the middle of this conversation the red-bearded face of Lebedetzky appeared in the window. He screwed up his short-sighted eyes, looking at the sleepy faces of the officers, and greeted them.

"Is everything all right?" he asked.

"One of the horses has a sore neck from the new collar," answered Lobytko, yawning.

The commander sighed, thought a moment, and said in a loud voice:

"I am thinking of going to see Alexandra Yevgrafovna. I

must call on her. Well, good-bye. I shall catch up with you in the evening."

A quarter of an hour later the brigade set off on its way. When it was moving along the road past the barns, Ryabovich looked at the house on the right. The blinds were down in all the windows. Evidently the household was still asleep. The one who had kissed Ryabovich the day before was asleep too. He tried to imagine her asleep. The wide-open window of the bedroom, the green branches peeping in, the morning freshness, the scent of the poplars, lilac, and roses, the bed, a chair, and on it the skirts that had rustled the day before, the little slippers, the little watch on the table—all this he pictured to himself clearly and distinctly, but the features of the face, the sweet sleepy smile, just what was characteristic and important, slipped through his imagination like quicksilver through the fingers. When he had ridden a third of a mile, he looked back: the yellow church, the house, and the river, were all bathed in light; the river with its bright green banks, with the blue sky reflected in it and glints of silver in the sunshine here and there, was very beautiful. Ryabovich gazed for the last time at Mestechki, and he felt as sad as though he were parting with something very near and dear to him.

And before him on the road were none but long familiar, uninteresting scenes. . . . To right and to left, fields of young rye and buckwheat with rooks hopping about in them; if one looked ahead, one saw dust and the backs of men's heads; if one looked back, one saw the same dust and faces. . . . Foremost of all marched four men with sabers —this was the vanguard. Next came the singers, and behind them the trumpeters on horseback. The vanguard and the singers, like torch-bearers in a funeral procession, often forgot to keep the regulation distance and pushed a long way ahead. . . . Ryabovich was with the first cannon of the fifth battery. He could see all the four batteries moving in front of him. To a civilian the long tedious procession which is a brigade on the move seems an intricate and un-

intelligible muddle; one cannot understand why there are
so many people round one cannon, and why it is drawn by
so many horses in such a strange network of harness, as
though it really were so terrible and heavy. To Ryabovich it
was all perfectly comprehensible and therefore uninteresting. He had known for ever so long why at the head of each
battery beside the officer there rode a stalwart noncom,
called bombardier; immediately behind him could be seen
the horsemen of the first and then of the middle units. Ryabovich knew that of the horses on which they rode, those
on the left were called one name, while those on the right
were called another—it was all extremely uninteresting. Behind the horsemen came two shaft-horses. On one of them
sat a rider still covered with the dust of yesterday and with
a clumsy and funny-looking wooden guard on his right leg.
Ryabovich knew the object of this guard, and did not think
it funny. All the riders waved their whips mechanically and
shouted from time to time. The cannon itself was not pre-
sentable. On the limber lay sacks of oats covered with a
tarpaulin, and the cannon itself was hung all over with
kettles, soldiers' knapsacks, bags, and looked like some small
harmless animal surrounded for some unknown reason by
men and horses. To the leeward of it marched six men, the
gunners, swinging their arms. After the cannon there came
again more bombardiers, riders, shaft-horses, and behind
them another cannon, as unpresentable and unimpressive
as the first. After the second came a third, a fourth; near
the fourth there was an officer, and so on. There were six
batteries in all in the brigade, and four cannon in each battery. The procession covered a third of a mile; it ended in
a string of wagons near which an extremely appealing creature—the ass, Magar, brought by a battery commander from
Turkey—paced pensively, his long-eared head drooping.

Ryabovich looked indifferently ahead and behind him, at
the backs of heads and at faces; at any other time he would
have been half asleep, but now he was entirely absorbed in
his new agreeable thoughts. At first when the brigade was

setting off on the march he tried to persuade himself that the incident of the kiss could only be interesting as a mysterious little adventure, that it was in reality trivial, and to think of it seriously, to say the least, was stupid; but now he bade farewell to logic and gave himself up to dreams. . . . At one moment he imagined himself in von Rabbeck's drawing-room beside a girl who was like the young lady in lilac and the blonde in black; then he would close his eyes and see himself with another, entirely unknown girl, whose features were very vague. In his imagination he talked, caressed her, leaned over her shoulder, pictured war, separation, then meeting again, supper with his wife, children. . . .

"Brakes on!" The word of command rang out every time they went downhill.

He, too, shouted "Brakes on!" and was afraid this shout would disturb his reverie and bring him back to reality. . . .

As they passed by some landowner's estate Ryabovich looked over the fence into the garden. A long avenue, straight as a ruler, strewn with yellow sand and bordered with young birch-trees, met his eyes. . . . With the eagerness of a man who indulges in daydreaming, he pictured to himself little feminine feet tripping along yellow sand, and quite unexpectedly had a clear vision in his imagination of her who had kissed him and whom he had succeeded in picturing to himself the evening before at supper. This image remained in his brain and did not desert him again.

At midday there was a shout in the rear near the string of wagons:

"Attention! Eyes to the left! Officers!"

The general of the brigade drove by in a carriage drawn by a pair of white horses. He stopped near the second battery, and shouted something which no one understood. Several officers, among them Ryabovich, galloped up to him.

"Well? How goes it?" asked the general, blinking his red eyes. "Are there any sick?"

Receiving an answer, the general, a little skinny man, chewed, thought for a moment and said, addressing one of the officers:

"One of your drivers of the third cannon has taken off his leg-guard and hung it on the fore part of the cannon, the rascal. Reprimand him."

He raised his eyes to Ryabovich and went on:

"It seems to me your breeching is too long."

Making a few other tedious remarks, the general looked at Lobytko and grinned.

"You look very melancholy today, Lieutenant Lobytko," he said. "Are you pining for Madame Lopukhova? Eh? Gentlemen, he is pining for Madame Lopukhova."

Madame Lopukhova was a very stout and very tall lady long past forty. The general, who had a predilection for large women, whatever their ages, suspected a similar taste in his officers. The officers smiled respectfully. The general, delighted at having said something very amusing and biting, laughed loudly, touched his coachman's back, and saluted. The carriage rolled on. . . .

"All I am dreaming about now which seems to me so impossible and unearthly is really quite an ordinary thing," thought Ryabovich, looking at the clouds of dust racing after the general's carriage. "It's all very ordinary, and everyone goes through it. . . . That general, for instance, was in love at one time; now he is married and has children. Captain Wachter, too, is married and loved, though the nape of his neck is very red and ugly and he has no waist. . . . Salmanov is coarse and too much of a Tartar, but he had a love affair that has ended in marriage. . . . I am the same as everyone else, and I, too, shall have the same experience as everyone else, sooner or later. . . ."

And the thought that he was an ordinary person and that his life was ordinary delighted him and gave him courage. He pictured *her* and his happiness boldly, just as he liked. . . .

When the brigade reached their halting-place in the evening, and the officers were resting in their tents, Ryabovich, Merzlyakov, and Lobytko were sitting round a chest having supper. Merzlyakov ate without haste, and, as he munched deliberately, read *The Messenger of Europe*, which he held on his knees. Lobytko talked incessantly and kept filling up his glass with beer, and Ryabovich, whose head was confused from dreaming all day long, drank and said nothing. After three glasses he got a little drunk, felt weak, and had an irresistible desire to relate his new sensations to his comrades.

"A strange thing happened to me at those von Rabbecks'," he began, trying to impart an indifferent and ironical tone to his voice. "You know I went into the billiard-room. . . ."

He began describing very minutely the incident of the kiss, and a moment later relapsed into silence. . . . In the course of that moment he had told everything, and it surprised him dreadfully to find how short a time it took him to tell it. He had imagined that he could have been telling the story of the kiss till next morning. Listening to him, Lobytko, who was a great liar and consequently believed no one, looked at him skeptically and laughed. Merzlyakov twitched his eyebrows and, without removing his eyes from *The Messenger of Europe*, said:

"That's an odd thing! How strange! . . . throws herself on a man's neck, without addressing him by name. . . . She must have been some sort of lunatic."

"Yes, she must," Ryabovich agreed.

"A similar thing once happened to me," said Lobytko, assuming a scared expression. "I was going last year to Kovno. . . . I took a second-class ticket. The train was crammed, and it was impossible to sleep. I gave the guard half a ruble; he took my luggage and led me to another compartment. . . . I lay down and covered myself with a blanket. . . . It was dark, you understand. Suddenly I felt someone touch me on the shoulder and breathe in my face. I made a movement with my hand and felt somebody's elbow. . . . I opened my eyes and only imagine—a woman. Black eyes, lips red as a prime salmon, nostrils breathing passionately —a bosom like a buffer. . . ."

"Excuse me," Merzlyakov interrupted calmly, "I understand about the bosom, but how could you see the lips if it was dark?"

Lobytko began trying to put himself right and laughing at Merzlyakov's being so dull-witted. It made Ryabovich wince. He walked away from the chest, got into bed, and vowed never to confide again.

Camp life began. . . . The days flowed by, one very much like another. All those days Ryabovich felt, thought, and behaved as though he were in love. Every morning when his orderly handed him what he needed for washing, and he sluiced his head with cold water, he recalled that there was something warm and delightful in his life.

In the evenings when his comrades began talking of love and women, he would listen, and draw up closer; and he wore the expression of a soldier listening to the description of a battle in which he has taken part. And on the evenings when the officers, out on a spree with the setter Lobytko at their head, made Don-Juanesque raids on the neighboring "suburb," and Ryabovich took part in such excursions, he always was sad, felt profoundly guilty, and inwardly begged *her* forgiveness. . . . In hours of leisure or on sleepless nights when he felt moved to recall his childhood, his father and mother—everything near and dear, in fact, he invariably thought of Mestechki, the queer horse, von Rabbeck, his wife who resembled Empress Eugénie, the dark room, the light in the crack of the door. . . .

On the thirty-first of August he was returning from the camp, not with the whole brigade, but with only two batteries. He was dreamy and excited all the way, as though he were going home. He had an intense longing to see again the queer horse, the church, the insincere family of the von Rabbecks, the dark room. The "inner voice," which so often deceives lovers, whispered to him for some reason

that he would surely see her. . . . And he was tortured by
the questions: How would he meet her? What would he
talk to her about? Had she forgotten the kiss? If the worst
came to the worst, he thought, even if he did not meet her,
it would be a pleasure to him merely to go through the dark
room and recall the past. . . .

Towards evening there appeared on the horizon the familiar church and white barns. Ryabovich's heart raced.
. . . He did not hear the officer who was riding beside him
and saying something to him, he forgot everything, and
looked eagerly at the river shining in the distance, at the
roof of the house, at the dovecote round which the pigeons
were circling in the light of the setting sun.

When they reached the church and were listening to the
quartermaster, he expected every second that a man on
horseback would come round the church enclosure and invite the officers to tea, but . . . the quartermaster ended
his report, the officers dismounted and strolled off to the
village, and the man on horseback did not appear.

"Von Rabbeck will hear at once from the peasants that
we have come and will send for us," thought Ryabovich,
as he went into the peasant cottage, unable to understand
why a comrade was lighting a candle and why the orderlies
were hastening to get the samovars going.

A crushing uneasiness took possession of him. He lay
down, then got up and looked out of the window to see
whether the messenger were coming. But there was no sign
of him.

He lay down again, but half an hour later he got up and,
unable to restrain his uneasiness, went into the street and
strode towards the church. It was dark and deserted in the
square near the church enclosure. Three soldiers were standing silent in a row where the road began to go down-hill.
Seeing Ryabovich, they roused themselves and saluted. He
returned the salute and began to go down the familiar path.

On the farther bank of the river the whole sky was
flooded with crimson: the moon was rising; two peasant

women, talking loudly, were pulling cabbage leaves in the kitchen garden; beyond the kitchen garden there were some cottages that formed a dark mass. . . . Everything on the near side of the river was just as it had been in May: the path, the bushes, the willows overhanging the water . . . but there was no sound of the brave nightingale and no scent of poplar and young grass.

Reaching the garden, Ryabovich looked in at the gate. The garden was dark and still. . . . He could see nothing but the white stems of the nearest birch-trees and a little bit of the avenue; all the rest melted together into a dark mass. Ryabovich looked and listened eagerly, but after waiting for a quarter of an hour without hearing a sound or catching a glimpse of a light, he trudged back. . . .

He went down to the river. The General's bathing cabin and the bath-sheets on the rail of the little bridge showed white before him. . . . He walked up on the bridge, stood a little, and quite unnecessarily touched a sheet. It felt rough and cold. He looked down at the water. . . . The river ran rapidly and with a faintly audible gurgle round the piles of the bathing cabin. The red moon was reflected near the left bank; little ripples ran over the reflection, stretching it out, breaking it into bits, and seemed trying to carry it away. . . .

"How stupid, how stupid!" thought Ryabovich, looking at the running water. "How unintelligent it all is!"

Now that he expected nothing, the incident of the kiss, his impatience, his vague hopes and disappointment, presented themselves to him in a clear light. It no longer seemed to him strange that the General's messenger never came and that he would never see the girl who had accidentally kissed him instead of someone else; on the contrary, it would have been strange if he had seen her. . . .

The water was running, he knew not where or why, just as it did in May. At that time it had flowed into a great river, from the great river into the sea; then it had risen in vapor, turned into rain, and perhaps the very same water

was running now before Ryabovich's eyes again. . . .
What for? Why?

And the whole world, the whole of life, seemed to Ryabovich an unintelligible, aimless jest. . . . And turning his eyes from the water and looking at the sky, he remembered again how Fate in the person of an unknown woman had by chance caressed him, he recalled his summer dreams and fancies, and his life struck him as extraordinarily meager, poverty-stricken, and drab. . . .

When he had returned to the cottage he did not find a single comrade. The orderly informed him that they had all gone to "General Fontryabkin, who had sent a messenger on horseback to invite them. . . ."

For an instant there was a flash of joy in Ryabovich's heart, but he quenched it at once, got into bed, and in his wrath with his fate, as though to spite it, did not go to the General's.

Gooseberries

THE SKY HAD been overcast since early morning; it was a
still day, not hot, but tedious, as it usually is when the
weather is gray and dull, when clouds have been hanging
over the fields for a long time, and you wait for the rain
that does not come. Ivan Ivanich, a veterinary, and Burkin,
a high school teacher, were already tired with walking, and
the plain seemed endless to them. Far ahead were the
scarcely visible windmills of the village of Mironositskoe; to
the right lay a range of hills that disappeared in the distance
beyond the village, and both of them knew that over there
were the river, and fields, green willows, homesteads, and
if you stood on one of the hills, you could see from there
another vast plain, telegraph poles, and a train that from
afar looked like a caterpillar crawling, and in clear weather
you could even see the town. Now, when it was still and
when nature seemed mild and pensive, Ivan Ivanich and
Burkin were filled with love for this plain, and both of them
thought what a beautiful land it was.

"Last time when we were in Elder Prokofi's barn," said
Burkin, "you were going to tell me a story."

"Yes; I wanted to tell you about my brother."

From *The Portable Chekhov*, translated by Avrahm Yarmolinsky. Copyright 1947 by The Viking Press, Inc. and reprinted with their permission.

28

Ivan Ivanich heaved a slow sigh and lit his pipe before beginning his story, but just then it began to rain. And five minutes later there was a downpour, and it was hard to tell when it would be over. The two men halted, at a loss; the dogs, already wet, stood with their tails between their legs and looked at them feelingly.

"We must find shelter somewhere," said Burkin. "Let's go to Alyokhin's; it's quite near."

"Let's."

They turned aside and walked across a mown meadow, now going straight ahead, now bearing to the right, until they reached the road. Soon poplars came into view, a garden, then the red roofs of barns; the river gleamed, and the view opened on a broad expanse of water with a mill and a white bathing cabin. That was Sofyino, Alyokhin's place.

The mill was going, drowning out the sound of the rain; the dam was shaking. Wet horses stood near the carts, their heads drooping, and men were walking about, their heads covered with sacks. It was damp, muddy, dreary; and the water looked cold and unkind. Ivan Ivanich and Burkin felt cold and messy and uncomfortable through and through; their feet were heavy with mud and when, having crossed the dam, they climbed up to the barns, they were silent as though they were cross with each other.

The noise of a winnowing machine came from one of the barns, the door was open, and clouds of dust were pouring from within. On the threshold stood Alyokhin himself, a man of forty, tall and rotund, with long hair, looking more like a professor or an artist than a gentleman farmer. He was wearing a white blouse, badly in need of washing, that was belted with a rope, and drawers, and his high boots were plastered with mud and straw. His eyes and nose were black with dust. He recognized Ivan Ivanich and Burkin and was apparently very glad to see them.

"Please go up to the house, gentlemen," he said, smiling; "I'll be there directly, in a moment."

It was a large structure of two stories. Alyokhin lived downstairs in what was formerly the stewards' quarters: two rooms that had arched ceilings and small windows; the furniture was plain, and the place smelled of rye bread, cheap vodka, and harness. He went into the showy rooms upstairs only rarely, when he had guests. Once in the house, the two visitors were met by a chambermaid, a young woman so beautiful that both of them stood still at the same moment and glanced at each other.

"You can't imagine how glad I am to see you, gentlemen," said Alyokhin, joining them in the hall. "What a surprise! Pelageya," he said, turning to the chambermaid, "give the guests a change of clothes. And, come to think of it, I will change, too. But I must go and bathe first, I don't think I've had a wash since spring. Don't you want to go into the bathing cabin? In the meanwhile things will be got ready here."

The beautiful Pelageya, with her soft, delicate air, brought them bath towels and soap, and Alyokhin went to the bathing cabin with his guests.

"Yes, it's a long time since I've bathed," he said, as he undressed. "I've an excellent bathing cabin, as you see—it was put up by my father—but somehow I never find time to use it." He sat down on the steps and lathered his long hair and neck, and the water around him turned brown.

"I say—" observed Ivan Ivanich significantly, looking at his head.

"I haven't had a good wash for a long time," repeated Alyokhin, embarrassed, and soaped himself once more; the water about him turned dark blue, the color of ink.

Ivan Ivanich came out of the cabin, plunged into the water with a splash and swam in the rain, thrusting his arms out wide; he raised waves on which white lilies swayed. He swam out to the middle of the river and dived and a minute later came up in another spot and swam on and kept diving, trying to touch bottom. "By God!" he kept repeating delightedly, "by God!" He swam to the mill, spoke to the

peasants there, and turned back and in the middle of the
river lay floating, exposing his face to the rain. Burkin and
Alyokhin were already dressed and ready to leave, but he
kept on swimming and diving. "By God!" he kept exclaiming. "Lord, have mercy on me."

"You've had enough!" Burkin shouted to him.

They returned to the house. And only when the lamp
was lit in the big drawing room upstairs, and the two guests,
in silk dressing gowns and warm slippers, were lounging in
armchairs, and Alyokhin himself, washed and combed,
wearing a new jacket, was walking about the room, evidently savoring the warmth, the cleanliness, the dry clothes
and light footwear, and when pretty Pelageya, stepping
noiselessly across the carpet and smiling softly, brought in
a tray with tea and jam, only then did Ivan Ivanich begin
his story, and it was as though not only Burkin and Alyokhin were listening, but also the ladies, old and young, and
the military men who looked down upon them, calmly and
severely, from their gold frames.

"We are two brothers," he began, "I, Ivan Ivanich, and
my brother, Nikolay Ivanich, who is two years my junior.
I went in for a learned profession and became a veterinary;
Nikolay at nineteen began to clerk in a provincial branch
of the Treasury. Our father was a *kantonist*, but he rose to
be an officer and so a nobleman, a rank that he bequeathed
to us together with a small estate. After his death there was
a lawsuit and we lost the estate to creditors, but be that as
it may, we spent our childhood in the country. Just like
peasant children we passed days and nights in the fields and
the woods, herded horses, stripped bast from the trees,
fished, and so on. And, you know, whoever even once in his
life has caught a perch or seen thrushes migrate in the autumn, when on clear, cool days they sweep in flocks over
the village, will never really be a townsman and to the day
of his death will have a longing for the open. My brother
was unhappy in the government office. Years passed, but
he went on warming the same seat, scratching away at the

same papers, and thinking of one and the same thing: how
to get away to the country. And little by little this vague
longing turned into a definite desire, into a dream of buying
a little property somewhere on the banks of a river or a lake.

"He was a kind and gentle soul and I loved him, but I
never sympathized with his desire to shut himself up for
the rest of his life on a little property of his own. It is a
common saying that a man needs only six feet of earth.
But six feet is what a corpse needs, not a man. It is also asserted that if our educated class is drawn to the land and
seeks to settle on farms, that's a good thing. But these farms
amount to the same six feet of earth. To retire from the
city, from the struggle, from the hubbub, to go off and hide
on one's own farm—that's not life, it is selfishness, sloth,
it is a kind of monasticism, but monasticism without works.
Man needs not six feet of earth, not a farm, but the whole
globe, all of Nature, where unhindered he can display all
the capacities and peculiarities of his free spirit.

"My brother Nikolay, sitting in his office, dreamed of
eating his own *shchi*, which would fill the whole farmyard
with a delicious aroma, of picnicking on the green grass, of
sleeping in the sun, of sitting for hours on the seat by the
gate gazing at field and forest. Books on agriculture and the
farming items in almanacs were his joy, the delight of his
soul. He liked newspapers too, but the only things he read
in them were advertisements of land for sale, so many
acres of tillable land and pasture, with house, garden, river,
mill, and millpond. And he pictured to himself garden
paths, flowers, fruit, birdhouses with starlings in them, cru-
cians in the pond, and all that sort of thing, you know.
These imaginary pictures varied with the advertisements he
came upon, but somehow gooseberry bushes figured in
every one of them. He could not picture to himself a single
countryhouse, a single rustic nook, without gooseberries.

"'Country life has its advantages,' he used to say. 'You
sit on the veranda having tea, and your ducks swim in the

pond, and everything smells delicious and—the gooseberries are ripening.'

"He would draw a plan of his estate and invariably it would contain the following features: a) the master's house; b) servants' quarters; c) kitchen garden; d) a gooseberry patch. He lived meagerly: he deprived himself of food and drink; he dressed God knows how, like a beggar, but he kept on saving and salting money away in the bank. He was terribly stingy. It was painful for me to see it, and I used to give him small sums and send him something on holidays, but he would put that away too. Once a man is possessed by an idea, there is no doing anything with him.

"Years passed. He was transferred to another province, he was already past forty, yet he was still reading newspaper advertisements and saving up money. Then I heard that he was married. Still for the sake of buying a property with a gooseberry patch he married an elderly, homely widow, without a trace of affection for her, but simply because she had money. After marrying her, he went on living parsimoniously, keeping her half-starved, and he put her money in the bank in his own name. She had previously been the wife of a postmaster, who had got her used to pies and cordials. This second husband did not even give her enough black bread. She began to sicken, and some three years later gave up the ghost. And, of course, it never for a moment occurred to my brother that he was to blame for her death. Money, like vodka, can do queer things to a man. Once in our town a merchant lay on his deathbed; before he died, he ordered a plateful of honey and he ate up all his money and lottery tickets with the honey, so that no one should get it. One day when I was inspecting a drove of cattle at a railway station, a cattle dealer fell under a locomotive and it sliced off his leg. We carried him in to the infirmary, the blood was gushing from the wound—a terrible business, but he kept begging us to find his leg and was very anxious about it: he had twenty rubles in the boot that was on that leg, and he was afraid they would be lost."

"That's a tune from another opera," said Burkin.

Ivan Ivanich paused a moment and then continued:

"After his wife's death, my brother began to look around for a property. Of course, you may scout about for five years and in the end make a mistake, and buy something quite different from what you have been dreaming of. Through an agent my brother bought a mortgaged estate of three hundred acres with a house, servants' quarters, a park, but with no orchard, no gooseberry patch, no duck pond. There was a stream, but the water in it was the color of coffee, for on one of its banks there was a brickyard and on the other a glue factory. But my brother was not at all disconcerted: he ordered a score of gooseberry bushes, planted them, and settled down to the life of a country gentleman.

"Last year I paid him a visit. I thought I would go and see how things were with him. In his letter to me my brother called his estate 'Chumbaroklov Waste, or Gimalayskoe' (our surname was Chimsha-Gimalaysky). I reached the place in the afternoon. It was hot. Everywhere there were ditches, fences, hedges, rows of fir trees, and I was at a loss as to how to get to the yard and where to leave my horse. I made my way to the house and was met by a fat dog with reddish hair that looked like a pig. It wanted to bark, but was too lazy. The cook, a fat, barelegged woman, who also looked like a pig, came out of the kitchen and said that the master was resting after dinner. I went in to see my brother, and found him sitting up in bed, with a quilt over his knees. He had grown older, stouter, flabby; his cheeks, his nose, his lips jutted out: it looked as though he might grunt into the quilt at any moment.

"We embraced and dropped tears of joy and also of sadness at the thought that the two of us had once been young, but were now gray and nearing death. He got dressed and took me out to show me his estate.

" 'Well, how are you getting on here?' I asked.

" 'Oh, all right, thank God. I am doing very well.'

"He was no longer the poor, timid clerk he used to be but a real landowner, a gentleman. He had already grown used to his new manner of living and developed a taste for it. He ate a great deal, steamed himself in the bathhouse, was growing stout, was already having a lawsuit with the village commune and the two factories and was very much offended when the peasants failed to address him as 'Your Honor.' And he concerned himself with his soul's welfare too in a substantial, upperclass manner, and performed good deeds not simply, but pompously. And what good works! He dosed the peasants with bicarbonate and castor oil for all their ailments and on his name day he had a thanksgiving service celebrated in the center of the village, and then treated the villagers to a gallon of vodka, which he thought was the thing to do. Oh, those horrible gallons of vodka! One day a fat landowner hauls the peasants up before the rural police officer for trespassing, and the next, to mark a feast day, treats them to a gallon of vodka, and they drink and shout 'Hurrah' and when they are drunk bow down at his feet. A higher standard of living, overeating and idleness develop the most insolent self-conceit in a Russian. Nikolay Ivanich, who when he was a petty official was afraid to have opinions of his own even if he kept them to himself, now uttered nothing but incontrovertible truths and did so in the tone of a minister of state: 'Education is necessary, but the masses are not ready for it; corporal punishment is generally harmful, but in some cases it is useful and nothing else will serve.'

" 'I know the common people, and I know how to deal with them,' he would say. 'They love me. I only have to raise my little finger, and they will do anything I want.'

"And all this, mark you, would be said with a smile that bespoke kindness and intelligence. Twenty times over he repeated: 'We, of the gentry,' 'I, as a member of the gentry.' Apparently he no longer remembered that our grandfather had been a peasant and our father just a private. Even our surname, 'Chimsha-Gimalaysky,' which in reality is grotesque, seemed to him sonorous, distinguished, and delightful.

"But I am concerned now not with him, but with me. I want to tell you about the change that took place in me during the few hours that I spent on his estate. In the evening when we were having tea, the cook served a plateful of gooseberries. They were not bought, they were his own gooseberries, the first ones picked since the bushes were planted. My brother gave a laugh and for a minute looked at the gooseberries in silence, with tears in his eyes—he could not speak for excitement. Then he put one berry in his mouth, glanced at me with the triumph of a child who has at last been given a toy he was longing for and said: 'How tasty!' And he ate the gooseberries greedily, and kept repeating: 'Ah, how delicious! Do taste them!'

"They were hard and sour, but as Pushkin has it,

> The falsehood that exalts we cherish more
> Than meaner truths that are a thousand strong.

I saw a happy man, one whose cherished dream had so obviously come true, who had attained his goal in life, who had got what he wanted, who was satisfied with his lot and with himself. For some reason an element of sadness had always mingled with my thoughts of human happiness, and now at the sight of a happy man I was assailed by an oppressive feeling bordering on despair. It weighed on me particularly at night. A bed was made up for me in a room next to my brother's bedroom, and I could hear that he was wakeful, and that he would get up again and again, go to the plate of gooseberries and eat one after another. I said to myself: how many contented, happy people there really are! What an overwhelming force they are! Look at life: the insolence and idleness of the strong, the ignorance and brutishness of the weak, horrible poverty everywhere, overcrowding, degeneration, drunkenness, hypocrisy, lying— Yet in all the houses and on all the streets there is peace and quiet; of the fifty thousand people who live in our town there is not one who would cry out, who would vent his indignation aloud. We see the people who go to market, eat by day, sleep by night, who babble nonsense, marry, grow old, good-naturedly drag their dead to the cemetery, but we do not see or hear those who suffer, and what is terrible in life goes on somewhere behind the scenes. Everything is peaceful and quiet and only mute statistics protest: so many people gone out of their minds, so many gallons of vodka drunk, so many children dead from malnutrition— And such a state of things is evidently necessary; obviously the happy man is at ease only because the unhappy ones bear their burdens in silence, and if there were not this silence, happiness would be impossible. It is a general hypnosis. Behind the door of every contented, happy man there ought to be someone standing with a little hammer and continually reminding him with a knock that there are unhappy people, that however happy he may be, life will sooner or later show him its claws, and trouble will come to him— illness, poverty, losses, and then no one will see or hear him, just as now he neither sees nor hears others. But there is no man with a hammer. The happy man lives at his ease, faintly fluttered by small daily cares, like an aspen in the wind—and all is well."

"That night I came to understand that I too had been contented and happy," Ivan Ivanich continued, getting up. "I too over the dinner table or out hunting would hold forth on how to live, what to believe, the right way to govern the people. I too would say that learning was the enemy of darkness, that education was necessary but that for the common people the three R's were sufficient for the time being. Freedom is a boon, I used to say, it is as essential as air, but we must wait awhile. Yes, that's what I used to say, and now I ask: Why must we wait?" said Ivan Ivanich, looking wrathfully at Burkin. "Why must we wait, I ask you? For what reason? I am told that nothing can be done all at once, that every idea is realized gradually, in its own time. But who is it that says so? Where is the proof that it is just? You cite the natural order of things, the law governing all phenomena, but is there law, is there order in the fact that I, a living, thinking man, stand beside a ditch and wait for it to close up of itself or fill up with silt, when I could jump over it or throw a bridge across it? And again, why must we wait? Wait, until we have no strength to live, and yet we have to live and are eager to live!

"I left my brother's place early in the morning, and ever since then it has become intolerable for me to stay in town. I am oppressed by the peace and the quiet, I am afraid to look at the windows, for there is nothing that pains me more than the spectacle of a happy family sitting at table having tea. I am an old man now and unfit for combat, I am not even capable of hating. I can only grieve inwardly, get irritated, worked up, and at night my head is ablaze with the rush of ideas and I cannot sleep. Oh, if I were young!"

Ivan Ivanich paced up and down the room excitedly and repeated, "If I were young!"

He suddenly walked up to Alyokhin and began to press now one of his hands, now the other.

"Pavel Konstantinich," he said imploringly, "don't quiet down, don't let yourself be lulled to sleep! As long as you are young, strong, alert, do not cease to do good! There is no happiness and there should be none, and if life has a meaning and a purpose, that meaning and purpose is not our happiness but something greater and more rational. Do good!"

All this Ivan Ivanich said with a pitiful, imploring smile, as though he were asking a personal favor.

Afterwards all three of them sat in armchairs in different corners of the drawing room and were silent. Ivan Ivanich's story satisfied neither Burkin nor Alyokhin. With the ladies and generals looking down from the golden frames, seeming alive in the dim light, it was tedious to listen to the story of the poor devil of a clerk who ate gooseberries. One felt like talking about elegant people, about women. And the fact that they were sitting in a drawing room where everything—the chandelier under its cover, the armchairs, the carpets underfoot—testified that the very people who were now looking down from the frames had once moved about here, sat and had tea, and the fact that lovely Pelageya was noiselessly moving about—that was better than any story.

Alyokhin was very sleepy; he had gotten up early, before three o'clock in the morning, to get some work done, and now he could hardly keep his eyes open, but he was afraid his visitors might tell an interesting story in his absence, and he would not leave. He did not trouble to ask himself if what Ivan Ivanich had just said was intelligent or right. The guests were not talking about groats, or hay, or tar, but about something that had no direct bearing on his life, and he was glad of it and wanted them to go on.

"However, it's bedtime," said Burkin, rising. "Allow me to wish you good night."

Alyokhin took leave of his guests and went downstairs to his own quarters, while they remained upstairs. They were installed for the night in a big room in which stood two old wooden beds decorated with carvings and in the corner was an ivory crucifix. The wide cool beds which had been made by the lovely Pelageya gave off a pleasant smell of clean linen.

Ivan Ivanich undressed silently and got into bed.

"Lord forgive us sinners!" he murmured, and drew the bedclothes over his head.

His pipe, which lay on the table, smelled strongly of burnt tobacco, and Burkin, who could not sleep for a long time, kept wondering where the unpleasant odor came from.

The rain beat against the window panes all night.

Fyodor Dostoevsky

[1821 — 1881]

RUSSIA'S MARQUIS DE SADE, the Dante of the North, a latter-day
Job—all these names characterize in part the fantastic life of
Dostoevsky, who seems more fictitious than his great creations
like Raskolnikov in *Crime and Punishment* (1866) and Dmitry
Karamazov in *The Brothers Karamazov* (1879–1880). Through
literature Dostoevsky made his confessions and sought the resurrected life; and though he never wrote his projected *Life of a
Great Sinner*, his stories and novels reflect his tortured anxieties
over heaven and hell.

Many people and events affected the soul of Dostoevsky. His
father, the son of a·poor nobleman turned priest, was an army
doctor; and Dostoevsky came to fear and hate this moody hypochondriac and religious fanatic who often harshly disciplined
his children. His mother, on the other hand, was gentle and
loving toward her son, who always cherished a memento of hers
inscribed with the prophetic words: "O heart! When will you
be filled with the love which alone is. man's salvation?" There
was some comfort too from the peasant women who intrigued
young Fyodor with stories, some of them terrifying. When his
father was murdered in 1839 by serfs he had maltreated, Dostoevsky seemed both relieved and horrified by the act, which
later played a significant role in his dream life.

Going to a military engineering school in Petersburg in 1838
increased Dostoevsky's fits of depression. Besides the harsh dis-

cipline of his masters, he hated scientific studies and was so
humiliated by his poverty and by his failure to be promoted
that he contemplated suicide. Literature gave him purpose and
meaning. Romantic writers like Hoffmann and Goethe and
dramatists like Shakespeare and Racine made him anxious to be
an artist dedicated to one philosophic theme: "Man is a mystery. It must be unraveled, and if you give your life to the task,
do not say that you have wasted it; I devote myself to this mystery because I wish to be a man."

With his first novel, *Poor Folk* (1846), written in imitation
of Gogol, Dostoevsky was acclaimed as a great artist. Like Gogol
he was deeply interested in the problems of the common man,
so he became involved with a liberal political group headed by
a socialist, Petrashevsky, and the critic Belinsky. In 1849, along
with others, he was arrested and sentenced to death for conspir-
ing against Emperor Nicholas I. He went through a mock execution and then was sent to Siberia. Dostoevsky turned his
prison life to advantage: close to death, he learned to love life
all the more; living with criminals of all types, including mur-
derers, he was awed by their spiritual strength; he read and
reread the New Testament and was inspired by Jesus Christ; his
dizzy spells turned out to be epilepsy, which gave him ecstatic
visions into the psyche. Without his hardships in Siberia, Dostoevsky might never have become a great writer. Even his unfortunate marriage to Marya Isayeva in 1857 added to his
understanding of women, to whom he was always attracted.

In 1859 Dostoevsky was permitted to leave Siberia and return
to Petersburg, where, two years later, he edited the periodical
Vremya. Though he was now "a complete monarchist," he
espoused many liberal causes, including the emancipation of
women. In 1862 he had the urge to travel (later he would be
forced into exile in order to escape debtor's prison), and he
went to England, France, Germany, and Italy. He developed a
great hatred of the West because he felt it was too materialistic and incapable of Christian brotherhood. He looked to his
own Russia as the future of a better Christianity. Ironically, his
continual need of money kept Dostoevsky in the casinos of the
West. But in his self-imposed exile he cried: "I feel that without the Russian earth all my strength, all my talent will dry up."
After the death of his wife in 1864 his luck changed; he mar-

ried Anna Snitkina, and with her help, he wrote his greatest fiction.

Once Dostoevsky said: "I have my own idea about art, and it is this: what most people regard as fantastic and lacking in universality, I hold to be the inmost essence of truth." When he turned from stories of incident to stories of men and women involved in fantasies and dreams he found his true forte. His ambivalent characters are usually hateful, criminal, sadistic, yet capable of love, compassion, and understanding. A master of the world of the senses and the unconscious and influenced by Kant and Hegel, Dostoevsky was often drawn to the individual's struggle between the intellect and the spirit. The form of his tense, concentrated stories rich in dialogue suggests the drama. Though a mediocre stylist who wrote much of his work in haste, and who sometimes resorted to padding and sensational effects, Dostoevsky has a genius for satiric humor which is overshadowed by his profound tragic vision.

An Honest Thief

ONE MORNING, just as I was about to set off to my office, Agravena, my cook, washerwoman and housekeeper, came in to me and, to my surprise, entered into conversation.

She had always been such a silent, simple creature that, except for her daily inquiry about dinner, she had not uttered a word for the last six years. I, at least, had heard nothing else from her.

"Here I have come in to have a word with you, sir," she began abruptly; "you really ought to let the little room."

"Which little room?"

"Why, the one next the kitchen, to be sure."

"What for?"

"What for? Why, because folks do take in lodgers, to be sure."

"But who would take it?"

"Who would take it? Why, a lodger would take it, to be sure."

"But, my good woman, one could not put a bedstead in it; there wouldn't be room to move! Who could live in it?"

The selection from Dostoevsky, *The Honest Thief and Other Stories*, trans. by Constance Garnett. Copyright 1923 by The Macmillan Company and used with their permission and with the permission of William Heinemann Ltd.

"Who wants to live there? As long as he has a place to sleep in. Why, he would live in the window."

"In what window?"

"In what window? As though you didn't know! The one in the passage, to be sure. He would sit there, sewing or doing anything else. Maybe he would sit on a chair, too. He's got a chair; and he has a table, too; he's got everything."

"Who is 'he,' then?"

"Oh, a good man, a man of experience. I will cook for him. And I'll ask him three roubles a month for his board and lodging."

After prolonged efforts I succeeded at last in learning from Agravena that an elderly man had somehow managed to persuade her to admit him into the kitchen as a lodger and boarder. Any notion Agravena took into her head had to be carried out; if not, I knew she would give me no peace. When anything was not to her liking, she at once began to brood, and sank into a deep dejection that would last for a fortnight or three weeks. During that period my dinners were spoiled, my linen was mislaid, my floors went unscrubbed; in short, I had a great deal to put up with. I had observed long ago that this inarticulate woman was incapable of conceiving a project, or originating an idea of her own. But if anything like a notion or a project was by some means put into her feeble brain, to prevent its being carried out meant, for a time, her moral assassination. And so, as I cared more for my peace of mind than for anything else, I consented forthwith.

"Has he a passport anyway, or something of the sort?"

"To be sure, he has. He is a good man, a man of experience; three roubles he's promised to pay."

The very next day the new lodger made his appearance in my modest bachelor quarters; but I was not put out by this, indeed I was inwardly pleased. I lead as a rule a very lonely hermit's existence. I have scarcely any friends; I hardly ever go anywhere. As I had spent ten years never coming out of my shell, I had, of course, grown used to solitude. But another ten or fifteen years or more of the same solitary existence, with the same Agravena, in the same bachelor quarters, was in truth a somewhat cheerless prospect. And therefore a new inmate, if well-behaved, was a heaven-sent blessing.

Agravena had spoken truly: my lodger was certainly a man of experience. From his passport it appeared that he was an old soldier, a fact which I should have known indeed from his face. An old soldier is easily recognized. Astafy Ivanovitch was a favorable specimen of his class. We got on very well together. What was best of all, Astafy Ivanovitch would sometimes tell a story, describing some incident in his own life. In the perpetual boredom of my existence such a story-teller was a veritable treasure. One day he told me one of these stories. It made an impression on me. The following event was what led to it.

I was left alone in the flat; both Astafy and Agravena were out on business of their own. All of a sudden I heard from the inner room somebody—I fancied a stranger—come in; I went out; there actually was a stranger in the passage, a short fellow wearing no overcoat in spite of the cold autumn weather.

"What do you want?"

"Does a clerk called Alexandrov live here?"

"Nobody of that name here, brother. Good-bye."

"Why, the dvornik told me it was here," said my visitor, cautiously retiring towards the door.

"Be off, be off, brother, get along."

Next day after dinner, while Astafy Ivanovitch was fitting on a coat which he was altering for me, again some one came into the passage. I half opened the door.

Before my very eyes my yesterday's visitor, with perfect composure, took my wadded greatcoat from the peg and, stuffing it under his arm, darted out of the flat. Agravena stood all the time staring at him, agape with astonishment and doing nothing for the protection of my property. Astafy

Ivanovitch flew in pursuit of the thief and ten minutes later came back out of breath and empty-handed. He had vanished completely.

"Well, there's a piece of luck, Astafy Ivanovitch!"

"It's a good job your cloak is left! Or he would have put you in a plight, the thief!"

But the whole incident had so impressed Astafy Ivanovitch that I forgot the theft as I looked at him. He could not get over it. Every minute or two he would drop the work upon which he was engaged, and would describe over again how it had all happened, how he had been standing, how the greatcoat had been taken down before his very eyes, not a yard away, and how it had come to pass that he could not catch the thief. Then he would sit down to his work again, then leave it once more, and at last I saw him go down to the dvornik to tell him all about it, and to upbraid him for letting such a thing happen in his domain. Then he came back again and began scolding Agravena. Then he sat down to his work again, and long afterwards he was still muttering to himself how it had all happened, how he stood there and I was here, how before our eyes, not a yard away, the thief took the coat off the peg, and so on. In short, though Astafy Ivanovitch understood his business, he was a terrible slow-coach and busybody.

"He's made fools of us, Astafy Ivanovitch," I said to him in the evening, as I gave him a glass of tea. I wanted to while away the time by recalling the story of the lost greatcoat, the frequent repetition of which, together with the great earnestness of the speaker, was beginning to become very amusing.

"Fools, indeed, sir! Even though it is no business of mine, I am put out. It makes me angry though it is not my coat that was lost. To my thinking there is no vermin in the world worse than a thief. Another takes what you can spare, but a thief steals the work of your hands, the sweat of your brow, your time . . . Ugh, it's nasty! One can't speak of it!

It's too vexing. How is it you don't feel the loss of your property, sir?"

"Yes, you are right, Astafy Ivanovitch, better if the thing had been burnt; it's annoying to let the thief have it, it's disagreeable."

"Disagreeable! I should think so! Yet, to be sure, there are thieves and thieves. And I have happened, sir, to come across an honest thief."

"An honest thief? But how can a thief be honest, Astafy Ivanovitch?"

"There you are right indeed, sir. How can a thief be honest? There are none such. I only meant to say that he was an honest man, sure enough, and yet he stole. I was simply sorry for him."

"Why, how was that, Astafy Ivanovitch?"

"It was about two years ago, sir. I had been nearly a year out of a place, and just before I lost my place I made the acquaintance of a poor lost creature. We got acquainted in a public-house. He was a drunkard, a vagrant, a beggar, he had been in a situation of some sort, but from his drinking habits he had lost his work. Such a ne'er-do-well! God only knows what he had on! Often you wouldn't be sure if he'd a shirt under his coat; everything he could lay his hands upon he would drink away. But he was not one to quarrel; he was a quiet fellow. A soft, good-natured chap. And he'd never ask, he was ashamed; but you could see for yourself the poor fellow wanted a drink, and you would stand it for him. And so we got friendly, that's to say, he stuck to me. . . . It was all one to me. And what a man he was, to be sure! Like a little dog he would follow me; wherever I went there he would be; and all that after our first meeting, and he as thin as a thread-paper! At first it was 'let me stay the night'; well, I let him stay.

"I looked at his passport, too; the man was all right.

"Well, the next day it was the same story, and then the third day he came again and sat all day in the window and stayed the night. Well, thinks I, he is sticking to me; give him food and drink and shelter at night, too—here am I, a poor man, and a hanger-on to keep as well! And before he came to me, he used to go in the same way to a government clerk's; he attached himself to him; they were always drinking together; but he, through trouble of some sort, drank himself into the grave. My man was called Emelyan Ilyitch. I pondered and pondered what I was to do with him. To drive him away I was ashamed. I was sorry for him; such a pitiful, Godforsaken creature I never did set eyes on. And not a word said, either; he does not ask, but just sits there and looks into your eyes like a dog. To think what drinking will bring a man down to!

"I keep asking myself how am I to say to him: 'You must be moving, Emelyanoushka, there's nothing for you here, you've come to the wrong place. I shall soon not have a bite for myself, how am I to keep you too?'

"I sat and wondered what he'd do when I said that to him. And I seemed to see how he'd stare at me, if he were to hear me say that, how long he would sit and not understand a word of it. And when it did get home to him at last, how he would get up from the window, would take up his bundle—I can see it now, the red-check handkerchief full of holes, with God knows what wrapped up in it, which he had always with him, and then how he would set his shabby old coat to rights, so that it would look decent and keep him warm, so that no holes would be seen—he was a man of delicate feelings! And how he'd open the door and go out with tears in his eyes. Well, there's no letting a man go to ruin like that. . . . One's sorry for him.

"And then again, I think, how am I off myself? Wait a bit, Emelyanoushka, says I to myself, you've not long to feast with me: I shall soon be going away and then you will not find me.

"Well, sir, our family made a move; and Alexander Filimonovitch, my master (now deceased, God rest his soul!) said, 'I am thoroughly satisfied with you, Astafy Ivanovitch;

when we come back from the country we will take you on again.' I had been butler with them; a nice gentleman he was, but he died that same year. Well, after seeing him off, I took my belongings, what little money I had, and I thought I'd have a rest for a time, so I went to an old woman I knew, and I took a corner in her room. There was only one corner free in it. She had been a nurse, so now she had a pension and a room of her own. Well, now good-bye, Emelyanoushka, thinks I, you won't find me now, my boy.

"And what do you think, sir? I had gone out to see a man I knew, and when I came back in the evening, the first thing I saw was Emelyanoushka! There he was, sitting on my box and his checked bundle beside him; he was sitting in his ragged old coat, waiting for me. And to while away the time he had borrowed a church book from the old lady, and was holding it wrong side upwards. He'd scented me out! My heart sank. Well, thinks I, there's no help for it —why didn't I turn him out at first? So I asked him straight off: 'Have you brought your passport, Emelyanoushka?'

"I sat down on the spot, sir, and began to ponder: will a vagabond like that be very much trouble to me? And on thinking it over it seemed he would not be much trouble. He must be fed, I thought. Well, a bit of bread in the morning, and to make it go down better I'll buy him an onion. At midday I should have to give him another bit of bread and an onion; and in the evening, onion again with kvass, with some more bread if he wanted it. And if some cabbage soup were to come our way, then we should both have had our fill. I am no great eater myself, and a drinking man, as we all know, never eats; all he wants is herb-brandy or green vodka. He'll ruin me with his drinking, I thought, but then another idea came into my head, sir, and took great hold on me. So much so that if Emelyanoushka had gone away I should have felt that I had nothing to live for, I do believe. . . . I determined on the spot to be a father and guardian to him. I'll keep him from ruin, I thought, I'll wean him from the glass! You wait a bit, thought I; very well, Emelyanoushka, you may stay, only you must behave yourself; you must obey orders.

"Well, thinks I to myself, I'll begin by training him to work of some sort, but not all at once; let him enjoy himself a little first, and I'll look round and find something you are fit for, Emelyanoushka. For every sort of work a man needs a special ability, you know, sir. And I began to watch him on the quiet; I soon saw Emelyanoushka was a desperate character. I began, sir, with a word of advice: I said this and that to him. 'Emelyanoushka,' said I, 'you ought to take a thought and mend your ways. Have done with drinking! Just look what rags you go about in: that old coat of yours, if I may make bold to say so, is fit for nothing but a sieve. A pretty state of things! It's time to draw the line, sure enough.' Emelyanoushka sat and listened to me with his head hanging down. Would you believe it, sir? It had come to such a pass with him, he'd lost his tongue through drink and could not speak a word of sense. Talk to him of cucumbers and he'd answer back about beans! He would listen and listen to me and then heave such a sigh. 'What are you sighing for, Emelyan Ilyitch?' I asked him.

" 'Oh, nothing; don't you mind me, Astafy Ivanovitch. Do you know there were two women fighting in the street today, Astafy Ivanovitch? One upset the other woman's basket of cranberries by accident.'

" 'Well, what of that?'

" 'And the second one upset the other's cranberries on purpose and trampled them under foot, too.'

" 'Well, and what of it, Emelyan Ilyitch?'

" 'Why, nothing, Astafy Ivanovitch, I just mentioned it.'

" ' "Nothing, I just mentioned it!" Emelyanoushka, my boy, I thought, you've squandered and drunk away your brains!'

" 'And do you know, a gentleman dropped a money-note on the pavement in Gorohovy Street; no, it was Sadovy

Street. And a peasant saw it and said, "That's my luck"; and at the same time another man saw it and said, "No, it's my bit of luck. I saw it before you did." '

" 'Well, Emelyan Ilyitch?'

" 'And the fellows had a fight over it, Astafy Ivanovitch. But a policeman came up, took away the note, gave it back to the gentleman and threatened to take up both the men.'

" 'Well, but what of that? What is there edifying about it, Emelyanoushka?'

" 'Why, nothing, to be sure. Folks laughed, Astafy Ivanovitch.'

" 'Ach, Emelyanoushka! What do the folks matter? You've sold your soul for a brass farthing! But do you know what I have to tell you, Emelyan Ilyitch?'

" 'What, Astafy Ivanovitch?'

" 'Take a job of some sort, that's what you must do. For the hundredth time I say to you, set to work, have some mercy on yourself!'

" 'What could I set to, Astafy Ivanovitch? I don't know what job I could set to, and there is no one who will take me on, Astafy Ivanovitch.'

" 'That's how you came to be turned off, Emelyanoushka, you drinking man!'

" 'And do you know Vlass, the waiter, was sent for to the office today, Astafy Ivanovitch?'

" 'Why did they send for him, Emelyanoushka?' I asked.

" 'I could not say why, Astafy Ivanovitch. I suppose they wanted him there, and that's why they sent for him.'

"A-ach, thought I, we are in a bad way, poor Emelyanoushka! The Lord is chastising us for our sins. Well, sir, what is one to do with such a man?

"But a cunning fellow he was, and no mistake. He'd listen and listen to me, but at last I suppose he got sick of it. As soon as he sees I am beginning to get angry, he'd pick up his old coat and out he'd slip and leave no trace. He'd wander about all day and come back at night drunk.

Where he got the money from, the Lord only knows; I had no hand in that.

" 'No,' said I, 'Emelyan Ilyitch, you'll come to a bad end. Give over drinking, mind what I say now, give it up! Next time you come home in liquor, you can spend the night on the stairs. I won't let you in!'

"After hearing that threat, Emelyanoushka sat at home that day and the next; but on the third he slipped off again. I waited and waited; he didn't come back. Well, at least, I don't mind owning, I was in a fright, and I felt for the man too. What have I done to him? I thought. I've scared him away. Where's the poor fellow gone to now? He'll get lost maybe. Lord have mercy upon us!

"Night came on; he did not come. In the morning I went out into the porch; I looked, and if he hadn't gone to sleep in the porch! There he was with his head on the step, and chilled to the marrow of his bones.

" 'What next, Emelyanoushka, God have mercy on you! Where will you get to next?'

" 'Why, you were—sort of—angry with me, Astafy Ivanovitch, the other day; you were vexed and promised to put me to sleep in the porch, so I didn't—sort of—venture to come in, Astafy Ivanovitch, and so I lay down here . . .'

"I did feel angry, and sorry too.

" 'Surely you might undertake some other duty, Emelyanoushka, instead of lying here guarding the steps,' I said.

" 'Why, what other duty, Astafy Ivanovitch?'

" 'You lost soul'—I was in such a rage, I called him that —'if you could but learn tailoring-work! Look at your old rag of a coat! It's not enough to have it in tatters, here you are sweeping the steps with it! You might take a needle and boggle up your rags, as decency demands. Ah, you drunken man!'

"What do you think, sir? He actually did take a needle. Of course I said it in jest, but he was so scared he set to work. He took off his coat and began threading the needle.

I watched him; as you may well guess, his eyes were all red and bleary, and his hands were all of a shake. He kept shoving and shoving the thread and could not get it through the eye of the needle; he kept screwing his eyes up and wetting the thread and twisting it in his fingers—it was no good! He gave it up and looked at me.

" 'Well,' said I, 'this is a nice way to treat me! If there had been folks by to see, I don't know what I should have done! Why, you simple fellow, I said it to you in joke, as a reproach. Give over your nonsense, God bless you! Sit quiet and don't put me to shame, don't sleep on my stairs and make a laughing-stock of me.'

" 'Why, what am I to do, Astafy Ivanovitch? I know very well I am a drunkard and good for nothing! I can do nothing but vex you, my bene-benefactor. . . .'

"And at that his blue lips began all of a sudden to quiver, and a tear ran down his white cheek and trembled on his stubby chin, and then poor Emelyanoushka burst into a regular flood of tears. Mercy on us! I felt as though a knife were thrust into my heart! The sensitive creature! I'd never have expected it! Who could have guessed it? No, Emelyanoushka, thought I, I shall give you up altogether. You can go your way like the rubbish you are.

"Well, sir, why make a long story of it? And the whole affair is so trifling; it's not worth wasting words upon. Why, you, for instance, sir, would not have given a thought to it, but I would have given a great deal—if I had a great deal to give—that it never should have happened at all.

"I had a pair of riding breeches by me, sir, deuce take them, fine, first-rate riding breeches they were, too, blue with a check on it. They'd been ordered by a gentleman from the country, but he would not have them after all; said they were not full enough, so they were left on my hands. It struck me they were worth something. At the second-hand dealer's I ought to get five silver roubles for them, or if not I could turn them into two pairs of trousers

for Petersburg gentlemen and have a piece over for a waistcoat for myself. Of course for poor people like us everything
comes in. And it happened just then that Emelyanoushka
was having a sad time of it. There he sat day after day; he
did not drink, not a drop passed his lips, but he sat and
moped like an owl. It was sad to see him—he just sat and
brooded. Well, thought I, either you've not got a copper
to spend, my lad, or else you're turning over a new leaf of
yourself, you've given it up, you've listened to reason. Well,
sir, that's how it was with us; and just then came a holiday.
I went to vespers; when I came home I found Emelyanoushka sitting in the window, drunk and rocking to and fro.

"Ah! so that's what you've been up to, my lad! And I
went to get something out of my chest. And when I looked
in, the breeches were not there. . . . I rummaged here and
there; they'd vanished. When I'd ransacked everywhere and
saw they were not there, something seemed to stab me to
the heart. I ran first to the old dame and began accusing
her; of Emelyanoushka I'd not the faintest suspicion,
though there was cause for it in his sitting there drunk.

" 'No,' said the old body, 'God be with you, my fine gentleman, what good are riding breeches to me? Am I going
to wear such things? Why, a skirt I had I lost the other day
through a fellow of your sort . . . I know nothing; I can
tell you nothing about it,' she said.

" 'Who has been here, who has been in?' I asked.

" 'Why, nobody has been, my good sir,' says she; 'I've
been here all the while; Emelyan Ilyitch went out and came
back again; there he sits, ask him.'

" 'Emelyanoushka,' said I, 'have you taken those new riding breeches for anything; you remember the pair I made
for that gentleman from the country?'

" 'No, Astafy Ivanovitch,' said he; 'I've not—sort of—
touched them.'

"I was in a state! I hunted high and low for them—they
were nowhere to be found. And Emelyanoushka sits there
rocking himself to and fro. I was squatting on my heels fac-

ing him and bending over the chest, and all at once I stole
a glance at him. . . . Alack, I thought; my heart suddenly
grew hot within me and I felt myself flushing up too. And
suddenly Emelyanoushka looked at me.

" 'No, Astafy Ivanovitch,' said he, 'those riding breeches
of yours, maybe, you are thinking, maybe, I took them, but
I never touched them.'

" 'But what can have become of them, Emelyan Ilyitch?'

" 'No, Astafy Ivanovitch,' said he, 'I've never seen them.'

" 'Why, Emelyan Ilyitch, I suppose they've run off of
themselves, eh?'

" 'Maybe they have, Astafy Ivanovitch.'

"When I heard him say that, I got up at once, went up
to him, lighted the lamp and sat down to work to my sewing. I was altering a waistcoat for a clerk who lived below
us. And wasn't there a burning pain and ache in my breast!
I shouldn't have minded so much if I had put all the clothes
I had in the fire. Emelyanoushka seemed to have an inkling
of what a rage I was in. When a man is guilty, you know,
sir, he scents trouble far off, like the birds of the air before
a storm.

" 'Do you know what, Astafy Ivanovitch,' Emelyanoushka began, and his poor old voice was shaking as he said
the words, 'Antip Prohoritch, the apothecary, married the
coachman's wife this morning, who died the other day—'

"I did give him a look, sir, a nasty look it was; Emelyanoushka understood it too. I saw him get up, go to the bed,
and begin to rummage there for something. I waited—he
was busy there a long time and kept muttering all the
while, 'No, not there, where can the blessed things have got
to?' I waited to see what he'd do; I saw him creep under
the bed on all fours. I couldn't bear it any longer. 'What are
you crawling about under the bed for, Emelyan Ilyitch?'
said I.

" 'Looking for the breeches, Astafy Ivanovitch. Maybe
they've dropped down there somewhere.'

" 'Why should you try to help a poor simple man like

me,' said I, 'crawling on your knees for nothing, sir?'—I called him that in my vexation.

" 'Oh, never mind, Astafy Ivanovitch, I'll just look. They'll turn up, maybe, somewhere.'

" 'H'm,' said I, 'look here, Emelyan Ilyitch!'

" 'What is it, Astafy Ivanovitch?' said he.

" 'Haven't you simply stolen them from me like a thief and a robber, in return for the bread and salt you've eaten here?' said I.

"I felt so angry, sir, at seeing him fooling about on his knees before me.

" 'No, Astafy Ivanovitch.'

"And he stayed lying as he was on his face under the bed. A long time he lay there and then at last he crept out. I looked at him, and the man was as white as a sheet. He stood up, and sat down near me in the window and sat so for some ten minutes.

" 'No, Astafy Ivanovitch,' he said, and all at once he stood up and came towards me, and I can see him now; he looked dreadful. 'No, Astafy Ivanovitch,' said he, 'I never —sort of—touched your breeches.'

"He was all of a shake, poking himself in the chest with a trembling finger, and his poor old voice shook so that I was frightened, sir, and sat as though I was rooted to the window-seat.

" 'Well, Emelyan Ilyitch,' said I, 'as you will, forgive me if I, in my foolishness, have accused you unjustly. As for the breeches, let them go hang; we can live without them. We've still our hands, thank God; we need not go thieving or begging from some other poor man; we'll earn our bread.'

"Emelyanoushka heard me out and went on standing there before me. I looked up, and he had sat down. And there he sat all evening without stirring. At last I lay down to sleep. Emelyanoushka went on sitting in the same place. When I looked out in the morning, he was lying curled up in his old coat on the bare floor; he felt too crushed even to come to bed. Well, sir, I felt no more liking for the fellow from that day, in fact for the first few days I hated him. I felt, as one may say, as though my own son had robbed me, and done me a deadly hurt. Ach, thought I, Emelyanoushka, Emelyanoushka! And Emelyanoushka, sir, went on drinking for a whole fortnight without stopping. He was drunk all the time, and regularly besotted. He went out in the morning and came back late at night, and for a whole fortnight I didn't get a word out of him. It was as though grief was gnawing at his heart, or as though he wanted to do for himself completely. At last he stopped; he must have come to the end of all he'd got, and then he sat in the window again. I remember he sat there without speaking for three days and three nights; all of a sudden I saw that he was crying. He was just sitting there, sir, and crying like anything; a perfect stream, as though he didn't know how his tears were flowing. And it's a sad thing, sir, to see a grown-up man and an old man, too, crying from woe and grief.

" 'What's the matter, Emelyanoushka?' said I.

"He began to tremble so that he shook all over. I spoke to him for the first time since that evening.

" 'Nothing, Astafy Ivanovitch.'

" 'God be with you, Emelyanoushka, what's lost is lost. Why are you moping about like this?' I felt sorry for him.

" 'Oh, nothing, Astafy Ivanovitch, it's no matter. I want to find some work to do, Astafy Ivanovitch.'

" 'And what sort of work, pray, Emelyanoushka?'

" 'Why, any sort; perhaps I could find a situation such as I used to have. I've been already to ask Fedosay Ivanitch. I don't like to be a burden on you, Astafy Ivanovitch. If I can find a situation, Astafy Ivanovitch, then I'll pay you it all back, and make you a return for all your hospitality.'

" 'Enough, Emelyanoushka, enough; let bygones be bygones—and no more to be said about it. Let us go on as we used to do before.'

" 'No, Astafy Ivanovitch, you, maybe, think—but I never touched your riding breeches.'

" 'Well, have it your own way; God be with you, Emelyanoushka.'

" 'No, Astafy Ivanovitch, I can't go on living with you, that's clear. You must excuse me, Astafy Ivanovitch.'

" 'Why, God bless you, Emelyan Ilyitch, who's offending you and driving you out of the place—am I doing it?'

" 'No, it's not the proper thing for me to live with you like this, Astafy Ivanovitch. I'd better be going.'

"He was so hurt, it seemed, he stuck to his point. I looked at him, and sure enough, up he got and pulled his old coat over his shoulders.

" 'But where are you going, Emelyan Ilyitch? Listen to reason: what are you about? Where are you off to?'

" 'No, good-bye, Astafy Ivanovitch, don't keep me now' —and he was blubbering again—'I'd better be going. You're not the same now.'

" 'Not the same as what? I am the same. But you'll be lost by yourself like a poor helpless babe, Emelyan Ilyitch.'

" 'No, Astafy Ivanovitch, when you go out now, you lock up your chest and it makes me cry to see it, Astafy Ivanovitch. You'd better let me go, Astafy Ivanovitch, and forgive me all the trouble I've given you while I've been living with you.'

"Well, sir, the man went away. I waited for a day; I expected he'd be back in the evening—no. Next day no sign of him, nor the third day either. I began to get frightened; I was so worried, I couldn't drink, I couldn't eat, I couldn't sleep. The fellow had quite disarmed me. On the fourth day I went out to look for him; I peeped into all the taverns, to inquire for him—but no, Emelyanoushka was lost. 'Have you managed to keep yourself alive, Emelyanoushka?' I wondered. 'Perhaps he is lying dead under some hedge, poor drunkard, like a sodden log.' I went home more dead than alive. Next day I went out to look for him again. And I kept

cursing myself that I'd been such a fool as to let the man
go off by himself. On the fifth day it was a holiday—in the
early morning I heard the door creak. I looked up and there
was my Emelyanoushka coming in. His face was blue and
his hair was covered with dirt as though he'd been sleeping
in the street; he was as thin as a match. He took off his old
coat, sat down on the chest, and looked at me. I was delighted to see him, but I felt more upset about him than
ever. For you see, sir, if I'd been overtaken in some sin, as
true as I am here, sir, I'd have died like a dog before I'd
have come back. But Emelyanoushka did come back. And
a sad thing it was, sure enough, to see a man sunk so low.
I began to look after him, to talk kindly to him, to comfort
him.

" 'Well, Emelyanoushka,' said I, 'I am glad you've come
back. Had you been away much longer I should have gone
to look for you in the taverns again today. Are you hungry?'

" 'No, Astafy Ivanovitch.'

" 'Come, now, aren't you really? Here, brother, is some
cabbage soup left over from yesterday; there was meat in
it; it is good stuff. And here is some bread and onion. Come,
eat it, it'll do you no harm.'

"I made him eat it, and I saw at once that the man had
not tasted food for maybe three days—he was as hungry
as a wolf. So it was hunger that had driven him to me. My
heart was melted looking at the poor fellow. 'Let me run to
the tavern,' thought I, 'I'll get something to ease his heart,
and then we'll make an end of it. I've no more anger in my
heart against you, Emelyanoushka!' I brought him some
vodka. 'Here, Emelyan Ilyitch, let us have a drink for the
holiday. Like a drink? And it will do you good.' He held
out his hand, held it out greedily; he was just taking it, and
then he stopped himself. But a minute after, I saw him
take it, and lift it to his mouth, spilling it on his sleeve.
But though he got it to his lips, he set it down on the table
again.

" 'What is it, Emelyanoushka?'

" 'Nothing, Astafy Ivanovitch, I—sort of—'

" 'Won't you drink it?'

" 'Well, Astafy Ivanovitch, I'm not—sort of—going to drink any more, Astafy Ivanovitch.'

" 'Do you mean you've given it up altogether, Emelyanoushka, or are you only not going to drink today?'

"He did not answer. A minute later I saw him rest his head on his hand.

" 'What's the matter, Emelyanoushka, are you ill?'

" 'Why, yes, Astafy Ivanovitch, I don't feel well.'

"I took him and laid him down on the bed. I saw that he really was ill: his head was burning hot and he was shivering with fever. I sat by him all day; towards night he was worse. I mixed him some oil and onion and kvass and bread broken up.

" 'Come, eat some of this,' said I, 'and perhaps you'll be better.' He shook his head. 'No,' said he, 'I won't have any dinner today, Astafy Ivanovitch.'

"I made some tea for him; I quite flustered our old woman—he was no better. Well, thinks I, it's a bad outlook! The third morning I went for a medical gentleman. There was one I knew living close by, Kostopravov by name. I'd made his acquaintance when I was in service with the Bosomyagins; he'd attended me. The doctor came and looked at him. 'He's in a bad way,' said he, 'it was no use sending for me. But if you like I can give him a powder.' Well, I didn't give him a powder, I thought that's just the doctor's little game; and then the fifth day came.

"He lay, sir, dying before my eyes. I sat in the window with my work in my hands. The old woman was heating the stove. We were all silent. My heart was simply breaking over him, the good-for-nothing fellow; I felt as if it were a son of my own I was losing. I knew that Emelyanoushka was looking at me. I'd seen the man all the day long making up his mind to say something and not daring to.

"At last I looked up at him; I saw such misery in the poor fellow's eyes. He had kept them fixed on me, but when he saw that I was looking at him, he looked down at once.

" 'Astafy Ivanovitch.'

" 'What is it, Emelyanoushka?'

" 'If you were to take my old coat to a secondhand dealer's, how much do you think they'd give you for it, Astafy Ivanovitch?'

" 'There's no knowing how much they'd give. Maybe they would give me a rouble for it, Emelyan Ilyitch.'

"But if I had taken it, they wouldn't have given a farthing for it, but would have laughed in my face for bringing such a trumpery thing. I simply said that to comfort the poor fellow, knowing the simpleton he was.

" 'But I was thinking, Astafy Ivanovitch, they might give you three roubles for it; it's made of cloth, Astafy Ivanovitch. How could they give only one rouble for a cloth coat?'

" 'I don't know, Emelyan Ilyitch,' said I, 'if you are thinking of taking it, you should certainly ask three roubles to begin with.'

"Emelyanoushka was silent for a time, and then he addressed me again—

" 'Astafy Ivanovitch.'

" 'What is it, Emelyanoushka?' I asked.

" 'Sell my coat when I die, and don't bury me in it. I can lie as well without it; and it's a thing of some value—it might come in useful.'

"I can't tell you how it made my heart ache to hear him. I saw that the death agony was coming on him. We were silent again for a bit. So an hour passed by. I looked at him again: he was still staring at me, and when he met my eyes he looked down again.

" 'Do you want some water to drink, Emelyan Ilyitch?' I asked.

" 'Give me some, God bless you, Astafy Ivanovitch.'

"I gave him a drink.

" 'Thank you, Astafy Ivanovitch,' said he.

" 'Is there anything else you would like, Emelyanoushka?'

" 'No, Astafy Ivanovitch, there's nothing I want, but I —sort of—'

" 'What?'

" 'I only—'

" 'What is it, Emelyanoushka?'

" 'Those riding breeches—it was—sort of—I who took them—Astafy Ivanovitch.'

" 'Well, God forgive you, Emelyanoushka,' said I, 'you poor, sorrowful creature. Depart in peace.'

"And I was choking myself, sir, and the tears were in my eyes. I turned aside for a moment.

" 'Astafy Ivanovitch—'

"I saw Emelyanoushka wanted to tell me something; he was trying to sit up, trying to speak, and mumbling something. He flushed red all over suddenly, looked at me . . . then I saw him turn white again, whiter and whiter, and he seemed to sink away all in a minute. His head fell back, he drew one breath, and gave up his soul to God."

A Christmas Tree
and a Wedding

THE OTHER DAY I saw a wedding . . . but no, I had better
tell you about the Christmas tree. The wedding was nice, I
liked it very much; but the other incident was better.
I don't know how it was that, looking at that wedding, I
thought of that Christmas tree. This was what happened.
Just five years ago, on New Year's Eve, I was invited to a
children's party. The giver of the party was a well-known
and businesslike personage, with connections, with a large
circle of acquaintances, and a good many schemes on hand,
so that it may be supposed that this party was an excuse
for getting the parents together and discussing various interesting matters in an innocent, casual way. I was an outsider;
I had no interesting matter to contribute, and so I spent
the evening rather independently. There was another gentleman present who was, I fancied, of no special rank or
family, and who, like me, had simply turned up at this

family festivity. He was the first to catch my eye. He was a tall, lanky man, very grave and very correctly dressed. But one could see that he was in no mood for merrymaking and family festivity; whenever he withdrew into a corner he left off smiling and knitted his bushy black brows. He had not a single acquaintance in the party except his host. One could see that he was fearfully bored, but that he was valiantly keeping up the part of a man perfectly happy and enjoying himself. I learned afterwards that this was a gentleman from the provinces, who had a critical and perplexing piece of business in Petersburg, who had brought a letter of introduction to our host, for whom our host was, by no means con amore, using his interest, and whom he had invited, out of civility, to his children's party. He did not play cards, cigars were not offered him, every one avoided entering into conversation with him, most likely recognizing the bird from its feathers; and so my gentleman was forced to sit the whole evening stroking his whiskers simply to have something to do with his hands. His whiskers were certainly very fine. But he stroked them so zealously that, looking at him, one might have supposed that the whiskers were created first and the gentleman only attached to them in order to stroke them.

In addition to this individual who assisted in this way at our host's family festivity (he had five fat, well-fed boys), I was attracted, too, by another gentleman. But he was quite of a different sort. He was a personage. He was called Yulian Mastakovitch. From the first glance one could see that he was an honoured guest, and stood in the same relation to our host as our host stood in relation to the gentleman who was stroking his whiskers. Our host and hostess said no end of polite things to him, waited on him hand and foot, pressed him to drink, flattered him, brought their visitors up to be introduced to him, but did not take him to be introduced to any one else. I noticed that tears glistened in our host's eyes when he remarked about the party that he had rarely spent an evening so agreeably. I felt as it

were frightened in the presence of such a personage, and
so, after admiring the children, I went away into a little
parlour, which was quite empty, and sat down in an arbour
of flowers which filled up almost half the room.

The children were all incredibly sweet, and resolutely refused to model themselves on the "grown-ups," regardless
of all the admonitions of their governesses and mammas.
They stripped the Christmas tree to the last sweetmeat in
the twinkling of an eye, and had succeeded in breaking half
the playthings before they knew what was destined for
which. Particularly charming was a black-eyed, curly-headed
boy, who kept trying to shoot me with his wooden gun. But
my attention was still more attracted by his sister, a girl of
eleven, quiet, dreamy, pale, with big, prominent, dreamy
eyes, exquisite as a little Cupid. The children hurt her feelings in some way, and so she came away from them to the
same empty parlour in which I was sitting, and played with
her doll in the corner. The visitors respectfully pointed out
her father, a wealthy contractor, and some one whispered
that three hundred thousand roubles were already set aside
for her dowry. I turned round to glance at the group who
were interested in such a circumstance, and my eye fell on
Yulian Mastakovitch, who, with his hands behind his back
and his head on one side, was listening with the greatest
attention to these gentlemen's idle gossip. Afterwards I
could not help admiring the discrimination of the host and
hostess in the distribution of the children's presents. The
little girl, who had already a portion of three hundred
thousand roubles, received the costliest doll. Then followed
presents diminishing in value in accordance with the rank
of the parents of these happy children; finally, the child of
lowest degree, a thin, freckled, red-haired little boy of ten,
got nothing but a book of stories about the marvels of nature and tears of devotion, etc., without pictures or even
woodcuts. He was the son of a poor widow, the governess of
the children of the house, an oppressed and scared little
boy. He was dressed in a short jacket of inferior nankin.

After receiving his book he walked round the other toys for a long time; he longed to play with the other children, but did not dare; it was evident that he already felt and understood his position. I love watching children. Their first independent approaches to life are extremely interesting. I noticed that the red-haired boy was so fascinated by the costly toys of the other children, especially by a theatre in which he certainly longed to take some part, that he made up his mind to sacrifice his dignity. He smiled and began playing with the other children, he gave away his apple to a fat-faced little boy who had a mass of goodies tied up in a pocket-handkerchief already, and even brought himself to carry another boy on his back, simply not to be turned away from the theatre, but an insolent youth gave him a heavy thump a minute later. The child did not dare to cry. Then the governess, his mother, made her appearance, and told him not to interfere with the other children's playing. The boy went away to the same room in which was the little girl. She let him join her, and the two set to work very eagerly dressing the expensive doll.

I had been sitting more than half an hour in the ivy arbour, listening to the little prattle of the red-haired boy and the beauty with the dowry of three hundred thousand, who was nursing her doll, when Yulian Mastakovitch suddenly walked into the room. He had taken advantage of the general commotion following a quarrel among the children to step out of the drawing room. I had noticed him a moment before talking very cordially to the future heiress's papa, whose acquaintance he had just made, of the superiority of one branch of the service over another. Now he stood in hesitation and seemed to be reckoning something on his fingers.

"Three hundred . . . three hundred," he was whispering. "Eleven . . . twelve . . . thirteen," and so on. "Sixteen—five years! Supposing it is at four per cent—five times twelve is sixty; yes, to that sixty . . . well, in five years we may assume it will be four hundred. Yes! . . . But he won't stick to four per cent, the rascal. He can get eight or ten. Well, five hundred, let us say, five hundred at least . . . that's certain; well, say a little more for frills. H'm! . . ."

His hesitation was at an end, he blew his nose and was on the point of going out of the room when he suddenly glanced at the little girl and stopped short. He did not see me behind the pots of greenery. It seemed to me that he was greatly excited. Either his calculations had affected his imagination or something else, for he rubbed his hands and could hardly stand still. This excitement reached its utmost limit when he stopped and bent another resolute glance at the future heiress. He was about to move forward, but first looked round, then moving on tiptoe, as though he felt guilty, he advanced towards the children. He approached with a little smile, bent down and kissed her on the head. The child, not expecting this attack, uttered a cry of alarm.

"What are you doing here, sweet child?" he asked in a whisper, looking round and patting the girl's cheek.

"We are playing."

"Ah! With him?" Yulian Mastakovitch looked askance at the boy. "You had better go into the drawing room, my dear," he said to him.

The boy looked at him open-eyed and did not utter a word. Yulian Mastakovich looked round him again, and again bent down to the little girl.

"And what is this you've got—a dolly, dear child?" he asked.

"Yes, a dolly," answered the child, frowning, and a little shy.

"A dolly . . . and do you know, dear child, what your dolly is made of?"

"I don't know . . ." the child answered in a whisper, hanging her head.

"It's made of rags, darling. You had better go into the drawing room to your playmates, boy," said Yulian Mastakovitch, looking sternly at the boy. The boy and girl frowned and clutched at each other. They did not want to be separated.

"And do you know why they gave you that doll?" asked Yulian Mastakovitch, dropping his voice to a softer and softer tone.

"I don't know."

"Because you have been a sweet and well-behaved child all the week."

At this point Yulian Mastakovitch, more excited than ever, speaking in most dulcet tones, asked at last, in a hardly audible voice choked with emotion and impatience—

"And will you love me, dear little girl, when I come and see your papa and mamma?"

Saying this, Yulian Mastakovitch tried once more to kiss "the dear little girl," but the red-haired boy, seeing that the little girl was on the point of tears, clutched her hand and began whimpering from sympathy for her. Yulian Mastakovitch was angry in earnest.

"Go away, go away from here, go away!" he said to the boy. "Go into the drawing room! Go in there to your playmates!"

"No, he needn't, he needn't! You go away," said the little girl. "Leave him alone, leave him alone," she said, almost crying.

Some one made a sound at the door. Yulian Mastakovitch instantly raised his majestic person and took alarm. But the red-haired boy was even more alarmed than Yulian Mastakovitch; he abandoned the little girl and, slinking along by the wall, stole out of the parlour into the dining room. To avoid arousing suspicion, Yulian Mastakovitch, too, went into the dining room. He was as red as a lobster, and, glancing into the looking glass, seemed to be ashamed at himself. He was perhaps vexed with himself for his impetuosity and hastiness. Possibly, he was at first so much impressed by his calculations, so inspired and fascinated by them, that in spite of his seriousness and dignity he made up his mind to behave like a boy, and directly approach the object of his attentions, even though she could not be really the object of his attentions for another five years at least. I followed the estimable gentleman into the dining room and there beheld a strange spectacle. Yulian Mastakovitch, flushed with vexation and anger, was frightening the red-haired boy, who, retreating from him, did not know where to run in his terror.

"Go away; what are you doing here? Go away, you scamp; are you after the fruit here, eh? Get along, you naughty boy! Get along, you sniveller, to your playmates!"

The panic-stricken boy in his desperation tried creeping under the table. Then his persecutor, in a fury, took out his large batiste handkerchief and began flicking it under the table at the child, who kept perfectly quiet. It must be observed that Yulian Mastakovitch was a little inclined to be fat. He was a sleek, red-faced, solidly built man, paunchy, with thick legs; what is called a fine figure of a man, round as a nut. He was perspiring, breathless, and fearfully flushed. At last he was almost rigid, so great was his indignation and perhaps—who knows?—his jealousy. I burst into loud laughter. Yulian Mastakovitch turned round and, in spite of all his consequence, was overcome with confusion. At that moment from the opposite door our host came in. The boy crept out from under the table and wiped his elbows and his knees. Yulian Mastakovitch hastened to put to his nose the handkerchief which he was holding in his hand by one end.

Our host looked at the three of us in some perplexity; but as a man who knew something of life, and looked at it from a serious point of view, he at once availed himself of the chance of catching his visitor by himself.

"Here, this is the boy," he said, pointing to the red-haired boy, "for whom I had the honour to solicit your influence."

"Ah!" said Yulian Mastakovitch, who had hardly quite recovered himself.

"The son of my children's governess," said our host, in a tone of a petitioner, "a poor woman, the widow of an honest civil servant; and therefore . . . and therefore, Yulian Mastakovitch, if it were possible . . ."

"Oh, no, no!" Yulian Mastakovitch made haste to answer; "no, excuse me, Filip Alexyevitch, it's quite impossible. I've made inquiries; there's no vacancy, and if there were, there are twenty applicants who have far more claim than he. . . . I am very sorry, very sorry. . . ."

"What a pity," said our host. "He is a quiet, well-behaved boy."

"A great rascal, as I notice," answered Yulian Mastakovitch, with a nervous twist of his lip. "Get along, boy; why are you standing there? Go to your playmates," he said, addressing the child.

At that point he could not contain himself, and glanced at me out of one eye. I, too, could not contain myself, and laughed straight in his face. Yulian Mastakovitch turned away at once, and in a voice calculated to reach my ear, asked who was that strange young man? They whispered together and walked out of the room. I saw Yulian Mastakovitch afterwards shaking his head incredulously as our host talked to him.

After laughing to my heart's content I returned to the drawing room. There the great man, surrounded by fathers and mothers of families, including the host and hostess, was saying something very warmly to a lady to whom he had just been introduced. The lady was holding by the hand the little girl with whom Yulian Mastakovitch had had the scene in the parlour a little while before. Now he was launching into praises and raptures over the beauty, the talents, the grace, and the charming manners of the charming child. He was unmistakably making up to the mamma. The mother listened to him almost with tears of delight. The father's lips were smiling. Our host was delighted at the general satisfaction. All the guests, in fact, were sympathetically gratified; even the children's games were checked that they might not hinder the conversation: the whole atmosphere was saturated with reverence. I heard afterwards

the mamma of the interesting child, deeply touched, beg
Yulian Mastakovitch, in carefully chosen phrases, to do her
the special honour of bestowing upon them the precious
gift of his acquaintance, and heard with what unaffected
delight Yulian Mastakovitch accepted the invitation, and
how afterwards the guests, dispersing in different directions,
moving away with the greatest propriety, poured out to one
another the most touchingly flattering comments upon the
contractor, his wife, his little girl, and, above all, upon
Yulian Mastakovitch.

"Is that gentleman married?" I asked, almost aloud, of
one of my acquaintances, who was standing nearest to
Yulian Mastakovitch. Yulian Mastakovitch flung a searching and vindictive glance at me.

"No!" answered my acquaintance, chagrined to the bottom of his heart by the awkwardness of which I had in-
tentionally been guilty. . . .

I passed lately by a certain church; I was struck by the
crowd of people in carriages. I heard people talking of the
wedding. It was a cloudy day, it was beginning to sleet. I
made my way through the crowd at the door and saw the
bridegroom. He was a sleek, well-fed, round, paunchy man,
very gorgeously dressed up. He was running fussily about,
giving orders. At last the news passed through the crowd
that the bride was coming. I squeezed my way through the
crowd and saw a marvellous beauty, who could scarcely have
reached her first season. But the beauty was pale and melancholy. She looked preoccupied; I even fancied that her
eyes were red with recent weeping. The classic severity of
every feature of her face gave a certain dignity and seriousness to her beauty. But through that sternness and dignity,
through that melancholy, could be seen the look of childish
innocence; something indescribably naïve, fluid, youthful,
which seemed mutely begging for mercy.

People were saying that she was only just sixteen. Glancing attentively at the bridegroom, I suddenly recognized

him as Yulian Mastakovitch, whom I had not seen for five years. I looked at her. My God! I began to squeeze my way as quickly as I could out of the church. I heard people saying in the crowd that the bride was an heiress, that she had a dowry of five hundred thousand . . . and a trousseau worth ever so much.

"It was a good stroke of business, though!" I thought as I made my way into the street.

Guy de Maupassant

[1850 — 1893]

"I HAVE COVETED everything and taken pleasure from nothing" says Maupassant's epitaph written by himself. He sought and won money, fame, and women but ended his life in a madhouse, his once handsome body destroyed by syphilis. The reading public, moreover, has taken the intensest pleasure in his mediocre short stories, like the trick-ending "Necklace" and the erotic jokes "That Pig Morin" and "The Signal." His best stories and his two excellent novels—A Woman's Life (1883) and Pierre and Jean (1888)—have too often been ignored. W. Somerset Maugham is the twentieth century's leading popularizer of the Maupassant type of story.

Initially Maupassant seemed destined to be a poet. But he could not escape France's rich heritage of storytelling, as seen in the medieval fabliau, with its robust, earthy humor, and the many oral tales of his native Normandy told by peasants with whom he mingled. He learned most from his mother, a good raconteur, who also encouraged him to read Shakespeare, whose rural descriptions made Maupassant even more conscious of the Normandy he loved. Later when he turned to writing fiction his stories laid in Italy and North Africa were distinct failures; like Dostoevsky he craved and needed the inspiration of his own native soil.

Yet Maupassant's home life was far from inspiring; it helped to make him a lifelong cynic. His parents, well-to-do bour-

73

geoisie, married in 1846, and Guy was born four years later in a village outside Dieppe. Their marriage disintegrated quickly, and 15 years later, they separated. To young Maupassant his father was the villain and his mother the wronged one. This incompatibility became important to his later fiction; he seemed to revenge himself on his father by choosing cuckoldry as one of his favorite themes. His rebellion and anxiety to shock turned elsewhere. He inherited this trait from his mother—a bohemian for her times—who smoked cigarettes, talked in agnostic terms, and wore short dresses. Studying in a Paris lycée at 9 and a seminary at Yvetot at 13, he read Rousseau as a welcome relief from the world of piety, and was expelled from the seminary for mocking a lecture by a holy father and for writing an "indecent" poem on marriage. Given extraordinary freedom by his mother, he became an idler. This freedom later wrecked him, making him even more cynical of love, of men and women.

It was Flaubert who saved Guy from a life of dissipation and turned his energies toward art. He firmly believed young Maupassant to have a great future as a poet; but at 23 his protégé gave up narrative poetry for fiction, probably because short stories were more easily salable to the newspapers. Sunday lunches with Flaubert convinced Maupassant that talent was a "long patience," and he went through a seven-year training period. Flaubert made him aware of many things. "If you have any originality . . . you must . . . bring it out; if you have not, you must acquire it." He also made him more conscious of a simple, rhythmic style, visual imagery, impersonality, and irony; he encouraged him to be independent of schools of writing like realism and naturalism.

There were other influences which affected the talent of Maupassant. His association with poetry made him doubly aware of the importance of a lucid style. His work for the newspapers became proving grounds for his anecdotes, which he eventually developed into stories full of sardonic wit and ribaldry. Readings in the philosophies of Herbert Spencer and Schopenhauer intensified his cynical view of life, though his service as a private in the Franco-Prussian War of 1870 made him almost fanatic in his devotion toward humiliated France. Following the war, his post as a government clerk gave him deeper insight into the bourgeoisie he was to mirror in his fiction.

In 1880 Maupassant contributed one of his earliest stories, "Boule de Suif," to Zola's collection, Les Soirées de Médan. Flaubert and the reading public instantly recognized the tale as "the work of a master." During the next 11 years Maupassant produced other classics among his 300 short stories.

Though widely read for his so-called immoral stories, Maupassant is really a moralist. Many of his tales, which seem spontaneously written and overly simple, draw upon the seven deadly sins—pride, covetousness, lust, anger, gluttony, envy, sloth—and show by a concealed psychology how the peasants, the bourgeoisie, the aristocracy fall far short of proper human conduct. With irony and satiric humor, Maupassant fills his compact tales with the sights, the sounds, and smells of the city and the town; and while his cynicism is unmistakable, there are clear evidences of compassion for the hard lot of humanity.

The Piece of String

ALONG ALL THE roads around Goderville the peasants and
their wives were coming toward the burgh because it was
market day. The men were proceeding with slow steps, the
whole body bent forward at each movement of their long
twisted legs, deformed by their hard work, by the weight
on the plow which, at the same time, raised the left shoulder and swerved the figure, by the reaping of the wheat
which made the knees spread to make a firm "purchase," by
all the slow and painful labors of the country. Their blouses,
blue, "stiff-starched," shining as if varnished, ornamented
with a little design in white at the neck and wrists, puffed
about their bony bodies, seemed like balloons ready to carry
them off. From each of them a head, two arms, and two
feet protruded.

Some led a cow or a calf by a cord, and their wives, walking behind the animal, whipped its haunches with a leafy
branch to hasten its progress. They carried large baskets on
their arms from which, in some cases, chickens and, in
others, ducks thrust out their heads. And they walked with

From *The Best Stories of Guy de Maupassant*, selected, with an introduction, by Saxe Commins. Copyright 1945 by Random House, Inc.

a quicker, livelier step than their husbands. Their spare straight figures were wrapped in a scanty little shawl, pinned over their flat bosoms, and their heads were enveloped in a white cloth glued to the hair and surmounted by a cap.

Then a wagon passed at the jerky trot of a nag, shaking strangely, two men seated side by side and a woman in the bottom of the vehicle, the latter holding on to the sides to lessen the hard jolts.

In the public square of Goderville there was a crowd, a throng of human beings and animals mixed together. The horns of the cattle, the tall hats with long nap of the rich peasants, and the headgear of the peasant women rose above the surface of the assembly. And the clamorous, shrill, screaming voices made a continuous and savage din which sometimes was dominated by the robust lungs of some countryman's laugh, or the long lowing of a cow tied to the wall of a house.

All that smacked of the stable, the dairy and the dirt heap, hay and sweat, giving forth that unpleasant odor, human and animal, peculiar to the people of the field.

Maître Hauchecome, of Breaute, had just arrived at Goderville, and he was directing his steps toward the public square, when he perceived upon the ground a little piece of string. Maître Hauchecome, economical like a true Norman, thought that everything useful ought to be picked up, and he bent painfully, for he suffered from rheumatism. He took the bit of thin cord from the ground and began to roll it carefully when he noticed Maître Malandain, the harness-maker, on the threshold of his door, looking at him. They had heretofore had business together on the subject of a halter, and they were on bad terms, being both good haters. Maître Hauchecome was seized with a sort of shame to be seen thus by his enemy, picking a bit of string out of the dirt. He concealed his "find" quickly under his blouse, then in his trousers' pocket; then he pretended to be still looking on the ground for something which he did not find, and he went toward the market, his head forward, bent double by his pains.

He was soon lost in the noisy and slowly moving crowd, which was busy with interminable bargainings. The peasants milked, went and came, perplexed, always in fear of being cheated, not daring to decide, watching the vender's eye, ever trying to find the trick in the man and the flaw in the beast.

The women, having placed their great baskets at their feet, had taken out the poultry which lay upon the ground, tied together by the feet, with terrified eyes and scarlet crests.

They heard offers, stated their prices with a dry air and impassive face, or perhaps, suddenly deciding on some proposed reduction, shouted to the customer who was slowly going away: "All right, Maître Authirne, I'll give it to you for that."

Then little by little the square was deserted, and the Angelus ringing at noon, those who had stayed too long scattered to their shops.

At Jourdain's the great room was full of people eating, as the big court was full of vehicles of all kinds, carts, gigs, wagons, dump carts, yellow with dirt, mended and patched, raising their shafts to the sky like two arms, or perhaps with their shafts in the ground and their backs in the air.

Just opposite the diners seated at the table, the immense fireplace, filled with bright flames, cast a lively heat on the backs of the row on the right. Three spits were turning on which were chickens, pigeons, and legs of mutton; and an appetizing odor of roast beef and gravy dripping over the nicely browned skin rose from the hearth, increased the jovialness, and made everybody's mouth water.

All the aristocracy of the plow ate there, at Maître Jourdain's, tavern keeper and horse dealer, a rascal who had money.

The dishes were passed and emptied, as were the jugs of

yellow cider. Everyone told his affairs, his purchases, and sales. They discussed the crops. The weather was favorable for the green things but not for the wheat.

Suddenly the drum beat in the court, before the house. Everybody rose, except a few indifferent persons, and ran to the door, or to the windows, their mouths still full and napkins in their hands.

After the public crier had ceased his drum-beating, he called out in a jerky voice, speaking his phrases irregularly:

"It is hereby made known to the inhabitants of Goderville, and in general to all persons present at the market, that there was lost this morning, on the road to Benzeville, between nine and ten o'clock, a black leather pocketbook containing five hundred francs and some business papers. The finder is requested to return same with all haste to the mayor's office or to Maître Fortune Houlbreque of Manneville; there will be twenty francs' reward."

Then the man went away. The heavy roll of the drum and the crier's voice were again heard at a distance.

Then they began to talk of this event, discussing the chances that Maître Houlbreque had of finding or not finding his pocketbook.

And the meal concluded. They were finishing their coffee when a chief of the gendarmes appeared upon the threshold.

He inquired:

"Is Maître Hauchecome, of Breaute, here?"

Maître Hauchecome, seated at the other end of the table, replied:

"Here I am."

And the officer resumed:

"Maître Hauchecome, will you have the goodness to accompany me to the mayor's office? The mayor would like to talk to you."

The peasant, surprised and disturbed, swallowed at a draught his tiny glass of brandy, rose, and, even more bent than in the morning, for the first steps after each rest were especially difficult, set out, repeating: "Here I am, here I am."

The mayor was awaiting him, seated on an armchair. He was the notary of the vicinity, a stout, serious man, with pompous phrases.

"Maître Hauchecome," said he, "you were seen this morning to pick up, on the road to Benzeville, the pocketbook lost by Maître Houlbreque, of Manneville."

The countryman, astounded, looked at the mayor, already terrified by this suspicion resting on him without his knowing why.

"Me? Me? Me pick up the pocketbook?"

"Yes, you, yourself."

"Word of honor, I never heard of it."

"But you were seen."

"I was seen, me? Who says he saw me?"

"Monsieur Malandain, the harness-maker."

The old man remembered, understood, and flushed with anger.

"Ah, he saw me, the clodhopper, he saw me pick up this string, here, M'sieu' the Mayor." And rummaging in his pocket he drew out the little piece of string.

But the mayor, incredulous, shook his head.

"You will not make me believe, Maître Hauchecome, that Monsieur Malandain, who is a man worthy of credence, mistook this cord for a pocketbook."

The peasant, furious, lifted his hand, spat at one side to attest his honor, repeating:

"It is nevertheless the truth of the good God, the sacred truth, M'sieu' the Mayor. I repeat it on my soul and my salvation."

The mayor resumed:

"After picking up the object, you stood like a stilt, looking a long while in the mud to see if any piece of money had fallen out."

The good old man choked with indignation and fear.

"How anyone can tell—how anyone can tell—such lies

to take away an honest man's reputation! How can anyone—"

There was no use in his protesting; nobody believed him.
He was confronted with Monsieur Malandain, who repeated and maintained his affirmation. They abused each
other for an hour. At his own request, Maître Hauchecome
was searched; nothing was found on him.

Finally the mayor, very much perplexed, discharged him
with the warning that he would consult the public prose-
cutor and ask for further orders.

The news had spread. As he left the mayor's office, the
old man was surrounded and questioned with a serious or
bantering curiosity, in which there was no indignation. He
began to tell the story of the string. No one believed him.
They laughed at him.

He went along, stopping his friends, beginning endlessly
his statements and his protestations, showing his pockets
turned inside out, to prove that he had nothing.

They said:

"Old rascal, get out!"

And he grew angry, becoming exasperated, hot and distressed at not being believed, not knowing what to do and
always repeating himself.

Night came. He must depart. He started on his way with
three neighbors to whom he pointed out the place where
he had picked up the bit of string; and all along the road
he spoke of his adventure.

In the evening he took a turn in the village of Breaute,
in order to tell it to everybody. He only met with incre-
dulity.

It made him ill at night.

The next day about one o'clock in the afternoon, Marius
Paumelle, a hired man in the employ of Maître Breton,
husbandman at Ymanville, returned the pocketbook and its
contents to Maître Houlbreque of Manneville.

This man claimed to have found the object in the road;
but not knowing how to read, he had carried it to the house

and given it to his employer.

The news spread through the neighborhood. Maître Hauchecome was informed of it. He immediately went the circuit and began to recount his story completed by the happy climax. He was in triumph.

"What grieved me so much was not the thing itself, as the lying. There is nothing so shameful as to be placed under a cloud on account of a lie."

He talked of his adventure all day long; he told it on the highway to people who were passing by, in the wineshop to people who were drinking there, and to persons coming out of church the following Sunday. He stopped strangers to tell them about it. He was calm now, and yet something disturbed him without his knowing exactly what it was. People had the air of joking while they listened. They did not seem convinced. He seemed to feel that remarks were being made behind his back.

On Tuesday of the next week he went to the market at Goderville, urged solely by the necessity he felt of discussing the case.

Malandain, standing at his door, began to laugh on seeing him pass. Why?

He approached a farmer from Crequetot, who did not let him finish, and giving him a thump in the stomach said to his face:

"You big rascal."

Then he turned his back on him.

Maître Hauchecome was confused; why was he called a big rascal?

When he was seated at the table in Jourdain's tavern he commenced to explain "the affair."

A horse dealer from Monvilliers called to him:

"Come, come, old sharper, that's an old trick; I know all about your piece of string!"

Hauchecome stammered:

"But the pocketbook was found."

But the other man replied:

"Shut up, papa, there is one that finds, and there is one that reports. At any rate you are mixed with it."

The peasant stood choking. He understood. They accused him of having had the pocketbook returned by a confederate, by an accomplice.

He tried to protest. All the table began to laugh.

He could not finish his dinner and went away in the midst of jeers.

He went home ashamed and indignant, choking with anger and confusion, the more dejected that he was capable with his Norman cunning of doing what they had accused him of, and even boasting of it as of a good turn. His innocence to him, in a confused way, was impossible to prove, as his sharpness was known. And he was stricken to the heart by the injustice of the suspicion.

Then he began to recount the adventures again, prolonging his history every day, adding each time new reasons, more energetic protestations, more solemn oaths which he imagined and prepared in his hours of solitude, his whole mind given up to the story of the string. He was believed so much the less as his defense was more complicated and his arguing more subtile.

"Those are lying excuses," they said behind his back.

He felt it, consumed his heart over it, and wore himself out with useless efforts. He wasted away before their very eyes.

The wags now made him tell about the string to amuse them, as they make a soldier who has been on a campaign tell about his battles. His mind, touched to the depth, began to weaken.

Toward the end of December he took to his bed.

He died in the first days of January, and in the delitium of his death struggles he kept claiming his innocence, reiterating:

"A piece of string, a piece of string—look—here it is, M'sieu' the Mayor."

Madame Tellier's Excursion

MEN WENT THERE every evening at about eleven o'clock, just as they went to the café. Six or eight of them used to meet there; always the same set, not fast men, but respectable tradesmen, and young men in government or some other employ; and they used to drink their Chartreuse, and tease the girls, or else they would talk seriously with Madame, whom everybody respected, and then would go home at twelve o'clock! The younger men would sometimes stay the night.

It was a small, comfortable house, at the corner of a street behind Saint Etienne's church. From the windows one could see the docks, full of ships which were being unloaded, and on the hill the old, gray chapel, dedicated to the Virgin.

Madame, who came of a respectable family of peasant proprietors in the department of the Eure, had taken up her profession, just as she would have become a milliner or dressmaker. The prejudice against prostitution, which is so violent and deeply rooted in large towns, does not exist in the country places in Normandy. The peasant simply

From *The Best Stories of Guy de Maupassant*, selected, with an introduction, by Saxe Commins. Copyright 1945 by Random House, Inc.

says: "It is a paying business," and sends his daughter to keep a harem of fast girls, just as he would send her to keep a girls' school.

She had inherited the house from an old uncle, to whom it had belonged. Monsieur and Madame, who had formerly been innkeepers near Yvetot, had immediately sold their house, as they thought that the business at Fécamp was more profitable. They arrived one fine morning to assume the direction of the enterprise, which was declining on account of the absence of a head. They were good people enough in their way, and soon made themselves liked by their staff and their neighbors.

Monsieur died of apoplexy two years later, for as his new profession kept him in idleness and without exercise, he had grown excessively stout, and his health had suffered. Since Madame had been a widow, all the frequenters of the establishment had wanted her; but people said that personally she was quite virtuous, and even the girls in the house could not discover anything against her. She was tall, stout, and affable, and her complexion, which had become pale in the dimness of her house, the shutters of which were scarcely ever opened, shone as if it had been varnished. She had a fringe of curly, false hair, which gave her a juvenile look, which in turn contrasted strongly with her matronly figure. She was always smiling and cheerful, and was fond of a joke, but there was a shade of reserve about her which her new occupation had not quite made her lose. Coarse words always shocked her, and when any young fellow who had been badly brought up called her establishment by its right name, she was angry and disgusted.

In a word, she had a refined mind, and although she treated her women as friends, yet she very frequently used to say that she and they were not made of the same stuff.

Sometimes during the week she would hire a carriage and take some of her girls into the country, where they used to enjoy themselves on the grass by the side of the little river. They behaved like a lot of girls let out from a school, and

used to run races, and play childish games. They would
have a cold dinner on the grass, and drink cider, and go
home at night with a delicious feeling of fatigue, and in the
carriage kiss Madame as a kind mother who was full of
goodness and complaisance.

The house had two entrances. At the corner there was a
sort of low café, which sailors and the lower orders frequented at night, and she had two girls whose special duty
it was to attend to that part of the business. With the as-
sistance of the waiter, whose name was Frederic, and who
was a short, light-haired, beardless fellow, as strong as a
horse, they set the half bottles of wine and the jugs of beer
on the shaky marble tables and then, sitting astride on the
customers' knees, would urge them to drink.

The three other girls (there were only five in all) formed
a kind of aristocracy, and were reserved for the company on
the first floor, unless they were wanted downstairs, and
there was nobody on the first floor. The salon of Jupiter,
where the tradesmen used to meet, was papered in blue,
and embellished with a large drawing representing Leda
stretched out under the swan. That room was reached by a
winding staircase, which ended at a narrow door opening
on to the street, and above it, all night long a little lamp
burned, behind wire bars, such as one still sees in some
towns, at the foot of the shrine of some saint.

The house, which was old and damp, rather smelled of
mildew. At times there was an odor of eau de Cologne in
the passages, or a half-open door downstairs allowed the
noise of the common men sitting and drinking downstairs
to reach the first floor, much to the disgust of the gentlemen
who were there. Madame, who was quite familiar with
those of her customers with whom she was on friendly
terms, did not leave the salon. She took much interest in
what was going on in the town, and they regularly told her
all the news. Her serious conversation was a change from
the ceaseless chatter of the three women; it was a rest from
the doubtful jokes of those stout individuals who every eve-

ning indulged in the commonplace amusement of drinking a glass of liquor in company with girls of easy virtue.

The names of the girls on the first floor were Fernande, Raphaelle, and Rosa "the Jade." As the staff was limited, Madame had endeavored that each member of it should be a pattern, an epitome of each feminine type, so that every customer might find, as nearly as possible, the realization of his ideal. Fernande represented the handsome blonde; she was very tall, rather fat, and lazy; a country girl, who could not get rid of her freckles, and whose short, light, almost colorless, tow-like hair, which was like combed-out flax, barely covered her head.

Raphaelle, who came from Marseilles, played the indispensable part of the handsome Jewess. She was thin, with high cheek-bones covered with rouge, and her black hair, which was always covered with pomatum, curled on to her forehead. Her eyes would have been handsome, if the right one had not had a speck in it. Her Roman nose came down over a square jaw, where two false upper teeth contrasted strangely with the bad color of the rest.

Rosa the Jade was a little roll of fat, nearly all stomach, with very short legs. From morning till night she sang songs, which were alternately indecent or sentimental, in a harsh voice, told silly, interminable tales, and only stopped talking in order to eat, or left off eating in order to talk. She was never still, was as active as a squirrel, in spite of her fat and her short legs; and her laugh, which was a torrent of shrill cries, resounded here and there, ceaselessly, in a bedroom, in the loft, in the café, everywhere, and always about nothing.

The two women on the ground floor were Louise, who was nicknamed "la Cocotte," and Flora, whom they called "Balançière," because she limped a little. The former always dressed as Liberty, with a tricolored sash, and the other as a Spanish woman, with a string of copper coins, which jingled at every step she took, in her carroty hair. Both looked like cooks dressed up for the carnival, and were like all other women of the lower orders, neither uglier nor better looking than they usually are. In fact they looked just like servants at an inn, and were generally called "the Two Pumps."

A jealous peace, very rarely disturbed, reigned among these five women, thanks to Madame's conciliatory wisdom and to her constant good humor; and the establishment, which was the only one of the kind in the little town, was very much frequented. Madame had succeeded in giving it such a respectable appearance; she was so amiable and obliging to everybody, her good heart was so well known, that she was treated with a certain amount of consideration. The regular customers spent money on her, and were delighted when she was especially friendly toward them. When they met during the day, they would say: "This evening, you know where," just as men say: "At the café, after dinner." In a word Madame Tellier's house was somewhere to go to, and her customers very rarely missed their daily meetings there.

One evening, toward the end of May, the first arrival, Monsieur Poulin, who was a timber merchant, and had been mayor, found the door shut. The little lantern behind the grating was not alight; there was not a sound in the house; everything seemed dead. He knocked, gently at first, and then more loudly, but nobody answered the door. Then he went slowly up the street, and when he got to the market place, he met Monsieur Duvert, the gun-maker, who was going to the same place, so they went back together, but did not meet with any better success. But suddenly they heard a loud noise close to them, and on going round the corner of the house, they saw a number of English and French sailors, who were hammering at the closed shutters of the café with their fists.

The two tradesmen immediately made their escape, for fear of being compromised, but a low *Pst* stopped them; it was Monsieur Tournevau, the fish-curer, who had recognized them, and was trying to attract their attention. They told him what had happened, and he was all the more vexed at it, as he, a married man, and father of a family, only went there on Saturdays—*securitatis causa*, as he said, alluding to a measure of sanitary policy, which his friend Doctor Borde had advised him to observe. That was his regular evening, and now he would be deprived of it for the whole week.

The three men went as far as the quay together, and on the way they met young Monsieur Philippe, the banker's son, who frequented the place regularly, and Monsieur Pinipesse, the collector. They all returned to the Rue aux Juifs together, to make a last attempt. But the exasperated sailors were besieging the house, throwing stones at the shutters, and shouting, and the five first-floor customers went away as quickly as possible, and walked aimlessly about the streets.

Presently they met Monsieur Dupuis, the insurance agent, and then Monsieur Vassi, the Judge of the Tribunal of Commerce, and they all took a long walk, going to the pier first of all. There they sat down in a row on the granite parapet, and watched the rising tide, and when the promenaders had sat there for some time, Monsieur Tournevau said: "This is not very amusing!"

"Decidedly not," Monsieur Pinipesse replied, and they started off to walk again.

After going through the street on the top of the hill, they returned over the wooden bridge which crosses the Retenue, passed close to the railway, and came out again on to the market place, when suddenly a quarrel arose between Monsieur Pinipesse and Monsieur Tournevau, about an edible fungus which one of them declared he had found in the neighborhood.

As they were out of temper already from annoyance, they would very probably have come to blows, if the others had not interfered. Monsieur Pinipesse went off furious, and soon another altercation arose between the ex-mayor, Monsieur Poulin, and Monsieur Dupuis, the insurance agent, on the subject of the tax-collector's salary, and the profits which he might make. Insulting remarks were freely passing between them, when a torrent of formidable cries were heard, and the body of sailors, who were tired of waiting so long outside a closed house, came into the square. They were walking arm-in-arm, two and two, and formed a long procession, and were shouting furiously. The landsmen went and hid themselves under a gateway, and the yelling crew disappeared in the direction of the abbey. For a long time they still heard the noise, which diminished like a storm in the distance, and then silence was restored. Monsieur Poulin and Monsieur Dupuis, who were enraged at each other, went in different directions, without wishing each other good-bye.

The other four set off again, and instinctively went in the direction of Madame Tellier's establishment, which was still closed, silent, impenetrable. A quiet, but obstinate, drunken man was knocking at the door of the *café*; then he stopped and called Frederic, the waiter, in a low voice, but finding that he got no answer, he sat down on the doorstep, and awaited the course of events.

The others were just going to retire, when the noisy band of sailors reappeared at the end of the street. The French sailors were shouting the "Marseillaise," and the Englishmen, "Rule Britannia." There was a general lurching against the wall, and then the drunken brutes went on their way toward the quay, where a fight broke out between the two nations, in the course of which an Englishman had his arm broken, and a Frenchman his nose split.

The drunken man, who had stopped outside the door, was crying by this time, as drunken men and children cry when they are vexed, and the others went away. By degrees, calm was restored in the noisy town; here and there at moments, the distant sound of voices could be heard, only to die away in the distance.

One man was still wandering about, Monsieur Tournevau, the fish-curer, who was vexed at having to wait until the next Saturday. He hoped for something to turn up, he did not know what; but he was exasperated at the police for thus allowing an establishment of such public utility, which they had under their control, to be thus closed.

He went back to it, examined the walls, and tried to find out the reason. On the shutter he saw a notice stuck up, so he struck a wax vesta, and read the following, in a large, uneven hand: "Closed on Account of the Confirmation."

Then he went away, as he saw it was useless to remain, and left the drunken man lying on the pavement fast asleep, outside the inhospitable door.

The next day, all the regular customers, one after the other, found some reason for going through the Rue aux Juifs with a bundle of papers under their arm, to keep them in countenance, and with a furtive glance they all read that mysterious notice:

CLOSED ON ACCOUNT OF THE CONFIRMATION.

II

Madame had a brother, who was a carpenter in their native place, Virville, in the department of Eure. When Madame had still kept the inn at Yvetot, she had stood godmother to that brother's daughter, who had received the name of Constance, Constance Rivet; she herself being a Rivet on her father's side. The carpenter, who knew that his sister was in a good position, did not lose sight of her, although they did not meet often, as they were both kept at home by their occupations, and lived a long way from each other. But when the girl was twelve years old, and about to be confirmed, he seized the opportunity to write to his sister, and ask her to come and be present at the ceremony. Their old parents were dead, and as Madame could not well refuse, she accepted the invitation. Her brother, whose name was Joseph, hoped that by dint of showing his sister attentions, she might be induced to make her will in the girl's favor, as she had no children of her own.

His sister's occupation did not trouble his scruples in the least, and, besides, nobody knew anything about it at Virville. When they spoke of her, they only said: "Madame Tellier is living at Fécamp," which might mean that she was living on her own private income. It was quite twenty leagues from Fécamp to Virville, and for a peasant, twenty leagues on land are more than is crossing the ocean to an educated person. The people at Virville had never been further than Rouen, and nothing attracted the people from Fécamp to a village of five hundred houses, in the middle of a plain, and situated in another department. At any rate, nothing was known about her business.

But the confirmation was coming on and Madame was in great embarrassment. She had no under-mistress, and did not at all dare to leave her house, even for a day. She feared the rivalries between the girls upstairs and those downstairs would certainly break out; that Frederic would get drunk, for when he was in that state, he would knock anybody down for a mere word. At last, however, she made up her mind to take them all with her, with the exception of the man, to whom she gave a holiday, until the next day but one.

When she asked her brother, he made no objection, but undertook to put them all up for a night. So on Saturday morning the eight o'clock express carried off Madame and her companions in a second-class carriage. As far as Beuzeille they were alone, and chattered like magpies, but at that station a couple got in. The man, an aged peasant dressed in a blue blouse with a folding collar, wide sleeves tight at the wrist, and ornamented with white embroidery, wore an old high hat with long nap. He held an enormous green umbrella in one hand, and a large basket in the other, from which the heads of three frightened ducks protruded.

The woman, who sat stiffly in her rustic finery, had a face like a fowl, and with a nose that was as pointed as a bill. She sat down opposite her husband and did not stir, as she was startled at finding herself in such smart company.

There was certainly an array of striking colors in the carriage. Madame was dressed in blue silk from head to foot, and had over her dress a dazzling red shawl of imitation French cashmere. Fernande was panting in a Scottish plaid dress, whose bodice, which her companions had laced as tight as they could, had forced up her falling bosom into a double dome, that was continually heaving up and down, and which seemed liquid beneath the material. Raphaelle, with a bonnet covered with feathers, so that it looked like a nest full of birds, had on a lilac dress with gold spots on it; there was something Oriental about it that suited her Jewish face. Rosa the Jade had on a pink petticoat with large flounces, and looked like a very fat child, an obese dwarf; while the Two Pumps looked as if they had cut their dresses out of old, flowered curtains, dating from the Restoration.

Perceiving that they were no longer alone in the compartment, the ladies put on staid looks, and began to talk of subjects which might give the others a high opinion of them. But at Bolbec a gentleman with light whiskers, with a gold chain, and wearing two or three rings, got in, and put several parcels wrapped in oil cloth into the net over his head. He looked inclined for a joke, and a good-natured fellow.

"Are you ladies changing your quarters?" he asked. The question embarrassed them all considerably. Madame, however, quickly recovered her composure, and said sharply, to avenge the honor of her corps:

"I think you might try to be polite!"

He excused himself, and said: "I beg your pardon, I ought to have said your nunnery."

As Madame could not think of a retort, or perhaps as

she thought herself justified sufficiently, she gave him a dignified bow, and pinched in her lips.

Then the gentleman, who was sitting between Rosa the Jade and the old peasant, began to wink knowingly at the ducks, whose heads were sticking out of the basket. When he felt that he had fixed the attention of his public, he began to tickle them under their bills, and spoke funnily to them, to make the company smile.

"We have left our little pond, qu-ack! qu-ack! to make the acquaintance of the little spit, qu-ack! qu-ack!"

The unfortunate creatures turned their necks away to avoid his caresses, and made desperate efforts to get out of their wicker prison, and then, suddenly, all at once, uttered the most lamentable quacks of distress. The women exploded with laughter. They leaned forward and pushed each other, so as to see better; they were very much interested in the ducks, and the gentleman redoubled his airs, his wit, and his teasing.

Rosa joined in, and leaning over her neighbor's legs, she kissed the three animals on the head. Immediately all the girls wanted to kiss them in turn, and the gentleman took them on to his knees, made them jump up and down and pinched them. The two peasants, who were even in greater consternation than their poultry, rolled their eyes as if they were possessed, without venturing to move, and their old wrinkled faces had not a smile nor a movement.

Then the gentleman, who was a commercial traveler, offered the ladies braces by way of a joke and taking up one of his packages, he opened it. It was a trick, for the parcel contained garters. There were blue silk, pink silk, red silk, violet silk, mauve silk garters, and the buckles were made of two gilt metal Cupids, embracing each other. The girls uttered exclamations of delight, and looked at them with that gravity which is natural to a woman when she is hankering after a bargain. They consulted one another by their looks or in a whisper, and replied in the same manner, and

Madame was longingly handling a pair of orange garters that were broader and more imposing than the rest; really fit for the mistress of such an establishment.

"Come, my kittens," he said, "you must try them on."

There was a torrent of exclamations, and they squeezed their petticoats between their legs, as if they thought he was going to ravish them, but he quietly waited his time, and said: "Well, if you will not, I shall pack them up again."

And he added cunningly: "I offer any pair they like, to those who will try them on."

But they would not, and sat up very straight, and looked dignified.

But the Two Pumps looked so distressed that he renewed the offer to them. Flora especially hesitated, and he pressed her:

"Come, my dear, a little courage! Just look at that lilac pair; it will suit your dress admirably."

That decided her, and pulling up her dress she showed a thick leg fit for a milk-maid, in a badly fitting, coarse stocking. The commercial traveler stooped down and fastened the garter below the knee first of all and then above it; and he tickled the girl gently, which made her scream and jump. When he had done, he gave her the lilac pair, and asked: "Who next?"

"I! I!" they all shouted at once, and he began on Rosa the Jade, who uncovered a shapeless, round thing without any ankle, a regular "sausage of a leg," as Raphaelle used to say.

The commercial traveler complimented Fernande, and grew quite enthusiastic over her powerful columns.

The thin tibias of the handsome Jewess met with less flattery, and Louise Cocotte, by way of a joke, put her petticoats over the man's head, so that Madame was obliged to interfere to check such unseemly behavior.

Lastly, Madame herself put out her leg, a handsome,

muscular, Norman leg, and in his surprise and pleasure the commercial traveler gallantly took off his hat to salute that master calf, like a true French cavalier.

The two peasants, who were speechless from surprise, looked askance, out of the corners of their eyes. They looked so exactly like fowls, that the man with the light whiskers, when he sat up, said "Co—co—ri—co," under their very noses, and that gave rise to another storm of amusement.

The old people got out at Motteville, with their basket, their ducks, and their umbrella, and they heard the woman say to her husband, as they went away:

"They are sluts, who are off to that cursed place, Paris."

The funny commercial traveler himself got out at Rouen, after behaving so coarsely that Madame was obliged sharply to put him into his right place. She added, as a moral: "This will teach us not to talk to the first comer."

At Oissel they changed trains, and at a little station further on Monsieur Joseph Rivet was waiting for them with a large cart with a number of chairs in it, which was drawn by a white horse.

The carpenter politely kissed all the ladies, and then helped them into his conveyance.

Three of them sat on three chairs at the back, Raphaelle, Madame, and her brother on the three chairs in front, and Rosa, who had no seat, settled herself as comfortably as she could on tall Fernande's knees, and then they set off.

But the horse's jerky trot shook the cart so terribly, that the chairs began to dance, throwing the travelers into the air, to the right and to the left, as if they had been dancing puppets. This made them make horrible grimaces and screams, which, however, were cut short by another jolt of the cart.

They clung to the sides of the vehicle, their bonnets fell on to their backs, their noses on their shoulders, and the white horse trotted on, stretching out his head and holding out his tail quite straight, a little hairless rat's tail, with which he whisked his buttocks from time to time.

Joseph Rivet, with one leg on the shafts and the other bent under him, held the reins with elbows high and kept uttering a kind of chuckling sound, which made the horse prick up its ears and go faster.

The green country extended on either side of the road, and here and there the colza in flower presented a waving expanse of yellow, from which there arose a strong, wholesome, sweet and penetrating smell, which the wind carried to some distance.

The cornflowers showed their little blue heads among the rye, and the women wanted to pick them, but Monsieur Rivet refused to stop.

Then sometimes a whole field appeared to be covered with blood, so thickly were the poppies growing, and the cart, which looked as if it were filled with flowers of more brilliant hue, drove on through the fields colored with wild flowers, to disappear behind the trees of a farm, then to reappear and go on again through the yellow or green standing crops studded with red or blue.

One o'clock struck as they drove up to the carpenter's door. They were tired out, and very hungry, as they had eaten nothing since they left home. Madame Rivet ran out, and made them alight, one after another, kissing them as soon as they were on the ground. She seemed as if she would never tire of kissing her sister-in-law, whom she apparently wanted to monopolize. They had lunch in the workshop, which had been cleared out for the next day's dinner.

A capital omelette, followed by boiled chitterlings, and washed down by good, sharp cider, made them all feel comfortable.

Rivet had taken a glass so that he might hob-nob with them, and his wife cooked, waited on them, brought in the dishes, took them out, and asked all of them in a whisper

whether they had everything they wanted. A number of
boards standing against the walls, and heaps of shavings
that had been swept into the corners, gave out the smell
of planed wood, of carpentering, that resinous odor which
penetrates the lungs.

They wanted to see the little girl, but she had gone to
church, and would not be back until evening, so they all
went out for a stroll in the country.

It was a small village, through which the high road
passed. Ten or a dozen houses on either side of the single
street had for tenants the butcher, the grocer, the carpenter,
the innkeeper, the shoemaker, and the baker, and others.

The church was at the end of the street. It was surrounded by a small churchyard, and four enormous lime-
trees, which stood just outside the porch, shaded it
completely. It was built of flint, in no particular style, and
had a slated steeple. When you got past it, you were in the
open country again, which was broken here and there by
clumps of trees which hid some homestead.

Rivet had given his arm to his sister, out of politeness,
although he was in his working clothes, and was walking
with her majestically. His wife, who was overwhelmed by
Raphaelle's gold-striped dress, was walking between her and
Fernande, and rotund Rosa was trotting behind with Louise
Cocotte and Flora, the Seesaw, who was limping along,
quite tired out.

The inhabitants came to their doors, the children left
off playing, and a window curtain would be raised, so as to
show a muslin cap, while an old woman with a crutch, who
was almost blind, crossed herself as if it were a religious
procession. They all looked for a long time after those
handsome ladies from the town, who had come so far to be
present at the confirmation of Joseph Rivet's little girl, and
the carpenter rose very much in the public estimation.

As they passed the church, they heard some children
singing; little shrill voices were singing a hymn, but Ma-

dame would not let them go in, for fear of disturbing the little cherubs.

After a walk, during which Joseph Rivet enumerated the principal landed proprietors, spoke about the yield of the land, and the productiveness of the cows and sheep, he took his flock of women home and installed them in his house, and as it was very small, he had to put them into the rooms, two and two.

Just for once, Rivet would sleep in the workshop on the shavings; his wife was going to share her bed with her sister-in-law, and Fernande and Raphaelle were to sleep together in the next room. Louise and Flora were put into the kitchen, where they had a mattress on the floor, and Rosa had a little dark cupboard at the top of the stairs to herself, close to the loft, where the candidate for confirmation was to sleep.

When the girl came in, she was overwhelmed with kisses; all the women wished to caress her, with that need of tender expression, that habit of professional wheedling, which had made them kiss the ducks in the railway carriage.

They took her on to their laps, stroked her soft, light hair, and pressed her in their arms with vehement and spontaneous outbursts of affection, and the child, who was very good-natured and docile, bore it all patiently.

As the day had been a fatiguing one for everybody, they all went to bed soon after dinner. The whole village was wrapped in that perfect stillness of the country, which is almost like a religious silence, and the girls, who were accustomed to the noisy evenings of their establishment, felt rather impressed by the perfect repose of the sleeping village. They shivered, not with cold, but with those little shivers of solitude which come over uneasy and troubled hearts.

As soon as they were in bed, two and two together, they clasped each other in their arms, as if to protect themselves against this feeling of the calm and profound slumber of the earth. But Rosa the Jade, who was alone in her little dark cupboard, felt a vague and painful emotion come over her.

She was tossing about in bed, unable to get to sleep, when she heard the faint sobs of a crying child close to her head, through the partition. She was frightened, and called out, and was answered by a weak voice, broken by sobs. It was the little girl who, being used to sleeping in her mother's room, was frightened in her small attic.

Rosa was delighted, got up softly so as not to awaken anyone, and went and fetched the child. She took her into her warm bed, kissed her and pressed her to her bosom, caressed her, lavished exaggerated manifestations of tenderness on her, and at last grew calmer herself and went to sleep. And till morning, the candidate for confirmation slept with her head on Rosa's naked bosom.

At five o'clock, the little church bell ringing the "Angelus" woke these women up, who as a rule slept the whole morning long.

The peasants were up already, and the women went busily from house to house, carefully bringing short, starched, muslin dresses in bandboxes, or very long wax tapers, with a bow of silk fringed with gold in the middle, and with dents in the wax for the fingers.

The sun was already high in the blue sky, which still had a rosy tint toward the horizon, like a faint trace of dawn, remaining. Families of fowls were walking about the hen-houses, and here and there a black cock, with a glistening breast, raised his head, crowned by his red comb, flapped his wings, and uttered his shrill crow, which the other cocks repeated.

Vehicles of all sorts came from neighboring parishes, and discharged tall, Norman women, in dark dresses, with neck-handkerchiefs crossed over the bosom, and fastened with silver brooches, a hundred years old.

The men had put on blouses over their new frock coats, or over their old dress coats of green cloth, the tails of which hung down below their blouses. When the horses

were in the stable, there was a double line of rustic convey-
ances along the road; carts, cabriolets, tilburies, char-à-bancs,
traps of every shape and age, resting on their shafts, or
pointing them in the air.

The carpenter's house was as busy as a beehive. The
ladies, in dressing jackets and petticoats, with their long,
thin, light hair, which looked as if it were faded and worn
by dyeing, were busy dressing the child, who was standing
motionless on a table, while Madame Tellier was directing
the movements of her battalion. They washed her, did her
hair, dressed her, and with the help of a number of pins,
they arranged the folds of her dress, and took in the waist,
which was too large.

Then, when she was ready, she was told to sit down and
not to move, and the women hurried off to get ready themselves.

The church bell began to ring again, and its tinkle was
lost in the air, like a feeble voice which is soon drowned in
space. The candidates came out of the houses, and went
toward the parochial building which contained the school
and the mansion house. This stood quite at one end of the
village, while the church was situated at the other.

The parents, in their very best clothes, followed their
children with awkward looks, and with the clumsy movements of bodies that are always bent at work.

The little girls disappeared in a cloud of muslin, which
looked like whipped cream, while the lads, who looked like
embryo waiters in a *café*, and whose heads shone with
pomatum, walked with their legs apart, so as not to get any
dust or dirt on to their black trousers.

It was something for the family to be proud of; a large
number of relatives from distant parts surrounded the child,
and, consequently, the carpenter's triumph was complete.

Madame Tellier's regiment, with its mistress at its head,
followed Constance; her father gave his arm to his sister,
her mother walked by the side of Raphaelle, Fernande with
Rosa, and the Two Pumps together. Thus they walked

majestically through the village, like a general's staff in full uniform, while the effect on the village was startling.

At the school, the girls arranged themselves under the Sister of Mercy, and the boys under the school-master, and they started off, singing a hymn as they went. The boys led the way, in two files, between the two rows of vehicles, from which the horses had been taken out, and the girls followed in the same order. As all the people in the village had given the town ladies the precedence out of politeness, they came immediately behind the girls, and lengthened the double line of the procession still more, three on the right and three on the left, while their dresses were as striking as a bouquet of fireworks.

When they went into the church, the congregation grew quite excited. They pressed against each other, they turned round, they jostled one another in order to see. Some of the devout ones almost spoke aloud, so astonished were they at the sight of these ladies, whose dresses were trimmed more elaborately than the priest's chasuble.

The Mayor offered them his pew, the first one on the right, close to the choir, and Madame Tellier sat there with her sister-in-law; Fernande and Raphaelle, Rosa the Jade, and the Two Pumps occupied the second seat, in company with the carpenter.

The choir was full of kneeling children, the girls on one side, and the boys on the other, and the long wax tapers which they held looked like lances, pointing in all directions. Three men were standing in front of the lectern, singing as loud as they could.

They prolonged the syllables of the sonorous Latin indefinitely, holding on to the Amens with interminable a— a's, which the serpent of the organ kept up in the monotonous, long-drawn-out notes, emitted by the deep-throated pipes.

A child's shrill voice took up the reply, and from time to time a priest sitting in a stall and wearing a biretta got up, muttered something, and sat down again. The three singers continued, with their eyes fixed on the big book of plainsong lying open before them on the outstretched wings of an eagle, mounted on a pivot.

Then silence ensued. The service went on, and toward the end of it, Rosa, with her head in both her hands, suddenly thought of her mother, and her village church on a similar occasion. She almost fancied that that day had returned, when she was so small, and almost hidden in her white dress, and she began to cry.

First of all she wept silently, the tears dropped slowly from her eyes, but her emotion increased with her recollections, and she began to sob. She took out her pocket-handkerchief, wiped her eyes, and held it to her mouth, so as not to scream, but it was useless.

A sort of rattle escaped her throat, and she was answered by two other profound, heart-breaking sobs; for her two neighbors, Louise and Flora, who were kneeling near her, overcome by similar recollections, were sobbing by her side. There was a flood of tears, and as weeping is contagious, Madame soon found that her eyes were wet, and on turning to her sister-in-law, she saw that all the occupants of the pew were crying.

Soon, throughout the church, here and there, a wife, a mother, a sister, seized by the strange sympathy of poignant emotion, and agitated by the grief of those handsome ladies on their knees, who were shaken by their sobs, was moistening her cambric pocket-handkerchief, and pressing her beating heart with her left hand.

Just as the sparks from an engine will set fire to dry grass, so the tears of Rosa and of her companions infected the whole congregation in a moment. Men, women, old men, and lads in new blouses were soon sobbing; something superhuman seemed to be hovering over their heads—a spirit, the powerful breath of an invisible and all-powerful being.

Suddenly a species of madness seemed to pervade the church, the noise of a crowd in a state of frenzy, a tempest of sobs and of stifled cries. It passed over the people like gusts of wind which bow the trees in a forest, and the priest, overcome by emotion, stammered out incoherent prayers, those inarticulate prayers of the soul, when it soars toward heaven.

The people behind him gradually grew calmer. The cantors, in all the dignity of their white surplices, went on in somewhat uncertain voices, and the organ itself seemed hoarse, as if the instrument had been weeping. The priest, however, raised his hand, as a sign for them to be still, and went to the chancel steps. All were silent, immediately.

After a few remarks on what had just taken place, which he attributed to a miracle, he continued, turning to the seats where the carpenter's guests were sitting:

"I especially thank you, my dear sisters, who have come from such a distance, and whose presence among us, whose evident faith and ardent piety have set such a salutary example to all. You have edified my parish; your emotion has warmed all hearts; without you, this day would not, perhaps, have had this really divine character. It is sufficient, at times, that there should be one chosen to keep in the flock, to make the whole flock blessed."

His voice failed him again, from emotion, and he said no more, but concluded the service.

They all left the church as quickly as possible; the children themselves were restless, tired with such a prolonged tension of the mind. Besides, the elders were hungry, and one after another left the churchyard, to see about dinner.

There was a crowd outside, a noisy crowd, a babel of loud voices, in which the shrill Norman accent was discernible. The villagers formed two ranks, and when the children appeared, each family seized their own.

The whole houseful of women caught hold of Constance, surrounded her and kissed her, and Rosa was especially demonstrative. At last she took hold of one hand, while Madame Tellier held the other, and Raphaelle and Fernande held up her long muslin petticoat, so that it might not drag in the dust. Louise and Flora brought up the rear with Madame Rivet, and the child, who was very silent and thoughtful, set off home, in the midst of this guard of honor.

The dinner was served in the workshop, on long boards supported by trestles, and through the open door they could see all the enjoyment that was going on. Everywhere people were feasting; through every window could be seen tables surrounded by people in their Sunday clothes. There was merriment, in every house—men sitting in their shirt sleeves, drinking cider, glass after glass.

In the carpenter's house the gaiety took on somewhat of an air of reserve, the consequence of the emotion of the girls in the morning. Rivet was the only one who was in good cue, and he was drinking to excess. Madame Tellier was looking at the clock every moment, for, in order not to lose two days following, they ought to take the 3:55 train, which would bring them to Fécamp by dark.

The carpenter tried very hard to distract her attention, so as to keep his guests until the next day. But he did not succeed, for she never joked when there was business to be done, and as soon as they had had their coffee she ordered her girls to make haste and get ready. Then, turning to her brother, she said:

"You must have the horse put in immediately," and she herself went to complete her preparations.

When she came down again, her sister-in-law was waiting to speak to her about the child, and a long conversation took place, in which, however, nothing was settled. The carpenter's wife finessed, and pretended to be very much moved, and Madame Tellier, who was holding the girl on her knees, would not pledge herself to anything definite, but merely gave vague promises: she would not forget her, there was plenty of time, and then, they were sure to meet again.

But the conveyance did not come to the door, and the women did not come downstairs. Upstairs, they even heard

loud laughter, falls, little screams, and much clapping of
hands, and so, while the carpenter's wife went to the stable
to see whether the cart was ready, Madame went upstairs.

Rivet, who was very drunk and half undressed, was vainly
trying to kiss Rosa, who was choking with laughter. The
Two Pumps were holding him by the arms and trying to
calm him, as they were shocked at such a scene after that
morning's ceremony; but Raphaelle and Fernande were
urging him on, writhing and holding their sides with laughter, and they uttered shrill cries at every useless attempt
that the drunken fellow made.

The man was furious, his face was red, his dress disordered, and he was trying to shake off the two women
who were clinging to him, while he was pulling Rosa's bodice, with all his might, and ejaculating: "Won't you, you
slut?"

But Madame, who was very indignant, went up to her
brother, seized him by the shoulders, and threw him out
of the room with such violence that he fell against a wall
in the passage, and a minute afterward, they heard him
pumping water on to his head in the yard. When he came
back with the cart, he was already quite calmed down.

They seated themselves in the same way as they had done
the day before, and the little white horse started off with
his quick, dancing trot. Under the hot sun, their fun, which
had been checked during dinner, broke out again. The girls
now were amused at the jolts which the wagon gave, pushed
their neighbors' chairs, and burst out laughing every moment, for they were in the vein for it, after Rivet's vain
attempt.

There was a haze over the country, the roads were glaring, and dazzled their eyes. The wheels raised up two trails
of dust, which followed the cart for a long time along the
highroad, and presently Fernande, who was fond of music,
asked Rosa to sing something. She boldly struck up the
"Gros Curé de Meudon," but Madame made her stop immediately as she thought it a song which was very unsuit-

able for such a day, and added:

"Sing us something of Béranger's."

After a moment's hesitation, Rosa began Béranger's song, "The Grandmother," in her worn-out voice, and all the girls, and even Madame herself, joined in the chorus:

> *How I regret*
> *My dimpled arms,*
> *My well-made legs,*
> *And my vanished charms!*

"That is first-rate," Rivet declared, carried away by the rhythm. They shouted the refrain to every verse, while Rivet beat time on the shafts with his foot, and on the horse's back with the reins. The animal, himself, carried away by the rhythm, broke into a wild gallop, and threw all the women in a heap, one on top of the other, in the bottom of the conveyance.

They got up, laughing as if they were crazy, and the song went on, shouted at the top of their voices, beneath the burning sky and among the ripening grain, to the rapid gallop of the little horse, who set off every time the refrain was sung, and galloped a hundred yards, to their great delight. Occasionally a stone breaker by the roadside sat up, and looked at the wild and shouting female load, through his wire spectacles.

When they got out at the station, the carpenter said:

"I am sorry you are going; we might have had some fun together."

But Madame replied very sensibly: "Everything has its right time, and we cannot always be enjoying ourselves."

And then he had a sudden inspiration: "Look here, I will come and see you at Fécamp next month." And he gave a knowing look, with his bright and roguish eyes.

"Come," Madame said, "you must be sensible; you may come if you like, but you are not to be up to any of your tricks."

He did not reply, and as they heard the whistle of the train he immediately began to kiss them all. When it came to Rosa's turn, he tried to get to her mouth, which she, however, smiling with her lips closed, turned away from him each time by a rapid movement of her head to one side. He held her in his arms, but he could not attain his object, as his large whip, which he was holding in his hand and waving behind the girl's back in desperation, interfered with his efforts.

"Passengers for Rouen, take your seats, please!" a guard cried, and they got in. There was a slight whistle followed by a loud one from the engine, which noisily puffed out its first jet of steam, while the wheels began to turn a little, with visible effort. Rivet left the station and went to the gate by the side of the line to get another look at Rosa, and as the carriage full of human merchandise passed him, he began to crack his whip and to jump, singing at the top of his voice:

> How I regret
> My dimpled arms,
> My well-made legs,
> And my vanished charms!

And then he watched a white pocket-handkerchief, which somebody was waving, as it disappeared in the distance.

III

They slept the peaceful sleep of quiet consciences, until they got to Rouen. When they returned to the house, refreshed and rested, Madame could not help saying:

"It was all very well, but I was already longing to get home."

They hurried over their supper, and then, when they had put on their usual light evening costumes, waited for their usual customers. The little colored lamp outside the door told the passers-by that the flock had returned to the fold, and in a moment the news spread, nobody knew how, or by whom.

Monsieur Philippe, the banker's son, even carried his audacity so far as to send a special messenger to Monsieur Tournevau who was in the bosom of his family.

The fish-curer used every Sunday to have several cousins to dinner, and they were having coffee, when a man came in with a letter in his hand. Monsieur Tournevau was much excited; he opened the envelope and grew pale; it only contained these words in pencil:

The cargo of fish has been found; the ship has come into port; good business for you. Come immediately.

He felt in his pockets, gave the messenger two-sous, and suddenly blushing to his ears, he said: "I must go out." He handed his wife the laconic and mysterious note, rang the bell, and when the servant came in, he asked her to bring him his hat and overcoat immediately. As soon as he was in the street, he began to run, and the way seemed to him to be twice as long as usual, in consequence of his impatience.

Madame Tellier's establishment had put on quite a holiday look. On the ground floor, a number of sailors were making a deafening noise, and Louise and Flora drank with one and the other, so as to merit their name of the Two Pumps more than ever. They were being called for everywhere at once; already they were not quite sober enough for their business, and the night bid fair to be a very jolly one.

The upstairs room was full by nine o'clock. Monsieur Vassi, the Judge of the Tribunal of Commerce, Madame's usual Platonic wooer, was talking to her in a corner, in a low voice, and they were both smiling, as if they were about to come to an understanding.

Monsieur Poulin, the ex-mayor, was holding Rosa on his knees; and she, with her nose close to his, was running her hands through the old gentleman's white whiskers.

Tall Fernande, who was lying on the sofa, had both her feet on Monsieur Pinipesse the tax-collector's stomach, and her back on young Monsieur Philippe's waistcoat; her right arm was round his neck, and she held a cigarette in her left.

Raphaelle appeared to be discussing matters with Monsieur Dupuis, the insurance agent, and she finished by saying: "Yes, my dear, I will."

Just then, the door opened suddenly, and Monsieur Tournevau came in. He was greeted with enthusiastic cries of: "Long live Tournevau!" and Raphaelle, who was twirling round, went and threw herself into his arms. He seized her in a vigorous embrace, and without saying a word, lifting her up as if she had been a feather, he carried her through the room.

Rosa was chatting to the ex-mayor, kissing him every moment, and pulling both his whiskers at the same time in order to keep his head straight.

Fernande and Madame remained with the four men, and Monsieur Philippe exclaimed: "I will pay for some champagne; get three bottles, Madame Tellier." And Fernande gave him a hug, and whispered to him: "Play us a waltz, will you?" So he rose and sat down at the old piano in the corner, and managed to get a hoarse waltz out of the entrails of the instrument.

The tall girl put her arms round the tax-collector, Madame asked Monsieur Vassi to take her in his arms, and the two couples turned round, kissing as they danced. Monsieur Vassi, who had formerly danced in good society, waltzed with such elegance that Madame was quite captivated.

Frederic brought the champagne; the first cork popped, and Monsieur Philippe played the introduction to a quadrille, through which the four dancers walked in society fashion, decorously, with propriety of deportment, with bows, and curtsies, and then they began to drink.

Monsieur Philippe next struck up a lively polka, and Monsieur Tournevau started off with the handsome Jewess, whom he held up in the air, without letting her feet touch the ground. Monsieur Pinipesse and Monsieur Vassi had started off with renewed vigor and from time to time one or another couple would stop to toss off a long glass of sparkling wine. The dance was threatening to become never-ending, when Rosa opened the door.

"I want to dance," she exclaimed. And she caught hold of Monsieur Dupuis, who was sitting idle on the couch, and the dance began again.

But the bottles were empty. "I will pay for one," Monsieur Tournevau said.

"So will I," Monsieur Vassi declared.

"And I will do the same," Monsieur Dupuis remarked.

They all began to clap their hands, and it soon became a regular ball. From time to time, Louise and Flora ran up-stairs quickly, had a few turns while their customers down-stairs grew impatient, and then they returned regretfully to the café. At midnight they were still dancing.

Madame shut her eyes to what was going on, and she had long private talks in corners with Monsieur Vassi, as if to settle the last details of something that had already been agreed upon.

At last, at one o'clock, the two married men, Monsieur Tournevau and Monsieur Pinipesse, declared that they were going home, and wanted to pay. Nothing was charged for except the champagne, and that only cost six francs a bottle, instead of ten, which was the usual price, and when they expressed their surprise at such generosity, Madame, who was beaming, said to them:

"We don't have a holiday every day."

Mademoiselle Fifi

THE MAJOR GRAF von Farlsberg, the Prussian commandant, was reading his newspaper, lying back in a great armchair, with his booted feet on the beautiful marble fireplace,
where his spurs had made two holes, which grew deeper
every day, during the three months that he had been in the
château of Urville.

A cup of coffee was smoking on a small, inlaid table,
which was stained with liquors, burnt by cigars, notched by
the penknife of the victorious officer, who occasionally
would stop while sharpening a pencil, to jot down figures,
or to make a drawing on it, just as it took his fancy.

When he had read his letters and the German newspapers, which his baggagemaster had brought him, he got
up, and after throwing three or four enormous pieces of
green wood on to the fire—for these gentlemen were gradually cutting down the park in order to keep themselves
warm—he went to the window. The rain was descending
in torrents, a regular Normandy rain, which looked as if it
were being poured out by some furious hand, a slanting
rain, which was as thick as a curtain, and which formed a

From *The Best Stories of Guy de Maupassant*, selected, with an introduction, by Saxe Commins. Copyright 1945 by Random House, Inc.

kind of wall with oblique stripes, and which deluged everything, a regular rain, such as one frequently experiences in the neighborhood of Rouen, which is the watering pot of France.

For a long time the officer looked at the sodden turf, and at the swollen Andelle beyond it, which was overflowing its banks, and he was drumming a waltz from the Rhine on the windowpanes, with his fingers, when a noise made him turn round; it was his second in command, Captain Baron von Kelweinstein.

The major was a giant, with broad shoulders, and a long, fair beard, which hung like a cloth on to his chest. His whole, solemn person suggested the idea of a military peacock, a peacock who was carrying his tail spread out on to his breast. He had cold, gentle, blue eyes, and the scar from a sword-cut, which he had received in the war with Austria; he was said to be an honorable man, as well as a brave officer.

The captain, a short, red-faced man, who was tightly girthed in at the waist, had his red hair cropped quite close to his head, and in certain lights almost looked as if he had been rubbed over with phosphorus. He had lost two front teeth one night, though he could not quite remember how. This defect made him speak so that he could not always be understood, and he had a bald patch on the top of his head, which made him look rather like a monk, with a fringe of curly, bright, golden hair round the circle of bare skin.

The commandant shook hands with him, and drank his cup of coffee (the sixth that morning) at a draught, while he listened to his subordinate's report of what had occurred; and then they both went to the window, and declared that it was a very unpleasant outlook. The major, who was a quiet man, with a wife at home, could accommodate himself to everything; but the captain, who was rather fast, being in the habit of frequenting low resorts, and much given to women, was mad at having been shut up for three months in the compulsory chastity of that wretched hole.

There was a knock at the door, and when the commandant said, "Come in," one of their automatic soldiers appeared, and by his mere presence announced that breakfast was ready. In the dining-room, they met three other officers of lower rank: a lieutenant, Otto von Grossling, and two sub-lieutenants, Fritz Scheunebarg, and Count von Eyrick, a very short, fair-haired man, who was proud and brutal toward men, harsh toward prisoners, and very violent.

Since he had been in France, his comrades had called him nothing but "Mademoiselle Fifi." They had given him that nickname on account of his dandified style and small waist, which looked as if he wore stays, from his pale face, on which his budding mustache scarcely showed, and on account of the habit he had acquired of employing the French expression, *fi, fi donc*, which he pronounced with a slight whistle, when he wished to express his sovereign contempt for persons or things.

The dining-room of the château was a magnificent long room, whose fine old mirrors, now cracked by pistol bullets, and Flemish tapestry, now cut to ribbons and hanging in rags in places, from sword-cuts, told too well what Mademoiselle Fifi's occupation was during his spare time.

There were three family portraits on the walls; a steel-clad knight, a cardinal, and a judge, who were all smoking long porcelain pipes, which had been inserted into holes in the canvas, while a lady in a long, pointed waist proudly exhibited an enormous pair of mustaches, drawn with a piece of charcoal.

The officers ate their breakfast almost in silence in that mutilated room, which looked dull in the rain, and melancholy under its vanquished appearance, although its old, oak floor had become as solid as the stone floor of a public house.

When they had finished eating, and were smoking and drinking, they began, as usual, to talk about the dull life they were leading. The bottles of brandy and of liquors passed from hand to hand, and all sat back in their chairs, taking repeated sips from their glasses, and scarcely removing the long, bent stems, which terminated in china bowls painted in a manner to delight a Hottentot, from their mouths.

As soon as their glasses were empty, they filled them again, with a gesture of resigned weariness, but Mademoiselle Fifi emptied his every minute, and a soldier immediately gave him another. They were enveloped in a cloud of strong tobacco smoke; they seemed to be sunk in a state of drowsy, stupid intoxication, in that dull state of drunkenness of men who have nothing to do, when suddenly, the baron sat up, and said: "By heavens! This cannot go on; we must think of something to do." And on hearing this, Lieutenant Otto and Sub-lieutenant Fritz, who preeminently possessed the grave, heavy German countenance, said: "What, captain?"

He thought for a few moments, and then replied: "What? Well, we must get up some entertainment, if the commandant will allow us."

"What sort of an entertainment, captain?" the major asked, taking his pipe out of his mouth.

"I will arrange all that, commandant," the baron said. "I will send *Le Devoir* to Rouen, who will bring us some ladies. I know where they can be found. We will have supper here, as all the materials are at hand, and, at least, we shall have a jolly evening."

Graf von Farlsberg shrugged his shoulders with a smile: "You must surely be mad, my friend."

But all the other officers got up, surrounded their chief, and said: "Let the captain have his own way, commandant; it is terribly dull here."

And the major ended by yielding. "Very well," he replied, and the baron immediately sent for *Le Devoir.*

The latter was an old corporal who had never been seen to smile, but who carried out all orders of his superiors to the letter, no matter what they might be. He stood there, with an impassive face, while he received the baron's instructions, and then went out; five minutes later a large wagon belonging to the military train, covered with a miller's tilt, galloped off as fast as four horses could take it, under the pouring rain, and the officers all seemed to awaken from their lethargy, their looks brightened, and they began to talk.

Although it was raining as hard as ever, the major declared that it was not so dull, and Lieutenant von Grossling said with conviction that the sky was clearing up, while Mademoiselle Fifi did not seem to be able to keep in his place. He got up, and sat down again, and his bright eyes seemed to be looking for something to destroy. Suddenly, looking at the lady with the mustaches, the young fellow pulled out his revolver, and said: "You shall not see it." And without leaving his seat he aimed, and with two successive bullets cut out both the eyes of the portrait.

"Let us make a mine!" he then exclaimed, and the conversation was suddenly interrupted, as if they had found some fresh and powerful subject of interest. The mine was his invention, his method of destruction, and his favorite amusement.

When he left the château, the lawful owner, Count Fernand d'Amoys d'Urville, had not had time to carry away or to hide anything, except the plate, which had been stowed away in a hole made in one of the walls, so that, as he was very rich and had good taste, the large drawing-room, which opened into the dining-room, had looked like the gallery in a museum, before his precipitate flight.

Expensive oil-paintings, water-colors, and drawings hung upon the walls, while on the tables, on the hanging shelves, and in elegant glass cupboards, there were a thousand knick-nacks: small vases, statuettes, groups in Dresden china, grotesque Chinese figures, old ivory, and Venetian glass, which filled the large room with their precious and fantastical array.

Scarcely anything was left now; not that the things had been stolen, for the major would not have allowed that, but

Mademoiselle Fifi *would have a mine,* and on that occasion all the officers thoroughly enjoyed themselves for
five minutes. The little marquis went into the drawing-
room to get what he wanted, and he brought back a small,
delicate china teapot, which he filled with gunpowder, and
carefully introduced a piece of German tinder into it,
through the spout. Then he lighted it, and took this infernal machine into the next room; but he came back immediately, and shut the door. The Germans all stood
expectantly, their faces full of childish, smiling curiosity,
and as soon as the explosion had shaken the château, they
all rushed in at once.

Mademoiselle Fifi, who got in first, clapped his hands
in delight at the sight of a terra-cotta Venus, whose head
had been blown off, and each picked up pieces of porcelain,
and wondered at the strange shape of the fragments, while
the major was looking with a paternal eye at the large
drawing-room which had been wrecked in such a Neronic
fashion, and which was strewn with the fragments of works
of art. He went out first, and said, with a smile: "He managed that very well!"

But there was such a cloud of smoke in the dining-room,
mingled with the tobacco smoke, that they could not
breathe, so the commandant opened the window, and all
the officers, who had gone into the room for a glass of
cognac, went up to it.

The moist air blew into the room, and brought a sort of
spray with it, which powdered their beards. They looked
at the tall trees which were dripping with the rain, at the
broad valley which was covered with mist, and at the church
spire in the distance, which rose up like a gray point in the
beating rain.

The bells had not rung since their arrival. That was the
only resistance which the invaders had met with in the
neighborhood. The parish priest had not refused to take in
and to feed the Prussian soldiers; he had several times even
drunk a bottle of beer or claret with the hostile com-

mandant, who often employed him as a benevolent inter-
mediary; but it was no use to ask him for a single stroke of
the bells; he would sooner have allowed himself to be shot.
That was his way of protesting against the invasion, a peaceful and silent protest, the only one, he said, which was suitable to a priest, who was a man of mildness, and not of
blood; and everyone, for twenty-five miles round, praised
Abbé Chantavoine's firmness and heroism, in venturing to
proclaim the public mourning by the obstinate silence of
his church bells.

The whole village grew enthusiastic over his resistance,
and was ready to back up their pastor and to risk anything, as
they looked upon that silent protest as the safeguard of the
national honor. It seemed to the peasants that thus they
had deserved better of their country than Belfort and Strass-
bourg, that they had set an equally valuable example, and
that the name of their little village would become immortalized by that; but with that exception, they refused
their Prussian conquerors nothing.

The commandant and his officers laughed among themselves at that inoffensive courage, and as the people in the
whole country round showed themselves obliging and com-
pliant toward them, they willingly tolerated their silent
patriotism. Only little Count Wilhelm would have liked
to have forced them to ring the bells. He was very angry at
his superior's politic compliance with the priest's scruples,
and every day he begged the commandant to allow him to
sound "ding-dong, ding-dong," just once, only just once,
just by way of a joke. And he asked it like a wheedling
woman, in the tender voice of some mistress who wishes to
obtain something, but the commandant would not yield,
and to console herself, Mademoiselle Fifi made a mine in
the château.

The five men stood there together for some minutes, inhaling the moist air, and at last, Lieutenant Fritz said, with
a laugh: "The ladies will certainly not have fine weather for
their drive." Then they separated, each to his own duties,

while the captain had plenty to do in seeing about the dinner.

When they met again, as it was growing dark, they began to laugh at seeing each other as dandified and smart as on the day of a grand review. The commandant's hair did not look as gray as it did in the morning, and the captain had shaved—had only kept his mustache on, which made him look as if he had a streak of fire under his nose.

In spite of the rain, they left the window open, and one of them went to listen from time to time. At a quarter past six the baron said he heard a rumbling in the distance. They all rushed down, and soon the wagon drove up at a gallop with its four horses, splashed up to their backs, steaming and panting. Five women got out at the bottom of the steps, five handsome girls whom a comrade of the captain, to whom *Le Devoir* had taken his card, had selected with care.

They had not required much pressing, as they were sure of being well treated, for they had got to know the Prussians in the three months during which they had had to do with them. So they resigned themselves to the men as they did to the state of affairs. "It is part of our business, so it must be done," they said as they drove along; no doubt to allay some slight, secret scruples of conscience.

They went into the dining-room immediately, which looked still more dismal in its dilapidated state, when it was lighted up; while the table covered with choice dishes, the beautiful china and glass, and the plate, which had been found in the hole in the wall where its owner had hidden it, gave to the place the look of a bandits' resort, where they were supping after committing a robbery. The captain was radiant; he took hold of the women as if he were familiar with them; appraising them, kissing them, valuing them for what they were worth as *ladies of pleasure*; and when the three young men wanted to appropriate one each, he opposed them authoritatively, reserving to himself the right to apportion them justly, according to their several ranks, so as not to wound the hierarchy. Therefore, so as to avoid all discussion, jarring, and suspicion of partiality, he placed them all in a line according to height, and addressing the tallest, he said in a voice of command:

"What is your name?"

"Pamela," she replied, raising her voice.

Then he said: "Number One, called Pamela, is adjudged to the commandant."

Then, having kissed Blondina, the second, as a sign of proprietorship, he proffered stout Amanda to Lieutenant Otto, Eva, "the Tomato," to Sub-lieutenant Fritz, and Rachel, the shortest of them all, a very young, dark girl, with eyes as black as ink, a Jewess, whose snub nose confirmed by exception the rule which allots hooked noses to all her race, to the youngest officer, frail Count Wilhelm von Eyrick.

They were all pretty and plump, without any distinctive features, and all were very much alike in look and person, from their daily dissipation, and the life common to houses of public accommodation.

The three younger men wished to carry off their women immediately, under the pretext of finding them brushes and soap; but the captain wisely opposed this, for he said they were quite fit to sit down to dinner, and that those who went up would wish for a change when they came down, and so would disturb the other couples, and his experience in such matters carried the day. There were only many kisses; expectant kisses.

Suddenly Rachel choked, and began to cough until the tears came into her eyes, while smoke came through her nostrils. Under pretense of kissing her, the count had blown a whiff of tobacco into her mouth. She did not fly into a rage, and did not say a word, but she looked at her possessor with latent hatred in her dark eyes.

They sat down to dinner. The commandant seemed delighted; he made Pamela sit on his right, and Blondina on his left, and said, as he unfolded his table napkin: "That was a delightful idea of yours, captain."

Lieutenants Otto and Fritz, who were as polite as if they had been with fashionable ladies, rather intimidated their neighbors, but Baron von Kelweinstein gave the reins to all his vicious propensities, beamed, made doubtful remarks, and seemed on fire with his crown of red hair. He paid them compliments in French from the other side of the Rhine, and sputtered out gallant remarks, only fit for a low pothouse, from between his two broken teeth.

They did not understand him, however, and their intelligence did not seem to be awakened until he uttered nasty words and broad expressions, which were mangled by his accent. Then all began to laugh at once, like mad women, and fell against each other, repeating the words, which the baron then began to say all wrong, in order that he might have the pleasure of hearing them say doubtful things. They gave him as much of that stuff as he wanted, for they were drunk after the first bottle of wine, and, becoming themselves once more, and opening the door to their usual habits, they kissed the mustaches on the right and left of them, pinched their arms, uttered furious cries, drank out of every glass, and sang French couplets, and bits of German songs, which they had picked up in their daily intercourse with the enemy.

Soon the men themselves, intoxicated by that which was displayed to their sight and touch, grew very amorous, shouted and broke the plates and dishes, while the soldiers behind them waited on them stolidly. The commandant was the only one who put any restraint upon himself.

Mademoiselle Fifi had taken Rachel onto his knees, and, getting excited, at one moment kissed the little black curls on her neck, inhaling the pleasant warmth of her body, and all the savor of her person, through the slight space there was between her dress and her skin, and at another pinched her furiously through the material, and made her scream, for he was seized with a species of ferocity, and tormented by his desire to hurt her. He often held her close to him, as if to make her part of himself, and put his lips in a long kiss on the Jewess's rosy mouth, until she lost her breath;

and at last he bit her until a stream of blood ran down her chin and on to her bodice.

For the second time, she looked at him full in the face, and as she bathed the wound, she said: "You will have to pay for that!"

But he merely laughed a hard laugh, and said: "I will pay."

At dessert, champagne was served, and the commandant rose, and in the same voice in which he would have drunk to the health of the Empress Augusta, he drank: "To our ladies!" Then a series of toasts began, toasts worthy of the lowest soldiers and of drunkards, mingled with filthy jokes, which were made still more brutal by their ignorance of the language. They got up, one after the other, trying to say something witty, forcing themselves to be funny, and the women, who were so drunk that they almost fell off their chairs, with vacant looks and clammy tongues, applauded madly each time.

The captain, who no doubt wished to impart an appearance of gallantry to the orgy, raised his glass again, and said: "To our victories over hearts!" Thereupon Lieutenant Otto, who was a species of bear from the Black Forest, jumped up, inflamed and saturated with drink, and seized by an access of alcoholic patriotism, cried: "To our victories over France!"

Drunk as they were, the women were silent, and Rachel turned round with a shudder, and said: "Look here, I know some Frenchmen, in whose presence you would not dare to say that." But the little count, still holding her on his knees, began to laugh, for the wine had made him very merry, and said: "Ha! ha! ha! I have never met any of them, myself. As soon as we show ourselves, they run away!"

The girl, who was in a terrible rage, shouted into his face: "You are lying, you dirty scoundrel!"

For a moment, he looked at her steadily, with his bright eyes upon her, as he had looked at the portrait before he destroyed it with revolver bullets, and then he began to laugh: "Ah! yes, talk about them, my dear! Should we be here now, if they were brave?" Then getting excited, he exclaimed: "We are the masters! France belongs to us!" She jumped off his knees with a bound, and threw herself into her chair, while he rose, held out his glass over the table, and repeated: "France and the French, the woods, the fields, and the houses of France belong to us!"

The others, who were quite drunk, and who were suddenly seized by military enthusiasm, the enthusiasm of brutes, seized their glasses, and shouting, "Long live Prussia!" emptied them at a draught.

The girls did not protest, for they were reduced to silence, and were afraid. Even Rachel did not say a word, as she had no reply to make, and then the little count put his champagne glass, which had just been refilled, onto the head of the Jewess, and exclaimed: "All the women in France belong to us, also!"

At that she got up so quickly that the glass upset, spilling the amber colored wine on to her black hair as if to baptize her, and broke into a hundred fragments as it fell on to the floor. With trembling lips, she defied the looks of the officer, who was still laughing, and she stammered out, in a voice choked with rage: "That—that—that—is not true —for you shall certainly not have any French women."

He sat down again, so as to laugh at his ease, and trying effectually to speak in the Parisian accent, he said: "That is good, very good! Then what did you come here for, my dear?"

She was thunderstruck, and made no reply for a moment, for in her agitation she did not understand him at first; but as soon as she grasped his meaning, she said to him indignantly and vehemently: "I! I am not a woman; I am only a strumpet, and that is all that Prussians want."

Almost before she had finished, he slapped her full in her face; but as he was raising his hand again, as if he would strike her, she, almost mad with passion, took up a small dessert knife from the table, and stabbed him right in the neck, just above the breastbone. Something that he was going to say was cut short in his throat, and he sat there, with his mouth half open, and a terrible look in his eyes.

All the officers shouted in horror, and leaped up tumultuously; but throwing her chair between Lieutenant Otto's legs, who fell down at full length, she ran to the window, opened it before they could seize her, and jumped out into the night and pouring rain.

In two minutes, Mademoiselle Fifi was dead. Fritz and Otto drew their swords and wanted to kill the women, who threw themselves at their feet and clung to their knees. With some difficulty the major stopped the slaughter, and had the four terrified girls locked up in a room under the care of two soldiers. Then he organized the pursuit of the fugitive, as carefully as if he were about to engage in a skirmish, feeling quite sure that she would be caught.

The table, which had been cleared immediately, now served as a bed on which to lay Fifi out, and the four officers made for the window, rigid and sobered, with the stern faces of soldiers on duty, and tried to pierce through the darkness of the night, amid the steady torrent of rain. Suddenly, a shot was heard, and then another, a long way off; and for four hours they heard from time to time near or distant reports and rallying cries, strange words uttered as a call, in guttural voices.

In the morning they all returned. Two soldiers had been killed and three others wounded by their comrades in the ardor of that chase, and in the confusion of such a nocturnal pursuit, but they had not caught Rachel.

Then the inhabitants of the district were terrorized, the houses were turned topsy-turvy, the country was scoured and beaten up, over and over again, but the Jewess did not seem to have left a single trace of her passage behind her.

When the general was told of it, he gave orders to hush up the affair, so as not to set a bad example to the army, but he severely censured the commandant, who in turn punished his inferiors. The general had said: "One does not go to war in order to amuse oneself, and to caress prostitutes." And Graf von Farlsberg, in his exasperation, made up his mind to have his revenge on the district, but as he required a pretext for showing severity, he sent for the priest, and ordered him to have the bell tolled at the funeral of Count von Eyrick.

Contrary to all expectation, the priest showed himself humble and most respectful, and when Mademoiselle Fifi's body left the Château d'Urville on its way to the cemetery, carried by soldiers, preceded, surrounded, and followed by soldiers, who marched with loaded rifles, for the first time the bell sounded its funereal knell in a lively manner, as if a friendly hand were caressing it. At night it sounded again, and the next day, and every day; it rang as much as anyone could desire. Sometimes even, it would start at night, and sound gently through the darkness, seized by strange joy, awakened, one could not tell why. All the peasants in the neighborhood declared that it was bewitched, and nobody, except the priest and the sacristan would now go near the church tower, and they went because a poor girl was living there in grief and solitude, secretly nourished by those two men.

She remained there until the German troops departed, and then one evening the priest borrowed the baker's cart, and himself drove his prisoner to Rouen. When they got there, he embraced her, and she quickly went back on foot to the establishment from which she had come, where the proprietress, who thought that she was dead, was very glad to see her.

A short time afterward, a patriot who had no prejudices, who liked her because of her bold deed, and who afterward loved her for herself, married her, and made a lady of her.

David Herbert Lawrence

[1885—1930]

"I SHALL ALWAYS be a priest of love," D. H. Lawrence once remarked, and while his life and fiction bear out this sacred
prophecy, his name has been linked periodically with obscene
literature. It may seem an amazing contradiction that as the
author of the once widely censored *Lady Chatterley's Lover*
(1928) he was shocked by the "vulgarities" of James Joyce's
Ulysses (1922).

One of the world's most perceptive masters of the riddle of
human relations—as seen in 10 novels, especially *Sons and Lovers* (1913), and more than 60 short stories—Lawrence learned
much from the incompatibility of his parents. His father was a
coal miner, a loud, uninhibited man who reveled in song and
drink. His mother was a former schoolteacher, a proud,
domineering, strict woman who tried to civilize her primitive
husband. Their endless quarrels affected young Lawrence so
profoundly that his life's work seemed at once clear: to understand and to resolve the complex wars within the souls of' men
and women.

His later frustrating relations with women were influenced
by ambivalent feelings toward his parents. Only when he escaped the conventional world in 1912 with a progressive, already married woman, Frieda Richthofen Weekley, did
Lawrence find his independence. Earlier his delicate condition
as a boy, which led later to fatal tuberculosis, made him a

temporary outcast from his schoolfellows, some of whom considered him effeminate, and brought him even closer to women. Many of his remarkable pre-Freudian insights into the psyche were intuitive; many others he learned by asking his women friends to write down what they felt in certain emotional situations.

Lawrence lived for his first 21 years in the village of Eastwood, 8 miles from Nottingham and the Sherwood Forest district. It was as incompatible to him as his domestic life. The rural landscape, now transformed by the industrial revolution, made him sensitive to the harsh effects of capital and labor, class distinctions, and money; and he analyzed their corrupting influence on life. His discouraging experiences as a clerk in 1901, a schoolteacher from 1902 to 1906, and a student at Nottingham University from 1906 to 1908 further convinced Lawrence that England was "the country of the damned," where one's creative and sexual life were stifled, even destroyed, by science and the intellect. Because of his fierce determination to live the religious-primitive life, he forsook England and traveled around the world in the 1920s—to the Continent, India, Australia, Mexico, and the United States—searching for his Utopia, "the old Homeric aristocracy, when the grandeur was inside the man and he lived in a simple wooden house."

Lawrence's life and art were also shaped by a wide variety of other forces. The family Bible he had "in his bones": the simple, direct, graceful, rapid majesty of its prose; the poetry which depended on repetitions and parallelisms; the imagery drawn from the domestic and the natural world; the fusion of reality and symbol; the appeal to both eye and ear; the drama and suspense—all these affected his art of writing. His love of botany, animals, anthropology, myths, and primitive art gave greater flexibility and range to his use of symbols and images. Poetry, especially Wordsworth's, the romances of James Fenimore Cooper, and the rural tales by Thomas Hardy added further dimensions to his insights into the religion of nature and man's relation to the cosmos. A student of drawing and painting, he developed the impressionist's love for color, for bold visual imagery. Readings in philosophers like Schopenhauer and William James made him more conscious of the role of man's will and freedom. Finally, the shock of World War I, with its many deaths and maimed lives, reaffirmed his prophetic destiny as a writer: ". . . the struggle shall not be for money or for power, but for individual freedom and common effort towards good."

With such an interest in humanity, it is not surprising to find Lawrence's fiction rooted in character. Many of his stories illuminate the baffling, contradictory interplay between the unconscious and the conscious self, where the deadened soul awakens to or yearns for the ideal, resurrected life. The character's conflicts are often between the head and the heart, the flesh and the spirit, the demonic and the angelic, the primitive and the civilized; and his backgrounds—the world of nature, a geographical place, the mystical realm—mirror the shifting moods within his soul. His conflicts relate to Lawrence's new religion (he thought Christianity a failure): "Life is only bearable when the mind and the body are in harmony, and there is a natural balance between them, and each has a natural respect for the other."

So dependent on character, Lawrence ignores the conventional plot. Many of his best short stories ("The Prussian Officer," "The Man Who Loved Islands," "The Fox"), unlike his sprawling novels, are instinctively correct. They are spontaneous overflows of feeling, powerful, intense, immediate, which merge with a cryptic, ironic, impressionistic style rich in symbolic and mythic associations to make for stories superbly unified through mood.

The Horse Dealer's Daughter

"WELL, MABEL, AND what are you going to do with yourself?" asked Joe, with foolish flippancy. He felt quite safe himself. Without listening for an answer, he turned aside, worked a grain of tobacco to the tip of his tongue, and spat it out. He did not care about anything, since he felt safe himself.

The three brothers and the sister sat round the desolate breakfast table, attempting some sort of desultory consultation. The morning's post had given the final tap to the family fortune, and all was over. The dreary dining-room itself, with its heavy mahogany furniture, looked as if it were waiting to be done away with.

But the consultation amounted to nothing. There was a strange air of ineffectuality about the three men, as they sprawled at table, smoking and reflecting vaguely on their own condition. The girl was alone, a rather short, sullen-looking young woman of twenty-seven. She did not share the same life as her brothers. She would have been good-looking, save for the impassive fixity of her face, "bull-dog," as her brothers called it.

There was a confused trampling of horses' feet outside. The three men all sprawled round in their chairs to watch. Beyond the dark holly-bushes that separated the strip of lawn from the highroad, they could see a cavalcade of shire horses swinging out of their own yard, being taken for exercise. This was the last time. These were the last horses that would go through their hands. The young men watched with critical, callous look. They were all frightened at the collapse of their lives, and the sense of disaster in which they were involved left them no inner freedom.

Yet they were three fine, well-set fellows enough. Joe, the eldest, was a man of thirty-three, broad and handsome in a hot, flushed way. His face was red, he twisted his black moustache over a thick finger, his eyes wcrc shallow and restless. He had a sensual way of uncovering his teeth when he laughed, and his bearing was stupid. Now he watched the horses with a glazed look of helplessness in his eyes, a certain stupor of downfall.

The great draught-horses swung past. They were tied head to tail, four of them, and they heaved along to where a lane branched off from the highroad, planting their great hoofs floutingly in the fine black mud, swinging their great rounded haunches sumptuously, and trotting a few sudden steps as they were led into the lane, round the corner. Every movement showed a massive, slumbrous strength, and a stupidity which held them in subjection. The groom at the head looked back, jerking the leading rope. And the caval-cade moved out of sight up the lane, the tail of the last horse, bobbed up tight and stiff, held out taut from the swinging great haunches as they rocked behind the hedges in a motion-like sleep.

Joe watched with glazed hopeless eyes. The horses were almost like his own body to him. He felt he was done for now. Luckily he was engaged to a woman as old as himself, and therefore her father, who was steward of a neighbouring estate, would provide him with a job. He would marry and go into harness. His life was over, he would be a subject animal now.

He turned uneasily aside, the retreating steps of the horses echoing in his ears. Then, with foolish restlessness, he reached for the scraps of bacon-rind from the plates, and making a faint whistling sound, flung them to the terrier that lay against the fender. He watched the dog swallow them, and waited till the creature looked into his eyes. Then a faint grin came on his face, and in a high, foolish voice he said:

"You won't get much more bacon, shall you, you little bitch?"

The dog faintly and dismally wagged its tail, then lowered its haunches, circled round, and lay down again.

There was another helpless silence at the table. Joe sprawled uneasily in his seat, not willing to go till the family conclave was dissolved. Fred Henry, the second brother, was erect, clean-limbed, alert. He had watched the passing of the horses with more sang-froid. If he was an animal, like Joe, he was an animal which controls, not one which is controlled. He was master of any horse, and he carried himself with a well-tempered air of mastery. But he was not master of the situations of life. He pushed his coarse brown moustache upwards, off his lip, and glanced irritably at his sister, who sat impassive and inscrutable.

"You'll go and stop with Lucy for a bit, shan't you?" he asked. The girl did not answer.

"I don't see what else you can do," persisted Fred Henry.

"Go as a skivvy," Joe interpolated laconically.

The girl did not move a muscle.

"If I was her, I should go in for training for a nurse," said Malcolm, the youngest of them all. He was the baby of the family, a young man of twenty-two, with a fresh, jaunty museau.

But Mabel did not take any notice of him. They had talked at her and round her for so many years, that she hardly heard them at all.

The marble clock on the mantelpiece softly chimed the half-hour, the dog rose uneasily from the hearthrug and looked at the party at the breakfast table. But still they sat on in ineffectual conclave.

"Oh, all right," said Joe suddenly, apropos of nothing. "I'll get a move on."

He pushed back his chair, straddled his knees with a downward jerk, to get them free, in horsey fashion, and went to the fire. Still he did not go out of the room; he was curious to know what the others would do or say. He began to charge his pipe, looking down at the dog and saying, in a high, affected voice:

"Going wi' me? Going wi' me are ter? Tha'rt goin' further than tha counts on just now, dost hear?"

The dog faintly wagged its tail, the man stuck out his jaw and covered his pipe with his hands, and puffed intently, losing himself in the tobacco, looking down all the while at the dog with an absent brown eye. The dog looked up at him in mournful distrust. Joe stood with his knees stuck out, in real horsey fashion.

"Have you had a letter from Lucy?" Fred Henry asked of his sister.

"Last week," came the neutral reply.

"And what does she say?"

There was no answer.

"Does she ask you to go and stop there?" persisted Fred Henry.

"She says I can if I like."

"Well, then, you'd better. Tell her you'll come on Monday."

This was received in silence.

"That's what you'll do then, is it?" said Fred Henry, in some exasperation.

But she made no answer. There was a silence of futility

and irritation in the room. Malcolm grinned fatuously.

"You'll have to make up your mind between now and next Wednesday," said Joe loudly, "or else find yourself lodgings on the kerbstone."

The face of the young woman darkened, but she sat on immutable.

"Here's Jack Fergusson!" exclaimed Malcolm, who was looking aimlessly out of the window.

"Where?" exclaimed Joe, loudly.

"Just gone past."

"Coming in?"

Malcolm craned his neck to see the gate.

"Yes," he said.

There was a silence. Mabel sat on like one condemned, at the head of the table. Then a whistle was heard from the kitchen. The dog got up and barked sharply. Joe opened the door and shouted:

"Come on."

After a moment a young man entered. He was muffled up in overcoat and a purple woollen scarf, and his tweed cap, which he did not remove, was pulled down on his head. He was of medium height, his face was rather long and pale, his eyes looked tired.

"Hello, Jack! Well, Jack!" exclaimed Malcolm and Joe. Fred Henry merely said, "Jack."

"What's doing?" asked the newcomer, evidently addressing Fred Henry.

"Same. We've got to be out by Wednesday. Got a cold?"

"I have—got it bad, too."

"Why don't you stop in?"

"Me stop in? When I can't stand on my legs, perhaps I shall have a chance." The young man spoke huskily. He had a slight Scotch accent.

"It's a knock-out, isn't it," said Joe, boisterously, "if a doctor goes round croaking with a cold. Looks bad for the patients, doesn't it?"

The young doctor looked at him slowly.

"Anything the matter with you, then?" he asked sarcastically.

"Not as I know of. Damn your eyes, I hope not. Why?"

"I thought you were very concerned about the patients, wondered if you might be one yourself."

"Damn it, no, I've never been patient to no flaming doctor, and hope I never shall be," returned Joe.

At this point Mabel rose from the table, and they all seemed to become aware of her existence. She began putting the dishes together. The young doctor looked at her, but did not address her. He had not greeted her. She went out of the room with the tray, her face impassive and unchanged.

"When are you off then, all of you?" asked the doctor.

"I'm catching the eleven-forty," replied Malcolm. "Are you goin' down wi' th' trap, Joe?"

"Yes, I've told you I'm going down wi' th' trap, haven't I?"

"We'd better be getting her in then. So long, Jack, if I don't see you before I go," said Malcolm, shaking hands.

He went out, followed by Joe, who seemed to have his tail between his legs.

"Well, this is the devil's own," exclaimed the doctor, when he was left alone with Fred Henry. "Going before Wednesday, are you?"

"That's the orders," replied the other.

"Where, to Northampton?"

"That's it."

"The devil!" exclaimed Fergusson, with quiet chagrin.

And there was silence between the two.

"All settled up, are you?" asked Fergusson.

"About."

There was another pause.

"Well, I shall miss yer, Freddy, boy," said the young doctor.

"And I shall miss thee, Jack," returned the other.

"Miss you like hell," mused the doctor.

Fred Henry turned aside. There was nothing to say. Mabel came in again, to finish clearing the table.

"What are you going to do, then, Miss Pervin?" asked Fergusson. "Going to your sister's, are you?"

Mabel looked at him with her steady, dangerous eyes, that always made him uncomfortable, unsettling his superficial ease.

"No," she said.

"Well, what in the name of fortune are you going to do? Say what you mean to do," cried Fred Henry, with futile intensity.

But she only averted her head, and continued her work. She folded the white table-cloth, and put on the chenille cloth.

"The sulkiest bitch that ever trod!" muttered her brother.

But she finished her task with perfectly impassive face, the young doctor watching her interestedly all the while. Then she went out.

Fred Henry stared after her, clenching his lips, his blue eyes fixing in sharp antagonism, as he made a grimace of sour exasperation.

"You could bray her into bits, and that's all you'd get out of her," he said in a small, narrowed tone.

The doctor smiled faintly.

"What's she *going* to do, then?" he asked.

"Strike me if *I* know!" returned the other.

There was a pause. Then the doctor stirred.

"I'll be seeing you to-night, shall I?" he said to his friend.

"Ay—where's it to be? Are we going over to Jessdale?"

"I don't know. I've got such a cold on me. I'll come round to the Moon and Stars, anyway."

"Let Lizzie and May miss their night for once, eh?"

"That's it—if I feel as I do now."

"All's one—"

The two young men went through the passage and down to the back door together. The house was large, but it was servantless now, and desolate. At the back was a small bricked house-yard, and beyond that a big square, gravelled fine and red, and having stables on two sides. Sloping, dank, winter-dark fields stretched away on the open sides.

But the stables were empty. Joseph Pervin, the father of the family, had been a man of no education, who had become a fairly large horse dealer. The stables had been full of horses, there was a great turmoil and come-and-go of horses and of dealers and grooms. Then the kitchen was full of servants. But of late things had declined. The old man had married a second time, to retrieve his fortunes. Now he was dead and everything was gone to the dogs, there was nothing but debt and threatening.

For months, Mabel had been servantless in the big house, keeping the home together in penury for her ineffectual brothers. She had kept house for ten years. But previously it was with unstinted means. Then, however brutal and coarse everything was, the sense of money had kept her proud, confident. The men might be foul-mouthed, the women in the kitchen might have bad reputations, her brothers might have illegitimate children. But so long as there was money, the girl felt herself established, and brutally proud, reserved.

No company came to the house, save dealers and coarse men. Mabel had no associates of her own sex, after her sister went away. But she did not mind. She went regularly to church, she attended to her father. And she lived in the memory of her mother, who had died when she was fourteen, and whom she had loved. She had loved her father, too, in a different way, depending upon him, and feeling secure in him, until at the age of fifty-four he married again. And then she had set hard against him. Now he had died and left them all hopelessly in debt.

She had suffered badly during the period of poverty. Nothing, however, could shake the curious sullen, animal pride that dominated each member of the family. Now, for Mabel, the end had come. Still she would not cast about her. She would follow her own way just the same. She would always hold the keys of her own situation. Mindless and persistent, she endured from day to day. Why should she think? Why should she answer anybody? It was enough that this was the end, and there was no way out. She need not pass any more darkly along the main street of the small town, avoiding every eye. She need not demean herself any more, going into the shops and buying the cheapest food. This was at an end. She thought of nobody, not even of herself. Mindless and persistent, she seemed in a sort of ecstasy to be coming near to her fulfilment, her own glorification, approaching her dead mother, who was glorified.

In the afternoon she took a little bag, with shears and sponge and a small scrubbing brush, and went out. It was a grey, wintry day, with saddened, dark green fields and an atmosphere blackened by the smoke of foundries not far off. She went quickly, darkly along the causeway, heeding nobody, through the town to the churchyard.

There she always felt secure, as if no one could see her, although as a matter of fact she was exposed to the stare of every one who passed along under the churchyard wall. Nevertheless, once under the shadow of the great looming church, among the graves, she felt immune from the world, reserved within the thick churchyard wall as in another country.

Carefully she clipped the grass from the grave, and arranged the pinky white, small chrysanthemums in the tin cross. When this was done, she took an empty jar from a neighbouring grave, brought water, and carefully, most scrupulously sponged the marble head-stone and the coping-stone.

It gave her sincere satisfaction to do this. She felt in immediate contact with the world of her mother. She took minute pains, went through the park in a state bordering on pure happiness, as if in performing this task she came into a subtle, intimate connection with her mother. For the life she followed here in the world was far less real than the world of death she inherited from her mother.

The doctor's house was just by the church. Fergusson, being a mere hired assistant, was slave to the country-side. As he hurried now to attend to the outpatients in the surgery, glancing across the graveyard with his quick eye, he saw the girl at her task at the grave. She seemed so intent and remote, it was like looking into another world. Some mystical element was touched in him. He slowed down as he walked, watching her as if spell-bound.

She lifted her eyes, feeling him looking. Their eyes met. And each looked away again at once, each feeling, in some way, found out by the other. He lifted his cap and passed on down the road. There remained distinct in his consciousness, like a vision, the memory of her face, lifted from the tombstone in the churchyard, and looking at him with slow, large, portentous eyes. It was portentous, her face. It seemed to mesmerize him. There was a heavy power in her eyes which laid hold of his whole being, as if he had drunk some powerful drug. He had been feeling weak and done before. Now the life came back into him, he felt delivered from his own fretted, daily self.

He finished his duties at the surgery as quickly as might be, hastily filling up the bottles of the waiting people with cheap drugs. Then, in perpetual haste, he set off again to visit several cases in another part of his round, before tea-time. At all times he preferred to walk if he could, but particularly when he was not well. He fancied the motion restored him.

The afternoon was falling. It was grey, deadened, and wintry, with a slow, moist, heavy coldness sinking in and deadening all the faculties. But why should he think or notice? He hastily climbed the hill and turned across the dark green fields, following the black cinder-track. In the distance, across a shallow dip in the country, the small town was clustered like smouldering ash, a tower, a spire, a heap of low, raw, extinct houses. And on the nearest fringe of the town, sloping into the dip, was Oldmeadow, the Pervins' house. He could see the stables and the outbuildings distinctly, as they lay towards him on the slope. Well, he would not go there many more times! Another resource would be lost to him, another place gone: the only company he cared for in the alien, ugly little town he was losing. Nothing but work, drudgery, constant hastening from dwelling to dwelling among the colliers and the iron-workers. It wore him out, but at the same time he had a craving for it. It was a stimulant to him to be in the homes of the working people, moving as it were through the innermost body of their life. His nerves were excited and gratified. He could come so near, into the very lives of the rough, inarticulate, powerfully emotional men and women. He grumbled, he said he hated the hellish hole. But as a matter of fact it excited him, the contact with the rough, strongly-feeling people was a stimulant applied direct to his nerves.

Below Oldmeadow, in the green, shallow, soddened hollow of fields, lay a square, deep pond. Roving across the landscape, the doctor's quick eye detected a figure in black passing through the gate of the field, down towards the pond. He looked again. It would be Mabel Pervin. His mind suddenly became alive and attentive.

Why was she going down there? He pulled up on the path on the slope above, and stood staring. He could just make sure of the small black figure moving in the hollow of the failing day. He seemed to see her in the midst of such obscurity, that he was like a clairvoyant, seeing rather with the mind's eye than with ordinary sight. Yet he could see her positively enough, whilst he kept his eye attentive. He felt, if he looked away from her, in the thick, ugly falling dusk, he would lose her altogether.

He followed her minutely as she moved, direct and intent, like something transmitted rather than stirring in voluntary activity, straight down the field towards the pond. There she stood on the bank for a moment. She never raised her head. Then she waded slowly into the water.

He stood motionless as the small black figure walked slowly and deliberately towards the centre of the pond, very slowly, gradually moving deeper into the motionless water, and still moving forward as the water got up to her breast. Then he could see her no more in the dusk of the dead afternoon.

"There!" he exclaimed. "Would you believe it?"

And he hastened straight down, running over the wet, soddened fields, pushing through the hedges, down into the depression of callous wintry obscurity. It took him several minutes to come to the pond. He stood on the bank, breathing heavily. He could see nothing. His eyes seemed to penetrate the dead water. Yes, perhaps that was the dark shadow of her black clothing beneath the surface of the water.

He slowly ventured into the pond. The bottom was deep, soft clay, he sank in, and the water clasped dead cold round his legs. As he stirred he could smell the cold, rotten clay that fouled up into the water. It was objectionable in his lungs. Still, repelled and yet not heeding, he moved deeper into the pond. The cold water rose over his thighs, over his loins, upon his abdomen. The lower part of his body was all sunk in the hideous cold element. And the bottom was so deeply soft and uncertain, he was afraid of pitching with his mouth underneath. He could not swim, and was afraid.

He crouched a little, spreading his hands under the water and moving them round, trying to feel for her. The dead cold pond swayed upon his chest. He moved again, a little deeper, and again, with his hands underneath, he felt all around under the water. And he touched her clothing. But it evaded his fingers. He made a desperate effort to grasp it.

And so doing he lost his balance and went under, horribly, suffocating in the foul earthy water, struggling madly for a few moments. At last, after what seemed an eternity, he got his footing, rose again into the air and looked around. He gasped, and knew he was in the world. Then he looked at the water. She had risen near him. He grasped her clothing, and drawing her nearer, turned to take his way to land again.

He went very slowly, carefully, absorbed in the slow progress. He rose higher, climbing out of the pond. The water was now only about his legs; he was thankful, full of relief to be out of the clutches of the pond. He lifted her and staggered on to the bank, out of the horror of wet, grey clay.

He laid her down on the bank. She was quite unconscious and running with water. He made the water come from her mouth, he worked to restore her. He did not have to work very long before he could feel the breathing begin again in her; she was breathing naturally. He worked a little longer. He could feel her live beneath his hands; she was coming back. He wiped her face, wrapped her in his overcoat, looked round into the dim, dark grey world, then lifted her and staggered down the bank and across the fields.

It seemed an unthinkably long way, and his burden so heavy he felt he would never get to the house. But at last he was in the stable-yard, and then in the house-yard. He opened the door and went into the house. In the kitchen he laid her down on the hearthrug, and called. The house was empty. But the fire was burning in the grate.

Then again he kneeled to attend to her. She was breathing regularly, her eyes were wide open and as if conscious, but there seemed something missing in her look. She was conscious in herself, but unconscious of her surroundings.

He ran upstairs, took blankets from a bed, and put them before the fire to warm. Then he removed her saturated, earthy-smelling clothing, rubbed her dry with a towel, and wrapped her naked in the blankets. Then he went into the dining-room, to look for spirits. There was a little whisky. He drank a gulp himself, and put some into her mouth.

The effect was instantaneous. She looked full into his face, as if she had been seeing him for some time, and yet had only just become conscious of him.

"Dr. Fergusson?" she said.

"What?" he answered.

He was divesting himself of his coat, intending to find some dry clothing upstairs. He could not bear the smell of the dead, clayey water, and he was mortally afraid for his own health.

"What did I do?" she asked.

"Walked into the pond," he replied. He had begun to shudder like one sick, and could hardly attend to her. Her eyes remained full on him, he seemed to be going dark in his mind, looking back at her helplessly. The shuddering became quieter in him, his life came back in him, dark and unknowing, but strong again.

"Was I out of my mind?" she asked, while her eyes were fixed on him all the time.

"Maybe, for the moment," he replied. He felt quiet, because his strength had come back. The strange fretful strain had left him.

"Am I out of my mind now?" she asked.

"Are you?" he reflected a moment. "No," he answered truthfully, "I don't see that you are." He turned his face aside. He was afraid now, because he felt dazed, and felt dimly that her power was stronger than his, in this issue. And she continued to look at him fixedly all the time. "Can you tell me where I shall find some dry things to put on?" he asked.

"Did you dive into the pond for me?" she asked.

"No," he answered. "I walked in. But I went in overhead as well."

There was silence for a moment. He hesitated. He very much wanted to go upstairs to get into dry clothing. But there was another desire in him. And she seemed to hold him. His will seemed to have gone to sleep, and left him, standing there slack before her. But he felt warm inside himself. He did not shudder at all, though his clothes were sodden on him.

"Why did you?" she asked.

"Because I didn't want you to do such a foolish thing," he said.

"It wasn't foolish," she said, still gazing at him as she lay on the floor, with a sofa cushion under her head. "It was the right thing to do. *I* knew best, then."

"I'll go and shift these wet things," he said. But still he had not the power to move out of her presence, until she sent him. It was as if she had the life of his body in her hands, and he could not extricate himself. Or perhaps he did not want to.

Suddenly she sat up. Then she became aware of her own immediate condition. She felt the blankets about her, she knew her own limbs. For a moment it seemed as if her reason were going. She looked round, with wild eye, as if seeking something. He stood still with fear. She saw her clothing lying scattered.

"Who undressed me?" she asked, her eyes resting full and inevitable on his face.

"I did," he replied, "to bring you round."

For some moments she sat and gazed at him awfully, her lips parted.

"Do you love me, then?" she asked.

He only stood and stared at her, fascinated. His soul seemed to melt.

She shuffled forward on her knees, and put her arms round him, round his legs, as he stood there, pressing her breasts against his knees and thighs, clutching him with strange, convulsive certainty, pressing his thighs against her, drawing him to her face, her throat, as she looked up at him with flaring, humble eyes of transfiguration, triumphant in first possession.

"You love me," she murmured, in strange transport, yearning and triumphant and confident. "You love me. I know you love me, I know."

And she was passionately kissing his knees, through the wet clothing, passionately and indiscriminately kissing his knees, his legs, as if unaware of everything.

He looked down at the tangled wet hair, the wild, bare, animal shoulders. He was amazed, bewildered, and afraid. He had never thought of loving her. He had never wanted to love her. When he rescued her and restored her, he was a doctor, and she was a patient. He had had no single personal thought of her. Nay, this introduction of the personal element was very distasteful to him, a violation of his professional honour. It was horrible to have her there embracing his knees. It was horrible. He revolted from it, violently. And yet—and yet—he had not the power to break away.

She looked at him again, with the same supplication of powerful love, and that same transcendent, frightening light of triumph. In view of the delicate flame which seemed to come from her face like a light, he was powerless. And yet he had never intended to love her. He had never intended. And something stubborn in him could not give way.

"You love me," she repeated, in a murmur of deep, rhapsodic assurance. "You love me."

Her hands were drawing him, drawing him down to her. He was afraid, even a little horrified. For he had, really, no intention of loving her. Yet her hands were drawing him towards her. He put out his hand quickly to steady himself, and grasped her bare shoulder. A flame seemed to burn the hand that grasped her soft shoulder. He had no intention of loving her: his whole will was against his yielding. It was horrible. And yet wonderful was the touch of her shoulders, beautiful the shining of her face. Was she perhaps mad? He had a horror of yielding to her. Yet something in him ached also.

He had been staring away at the door, away from her. But his hand remained on her shoulder. She had gone suddenly very still. He looked down at her. Her eyes were now wide with fear, with doubt, the light was dying from her face, a shadow of terrible greyness was returning. He could not bear the touch of her eyes' question upon him, and the look of death behind the question.

With an inward groan he gave way, and let his heart

yield towards her. A sudden gentle smile came on his face. And her eyes, which never left his face, slowly, slowly filled with tears. He watched the strange water rise in her eyes, like some slow fountain coming up. And his heart seemed to burn and melt away in his breast.

He could not bear to look at her any more. He dropped on his knees and caught her head with his arms and pressed her face against his throat. She was very still. His heart, which seemed to have broken, was burning with a kind of agony in his breast. And he felt her slow, hot tears wetting his throat. But he could not move.

He felt the hot tears wet his neck and the hollows of his neck, and he remained motionless, suspended through one of man's eternities. Only now it had become indispensable to him to have her face pressed close to him; he could never let her go again. He could never let her head go away from the close clutch of his arm. He wanted to remain like that for ever, with his heart hurting him in a pain that was also life to him. Without knowing, he was looking down on her damp, soft brown hair.

Then, as it were suddenly, he smelt the horrid stagnant smell of that water. And at the same moment she drew away from him and looked at him. Her eyes were wistful and unfathomable. He was afraid of them, and he fell to kissing her, not knowing what he was doing. He wanted her eyes not to have that terrible, wistful, unfathomable look.

When she turned her face to him again, a faint delicate flush was glowing, and there was again dawning that terrible shining of joy in her eyes, which really terrified him, and yet which he now wanted to see, because he feared the look of doubt still more.

"You love me?" she said, rather faltering.

"Yes." The word cost him a painful effort. Not because it wasn't true. But because it was too newly true, the *saying* seemed to tear open again his newly torn heart. And he hardly wanted it to be true, even now.

She lifted her face to him, and he bent forward and kissed

her on the mouth, gently, with the one kiss that is an eternal pledge. And as he kissed her his heart strained again in his breast. He never intended to love her. But now it was over. He had crossed over the gulf to her, and all that he had left behind had shrivelled and become void.

After the kiss, her eyes again slowly filled with tears. She sat still, away from him, with her face drooped aside, and her hands folded in her lap. The tears fell very slowly. There was complete silence. He too sat there motionless and silent on the hearthrug. The strange pain of his heart that was broken seemed to consume him. That he should love her? That this was love! That he should be ripped open in this way! Him, a doctor! How they would all jeer if they knew! It was agony to him to think they might know.

In the curious naked pain of the thought he looked again to her. She was sitting there drooped into a muse. He saw a tear fall, and his heart flared hot. He saw for the first time that one of her shoulders was quite uncovered, one arm bare, he could see one of her small breasts; dimly, because it had become almost dark in the room.

"Why are you crying?" he asked, in an altered voice.

She looked up at him, and behind her tears the consciousness of her situation for the first time brought a dark look of shame to her eyes.

"I'm not crying, really," she said, watching him half frightened.

He reached his hand, and softly closed it on her bare arm.

"I love you! I love you!" he said in a soft, low vibrating voice, unlike himself.

She shrank, and dropped her head. The soft, penetrating grip of his hand on her arm distressed her. She looked up at him.

"I want to go," she said. "I want to go and get you some dry things."

"Why?" he said. "I'm all right."

"But I want to go," she said. "And I want you to change your things."

He released her arm, and she wrapped herself in the

blanket, looking at him rather frightened. And still she did not rise.

"Kiss me," she said wistfully.

He kissed her, but briefly, half in anger.

Then, after a second, she rose nervously, all mixed up in the blanket. He watched her in her confusion, as she tried to extricate herself and wrap herself up so that she could walk. He watched her relentlessly, as she knew. And as she went, the blanket trailing, and as he saw a glimpse of her feet and her white leg, he tried to remember her as she was when he had wrapped her in the blanket. But then he didn't want to remember, because she had been nothing to him then, and his nature revolted from remembering her as she was when she was nothing to him.

A tumbling, muffled noise from within the dark house startled him. Then he heard her voice:—"There are clothes." He rose and went to the foot of the stairs, and gathered up the garments she had thrown down. Then he came back to the fire, to rub himself down and dress. He grinned at his own appearance when he had finished.

The fire was sinking, so he put on coal. The house was now quite dark, save for the light of a street-lamp that shone in faintly from beyond the holly-trees. He lit the gas with matches he found on the mantelpiece. Then he emptied the pockets of his own clothes, and threw all his wet things in a heap into the scullery. After which he gathered up her sodden clothes, gently, and put them in a separate heap on the copper-top in the scullery.

It was six o'clock on the clock. His own watch had stopped. He ought to go back to the surgery. He waited, and still she did not come down. So he went to the foot of the stairs and called:

"I shall have to go."

Almost immediately he heard her coming down. She had on her best dress of black voile, and her hair was tidy, but still damp. She looked at him—and in spite of herself, smiled.

"I don't like you in those clothes," she said.

"Do I look a sight?" he answered.

They were shy of one another.

"I'll make you some tea," she said.

"No, I must go."

"Must you?" And she looked at him again with the wide, strained, doubtful eyes. And again, from the pain of his breast, he knew how he loved her. He went and bent to kiss her, gently, passionately, with his heart's painful kiss.

"And my hair smells so horrible," she murmured in distraction. "And I'm so awful, I'm so awful! Oh, no, I'm too awful." And she broke into bitter, heart-broken sobbing. "You can't want to love me, I'm horrible."

"Don't be silly, don't be silly," he said, trying to comfort her, kissing her, holding her in his arms. "I want you, I want to marry you, we're going to be married, quickly, quickly—tomorrow if I can."

But she only sobbed terribly, and cried:

"I feel awful. I feel awful. I feel I'm horrible to you."

"No, I want you, I want you," was all he answered, blindly, with that terrible intonation which frightened her almost more than her horror lest he should *not* want her.

Things

THEY WERE TRUE idealists, from New England. But that is some time ago: before the war. Several years before the war, they met and married; he a tall, keen-eyed young man from Connecticut, she a smallish, demure, Puritan-looking young woman from Massachusetts. They both had a little money. Not much, however. Even added together, it didn't make three thousand dollars a year. Still—they were free. Free!

Ah! Freedom! To be free to live one's own life! To be twenty-five and twenty-seven, a pair of true idealists with a mutual love of beauty, and an inclination towards "Indian thought"—meaning alas, Mrs. Besant—and an income a little under three thousand dollars a year! But what is money? All one wishes to do is to live a full and beautiful life. In Europe, of course, right at the fountainhead of tradition. It might possibly be done in America: in New England, for example. But at a forfeiture of a certain amount of "beauty." True beauty takes a long time to mature. The baroque is only half-beautiful, half-matured. No, the real silver bloom, the real golden-sweet bouquet of

From *The Lovely Lady* by D. H. Lawrence. Copyright 1933 by the Estate of D. H. Lawrence. Reprinted by permission of The Viking Press, Inc.

beauty had its roots in the Renaissance, not in any later or shallower period.

Therefore the two idealists, who were married in New Haven, sailed at once to Paris: Paris of the old days. They had a studio apartment on the Boulevard Montparnasse, and they became real Parisians, in the old, delightful sense, not in the modern, vulgar. It was the shimmer of the pure impressionists, Monet and his followers, the world seen in terms of pure light, light broken and unbroken. How lovely! How lovely the nights, the river, the mornings in the old streets and by the flower-stalls and the book-stalls, the afternoons up on Montmartre or in the Tuileries, the evenings on the boulevards!

They both painted, but not desperately. Art had not taken them by the throat, and they did not take Art by the throat. They painted: that's all. They knew people—nice people, if possible, though one had to take them mixed. And they were happy.

Yet it seems as if human beings must set their claws in *something*. To be "free," to be "living a full and beautiful life," you must, alas, be attached to something. A "full and beautiful life" means a tight attachment to *something*— at least, it is so for all idealists—or else a certain boredom supervenes; there is a certain waving of loose ends upon the air, like the waving, yearning tendrils of the vine that spread and rotate, seeking something to clutch, something up which to climb towards the necessary sun. Finding nothing, the vine can only trail, half-fulfilled, upon the ground. Such is freedom!—a clutching of the right pole. And human beings are all vines. But especially the idealist. He is a vine, and he needs to clutch and climb. And he despises the man who is a mere *potato*, or turnip, or lump of wood.

Our idealists were frightfully happy, but they were all the time reaching out for something to cotton on to. At first, Paris was enough. They explored Paris *thoroughly*. And they learned French till they almost felt like French people, they could speak it so glibly.

Still, you know, you never talk French with your *soul*. It can't be done. And though it's very thrilling, at first, talking in French to clever Frenchmen—they seem *so* much cleverer than oneself—still, in the long run, it is not satisfying. The endlessly clever *materialism* of the French leaves you cold, in the end, gives a sense of barrenness and incompatibility with true New England depth. So our two idealists felt.

They turned away from France—but ever so gently. France had disappointed them. "We've loved it, and we've got a great deal out of it. But after a while, after a considerable while, several years, in fact, Paris leaves one feeling disappointed. It hasn't quite got what one wants."

"But Paris isn't France."

"No, perhaps not. France is quite different from Paris. And France is lovely—quite lovely. But *to us*, though we love it, it doesn't say a great deal."

So, when the war came, the idealists moved to Italy. And they loved Italy. They found it beautiful, and more poignant than France. It seemed much nearer to the New England conception of beauty: something pure, and full of sympathy, without the *materialism* and the *cynicism* of the French. The two idealists seemed to breathe their own true air in Italy.

And in Italy, much more than in Paris, they felt they could thrill to the teachings of the Buddha. They entered the swelling stream of modern Buddhistic emotion, and they read the books, and they practised meditation, and they deliberately set themselves to eliminate from their own souls greed, pain, and sorrow. They did not realize—yet— that Buddha's very eagerness to free himself from pain and sorrow is in itself a sort of greed. No, they dreamed of a perfect world, from which all greed, and nearly all pain, and a great deal of sorrow, were eliminated.

But America entered the war, so the two idealists had to help. They did hospital work. And though their experience made them realize more than ever that greed, pain, and sorrow *should* be eliminated from the world, nevertheless the Buddhism, or the theosophy, didn't emerge very triumphant from the long crisis. Somehow, somewhere, in some part of themselves, they felt that greed, pain, and sorrow would never be eliminated, because most people don't care about eliminating them, and never will care. Our idealists were far too western to think of abandoning all the world to damnation, while they saved their two selves. They were far too unselfish to sit tight under a bho-tree and reach Nirvana in a mere couple.

It was more than that, though. They simply hadn't enough *Sitzfleisch* to squat under a bho-tree and get to Nirvana by contemplating anything, least of all their own navel. If the whole wide world was not going to be saved, they, personally, were not so very keen on being saved just by themselves. No, it would be so lonesome. They were New Englanders, so it must be all or nothing. Greed, pain, and sorrow must either be eliminated from *all the world*, or else, what was the use of eliminating them from oneself? No use at all! One was just a victim.

And so, although they still *loved* "Indian thought," and felt very tender about it: well, to go back to our metaphor, the pole up which the green and anxious vines had clambered so far now proved dry-rotten. It snapped, and the vines came slowly subsiding to earth again. There was no crack and crash. The vines held themselves up by their own foliage, for a while. But they subsided. The beanstalk of "Indian thought" had given way before Jack and Jill had climbed off the tip of it to a further world.

They subsided with a slow rustle back to earth again. But they made no outcry. They were again "disappointed." But they never admitted it. "Indian thought" had let them down. But they never complained. Even to one another, they never said a word. They were disappointed, faintly but deeply disillusioned, and they both knew it. But the knowledge was tacit.

And they still had so much in their lives. They still had

Italy—dear Italy. And they still had freedom, the priceless treasure. And they still had so much "beauty." About the fulness of their lives they were not quite so sure. They had one little boy, whom they loved as parents should love their children, but whom they wisely refrained from fastening upon, to build their lives on him. No, no, they must live their own lives! They still had strength of mind to know that.

But they were now no longer so very young. Twenty-five and twenty-seven had become thirty-five and thirty-seven. And though they had had a very wonderful time in Europe, and though they still loved Italy—dear Italy!—yet: they were disappointed. They had got a lot out of it: oh, a very great deal indeed! Still, it hadn't given them quite, not *quite*, what they had expected. Europe was lovely, but it was dead. Living in Europe, you were living on the past. And Europeans, with all their superficial charm, were not *really* charming. They were materialistic, they had no *real* soul. They just did not understand the inner urge of the spirit, because the inner urge was dead in them, they were all survivals. There, that was the truth about Europeans: they were survivals, with no more getting ahead in them.

It was another bean-pole, another vine-support crumbled under the green life of the vine. And very bitter it was, this time. For up the old tree-trunk of Europe the green vine had been clambering silently for more than ten years, ten hugely important years, the years of real living. The two idealists had *lived* in Europe, lived on Europe and on European life and European things as vines in an everlasting vineyard.

They had made their home here: a home such as you could never make in America. Their watchword had been "beauty." They had rented, the last four years, the second floor of an old palazzo on the Arno, and here they had all their "things." And they derived a profound, profound satisfaction from their apartment: the lofty, silent, ancient rooms with windows on the river, with glistening dark-red floors, and the beautiful furniture that the idealists had "picked up."

Yes, unknown to themselves, the lives of the idealists had been running with a fierce swiftness horizontally, all the time. They had become tense, fierce hunters of "things" for their home. While their souls were climbing up to the sun of old European culture or old Indian thought, their passions were running horizontally, clutching at "things." Of course they did not buy the things for the things' sakes, but for the sake of "beauty." They looked upon their home as a place entirely furnished by loveliness, not by "things" at all. Valerie had some very lovely curtains at the windows of the long *salotto*, looking on the river: curtains of queer ancient material that looked like finely knitted silk, most beautifully faded down from vermilion and orange, and gold, and black, down to a sheer soft glow. Valerie hardly ever came into the *salotto* without mentally falling on her knees before the curtains. "Chartres!" she said. "To me they are Chartres!" And Melville never turned and looked at his sixteenth-century Venetian bookcase, with its two or three dozen of choice books, without feeling his marrow stir in his bones. The holy of holies!

The child silently, almost sinisterly, avoided any rude contact with these ancient monuments of furniture, as if they had been nests of sleeping cobras, or that "thing" most perilous to the touch, the Ark of the Covenant. His childish awe was silent and cold, but final.

Still, a couple of New England idealists cannot live merely on the bygone glory of their furniture. At least, one couple could not. They got used to the marvellous Bologna cupboard, they got used to the wonderful Venetian bookcase, and the books, and the Siena curtains and bronzes, and the lovely sofas and side-tables and chairs they had "picked up" in Paris. Oh, they had been picking things up since the first day they landed in Europe. And they were still at it. It is the last interest Europe can offer to an outsider: or to an insider either.

When people came, and were thrilled by the Melville interior, then Valerie and Erasmus felt they had not lived in vain: that they still were living. But in the long mornings, when Erasmus was desultorily working at Renaissance Florentine literature, and Valerie was attending to the apartment: and in the long hours after lunch; and in the long, usually very cold and oppressive evenings in the ancient palazzo: then the halo died from around the furniture, and the things became things, lumps of matter that just stood there or hung there, *ad infinitum*, and said nothing; and Valerie and Erasmus almost hated them. The glow of beauty, like every other glow, dies down unless it is fed. The idealists still dearly loved their things. But they had got them. And the sad fact is, things that glow vividly while you're getting them, go almost quite cold after a year or two. Unless, of course, people envy them very much, and the museums are pining for them. And the Melvilles' "things," though very good, were not quite so good as that.

So, the glow gradually went out of everything, out of Europe, out of Italy—"the Italians are *dears*"—even out of that marvellous apartment on the Arno. "Why, if I had this apartment, I'd never, never even want to go out of doors! It's too lovely and perfect." That was something, of course—to hear that.

And yet Valerie and Erasmus went out of doors: they even went out to get away from its ancient, cold-floored, stone-heavy silence and dead dignity. "We're living on the past, you know, Dick," said Valerie to her husband. She called him Dick.

They were grimly hanging on. They did not like to give in. They did not like to own up that they were through. For twelve years now, they had been "free" people living a "full and beautiful life." And America for twelve years had been their anathema, the Sodom and Gomorrah of industrial materialism.

It wasn't easy to own that you were "through." They hated to admit that they wanted to go back. But at last, reluctantly, they decided to go, "for the boy's sake."—"We can't *bear* to leave Europe. But Peter is an American, so he had better look at America while he's young." The Melvilles had an entirely English accent and manner; almost; a little Italian and French here and there.

They left Europe behind, but they took as much of it along with them as possible. Several van-loads, as a matter of fact. All those adorable and irreplaceable "things." And all arrived in New York, idealists, child, and the huge bulk of Europe they had lugged along.

Valerie had dreamed of a pleasant apartment, perhaps on Riverside Drive, where it was not so expensive as east of Fifth Avenue, and where all their wonderful things would look marvellous. She and Erasmus house-hunted. But alas! their income was quite under three thousand dollars a year. They found—well, everybody knows what they found. Two small rooms and a kitchenette, and don't let us unpack a *thing!*

The chunk of Europe which they had bitten off went into a warehouse, at fifty dollars a month. And they sat in two small rooms and a kitchenette, and wondered why they'd done it.

Erasmus, of course, ought to get a job. This was what was written on the wall, and what they both pretended not to see. But it had been the strange, vague threat that the Statue of Liberty had always held over them: "Thou shalt get a job!" Erasmus had the tickets, as they say. A scholastic career was still possible for him. He had taken his exams brilliantly at Yale, and had kept up his "researches," all the time he had been in Europe.

But both he and Valerie shuddered. A scholastic career! The scholastic world! The American scholastic world! Shudder upon shudder! Give up their freedom, their full and beautiful life? Never! Never! Erasmus would be forty next birthday.

The "things" remained in warehouse. Valerie went to look at them. It cost her a dollar an hour, and horrid pangs.

The "things," poor things, looked a bit shabby and wretched, in that warehouse.

However, New York was not all America. There was the great clean West. So the Melvilles went West, with Peter, but without the things. They tried living the simple life, in the mountains. But doing their own chores became almost a nightmare. "Things" are all very well to look at, but it's awful handling them, even when they're beautiful. To be the slave of hideous things, to keep a stove going, cook meals, wash dishes, carry water and clean floors: pure horror of sordid anti-life!

In the cabin on the mountains, Valerie dreamed of Florence, the lost apartment; and her Bologna cupboard and Louis-Quinze chairs, above all, her "Chartres" curtains, stood in New York and costing fifty dollars a month.

A millionaire friend came to the rescue, offering them a cottage on the California coast—California! Where the new soul is to be born in man. With joy the idealists moved a little farther west, catching at new vine-props of hope.

And finding them straws! The millionaire cottage was perfectly equipped. It was perhaps as labour-savingly perfect as is possible: electric heating and cooking, a white-and-pearl enameled kitchen, nothing to make dirt except the human being himself. In an hour or so the idealists had got through their chores. They were "free"—free to hear the great Pacific pounding the coast, and to feel a new soul filling their bodies.

Alas! the Pacific pounded the coast with hideous brutality, brute force itself! And the new soul, instead of sweetly stealing into their bodies, seemed only meanly to gnaw the old soul out of their bodies. To feel you are under the fist of the most blind and crunching brute force: to feel that your cherished idealist's soul is being gnawed out of you, and only irritation left in place of it: well, it isn't good enough.

After about nine months, the idealists departed from the California west. It had been a great experience, they were glad to have had it. But, in the long run, the West was not the place for them, and they knew it. No, the people who wanted new souls had better get them. They, Valerie and Erasmus Melville, would like to develop the old soul a little further. Anyway, they had not felt any influx of new soul, on the California coast. On the contrary.

So, with a slight hole in their material capital, they returned to Massachusetts and paid a visit to Valerie's parents, taking the boy along. The grandparents welcomed the child—poor expatriated boy—and were rather cold to Valerie, but really cold to Erasmus. Valerie's mother definitely said to Valerie, one day, that Erasmus ought to take a job, so that Valerie could live decently. Valerie haughtily reminded her mother of the beautiful apartment on the Arno, and the "wonderful" things in store in New York, and of the "marvellous and satisfying life" she and Erasmus had led. Valerie's mother said that she didn't think her daughter's life looked so very marvellous at present: homeless, with a husband idle at the age of forty, a child to educate, and a dwindling capital: looked the reverse of marvellous to her. Let Erasmus take some post in one of the universities.

"What post? What university?" interrupted Valerie.

"That could be found, considering your father's connections and Erasmus's qualifications," replied Valerie's mother. "And you could get all your valuable things out of store, and have a really lovely home, which everybody in America would be proud to visit. As it is, your furniture is eating up your income, and you are living like rats in a hole, with nowhere to go to."

This was very true. Valerie was beginning to pine for a home, with her "things." Of course she could have sold her furniture for a substantial sum. But nothing would have induced her to. Whatever else passed away, religions, cultures, continents, and hopes, Valerie would never part from the "things" which she and Erasmus had collected with such passion. To these she was nailed.

But she and Erasmus still would not give up that freedom, that full and beautiful life they had so believed in. Erasmus cursed America. He did not *want* to earn a living. He panted for Europe.

Leaving the boy in charge of Valerie's parents, the two idealists once more set off for Europe. In New York they paid two dollars and looked for a brief, bitter hour at their "things." They sailed "student class"—that is, third. Their income now was less than two thousand dollars, instead of three. And they made straight for Paris—cheap Paris.

They found Europe, this time, a complete failure. "We have returned like dogs to our vomit," said Erasmus; "but the vomit has staled in the meantime." He found he couldn't stand Europe. It irritated every nerve in his body. He hated America too. But America at least was a darn sight better than this miserable, dirt-eating continent; which was by no means cheap any more, either.

Valerie, with her heart on her things—she had really burned to get them out of that warehouse, where they had stood now for three years, eating up two thousand dollars —wrote to her mother she thought Erasmus would come back if he could get some suitable work in America. Erasmus, in a state of frustration bordering on rage and insanity, just went round Italy in a poverty-stricken fashion, his coat-cuffs frayed, hating everything with intensity. And when a post was found for him in Cleveland University, to teach French, Italian, and Spanish literature, his eyes grew more beady, and his long, queer face grew sharper and more rat-like, with utter baffled fury. He was forty, and the job was upon him.

"I think you'd better accept, dear. You don't care for Europe any longer. As you say, it's dead and finished. They offer us a house on the college lot, and mother says there's room in it for all our things. I think we'd better cable 'Accept.' "

He glowered at her like a cornered rat. One almost expected to see rat's whiskers twitching at the sides of the sharp nose.

"Shall I send the cablegram?" she asked.

"Send it!" he blurted.

And she went out and sent it.

He was a changed man, quieter, much less irritable. A load was off him. He was inside the cage.

But when he looked at the furnaces of Cleveland, vast and like the greatest of black forests, with red and white-hot cascades of gushing metal, and tiny gnomes of men, and terrific noises, gigantic, he said to Valerie:

"Say what you like, Valerie, this is the biggest thing the modern world has to show."

And when they were in their up-to-date little house on the college lot of Cleveland University and that woebegone débris of Europe, Bologna cupboard, Venice book-shelves, Ravenna bishop's chair, Louis-Quinze side-tables, "Chartres" curtains, Siena bronze lamps, all were arrayed, and all looked perfectly out of keeping, and therefore very impressive; and when the idealists had had a bunch of gaping people in, and Erasmus had showed off in his best European manner, but still quite cordial and American; and Valerie had been most ladylike, but for all that, "we prefer America"; then Erasmus said, looking at her with the queer sharp eyes of a rat:

"Europe's the mayonnaise all right, but America supplies the good old lobster—what?"

"Every time!" she said, with satisfaction.

And he peered at her. He was in the cage: but it was safe inside. And she, evidently, was her real self at last. She had got the goods. Yet round his nose was a queer, evil, scholastic look, of pure scepticism. But he liked lobster.

Joseph Conrad

[1857 — 1924]

JOSEF TEODOR KONRAD KORZENIOWSKI was barely 5 when he accompanied his parents, who were illustrious Polish gentry but rebels against the Czar, into Russian exile. After their death from barbarous treatment, he returned to his mother's family in Poland until he was 17. At his relatives' urging he left the country but, to their surprise, joined the merchant marine in Marseilles, carrying cargo to the West Indies and running guns to the Carlists in Spain. Not until 1878 did he ship aboard a British vessel and land in England. Nevertheless, he was naturalized in 1886, the year he received his master's ticket; and ten years later had married an Englishwoman.

Life at sea or in distant ports could hardly have been unqualified adventure for the young man who spoke many times of a "private gnawing worm" inside him. Ambitions that no naval career could satisfy agitated him. Perhaps he could not forget that his father had been a poet, dramatist, and translator of Hugo and Shakespeare. To satisfy that inner claim, between watches in his cabin in 1889 he began to write of an outcast Pacific trader named Almayer. The following year he took temporary command of a small Congo steamboat: and although the illness which he contracted harassed his health for the rest of his life, his belief that even doomed men have a duty was strengthened. "Before the Congo," he once said, "I was just a mere animal." In 1895 he published *Almayer's Folly*; and never sailed again.

His youthful devotion to Dickens, the naïve reformist, and to the adventure-fantasies of Cooper was rapidly transformed as he fell under the influence of Flaubert's and Turgenev's fuller realism. As early as 1897 he was declaring his obligation to "render the highest kind of justice to the visible universe, by bringing to light the truth, manifold and one, underlying its every aspect." Perhaps because even his earliest stories were serious, ironic considerations, encouragement came to Conrad largely from other writers such as Henry James and Stephen Crane, and not from the public.

"The Lagoon" (*Tales of Unrest*, 1898) is prophetic of questions reappearing in *Lord Jim* (1900): what sanctions can be found for human action when traditions are overthrown; is freedom possible without an accompanying sense of guilt for the endless consequences of even the minor acts of a man; how can the onlooker even understand, much less judge, the stricken, lonely conscience of another? "The Heart of Darkness" (*Youth*, 1902) extends the dramatization of dissolving ideals, the admission of psychically divided selves and cultures. The same motifs recur in Conrad's novels of political jungles, *The Secret Agent* (1907) and *Under Western Eyes* (1911), and again in "The Secret Sharer" (*'Twixt Land and Sea*, 1912). In such works, the world between great wars as well as postwar worlds have finally recognized images of modern man's travail.

Not until 1914, with the publication of *Chance*, did Conrad receive widespread public recognition. By then his son's enlistment in the British army, added to his anxiety for the future of his adopted country, made personal prosperity seem irrelevant. His last works were reminiscences, a communing with the dead.

Conrad's career as a responsible ship's master undoubtedly confirmed his conviction that fidelity is man's greatest virtue, and betrayal the blackest crime. However, the trials of his personal life also made him see how difficult it sometimes is for a man to distinguish his duty. At what point does image become mirage; does wilful faith become self-delusion and imposture? Confronted by such dilemmas, Conrad required that human truth be validated in action: "to the destructive element submit yourself, and with the exertions of your hands and feet in the water make the deep, deep sea keep you up." To convey this sense that man's hope, like life itself, is a calculated risk, Conrad developed a method of narration impressionistic in texture and piecemeal in structure. Seemingly disconnected persons are presented, each in his own compartment of experience; but a continuity of sorts is provided through the unrelenting intensity of the author's graphic concern. Conradian descriptions have rarely been surpassed—perhaps because the original strangeness of the language made him settle for nothing less than the thing itself behind the word. Yet even this clarity proved an illusion, or only a partial dimension in some larger measure. More and more Conrad employed what James called "central intelligences"—the professionally expert but nevertheless detached observer, such as Marlow, who sees the bright sense-image as symbol for deeper realities. If Conrad rarely employs interior monologue, it may be that even the most introspective of his agonizing characters—the outcast, the political refugee, the outpost *isolé*—is as much a stranger to himself as to others.

Before the irrational, Conrad felt uneasy. He admitted, "I have a positive horror of losing even for one moving moment that full possession of myself which is the first condition of good service." Despite this fear, his whole effort was to recover those primitive selves which he found in the dark interior, the preconscious, of his characters. Sometimes when he wondered if his own life's choices, made from the multitude of daily alternatives, had been proper ones, he was tempted to return to the sea as a Suez pilot. But, following the example of those displaced men whose stoic search for self-command he had dramatized, each time Conrad accepted his ordeal. Dedicated to sacrifice without reward, typically he refused the knighthood offered him the last year of his life.

Amy Foster

KENNEDY IS A country doctor, and lives in Colebrook, on the shores of Eastbay. The high ground rising abruptly behind the red roofs of the little town crowds the quaint High Street against the wall which defends it from the sea. Beyond the sea wall there curves for miles in a vast and regular sweep the barren beach of shingle, with the village of Brenzett standing out darkly across the water, a spire in a clump of trees; and still farther out the perpendicular column of a lighthouse, looking in the distance no bigger than a lead pencil, marks the vanishing point of the land. The country at the back of Brenzett is low and flat; but the bay is fairly well sheltered from the seas, and occasionally a big ship, windbound or through stress of weather, makes use of the anchoring ground a mile and a half due north from you as you stand at the back door of the "Ship Inn" in Brenzett. A dilapidated windmill near by, lifting its shattered arms from a mount no loftier than a rubbish heap, and a Martello tower squatting at the water's edge half a mile to the south of the Coastguard cottages, are familiar to the skippers of small craft. These are the official

From *Typhoon and Other Stories*, Doubleday, Page & Company, 1924. Reprinted by permission of The Trustees of the Joseph Conrad Estate, Doubleday & Company of New York and J. M. Dent & Sons Ltd. London.

seamarks for the patch of trustworthy bottom represented
on the Admiralty charts by an irregular oval of dots enclosing several figure sixes, with a tiny anchor engraved
among them, and the legend "mud and shells" over all.

The brow of the upland overtops the square tower of the
Colebrook Church. The slope is green and looped by a
white road. Ascending along this road, you open a valley
broad and shallow, a wide green trough of pastures and
hedges merging inland into a vista of purple tints and flowing lines closing the view.

In this valley down to Brenzett and Colebrook and up
to Darnford, the market town fourteen miles away, lies the
practice of my friend Kennedy. He had begun life as sur-
geon in the Navy, and afterwards had been the companion
of a famous traveler, in the days when there were continents with unexplored interiors. His papers on the fauna
and flora made him known to scientific societies. And now
he had come to a country practice—from choice. The penetrating power of his mind, acting like a corrosive fluid, had
destroyed his ambition, I fancy. His intelligence is of a
scientific order, of an investigating habit, and of that un-
appeasable curiosity which believes that there is a particle
of a general truth in every mystery.

A good many years ago now, on my return from abroad,
he invited me to stay with him. I came readily enough, and
as he could not neglect his patients to keep me company,
he took me on his rounds—thirty miles or so of an afternoon, sometimes. I waited for him on the roads; the horse
reached after the leafy twigs, and, sitting high in the dog-
cart, I could hear Kennedy's laugh through the half-open
door of some cottage. He had a big, hearty laugh that would
have fitted a man twice his size, a brisk manner, a bronzed
face, and a pair of gray, profoundly attentive eyes. He had
the talent of making people talk to him freely, and an in-
exhaustible patience in listening to their tales.

One day, as we trotted out of a large village into a shady
bit of road, I saw on our left hand a low, black cottage, with

diamond panes in the windows, a creeper on the end wall, a roof of shingle, and some roses climbing on the rickety trelliswork of the tiny porch. Kennedy pulled up to a walk. A woman, in full sunlight, was throwing a dripping blanket over a line stretched between two old apple trees. And as the bobtailed, long-necked chestnut, trying to get his head, jerked the left hand, covered by a thick dogskin glove, the doctor raised his voice over the hedge: "How's your child, Amy?"

I had time to see her dull face, red, not with a mantling blush, but as if her flat cheeks had been vigorously slapped, and to take in the squat figure, the scanty, dusty brown hair drawn into a tight knot at the back of the head. She looked quite young. With a distinct catch in her breath, her voice sounded low and timid.

"He's well, thank you."

We trotted again. "A young patient of yours," I said; and the doctor, flicking the chestnut absently, muttered, "Her husband used to be."

"She seems a dull creature," I remarked, listlessly.

"Precisely," said Kennedy. "She is very passive. It's enough to look at the red hands hanging at the end of those short arms, at those slow, prominent brown eyes, to know the inertness of her mind—an inertness that one would think made it everlastingly safe from all the surprises of imagination. And yet which of us is safe? At any rate, such as you see her, she had enough imagination to fall in love. She's the daughter of one Isaac Foster, who from a small farmer has sunk into a shepherd; the beginning of his misfortunes dating from his runaway marriage with the cook of his widowed father—a well-to-do, apoplectic grazier, who passionately struck his name off his will, and had been heard to utter threats against his life. But this old affair, scandalous enough to serve as a motive for a Greek tragedy, arose from the similarity of their characters. There are other tragedies, less scandalous and of a subtler poignancy, arising from irreconcilable differences and from that fear of the Incomprehensible that hangs over all our heads—over all our heads. . . ."

The tired chestnut dropped into a walk; and the rim of the sun, all red in a speckless sky, touched familiarly the smooth top of a plowed rise near the road as I had seen it times innumerable touch the distant horizon of the sea. The uniform brownness of the harrowed field glowed with a rose tinge, as though the powdered clods had sweated out in minute pearls of blood the toil of uncounted plowmen. From the edge of a copse a wagon with two horses was rolling gently along the ridge. Raised above our heads upon the skyline, it loomed up against the red sun, triumphantly big, enormous, like a chariot of giants drawn by two slow-stepping steeds of legendary proportions. And the clumsy figure of the man plodding at the head of the leading horse projected itself on the background of the Infinite with a heroic uncouthness. The end of his carter's whip quivered high up in the blue. Kennedy discoursed.

"She's the eldest of a large family. At the age of fifteen they put her out to service at the New Barns Farm. I attended Mrs. Smith, the tenant's wife, and saw that girl there for the first time. Mrs. Smith, a genteel person with a sharp nose, made her put on a black dress every afternoon. I don't know what induced me to notice her at all. There are faces that call your attention by a curious want of definiteness in their whole aspect, as, walking in a mist, you peer attentively at a vague shape which, after all, may be nothing more curious or strange than a signpost. The only peculiarity I perceived in her was a slight hesitation in her utterance, a sort of preliminary stammer which passes away with the first word. When sharply spoken to, she was apt to lose her head at once; but her heart was of the kindest. She had never been heard to express a dislike for a single human being, and she was tender to every living creature. She was devoted to Mrs. Smith, to Mr. Smith, to their dogs, cats, canaries; and as to Mrs. Smith's gray parrot, its peculiarities exercised upon her a positive fascination. Nevertheless, when that outlandish bird, attacked by the cat, shrieked for help in human accents, she ran out into the yard stopping her ears, and did not prevent the crime. For Mrs. Smith this was another evidence of her stupidity; on the other hand, her want of charm, in view of Smith's well-known frivolousness, was a great recommendation. Her shortsighted eyes would swim with pity for a poor mouse in a trap, and she had been seen once by some boys on her knees in the wet grass helping a toad in difficulties. If it's true, as some German fellow has said, that without phosphorus there is no thought, it is still more true that there is no kindness of heart without a certain amount of imagination. She had some. She had even more than is necessary to understand suffering and to be moved by pity. She fell in love under circumstances that leave no room for doubt in the matter; for you need imagination to form a notion of beauty at all, and still more to discover your ideal in an unfamiliar shape.

"How this aptitude came to her, what it did feed upon, is an inscrutable mystery. She was born in the village, and had never been farther away from it than Colebrook or perhaps Darnford. She lived for four years with the Smiths. New Barns is an isolated farmhouse a mile away from the road, and she was content to look day after day at the same fields, hollows, rises; at the trees and the hedgerows; at the faces of the four men about the farm, always the same—day after day, month after month, year after year. She never showed a desire for conversation, and, as it seemed to me, she did not know how to smile. Sometimes of a fine Sunday afternoon she would put on her best dress, a pair of stout boots, a large gray hat trimmed with a black feather (I've seen her in that finery), seize an absurdly slender parasol, climb over two stiles, tramp over three fields and along two hundred yards of road—never farther. There stood Foster's cottage. She would help her mother to give their tea to the younger children, wash up the crockery, kiss the little ones, and go back to the farm. That was all. All the

rest, all the change, all the relaxation. She never seemed
to wish for anything more. And then she fell in love. She
fell in love silently, obstinately—perhaps helplessly. It came
slowly, but when it came it worked like a powerful spell; it
was love as the ancients understood it: an irresistible and
fateful impulse—a possession! Yes, it was in her to become
haunted and possessed by a face, by a presence, fatally, as
though she had been a pagan worshiper of form under a
joyous sky—and to be awakened at last from that mysterious
forgetfulness of self, from that enchantment, from that
transport, by a fear resembling the unaccountable terror of
a brute. . . ."

With the sun hanging low on its western limit, the expanse of the grasslands framed in the counterscarps of the
rising ground took on a gorgeous and somber aspect. A
sense of penetrating sadness, like that inspired by a grave
strain of music, disengaged itself from the silence of the
fields. The men we met walked past, slow, unsmiling, with
downcast eyes, as if the melancholy of an overburdened
earth had weighted their feet, bowed their shoulders, borne
down their glances.

"Yes," said the doctor to my remark, "one would think
the earth is under a curse, since of all her children these
that cling to her the closest are uncouth in body and as
leaden of gait as if their very hearts were loaded with chains.
But here on this same road you might have seen amongst
these heavy men a being lithe, supple and long-limbed,
straight like a pine, with something striving upwards in his
appearance as though the heart within him had been
buoyant. Perhaps it was only the force of the contrast, but
when he was passing one of these villagers here, the soles of
his feet did not seem to me to touch the dust of the road.
He vaulted over the stiles, paced these slopes with a long
elastic stride that made him noticeable at a great distance,
and had lustrous black eyes. He was so different from the
mankind around that, with his freedom of movement, his
soft—a little startled—glance, his olive complexion and

graceful bearing, his humanity suggested to me the nature of a woodland creature. He came from there."

The doctor pointed with his whip, and from the summit of the descent seen over the rolling tops of the trees in a park by the side of the road, appeared the level sea far below us, like the floor of an immense edifice inlaid with bands of dark ripple, with still trails of glitter, ending in a belt of glassy water at the foot of the sky. The light blur of smoke, from an invisible steamer, faded on the great clearness of the horizon like the mist of a breath on a mirror; and, inshore, the white sails of a coaster, with the appearance of disentangling themselves slowly from under the branches, floated clear of the foliage of the trees.

"Shipwrecked in the bay?" I said.

"Yes; he was a castaway. A poor emigrant from Central Europe bound to America and washed ashore here in a storm. And for him, who knew nothing of the earth, England was an undiscovered country. It was some time before he learned its name; and for all I know he might have expected to find wild beasts or wild men here, when, crawling in the dark over the sea wall, he rolled down the other side into a dyke, where it was another miracle he didn't get drowned. But he struggled instinctively like an animal under a net, and this blind struggle threw him out into a field. He must have been, indeed, of a tougher fiber than he looked to withstand without expiring such buffetings, the violence of his exertions, and so much fear. Later on, in his broken English that resembled curiously the speech of a young child, he told me himself that he put his trust in God, believing he was no longer in this world. And truly— he would add—how was he to know? He fought his way against the rain and the gale on all fours, and crawled at last among some sheep huddled close under the lee of a hedge. They ran off in all directions, bleating in the darkness, and he welcomed the first familiar sound he heard on these shores. It must have been two in the morning then. And this is all we know of the manner of his landing, though he did not arrive unattended by any means. Only his grisly company did not begin to come ashore till much later in the day. . . ."

The doctor gathered the reins, clicked his tongue; we trotted down the hill. Then turning, almost directly, a sharp corner into High Street, we rattled over the stones and were home.

Late in the evening Kennedy, breaking a spell of moodiness that had come over him, returned to the story. Smoking his pipe, he paced the long room from end to end. A reading lamp concentrated all its light upon the papers on his desk; and, sitting by the open window, I saw, after the windless, scorching day, the frigid splendor of a hazy sea lying motionless under the moon. Not a whisper, not a splash, not a stir of the shingle, not a footstep, not a sigh came up from the earth below—never a sign of life but the scent of climbing jasmine; and Kennedy's voice, speaking behind me, passed through the wide casement, to vanish outside in a chill and sumptuous stillness.

". . . The relations of shipwrecks in the olden times tell us of much suffering. Often the castaways were only saved from drowning to die miserably from starvation on a barren coast; others suffered violent death or else slavery, passing through years of precarious existence with people to whom their strangeness was an object of suspicion, dislike or fear. We read about these things, and they are very pitiful. It is indeed hard upon a man to find himself a lost stranger, helpless, incomprehensible, and of a mysterious origin, in some obscure corner of the earth. Yet amongst all the adventurers shipwrecked in all the wild parts of the world, there is not one, it seems to me, that ever had to suffer a fate so simply tragic as the man I am speaking of, the most innocent of adventurers cast out by the sea in the bight of this bay, almost within sight from this very window.

"He did not know the name of his ship. Indeed, in the course of time we discovered he did not even know that ships had names—'like Christian people'; and when, one

day, from the top of Talfourd Hill, he beheld the sea lying
open to his view, his eyes roamed afar, lost in an air of wild
surprise, as though he had never seen such a sight before.
And probably he had not. As far as I could make out, he
had been hustled together with many others on board an
emigrant ship at the mouth of the Elbe, too bewildered to
take note of his surroundings, too weary to see anything,
too anxious to care. They were driven below into the
'tween-deck and battened down from the very start. It was
a low timber dwelling—he would say—with wooden beams
overhead, like the houses in his country, but you went into
it down a ladder. It was very large, very cold, damp and
somber, with places in the manner of wooden boxes where
people had to sleep one above another, and it kept on rocking all ways at once all the time. He crept into one of these
boxes and lay down there in the clothes in which he had
left his home many days before, keeping his bundle and
his stick by his side. People groaned, children cried, water
dripped, the lights went out, the walls of the place creaked,
and everything was being shaken so that in one's little box
one dared not lift one's head. He had lost touch with his
only companion (a young man from the same valley, he
said), and all the time a great noise of wind went on outside and heavy blows fell—boom! boom! An awful sickness
overcame him, even to the point of making him neglect his
prayers. Besides, one could not tell whether it was morning
or evening. It seemed always to be night in that place.

"Before that he had been traveling a long, long time on
the iron track. He looked out of the window, which had a
wonderfully clear glass in it, and the trees, the houses, the
fields, and the long roads seemed to fly round and round
about him till his head swam. He gave me to understand
that he had on his passage beheld uncounted multitudes of
people—whole nations—all dressed in such clothes as the
rich wear. Once he was made to get out of the carriage, and
slept through a night on a bench in a house of bricks with
his bundle under his head; and once for many hours he had

to sit on a floor of flat stones, dozing, with his knees up and with his bundle between his feet. There was a roof over him, which seemed made of glass, and was so high that the tallest mountain pine he had ever seen would have had room to grow under it. Steam machines rolled in at one end and out at the other. People swarmed more than you can see on a feast day round the miraculous Holy Image in the yard of the Carmelite Convent down in the plains where, before he left his home, he drove his mother in a wooden cart—a pious old woman who wanted to offer prayers and make a vow for his safety. He could not give me an idea of how large and lofty and full of noise and smoke and gloom, and clang of iron, the place was, but someone had told him it was called Berlin. Then they rang a bell, and another steam machine came in, and again he was taken on and on through a land that wearied his eyes by its flatness without a single bit of a hill to be seen anywhere. One more night he spent shut up in a building like a good stable with a litter of straw on the floor, guarding his bundle amongst a lot of men, of whom not one could understand a single word he said. In the morning they were all led down to the stony shores of an extremely broad muddy river, flowing not between hills but between houses that seemed immense. There was a steam machine that went on the water, and they all stood upon it packed tight, only now there were with them many women and children who made much noise. A cold rain fell, the wind blew in his face; he was wet through, and his teeth chattered. He and the young man from the same valley took each other by the hand.

"They thought they were being taken to America straight away, but suddenly the steam machine bumped against the side of a thing like a great house on the water. The walls were smooth and black, and there uprose, growing from the roof as it were, bare trees in the shape of crosses, extremely high. That's how it appeared to him then, for he had never seen a ship before. This was the ship that was

going to swim all the way to America. Voices shouted,
everything swayed; there was a ladder dipping up and down.
He went up on his hands and knees in mortal fear of falling
into the water below, which made a great splashing. He got
separated from his companion, and when he descended into
the bottom of that ship his heart seemed to melt suddenly
within him.

"It was then also, as he told me, that he lost contact for
good and all with one of those three men who the summer
before had been going about through all the little towns
in the foothills of his country. They would arrive on market
days driving in a peasant's cart, and would set up an office
in an inn or some other Jew's house. There were three of
them, of whom one with a long beard looked venerable;
and they had red cloth collars round their necks and gold
lace on their sleeves like Government officials. They sat
proudly behind a long table; and in the next room, so that
the common people shouldn't hear, they kept a cunning
telegraph machine, through which they could talk to the
Emperor of America. The fathers hung about the door, but
the young men of the mountains would crowd up to the
table asking many questions, for there was work to be got
all the year round at three dollars a day in America, and no
military service to do.

"But the American Kaiser would not take everybody. Oh,
no! He himself had great difficulty in getting accepted, and
the venerable man in uniform had to go out of the room
several times to work the telegraph on his behalf. The
American Kaiser engaged him at last at three dollars, he
being young and strong. However, many able young men
backed out, afraid of the great distance; besides, those only
who had some money could be taken. There were some
who sold their huts and their land because it cost a lot of
money to get to America; but then, once there, you had
three dollars a day, and if you were clever you could find
places where true gold could be picked up on the ground.
His father's house was getting over-full. Two of his brothers

were married and had children. He promised to send money home from America by post twice a year. His father sold an old cow, a pair of piebald mountain ponies of his own raising, and a cleared plot of fair pasture land on the sunny slope of a pineclad pass to a Jew innkeeper, in order to pay the people of the ship that took men to America to get rich in a short time.

"He must have been a real adventurer at heart, for how many of the greatest enterprises in the conquest of the earth had for their beginning just such a bargaining away of the paternal cow for the mirage or true gold far away! I have been telling you more or less in my own words what I learned fragmentarily in the course of two or three years, during which I seldom missed an opportunity of a friendly chat with him. He told me this story of his adventure with many flashes of white teeth and lively glances of black eyes, at first in a sort of anxious baby-talk, then, as he acquired the language, with great fluency, but always with that singing, soft, and at the same time vibrating intonation that instilled a strangely penetrating power into the sound of the most familiar English words, as if they had been the words of an unearthly language. And he always would come to an end, with many emphatic shakes of his head, upon that awful sensation of his heart melting within him directly he set foot on board that ship. Afterwards there seemed to come for him a period of blank ignorance, at any rate as to facts. No doubt he must have been abominably seasick and abominably unhappy—this soft and passionate adventurer, taken thus out of his knowledge, and feeling bitterly as he lay in his emigrant bunk his utter loneliness; for his was a highly sensitive nature. The next thing we know of him for certain is that he had been hiding in Hammond's pigpound by the side of the road to Norton, six miles, as the crow flies, from the sea. Of these experiences he was unwilling to speak: they seemed to have seared into his soul a somber sort of wonder and indignation. Through the rumors of the countryside, which lasted for a good many

days after his arrival, we know that the fishermen of West
Colebrook had been disturbed and startled by heavy knocks
against the walls of weatherboard cottages, and by a voice
crying piercingly strange words in the night. Several of
them turned out even, but, no doubt, he had fled in sudden
alarm at their rough angry tones hailing each other in the
darkness. A sort of frenzy must have helped him up the
steep Norton hill. It was he, no doubt, who early the following morning had been seen lying (in a swoon, I should
say) on the roadside grass by the Brenzett carrier, who actually got down to have a nearer look, but drew back, intimidated by the perfect immobility, and by something
queer in the aspect of that tramp, sleeping so still under
the showers. As the day advanced, some children came
dashing into school at Norton in such a fright that the
schoolmistress went out and spoke indignantly to a 'horrid-
looking man' on the road. He edged away, hanging his
head, for a few steps, and then suddenly ran off with extraordinary fleetness. The driver of Mr. Bradley's milk cart
made no secret of it that he had lashed with his whip at
a hairy sort of gypsy fellow who, jumping up at a turn of
the road by the Vents, made a snatch at the pony's bridle.
And he caught him a good one, too, right over the face, he
said, that made him drop down in the mud a jolly sight
quicker than he had jumped up; but it was a good half a
mile before he could stop the pony. Maybe that in his
desperate endeavors to get help, and in his need to get in
touch with someone, the poor devil had tried to stop the
cart. Also three boys confessed afterwards to throwing
stones at a funny tramp, knocking about all wet and muddy,
and, it seemed, very drunk, in the narrow deep lane by the
limekilns. All this was the talk of three villages for days;
but we have Mrs. Finn's (the wife of Smith's wagoner) un-
impeachable testimony that she saw him get over the low
wall of Hammond's pigpound and lurch straight at her,
babbling aloud in a voice that was enough to make one
die of fright. Having the baby with her in a perambulator,

Mrs. Finn called out to him to go away, and as he persisted in coming nearer, she hit him courageously with her umbrella over the head, and, without once looking back, ran like the wind with the perambulator as far as the first house in the village. She stopped then, out of breath, and spoke to old Lewis, hammering there at a heap of stones; and the old chap, taking off his immense black wire goggles, got up on his shaky legs to look where she pointed. Together they followed with their eyes the figure of the man running over a field; they saw him fall down, pick himself up, and run on again, staggering and waving his long arms above his head, in the direction of the New Barns Farm. From that moment he is plainly in the toils of his obscure and touching destiny. There is no doubt after this of what happened to him. All is certain now: Mrs. Smith's intense terror; Amy Foster's stolid conviction held against the other's nervous attack, that the man 'meant no harm'; Smith's exasperation (on his return from Darnford Market) at finding the dog barking himself into a fit, the back door locked, his wife in hysterics; and all for an unfortunate dirty tramp, supposed to be even then lurking in his stackyard. Was he? He would teach him to frighten women.

"Smith is notoriously hot-tempered, but the sight of some nondescript and miry creature sitting cross-legged amongst a lot of loose straw, and swinging itself to and fro like a bear in a cage, made him pause. Then this tramp stood up silently before him, one mass of mud and filth from head to foot. Smith, alone amongst his stacks with this apparition, in the stormy twilight ringing with the infuriated barking of the dog, felt the dread of an inexplicable strangeness. But when that being, parting with his black hands the long matted locks that hung before his face, as you part the two halves of a curtain, looked out at him with glistening, wild, black-and-white eyes, the weirdness of this silent encounter fairly staggered him. He has admitted since (for the story has been a legitimate subject of conversation about here for years) that he made more than

one step backwards. Then a sudden burst of rapid, sense-
less speech persuaded him at once that he had to do with
an escaped lunatic. In fact, that impression never wore off
completely. Smith has not in his heart given up his secret
conviction of the man's essential insanity to this very day.

"As the creature approached him, jabbering in a most
discomposing manner, Smith (unaware that he was being
addressed as 'gracious lord,' and adjured in God's name to
afford food and shelter) kept on speaking firmly but gently
to it, and retreating all the time into the other yard. At last,
watching his chance, by a sudden charge he bundled him
headlong into the wood-lodge, and instantly shot the bolt.
Thereupon he wiped his brow, though the day was cold.
He had done his duty to the community by shutting up a
wandering and probably dangerous maniac. Smith isn't
a hard man at all, but he had room in his brain only for
that one idea of lunacy. He was not imaginative enough to
ask himself whether the man might not be perishing with
cold and hunger. Meantime, at first, the maniac made a
great deal of noise in the lodge. Mrs. Smith was screaming
upstairs, where she had locked herself in her bedroom; but
Amy Foster sobbed piteously at the kitchen door, wringing
her hands and muttering, 'Don't! don't!' I daresay Smith
had a rough time of it that evening with one noise and
another, and this insane, disturbing voice crying obstinately
through the door only added to his irritation. He couldn't
possibly have connected this troublesome lunatic with the
sinking of a ship in Eastbay, of which there had been a
rumor in the Darnford market place. And I dare say the
man inside had been very near to insanity on that night.
Before his excitement collapsed and he became unconscious
he was throwing himself violently about in the dark, rolling
on some dirty sacks, and biting his fists with rage, cold,
hunger, amazement, and despair.

"He was a mountaineer of the eastern range of the Car-
pathians, and the vessel sunk the night before in Eastbay

was the Hamburg emigrant ship *Herzogin Sophia-Dorothea*, of appalling memory.

"A few months later we could read in the papers the accounts of the bogus 'Emigration Agencies' among the Slavic peasantry in the more remote provinces of Austria. The object of these scoundrels was to get hold of the poor ignorant people's homesteads, and they were in league with the local usurers. They exported their victims through Hamburg mostly. As to the ship, I had watched her out of this very window, reaching close-hauled under short canvas into the bay on a dark, threatening afternoon. She came to an anchor, correctly by the chart, off the Brenzett Coastguard station. I remember before the night fell looking out again at the outlines of her spars and rigging that stood out dark and pointed on a background of ragged, slaty clouds like another and a slighter spire to the left of the Brenzett churchtower. In the evening the wind rose. At midnight I could hear in my bed the terrific gusts and the sounds of a driving deluge.

"About that time the Coastguardsmen thought they saw the lights of a steamer over the anchoring ground. In a moment they vanished; but it is clear that another vessel of some sort had tried for shelter in the bay on that awful, blind night, had rammed the German ship amidships ('a breach'—as one of the divers told me afterwards—'that you could sail a Thames barge through'), and then had gone out either scatheless or damaged, who shall say; but had gone out, unknown, unseen, and fatal, to perish mysteriously at sea. Of her nothing ever came to light, and yet the hue and cry that was raised all over the world would have found her out if she had been in existence anywhere on the face of the waters.

"A completeness without a clue, and a stealthy silence as of a neatly executed crime, characterize this murderous disaster, which, as you may remember, had its gruesome celebrity. The wind would have prevented the loudest out-

cries from reaching the shore; there had been evidently no
time for signals of distress. It was death without any sort of
fuss. The Hamburg ship, filling all at once, capsized as she
sank, and at daylight there was not even the end of a spar
to be seen above water. She was missed, of course, and at
first the Coastguardsmen surmised that she had either
dragged her anchor or parted her cable sometime during
the night, and had been blown out to sea. Then, after the
tide turned, the wreck must have shifted a little and released some of the bodies, because a child—a little fair-
haired child in a red frock—came ashore abreast of the
Martello tower. By the afternoon you could see along three
miles of beach dark figures with bare legs dashing in and
out of the tumbling foam, and rough-looking men, women
with hard faces, children, mostly fair-haired, were being
carried, stiff and dripping, on stretchers, on wattles, on lad-
ders, in a long procession past the door of the 'Ship Inn,'
to be laid out in a row under the north wall of the Brenzett
Church.

"Officially, the body of the little girl in the red frock is
the first thing that came ashore from that ship. But I have
patients amongst the seafaring population of West Colebrook, and, unofficially, I am informed that very early that
morning two brothers, who went down to look after their
cobble hauled up on the beach, found a good way from
Brenzett, an ordinary ship's hencoop, lying high and dry
on the shore, with eleven drowned ducks inside. Their
families ate the birds, and the hencoop was split into firewood with a hatchet. It is possible that a man (supposing
he happened to be on deck at the time of the accident)
might have floated ashore on that hencoop. He might. I
admit it is improbable, but there was the man—and for
days, nay, for weeks—it didn't enter our heads that we had
amongst us the only living soul that had escaped from that
disaster. The man himself, even when he learned to speak
intelligibly, could tell us very little. He remembered he had
felt better (after the ship had anchored, I suppose), and

that the darkness, the wind, and the rain took his breath away. This looks as if he had been on deck sometime during that night. But we mustn't forget he had been taken out of his knowledge, that he had been seasick and battened down below for four days, that he had no general notion of a ship or of the sea, and therefore could have no definite idea of what was happening to him. The rain, the wind, the darkness he knew; he understood the bleating of the sheep, and he remembered the pain of his wretchedness and misery, his heartbroken astonishment that it was neither seen nor understood, his dismay at finding all the men angry and all the women fierce. He had approached them as a beggar, it is true, he said; but in his country, even if they gave nothing, they spoke gently to beggars. The children in his country were not taught to throw stones at those who asked for compassion. Smith's strategy overcame him completely. The wood-lodge presented the horrible aspect of a dungeon. What would be done to him next? . . . No wonder that Amy Foster appeared to his eyes with the aureole of an angel of light. The girl had not been able to sleep for thinking of the poor man, and in the morning, before the Smiths were up, she slipped out across the back yard. Holding the door of the wood-lodge ajar, she looked in and extended to him half a loaf of white bread—'such bread as the rich eat in my country,' he used to say.

"At this he got up slowly from amongst all sorts of rubbish, stiff, hungry, trembling, miserable, and doubtful. 'Can you eat this?' she asked in her soft and timid voice. He must have taken her for a 'gracious lady.' He devoured ferociously, and tears were falling on the crust. Suddenly he dropped the bread, seized her wrist, and imprinted a kiss on her hand. She was not frightened. Through his forlorn condition she had observed that he was good-looking. She shut the door and walked back slowly to the kitchen. Much later on, she told Mrs. Smith, who shuddered at the bare idea of being touched by that creature.

"Through this act of impulsive pity he was brought back

again within the pale of human relations with his new surroundings. He never forgot it—never.

"That very same morning old Mr. Swaffer (Smith's nearest neighbor) came over to give his advice, and ended by carrying him off. He stood, unsteady on his legs, meek, and caked over in half-dried mud, while the two men talked around him in an incomprehensible tongue. Mrs. Smith had refused to come downstairs till the madman was off the premises; Amy Foster, far from within the dark kitchen, watched through the open back door; and he obeyed the signs that were made to him to the best of his ability. But Smith was full of mistrust. 'Mind, sir! It may be all his cunning,' he cried repeatedly in a tone of warning. When Mr. Swaffer started the mare, the deplorable being sitting humbly by his side, through weakness, nearly fell out over the back of the high two-wheeled cart. Swaffer took him straight home. And it is then that I come upon the scene.

"I was called in by the simple process of the old man beckoning to me with his forefinger over the gate of his house as I happened to be driving past. I got down, of course.

"'I've got something here,' he mumbled, leading the way to an outhouse at a little distance from his other farm buildings.

"It was there that I saw him first, in a long, low room taken upon the space of that sort of coach-house. It was bare and whitewashed, with a small square aperture glazed with one cracked, dusty pane at its further end. He was lying on his back upon a straw pallet; they had given him a couple of horse blankets, and he seemed to have spent the remainder of his strength in the exertion of cleaning himself. He was almost speechless; his quick breathing under the blankets pulled up to his chin, his glittering, restless black eyes reminded me of a wild bird caught in a snare. While I was examining him, old Swaffer stood silently by the door, passing the tips of his fingers along his shaven upper lip. I gave some directions, promised to send a bottle of medicine, and naturally made some inquiries.

" 'Smith caught him in the stackyard at New Barns,' said the old chap in his deliberate, unmoved manner, and as if the other had been indeed a sort of wild animal. 'That's how I came by him. Quite a curiosity, isn't he? Now tell me, doctor—you've been all over the world—don't you think that's a bit of a Hindoo we've got hold of here?'

"I was greatly surprised. His long black hair scattered over the straw bolster contrasted with the olive pallor of his face. It occurred to me he might be a Basque. It didn't necessarily follow that he should understand Spanish; but I tried him with the few words I know, and also with some French. The whispered sounds I caught by bending my ear to his lips puzzled me utterly. That afternoon the young ladies from the rectory (one of them read Goethe with a dictionary, and the other had struggled with Dante for years), coming to see Miss Swaffer, tried their German and Italian on him from the doorway. They retreated, just the least bit scared by the flood of passionate speech which, turning on his pallet, he let out at them. They admitted that the sound was pleasant, soft, musical—but, in conjunction with his looks perhaps, it was startling—so excitable, so utterly unlike anything one had ever heard. The village boys climbed up the bank to have a peep through the little square aperture. Everybody was wondering what Mr. Swaffer would do with him.

"He simply kept him.

"Swaffer would be called eccentric were he not so much respected. They will tell you that Mr. Swaffer sits up as late as ten o'clock at night to read books, and they will tell you also that he can write a check for two hundred pounds without thinking twice about it. He himself would tell you that the Swaffers had owned land between this and Darnford for these three hundred years. He must be eighty-five today, but he does not look a bit older than when I first came here. He is a great breeder of sheep, and deals extensively in cattle. He attends market days for miles around in every sort of weather, and drives sitting bowed low over the reins, his lank gray hair curling over the collar of his warm coat, and with a green plaid rug round his legs. The calmness of advanced age gives a solemnity to his manner. He is clean-shaved; his lips are thin and sensitive; something rigid and monachal in the set of his features lends a certain elevation to the character of his face. He has been known to drive miles in the rain to see a new kind of rose in somebody's garden, or a monstrous cabbage grown by a cottager. He loves to hear tell of or to be shown something that he calls 'outlandish.' Perhaps it was just that outlandishness of the man which influenced old Swaffer. Perhaps it was only an inexplicable caprice. All I know is that at the end of three weeks I caught sight of Smith's lunatic digging in Swaffer's kitchen garden. They had found out he could use a spade. He dug barefooted.

"His black hair flowed over his shoulders. I suppose it was Swaffer who had given him the striped old cotton shirt; but he wore still the national brown cloth trousers (in which he had been washed ashore) fitting to the leg almost like tights; was belted with a broad leather belt studded with little brass discs; and had never yet ventured into the village. The land he looked upon seemed to him kept neatly, like the grounds round a landowner's house; the size of the cart horses struck him with astonishment; the roads resembled garden walks, and the aspect of the people, especially on Sundays, spoke of opulence. He wondered what made them so hardhearted and their children so bold. He got his food at the back door, carried it in both hands, carefully, to his outhouse, and, sitting alone on his pallet, would make the sign of the cross before he began. Beside the same pallet, kneeling in the early darkness of the short days, he recited aloud the Lord's Prayer before he slept. Whenever he saw old Swaffer he would bow with veneration from the waist, and stand erect while the old man, with his fingers over his upper lip, surveyed him silently. He bowed also to Miss Swaffer, who kept house frugally for her father—a broad-shouldered, big-boned woman of forty-five, with the pocket of her dress full of keys, and a gray, steady eye. She was Church—as people said (while her father was one of the trustees of the Baptist Chapel) —and wore a little steel cross at her waist. She dressed severely in black, in memory of one of the innumerable Bradleys of the neighborhood, to whom she had been engaged some twenty-five years ago—a young farmer who broke his neck out hunting on the eve of the wedding day. She had the unmoved countenance of the deaf, spoke very seldom, and her lips, thin like her father's, astonished one sometimes by a mysteriously ironic curl.

"These were the people to whom he owed allegiance, and an overwhelming loneliness seemed to fall from the leaden sky of that winter without sunshine. All the faces were sad. He could talk to no one, and had no hope of ever understanding anybody. It was as if these had been the faces of people from the other world—dead people—he used to tell me years afterwards. Upon my word, I wonder he did not go mad. He didn't know where he was. Somewhere very far from his mountains—somewhere over the water. Was this America, he wondered?

"If it hadn't been for the steel cross at Miss Swaffer's belt he would not, he confessed, have known whether he was in a Christian country at all. He used to cast stealthy glances at it, and feel comforted. There was nothing here the same as in his country! The earth and the water were different; there were no images of the Redeemer by the roadside. The very grass was different, and the trees. All the trees but the three old Norway pines on the bit of lawn before Swaffer's house, and these reminded him of his country. He had been detected once, after dusk, with his forehead against the trunk of one of them, sobbing, and talking to himself. They had been like brothers to him at that time, he affirmed. Everything else was strange. Conceive you the

kind of an existence overshadowed, oppressed, by the everyday material appearances, as if by the visions of a nightmare. At night, when he could not sleep, he kept on
thinking of the girl who gave him the first piece of bread
he had eaten in this foreign land. She had been neither
fierce nor angry, nor frightened. Her face he remembered
as the only comprehensible face amongst all these faces
that were as closed, as mysterious, and as mute as the faces
of the dead who are possessed of a knowledge beyond the
comprehension of the living. I wonder whether the memory
of her compassion prevented him from cutting his throat.
But there! I suppose I am an old sentimentalist, and forget
the instinctive love of life which it takes all the strength
of an uncommon despair to overcome.

"He did the work which was given him with an intelligence which surprised old Swaffer. By and by it was discovered that he could help at the plowing, could milk
the cows, feed the bullocks in the cattleyard, and was of
some use with the sheep. He began to pick up words, too,
very fast; and suddenly, one fine morning in spring, he
rescued from an untimely death a grandchild of old Swaffer.

"Swaffer's younger daughter is married to Willcox, a
solicitor and the town clerk of Colebrook. Regularly twice
a year they come to stay with the old man for a few days.
Their only child, a little girl not three years old at the time,
ran out of the house alone in her little white pinafore, and,
toddling across the grass of a terraced garden, pitched herself over a low wall head first into the horsepond in the
yard below.

"Our man was out with the wagoner and the plow in
the field nearest to the house, and as he was leading the team
round to begin a fresh furrow, he saw, through the gap of
a gate, what for anybody else would have been a mere flutter
of something white. But he had straight-glancing, quick,
far-reaching eyes, that only seemed to flinch and lose their
amazing power before the immensity of the sea. He was
barefooted, and looking as outlandish as the heart of Swaffer

could desire. Leaving the horses on the turn, to the inexpressible disgust of the wagoner he bounded off, going over the plowed ground in long leaps, and suddenly appeared before the mother, thrust the child into her arms, and strode away.

"The pond was not very deep; but still, if he had not had such good eyes, the child would have perished—miserably suffocated in the foot or so of sticky mud at the bottom. Old Swaffer walked out slowly into the field, waited till the plow came over to his side, had a good look at him, and without saying a word went back to the house. But from that time they laid out his meals on the kitchen table; and at first, Miss Swaffer, all in black and with an inscrutable face, would come and stand in the doorway of the living room to see him make a big sign of the cross before he fell to. I believe that from that day, too, Swaffer began to pay him regular wages.

"I can't follow step by step his development. He cut his hair short, was seen in the village and along the road going to and fro to his work like any other man. Children ceased to shout after him. He became aware of social differences, but remained for a long time surprised at the bare poverty of the churches among so much wealth. He couldn't understand either why they were kept shut up on weekdays. There was nothing to steal in them. Was it to keep people from praying too often? The rectory took much notice of him about that time, and I believe the young ladies attempted to prepare the ground for his conversion. They could not, however, break him of his habit of crossing himself, but he went so far as to take off the string with a couple of brass medals the size of a sixpence, a tiny metal cross, and a square sort of scapulary which he wore round his neck. He hung them on the wall by the side of his bed, and he was still to be heard every evening reciting the Lord's Prayer, in incomprehensible words and in a slow, fervent tone, as he had heard his old father do at the head of all the kneeling family, big and little, on every evening of his life. And though he wore corduroys at work, and a slop-made pepper-and-salt suit on Sundays, strangers would turn round to look after him on the road. His foreignness had a peculiar and indelible stamp. At last people became used to seeing him. But they never became used to him. His rapid, skimming walk; his swarthy complexion; his hat cocked on the left ear; his habit, on warm evenings, of wearing his coat over one shoulder, like a hussar's dolman; his manner of leaping over the stiles, not as a feat of agility, but in the ordinary course of progression—all these peculiarities were, as one may say, so many causes of scorn and offense to the inhabitants of the village. They wouldn't in their dinner hour lie flat on their backs on the grass to stare at the sky. Neither did they go about the fields screaming dismal tunes. Many times I have heard his high-pitched voice from behind the ridge of some sloping sheep-walk, a voice light and soaring, like a lark's, but with a melancholy human note, over our fields that hear only the song of birds. And I would be startled myself. Ah! He was different; innocent of heart, and full of good will, which nobody wanted, this castaway, that, like a man transplanted into another planet, was separated by an immense space from his past and by an immense ignorance from his future. His quick, fervent utterance positively shocked everybody. 'An excitable devil,' they called him. One evening, in the taproom of the Coach and Horses (having drunk some whisky), he upset them all by singing a love song of his country. They hooted him down, and he was pained; but Preble, the lame wheelwright, and Vincent, the fat blacksmith, and the other notables, too, wanted to drink their evening beer in peace. On another occasion he tried to show them how to dance. The dust rose in clouds from the sanded floor; he leaped straight up amongst the deal tables, struck his heels together, squatted on one heel in front of old Preble, shooting out the other leg, uttered wild and exulting cries, jumped up to whirl on one foot, snapping his fingers above his head—and a strange carter who was

having a drink in there began to swear, and cleared out
with his half-pint in his hand into the bar. But when suddenly he sprang upon a table and continued to dance among
the glasses, the landlord interfered. He didn't want any
'acrobat tricks in the taproom.' They laid their hands on
him. Having had a glass or two, Mr. Swaffer's foreigner tried
to expostulate: was ejected forcibly: got a black eye.

"I believe he felt the hostility of his human surroundings.
But he was tough—tough in spirit, too, as well as in body.
Only the memory of the sea frightened him, with that
vague terror that is left by a bad dream. His home was far
away; and he did not want now to go to America. I had
often explained to him that there is no place on earth where
true gold can be found lying ready and to be got for the
trouble of the picking up. How, then, he asked, could he
ever return home with empty hands when there had been
sold a cow, two ponies, and a bit of land to pay for his
going? His eyes would fill with tears, and, averting them
from the immense shimmer of the sea, he would throw
himself face down on the grass. But sometimes, cocking his
hat with a little conquering air, he would defy my wisdom.
He had found his bit of true gold. That was Amy Foster's
heart; which was 'a golden heart, and soft to people's misery,' he would say in the accents of overwhelming conviction.

"He was called Yanko. He had explained that this meant
Little John; but as he would also repeat very often that he
was a mountaineer (some word sounding in the dialect of
his country like Goorall) he got it for his surname. And this
is the only trace of him that the succeeding ages may find
in the marriage register of the parish. There it stands—
Yanko Goorall—in the rector's handwriting. The crooked
cross made by the castaway, a cross whose tracing no doubt
seemed to him the most solemn part of the whole ceremony, is all that remains now to perpetuate the memory
of his name.

"His courtship had lasted some time—ever since he got

his precarious footing in the community. It began by his
buying for Amy Foster a green satin ribbon in Darnford.
This was what you did in his country. You bought a ribbon
at a Jew's stall on a fair-day. I don't suppose the girl knew
what to do with it, but he seemed to think that his honorable intentions could not be mistaken.

"It was only when he declared his purpose to get married that I fully understood how, for a hundred futile and
inappreciable reasons, how—shall I say odious?—he was to
all the countryside. Every old woman in the village was up
in arms. Smith, coming upon him near the farm, promised
to break his head for him if he found him about again.
But he twisted his little black mustache with such a bel-
licose air and rolled such big, black fierce eyes at Smith
that this promise came to nothing. Smith, however, told
the girl that she must be mad to take up with a man who
was surely wrong in his head. All the same, when she heard
him in the gloaming whistle from beyond the orchard a
couple of bars of a weird and mournful tune, she would
drop whatever she had in her hand—she would leave Mrs.
Smith in the middle of a sentence—and she would run out
to his call. Mrs. Smith called her a shameless hussy. She
answered nothing. She said nothing at all to anybody, and
went on her way as if she had been deaf. She and I alone
in all the land, I fancy, could see his very real beauty. He
was very good-looking, and most graceful in his bearing,
with that something wild as of a woodland creature in his
aspect. Her mother moaned over her dismally whenever the
girl came to see her on her day out. The father was surly,
but pretended not to know; and Mrs. Finn once told her
plainly that 'this man, my dear, will do you some harm
some day yet.' And so it went on. They could be seen on
the roads, she tramping stolidly in her finery—gray dress,
black feather, stout boots, prominent white cotton gloves
that caught your eye a hundred yards away; and he, his
coat slung picturesquely over one shoulder, pacing by her
side, gallant of bearing and casting tender glances upon the

girl with the golden heart. I wonder whether he saw how
plain she was. Perhaps among types so different from what
he had ever seen, he had not the power to judge; or perhaps he was seduced by the divine quality of her pity.

"Yanko was in great trouble meantime. In his country
you get an old man for an ambassador in marriage affairs.
He did not know how to proceed. However, one day in
the midst of sheep in a field (he was now Swaffer's under-
shepherd with Foster) he took off his hat to the father and
declared himself humbly. 'I daresay she's fool enough to
marry you,' was all Foster said. 'And then,' he used to relate, 'he puts his hat on his head, looks black at me as if
he wanted to cut my throat, whistles the dog, and off he
goes, leaving me to do the work.' The Fosters, of course,
didn't like to lose the wages the girl earned: Amy used to
give all her money to her mother. But there was in Foster
a very genuine aversion to that match. He contended that
the fellow was very good with sheep, but was not fit for
any girl to marry. For one thing, he used to go along the
hedges muttering to himself like a dam' fool; and then,
these foreigners behave very queerly to women sometimes.
And perhaps he would want to carry her off somewhere—
or run off himself. It was not safe. He preached it to his
daughter that the fellow might ill-use her in some way.
She made no answer. It was, they said in the village, as if
the man had done something to her. People discussed the
matter. It was quite an excitement, and the two went on
'walking out' together in the face of opposition. Then something unexpected happened.

"I don't know whether old Swaffer ever understood how
much he was regarded in the light of a father by his foreign
retainer. Anyway the relation was curiously feudal. So when
Yanko asked formally for an interview—'and the Miss, too'
(he called the severe, deaf Miss Swaffer simply *Miss*)—it
was to obtain their permission to marry. Swaffer heard him
unmoved, dismissed him by a nod, and then shouted the
intelligence into Miss Swaffer's best ear. She showed no

surprise, and only remarked grimly, in a veiled blank voice, 'He certainly won't get any other girl to marry him.'

"It is Miss Swaffer who has all the credit for the munificence: but in a very few days it came out that Mr. Swaffer had presented Yanko with a cottage (the cottage you've seen this morning) and something like an acre of ground —had made it over to him in absolute property. Willcox expedited the deed, and I remember him telling me he had a great pleasure in making it ready. It recited: 'In consideration of saving the life of my beloved grandchild, Bertha Willcox.'

"Of course, after that no power on earth could prevent them from getting married.

"Her infatuation endured. People saw her going out to meet him in the evening. She stared with unblinking, fascinated eyes up the road where he was expected to appear, walking freely, with a swing from the hip, and humming one of the love tunes of his country. When the boy was born, he got elevated at the 'Coach and Horses,' essayed again a song and a dance, and was again ejected. People expressed their commiseration for a woman married to that jack-in-the-box. He didn't care. There was a man now (he told me boastfully) to whom he could sing and talk in the language of his country, and show how to dance by and by.

"But I don't know. To me he appeared to have grown less springy of step, heavier in body, less keen of eye. Imagination, no doubt; but it seems to me now as if the net of fate had been drawn closer round him already.

"One day I met him on the footpath over the Talfourd Hill. He told me that 'women were funny.' I had heard already of domestic differences. People were saying that Amy Foster was beginning to find out what sort of man she had married. He looked upon the sea with indifferent, unseeing eyes. His wife had snatched the child out of his arms one day as he sat on the doorstep crooning to it a song such as the mothers sing to babies in his mountains. She seemed to think he was doing it some harm. Women are funny.

And she had objected to him praying aloud in the evening. Why? He expected the boy to repeat the prayer aloud after him by and by, as he used to do after his old father when he was a child—in his own country. And I discovered he longed for their boy to grow up so that he could have a man to talk with in that language that to our ears sounded so disturbing, so passionate, and so bizarre. Why his wife should dislike the idea he couldn't tell. But that would pass, he said. And tilting his head knowingly, he tapped his breastbone to indicate that she had a good heart: not hard, not fierce, open to compassion, charitable to the poor!

"I walked away thoughtfully; I wondered whether his difference, his strangeness, were not penetrating with repulsion that dull nature they had begun by irresistibly attracting. I wondered. . . ."

The doctor came to the window and looked out at the frigid splendor of the sea, immense in the haze, as if enclosing all the earth with all the hearts lost among the passions of love and fear.

"Physiologically, now," he said, turning away abruptly, "it was possible. It was possible."

He remained silent. Then went on—

"At all events, the next time I saw him he was ill—lung trouble. He was tough, but I dare say he was not acclimatized as well as I had supposed. It was a bad winter; and, of course, these mountaineers do get fits of homesickness; and a state of depression would make him vulnerable. He was lying half dressed on a couch downstairs.

"A table covered with a dark oilcloth took up all the middle of the little room. There was a wicker cradle on the floor, a kettle spouting steam on the hob, and some child's linen lay drying on the fender. The room was warm, but the door opens right into the garden, as you noticed perhaps.

"He was very feverish, and kept on muttering to himself. She sat on a chair and looked at him fixedly across the table with her brown, blurred eyes. 'Why don't you have him upstairs?' I asked. With a start and a confused stammer she said, 'Oh! ah! I couldn't sit with him upstairs, sir.'

"I gave her certain directions; and going outside, I said again that he ought to be in bed upstairs. She wrung her hands. 'I couldn't. I couldn't. He keeps on saying something—I don't know what.' With the memory of all the talk against the man that had been dinned into her ears, I looked at her narrowly. I looked into her short-sighted eyes, at her dumb eyes that once in her life had seen an enticing shape, but seemed, staring at me, to see nothing at all now. But I saw she was uneasy.

" 'What's the matter with him?' she asked in a sort of vacant trepidation. 'He doesn't look very ill. I never did see anybody look like this before. . . .'

" 'Do you think,' I asked indignantly, 'he is shamming?'

" 'I can't help it, sir,' she said, stolidly. And suddenly she clapped her hands and looked right and left. 'And there's the baby. I am so frightened. He wanted me just now to give him the baby. I can't understand what he says to it.'

" 'Can't you ask a neighbor to come in tonight?' I asked.

" 'Please, sir, nobody seems to care to come,' she muttered, dully resigned all at once.

"I impressed upon her the necessity of the greatest care, and then had to go. There was a good deal of sickness that winter. 'Oh, I hope he won't talk!' she exclaimed softly just as I was going away.

"I don't know how it is I did not see—but I didn't. And yet, turning in my trap, I saw her lingering before the door, very still, and as if meditating a flight up the miry road.

"Towards the night his fever increased.

"He tossed, moaned, and now and then muttered a complaint. And she sat with the table between her and the couch, watching every movement and every sound, with the terror, the unreasonable terror, of that man she could not understand creeping over her. She had drawn the wicker cradle close to her feet. There was nothing in her now but the maternal instinct and that unaccountable fear.

"Suddenly coming to himself, parched, he demanded a drink of water. She did not move. She had not understood, though he may have thought he was speaking in English. He waited, looking at her, burning with fever, amazed at her silence and immobility, and then he shouted impatiently, 'Water! Give me water!'

"She jumped to her feet, snatched up the child, and stood still. He spoke to her, and his passionate remonstrances only increased her fear of that strange man. I believe he spoke to her for a long time, entreating, wondering, pleading, ordering, I suppose. She says she bore it as long as she could. And then a gust of rage came over him.

"He sat up and called out terribly one word—some word. Then he got up as though he hadn't been ill at all, she says. And as in fevered dismay, indignation, and wonder he tried to get to her round the table, she simply opened the door and ran out with the child in her arms. She heard him call twice after her down the road in a terrible voice—and fled. . . . Ah! but you should have seen stirring behind the dull, blurred glance of those eyes the specter of the fear which had haunted her on that night three miles and a half to the door of Foster's cottage! I did the next day.

"And it was I who found him lying face down and his body in a puddle, just outside the little wicker gate.

"I had been called out that night to an urgent case in the village, and on my way home at daybreak passed by the cottage. The door stood open. My man helped me to carry him in. We laid him on the couch. The lamp smoked, the fire was out, the chill of the stormy night oozed from the cheerless yellow paper on the wall. 'Amy!' I called aloud, and my voice seemed to lose itself in the emptiness of this tiny house as if I had cried in a desert. He opened his eyes. 'Gone!' he said, distinctly. 'I had only asked for water—only for a little water. . . .'

"He was muddy. I covered him up and stood waiting in silence, catching a painfully gasped word now and then. They were no longer in his own language. The fever had left him, taking with it the heat of life. And with his panting breast and lustrous eyes he reminded me again of a wild creature under the net; of a bird caught in a snare. She had left him. She had left him—sick—helpless—thirsty. The spear of the hunter had entered his very soul. 'Why?' he cried, in the penetrating and indignant voice of a man calling to a responsible Maker. A gust of wind and a swish of rain answered.

"And as I turned away to shut the door he pronounced the word 'Merciful!' and expired.

"Eventually I certified heart failure as the immediate cause of death. His heart must have indeed failed him, or else he might have stood this night of storm and exposure, too. I closed his eyes and drove away. Not very far from the cottage I met Foster walking sturdily between the dripping hedges with his collie at his heels.

" 'Do you know where your daughter is?' I asked.

" 'Don't I!' he cried. 'I am going to talk to him a bit. Frightening a poor woman like this.'

" 'He won't frighten her any more,' I said. 'He is dead.'

"He struck with his stick at the mud.

" 'And there's the child.'

"Then, after thinking deeply for a while—

" 'I don't know that it isn't for the best.'

"That's what he said. And she says nothing at all now. Not a word of him. Never. Is his image as utterly gone from her mind as his lithe and striding figure, his caroling voice are gone from our fields? He is no longer before her eyes to excite her imagination into a passion of love or fear; and his memory seems to have vanished from her dull brain as a shadow passes away upon a white screen. She lives in the cottage and works for Miss Swaffer. She is Amy Foster for everybody, and the child is 'Amy Foster's boy.' She calls him Johnny—which means Little John.

"It is impossible to say whether this name recalls anything to her. Does she ever think of the past? I have seen her hanging over the boy's cot in a very passion of maternal tenderness. The little fellow was lying on his back, a little frightened at me, but very still, with his big black eyes, with his fluttered air of a bird in a snare. And looking at him I seemed to see again the other one—the father, cast out mysteriously by the sea to perish in the supreme disaster of loneliness and despair."

The Lagoon

THE WHITE MAN, leaning with both arms over the roof of
the little house in the stern of the boat, said to the steersman:

"We will pass the night in Arsat's clearing. It is late."

The Malay only grunted, and went on looking fixedly at
the river. The white man rested his chin on his crossed
arms and gazed at the wake of the boat. At the end of the
straight avenue of forests cut by the intense glitter of the
river, the sun appeared unclouded and dazzling, poised low
over the water that shone smoothly like a band of metal.
The forests, somber and dull, stood motionless and silent
on each side of the broad stream. At the foot of big, towering trees, trunkless nipa palms rose from the mud of the
bank, in bunches of leaves enormous and heavy, that hung
unstirring over the brown swirl of eddies. In the stillness
of the air every tree, every leaf, every bough, every tendril
of creeper and every petal of minute blossoms seemed to
have been bewitched into an immobility perfect and final.
Nothing moved on the river but the eight paddles that rose
flashing regularly, dipped together with a single splash;

From *Tales of Unrest*, Doubleday, Page & Company, 1924. Reprinted
by permission of The Trustees of the Joseph Conrad Estate, Doubleday
& Company of New York and J. M. Dent & Sons Ltd. London.

while the steersman swept right and left with a periodic and sudden flourish of his blade describing a glinting semicircle above his head. The churned-up water frothed alongside with a confused murmur. And the white man's canoe, advancing upstream in the short-lived disturbance of its own making, seemed to enter the portals of a land from which the very memory of motion had forever departed.

The white man, turning his back upon the setting sun, looked along the empty and broad expanse of the sea-reach. For the last three miles of its course the wandering, hesitating river, as if enticed irresistibly by the freedom of an open horizon, flows straight into the sea, flows straight to the east—to the east that harbors both light and darkness. Astern of the boat the repeated call of some bird, a cry discordant and feeble, skipped along over the smooth water and lost itself, before it could reach the other shore, in the breathless silence of the world.

The steersman dug his paddle into the stream, and held hard with stiffened arms, his body thrown forward. The water gurgled aloud; and suddenly the long straight reach seemed to pivot on its center, the forests swung in a semicircle, and the slanting beams of sunset touched the broadside of the canoe with a fiery glow, throwing the slender and distorted shadows of its crew upon the streaked glitter of the river. The white man turned to look ahead. The course of the boat had been altered at right angles to the stream, and the carved dragon head of its prow was pointing now at a gap in the fringing bushes of the bank. It glided through, brushing the overhanging twigs, and disappeared from the river like some slim and amphibious creature leaving the water for its lair in the forests.

The narrow creek was like a ditch: tortuous, fabulously deep; filled with gloom under the thin strip of pure and shining blue of the heaven. Immense trees soared up, invisible behind the festooned draperies of creepers. Here and there, near the glistening blackness of the water, a twisted root of some tall tree showed amongst the tracery of small ferns, black and dull, writhing and motionless, like an arrested snake. The short words of the paddlers reverberated loudly between the thick and somber walls of vegetation. Darkness oozed out from between the trees, through the tangled maze of the creepers, from behind the great fantastic and unstirring leaves; the darkness, mysterious and invincible; the darkness scented and poisonous of impenetrable forests.

The men poled in the shoaling water. The creek broadened, opening out into a wide sweep of a stagnant lagoon. The forests receded from the marshy bank, leaving a level strip of bright green, reedy grass to frame the reflected blueness of the sky. A fleecy pink cloud drifted high above, trailing the delicate coloring of its image under the floating leaves and the silvery blossoms of the lotus. A little house, perched on high piles, appeared black in the distance. Near it, two tall nibong palms, that seemed to have come out of the forests in the background, leaned slightly over the ragged roof, with a suggestion of sad tenderness and care in the droop of their leafy and soaring heads.

The steersman, pointing with his paddle, said, "Arsat is there. I see his canoe fast between the piles."

The polers ran along the sides of the boat glancing over their shoulders at the end of the day's journey. They would have preferred to spend the night somewhere else than on this lagoon of weird aspect and ghostly reputation. Moreover, they disliked Arsat, first as a stranger, and also because he who repairs a ruined house, and dwells in it, proclaims that he is not afraid to live amongst the spirits that haunt the places abandoned by mankind. Such a man can disturb the course of fate by glances or words; while his familiar ghosts are not easy to propitiate by casual wayfarers upon whom they long to wreak the malice of their human master. White men care not for such things, being unbelievers and in league with the Father of Evil, who leads them unharmed through the invisible dangers of this world. To the warnings of the righteous they oppose an offensive pretense of disbelief. What is there to be done?

So they thought, throwing their weight on the end of their long poles. The big canoe glided on swiftly, noiselessly, and smoothly, towards Arsat's clearing, till, in a great rattling of poles thrown down, and the loud murmurs of "Allah be praised!" it came with a gentle knock against the crooked piles below the house.

The boatmen with uplifted faces shouted discordantly, "Arsat! O Arsat!" Nobody came. The white man began to climb the rude ladder giving access to the bamboo platform before the house. The juragan of the boat said sulkily, "We will cook in the sampan, and sleep on the water."

"Pass my blankets and the basket," said the white man, curtly.

He knelt on the edge of the platform to receive the bundle. Then the boat shoved off, and the white man, standing up, confronted Arsat, who had come out through the low door of his hut. He was a man young, powerful, with broad chest and muscular arms. He had nothing on but his sarong. His head was bare. His big, soft eyes stared eagerly at the white man, but his voice and demeanor were composed as he asked, without any words of greeting:

"Have you medicine, Tuan?"

"No," said the visitor in a startled tone. "No. Why? Is there sickness in the house?"

"Enter and see," replied Arsat, in the same calm manner, and turning short round, passed again through the small doorway. The white man, dropping his bundles, followed.

In the dim light of the dwelling he made out on a couch of bamboos a woman stretched on her back under a broad sheet of red cotton cloth. She lay still, as if dead; but her big eyes, wide open, glittered in the gloom, staring upwards at the slender rafters, motionless and unseeing. She was in a high fever, and evidently unconscious. Her cheeks were sunk slightly, her lips were partly open, and on the young face there was the ominous and fixed expression—the absorbed, contemplating expression of the unconscious who are going to die. The two men stood looking down at her in silence.

"Has she been long ill?" asked the traveler.

"I have not slept for five nights," answered the Malay, in a deliberate tone. "At first she heard voices calling her from the water and struggled against me who held her. But since the sun of today rose she hears nothing—she hears not me. She sees nothing. She sees not me—me!"

He remained silent for a minute, then asked softly: "Tuan, will she die?"

"I fear so," said the white man, sorrowfully. He had known Arsat years ago, in a far country in times of trouble and danger, when no friendship is to be despised. And since his Malay friend had come unexpectedly to dwell in the hut on the lagoon with a strange woman, he had slept many times there, in his journeys up and down the river. He liked the man who knew how to keep faith in council and how to fight without fear by the side of his white friend. He liked him—not so much perhaps as a man likes his favorite dog—but still he liked him well enough to help and ask no questions, to think sometimes vaguely and hazily in the midst of his own pursuits, about the lonely man and the long-haired woman with audacious face and triumphant eyes, who lived together hidden by the forests—alone and feared.

The white man came out of the hut in time to see the enormous conflagration of sunset put out by the swift and stealthy shadows that, rising like a black and impalpable vapor above the treetops, spread over the heaven, extinguishing the crimson glow of floating clouds and the red brilliance of departing daylight. In a few moments all the stars came out above the intense blackness of the earth and the great lagoon gleaming suddenly with reflected lights resembled an oval patch of night sky flung down into the hopeless and abysmal night of the wilderness. The white man had some supper out of the basket, then collecting a few sticks that lay about the platform, made up a small fire, not for warmth, but for the sake of the smoke, which would keep off the mosquitoes. He wrapped himself in the blankets and sat with his back against the reed wall of the house, smoking thoughtfully.

Arsat came through the doorway with noiseless steps and squatted down by the fire. The white man moved his outstretched legs a little.

"She breathes," said Arsat in a low voice, anticipating the expected question. "She breathes and burns as if with a great fire. She speaks not; she hears not—and burns!"

He paused for a moment, then asked in a quiet, incurious tone:

"Tuan . . . will she die?"

The white man moved his shoulders uneasily and muttered in a hesitating manner:

"If such is her fate."

"No, Tuan," said Arsat, calmly. "If such is my fate. I hear, I see, I wait. I remember . . . Tuan, do you remember the old days? Do you remember my brother?"

"Yes," said the white man. The Malay rose suddenly and went in. The other, sitting still outside, could hear the voice in the hut. Arsat said: "Hear me! Speak!" His words were succeeded by a complete silence. "O Diamelen!" he cried, suddenly. After that cry there was a deep sigh. Arsat came out and sank down again in his old place.

They sat in silence before the fire. There was no sound within the house, there was no sound near them; but far away on the lagoon they could hear the voices of the boatmen ringing fitful and distinct on the calm water. The fire in the bows of the sampan shone faintly in the distance with a hazy red glow. Then it died out. The voices ceased. The land and the water slept invisible, unstirring and mute. It was as though there had been nothing left in the world but the glitter of stars streaming, ceaseless and vain, through the black stillness of the night.

The white man gazed straight before him into the darkness with wide-open eyes. The fear and fascination, the inspiration and the wonder of death—of death near, unavoidable, and unseen, soothed the unrest of his race and stirred the most indistinct, the most intimate of his thoughts. The ever-ready suspicion of evil, the gnawing suspicion that lurks in our hearts, flowed out into the stillness round him—into the stillness profound and dumb, and made it appear untrustworthy and infamous, like the placid and impenetrable mask of an unjustifiable violence. In that fleeting and powerful disturbance of his being the earth enfolded in the starlight peace became a shadowy country of inhuman strife, a battlefield of phantoms terrible and charming, august or ignoble, struggling ardently for the possession of our helpless hearts. An unquiet and mysterious country of inextinguishable desires and fears.

A plaintive murmur rose in the night; a murmur saddening and startling, as if the great solitudes of surrounding woods had tried to whisper into his ear the wisdom of their immense and lofty indifference. Sounds hesitating and vague floated in the air round him, shaped themselves slowly into words; and at last flowed on gently in a murmuring stream of soft and monotonous sentences. He stirred like a man waking up and changed his position slightly. Arsat, motionless and shadowy, sitting with bowed head under the stars, was speaking in a low and dreamy tone:

". . . for where can we lay down the heaviness of our trouble but in a friend's heart? A man must speak of war and of love. You, Tuan, know what war is, and you have seen me in time of danger seek death as other men seek life! A writing may be lost; a lie may be written; but what the eye has seen is truth and remains in the mind!"

"I remember," said the white man, quietly. Arsat went on with mournful composure:

"Therefore I shall speak to you of love. Speak in the night. Speak before both night and love are gone—and the eye of day looks upon my sorrow and my shame; upon my blackened face; upon my burnt-up heart."

A sigh, short and faint, marked an almost imperceptible pause, and then his words flowed on, without a stir, without a gesture.

"After the time of trouble and war was over and you went away from my country in the pursuit of your desires, which we, men of the islands, cannot understand, I and my brother became again, as we had been before, the sword bearers of the Ruler. You know we were men of family, belonging to a ruling race, and more fit than any to carry on our right shoulder the emblem of power. And in the time of prosperity Si Dendring showed us favor, as we, in time of sorrow, had showed to him the faithfulness of our courage. It was a time of peace. A time of deer hunts and cock fights; of idle talks and foolish squabbles between men whose bellies are full and weapons are rusty. But the sower watched the young rice shoots grow up without fear, and the traders came and went, departed lean and returned fat into the river of peace. They brought news, too. Brought lies and truth mixed together, so that no man knew when to rejoice and when to be sorry. We heard from them about you also. They had seen you here and had seen you there. And I was glad to hear, for I remembered the stirring times, and I always remembered you, Tuan, till the time came when my eyes could see nothing in the past, because they had looked upon the one who is dying there—in the house."

He stopped to exclaim in an intense whisper, "O Mara bahia! O Calamity!" then went on speaking a little louder:

"There's no worse enemy and no better friend than a brother, Tuan, for one brother knows another, and in perfect knowledge is strength for good or evil. I loved my brother. I went to him and told him that I could see nothing but one face, hear nothing but one voice. He told me: 'Open your heart so that she can see what is in it—and wait. Patience is wisdom. Inchi Midah may die or our Ruler may throw off his fear of a woman!' . . . I waited! . . .

You remember the lady with the veiled face, Tuan, and
the fear of our Ruler before her cunning and temper. And
if she wanted her servant, what could I do? But I fed the
hunger of my heart on short glances and stealthy words. I
loitered on the path to the bathhouses in the daytime, and
when the sun had fallen behind the forest I crept along
the jasmine hedges of the women's courtyard. Unseeing,
we spoke to one another through the scent of flowers,
through the veil of leaves, through the blades of long grass
that stood still before our lips; so great was our prudence,
so faint was the murmur of our great longing. The time
passed swiftly . . . and there were whispers amongst
women—and our enemies watched—my brother was
gloomy, and I began to think of killing and of a fierce
death. . . . We are of a people who take what they want
—like you whites. There is a time when a man should forget loyalty and respect. Might and authority are given to
rulers, but to all men is given love and strength and courage. My brother said, 'You shall take her from their midst.
We are two who are like one.' And I answered, 'Let it be
soon, for I find no warmth in sunlight that does not shine
upon her.' Our time came when the Ruler and all the great
people went to the mouth of the river to fish by torchlight.
There were hundreds of boats, and on the white sand, between the water and the forests, dwellings of leaves were
built for the households of the Rajahs. The smoke of cooking fires was like a blue mist of the evening, and many
voices rang in it joyfully. While they were making the boats
ready to beat up the fish, my brother came to me and said,
'Tonight!' I looked to my weapons, and when the time
came our canoe took its place in the circle of boats carrying
the torches. The lights blazed on the water, but behind the
boats there was darkness. When the shouting began and the
excitement made them like mad we dropped out. The water
swallowed our fire, and we floated back to the shore that
was dark with only here and there the glimmer of embers.
We could hear the talk of slave girls amongst the sheds.

Then we found a place deserted and silent. We waited there. She came. She came running along the shore, rapid and leaving no trace, like a leaf driven by the wind into the sea. My brother said gloomily, 'Go and take her; carry her into our boat.' I lifted her in my arms. She panted. Her heart was beating against my breast. I said, 'I take you from those people. You came to the cry of my heart, but my arms take you into my boat against the will of the great!' 'It is right,' said my brother. 'We are men who take what we want and can hold it against many. We should have taken her in daylight.' I said, 'Let us be off'; for since she was in my boat I began to think of our Ruler's many men. 'Yes. Let us be off,' said my brother. 'We are cast out and this boat is our country now—and the sea is our refuge.' He lingered with his foot on the shore, and I entreated him to hasten, for I remembered the strokes of her heart against my breast and thought that two men cannot withstand a hundred. We left, paddling downstream close to the bank; and as we passed by the creek where they were fishing, the great shouting had ceased, but the murmur of voices was loud like the humming of insects flying at noonday. The boats floated, clustered together, in the red light of torches, under a black roof of smoke; and men talked of their sport. Men that boasted, and praised, and jeered—men that would have been our friends in the morning, but on that night were already our enemies. We paddled swiftly past. We had no more friends in the country of our birth. She sat in the middle of the canoe with covered face; silent as she is now; unseeing as she is now—and I had no regret at what I was leaving because I could hear her breathing close to me—as I can hear her now."

He paused, listened with his ear turned to the doorway, then shook his head and went on:

"My brother wanted to shout the cry of challenge—one cry only—to let the people know we were freeborn robbers who trusted our arms and the great sea. And again I begged him in the name of our love to be silent. Could I not hear her breathing close to me? I knew the pursuit would come quick enough. My brother loved me. He dipped his paddle without a splash. He only said, 'There is half a man in you now—the other half is in that woman. I can wait. When you are a whole man again, you will come back with me here to shout defiance. We are sons of the same mother.' I made no answer. All my strength and all my spirit were in my hands that held the paddle—for I longed to be with her in a safe place beyond the reach of men's anger and of women's spite. My love was so great, that I thought it could guide me to a country where death was unknown, if I could only escape from Inchi Midah's fury and from our Ruler's sword. We paddled with haste, breathing through our teeth. The blades bit deep into the smooth water. We passed out of the river; we flew in clear channels amongst the shallows. We skirted the black coast; we skirted the sand beaches where the sea speaks in whispers to the land; and the gleam of white sand flashed back past our boat, so swiftly she ran upon the water. We spoke not. Only once I said, 'Sleep, Diamelen, for soon you may want all your strength.' I heard the sweetness of her voice, but I never turned my head. The sun rose and still we went on. Water fell from my face like rain from a cloud. We flew in the light and heat. I never looked back, but I knew that my brother's eyes, behind me, were looking steadily ahead, for the boat went as straight as a bushman's dart, when it leaves the end of the sumpitan. There was no better paddler, no better steersman than my brother. Many times, together, we had won races in that canoe. But we never had put out our strength as we did then—then, when for the last time we paddled together! There was no braver or stronger man in our country than my brother. I could not spare the strength to turn my head and look at him, but every moment I heard the hiss of his breath getting louder behind me. Still he did not speak. The sun was high. The heat clung to my back like a flame of fire. My ribs were ready to burst, but I could no longer get enough air into my chest. And then I felt I must cry out with my last breath, 'Let us rest!' . . . 'Good!' he answered; and his voice was firm. He was strong. He was brave. He knew not fear and no fatigue. . . . My brother!"

A murmur powerful and gentle, a murmur vast and faint; the murmur of trembling leaves, of stirring boughs, ran through the tangled depths of the forests, ran over the starry smoothness of the lagoon, and the water between the piles lapped the slimy timber once with a sudden splash. A breath of warm air touched the two men's faces and passed on with a mournful sound—a breath loud and short like an uneasy sigh of the dreaming earth.

Arsat went on in an even, low voice.

"We ran our canoe on the white beach of a little bay close to a long tongue of land that seemed to bar our road; a long wooded cape going far into the sea. My brother knew that place. Beyond the cape a river has its entrance, and through the jungle of that land there is a narrow path. We made a fire and cooked rice. Then we lay down to sleep on the soft sand in the shade of our canoe, while she watched. No sooner had I closed my eyes than I heard her cry of alarm. We leaped up. The sun was halfway down the sky already, and coming in sight in the opening of the bay we saw a prau manned by many paddlers. We knew it at once; it was one of our Rajah's praus. They were watching the shore, and saw us. They beat the gong, and turned the head of the prau into the bay. I felt my heart become weak within my breast. Diamelen sat on the sand and covered her face. There was no escape by sea. My brother laughed. He had the gun you had given him, Tuan, before you went away, but there was only a handful of powder. He spoke to me quickly: 'Run with her along the path. I shall keep them back, for they have no firearms, and landing in the face of a man with a gun is certain death for some. Run with her. On the other side of that wood there is a fisherman's house—and a canoe. When I have fired all the shots I will follow. I am a great runner, and before they can come up we shall be gone. I will hold out as long as I can, for she is but a woman—that can neither run nor fight, but she has your heart in her weak hands.' He dropped behind the canoe. The prau was coming. She and I ran, and as we rushed along the path I heard shots. My brother fired— once—twice—and the booming of the gong ceased. There was silence behind us. That neck of land is narrow. Before I heard my brother fire the third shot I saw the shelving shore, and I saw the water again; the mouth of a broad river. We crossed a grassy glade. We ran down to the water. I saw a low hut above the black mud, and a small canoe hauled up. I heard another shot behind me. I thought, 'That is his last charge.' We rushed down to the canoe; a man came running from the hut, but I leaped on him, and we rolled together in the mud. Then I got up, and he lay still at my feet. I don't know whether I had killed him or not. I and Diamelen pushed the canoe afloat. I heard yells behind me, and I saw my brother run across the glade. Many men were bounding after him. I took her in my arms and threw her into the boat, then leaped in myself. When I looked back I saw that my brother had fallen. He fell and was up again, but the men were closing round him. He shouted, 'I am coming!' The men were close to him. I looked. Many men. Then I looked at her. Tuan, I pushed the canoe! I pushed it into deep water. She was kneeling forward looking at me, and I said, 'Take your paddle,' while I struck the water with mine. Tuan, I heard him cry. I heard him cry my name twice; and I heard voices shouting, 'Kill! Strike!' I never turned back. I heard him calling my name again with a great shriek, as when life is going out together with the voice—and I never turned my head. My own name! . . . My brother! Three times he called—but I was not afraid of life. Was she not there in that canoe? And could I not with her find a country where death is forgotten—where death is unknown!"

The white man sat up. Arsat rose and stood, an indistinct and silent figure above the dying embers of the fire.

Over the lagoon a mist drifting and low had crept, erasing slowly the glittering images of the stars. And now a great expanse of white vapor covered the land: it flowed cold and gray in the darkness, eddied in noiseless whirls round the tree trunks and about the platform of the house, which seemed to float upon a restless and impalpable illusion of a sea. Only far away the tops of the trees stood outlined on the twinkle of heaven, like a somber and forbidding shore —a coast deceptive, pitiless and black.

Arsat's voice vibrated loudly in the profound peace.

"I had her there! I had her! To get her I would have faced all mankind. But I had her—and—"

His words went out ringing into the empty distances. He paused, and seemed to listen to them dying away very far—beyond help and beyond recall. Then he said quietly: "Tuan, I loved my brother."

A breath of wind made him shiver. High above his head, high above the silent sea of mist the drooping leaves of the palms rattled together with a mournful and expiring sound. The white man stretched his legs. His chin rested on his chest, and he murmured sadly without lifting his head:

"We all love our brothers."

Arsat burst out with an intense whispering violence:

"What did I care who died? I wanted peace in my own heart."

He seemed to hear a stir in the house—listened—then stepped in noiselessly. The white man stood up. A breeze was coming in fitful puffs. The stars shone paler as if they had retreated into the frozen depths of immense space. After a chill gust of wind there were a few seconds of perfect calm and absolute silence. Then from behind the black and wavy line of the forests a column of golden light shot up into the heavens and spread over the semicircle of the eastern horizon. The sun had risen. The mist lifted, broke into drifting patches, vanished into thin flying wreaths; and the unveiled lagoon lay, polished and black, in the heavy shadows at the foot of the wall of trees. A white eagle rose over it with a slanting and ponderous flight, reached the clear sunshine and appeared dazzlingly brilliant for a moment, then soaring higher, became a dark and motionless speck before it vanished into the blue as if it had left the earth forever. The white man, standing gazing upwards before the doorway, heard in the hut a confused and broken murmur of distracted words ending with a loud groan. Suddenly Arsat stumbled out with outstretched hands, shivered, and stood still for some time with fixed eyes. Then he said:

"She burns no more."

Before his face the sun showed its edge above the treetops rising steadily. The breeze freshened; a great brilliance burst upon the lagoon, sparkled on the rippling water. The forests came out of the clear shadows of the morning, became distinct, as if they had rushed nearer—to stop short in a great stir of leaves, of nodding boughs, of swaying branches. In the merciless sunshine the whisper of unconscious life grew louder, speaking in an incomprehensible voice round the dumb darkness of that human sorrow. Arsat's eyes wandered slowly, then stared at the rising sun.

"I can see nothing," he said half aloud to himself.

"There is nothing," said the white man, moving to the edge of the platform and waving his hand to his boat. A shout came faintly over the lagoon and the sampan began to glide towards the abode of the friend of ghosts.

"If you want to come with me, I will wait all the morning," said the white man, looking away upon the water.

"No, Tuan," said Arsat, softly. "I shall not eat or sleep in this house, but I must first see my road. Now I can see nothing—see nothing! There is no light and no peace in the world; but there is death—death for many. We are sons of the same mother—and I left him in the midst of enemies; but I am going back now."

He drew a long breath and went on in a dreamy tone:

"In a little while I shall see clear enough to strike—to strike. But she has died, and . . . now . . . darkness."

He flung his arms wide open, let them fall along his body, then stood still with unmoved face and stony eyes, staring at the sun. The white man got down into his canoe. The polers ran smartly along the sides of the boat, looking over their shoulders at the beginning of a weary journey. High in the stern, his head muffled up in white rags, the juragan sat moody, letting his paddle trail in the water. The white man, leaning with both arms over the grass roof of the little cabin, looked back at the shining ripple of the boat's wake. Before the sampan passed out of the lagoon into the creek he lifted his eyes. Arsat had not moved. He stood lonely in the searching sunshine; and he looked beyond the great light of a cloudless day into the darkness of a world of illusions.

Stephen Crane

[1871—1900]

NAMED FOR AN ancestor who signed the Declaration of Independence, Stephen Crane was a one-man literary revolution. William Dean Howells felt certain he came into life "fully armed"; Sherwood Anderson called him "an explosion." Martial images such as these reflect the bold words Crane once wrote into his unpublished notebook: "Congratulate yourselves if you have done something strange and extravagant and have broken the monotony of a decorous age." He did something extravagant; he is—more than Mark Twain—the first "modern" American writer, and his best short stories are today as "modern" as ever. In his brief life (he died at 28 of tuberculosis) he helped to kill sentimental writing and gave American fiction renewed dignity as an art form. His most illustrious protégé was Ernest Hemingway.

Everywhere he turned, Crane displayed his independent and rebellious nature. He reacted against the narrow-minded, puritanical ways of his father, a Methodist minister, and his mother, the daughter of one, though he was deeply moved by his father's death in 1880. In 1888, as a student at Hudson River Institute in New York, he seemed to work hard to earn the epithet, "the minister's wild son": he drank, swore, smoked cigars, cigarettes, and showed a ready interest in women. Almost by instinct he championed the underdog and rallied against the conventions of society. Siding with the outcast

Cuban students at Hudson, he was a "little David throwing stones at the collective Goliath." In 1896 he showed the same trait by condemning the police of New York City for their rough treatment of prostitutes, and even sent a telegram to Theodore Roosevelt, then police commissioner. His "Monster" (1898) and *Whilomville Stories* (1900) reflect some of the conflicts between himself and the "savage" societies he confronted in the small towns and cities of New York and New Jersey.

The religion which was so important to his parents he came to hate. During the summer months in the 1880s he was forced by his mother, who "lived in and for religion," to attend camp meetings at Ocean Grove, New Jersey. Listening to the hell-fire and day-of-doom sermons, he became skeptical of God and termed Methodism a "holy show." But he never could escape the Bible readings at home and at Hudson, Lafayette College, and Syracuse University. Much of the cosmic irony in his later writings stems from his hostility to a stern religion; clear evidences of this can be seen in his anarchistic poems, *The Black Riders* (1895) and *War Is Kind* (1899).

Some of Crane's personal battles were more subtle and inward. Fear was always with him. At 4, he was frightened by dreams of black riders charging up from the sea. At 12, he was terrorized by a stabbing incident. As a student at Lafayette College, he was awed by hazing and tried to defend himself with a shaking revolver. This intense fear is closely related to his growing obsession with war and death, and with courage and cowardice. As a child he read military histories and romantic war tales, plotted battle campaigns with rows of buttons, proudly recalled the military feats of his ancestors, listened to Civil War veterans, took a fanatic interest in his rank as first lieutenant at Hudson, and played football as though it were war. The remarkable psychological insights in his war novel, *The Red Badge of Courage* (1895), written before he saw real war in Greece and Cuba as a foreign correspondent, he claimed he got from his experience on the football field. In a sense this is true; Crane learned by "feeling" himself in situations and testing his own responses to fear, death, courage, and cowardice, all central themes in his fiction.

His most curious tension was between romance and reality. He yearned for perfection in courage and honor but continually he met with fear and shame, and this filled his soul with irony. His idyllic love affairs with genteel women failed; his reality was the prostitute (he finally eloped with Cora Taylor, the madam of a bawdy house). He protested against the conditions of the poor in the Bowery and fought the smugness of the rich, but in time he came to enjoy the life of a baron at Brede Place, England, in 1899. Even the hardboiled realism of his fiction has romantic overtones.

These tensions became the fabric of Crane's novels and short stories. Usually linked with European naturalism (Zola, Tolstoy, and Flaubert) and with Poe, Bierce, and Twain, he once proclaimed: "Away with literary cads and canons. Be yourself!" To use his own honest vision was his artistic aim. Most often he satisfied it by personal experience: he slept in a flophouse to get the atmosphere for "Experiment in Misery"; he lived the life of "The Open Boat" before he wrote it. Crane also craved originality in style (he was hostile to the "mildewed" phrases of earlier writers), and his revolutionary style—tense, darting, abrupt, ironic—blends with an impressionistic technique (learned from artist friends in New York) to present a series of richly colored episodes packed with emotional, psychological, and symbolical suggestiveness. The techniques of poetry and drama can be seen in his use of refrains and dramatic scenes. Most important are his anonymous characters, whose states of mind are explored in a naturalistic jungle of violence and death where heredity, environment, nature, and fate play ironic roles. Though the tales are pessimistic, there are momentary bits of grotesque humor and a short-lived optimism.

The Open Boat

A Tale Intended To Be After the Fact: Being the Experience of Four Men from the Sunk Steamer *Commodore*

I

None of them knew the color of the sky. Their eyes glanced level, and were fastened upon the waves that swept toward them. These waves were of the hue of slate, save for the tops, which were of foaming white, and all of the men knew the colors of the sea. The horizon narrowed and widened, and dipped and rose, and at all times its edge was jagged with waves that seemed thrust up in points like rocks.

Many a man ought to have a bathtub larger than the boat which here rode upon the sea. These waves were most wrongfully and barbarously abrupt and tall, and each froth-top was a problem in small-boat navigation.

From *Stephen Crane: An Omnibus*, edited by Robert W. Stallman. Published by Alfred A. Knopf, Inc., 1952.

The cook squatted in the bottom, and looked with both eyes at the six inches of gunwale which separated him from the ocean. His sleeves were rolled over his fat forearms, and the two flaps of his unbuttoned vest dangled as he bent to bail out the boat. Often he said, "Gawd! that was a narrow clip." As he remarked it he invariably gazed eastward over the broken sea.

The oiler, steering with one of the two oars in the boat, sometimes raised himself suddenly to keep clear of water that swirled in over the stern. It was a thin little oar, and it seemed often ready to snap.

The correspondent, pulling at the other oar, watched the waves and wondered why he was there.

The injured captain, lying in the bow, was at this time buried in that profound dejection and indifference which comes, temporarily at least, to even the bravest and most enduring when, willy-nilly, the firm fails, the army loses, the ship goes down. The mind of the master of a vessel is rooted deep in the timbers of her, though he command for a day or a decade; and this captain had on him the stern impression of a scene in the grays of dawn of seven turned faces, and later a stump of a topmast with a white ball on it, that slashed to and fro at the waves, went low and lower, and down. Thereafter there was something strange in his voice. Although steady, it was deep with mourning, and of a quality beyond oration or tears.

"Keep 'er a little more south, Billie," said he.

"A little more south, sir," said the oiler in the stern.

A seat in this boat was not unlike a seat upon a bucking broncho, and, by the same token, a broncho is not much smaller. The craft pranced and reared and plunged like an animal. As each wave came, and she rose for it, she seemed like a horse making at a fence outrageously high. The manner of her scramble over these walls of water is a mystic thing, and, moreover, at the top of them were ordinarily these problems in white water, the foam racing down from the summit of each wave requiring a new leap, and a leap from the air. Then, after scornfully bumping a crest, she would slide and race and splash down a long incline, and arrive bobbing and nodding in front of the next menace.

A singular disadvantage of the sea lies in the fact that, after successfully surmounting one wave, you discover that there is another behind it just as important and just as nervously anxious to do something effective in the way of swamping boats. In a ten-foot dinghy one can get an idea of the resources of the sea in the line of waves that is not probable to the average experience, which is never at sea in a dinghy. As each slaty wall of water approached, it shut all else from the view of the men in the boat, and it was not difficult to imagine that this particular wave was the final outburst of the ocean, the last effort of the grim water. There was a terrible grace in the move of the waves, and they came in silence, save for the snarling of the crests.

In the wan light the faces of the men must have been gray. Their eyes must have glinted in strange ways as they gazed steadily astern. Viewed from a balcony, the whole thing would, doubtless, have been weirdly picturesque. But the men in the boat had no time to see it, and if they had had leisure, there were other things to occupy their minds. The sun swung steadily up the sky, and they knew it was broad day because the color of the sea changed from slate to emerald-green streaked with amber lights, and the foam was like tumbling snow. The process of the breaking day was unknown to them. They were aware only of this effect upon the color of the waves that rolled toward them.

In disjointed sentences the cook and the correspondent argued as to the difference between a life-saving station and a house of refuge. The cook had said: "There's a house of refuge just north of the Mosquito Inlet Light, and as soon as they see us they'll come off in their boat and pick us up."

"As soon as who see us?" said the correspondent.

"The crew," said the cook.

"Houses of refuge don't have crews," said the correspondent. "As I understand them, they are only places where clothes and grub are stored for the benefit of ship-wrecked people. They don't carry crews."

"Oh, yes, they do," said the cook.

"No, they don't," said the correspondent.

"Well, we're not there yet, anyhow," said the oiler in the stern.

"Well," said the cook, "perhaps it's not a house of refuge that I'm thinking of as being near Mosquito Inlet Light; perhaps it's a life-saving station."

"We're not there yet," said the oiler in the stern.

II

As the boat bounced from the top of each wave the wind tore through the hair of the hatless men, and as the craft plopped her stern down again the spray splashed past them. The crest of each of these waves was a hill, from the top of which the men surveyed for a moment a broad, tumultuous expanse, shining and wind-riven. It was probably splendid, it was probably glorious, this play of the free sea, wild with lights of emerald and white and amber.

"Bully good thing it's an on-shore wind," said the cook. "If not, where would we be? Wouldn't have a show."

"That's right," said the correspondent.

The busy oiler nodded his assent.

Then the captain, in the bow, chuckled in a way that ex-pressed humor, contempt, tragedy, all in one. "Do you think we've got much of a show now, boys?" said he.

Whereupon the three were silent, save for a trifle of hemming and hawing. To express any particular optimism at this time they felt to be childish and stupid, but they all doubtless possessed this sense of the situation in their minds. A young man thinks doggedly at such times. On the other hand, the ethics of their condition was decidedly against any open suggestion of hopelessness. So they were silent.

"Oh, well," said the captain, soothing his children, "we'll get ashore all right."

But there was that in his tone which made them think; so the oiler quoth, "Yes! if this wind holds."

The cook was bailing. "Yes! if we don't catch hell in the surf."

Canton-flannel gulls flew near and far. Sometimes they sat down on the sea, near patches of brown seaweed that rolled over the waves with a movement like carpets on a line in a gale. The birds sat comfortably in groups, and they were envied by some in the dinghy, for the wrath of the sea was no more to them than it was to a covey of prairie chickens a thousand miles inland. Often they came very close and stared at the men with black, bead-like eyes. At these times they were uncanny and sinister in their unblinking scrutiny, and the men hooted angrily at them, telling them to be gone. One came, and evidently decided to alight on the top of the captain's head. The bird flew parallel to the boat and did not circle, but made short sidelong jumps in the air in chicken fashion. His black eyes were wistfully fixed upon the captain's head. "Ugly brute," said the oiler to the bird. "You look as if you were made with a jackknife." The cook and the correspondent swore darkly at the creature. The captain naturally wished to knock it away with the end of the heavy painter, but he did not dare do it, because anything resembling an emphatic gesture would have capsized this freighted boat; and so, with his open hand, the captain gently and carefully waved the gull away. After it had been discouraged from the pursuit the captain breathed easier on account of his hair, and others breathed easier because the bird struck their minds at this time as being somehow gruesome and ominous.

In the meantime the oiler and the correspondent rowed. And also they rowed. They sat together in the same seat, and each rowed an oar. Then the oiler took both oars; then the correspondent took both oars; then the oiler; then the correspondent. They rowed and they rowed. The very ticklish part of the business was when the time came for the reclining one in the stern to take his turn at the oars. By the very last star of truth, it is easier to steal eggs from under a hen than it was to change seats in the dinghy. First the man in the stern slid his hand along the thwart and moved with care, as if he were of Sèvres. Then the man in the rowing-seat slid his hand along the other thwart. It was all done with the most extraordinary care. As the two sidled past each other, the whole party kept watchful eyes on the coming wave, and the captain cried: "Look out, now! Steady, there!"

The brown mats of seaweed that appeared from time to time were like islands, bits of earth. They were travelling, apparently, neither one way nor the other. They were, to all intents, stationary. They informed the men in the boat that it was making progress slowly toward the land.

The captain, rearing cautiously in the bow after the dinghy soared on a great swell, said that he had seen the lighthouse at Mosquito Inlet. Presently the cook remarked that he had seen it. The correspondent was at the oars then, and for some reason he too wished to look at the lighthouse; but his back was toward the far shore, and the waves were important, and for some time he could not seize an opportunity to turn his head. But at last there came a wave more gentle than the others, and when at the crest of it he swiftly scoured the western horizon.

"See it?" said the captain.

"No," said the correspondent, slowly; "I didn't see anything."

"Look again," said the captain. He pointed. "It's exactly in that direction."

At the top of another wave the correspondent did as he was bid, and this time his eyes chanced on a small, still thing on the edge of the swaying horizon. It was precisely like the point of a pin. It took an anxious eye to find a lighthouse so tiny.

"Think we'll make it, Captain?"

"If this wind holds and the boat don't swamp, we can't do much else," said the captain.

The little boat, lifted by each towering sea and splashed viciously by the crests, made progress that in the absence of seaweed was not apparent to those in her. She seemed just a wee thing wallowing, miraculously top up, at the mercy of five oceans. Occasionally a great spread of water, like white flames, swarmed into her.

"Bail her, cook," said the captain, serenely.

"All right, Captain," said the cheerful cook.

III

It would be difficult to describe the subtle brotherhood of men that was here established on the seas. No one said that it was so. No one mentioned it. But it dwelt in the boat, and each man felt it warm him. They were a captain, an oiler, a cook, and a correspondent, and they were friends —friends in a more curiously iron-bound degree than may be common. The hurt captain, lying against the water jar in the bow, spoke always in a low voice and calmly; but he could never command a more ready and swiftly obedient crew than the motley three of the dinghy. It was more than a mere recognition of what was best for the common safety. There was surely in it a quality that was personal and heartfelt. And after this devotion to the commander of the boat, there was this comradeship, that the correspondent, for instance, who had been taught to be cynical of men, knew even at the time was the best experience of his life. But no one said that it was so. No one mentioned it.

"I wish we had a sail," remarked the captain. "We might try my overcoat on the end of an oar, and give you two boys a chance to rest." So the cook and the correspondent

held the mast and spread wide the overcoat; the oiler
steered; and the little boat made good way with her new
rig. Sometimes the oiler had to scull sharply to keep a sea
from breaking into the boat, but otherwise sailing was a
success.

Meanwhile the lighthouse had been growing slowly
larger. It had now almost assumed color, and appeared like
a little gray shadow on the sky. The man at the oars could
not be prevented from turning his head rather often to try
for a glimpse of this little gray shadow.

At last, from the top of each wave, the men in the tossing boat could see land. Even as the lighthouse was an upright shadow on the sky, this land seemed but a long black
shadow on the sea. It certainly was thinner than paper.
"We must be about opposite New Smyrna," said the cook,
who had coasted this shore often in schooners. "Captain,
by the way, I believe they abandoned that life-saving station
there about a year ago."

"Did they?" said the captain.

The wind slowly died away. The cook and the correspondent were not now obliged to slave in order to hold
high the oar. But the waves continued their old impetuous
swooping at the dinghy, and the little craft, no longer under way, struggled woundily over them. The oiler or the
correspondent took the oars again.

Shipwrecks are apropos of nothing. If men could only
train for them and have them occur when the men had
reached pink condition, there would be less drowning at
sea. Of the four in the dinghy none had slept any time
worth mentioning for two days and two nights previous to
embarking in the dinghy, and in the excitement of clambering about the deck of a foundering ship they had also forgotten to eat heartily.

For these reasons, and for others, neither the oiler nor
the correspondent was fond of rowing at this time. The
correspondent wondered ingenuously how in the name of
all that was sane could there be people who thought it

amusing to row a boat. It was not an amusement; it was a diabolical punishment, and even a genius of mental aberrations could never conclude that it was anything but a horror to the muscles and a crime against the back. He mentioned to the boat in general how the amusement of rowing struck him, and the weary-faced oiler smiled in full sympathy. Previously to the foundering, by the way, the oiler had worked double watch in the engine-room of the ship.

"Take her easy now, boys," said the captain. "Don't spend yourselves. If we have to run a surf you'll need all your strength, because we'll sure have to swim for it. Take your time."

Slowly the land arose from the sea. From a black line it became a line of black and a line of white—trees and sand. Finally the captain said that he could make out a house on the shore. "That's the house of refuge, sure," said the cook. "They'll see us before long, and come out after us."

The distant lighthouse reared high. "The keeper ought to be able to make us out now, if he's looking through a glass," said the captain. "He'll notify the life-saving people."

"None of those other boats could have got ashore to give word of the wreck," said the oiler, in a low voice, "else the life boat would be out hunting us."

Slowly and beautifully the land loomed out of the sea. The wind came again. It had veered from the northeast to the southeast. Finally a new sound struck the ears of the men in the boat. It was the low thunder of the surf on the shore. "We'll never be able to make the lighthouse now," said the captain. "Swing her head a little more north, Billie."

"A little more north, sir," said the oiler.

Whereupon the little boat turned her nose once more down the wind, and all but the oarsman watched the shore grow. Under the influence of this expansion doubt and direful apprehension were leaving the minds of the men. The management of the boat was still most absorbing, but it could not prevent a quiet cheerfulness. In an hour, perhaps, they would be ashore.

Their backbones had become thoroughly used to balancing in the boat, and they now rode this wild colt of a dinghy like circus men. The correspondent thought that he had been drenched to the skin, but happening to feel in the top pocket of his coat, he found therein eight cigars. Four of them were soaked with sea water; four were perfectly scatheless. After a search, somebody produced three dry matches; and thereupon the four waifs rode impudently in their little boat and, with an assurance of an impending rescue shining in their eyes, puffed at the big cigars, and judged well and ill of all men. Everybody took a drink of water.

IV

"Cook," remarked the captain, "there don't seem to be any signs of life about your house of refuge."

"No," replied the cook. "Funny they don't see us!"

A broad stretch of lowly coast lay before the eyes of the men. It was of low dunes topped with dark vegetation. The roar of the surf was plain, and sometimes they could see the white lip of a wave as it spun up the beach. A tiny house was blocked out black upon the sky. Southward, the slim lighthouse lifted its little gray length.

Tide, wind, and waves were swinging the dinghy northward. "Funny they don't see us," said the men.

The surf's roar was here dulled, but its tone was nevertheless thunderous and mighty. As the boat swam over the great rollers the men sat listening to this roar. "We'll swamp sure," said everybody.

It is fair to say here that there was not a life-saving station within twenty miles in either direction; but the men did not know this fact, and in consequence they made dark and opprobrious remarks concerning the eyesight of the nation's life savers. Four scowling men sat in the dinghy and surpassed records in the invention of epithets.

"Funny they don't see us."

The light-heartedness of a former time had completely faded. To their sharpened minds it was easy to conjure pictures of all kinds of incompetency and blindness and, indeed, cowardice. There was the shore of the populous land, and it was bitter and bitter to them that from it came no sign.

"Well," said the captain, ultimately, "I suppose we'll have to make a try for ourselves. If we stay out here too long, we'll none of us have strength left to swim after the boat swamps."

And so the oiler, who was at the oars, turned the boat straight for the shore. There was a sudden tightening of muscles. There was some thinking.

"If we don't all get ashore," said the captain—"if we don't all get ashore, I suppose you fellows know where to send news of my finish?"

They then briefly exchanged some addresses and admonitions. As for the reflections of the men, there was a great deal of rage in them. Perchance they might be formulated thus: "If I am going to be drowned—if I am going to be drowned—if I am going to be drowned, why, in the name of the seven mad gods who rule the sea, was I allowed to come thus far and contemplate sand and trees? Was I brought here merely to have my nose dragged away as I was about to nibble the sacred cheese of life? It is preposterous. If this old ninny woman, Fate, cannot do better than this, she should be deprived of the management of men's fortunes. She is an old hen who knows not her intention. If she has decided to drown me, why did she not do it in the beginning and save me all this trouble? The whole affair is absurd. . . . But no; she cannot mean to drown me. She dare not drown me. She cannot drown me. Not after all this work." Afterward the man might have had an impulse to shake his fist at the clouds. "Just you drown me, now, and then hear what I call you!"

The billows that came at this time were more formidable. They seemed always just about to break and roll over the little boat in a turmoil of foam. There was a preparatory and long growl in the speech of them. No mind unused to the sea would have concluded that the dinghy could ascend these sheer heights in time. The shore was still afar. The oiler was a wily surfman. "Boys," he said swiftly, "she won't live three minutes more, and we're too far out to swim. Shall I take her to sea again, Captain?"

"Yes; go ahead!" said the captain.

This oiler, by a series of quick miracles and fast and steady oarsmanship, turned the boat in the middle of the surf and took her safely to sea again.

There was a considerable silence as the boat bumped over the furrowed sea to deeper water. Then somebody in gloom spoke: "Well, anyhow, they must have seen us from the shore by now."

The gulls went in slanting flight up the wind toward the gray, desolate east. A squall, marked by dingy clouds and clouds brick-red, like smoke from a burning building, appeared from the southeast.

"What do you think of those life-saving people? Ain't they peaches?"

"Funny they haven't seen us."

"Maybe they think we're out here for sport! Maybe they think we're fishin'. Maybe they think we're damned fools."

It was a long afternoon. A changed tide tried to force them southward, but wind and wave said northward. Far ahead, where coast-line, sea, and sky formed their mighty angle, there were little dots which seemed to indicate a city on the shore.

"St. Augustine?"

The captain shook his head. "Too near Mosquito Inlet."

And the oiler rowed, and then the correspondent rowed; then the oiler rowed. It was a weary business. The human back can become the seat of more aches and pains than are registered in books for the composite anatomy of a regiment. It is a limited area, but it can become the theater of innumerable muscular conflicts, tangles, wrenches, knots, and other comforts.

"Did you ever like to row, Billie?" asked the correspondent.

"No," said the oiler; "hang it!"

When one exchanged the rowing-seat for a place in the bottom of the boat, he suffered a bodily depression that caused him to be careless of everything save an obligation to wiggle one finger. There was cold sea water swashing to and fro in the boat, and he lay in it. His head, pillowed on a thwart, was within an inch of the swirl of a wave crest, and sometimes a particularly obstreperous sea came inboard and drenched him once more. But these matters did not annoy him. It is almost certain that if the boat had capsized he would have tumbled comfortably out upon the ocean as if he felt sure that it was a great soft mattress.

"Look! There's a man on the shore!"

"Where?"

"There! See 'im? See 'im?"

"Yes, sure! He's walking along."

"Now he's stopped. Look! He's facing us!"

"He's waving at us!"

"So he is! By thunder!"

"Ah, now we're all right! Now we're all right! There'll be a boat out here for us in half an hour."

"He's going on. He's running. He's going up to that house there."

The remote beach seemed lower than the sea, and it required a searching glance to discern the little black figure. The captain saw a floating stick, and they rowed to it. A bath towel was by some weird chance in the boat, and, tying this on the stick, the captain waved it. The oarsman did not dare turn his head, so he was obliged to ask questions.

"What's he doing now?"

"He's standing still again. He's looking, I think. . . ."

There he goes again—toward the house. . . . Now he's stopped again."

"Is he waving at us?"

"No, not now; he was, though."

"Look! There comes another man!"

"He's running."

"Look at him go, would you!"

"Why, he's on a bicycle. Now he's met the other man. They're both waving at us. Look!"

"There comes something up the beach."

"What the devil is that thing?"

"Why, it looks like a boat."

"Why, certainly, it's a boat."

"No; it's on wheels."

"Yes, so it is. Well, that must be the life boat. They drag them along shore on a wagon."

"That's the life boat, sure."

"No, by God, it's—it's an omnibus."

"I tell you it's a life boat."

"It is not! It's an omnibus. I can see it plain. See? One of these big hotel omnibuses."

"By thunder, you're right. It's an omnibus, sure as fate. What do you suppose they are doing with an omnibus? Maybe they are going around collecting the life crew, hey?"

"That's it, likely. Look! There's a fellow waving a little black flag. He's standing on the steps of the omnibus. There come those other two fellows. Now they're all talking together. Look at the fellow with the flag. Maybe he ain't waving it!"

"That ain't a flag, is it? That's his coat. Why, certainly, that's his coat."

"So it is; it's his coat. He's taken it off and is waving it around his head. But would you look at him swing it!"

"Oh, say, there isn't any life-saving station there. That's just a winter-resort hotel omnibus that has brought over some of the boarders to see us drown."

"What's that idiot with the coat mean? What's he signalling, anyhow?"

"It looks as if he were trying to tell us to go north. There must be a life-saving station up there."

"No; he thinks we're fishing. Just giving us a merry hand. See? Ah, there, Willie!"

"Well, I wish I could make something out of those signals. What do you suppose he means?"

"He don't mean anything; he's just playing."

"Well, if he'd just signal us to try the surf again, or to go to sea and wait, or go north, or south, or go to hell, there would be some reason in it. But look at him! He just stands there and keeps his coat revolving like a wheel. The ass!"

"There come more people."

"Now there's quite a mob. Look! Isn't that a boat?"

"Where? Oh, I see where you mean. No, that's no boat."

"That fellow is still waving his coat."

"He must think we like to see him do that. Why don't he quit it? It don't mean anything."

"I don't know. I think he is trying to make us go north. It must be that there's a life-saving station there somewhere."

"Say, he ain't tired yet. Look at 'im wave!"

"Wonder how long he can keep that up. He's been revolving his coat ever since he caught sight of us. He's an idiot. Why aren't they getting men to bring a boat out? A fishing boat—one of those big yawls—could come out here all right. Why don't he do something?"

"Oh, it's all right now."

"They'll have a boat out here for us in less than no time, now that they've seen us."

A faint yellow tone came into the sky over the low land. The shadows on the sea slowly deepened. The wind bore coldness with it, and the men began to shiver.

"Holy smoke!" said one, allowing his voice to express his

impious mood, "if we keep on monkeying out here! If we've got to flounder out here all night!"

"Oh, we'll never have to stay here all night! Don't you worry. They've seen us now, and it won't be long before they'll come chasing out after us."

The shore grew dusky. The man waving a coat blended gradually into this gloom, and it swallowed in the same manner the omnibus and the group of people. The spray, when it dashed uproariously over the side, made the voyagers shrink and swear like men who were being branded.

"I'd like to catch the chump who waved the coat. I feel like soaking him one, just for luck."

"Why? What did he do?"

"Oh, nothing, but then he seemed so damned cheerful."

In the meantime the oiler rowed, and then the correspondent rowed, and then the oiler rowed. Gray-faced and bowed forward, they mechanically, turn by turn, plied the leaden oars. The form of the lighthouse had vanished from the southern horizon, but finally a pale star appeared, just lifting from the sea. The streaked saffron in the west passed before the all-merging darkness, and the sea to the east was black. The land had vanished, and was expressed only by the low and drear thunder of the surf.

"If I am going to be drowned—if I am going to be drowned—if I am going to be drowned, why, in the name of the seven mad gods who rule the sea, was I allowed to come thus far and contemplate sand and trees? Was I brought here merely to have my nose dragged away as I was about to nibble the sacred cheese of life?"

The patient captain, drooped over the water jar, was sometimes obliged to speak to the oarsman.

"Keep her head up! Keep her head up!"

"Keep her head up, sir." The voices were weary and low.

This was surely a quiet evening. All save the oarsman lay heavily and listlessly in the boat's bottom. As for him, his eyes were just capable of noting the tall black waves that swept forward in a most sinister silence, save for an occasional subdued growl of a crest.

The cook's head was on a thwart, and he looked without interest at the water under his nose. He was deep in other scenes. Finally he spoke. "Billie," he murmured dreamfully, "what kind of pie do you like best?"

V

"Pie!" said the oiler and the correspondent, agitatedly. "Don't talk about those things, blast you!"

"Well," said the cook, "I was just thinking about ham sandwiches, and—"

A night on the sea in an open boat is a long night. As darkness settled finally, the shine of the light, lifting from the sea in the south, changed to full gold. On the northern horizon a new light appeared, a small bluish gleam on the edge of the waters. These two lights were the furniture of the world. Otherwise there was nothing but waves.

Two men huddled in the stern, and distances were so magnificent in the dinghy that the rower was enabled to keep his feet partly warm by thrusting them under his companions. Their legs indeed extended far under the rowing-seat until they touched the feet of the captain forward. Sometimes, despite the efforts of the tired oarsman, a wave came piling into the boat, an icy wave of the night, and the chilling water soaked them anew. They would twist their bodies for a moment and groan, and sleep the dead sleep once more, while the water in the boat gurgled about them as the craft rocked.

The plan of the oiler and the correspondent was for one to row until he lost the ability, and then arouse the other from his seawater couch in the bottom of the boat.

The oiler plied the oars until his head drooped forward and the overpowering sleep blinded him; and he rowed yet afterward. Then he touched a man in the bottom of the boat, and called his name. "Will you spell me for a little while?" he said meekly.

"Sure, Billie," said the correspondent, awaking and dragging himself to a sitting position. They exchanged places carefully, and the oiler, cuddling down in the sea water at the cook's side, seemed to go to sleep instantly.

The particular violence of the sea had ceased. The waves came without snarling. The obligation of the man at the oars was to keep the boat headed so that the tilt of the rollers would not capsize her, and to preserve her from filling when the crests rushed past. The black waves were silent and hard to be seen in the darkness. Often one was almost upon the boat before the oarsman was aware.

In a low voice the correspondent addressed the captain. He was not sure that the captain was awake, although this iron man seemed to be always awake. "Captain, shall I keep her making for that light north, sir?"

The same steady voice answered him. "Yes. Keep it about two points off the port bow."

The cook had tied a life belt around himself in order to get even the warmth which this clumsy cork contrivance could donate, and he seemed almost stove-like when a rower, whose teeth invariably chattered wildly as soon as he ceased his labor, dropped down to sleep.

The correspondent, as he rowed, looked down at the two men sleeping underfoot. The cook's arm was around the oiler's shoulders, and, with their fragmentary clothing and haggard faces, they were the babes of the sea—a grotesque rendering of the old babes in the wood.

Later he must have grown stupid at his work, for suddenly there was a growling of water, and a crest came with a roar and a swash into the boat, and it was a wonder that it did not set the cook afloat in his life belt. The cook continued to sleep, but the oiler sat up, blinking his eyes and shaking with the new cold.

"Oh, I'm awful sorry, Billie," said the correspondent, contritely.

"That's all right, old boy," said the oiler, and lay down again and was asleep.

Presently it seemed that even the captain dozed, and the correspondent thought that he was the one man afloat on all the oceans. The wind had a voice as it came over the waves, and it was sadder than the end.

There was a long, loud swishing astern of the boat, and a gleaming trail of phosphorescence, like blue flame, was furrowed on the black waters. It might have been made by a monstrous knife.

Then there came a stillness, while the correspondent breathed with open mouth and looked at the sea.

Suddenly there was another swish and another long flash of bluish light, and this time it was alongside the boat, and might almost have been reached with an oar. The correspondent saw an enormous fin speed like a shadow through the water, hurling the crystalline spray and leaving the long glowing trail.

The correspondent looked over his shoulder at the captain. His face was hidden, and he seemed to be asleep. He looked at the babes of the sea. They certainly were asleep. So, being bereft of sympathy, he leaned a little way to one side and swore softly into the sea.

But the thing did not then leave the vicinity of the boat. Ahead or astern, on one side or the other, at intervals long or short, fled the long sparkling streak, and there was to be heard the whirroo of the dark fin. The speed and power of the thing was greatly to be admired. It cut the water like a gigantic and keen projectile.

The presence of this biding thing did not affect the man with the same horror that it would if he had been a picnicker. He simply looked at the sea dully and swore in an undertone.

Nevertheless, it is true that he did not wish to be alone with the thing. He wished one of his companions to awake by chance and keep him company with it. But the captain hung motionless over the water jar, and the oiler and the cook in the bottom of the boat were plunged in slumber.

VI

"If I am going to be drowned—if I am going to be drowned—if I am going to be drowned, why, in the name of the seven mad gods who rule the sea, was I allowed to come thus far and contemplate sand and trees?"

During this dismal night, it may be remarked that a man would conclude that it was really the intention of the seven mad gods to drown him, despite the abominable injustice of it. For it was certainly an abominable injustice to drown a man who had worked so hard, so hard. The man felt it would be a crime most unnatural. Other people had drowned at sea since galleys swarmed with painted sails, but still—

When it occurs to a man that nature does not regard him as important, and that she feels she would not maim the universe by disposing of him, he at first wishes to throw bricks at the temple, and he hates deeply the fact that there are no bricks and no temples. Any visible expression of nature would surely be pelleted with his jeers.

Then, if there be no tangible thing to hoot, he feels, perhaps, the desire to confront a personification and indulge in pleas, bowed to one knee, and with hands supplicant, saying, "Yes, but I love myself."

A high cold star on a winter's night is the word he feels that she says to him. Thereafter he knows the pathos of his situation.

The men in the dinghy had not discussed these matters, but each had, no doubt, reflected upon them in silence and according to his mind. There was seldom any expression upon their faces save the general one of complete weariness. Speech was devoted to the business of the boat.

To chime the notes of his emotion, a verse mysteriously entered the correspondent's head. He had even forgotten that he had forgotten this verse, but it suddenly was in his mind.

A soldier of the Legion lay dying in Algiers;
There was lack of woman's nursing, there was dearth of woman's
tears;
But a comrade stood beside him, and he took that comrade's
hand,
And he said, "I never more shall see my own, my native land."

In his childhood the correspondent had been made acquainted with the fact that a soldier of the Legion lay dying in Algiers, but he had never regarded it as important. Myriads of his schoolfellows had informed him of the soldier's plight, but the dinning had naturally ended by making him perfectly indifferent. He had never considered it his affair that a soldier of the Legion lay dying in Algiers, nor had it appeared to him as a matter for sorrow. It was less to him than the breaking of a pencil's point.

Now, however, it quaintly came to him as a human, living thing. It was no longer merely a picture of a few throes in the breast of a poet, meanwhile drinking tea and warming his feet at the grate; it was an actuality—stern, mournful, and fine.

The correspondent plainly saw the soldier. He lay on the sand with his feet out straight and still. While his pale left hand was upon his chest in an attempt to thwart the going of his life, the blood came between his fingers. In the far Algerian distance, a city of low square forms was set against a sky that was faint with the last sunset hues. The correspondent, plying the oars and dreaming of the slow and slower movements of the lips of the soldier, was moved by a profound and perfectly impersonal comprehension. He was sorry for the soldier of the Legion who lay dying in Algiers.

The thing which had followed the boat and waited had evidently grown bored at the delay. There was no longer to be heard the slash of the cutwater, and there was no longer the flame of the long trail. The light in the north still glimmered, but it was apparently no nearer to the boat. Sometimes the boom of the surf rang in the correspondent's ears, and he turned the craft seaward then and rowed harder. Southward, some one had evidently built a watch fire on the beach. It was too low and too far to be seen, but it made a shimmering, roseate reflection upon the bluff back of it, and this could be discerned from the boat. The wind came stronger, and sometimes a wave suddenly raged out like a mountain cat, and there was to be seen the sheen and sparkle of a broken crest.

The captain, in the bow, moved on his water jar and sat erect. "Pretty long night," he observed to the correspondent. He looked at the shore. "Those life-saving people take their time."

"Did you see that shark playing around?"

"Yes, I saw him. He was a big fellow, all right."

"Wish I had known you were awake."

Later the correspondent spoke into the bottom of the boat. "Billie!" There was a slow and gradual disentanglement. "Billie, will you spell me?"

"Sure," said the oiler.

As soon as the correspondent touched the cold, comfortable sea water in the bottom of the boat and had huddled close to the cook's life belt he was deep in sleep, despite the fact that his teeth played all the popular airs. This sleep was so good to him that it was but a moment before he heard a voice call his name in a tone that demonstrated the last stages of exhaustion. "Will you spell me?"

"Sure, Billie."

The light in the north had mysteriously vanished, but the correspondent took his course from the wide-awake captain.

Later in the night they took the boat farther out to sea, and the captain directed the cook to take one oar at the stern and keep the boat facing the seas. He was to call out if he should hear the thunder of the surf. This plan enabled the oiler and the correspondent to get respite together. "We'll give those boys a chance to get into shape again," said the captain. They curled down and, after a few pre-

liminary chatterings and trembles, slept once more the
dead sleep. Neither knew they had bequeathed to the cook
the company of another shark, or perhaps the same shark.

As the boat caroused on the waves, spray occasionally
bumped over the side and gave them a fresh soaking, but
this had no power to break their repose. The ominous slash
of the wind and the water affected them as it would have
affected mummies.

"Boys," said the cook, with the notes of every reluctance
in his voice, "she's drifted in pretty close. I guess one of
you had better take her to sea again." The correspondent,
aroused, heard the crash of the toppled crests.

As he was rowing, the captain gave him some whisky-and-
water, and this steadied the chills out of him. "If I ever get
ashore and anybody shows me even a photograph of an
oar—"

At last there was a short conversation.

"Billie! . . . Billie, will you spell me?"

"Sure," said the oiler.

VII

When the correspondent again opened his eyes, the sea
and the sky were each of the gray hue of the dawning. Later,
carmine and gold was painted upon the waters. The morning appeared finally, in its splendor, with a sky of pure blue,
and the sunlight flamed on the tips of the waves.

On the distant dunes were set many little black cottages,
and a tall white windmill reared above them. No man, nor
dog, nor bicycle appeared on the beach. The cottages might
have formed a deserted village.

The voyagers scanned the shore. A conference was held
in the boat. "Well," said the captain, "if no help is coming,
we might better try a run through the surf right away. If
we stay out here much longer we will be too weak to do
anything for ourselves at all." The others silently acquiesced
in this reasoning. The boat was headed for the beach. The

correspondent wondered if none ever ascended the tall wind-tower, and if then they never looked seaward. This tower was a giant, standing with its back to the plight of the ants. It represented in a degree, to the correspondent, the serenity of nature amid the struggles of the individual —nature in the wind, and nature in the vision of men. She did not seem cruel to him then, nor beneficent, nor treacherous, nor wise. But she was indifferent, flatly indifferent. It is, perhaps, plausible that a man in this situation, impressed with the unconcern of the universe, should see the innumerable flaws of his life and have them taste wickedly in his mind, and wish for another chance. A distinction between right and wrong seems absurdly clear to him, then, in this new ignorance of the grave-edge, and he understands that if he were given another opportunity he would mend his conduct and his words, and be better and brighter during an introduction or at a tea.

"Now, boys," said the captain, "she is going to swamp sure. All we can do is to work her in as far as possible, and then when she swamps, pile out and scramble for the beach. Keep cool now, and don't jump until she swamps sure."

The oiler took the oars. Over his shoulders he scanned the surf. "Captain," he said, "I think I'd better bring her about and keep her head-on to the seas and back her in."

"All right, Billie," said the captain. "Back her in." The oiler swung the boat then, and, seated in the stern, the cook and the correspondent were obliged to look over their shoulders to contemplate the lonely and indifferent shore.

The monstrous inshore rollers heaved the boat high until the men were again enabled to see the white sheets of water scudding up the slanted beach. "We won't get in very close," said the captain. Each time a man could wrest his attention from the rollers, he turned his glance toward the shore, and in the expression of the eyes during this contemplation there was a singular quality. The correspondent, observing the others, knew that they were not afraid, but the full meaning of their glances was shrouded.

As for himself, he was too tired to grapple fundamentally

with the fact. He tried to coerce his mind into thinking of it, but the mind was dominated at this time by the muscles, and the muscles said they did not care. It merely occurred to him that if he should drown it would be a shame.

There were no hurried words, no pallor, no plain agitation. The men simply looked at the shore. "Now, remember to get well clear of the boat when you jump," said the captain.

Seaward the crest of a roller suddenly fell with a thunderous crash, and the long white comber came roaring down upon the boat.

"Steady now," said the captain. The men were silent. They turned their eyes from the shore to the comber and waited. The boat slid up the incline, leaped at the furious top, bounced over it, and swung down the long back of the wave. Some water had been shipped, and the cook bailed it out.

But the next crest crashed also. The tumbling, boiling flood of white water caught the boat and whirled it almost perpendicular. Water swarmed in from all sides. The correspondent had his hands on the gunwale at this time, and when the water entered at that place he swiftly withdrew his fingers, as if he objected to wetting them.

The little boat, drunken with this weight of water, reeled and snuggled deeper into the sea.

"Bail her out, cook! Bail her out!" said the captain.

"All right, Captain," said the cook.

"Now, boys, the next one will do for us sure," said the oiler. "Mind to jump clear of the boat."

The third wave moved forward, huge, furious, implacable. It fairly swallowed the dinghy, and almost simultaneously the men tumbled into the sea. A piece of life belt had lain in the bottom of the boat, and as the correspondent went overboard he held this to his chest with his left hand.

The January water was icy, and he reflected immediately that it was colder than he had expected to find it off the coast of Florida. This appeared to his dazed mind as a fact

important enough to be noted at the time. The coldness of
the water was sad; it was tragic. This fact was somehow
mixed and confused with his opinion of his own situation,
so that it seemed almost a proper reason for tears. The
water was cold.

When he came to the surface he was conscious of little
but the noisy water. Afterward he saw his companions in
the sea. The oiler was ahead in the race. He was swimming
strongly and rapidly. Off to the correspondent's left, the
cook's great white and corked back bulged out of the water;
and in the rear the captain was hanging with one good hand
to the keel of the overturned dinghy.

There is a certain immovable quality to a shore, and the
correspondent wondered at it amid the confusion of the sea.

It seemed also very attractive; but the correspondent knew
that it was a long journey, and he paddled leisurely. The
piece of life preserver lay under him, and sometimes he
whirled down the incline of a wave as if he were on a
hand-sled.

But finally he arrived at a place in the sea where the
travel was beset with difficulty. He did not pause swimming
to inquire what manner of current had caught him, but
there his progress ceased. The shore was set before him
like a bit of scenery on a stage, and he looked at it and
understood with his eyes each detail of it.

As the cook passed, much farther to the left, the captain
was calling to him, "Turn over on your back, cook! Turn
over on your back and use the oar."

"All right, sir." The cook turned on his back, and, paddling with an oar, went ahead as if he were a canoe.

Presently the boat also passed to the left of the correspondent, with the captain clinging with one hand to the
keel. He would have appeared like a man raising himself to
look over a board fence if it were not for the extraordinary
gymnastics of the boat. The correspondent marvelled that
the captain could still hold to it.

They passed on nearer to shore—the oiler, the cook, the captain—and following them went the water jar, bouncing gaily over the seas.

The correspondent remained in the grip of this strange new enemy, a current. The shore, with its white slope of sand and its green bluff, topped with little silent cottages, was spread like a picture before him. It was very near to him then, but he was impressed as one who, in a gallery, looks at a scene from Brittany or Algiers.

He thought: "I am going to drown? Can it be possible? Can it be possible? Can it be possible?" Perhaps an individual must consider his own death to be the final phenomenon of nature.

But later a wave perhaps whirled him out of this small deadly current, for he found suddenly that he could again make progress toward the shore. Later still he was aware that the captain, clinging with one hand to the keel of the dinghy, had his face turned away from the shore and toward him and was calling his name. "Come to the boat! Come to the boat!"

In his struggle to reach the captain and the boat, he reflected that when one gets properly wearied drowning must really be a comfortable arrangement—a cessation of hostilities accompanied by a large degree of relief; and he was glad of it, for the main thing in his mind for some moments had been horror of the temporary agony. He did not wish to be hurt.

Presently he saw a man running along the shore. He was undressing with most remarkable speed. Coat, trousers, shirt, everything flew magically off him.

"Come to the boat!" called the captain.

"All right, Captain." As the correspondent paddled, he saw the captain let himself down to bottom and leave the boat. Then the correspondent performed his one little marvel of the voyage. A large wave caught him and flung him with ease and supreme speed completely over the boat and far beyond it. It struck him even then as an event in gymnastics and a true miracle of the sea. An overturned boat in the surf is not a plaything to a swimming man.

The correspondent arrived in water that reached only to his waist, but his condition did not enable him to stand for more than a moment. Each wave knocked him into a heap, and the undertow pulled at him.

Then he saw the man who had been running and undressing, and undressing and running, come bounding into the water. He dragged ashore the cook, and then waded toward the captain; but the captain waved him away and sent him to the correspondent. He was naked—naked as a tree in winter; but a halo was about his head, and he shone like a saint. He gave a strong pull, and a long drag, and a bully heave at the correspondent's hand. The correspondent, schooled in the minor formulae, said, "Thanks, old man." But suddenly the man cried, "What's that?" He pointed a swift finger. The correspondent said, "Go."

In the shallows, face downward, lay the oiler. His forehead touched sand that was periodically, between each wave, clear of the sea.

The correspondent did not know all that transpired afterward. When he achieved safe ground he fell, striking the sand with each particular part of his body. It was as if he had dropped from a roof, but the thud was grateful to him.

It seems that instantly the beach was populated with men with blankets, clothes, and flasks, and women with coffee pots and all the remedies sacred to their minds. The welcome of the land to the men from the sea was warm and generous; but a still and dripping shape was carried slowly up the beach, and the land's welcome for it could only be the different and sinister hospitality of the grave.

When it came night, the white waves paced to and fro in the moonlight, and the wind brought the sound of the great sea's voice to the men on the shore, and they felt that they could then be interpreters.

The Bride Comes to Yellow Sky

I

THE GREAT PULLMAN was whirling onward with such dignity of motion that a glance from the window seemed simply to prove that the plains of Texas were pouring eastward. Vast flats of green grass, dull-hued spaces of mesquit and cactus, little groups of frame houses, woods of light and tender trees, all were sweeping into the east, sweeping over the horizon, a precipice.

A newly married pair had boarded this coach at San Antonio. The man's face was reddened from many days in the wind and sun, and a direct result of his new black clothes was that his brick-colored hands were constantly performing in a most conscious fashion. From time to time he looked down respectfully at his attire. He sat with a hand on each knee, like a man waiting in a barber's shop. The glances he devoted to other passengers were furtive and shy.

The bride was not pretty, nor was she very young. She wore a dress of blue cashmere, with small reservations of

From *Stephen Crane: An Omnibus*, edited by Robert W. Stallman. Published by Alfred A. Knopf, Inc., 1952.

velvet here and there, and with steel buttons abounding.
She continually twisted her head to regard her puff sleeves,
very stiff, straight, and high. They embarrassed her. It was
quite apparent that she had cooked, and that she expected
to cook, dutifully. The blushes caused by the careless scrutiny of some passengers as she had entered the car were
strange to see upon this plain, under-class countenance,
which was drawn in placid, almost emotionless lines.

They were evidently very happy. "Ever been in a parlor
car before?" he asked, smiling with delight.

"No," she answered; "I never was. It's fine, ain't it?"

"Great! And then after a while we'll go forward to the
diner, and get a big lay-out. Finest meal in the world.
Charge a dollar."

"Oh, do they?" cried the bride. "Charge a dollar? Why,
that's too much—for us—ain't it, Jack?"

"Not this trip, anyhow," he answered bravely. "We're
going to go the whole thing."

Later he explained to her about the trains. "You see, it's
a thousand miles from one end of Texas to the other; and
this train runs right across it, and never stops but four
times." He had the pride of an owner. He pointed out to
her the dazzling fittings of the coach; and in truth her eyes
opened wider as she contemplated the sea-green figured
velvet, the shining brass, silver, and glass, the wood that
gleamed as darkly brilliant as the surface of a pool of oil.
At one end a bronze figure sturdily held a support for a
separated chamber, and at convenient places on the ceiling
were frescos in olive and silver.

To the minds of the pair, their surroundings reflected the
glory of their marriage that morning in San Antonio; this
was the environment of their new estate; and the man's
face in particular beamed with an elation that made him
appear ridiculous to the Negro porter. This individual at
times surveyed them from afar with an amused and superior
grin. On other occasions he bullied them with skill in ways
that did not make it exactly plain to them that they were

being bullied. He subtly used all the manners of the most unconquerable kind of snobbery. He oppressed them; but of this oppression they had small knowledge, and they speedily forgot that infrequently a number of travelers covered them with stares of derisive enjoyment. Historically there was supposed to be something infinitely humorous in their situation.

"We are due in Yellow Sky at 3:42," he said, looking tenderly into her eyes.

"Oh, are we?" she said, as if she had not been aware of it. To evince surprise at her husband's statement was part of her wifely amiability. She took from a pocket a little silver watch; and as she held it before her, and stared at it with a frown of attention, the new husband's face shone.

"I bought it in San Anton' from a friend of mine," he told her gleefully.

"It's seventeen minutes past twelve," she said, looking up at him with a kind of shy and clumsy coquetry. A passenger, noting this play, grew excessively sardonic, and winked at himself in one of the numerous mirrors.

At last they went to the dining car. Two rows of Negro waiters, in glowing white suits, surveyed their entrance with the interest, and also the equanimity, of men who had been forewarned. The pair fell to the lot of a waiter who happened to feel pleasure in steering them through their meal. He viewed them with the manner of a fatherly pilot, his countenance radiant with benevolence. The patronage, entwined with the ordinary deference, was not plain to them. And yet, as they returned to their coach, they showed in their faces a sense of escape.

To the left, miles down a long purple slope, was a little ribbon of mist where moved the keening Rio Grande. The train was approaching it at an angle, and the apex was Yellow Sky. Presently it was apparent that, as the distance from Yellow Sky grew shorter, the husband became commensurately restless. His brick-red hands were more insistent in their prominence. Occasionally he was even rather

absent-minded and faraway when the bride leaned forward
and addressed him.

As a matter of truth, Jack Potter was beginning to find
the shadow of a deed weigh upon him like a leaden slab.
He, the town marshal of Yellow Sky, a man known, liked,
and feared in his corner, a prominent person, had gone to
San Antonio to meet a girl he believed he loved, and there,
after the usual prayers, had actually induced her to marry
him, without consulting Yellow Sky for any part of the
transaction. He was now bringing his bride before an innocent and unsuspecting community.

Of course people in Yellow Sky married as it pleased
them, in accordance with a general custom; but such was
Potter's thought of his duty to his friends, or of their idea
of his duty, or of an unspoken form which does not control
men in these matters, that he felt he was heinous. He had
committed an extraordinary crime. Face to face with this
girl in San Antonio, and spurred by his sharp impulse, he
had gone headlong over all the social hedges. At San Antonio he was like a man hidden in the dark. A knife to sever
any friendly duty, any form, was easy to his hand in that remote city. But the hour of Yellow Sky—the hour of daylight—was approaching.

He knew full well that his marriage was an important
thing to his town. It could only be exceeded by the burning
of the new hotel. His friends could not forgive him. Frequently he had reflected on the advisability of telling them
by telegraph, but a new cowardice had been upon him. He
feared to do it. And now the train was hurrying him toward
a scene of amazement, glee, and reproach. He glanced out
of the window at the line of haze swinging slowly in toward
the train.

Yellow Sky had a kind of brass band, which played painfully, to the delight of the populace. He laughed without
heart as he thought of it. If the citizens could dream of his
prospective arrival with his bride, they would parade the

band at the station and escort them, amid cheers and laughing congratulations, to his adobe home.

He resolved that he would use all the devices of speed and plainscraft in making the journey from the station to his house. Once within that safe citadel, he could issue some sort of vocal bulletin, and then not go among the citizens until they had time to wear off a little of their enthusiasm.

The bride looked anxiously at him. "What's worrying you, Jack?"

He laughed again. "I'm not worrying, girl; I'm only thinking of Yellow Sky."

She flushed in comprehension.

A sense of mutual guilt invaded their minds and developed a finer tenderness. They looked at each other with eyes softly aglow. But Potter often laughed the same nervous laugh; the flush upon the bride's face seemed quite permanent.

The traitor to the feelings of Yellow Sky narrowly watched the speeding landscape. "We're nearly there," he said.

Presently the porter came and announced the proximity of Potter's home. He held a brush in his hand, and, with all his airy superiority gone, he brushed Potter's new clothes as the latter slowly turned this way and that way. Potter fumbled out a coin and gave it to the porter, as he had seen others do. It was a heavy and muscle-bound business, as that of a man shoeing his first horse.

The porter took their bag, and as the train began to slow they moved forward to the hooded platform of the car. Presently the two engines and their long string of coaches rushed into the station of Yellow Sky.

"They have to take water here," said Potter, from a constricted throat and in mournful cadence, as one announcing death. Before the train stopped his eye had swept the length of the platform, and he was glad and astonished to see there

was none upon it but the station agent, who, with a slightly
hurried and anxious air, was walking toward the water tanks.
When the train had halted, the porter alighted first, and
placed in position a little temporary step.

"Come on, girl," said Potter, hoarsely. As he helped her
down they each laughed on a false note. He took the bag
from the Negro, and bade his wife cling to his arm. As they
slunk rapidly away, his hangdog glance perceived that they
were unloading the two trunks, and also that the station
agent, far ahead near the baggage car, had turned and was
running toward him, making gestures. He laughed, and
groaned as he laughed, when he noted the first effect of his
marital bliss upon Yellow Sky. He gripped his wife's arm
firmly to his side, and they fled. Behind them the porter
stood, chuckling fatuously.

II

The California express on the Southern Railway was due
at Yellow Sky in twenty-one minutes. There were six men
at the bar of the Weary Gentleman saloon. One was a
drummer who talked a great deal and rapidly; three were
Texans who did not care to talk at that time; and two were
Mexican sheep-herders, who did not talk as a general practice in the Weary Gentleman saloon. The barkeeper's dog
lay on the boardwalk that crossed in front of the door. His
head was on his paws, and he glanced drowsily here and
there with the constant vigilance of a dog that is kicked on
occasion. Across the sandy street were some vivid green
grass-plots, so wonderful in appearance, amid the sands that
burned near them in a blazing sun, that they caused a
doubt in the mind. They exactly resembled the grass mats
used to represent lawns on the stage. At the cooler end of
the railway station, a man without a coat sat in a tilted
chair and smoked his pipe. The fresh-cut bank of the Rio
Grande circled near the town, and there could be seen be-

yond it a great plum-colored plain of mesquit.
Save for the busy drummer and his companions in the
saloon, Yellow Sky was dozing. The newcomer leaned grace-
fully upon the bar, and recited many tales with the confidence of a bard who has come upon a new field.

"—and at the moment that the old man fell downstairs
with the bureau in his arms, the old woman was coming up
with two scuttles of coal, and of course—"

The drummer's tale was interrupted by a young man who
suddenly appeared in the open door. He cried: "Scratchy
Wilson's drunk, and has turned loose with both hands."
The two Mexicans at once set down their glasses and faded
out of the rear entrance of the saloon.

The drummer, innocent and jocular, answered: "All
right, old man. S'pose he has? Come in and have a drink,
anyhow."

But the information had made such an obvious cleft in
every skull in the room that the drummer was obliged to
see its importance. All had become instantly solemn. "Say,"
said he, mystified, "what is this?" His three companions
made the introductory gesture of eloquent speech; but the
young man at the door forestalled them.

"It means, my friend," he answered, as he came into the
saloon, "that for the next two hours this town won't be a
health resort."

The barkeeper went to the door, and locked and barred
it; reaching out of the window, he pulled in heavy wooden
shutters, and barred them. Immediately a solemn, chapel-
like gloom was upon the place. The drummer was looking
from one to another.

"But say," he cried, "what is this, anyhow? You don't
mean there is going to be a gun fight?"

"Don't know whether there'll be a fight or not," answered one man, grimly, "but there'll be some shootin'—
some good shootin'."

The young man who had warned them waved his hand.
"Oh, there'll be a fight fast enough, if any one wants it.

Anybody can get a fight out there in the street. There's a fight just waiting."

The drummer seemed to be swayed between the interest of a foreigner and a perception of personal danger. "What did you say his name was?" he asked.

"Scratchy Wilson," they answered in chorus.

"And will he kill anybody? What are you going to do? Does this happen often? Does he rampage around like this once a week or so? Can he break in that door?"

"No; he can't break down that door," replied the barkeeper. "He's tried it three times. But when he comes you'd better lay down on the floor, stranger. He's dead sure to shoot at it, and a bullet may come through."

Thereafter the drummer kept a strict eye upon the door. The time had not yet been called for him to hug the floor, but, as a minor precaution, he sidled near to the wall. "Will he kill anybody?" he said again.

The men laughed low and scornfully at the question.

"He's out to shoot, and he's out for trouble. Don't see any good in experimentin' with him."

"But what do you do in a case like this? What do you do?"

A man responded: "Why, he and Jack Potter—"

"But," in chorus the other men interrupted, "Jack Potter's in San Anton'."

"Well, who is he? What's he got to do with it?"

"Oh, he's the town marshal. He goes out and fights Scratchy when he gets on one of these tears."

"Wow!" said the drummer, mopping his brow. "Nice job he's got."

The voices had toned away to mere whisperings. The drummer wished to ask further questions, which were born of an increasing anxiety and bewilderment; but when he attempted them, the men merely looked at him in irritation and motioned him to remain silent. A tense waiting hush was upon them. In the deep shadows of the room their eyes shone as they listened for sounds from the street. One man made three gestures at the barkeeper; and the latter, moving like a ghost, handed him a glass and a bottle. The man poured a full glass of whisky, and set down the bottle noiselessly. He gulped the whisky in a swallow, and turned again toward the door in immovable silence. The drummer saw that the barkeeper, without a sound, had taken a Winchester from beneath the bar. Later he saw this individual beckoning to him, so he tiptoed across the room.

"You better come with me back of the bar."

"No, thanks," said the drummer, perspiring; "I'd rather be where I can make a break for the back door."

Whereupon the man of bottles made a kindly but peremptory gesture. The drummer obeyed it, and, finding himself seated on a box with his head below the level of the bar, balm was laid upon his soul at sight of various zinc and copper fittings that bore a resemblance to armor plate. The barkeeper took a seat comfortably upon an adjacent box.

"You see," he whispered, "this here Scratchy Wilson is a wonder with a gun—a perfect wonder; and when he goes on the war-trail, we hunt our holes—naturally. He's about the last one of the old gang that used to hang out along the river here. He's a terror when he's drunk. When he's sober he's all right—kind of simple—wouldn't hurt a fly—nicest fellow in town. But when he's drunk—whoo!"

There were periods of stillness. "I wish Jack Potter was back from San Anton'," said the barkeeper. "He shot Wilson up once—in the leg—and he would sail in and pull out the kinks in this thing."

Presently they heard from a distance the sound of a shot, followed by three wild yowls. It instantly removed a bond from the men in the darkened saloon. There was a shuffling of feet. They looked at each other. "Here he comes," they said.

III

A man in a maroon-colored flannel shirt, which had been

purchased for purposes of decoration, and made principally by some Jewish women on the East Side of New York, rounded a corner and walked into the middle of the main street of Yellow Sky. In either hand the man held a long, heavy, blue-black revolver. Often he yelled, and these cries rang through a semblance of a deserted village, shrilly flying over the roofs in a volume that seemed to have no relation to the ordinary vocal strength of a man. It was as if the surrounding stillness formed the arch of a tomb over him. These cries of ferocious challenge rang against walls of silence. And his boots had red tops with gilded imprints, of the kind beloved in winter by little sledding boys on the hillsides of New England.

The man's face flamed in a rage begot of whisky. His eyes, rolling, and yet keen for ambush, hunted the still doorways and windows. He walked with the creeping movement of the midnight cat. As it occurred to him, he roared menacing information. The long revolvers in his hands were as easy as straws; they were moved with an electric swiftness. The little fingers of each hand played sometimes in a musician's way. Plain from the low collar of the shirt, the cords of his neck straightened and sank, straightened and sank, as passion moved him. The only sounds were his terrible invitations. The calm adobes preserved their demeanor at the passing of this small thing in the middle of the street.

There was no offer of fight—no offer of fight. The man called to the sky. There were no attractions. He bellowed and fumed and swayed his revolvers here and everywhere.

The dog of the barkeeper of the Weary Gentleman saloon had not appreciated the advance of events. He yet lay dozing in front of his master's door. At sight of the dog, the man paused and raised his revolver humorously. At sight of the man, the dog sprang up and walked diagonally away, with a sullen head, and growling. The man yelled, and the dog broke into a gallop. As it was about to enter an alley, there was a loud noise, a whistling, and something spat the ground directly before it. The dog screamed, and, wheeling in terror, galloped headlong in a new direction. Again there was a noise, a whistling, and sand was kicked viciously before it. Fear-stricken, the dog turned and flurried like an animal in a pen. The man stood laughing, his weapons at his hips.

Ultimately the man was attracted by the closed door of the Weary Gentleman saloon. He went to it and, hammering with a revolver, demanded drink.

The door remaining imperturbable, he picked a bit of paper from the walk, and nailed it to the framework with a knife. He then turned his back contemptuously upon this popular resort and, walking to the opposite side of the street and spinning there on his heel quickly and lithely, fired at the bit of paper. He missed it by a half-inch. He swore at himself, and went away. Later he comfortably fusilladed the windows of his most intimate friend. The man was playing with this town; it was a toy for him.

But still there was no offer of fight. The name of Jack Potter, his ancient antagonist, entered his mind, and he concluded that it would be a glad thing if he should go to Potter's house, and by bombardment induce him to come out and fight. He moved in the direction of his desire, chanting Apache scalp-music.

When he arrived at it, Potter's house presented the same still front as had the other adobes. Taking up a strategic position, the man howled a challenge. But this house regarded him as might a great stone god. It gave no sign. After a decent wait, the man howled further challenges, mingling with them wonderful epithets.

Presently there came the spectacle of a man churning himself into deepest rage over the immobility of a house. He fumed at it as the winter wind attacks a prairie cabin in the North. To the distance there should have gone the sound of a tumult like the fighting of two hundred Mexicans. As necessity bade him, he paused for breath or to re-load his revolvers.

IV

Potter and his bride walked sheepishly and with speed. Sometimes they laughed together shamefacedly and low.

"Next corner, dear," he said finally.

They put forth the efforts of a pair walking bowed against a strong wind. Potter was about to raise a finger to point the first appearance of the new home when, as they circled the corner, they came face to face with a man in a maroon-colored shirt, who was feverishly pushing cartridges into a large revolver. Upon the instant the man dropped his re-volver to the ground and, like lightning, whipped another from its holster. The second weapon was aimed at the bridegroom's chest.

There was a silence. Potter's mouth seemed to be merely a grave for his tongue. He exhibited an instinct to at once loosen his arm from the woman's grip, and he dropped the bag to the sand. As for the bride, her face had gone as yellow as old cloth. She was a slave to hideous rites, gazing at the apparitional snake.

The two men faced each other at a distance of three paces. He of the revolver smiled with a new and quiet ferocity.

"Tried to sneak up on me," he said. "Tried to sneak up on me!" His eyes grew more baleful. As Potter made a slight movement, the man thrust his revolver venomously forward. "No; don't you do it, Jack Potter. Don't you move a finger toward a gun just yet. Don't you move an eyelash. The time has come for me to settle with you, and I'm goin' to do it my own way, and loaf along with no inter-ferin'. So if you don't want a gun bent on you, just mind what I tell you."

Potter looked at his enemy. "I ain't got a gun on me, Scratchy," he said. "Honest, I ain't." He was stiffening and steadying, but yet somewhere at the back of his mind a vision of the Pullman floated: the sea-green figured velvet, the shining brass, silver, and glass, the wood that gleamed as darkly brilliant as the surface of a pool of oil—all the glory of the marriage, the environment of the new estate. "You know I fight when it comes to fighting, Scratchy Wilson; but I ain't got a gun on me. You'll have to do all the shootin' yourself."

His enemy's face went livid. He stepped forward, and lashed his weapon to and fro before Potter's chest. "Don't you tell me you ain't got no gun on you, you whelp. Don't tell me no lie like that. There ain't a man in Texas ever seen you without no gun. Don't take me for no kid." His eyes blazed with light, and his throat worked like a pump.

"I ain't takin' you for no kid," answered Potter. His heels had not moved an inch backward. "I'm takin' you for a damn fool. I tell you I ain't got a gun, and I ain't. If you're goin' to shoot me up, you better begin now; you'll never get a chance like this again."

So much enforced reasoning had told on Wilson's rage; he was calmer. "If you ain't got a gun, why ain't you got a gun?" he sneered. "Been to Sunday school?"

"I ain't got a gun because I've just come from San Anton' with my wife. I'm married," said Potter. "And if I'd thought there was going to be any galoots like you prowling around when I brought my wife home, I'd had a gun, and don't you forget it."

"Married!" said Scratchy, not at all comprehending.

"Yes, married. I'm married," said Potter, distinctly.

"Married?" said Scratchy. Seemingly for the first time, he saw the drooping, drowning woman at the other man's side. "No!" he said. He was like a creature allowed a glimpse of another world. He moved a pace backward, and his arm, with the revolver, dropped to his side. "Is this the lady?" he asked.

"Yes; this is the lady," answered Potter.

There was another period of silence.

"Well," said Wilson at last, slowly, "I s'pose it's all off now."

"It's all off if you say so, Scratchy. You know I didn't make the trouble." Potter lifted his valise.

"Well, I 'low it's off, Jack," said Wilson. He was looking at the ground. "Married!" He was not a student of chivalry; it was merely that in the presence of this foreign condition he was a simple child of the earlier plains. He picked up his starboard revolver, and, placing both weapons in their holsters, he went away. His feet made funnel-shaped tracks in the heavy sand.

Katherine Anne Porter

[1894 –   ]

ALTHOUGH FOR MORE than ten years Katherine Anne Porter has been writing her longer works in progress—a biography of Cotton Mather and a first novel, *Ship of Fools* (1962)—most of her short stories have been completed in one draft, and some in one sitting. These facts testify to the minute caution of her craft and validate her remark that "my one aim is to tell a straight story and to give true testimony." Nevertheless, they ought not to be interpreted to mean that he vision is infinitesimal or discontinuous. Everywhere present in her work is a Southerner's sense of enduring history and of personal heritage; and she herself has insisted that each story is part of some larger design, just as Faulkner's individual novels might be considered fragments of an epic.

Certainly it is significant that, as girl and growing woman, her fictional self, Miranda, pursues her brave new world through more than a third of the stories in Miss Porter's collections. Moreover, from volume to volume Miranda moves towards completion of a complex cycle: childish dependence on her grandmother; adolescent rebellion and confused excursion; final recapitulation of her grandmother's character—joyless but courageous—in her mature self. In her book of essays, *The Days Before* (1952), Miss Porter has explained that "my material consists of memory, legend, personal experience, and acquired knowledge. They combine in a constant process of re-creation."

Correspondences between the lives of author and character are undeniable: the terrible clarity, for example, of the influenza epidemic in "Pale Horse, Pale Rider" reflects her own severe illness in 1918, while she was a reporter in Denver. Nevertheless, the progress towards self-recognition which she traces is more than personal.

Katherine Anne Porter was raised in Texas by a grandmother who had lived with all the lavish splendor but also the provident responsibility of her class, in Kentucky, before the Civil War. When her husband died young in the desperate Reconstruction days, she was sufficiently trained in her obligations not to flinch. First in Louisiana and then in Texas she brought up her own children and later their children. Although she was reduced to "coffee" made from ground sweet potato and dried corn, her fortitude under such circumstances was visible proof that the grandeur due her family was not forever lost but merely interrupted. At night the grandchildren gathered at her knee to pray and to be reminded that bad morals and bad manners were kin to each other. The aging matriarch loved to dress in mourning, but rode horseback at a gallop until the year she died.

Such an ancestry, similar to Miranda's, Miss Porter found inescapable. At first her grandmother seemed a figure of unshakable confidence; then, a figure of tyranny that threatened the very egos it had nurtured; but later, after attempted flight, a figure of calm—a benchmark in a changing landscape. Ironically it was the inherited image of a recoverable past which made Miss Porter wander from home, in search of home. After leaving the convent schools of her early years, she had watched the Madero revolution from the window of a cathedral across the Mexican border from Indian Creek, her birthplace. Later she came to know intimately Cajuns in Louisiana and Germans in Texas: "it seemed to me that all my life I had lived among people who spoke broken, laboring tongues. . . ." For these beseeching half-mutes, the inarticulate, her symbols are spokesmen.

Writing not as onlooker but as participant, Miss Porter provides each story with a surprise and precision founded on and inseparable from her experience. *Flowering Judas and Other Stories* (1930: four additions were made in 1935); *Pale Horse, Pale Rider* (1939); *The Leaning Tower and Other Stories*

(1944)—all these respect the importance of discovering and distilling other people's motives, whether the most majestic or the most threatening. "I have never known an uninteresting human being," she wrote, "and I have never known two alike. . . . I am interested in the thumbprint. I am passionately involved with these individuals who populate all these enormous migrations, calamities; who fight wars and furnish life for the future; these beings without which, one by one, all the 'broad movements of history' could never take place. One by one—as they were born."

Far from living in a moral vacuum, as she has accused Gertrude Stein of doing, Katherine Anne Porter is very much aware of the individual's vulnerability in a world that grows increasingly authoritarian. She has referred to herself as "the grandchild of a lost War"—over states' rights and slavery. In 1940, with the Nazis on the brink of France, she wrote that "all the conscious and recollected years of my life have been lived to this day under the heavy threat of world catastrophe. . . ." Before it however she did not quail but agreed with E. M. Forster that only in art and religion is real order possible. Just as Miranda does not despair but comes away from innocence humbled and transmuted, so the commission of the artist, her everyday care, is to find that reason which justifies belief in human worth, in the midst of vileness.

The Grave

THE GRANDFATHER, dead for more than thirty years, had been twice disturbed in his long repose by the constancy and possessiveness of his widow. She removed his bones first to Louisiana and then to Texas as if she had set out to find her own burial place, knowing well she would never return to the places she had left. In Texas she set up a small cemetery in a corner of her first farm, and as the family connection grew, and oddments of relations came over from Kentucky to settle, it contained at last about twenty graves. After the grandmother's death, part of her land was to be sold for the benefit of certain of her children, and the cemetery happened to lie in the part set aside for sale. It was necessary to take up the bodies and bury them again in the family plot in the big new public cemetery, where the grandmother had been buried. At last her husband was to lie beside her for eternity, as she had planned.

The family cemetery had been a pleasant small neglected garden of tangled rose bushes and ragged cedar trees and cypress, the simple flat stones rising out of uncropped sweet-

From *The Leaning Tower and Other Stories*, copyright, 1944, by Katherine Anne Porter. Reprinted by permission of Harcourt, Brace & World, Inc.

smelling wild grass. The graves were lying open and empty one burning day when Miranda and her brother Paul, who often went together to hunt rabbits and doves, propped their twenty-two Winchester rifles carefully against the rail fence, climbed over and explored among the graves. She was nine years old and he was twelve.

They peered into the pits all shaped alike with such purposeful accuracy, and looking at each other with pleased adventurous eyes, they said in solemn tones: "These were graves!" trying by words to shape a special, suitable emotion in their minds, but they felt nothing except an agreeable thrill of wonder: they were seeing a new sight, doing something they had not done before. In them both there was also a small disappointment at the entire commonplaceness of the actual spectacle. Even if it had once contained a coffin for years upon years, when the coffin was gone a grave was just a hole in the ground. Miranda leaped into the pit that had held her grandfather's bones. Scratching around aimlessly and pleasurably as any young animal, she scooped up a lump of earth and weighed it in her palm. It had a pleasantly sweet, corrupt smell, being mixed with cedar needles and small leaves, and as the crumbs fell apart, she saw a silver dove no larger than a hazel nut, with spread wings and a neat fan-shaped tail. The breast had a deep round hollow in it. Turning it up to the fierce sunlight, she saw that the inside of the hollow was cut in little whorls. She scrambled out, over the pile of loose earth that had fallen back into one end of the grave, calling to Paul that she had found something, he must guess what. . . His head appeared smiling over the rim of another grave. He waved a closed hand at her. "I've got something too!" They ran to compare treasures, making a game of it, so many guesses each, all wrong, and a final showdown with opened palms. Paul had found a thin wide gold ring carved with intricate flowers and leaves. Miranda was smitten at sight of the ring and wished to have it. Paul seemed more impressed by the dove. They made a trade, with some little bickering. After he had got the dove in his hand, Paul said, "Don't you know what this is? This is a screw head for a coffin! . . . I'll bet nobody else in the world has one like this!"

Miranda glanced at it without covetousness. She had the gold ring on her thumb; it fitted perfectly. "Maybe we ought to go now," she said, "maybe one of the niggers 'll see us and tell somebody." They knew the land had been sold, the cemetery was no longer theirs, and they felt like trespassers. They climbed back over the fence, slung their rifles loosely under their arms—they had been shooting at targets with various kinds of firearms since they were seven years old—and set out to look for the rabbits and doves or whatever small game might happen along. On these expeditions Miranda always followed at Paul's heels along the path, obeying instructions about handling her gun when going through fences; learning how to stand it up properly so it would not slip and fire unexpectedly; how to wait her time for a shot and not just bang away in the air without looking, spoiling shots for Paul, who really could hit things if given a chance. Now and then, in her excitement at seeing birds whizz up suddenly before her face, or a rabbit leap across her very toes, she lost her head, and almost without sighting she flung her rifle up and pulled the trigger. She hardly ever hit any sort of mark. She had no proper sense of hunting at all. Her brother would be often completely disgusted with her. "You don't care whether you get your bird or not," he said. "That's no way to hunt." Miranda could not understand his indignation. She had seen him smash his hat and yell with fury when he had missed his aim. "What I like about shooting," said Miranda, with exasperating inconsequence, "is pulling the trigger and hearing the noise."

"Then, by golly," said Paul, "whyn't you go back to the range and shoot at bulls-eyes?"

"I'd just as soon," said Miranda, "only like this, we walk around more."

"Well, you just stay behind and stop spoiling my shots," said Paul, who, when he made a kill, wanted to be certain he had made it. Miranda, who alone brought down a bird once in twenty rounds, always claimed as her own any game they got when they fired at the same moment. It was tiresome and unfair and her brother was sick of it.

"Now, the first dove we see, or the first rabbit, is mine," he told her. "And the next will be yours. Remember that and don't get smarty."

"What about snakes?" asked Miranda idly. "Can I have the first snake?"

Waving her thumb gently and watching her gold ring glitter, Miranda lost interest in shooting. She was wearing her summer roughing outfit: dark blue overalls, a light blue shirt, a hired-man's straw hat and thick brown sandals. Her brother had the same outfit except his was a sober hickory-nut color. Ordinarily Miranda preferred her overalls to any other dress, though it was making rather a scandal in the countryside, for the year was 1903, and in the back country the law of female decorum had teeth in it. Her father had been criticized for letting his girls dress like boys and go careering around astride barebacked horses. Big sister Maria, the really independent and fearless one, in spite of her rather affected ways, rode at a dead run with only a rope knotted around her horse's nose. It was said the motherless family was running down, with the grandmother no longer there to hold it together. It was known that she had discriminated against her son Harry in her will, and that he was in straits about money. Some of his old neighbors reflected with vicious satisfaction that now he would probably not be so stiffnecked, nor have any more high-stepping horses either. Miranda knew this, though she could not say how. She had met along the road old women of the kind who smoked corn cob pipes, who had treated her grandmother with most sincere respect. They slanted their gummy old eyes side-ways at the granddaughter and said, "Ain't you ashamed of yoself, Missy? It's aginst the Scrip-

tures to dress like that. Whut yo Pappy thinkin about?"
Miranda, with her powerful social sense, which was like a
fine set of antennae radiating from every pore of her skin,
would feel ashamed because she knew well it was rude and
ill-bred to shock anybody, even bad-tempered old crones,
though she had faith in her father's judgment and was
perfectly comfortable in the clothes. Her father had said,
"They're just what you need, and they'll save your dresses
for school. . ." This sounded quite simple and natural
to her. She had been brought up in rigorous economy.
Wastefulness was vulgar. It was also a sin. These were
truths; she had heard them repeated many times and never
once disputed.

Now the ring, shining with the serene purity of fine gold
on her rather grubby thumb, turned her feelings against her
overalls and sockless feet, toes sticking through the thick
brown leather straps. She wanted to go back to the farmhouse, take a good cold bath, dust herself with plenty of
Maria's violet talcum powder—provided Maria was not present to object, of course—put on the thinnest, most becoming dress she owned, with a big sash, and sit in a
wicker chair under the trees. . . These things were not
all she wanted, of course; she had vague stirrings of desire
for luxury and a grand way of living which could not take
precise form in her imagination but were founded on family
legend of past wealth and leisure. These immediate comforts were what she could have, and she wanted them at
once. She lagged rather far behind Paul, and once she
thought of just turning back without a word and going
home. She stopped, thinking that Paul would never do
that to her, and so she would have to tell him. When a
rabbit leaped, she let Paul have it without dispute. He
killed it with one shot.

When she came up with him, he was already kneeling,
examining the wound, the rabbit trailing from his hands.
"Right through the head," he said complacently, as if he
had aimed for it. He took out his sharp, competent bowie

knife and started to skin the body. He did it very cleanly
and quickly. Uncle Jimbilly knew how to prepare the skins
so that Miranda always had fur coats for her dolls, for
though she never cared much for her dolls she liked seeing
them in fur coats. The children knelt facing each other
over the dead animal. Miranda watched admiringly while
her brother stripped the skin away as if he were taking off
a glove. The flayed flesh emerged dark scarlet, sleek, firm;
Miranda with thumb and finger felt the long fine muscles
with the silvery flat strips binding them to the joints.
Brother lifted the oddly bloated belly. "Look," he said, in
a low amazed voice. "It was going to have young ones."

Very carefully he slit the thin flesh from the center ribs
to the flanks, and a scarlet bag appeared. He slit again and
pulled the bag open, and there lay a bundle of tiny rabbits,
each wrapped in a thin scarlet veil. The brother pulled these
off and there they were, dark gray, their sleek wet down
lying in minute even ripples, like a baby's head just washed,
their unbelievably small delicate ears folded close, their
little blind faces almost featureless.

Miranda said, "Oh, I want to see," under her breath.
She looked and looked—excited but not frightened, for she
was accustomed to the sight of animals killed in hunting—
filled with pity and astonishment and a kind of shocked
delight in the wonderful little creatures for their own sakes,
they were so pretty. She touched one of them ever so carefully. "Ah, there's blood running over them," she said and
began to tremble without knowing why. Yet she wanted
most deeply to see and to know. Having seen, she felt at
once as if she had known all along. The very memory of
her former ignorance faded, she had always known just
this. No one had ever told her anything outright, she had
been rather unobservant of the animal life around her because she was so accustomed to animals. They seemed
simply disorderly and unaccountably rude in their habits,
but altogether natural and not very interesting. Her brother
had spoken as if he had known about everything all along.

He may have seen all this before. He had never said a word to her, but she knew now a part at least of what he knew. She understood a little of the secret, formless intuitions in her own mind and body, which had been clearing up, taking form, so gradually and so steadily she had not realized that she was learning what she had to know. Paul said cautiously, as if he were talking about something forbidden: "They were just about ready to be born." His voice dropped on the last word. "I know," said Miranda, "like kittens. I know, like babies." She was quietly and terribly agitated, standing again with her rifle under her arm, looking down at the bloody heap. "I don't want the skin," she-said, "I won't have it." Paul buried the young rabbits again in their mother's body, wrapped the skin around her, carried her to a clump of sage bushes, and hid her away. He came out again at once and said to Miranda, with an eager friendliness, a confidential tone quite unusual in him, as if he were taking her into an important secret on equal terms: "Listen now. Now you listen to me, and don't ever forget. Don't you ever tell a living soul that you saw this. Don't tell a soul. Don't tell Dad because I'll get into trouble. He'll say I'm leading you into things you ought not to do. He's always saying that. So now don't you go and forget and blab out sometime the way you're always doing. . . Now, that's a secret. Don't you tell."

Miranda never told, she did not even wish to tell anybody. She thought about the whole worrisome affair with confused unhappiness for a few days. Then it sank quietly into her mind and was heaped over by accumulated thousands of impressions, for nearly twenty years. One day she was picking her path among the puddles and crushed refuse of a market street in a strange city of a strange country, when without warning, plain and clear in its true colors as if she looked through a frame upon a scene that had not stirred nor changed since the moment it happened, the episode of that far-off day leaped from its burial place before her mind's eye. She was so reasonlessly horrified she halted suddenly staring, the scene before her eyes dimmed by the vision back of them. An Indian vendor had held up before her a tray of dyed sugar sweets, in the shapes of all kinds of small creatures: birds, baby chicks, baby rabbits, lambs, baby pigs. They were in gay colors and smelled of vanilla, maybe. . . . It was a very hot day and the smell in the market, with its piles of raw flesh and wilting flowers, was like the mingled sweetness and corruption she had smelled that other day in the empty cemetery at home: the day she had remembered always until now vaguely as the time she and her brother had found treasure in the opened graves. Instantly upon this thought the dreadful vision faded, and she saw clearly her brother, whose childhood face she had forgotten, standing again in the blazing sunshine, again twelve years old, a pleased sober smile in his eyes, turning the silver dove over and over in his hands.

Flowering Judas

BRAGGIONI SITS HEAPED upon the edge of a straight-backed chair much too small for him, and sings to Laura in a furry, mournful voice. Laura has begun to find reasons for avoiding her own house until the latest possible moment, for Braggioni is there almost every night. No matter how late she is, he will be sitting there with a surly, waiting expression, pulling at his kinky yellow hair, thumbing the strings of his guitar, snarling a tune under his breath. Lupe the Indian maid meets Laura at the door, and says with a flicker of a glance towards the upper room, "He waits."

Laura wishes to lie down, she is tired of her hairpins and the feel of her long tight sleeves, but she says to him, "Have you a new song for me this evening?" If he says yes, she asks him to sing it. If he says no, she remembers his favorite one, and asks him to sing it again. Lupe brings her a cup of chocolate and a plate of rice, and Laura eats at the small table under the lamp, first inviting Braggioni, whose answer is always the same: "I have eaten, and besides, chocolate thickens the voice."

Laura says, "Sing, then," and Braggioni heaves himself

into song. He scratches the guitar familiarly as though it were a pet animal, and sings passionately off key, taking the high notes in a prolonged painful squeal. Laura, who haunts the markets listening to the ballad singers, and stops every day to hear the blind boy playing his reed-flute in Sixteenth of September Street, listens to Braggioni with pitiless courtesy, because she dares not smile at his miserable performance. Nobody dares to smile at him. Braggioni is cruel to everyone, with a kind of specialized insolence, but he is so vain of his talents, and so sensitive to slights, it would require a cruelty and vanity greater than his own to lay· a finger on the vast cureless wound of his self-esteem. It would require courage, too, for it is dangerous to offend him, and nobody has this courage.

Braggioni loves himself with such tenderness and amplitude and eternal charity that his followers—for he is a leader of men, a skilled revolutionist, and his skin has been punctured in honorable warfare—warm themselves in the reflected glow, and say to each other: "He has a real nobility, a love of humanity raised above mere personal affections." The excess of this self-love has flowed out, inconveniently for her, over Laura, who, with so many others, owes her comfortable situation and her salary to him. When he is in a very good humor, he tells her, "I am tempted to forgive you for being a *gringa*. *Gringita!*" and Laura, burning, imagines herself leaning forward suddenly, and with a sound back-handed slap wiping the suety smile from his face. If he notices her eyes at these moments he gives no sign.

She knows what Braggioni would offer her, and she must resist tenaciously without appearing to resist, and if she could avoid it she would not admit even to herself the slow drift of his intention. During these long evenings which have spoiled a long month for her, she sits in her deep chair with an open book on her knees, resting her eyes on the consoling rigidity of the printed page when the sight and sound of Braggioni singing threaten to identify themselves with all her remembered afflictions and to add their weight to her uneasy premonitions of the future. The gluttonous bulk of Braggioni has become a symbol of her many disillusions, for a revolutionist should be lean, animated by heroic faith, a vessel of abstract virtues. This is nonsense, she knows it now and is ashamed of it. Revolution must have leaders, and leadership is a career for energetic men. She is, her comrades tell her, full of romantic error, for what she defines as cynicism in them is merely "a developed sense of reality." She is almost too willing to say, "I am wrong, I suppose I don't really understand the principles," and afterward she makes a secret truce with herself, determined not to surrender her will to such expedient logic. But she cannot help feeling that she has been betrayed irreparably by the disunion between her way of living and her feeling of what life should be, and at times she is almost contented to rest in this sense of grievance as a private store of consolation. Sometimes she wishes to run away, but she stays. Now she longs to fly out of this room, down the narrow stairs, and into the street where the houses lean together like conspirators under a single mottled lamp, and leave Braggioni singing to himself.

Instead she looks at Braggioni, frankly and clearly, like a good child who understands the rules of behavior. Her knees cling together under sound blue serge, and her round white collar is not purposely nun-like. She wears the uniform of an idea, and has renounced vanities. She was born Roman Catholic, and in spite of her fear of being seen by someone who might make a scandal of it, she slips now and again into some crumbling little church, kneels on the chilly stone, and says a Hail Mary on the gold rosary she bought in Tehuantepec. It is no good and she ends by examining the altar with its tinsel flowers and ragged brocades, and feels tender about the battered doll-shape of some male saint whose white, lace-trimmed drawers hang limply around his ankles below the hieratic dignity of his velvet robe. She has encased herself in a set of principles derived from her early training, leaving no detail of gesture or of personal taste untouched, and for this reason she will not wear lace made on machines. This is her private heresy, for in her special group the machine is sacred, and will be the salvation of the workers. She loves fine lace, and there is a tiny edge of fluted cobweb on this collar, which is one of twenty precisely alike, folded in blue tissue paper in the upper drawer of her clothes chest.

Braggioni catches her glance solidly as if he had been waiting for it, leans forward, balancing his paunch between his spread knees, and sings with tremendous emphasis, weighing his words. He has, the song relates, no father and no mother, nor even a friend to console him; lonely as a wave of the sea he comes and goes, lonely as a wave. His mouth opens round and yearns sideways, his balloon cheeks grow oily with the labor of song. He bulges marvelously in his expensive garments. Over his lavender collar, crushed upon a purple necktie, held by a diamond hoop: over his ammunition belt of tooled leather worked in silver, buckled cruelly around his gasping middle: over the tops of his glossy yellow shoes Braggioni swells with ominous ripeness, his mauve silk hose stretched taut, his ankles bound with the stout leather thongs of his shoes.

When he stretches his eyelids at Laura she notes again that his eyes are the true tawny yellow cat's eyes. He is rich, not in money, he tells her, but in power, and this power brings with it the blameless ownership of things, and the right to indulge his love of small luxuries. "I have a taste for the elegant refinements," he said once, flourishing a yellow silk handkerchief before her nose. "Smell that? It is Jockey Club, imported from New York." Nonetheless he is wounded by life. He will say so presently. "It is true everything turns to dust in the hand, to gall on the tongue." He sighs and his leather belt creaks like a saddle girth. "I am disappointed in everything as it comes. Everything." He shakes his head. "You, poor thing, you will be disappointed too. You are born for it. We are more alike than you realize in some things. Wait and see. Some day you will remember what I have told you, you will know that Braggioni was your friend."

Laura feels a slow chill, a purely physical sense of danger, a warning in her blood that violence, mutilation, a shocking death, wait for her with lessening patience. She has translated this fear into something homely, immediate, and sometimes hesitates before crossing the street. "My personal fate is nothing, except as the testimony of a mental attitude," she reminds herself, quoting from some forgotten philosophic primer, and is sensible enough to add, "Anyhow, I shall not be killed by an automobile if I can help it."

"It may be true I am as corrupt, in another way, as Braggioni," she thinks in spite of herself, "as callous, as incomplete," and if this is so, any kind of death seems preferable. Still she sits quietly, she does not run. Where could she go? Uninvited she has promised herself to this place; she can no longer imagine herself as living in another country, and there is no pleasure in remembering her life before she came here.

Precisely what is the nature of this devotion, its true motives, and what are its obligations? Laura cannot say. She spends part of her days in Xochimilco, near by, teaching Indian children to say in English, "The cat is on the mat." When she appears in the classroom they crowd about her with smiles on their wise, innocent, clay-colored faces, crying, "Good morning, my titcher!" in immaculate voices, and they make of her desk a fresh garden of flowers every day.

During her leisure she goes to union meetings and listens to busy important voices quarreling over tactics, methods, internal politics. She visits the prisoners of her own political faith in their cells, where they entertain themselves with counting cockroaches, repenting of their indiscretions, composing their memoirs, writing out manifestoes and plans for their comrades who are still walking about free,

hands in pockets, sniffing fresh air. Laura brings them food
and cigarettes and a little money, and she brings messages
disguised in equivocal phrases from the men outside who
dare not set foot in the prison for fear of disappearing into
the cells kept empty for them. If the prisoners confuse
night and day, and complain, "Dear little Laura, time
doesn't pass in this infernal hole, and I won't know when
it is time to sleep unless I have a reminder," she brings
them their favorite narcotics, and says in a tone that does
not wound them with pity, "Tonight will really be night
for you," and though her Spanish amuses them, they find
her comforting, useful. If they lose patience and all faith,
and curse the slowness of their friends in coming to their
rescue with money and influence, they trust her not to repeat everything, and if she inquires, "Where do you think
we can find money, or influence?" they are certain to answer, "Well, there is Braggioni, why doesn't he do something?"

She smuggles letters from headquarters to men hiding
from firing squads in back streets in mildewed houses,
where they sit in tumbled beds and talk bitterly as if all
Mexico were at their heels, when Laura knows positively
they might appear at the band concert in the Alameda on
Sunday morning, and no one would notice them. But
Braggioni says, "Let them sweat a little. The next time
they may be careful. It is very restful to have them out
of the way for a while." She is not afraid to knock on any
door in any street after midnight, and enter in the darkness,
and say to one of these men who is really in danger: "They
will be looking for you—seriously—tomorrow morning after
six. Here is some money from Vicente. Go to Vera Cruz
and wait."

She borrows money from the Roumanian agitator to give
to his bitter enemy the Polish agitator. The favor of Braggioni is their disputed territory, and Braggioni holds the
balance nicely, for he can use them both. The Polish agitator talks love to her over café tables, hoping to exploit

what he believes is her secret sentimental preference for him, and he gives her misinformation which he begs her to repeat as the solemn truth to certain persons. The Roumanian is more adroit. He is generous with his money in all good causes, and lies to her with an air of ingenuous candor, as if he were her good friend and confidant. She never repeats anything they may say. Braggioni never asks questions. He has other ways to discover all that he wishes to know about them.

Nobody touches her, but all praise her gray eyes, and the soft, round under lip which promises gayety, yet is always grave, nearly always firmly closed: and they cannot understand why she is in Mexico. She walks back and forth on her errands, with puzzled eyebrows, carrying her little folder of drawings and music and school papers. No dancer dances more beautifully than Laura walks, and she inspires some amusing, unexpected ardors, which cause little gossip, because nothing comes of them. A young captain who had been a soldier in Zapata's army attempted, during a horseback ride near Cuernavaca, to express his desire for her with the noble simplicity befitting a rude folk-hero: but gently, because he was gentle. This gentleness was his defeat, for when he alighted, and removed her foot from the stirrup, and essayed to draw her down into his arms, her horse, ordinarily a tame one, shied fiercely, reared and plunged away. The young hero's horse careered blindly after his stablemate, and the hero did not return to the hotel until rather late that evening. At breakfast he came to her table in full charro dress, gray buckskin jacket and trousers with strings of silver buttons down the leg, and he was in a humorous, careless mood. "May I sit with you?" and "You are a wonderful rider. I was terrified that you might be thrown and dragged. I should never have forgiven myself. But I cannot admire you enough for your riding!"

"I learned to ride in Arizona," said Laura.

"If you will ride with me again this morning, I promise you a horse that will not shy with you," he said. But Laura remembered that she must return to Mexico City at noon. Next morning the children made a celebration and spent their playtime writing on the blackboard, "We lóv ar ticher," and with tinted chalks they drew wreaths of flowers around the words. The young hero wrote her a letter: "I am a very foolish, wasteful, impulsive man. I should have first said I love you, and then you would not have run away. But you shall see me again." Laura thought, "I must send him a box of colored crayons," but she was trying to forgive herself for having spurred her horse at the wrong moment.

A brown, shock-haired youth came and stood in her patio one night and sang like a lost soul for two hours, but Laura could think of nothing to do about it. The moonlight spread a wash of gauzy silver over the clear spaces of the garden, and the shadows were cobalt blue. The scarlet blossoms of the Judas tree were dull purple, and the names of the colors repeated themselves automatically in her mind, while she watched not the boy, but his shadow, fallen like a dark garment across the fountain rim, trailing in the water. Lupe came silently and whispered expert counsel in her ear: "If you will throw him one little flower, he will sing another song or two and go away." Laura threw the flower, and he sang a last song and went away with the flower tucked in the band of his hat. Lupe said, "He is one of the organizers of the Typographers Union, and before that he sold corridos in the Merced market, and before that, he came from Guanajuato, where I was born. I would not trust any man, but I trust least those from Guanajuato."

She did not tell Laura that he would be back again the next night, and the next, nor that he would follow her at a certain fixed distance around the Merced market, through the Zócolo, up Francisco I. Madero Avenue, and so along the Paseo de la Reforma to Chapultepec Park, and into the Philosopher's Footpath, still with that flower withering in his hat, and an indivisible attention in his eyes.

Now Laura is accustomed to him, it means nothing except that he is nineteen years old and is observing a convention with all propriety, as though it were founded on a law of nature, which in the end it might well prove to be. He is beginning to write poems which he prints on a wooden press, and he leaves them stuck like handbills in her door. She is pleasantly disturbed by the abstract, unhurried watchfulness of his black eyes which will in time turn easily towards another object. She tells herself that throwing the flower was a mistake, for she is twenty-two years old and knows better; but she refuses to regret it, and persuades herself that her negation of all external events as they occur is a sign that she is gradually perfecting herself in the stoicism she strives to cultivate against that disaster she fears, though she cannot name it.

She is not at home in the world. Every day she teaches children who remain strangers to her, though she loves their tender round hands and their charming opportunist savagery. She knocks at unfamiliar doors not knowing whether a friend or a stranger shall answer, and even if a known face emerges from the sour gloom of that unknown interior, still it is the face of a stranger. No matter what this stranger says to her, nor what her message to him, the very cells of her flesh reject knowledge and kinship in one monotonous word. No. No. No. She draws her strength from this one holy talismanic word which does not suffer her to be led into evil. Denying everything, she may walk anywhere in safety, she looks at everything without amazement.

No, repeats this firm unchanging voice of her blood; and she looks at Braggioni without amazement. He is a great man, he wishes to impress this simple girl who covers her great round breasts with thick dark cloth, and who hides long, invaluably beautiful legs under a heavy skirt. She is almost thin except for the incomprehensible fullness of her breasts, like a nursing mother's, and Braggioni, who considers himself a judge of women, speculates again on the puzzle of her notorious virginity, and takes the liberty of speech which she permits without a sign of modesty, indeed, without any sort of sign, which is disconcerting. "You think you are so cold, *gringita!* Wait and see. You will surprise yourself some day! May I be there to advise you!" He stretches his eyelids at her, and his ill-humored cat's eyes waver in a separate glance for the two points of light marking the opposite ends of a smoothly drawn path between the swollen curve of her breasts. He is not put off by that blue serge, nor by her resolutely fixed gaze. There is all the time in the world. His cheeks are bellying with the wind of song. "O girl with the dark eyes," he sings, and reconsiders. "But yours are not dark. I can change all that. O girl with the green eyes, you have stolen my heart away!" then his mind wanders to the song, and Laura feels the weight of his attention being shifted elsewhere. Singing thus, he seems harmless, he is quite harmless, there is nothing to do but sit patiently and say "No," when the moment comes. She draws a full breath, and her mind wanders also, but not far. She dares not wander too far.

Not for nothing has Braggioni taken pains to be a good revolutionist and a professional lover of humanity. He will never die of it. He has the malice, the cleverness, the wickedness, the sharpness of wit, the hardness of heart, stipulated for loving the world profitably. *He will never die of it.* He will live to see himself kicked out from his feeding trough by other hungry world-saviors. Traditionally he must sing in spite of his life which drives him to bloodshed, he tells Laura, for his father was a Tuscany peasant who drifted to Yucatan and married a Maya woman: a woman of race, an aristocrat. They gave him the love and knowledge of music, thus: and under the rip of his thumbnail, the strings of the instrument complain like exposed nerves.

Once he was called Delgadito by all the girls and married women who ran after him; he was so scrawny all his bones showed under his thin cotton clothing, and he could squeeze his emptiness to the very backbone with his two hands. He was a poet and the revolution was only a dream then; too many women loved him and sapped away his youth, and he could never find enough to eat anywhere, anywhere! Now he is a leader of men, crafty men who whisper in his ear, hungry men who wait for hours outside his office for a word with him, emaciated men with wild faces who waylay him at the street gate with a timid, "Comrade, let me tell you . . ." and they blow the foul breath from their empty stomachs in his face.

He is always sympathetic. He gives them handfuls of small coins from his own pocket, he promises them work, there will be demonstrations, they must join the unions and attend the meetings, above all they must be on the watch for spies. They are closer to him than his own brothers, without them he can do nothing—until tomorrow, comrade!

Until tomorrow. "They are stupid, they are lazy, they are treacherous, they would cut my throat for nothing," he says to Laura. He has good food and abundant drink, he hires an automobile and drives in the Paseo on Sunday morning, and enjoys plenty of sleep in a soft bed beside a wife who dares not disturb him; and he sits pampering his bones in easy billows of fat, singing to Laura, who knows and thinks these things about him. When he was fifteen, he tried to drown himself because he loved a girl, his first love, and she laughed at him. "A thousand women have paid for that," and his tight little mouth turns down at the corners. Now he perfumes his hair with Jockey Club, and confides to Laura: "One woman is really as good as another for me, in the dark. I prefer them all."

His wife organizes unions among the girls in the cigarette factories, and walks in picket lines, and even speaks at meetings in the evening. But she cannot be brought to acknowledge the benefits of true liberty. "I tell her I must have my freedom, net. She does not understand my point of view." Laura has heard this many times. Braggioni scratches the guitar and meditates. "She is an instinctively virtuous woman, pure gold, no doubt of that. If she were not, I should lock her up, and she knows it."

His wife, who works so hard for the good of the factory girls, employs part of her leisure lying on the floor weeping because there are so many women in the world, and only one husband for her, and she never knows where nor when to look for him. He told her: "Unless you can learn to cry when I am not here, I must go away for good." That day he went away and took a room at the Hotel Madrid.

It is this month of separation for the sake of higher principles that has been spoiled not only for Mrs. Braggioni, whose sense of reality is beyond criticism, but for Laura, who feels herself bogged in a nightmare. Tonight Laura envies Mrs. Braggioni, who is alone, and free to weep as much as she pleases about a concrete wrong. Laura has just come from a visit to the prison, and she is waiting for tomorrow with a bitter anxiety as if tomorrow may not come, but time may be caught immovably in this hour, with herself transfixed, Braggioni singing on forever, and Eugenio's body not yet discovered by the guard.

Braggioni says: "Are you going to sleep?" Almost before she can shake her head, he begins telling her about the May-day disturbances coming on in Morelia, for the Catholics hold a festival in honor of the Blessed Virgin, and the Socialists celebrate their martyrs on that day. "There will be two independent processions, starting from either end of town, and they will march until they meet, and the rest depends . . ." He asks her to oil and load his pistols. Standing up, he unbuckles his ammunition belt, and spreads it laden across her knees. Laura sits with the shells slipping through the cleaning cloth dipped in oil, and he says again he cannot understand why she works so hard for the revolutionary idea unless she loves some man who is in it. "Are you not in love with someone?" "No," says Laura. "And no one is in love with you?" "No." "Then it is your own fault. No woman need go begging. Why, what is the matter with you? The legless beggar woman in the Alameda has a perfectly faithful lover. Did you know that?"

Laura peers down the pistol barrel and says nothing, but a long, slow faintness rises and subsides in her; Braggioni curves his swollen fingers around the throat of the guitar and softly smothers the music out of it, and when she hears him again he seems to have forgotten her, and is speaking in the hypnotic voice he uses when talking in small rooms to a listening, close-gathered crowd. Some day this world, now seemingly so composed and eternal, to the edges of every sea shall be merely a tangle of gaping trenches, of crashing walls and broken bodies. Everything must be torn from its accustomed place where it has rotted for centuries, hurled skyward and distributed, cast down again clean as rain, without separate identity. Nothing shall survive that the stiffened hands of poverty have created for the rich and no one shall be left alive except the elect spirits destined to procreate a new world cleansed of cruelty and injustice, ruled by benevolent anarchy: "Pistols are good, I love them, cannon are even better, but in the end I pin my faith to good dynamite," he concludes, and strokes the pistol lying in her hands. "Once I dreamed of destroying this city, in case it offered resistance to General Ortíz, but it fell into his hands like an overripe pear."

He is made restless by his own words, rises and stands waiting. Laura holds up the belt to him: "Put that on, and go kill somebody in Morelia, and you will be happier," she says softly. The presence of death in the room makes her bold. "Today, I found Eugenio going into a stupor. He refused to allow me to call the prison doctor. He had taken all the tablets I brought him yesterday. He said he took them because he was bored."

"He is a fool, and his death is his own business," says Braggioni, fastening his belt carefully.

"I told him if he had waited only a little while longer, you would have got him set free," says Laura. "He said he did not want to wait."

"He is a fool and we are well rid of him," says Braggioni, reaching for his hat.

He goes away. Laura knows his mood has changed, she will not see him any more for a while. He will send word when he needs her to go on errands into strange streets, to speak to the strange faces that will appear, like clay masks with the power of human speech, to mutter their thanks to Braggioni for his help. Now she is free, and she thinks, I must run while there is time. But she does not go.

Braggioni enters his own house where for a month his wife has spent many hours every night weeping and tangling her hair upon her pillow. She is weeping now, and she weeps more at the sight of him, the cause of all her sorrows. He looks about the room. Nothing is changed, the smells are good and familiar, he is well acquainted with the woman who comes toward him with no reproach except grief on her face. He says to her tenderly: "You are so good, please don't cry any more, you dear good creature." She says, "Are you tired, my angel? Sit here and I will wash your feet." She brings a bowl of water, and kneeling, unlaces his shoes, and when from her knees she raises her sad eyes under her blackened lids, he is sorry for everything, and bursts into tears. "Ah, yes, I am hungry, I am tired, let us eat something together," he says, between sobs. His wife leans her head on his arm and says, "Forgive me!" and this time he is refreshed by the solemn, endless rain of her tears.

Laura takes off her serge dress and puts on a white linen nightgown and goes to bed. She turns her head a little to one side, and lying still, reminds herself that it is time to sleep. Numbers tick in her brain like little clocks, soundless doors close of themselves around her. If you would sleep, you must not remember anything, the children will say tomorrow, good morning, my teacher, the poor prisoners who come every day bringing flowers to their jailor. 1-2-3-4-5 —it is monstrous to confuse love with revolution, night with day, life with death—ah, Eugenio!

The tolling of the midnight bell is a signal, but what

does it mean? Get up, Laura, and follow me: come out of your sleep, out of your bed, out of this strange house. What are you doing in this house? Without a word, without fear she rose and reached for Eugenio's hand, but he eluded her with a sharp, sly smile and drifted away. This is not all, you shall see—Murderer, he said, follow me, I will show you a new country, but it is far away and we must hurry. No, said Laura, not unless you take my hand, no; and she clung first to the stair rail, and then to the topmost branch of the Judas tree that bent down slowly and set her upon the earth, and then to the rocky ledge of a cliff, and then to the jagged wave of a sea that was not water but a desert of crumbling stone. Where are you taking me, she asked in wonder but without fear. To death, and it is a long way off, and we must hurry, said Eugenio. No, said Laura, not unless you take my hand. Then eat these flowers, poor prisoner, said Eugenio in a voice of pity, take and eat: and from the Judas tree he stripped the warm bleeding flowers, and held them to her lips. She saw that his hand was flesh-less, a cluster of small white petrified branches, and his eye sockets were without light, but she ate the flowers greedily for they satisfied both hunger and thirst. Murderer! said Eugenio, and Cannibal! This is my body and my blood. Laura cried No! and at the sound of her own voice, she awoke trembling, and was afraid to sleep again.

James Joyce

[1882 — 1941]

WHEN JAMES JOYCE in early manhood became an apostate Catholic and an expatriate Irishman, his was an act of bitter criticism, not of repudiation. Although most of his mature life was spent on the Continent, his writing never deserted the Dublin of his youth. He wrote constantly to his friends for the exact location and description of trees or buildings at home, and the mannerisms of old acquaintances: while his art tried to elevate these to the level of myth or of Everyman's epic.

Because his allegiances were too large to sympathize with the terrorism of Irish nationalists, Joyce filtered the wit and human subtleties, only, out of endless political discussions which filled his father's parlor conversations. Despite his Jesuit education, he blamed the Irish clergy, too, and their counsel of acceptance for contributing to the betrayal of genuine local aspirations. Consequently, even the pity he felt for his mother's hard life (she died at 44, a year after Joyce's self-exile) could not restore him to the sacraments—because, paradoxically, the "unwilling unbeliever" would have considered this a sacrilege. The conscience-stricken remorse, that "agenbite of inwit" which Stephen Dedalus suffered for similar scruples, is recorded in *Ulysses*; and the satire in Joyce's short stories tempers savage disdain with earnest compassion.

Gradually Joyce became convinced that only in art could he recover those Aquinian attributes of beauty—integrity, sym-

metry, and radiance—which Ireland, "the sow that eats her
farrow," denied him. He sailed first for Paris and then for
Trieste where he taught at a Berlitz Language School. Meanwhile he obsessively collected details about Dublin and innumerable "epiphanies"—those unprepared revelations of inner man
—with which he planned finally to "forge the uncreated conscience of my race." The group of stories which resulted was
contracted to a Dublin publisher who, however, after years of
delaying finally broke up the type and burned the few copies
which had already been printed. Undaunted, in 1914 Joyce published *Dubliners* in alien London. Joyce's favorite in that collection was "Ivy Day in the Committee Room," according to
his brother who had accumulated many of its ironic details
while accompanying their father as an election canvasser. So
close to Joyce were even the secondhand experiences com-
memorated in *Dubliners* that its people are respected at the
same time that he rejects the utter sterility of their beliefs and
customs.

The monastically austere style and underdeveloped drama
so appropriate to these stories about Ireland's lonely ones, who
are lost in human vanity and parochial self-righteousness, were
helpful to Joyce during revision of his unfinished novel, *Stephen
Hero*, which he had begun about 1904. By the time of its publication as *Portrait of the Artist as a Young Man*, in 1916, it
had shrunk by two-thirds and, although still autobiographical,
had become far less personal. It had moved closer to that static
condition which Joyce considered proper to literature and which
he had illustrated in the truncated form of his stories. T. S.
Eliot considered *Dubliners'* epiphanies as revealing as the supposedly more intimate stream-of-consciousness developed in
Ulysses.

As if reduced to conversations with himself by the failure
of his society to understand him, young Stephen Dedalus ends
Portrait with asides to himself in his diary. *Ulysses* (1922) too
depends on introspection and soliloquy, while tracing the gradual convergence of two lives, Stephen's and Leopold Bloom's,
on a single day in Dublin. Outcast artist and fallen-away Jew,
both are misfits. In part they represent those ancient cultures,
the Hebraic and the Hellenic, brought to a dead end in an insensitive modern world. In their brief last-minute encounter at

Bloom's house, the two men might have found consolation in their common loneliness, had the search of these fellow wanderers for recognition and completion been less concealed even from themselves. Their psychological kinship is made implicit through a montage of symbols and parallel scenes. Yet the constant frustration of their meeting produces an episodic structure more complex but no less static than the collection of snapshots that constitutes Dubliners.

After World War I, Joyce returned from Zurich to Trieste and to his immense work-in-progress, Finnegans Wake. It became if not "the uncreated conscience" which Stephen Dedalus intended to forge for his people, then their created unconscious. The virtuoso style of Ulysses is here elaborated until it suggests vast cross-indexes of the secret mind. A sort of internationalized language is welded together out of compound (portmanteau) words; and even the characters, at first defined only as one another's opposite, ultimately are seen as conflicting traits in a single personality, a kind of generic man or Over-self. The action is organized into a four-part cycle, to suggest that the history of human culture has its seasons too and that patterns of change, never accidental, are as predictable as the stages in some grand insect's prolonged metamorphosis. Indicative of just such recurrence, the novel's final run-on sentence is completed in the opening fragment of Finnegans Wake. However, precisely because the movement of these human cycles is repetitive and because the action within each cycle is infinitely subdivided into images from the collective unconscious, once again the total effect is static. If Finnegans Wake is interpreted as the nighttime counterpart of Ulysses' epic day, then each of Joyce's works can be described as one sweeping arc in an imposing, closed circle.

Joyce had once told his brother, "Isolation is the first principle of artistic economy"; and his brother subsequently had spoken of him, not without affection, as a Faust-figure to whom only art mattered. From the first, too, Joyce had admired Ibsen for that playwright's aloofness from critics. Nevertheless, his outsiders—the boy in "Araby"; Dedalus; Bloom; HCE (Here Comes Everybody)—long to be identified and restored, though only to a society reformed and transfigured. Finnegans Wake (1939) is an attempt to dramatize this agony of exile even while it prophesies the return of the artist-"egoarch" to his destined place in some future cyclic stage.

In spite of this qualified truce, Joyce was once more a refugee from violence and human hypocrisies when he died in 1941, having fled to neutral Switzerland from the Nazi invasion of France.

Araby

NORTH RICHMOND STREET, being blind, was a quiet street except at the hour when the Christian Brothers' School set the boys free. An uninhabited house of two stories stood at the blind end, detached from its neighbours in a square ground. The other houses of the street, conscious of decent lives within them, gazed at one another with brown imperturbable faces.

The former tenant of our house, a priest, had died in the back drawing-room. Air, musty from having been long enclosed, hung in all the rooms, and the waste room behind the kitchen was littered with old useless papers. Among these I found a few paper-covered books, the pages of which were curled and damp: *The Abbot*, by Walter Scott, *The Devout Communicant* and *The Memoirs of Vidocq*. I liked the last best because its leaves were yellow. The wild garden behind the house contained a central apple-tree and a few straggling bushes under one of which I found the late tenant's rusty bicycle-pump. He had been a very charitable priest; in his will he had left all his money to institutions and the furniture of his house to his sister.

From *Dubliners* by James Joyce, Viking Compass edition, 1958. Reprinted by permission of The Viking Press, Inc.

When the short days of winter came, dusk fell before we had well eaten our dinner. When we met in the streets the houses had grown somber. The space of sky above us was the color of ever-changing violet and towards it the lamps of the street lifted their feeble lanterns. The cold air stung us and we played till our bodies glowed. Our shouts echoed in the silent street. The career of our play brought us through the dark muddy lanes behind the houses where we ran the gauntlet of the rough tribes from the cottages, to the back doors of the dark dripping gardens where odours arose from the ashpits, to the dark odourous stables where a coachman smoothed and combed the horse or shook music from the buckled harness. When we returned to the street, light from the kitchen windows had filled the areas. If my uncle was seen turning the corner we hid in the shadow until we had seen him safely housed. Or if Mangan's sister came out on the doorstep to call her brother in to his tea we watched her from our shadow peer up and down the street. We waited to see whether she would remain or go in and, if she remained, we left our shadow and walked up to Mangan's steps resignedly. She was waiting for us, her figure defined by the light from the half-opened door. Her brother always teased her before he obeyed and I stood by the railings looking up at her. Her dress swung as she moved her body and the soft rope of her hair tossed from side to side.

Every morning I lay on the floor in the front parlour watching her door. The blind was pulled down to within an inch of the sash so that I could not be seen. When she came out on the doorstep my heart leaped. I ran to the hall, seized my books and followed her. I kept her brown figure always in my eye and, when we came near the point at which our ways diverged, I quickened my pace and passed her. This happened morning after morning. I had never spoken to her, except for a few casual words, and yet her name was like a summons to all my foolish blood.

Her image accompanied me even in places the most hostile to romance. On Saturday evenings when my aunt went marketing I had to go to carry some of the parcels. We walked through the flaring streets, jostled by drunken men and bargaining women, amid the curses of labourers, the shrill litanies of shop-boys who stood on guard by the barrels of pigs' cheeks, the nasal chanting of street-singers, who sang a *come-all-you* about O'Donovan Rossa, or a ballad about the troubles in our native land. These noises converged in a single sensation of life for me: I imagined that I bore my chalice safely through a throng of foes. Her name sprang to my lips at moments in strange prayers and praises which I myself did not understand. My eyes were often full of tears (I could not tell why) and at times a flood from my heart seemed to pour itself out into my bosom. I thought little of the future. I did not know whether I would ever speak to her or not or, if I spoke to her, how I could tell her of my confused adoration. But my body was like a harp and her words and gestures were like fingers running upon the wires.

One evening I went into the back drawing-room in which the priest had died. It was a dark rainy evening and there was no sound in the house. Through one of the broken panes I heard the rain impinge upon the earth, the fine incessant needles of water playing in the sodden beds. Some distant lamp or lighted window gleamed below me. I was thankful that I could see so little. All my senses seemed to desire to veil themselves and, feeling that I was about to slip from them, I pressed the palms of my hands together until they trembled, murmuring: "O love! O love!" many times.

At last she spoke to me. When she addressed the first words to me I was so confused that I did not know what to answer. She asked me was I going to *Araby*. I forgot whether I answered yes or no. It would be a splendid bazaar, she said; she would love to go.

"And why can't you?" I asked.

While she spoke she turned a silver bracelet round and

round her wrist. She could not go, she said, because there would be a retreat that week in her convent. Her brother and two other boys were fighting for their caps and I was alone at the railings. She held one of the spikes, bowing her head towards me. The light from the lamp opposite our door caught the white curve of her neck, lit up her hair that rested there and, falling, lit up the hand upon the railing. It fell over one side of her dress and caught the white border of a petticoat, just visible as she stood at ease.

"It's well for you," she said.

"If I go," I said, "I will bring you something."

What innumerable follies laid waste my waking and sleeping thoughts after that evening! I wished to annihilate the tedious intervening days. I chafed against the work of school. At night in my bedroom and by day in the class-room her image came between me and the page I strove to read. The syllables of the word *Araby* were called to me through the silence in which my soul luxuriated and cast an Eastern enchantment over me. I asked for leave to go to the bazaar on Saturday night. My aunt was surprised and hoped it was not some Freemason affair. I answered few questions in class. I watched my master's face pass from amiability to sternness; he hoped I was not beginning to idle. I could not call my wandering thoughts together. I had hardly any patience with the serious work of life which, now that it stood between me and my desire, seemed to me child's play, ugly monotonous child's play.

On Saturday morning I reminded my uncle that I wished to go to the bazaar in the evening. He was fussing at the hallstand, looking for the hat-brush, and answered me curtly:

"Yes, boy, I know."

As he was in the hall I could not go into the front par-lour and lie at the window. I left the house in bad humor and walked slowly towards the school. The air was pitilessly raw and already my heart misgave me.

When I came home to dinner my uncle had not yet been

home. Still it was early. I sat staring at the clock for some
time and, when its ticking began to irritate me, I left the
room. I mounted the staircase and gained the upper part
of the house. The high cold empty gloomy rooms liberated
me and I went from room to room singing. From the front
window I saw my companions playing below in the street.
Their cries reached me weakened and indistinct and, leaning my forehead against the cool glass, I looked over at the
dark house where she lived. I may have stood there for an
hour, seeing nothing but the brown-clad figure cast by my
imagination, touched discreetly by the lamplight at the
curved neck, at the hand upon the railings and at the border
below the dress.

When I came downstairs again I found Mrs. Mercer sitting at the fire. She was an old garrulous woman, a pawn-
broker's widow, who collected used stamps for some pious
purpose. I had to endure the gossip of the tea-table. The
meal was prolonged beyond an hour and still my uncle did
not come. Mrs. Mercer stood up to go: she was sorry she
couldn't wait any longer, but it was after eight o'clock and
she did not like to be out late, as the night air was bad for
her. When she had gone I began to walk up and down the
room, clenching my fists. My aunt said:

"I'm afraid you may put off your bazaar for this night of
Our Lord."

At nine o'clock I heard my uncle's latchkey in the hall
door. I heard him talking to himself and heard the hallstand
rocking when it had received the weight of his overcoat. I
could interpret these signs. When he was midway through
his dinner I asked him to give me the money to go to the
bazaar. He had forgotten.

"The people are in bed and after their first sleep now,"
he said.

I did not smile. My aunt said to him energetically:

"Can't you give him the money and let him go? You've
kept him late enough as it is."

My uncle said he was very sorry he had forgotten. He

said he believed in the old saying, "All work and no play makes Jack a dull boy." He asked me where I was going and, when I had told him a second time, he asked me did I know *The Arab's Farewell to his Steed*. When I left the kitchen he was about to recite the opening lines of the piece to my aunt.

I held a florin tightly in my hand as I strode down Buckingham Street towards the station. The sight of the streets thronged with buyers and glaring with gas recalled to me the purpose of my journey. I took my seat in a third-class carriage of a deserted train. After an intolerable delay the train moved out of the station slowly. It crept onward among ruinous houses and over the twinkling river. At Westland Row Station a crowd of people pressed to the carriage doors; but the porters moved them back, saying that it was a special train for the bazaar. I remained alone in the bare carriage. In a few minutes the train drew up beside an improvised wooden platform. I passed out on to the road and saw by the lighted dial of a clock that it was ten minutes to ten. In front of me was a large building which displayed the magical name.

I could not find any sixpenny entrance and, fearing that the bazaar would be closed, I passed in quickly through a turnstile, handing a shilling to a weary-looking man. I found myself in a big hall girdled at half its height by a gallery. Nearly all the stalls were closed and the greater part of the hall was in darkness. I recognized a silence like that which pervades a church after a service. I walked into the center of the bazaar timidly. A few people were gathered about the stalls which were still open. Before a curtain, over which the words *Café Chantant* were written in coloured lamps, two men were counting money on a salver. I listened to the fall of the coins.

Remembering with difficulty why I had come I went over to one of the stalls and examined porcelain vases and flowered tea-sets. At the door of the stall a young lady was talking and laughing with two young gentlemen. I remarked their English accents and listened vaguely to their conversation.

"O, I never said such a thing!"

"O, but you did!"

"O, but I didn't!"

"Didn't she say that?"

"Yes. I heard her."

"O, there's a . . . fib!"

Observing me the young lady came over and asked me did I wish to buy anything. The tone of her voice was not encouraging; she seemed to have spoken to me out of a sense of duty. I looked humbly at the great jars that stood like eastern guards at either side of the dark entrance to the stall and murmured:

"No, thank you."

The young lady changed the position of one of the vases and went back to the two young men. They began to talk of the same subject. Once or twice the young lady glanced at me over her shoulder.

I lingered before her stall, though I knew my stay was useless, to make my interest in her wares seem the more real. Then I turned away slowly and walked down the middle of the bazaar. I allowed the two pennies to fall against the sixpence in my pocket. I heard a voice call from one end of the gallery that the light was out. The upper part of the hall was now completely dark.

Gazing up into the darkness I saw myself as a creature driven and derided by vanity; and my eyes burned with anguish and anger.

Clay

THE MATRON HAD given her leave to go out as soon as the women's tea was over and Maria looked forward to her evening out. The kitchen was spick and span: the cook said you could see yourself in the big copper boilers. The fire was nice and bright and on one of the sidetables were four very big barmbracks. These barmbracks seemed uncut; but if you went closer you would see that they had been cut into long thick even slices and were ready to be handed round at tea. Maria had cut them herself.

Maria was a very, very small person indeed but she had a very long nose and a very long chin. She talked a little through her nose, always soothingly: "Yes, my dear," and "No, my dear." She was always sent for when the women quarrelled over their tubs and always succeeded in making peace. One day the matron had said to her:

"Maria, you are a veritable peace-maker!"

And the sub-matron and two of the Board ladies had heard the compliment. And Ginger Mooney was always saying what she wouldn't do to the dummy who had charge of the irons if it wasn't for Maria. Everyone was so fond of Maria.

From *Dubliners* by James Joyce, Viking Compass edition, 1958. Reprinted by permission of The Viking Press, Inc.

The women would have their tea at six o'clock and she would be able to get away before seven. From Ballsbridge to the Pillar, twenty minutes; from the Pillar to Drumcondra, twenty minutes; and twenty minutes to buy the things. She would be there before eight. She took out her purse with the silver clasps and read again the words *A Present from Belfast*. She was very fond of that purse because Joe had brought it to her five years before when he and Alphy had gone to Belfast on a Whit-Monday trip. In the purse were two half-crowns and some coppers. She would have five shillings clear after paying tram fare. What a nice evening they would have, all the children singing! Only she hoped that Joe wouldn't come in drunk. He was so different when he took any drink.

Often he had wanted her to go and live with them; but she would have felt herself in the way (though Joe's wife was ever so nice with her) and she had become accustomed to the life of the laundry. Joe was a good fellow. She had nursed him and Alphy too; and Joe used often say:

"Mamma is mamma but Maria is my proper mother."

After the break-up at home the boys had got her that position in the *Dublin by Lamplight* laundry, and she liked it. She used to have such a bad opinion of Protestants but now she thought they were very nice people, a little quiet and serious, but still very nice people to live with. Then she had her plants in the conservatory and she liked looking after them. She had lovely ferns and wax-plants and, whenever anyone came to visit her, she always gave the visitor one or two slips from her conservatory. There was one thing she didn't like and that was the tracts on the walls; but the matron was such a nice person to deal with, so genteel.

When the cook told her everything was ready she went into the women's room and began to pull the big bell. In a few minutes the women began to come in by twos and threes, wiping their steaming hands in their petticoats and pulling down the sleeves of their blouses over their red steaming arms. They settled down before their huge mugs which the cook and the dummy filled up with hot tea, already mixed with milk and sugar in huge tin cans. Maria superintended the distribution of the barmbrack and saw that every woman got her four slices. There was a great deal of laughing and joking during the meal. Lizzie Fleming said Maria was sure to get the ring and, though Fleming had said that for so many Hallow Eves, Maria had to laugh and say she didn't want any ring or man either; and when she laughed her grey-green eyes sparkled with disappointed shyness and the tip of her nose nearly met the tip of her chin. Then Ginger Mooney lifted up her mug of tea and proposed Maria's health while all the other women clattered with their mugs on the table, and said she was sorry she hadn't a sup of porter to drink it in. And Maria laughed again till the tip of her nose nearly met the tip of her chin and till her minute body nearly shook itself asunder because she knew that Mooney meant well though, of course, she had the notions of a common woman.

But wasn't Maria glad when the women had finished their tea and the cook and the dummy had begun to clear away the tea-things! She went into her little bedroom and, remembering that the next morning was a mass morning, changed the hand of the alarm from seven to six. Then she took off her working skirt and her house-boots and laid her best skirt out on the bed and her tiny dress-boots beside the foot of the bed. She changed her blouse too and, as she stood before the mirror, she thought of how she used to dress for mass on Sunday morning when she was a young girl; and she looked with quaint affection at the diminutive body which she had so often adorned. In spite of its years she found it a nice tidy little body.

When she got outside the streets were shining with rain and she was glad of her old brown waterproof. The tram was full and she had to sit on the little stool at the end of the car, facing all the people, with her toes barely touching the floor. She arranged in her mind all she was going to do and thought how much better it was to be independent and to have your own money in your pocket. She hoped they would have a nice evening. She was sure they would but she could not help thinking what a pity it was Alphy and Joe were not speaking. They were always falling out now but when they were boys together they used to be the best of friends: but such was life.

She got out of her tram at the Pillar and ferreted her way quickly among the crowds. She went into Downes's cake-shop but the shop was so full of people that it was a long time before she could get herself attended to. She bought a dozen of mixed penny cakes, and at last came out of the shop laden with a big bag. Then she thought what else would she buy: she wanted to buy something really nice. They would be sure to have plenty of apples and nuts. It was hard to know what to buy and all she could think of was cake. She decided to buy some plumcake but Downes's plumcake had not enough almond icing on top of it so she went over to a shop in Henry Street. Here she was a long time in suiting herself and the stylish young lady behind the counter, who was evidently a little annoyed by her, asked her was it wedding-cake she wanted to buy. That made Maria blush and smile at the young lady; but the young lady took it all very seriously and finally cut a thick slice of plumcake, parcelled it up and said:

"Two-and-four, please."

She thought she would have to stand in the Drumcondra tram because none of the young men seemed to notice her but an elderly gentleman made room for her. He was a stout gentleman and he wore a brown hard hat; he had a square red face and a greyish moustache. Maria thought he was a colonel-looking gentleman and she reflected how much more polite he was than the young men who simply stared straight before them. The gentleman began to chat with her about Hallow Eve and the rainy weather. He supposed the bag was full of good things for the little ones and said it was only right that the youngsters should enjoy

themselves while they were young. Maria agreed with him
and favoured him with demure nods and hems. He was
very nice with her, and when she was getting out at the
Canal Bridge she thanked him and bowed, and he bowed
to her and raised his hat and smiled agreeably; and while
she was going up along the terrace, bending her tiny head
under the rain, she thought how easy it was to know a
gentleman even when he has a drop taken.

Everybody said: "O, here's Maria!" when she came to
Joe's house. Joe was there, having come home from business, and all the children had their Sunday dresses on.
There were two big girls in from next door and games were
going on. Maria gave the bag of cakes to the eldest boy,
Alphy, to divide and Mrs. Donnelly said it was too good
of her to bring such a big bag of cakes and made all the
children say:

"Thanks, Maria."

But Maria said she had brought something special for
papa and mamma, something they would be sure to like,
and she began to look for her plumcake. She tried in
Downes's bag and then in the pockets of her waterproof
and then on the hallstand but nowhere could she find it.
Then she asked all the children had any of them eaten it
—by mistake, of course—but the children all said no and
looked as if they did not like to eat cakes if they were
to be accused of stealing. Everybody had a solution for
the mystery and Mrs. Donnelly said it was plain that Maria
had left it behind her in the tram. Maria, remembering
how confused the gentleman with the greyish moustache
had made her, coloured with shame and vexation and disappointment. At the thought of the failure of her little
surprise and of the two and four-pence she had thrown
away for nothing she nearly cried outright.

But Joe said it didn't matter and made her sit down
by the fire. He was very nice with her. He told her all
that went on in his office, repeating for her a smart answer
which he had made to the manager. Maria did not under-

stand why Joe laughed so much over the answer he had made but she said that the manager must have been a very overbearing person to deal with. Joe said he wasn't so bad when you knew how to take him, that he was a decent sort so long as you didn't rub him the wrong way. Mrs. Donnelly played the piano for the children and they danced and sang. Then the two next-door girls handed round the nuts. Nobody could find the nutcrackers and Joe was nearly getting cross over it and asked how did they expect Maria to crack nuts without a nutcracker. But Maria said she didn't like nuts and that they weren't to bother about her. Then Joe asked would she take a bottle of stout and Mrs. Donnelly said there was port wine too in the house if she would prefer that. Maria said she would rather they didn't ask her to take anything: but Joe insisted.

So Maria let him have his way and they sat by the fire talking over old times and Maria thought she would put in a good word for Alphy. But Joe cried that God might strike him stone dead if ever he spoke a word to his brother again and Maria said she was sorry she had mentioned the matter. Mrs. Donnelly told her husband it was a great shame for him to speak that way of his own flesh and blood but Joe said that Alphy was no brother of his and there was nearly being a row on the head of it. But Joe said he would not lose his temper on account of the night it was and asked his wife to open some more stout. The two next-door girls had arranged some Hallow Eve games and soon everything was merry again. Maria was delighted to see the children so merry and Joe and his wife in such good spirits. The next-door girls put some saucers on the table and then led the children up to the table, blindfold. One got the prayer-book and the other three got the water; and when one of the next-door girls got the ring Mrs. Donnelly shook her finger at the blushing girl as much as to say: *O, I know all about it!* They insisted then on blindfolding Maria and leading her up to the table to see what she would get; and, while they were putting on the bandage, Maria laughed and laughed again till the tip of her nose nearly met the tip of her chin.

They led her up to the table amid laughing and joking and she put her hand out in the air as she was told to do. She moved her hand about here and there in the air and descended on one of the saucers. She felt a soft wet substance with her fingers and was surprised that nobody spoke or took off her bandage. There was a pause for a few seconds; and then a great deal of scuffling and whispering. Somebody said something about the garden, and at last Mrs. Donnelly said something very cross to one of the next-door girls and told her to throw it out at once: that was no play. Maria understood that it was wrong that time and so she had to do it over again: and this time she got the prayer-book.

After that Mrs. Donnelly played Miss McCloud's Reel for the children and Joe made Maria take a glass of wine. Soon they were all quite merry again and Mrs. Donnelly said Maria would enter a convent before the year was out because she had got the prayer-book. Maria had never seen Joe so nice to her as he was that night, so full of pleasant talk and reminiscences. She said they were all very good to her.

At last the children grew tired and sleepy and Joe asked Maria would she not sing some little song before she went, one of the old songs. Mrs. Donnelly said "Do, please, Maria!" and so Maria had to get up and stand beside the piano. Mrs. Donnelly bade the children be quiet and listen to Maria's song. Then she played the prelude and said "Now, Maria!" and Maria, blushing very much, began to sing in a tiny quavering voice. She sang I Dreamt that I Dwelt, and when she came to the second verse she sang again:

> "I dreamt that I dwelt in marble halls
> With vassals and serfs at my side
> And of all who assembled within those walls
> That I was the hope and the pride.

> I had riches too great to count, could boast
> Of a high ancestral name,
> But I also dreamt, which pleased me most,
> That you loved me still the same."

But no one tried to show her her mistake; and when she had ended her song Joe was very much moved. He said that there was no time like the long ago and no music for him like poor old Balfe, whatever other people might say; and his eyes filled up so much with tears that he could not find what he was looking for and in the end he had to ask his wife to tell him where the corkscrew was.

Ivy Day in the Committee Room

OLD JACK RAKED the cinders together with a piece of cardboard and spread them judiciously over the whitening dome of coals. When the dome was thinly covered his face lapsed into darkness but, as he set himself to fan the fire again, his crouching shadow ascended the opposite wall and his face slowly re-emerged into light. It was an old man's face, very bony and hairy. The moist blue eyes blinked at the fire and the moist mouth fell open at times, munching once or twice mechanically when it closed. When the cinders had caught he laid the piece of cardboard against the wall, sighed and said:

"That's better now, Mr. O'Connor."

Mr. O'Connor, a grey-haired young man, whose face was disfigured by many blotches and pimples, had just brought the tobacco for a cigarette into a shapely cylinder but when spoken to he undid his handiwork meditatively. Then he began to roll the tobacco again meditatively and after a moment's thought decided to lick the paper.

From *Dubliners* by James Joyce, Viking Compass edition, 1958. Reprinted by permission of The Viking Press, Inc.

"Did Mr. Tierney say when he'd be back?" he asked in a husky falsetto.

"He didn't say."

Mr. O'Connor put his cigarette into his mouth and began to search his pockets. He took out a pack of thin pasteboard cards.

"I'll get you a match," said the old man.

"Never mind, this'll do," said Mr. O'Connor.

He selected one of the cards and read what was printed on it:

MUNICIPAL ELECTIONS

Royal Exchange Ward

Mr. Richard J. Tierney, P.L.G., respectfully solicits the favour of your vote and influence at the coming election in the Royal Exchange Ward.

Mr. O'Connor had been engaged by Tierney's agent to canvass one part of the ward but, as the weather was inclement and his boots let in the wet, he spent a great part of the day sitting by the fire in the Committee Room in Wicklow Street with Jack, the old caretaker. They had been sitting thus since the short day had grown dark. It was the sixth of October, dismal and cold out of doors.

Mr. O'Connor tore a strip off the card and, lighting it, lit his cigarette. As he did so the flame lit up a leaf of dark glossy ivy in the lapel of his coat. The old man watched him attentively and then, taking up the piece of cardboard again, began to fan the fire slowly while his companion smoked.

"Ah, yes," he said, continuing, "it's hard to know what way to bring up children. Now who'd think he'd turn out like that! I sent him to the Christian Brothers and I done what I could for him, and there he goes boosing about. I tried to make him someway decent."

He replaced the cardboard wearily.

"Only I'm an old man now I'd change his tune for him. I'd take the stick to his back and beat him while I could stand over him—as I done many a time before. The mother, you know, she cocks him up with this and that. . . ."

"That's what ruins children," said Mr. O'Connor.

"To be sure it is," said the old man. "And little thanks you get for it, only impudence. He takes th'upper hand of me whenever he sees I've a sup taken. What's the world coming to when sons speaks that way to their fathers?"

"What age is he?" said Mr. O'Connor.

"Nineteen," said the old man.

"Why don't you put him to something?"

"Sure, amn't I never done at the drunken bowsy ever since he left school? 'I won't keep you,' I says. 'You must get a job for yourself.' But, sure, it's worse whenever he gets a job; he drinks it all."

Mr. O'Connor shook his head in sympathy, and the old man fell silent, gazing into the fire. Someone opened the door of the room and called out:

"Hello! Is this a Freemason's meeting?"

"Who's that?" said the old man.

"What are you doing in the dark?" asked a voice.

"Is that you, Hynes?" asked Mr. O'Connor.

"Yes. What are you doing in the dark?" said Mr. Hynes, advancing into the light of the fire.

He was a tall, slender young man with a light brown moustache. Imminent little drops of rain hung at the brim of his hat and the collar of his jacket-coat was turned up.

"Well, Mat," he said to Mr. O'Connor, "how goes it?"

Mr. O'Connor shook his head. The old man left the hearth, and after stumbling about the room returned with two candlesticks which he thrust one after the other into the fire and carried to the table. A denuded room came into view and the fire lost all its cheerful colour. The walls of the room were bare except for a copy of an election address. In the middle of the room was a small table on which papers were heaped.

Mr. Hynes leaned against the mantelpiece and asked: "Has he paid you yet?"

"Not yet," said Mr. O'Connor. "I hope to God he'll not leave us in the lurch to-night."

Mr. Hynes laughed.

"O, he'll pay you. Never fear," he said.

"I hope he'll look smart about it if he means business," said Mr. O'Connor.

"What do you think, Jack?" said Mr. Hynes satirically to the old man.

The old man returned to his seat by the fire, saying:

"It isn't but he has it, anyway. Not like the other tinker."

"What other tinker?" said Mr. Hynes.

"Colgan," said the old man scornfully.

"It is because Colgan's a working-man you say that? What's the difference between a good honest bricklayer and a publican—eh? Hasn't the working-man as good a right to be in the Corporation as anyone else—ay, and a better right than those shoneens that are always hat in hand before any fellow with a handle to his name? Isn't that so, Mat?" said Mr. Hynes, addressing Mr. O'Connor.

"I think you're right," said Mr. O'Connor.

"One man is a plain honest man with no hunker-sliding about him. He goes in to represent the labour classes. This fellow you're working for only wants to get some job or other."

"Of course, the working-classes should be represented," said the old man.

"The working-man," said Mr. Hynes, "gets all kicks and no halfpence. But it's labour produces everything. The working-man is not looking for fat jobs for his sons and nephews and cousins. The working-man is not going to drag the honour of Dublin in the mud to please a German monarch."

"How's that?" said the old man.

"Don't you know they want to present an address of welcome to Edward Rex if he comes here next year? What do we want kowtowing to a foreign king?"

"Our man won't vote for the address," said Mr. O'Connor. "He goes in on the Nationalist ticket."

"Won't he?" said Mr. Hynes. "Wait till you see whether he will or not. I know him. Is it Tricky Dicky Tierney?"

"By God! perhaps you're right, Joe," said Mr. O'Connor. "Anyway, I wish he'd turn up with the spondulics."

The three men fell silent. The old man began to rake more cinders together. Mr. Hynes took off his hat, shook it and then turned down the collar of his coat, displaying, as he did so, an ivy leaf in the lapel.

"If this man was alive," he said, pointing to the leaf, "we'd have no talk of an address of welcome."

"That's true," said Mr. O'Connor.

"Musha, God be with them times!" said the old man. "There was some life in it then."

The room was silent again. Then a bustling little man with a snuffling nose and very cold ears pushed in the door. He walked over quickly to the fire, rubbing his hands as if he intended to produce a spark from them.

"No money, boys," he said.

"Sit down here, Mr. Henchy," said the old man, offering him his chair.

"O, don't stir, Jack, don't stir," said Mr. Henchy.

He nodded curtly to Mr. Hynes and sat down on the chair which the old man vacated.

"Did you serve Aungier Street?" he asked Mr. O'Connor.

"Yes," said Mr. O'Connor, beginning to search his pockets for memoranda.

"Did you call on Grimes?"

"I did."

"Well? How does he stand?"

"He wouldn't promise. He said: 'I won't tell anyone what way I'm going to vote.' But I think he'll be all right."

"Why so?"

"He asked me who the nominators were; and I told him.

I mentioned Father Burke's name. I think it'll be all right."

Mr. Henchy began to snuffle and to rub his hands over the fire at a terrific speed. Then he said:

"For the love of God, Jack, bring us a bit of coal. There must be some left."

The old man went out of the room.

"It's no go," said Mr. Henchy, shaking his head. "I asked the little shoeboy, but he said: 'O, now, Mr. Henchy, when I see the work going on properly I won't forget you, you may be sure.' Mean little tinker! 'Usha, how could he be anything else?"

"What did I tell you, Mat?" said Mr. Hynes. "Tricky Dicky Tierney."

"O, he's as tricky as they make 'em," said Mr. Henchy. "He hasn't got those little pigs' eyes for nothing. Blast his soul! Couldn't he pay up like a man instead of: 'O, now, Mr. Henchy, I must speak to Mr. Fanning. . . . I've spent a lot of money'? Mean little schoolboy of hell! I suppose he forgets the time his little old father kept the hand-me-down shop in Mary's Lane."

"But is that a fact?" asked Mr. O'Connor.

"God, yes," said Mr. Henchy. "Did you never hear that? And the men used to go in on Sunday morning before the houses were open to buy a waistcoat or a trousers—moya! But Tricky Dicky's little old father always had a tricky little black bottle up in a corner. Do you mind now? That's that. That's where he first saw the light."

The old man returned with a few lumps of coal which he placed here and there on the fire.

"That's a nice how-do-you-do," said Mr. O'Connor. "How does he expect us to work for him if he won't stump up?"

"I can't help it," said Mr. Henchy. "I expect to find the bailiffs in the hall when I go home."

Mr. Hynes laughed and, shoving himself away from the mantelpiece with the aid of his shoulders, made ready to leave.

"It'll be all right when King Eddie comes," he said. "Well, boys, I'm off for the present. See you later. 'Bye, 'bye."

He went out of the room slowly. Neither Mr. Henchy nor the old man said anything, but, just as the door was closing, Mr. O'Connor, who had been staring moodily into the fire, called out suddenly:

" 'Bye, Joe."

Mr. Henchy waited a few moments and then nodded in the direction of the door.

"Tell me," he said across the fire, "what brings our friend in here? What does he want?"

" 'Usha, poor Joe!" said Mr. O'Connor, throwing the end of his cigarette into the fire, "he's hard up, like the rest of us."

Mr. Henchy snuffled vigorously and spat so copiously that he nearly put out the fire, which uttered a hissing protest.

"To tell you my private and candid opinion," he said, "I think he's a man from the other camp. He's a spy of Colgan's, if you ask me. Just go round and try and find out how they're getting on. They won't suspect you. Do you twig?"

"Ah, poor Joe is a decent skin," said Mr. O'Connor.

"His father was a decent, respectable man," Mr. Henchy admitted. "Poor old Larry Hynes! Many a good turn he did in his day! But I'm greatly afraid our friend is not nineteen carat. Damn it, I can understand a fellow being hard up, but what I can't understand is a fellow sponging. Couldn't he have some spark of manhood about him?"

"He doesn't get a warm welcome from me when he comes," said the old man. "Let him work for his own side and not come spying around here."

"I don't know," said Mr. O'Connor dubiously, as he took out cigarette-papers and tobacco. "I think Joe Hynes is a straight man. He's a clever chap, too, with the pen. Do you remember that thing he wrote . . . ?"

"Some of these hillsiders and fenians are a bit too clever if you ask me," said Mr. Henchy. "Do you know what my private and candid opinion is about some of those little jokers? I believe half of them are in the pay of the Castle."

"There's no knowing," said the old man.

"O, but I know it for a fact," said Mr. Henchy. "They're Castle hacks. . . . I don't say Hynes. . . . No, damn it, I think he's a stroke above that. . . . But there's a certain little nobleman with a cock-eye—you know the patriot I'm alluding to?"

Mr. O'Connor nodded.

"There's a lineal descendant of Major Sirr for you if you like! O, the heart's blood of a patriot! That's a fellow now that'd sell his country for fourpence—ay—and go down on his bended knees and thank the Almighty Christ he had a country to sell."

There was a knock at the door.

"Come in!" said Mr. Henchy.

A person resembling a poor clergyman or a poor actor appeared in the doorway. His black clothes were tightly buttoned on his short body and it was impossible to say whether he wore a clergyman's collar or a layman's, because the collar of his shabby frock-coat, the uncovered buttons of which reflected the candlelight, was turned up about his neck. He wore a round hat of hard black felt. His face, shining with raindrops, had the appearance of damp yellow cheese save where two rosy spots indicated the cheekbones. He opened his very long mouth suddenly to express disappointment and at the same time opened wide his very bright blue eyes to express pleasure and surprise.

"O Father Keon!" said Mr. Henchy, jumping up from his chair. "Is that you? Come in!"

"O, no, no, no!" said Father Keon quickly, pursing his lips as if he were addressing a child.

"Won't you come in and sit down?"

"No, no, no!" said Father Keon, speaking in a discreet, indulgent, velvety voice. "Don't let me disturb you now! I'm just looking for Mr. Fanning. . . ."

"He's round at the *Black Eagle*," said Mr. Henchy. "But won't you come in and sit down a minute?"

"No, no, thank you. It was just a little business matter," said Father Keon. "Thank you, indeed."

He retreated from the doorway and Mr. Henchy, seizing one of the candlesticks, went to the door to light him downstairs.

"O, don't trouble, I beg!"

"No, but the stairs is so dark."

"No, no, I can see. . . . Thank you, indeed."

"Are you right now?"

"All right, thanks. . . . Thanks."

Mr. Henchy returned with the candlestick and put it on the table. He sat down again at the fire. There was silence for a few moments.

"Tell me, John," said Mr. O'Connor, lighting his cigarette with another pasteboard card.

"Hm?"

"What he is exactly?"

"Ask me an easier one," said Mr. Henchy.

"Fanning and himself seem to me very thick. They're often in Kavanagh's together. Is he a priest at all?"

"'Mmmyes, I believe so. . . . I think he's what you call a black sheep. We haven't many of them, thank God! but we have a few. . . . He's an unfortunate man of some kind. . . ."

"And how does he knock it out?" asked Mr. O'Connor.

"That's another mystery."

"Is he attached to any chapel or church or institution or—"

"No," said Mr. Henchy, "I think he's travelling on his own account. . . . God forgive me," he added, "I thought he was the dozen of stout."

"Is there any chance of a drink itself?" asked Mr. O'Connor.

"I'm dry too," said the old man.

"I asked that little shoeboy three times," said Mr. Henchy, "would he send up a dozen of stout. I asked him again now, but he was leaning on the counter in his shirt-sleeves having a deep goster with Alderman Cowley."

"Why didn't you remind him?" said Mr. O'Connor.

"Well, I couldn't go over while he was talking to Alderman Cowley. I just waited till I caught his eye, and said: 'About that little matter I was speaking to you about. . . .' 'That'll be all right, Mr. H.,' he said. Yerra, sure the little hop-o'-my-thumb has forgotten all about it."

"There's some deal on in that quarter," said Mr. O'Connor thoughtfully. "I saw the three of them hard at it yesterday at Suffolk Street corner."

"I think I know the little game they're at," said Mr. Henchy. "You must owe the City Fathers money nowadays if you want to be made Lord Mayor. Then they'll make you Lord Mayor. By God! I'm thinking seriously of becoming a City Father myself. What do you think? Would I do for the job?"

Mr. O'Connor laughed.

"So far as owing money goes. . . ."

"Driving out of the Mansion House," said Mr. Henchy, "in all my vermin, with Jack here standing up behind me in a powdered wig—eh?"

"And make me your private secretary, John."

"Yes. And I'll make Father Keon my private chaplain. We'll have a family party."

"Faith, Mr. Henchy," said the old man, "you'd keep up better style than some of them. I was talking one day to old Keegan, the porter. 'And how do you like your new master, Pat?' says I to him. 'You haven't much entertaining now,' says I. 'Entertaining!' says he. 'He'd live on the smell of an oil-rag.' And do you know what he told me? Now, I declare to God, I didn't believe him."

"What?" said Mr. Henchy and Mr. O'Connor.

"He told me: 'What do you think of a Lord Mayor of Dublin sending out for a pound of chops for his dinner? How's that for high living?' says he. 'Wisha! wisha," says I. 'A pound of chops,' says he, 'coming into the Mansion House.' 'Wisha!' says I, 'what kind of people is going at all now?'"

At this point there was a knock at the door, and a boy put in his head.

"What is it?" said the old man.

"From the *Black Eagle*," said the boy, walking in sideways and depositing a basket on the floor with a noise of shaken bottles.

The old man helped the boy to transfer the bottles from the basket to the table and counted the full tally. After the transfer the boy put his basket on his arm and asked:

"Any bottles?"

"What bottles?" said the old man.

"Won't you let us drink them first?" said Mr. Henchy.

"I was told to ask for bottles."

"Come back to-morrow," said the old man.

"Here, boy!" said Mr. Henchy, "will you run over to O'Farrell's and ask him to lend us a corkscrew—for Mr. Henchy, say. Tell him we won't keep it a minute. Leave the basket there."

The boy went out and Mr. Henchy began to rub his hands cheerfully, saying:

"Ah, well, he's not so bad after all. He's as good as his word, anyhow."

"There's no tumblers," said the old man.

"O, don't let that trouble you, Jack," said Mr. Henchy. "Many's the good man before now drank out of the bottle."

"Anyway, it's better than nothing," said Mr. O'Connor.

"He's not a bad sort," said Mr. Henchy, "only Fanning has such a loan of him. He means well, you know, in his own tinpot way."

The boy came back with the corkscrew. The old man opened three bottles and was handing back the corkscrew when Mr. Henchy said to the boy:

"Would you like a drink, boy?"

"If you please, sir," said the boy.

The old man opened another bottle grudgingly, and handed it to the boy.

"What age are you?" he asked.

"Seventeen," said the boy.

As the old man said nothing further, the boy took the bottle, said: "Here's my best respects, sir, to Mr. Henchy," drank the contents, put the bottle back on the table and wiped his mouth with his sleeve. Then he took up the corkscrew and went out of the door sideways, muttering some form of salutation.

"That's the way it begins," said the old man.

"The thin edge of the wedge," said Mr. Henchy.

The old man distributed the three bottles which he had opened and the men drank from them simultaneously. After having drunk each placed his bottle on the mantelpiece within hand's reach and drew in a long breath of satisfaction.

"Well, I did a good day's work to-day," said Mr. Henchy, after a pause.

"That so, John?"

"Yes. I got him one or two sure things in Dawson Street, Crofton and myself. Between ourselves, you know, Crofton (he's a decent chap, of course), but he's not worth a damn as a canvasser. He hasn't a word to throw to a dog. He stands and looks at the people while I do the talking."

Here two men entered the room. One of them was a very fat man, whose blue serge clothes seemed to be in danger of falling from his sloping figure. He had a big face which resembled a young ox's face in expression, staring blue eyes and a grizzled moustache. The other man, who was much younger and frailer, had a thin, clean-shaven face. He wore a very high double collar and a wide-brimmed bowler hat.

"Hello, Crofton!" said Mr. Henchy to the fat man. "Talk of the devil. . ."

"Where did the boose come from?" asked the young man. "Did the cow calve?"

"O, of course, Lyons spots the drink first thing!" said Mr. O'Connor, laughing.

"Is that the way you chaps canvass," said Mr. Lyons, "and Crofton and I out in the cold and rain looking for votes?"

"Why, blast your soul," said Mr. Henchy, "I'd get more votes in five minutes than you two'd get in a week."

"Open two bottles of stout, Jack," said Mr. O'Connor.

"How can I?" said the old man, "when there's no corkscrew?"

"Wait now, wait now!" said Mr. Henchy, getting up quickly. "Did you ever see this little trick?"

He took two bottles from the table and, carrying them to the fire, put them on the hob. Then he sat down again by the fire and took another drink from his bottle. Mr. Lyons sat on the edge of the table, pushed his hat towards the nape of his neck and began to swing his legs.

"Which is my bottle?" he asked.

"This, lad," said Mr. Henchy.

Mr. Crofton sat down on a box and looked fixedly at the other bottle on the hob. He was silent for two reasons. The first reason, sufficient in itself, was that he had nothing to say; the second reason was that he considered his companions beneath him. He had been a canvasser for Wilkins, the Conservative, but when the Conservatives had withdrawn their man and, choosing the lesser of two evils, given their support to the Nationalist candidate, he had been engaged to work for Mr. Tierney.

In a few minutes an apologetic "Pok!" was heard as the cork flew out of Mr. Lyons' bottle. Mr. Lyons jumped off the table, went to the fire, took his bottle and carried it back to the table.

"I was just telling them, Crofton," said Mr. Henchy, "that we got a good few votes to-day."

"Who did you get?" asked Mr. Lyons.

"Well, I got Parkes for one, and I got Atkinson for two, and I got Ward of Dawson Street. Fine old chap he is, too —regular old toff, old Conservative! 'But isn't your candidate a Nationalist?' said he. 'He's a respectable man,' said I. 'He's in favour of whatever will benefit this country. He's a big ratepayer,' I said. 'He has extensive house property in the city and three places of business and isn't it to his own advantage to keep down the rates? He's a prominent and respected citizen,' said I, 'and a Poor Law Guardian, and he doesn't belong to any party, good, bad, or indifferent.' That's the way to talk to 'em."

"And what about the address to the King?" said Mr. Lyons, after drinking and smacking his lips.

"Listen to me," said Mr. Henchy. "What we want in this country, as I said to old Ward, is capital. The King's coming here will mean an influx of money into this country. The citizens of Dublin will benefit by it. Look at all the factories down by the quays there, idle! Look at all the money there is in the country if we only worked the old industries, the mills, the ship-building yards and factories. It's capital we want."

"But look here, John," said Mr. O'Connor. "Why should we welcome the King of England? Didn't Parnell himself . . ."

"Parnell," said Mr. Henchy, "is dead. Now, here's the way I look at it. Here's this chap come to the throne after his old mother keeping him out of it till the man was grey. He's a man of the world, and he means well by us. He's a jolly fine decent fellow, if you ask me, and no damn nonsense about him. He just says to himself: 'The old one never went to see these wild Irish. By Christ, I'll go myself and see what they're like.' And are we going to insult the man when he comes over here on a friendly visit? Eh? Isn't that right, Crofton?"

Mr. Crofton nodded his head.

"But after all now," said Mr. Lyons argumentatively, "King Edward's life, you know, is not the very . . ."

"Let bygones be bygones," said Mr. Henchy. "I admire the man personally. He's just an ordinary knockabout like you and me. He's fond of his glass of grog and he's a bit of a rake, perhaps, and he's a good sportsman. Damn it, can't we Irish play fair?"

"That's all very fine," said Mr. Lyons. "But look at the case of Parnell now."

"In the name of God," said Mr. Henchy, "where's the analogy between the two cases?"

"What I mean," said Mr. Lyons, "is we have our ideals. Why, now, would we welcome a man like that? Do you think now after what he did Parnell was a fit man to lead us? And why, then, would we do it for Edward the Seventh?"

"This is Parnell's anniversary," said Mr. O'Connor, "and don't let us stir up any bad blood. We all respect him now that he's dead and gone—even the Conservatives," he added, turning to Mr. Crofton.

Pok! The tardy cork flew out of Mr. Crofton's bottle. Mr. Crofton got up from his box and went to the fire. As he returned with his capture he said in a deep voice:

"Our side of the house respects him, because he was a gentleman."

"Right you are, Crofton!" said Mr. Henchy fiercely. "He was the only man that could keep that bag of cats in order. 'Down, ye dogs! Lie down, ye curs!' That's the way he treated them. Come in, Joe! Come in!" he called out, catching sight of Mr. Hynes in the doorway.

Mr. Hynes came in slowly.

"Open another bottle of stout, Jack," said Mr. Henchy. "O, I forgot there's no corkscrew! Here, show me one here and I'll put it at the fire."

The old man handed him another bottle and he placed it on the hob.

"Sit down, Joe," said Mr. O'Connor, "we're just talking about the Chief."

"Ay, ay!" said Mr. Henchy.

Mr. Hynes sat on the side of the table near Mr. Lyons but said nothing.

"There's one of them, anyhow," said Mr. Henchy, "that didn't renege him. By God, I'll say for you, Joe! No, by God, you stuck to him like a man!"

"O, Joe," said Mr. O'Connor suddenly. "Give us that thing you wrote—do you remember? Have you got it on you?"

"O, ay!" said Mr. Henchy. "Give us that. Did you ever hear that, Crofton? Listen to this now: splendid thing."

"Go on," said Mr. O'Connor. "Fire away, Joe."

Mr. Hynes did not seem to remember at once the piece to which they were alluding, but, after reflecting a' while, he said:

"O, that thing is it. . . . Sure, that's old now."

"Out with it, man!" said Mr. O'Connor.

" 'Sh, 'sh," said Mr. Henchy. "Now, Joe!"

Mr. Hynes hesitated a little longer. Then amid the silence he took off his hat, laid it on the table and stood up. He seemed to be rehearsing the piece in his mind. After a rather long pause he announced:

THE DEATH OF PARNELL
6th October, 1891

He cleared his throat once or twice and then began to recite:

He is dead. Our Uncrowned King is dead.
    O, Erin, mourn with grief and woe
For he lies dead whom the fell gang
    Of modern hypocrites laid low.

He lies slain by the coward hounds
    He raised to glory from the mire;
And Erin's hopes and Erin's dreams
    Perish upon her monarch's pyre.

In palace, cabin or in cot
   The Irish heart where'er it be
Is bowed with woe—for he is gone
   Who would have wrought her destiny.

He would have had his Erin famed,
   The green flag gloriously unfurled,
Her statesmen, bards and warriors raised
   Before the nations of the World.

He dreamed (alas, 'twas but a dream!)
   Of Liberty: but as he strove
To clutch that idol, treachery
   Sundered him from the thing he loved.

Shame on the coward, caitiff hands
   That smote their Lord or with a kiss
Betrayed him to the rabble-rout
   Of fawning priests—no friends of his.

May everlasting shame consume
   The memory of those who tried
To befoul and smear the exalted name
   Of one who spurned them in his pride.

He fell as fall the mighty ones,
   Nobly undaunted to the last,
And death has now united him
   With Erin's heroes of the past.

No sound of strife disturb his sleep!
   Calmly he rests: no human pain
Or high ambition spurs him now
   The peaks of glory to attain.

They had their way: they laid him low.
   But Erin, list, his spirit may
Rise, like the Phoenix from the flames,
   When breaks the dawning of the day,

The day that brings us Freedom's reign.
   And on that day may Erin well
Pledge in the cup she lifts to Joy
   One grief—the memory of Parnell.

Mr. Hynes sat down again on the table. When he had finished his recitation there was a silence and then a burst of clapping: even Mr. Lyons clapped. The applause continued for a little time. When it had ceased all the auditors drank from their bottles in silence.

Pok! The cork flew out of Mr. Hynes' bottle, but Mr. Hynes remained sitting flushed and bareheaded on the table. He did not seem to have heard the invitation.

"Good man, Joe!" said Mr. O'Connor, taking out his cigarette papers and pouch the better to hide his emotion.

"What do you think of that, Crofton?" cried Mr. Henchy. "Isn't that fine? What?"

Mr. Crofton said that it was a very fine piece of writing.

Luigi Pirandello

[1867 — 1936]

THE MEDIEVAL TORPOR of Sicily at the time of Luigi Pirandello's birth might have suggested to his imagination some sense of the inescapable, but little of that quality of unpredictable quick-change which is identifiable in all his mature writings. Nominally, Italy achieved national unity during his childhood; but Sicilians—inbred, taciturn, isolated—continued to speak of travel to Florence as "going to the Continent." Moreover, young Pirandello was raised quietly to assume his wealthy father's business, ownership of island sulphur mines. At 18 he would have quit his studies, in order to support his fiancée; but his father insisted that he enter the University of Rome and, later, Bonn University, after he complained of the incompetence of Roman instruction. Since his own engagement dissolved during the next few years, Pirandello agreed in 1894 to marry his father's choice, a girl whom he hardly knew except as the daughter of his father's business partner. They were settled in Rome on generous family allowances.

Suddenly, floods destroyed the Sicilian sulphur mines; the severe shock unsettled his wife's mind. For years, while he supported his family as professor of Italian literature at the Roman Normal School, his wife filled his hours at home with wild accusations of infidelity. Gradually he saw himself becoming only the shadow of the image her mind held. He was tortured too by thoughts of lives he might have led. But not until after

322

World War I would he allow his wife to be taken from him and to be placed in a nursing home.

By then his importance as a writer was beginning to be recognized. Between 1889 and 1912, he had published five collections of verse whose cynicism was disciplined by epigrammatic humor. A deeper, more relentless kind of tragic humor, however, is evident in his short stories, written at the suggestion of Capuana and Verga, fellow Sicilian writers in Rome who had already found provincial life, however squalid or incongruous, worthy of art. He began to plan 24 volumes of 15 stories apiece; but because later his interests turned to the drama, only 15 volumes were completed in his lifetime. Mostly they are stories of harrowing peasant life in Sicily and of bourgeois illusions: but the torment of self-division is already as significant as any class divisions in these stories. The land of volcanic ash and sulphur offers a natural symbol for a wasteland which the errant knight, time and again, fails to redeem. Pirandello's men of impulse and quiet perplexities contrast ironically with the cult of the pompous strong man in the work of his contemporary, D'Annunzio. Yet his characters often possess a native grace and dignity which elevate them above naturalistic primitives. Old comedies of error and mistaken identity become, in Pirandello, quests for truth amid the transitory acts of man. During these same years, the problem of plural personality reappears in the seven novels on which Pirandello was working. Always, a kind of introspective patience tries to outwait dilemmas that cannot be outwitted.

By 1915 James Joyce had helped Pirandello find a publisher; but only those, later, who survived World War I could fully appreciate Pirandello's downward journey into the maze that man had become. They could believe in the dark functions of man's unconscious will, explored in postwar decades by Freud and Jung, because they had seen the reversion of civilized nations to mass slaughter.

Pirandello had already written five plays—mainly Sicilian folk dramas—before the war. Afterwards (at the urging of a comic actor!) the stage occupied his imagination thoroughly, resulting in such unrivaled philosophical plays as *Six Characters in Search of an Author* and *Henry IV*, both written within a five-week period. Half of his 50-odd plays are dramatizations of his stories, with occasional commentators added and lengthy stage directions inserted to overcome the difficulties inherent in a drama of ideas—solutions employed by George Bernard Shaw and Eugene O'Neill as well. The theater, which depends on roles assumed and discarded and which filters the playwright's intentions through actor and director, was the perfect medium for Pirandello's concern with truth's transitory nature.

His esthetic had already been presented in 1908, through two volumes of essays, *Art and Science* and *Humor*. In these, the creative act of the artist is equated with the personal mythmaking and self-idealization of everyman; and the failure of complete self-knowledge in any man, when "being and seeming" contradict each other, results in a profound comedy of the absurd. Trying to dramatize this philosophy, Pirandello wrote quickly, driven more now by its desperate elusiveness than by poverty.

In 1934 Pirandello received the Nobel prize for literature. But his search, not for success but for certainty, could never stop. Publicly he accepted Mussolini; yet his last plays betray an "inward exile" from fascist politics, confirmed by his refusal to be buried in a "black shirt" uniform.

Bombolo

BOMBOLO SAT IN the café all day long, a red fez on his big curly head, his legs straddling the table base, one commanding fist on the marble top and the other on his hip. He would look around, not defiantly but with a stern expression that said flatly, "Make no mistake about it: here you deal with me!"

Landowners came one after another, not only from Montelusa but from all the surrounding countryside. Even the old Marchese, Don Nicolino Nigrelli, who always carried an ebony cane and held the round ivory ball of the handle against his puckered lips as if he were playing a flute. Then there were Baron Don Mauro Ragona, Tavella, too—all of them respectfully baring their heads.

"Don Zuli, please do me a favor."

Before this deference, Bombolo would jump to his feet, pull off his fez and stand at attention, head high, eyes lowered.

"At your service, Excellency," he would say.

The usual complaints, on the one hand, and exhortations, on the other, would soon follow. Nigrelli had lost four head

From *Short Stories by Pirandello*, translated by Lily Duplaix. Copyright, 1959, by Gli Eredi Di Luigi Pirandello. Reprinted by permission of Simon and Schuster, Inc.

of cattle on the hill; Ragona eight from the sheep fold;
Tavella five from the stable. One came to tell him that the
boy watching over his herd had been tied to a tree. Another
said his cow had been taken and the newborn calf left to
die of starvation.

Bombolo would, at first, show indignation over such out-
rages, exclaiming, "The villains!"

Then lifting clasped hands, he would go on: "But, sir,
we call them villains, yet in all conscience, how much do
these poor villains earn a day? Three tari—one lira and a
quarter! That's what they're paid, isn't it? And what's three
tari for a man? One of God's poor creatures baptized like
you—not like me, a heathen Turk, as you can see," he
would say, pointing to his fez. "Tell me, sir, isn't it a moral
crime to pay three tari a day to a man who wields a shovel
and sweats blood from sunrise to sunset, without pause except at noon, when he takes time out to munch a crust of
bread with saliva for a chaser, and then returns to work
still chewing his last mouthful? Look at Cosimo Lopes.
Since he's been paying his peasants three lire a day, has he
had anything to complain about?" Quickly, he pulled a
hair from his head and held it up as if it were a talisman.
"Three lire, sir, is only right! Do as I say and if tomorrow
anyone mistreats you or your animals, you may come and
spit in my face. I'll be here."

In the end, changing both his manner and tone of voice,
he would ask, "How many head did you say? Four? Leave it
to me. I'll go saddle my horse now."

For two or three days he would pretend to scour the
countryside for the missing cattle, riding all night, or so
he said, in the rain or under the stars. No one believed it,
of course. He well knew that they didn't believe it. But
when, upon his return, he would reappear before old Marchese Nigrelli, or Ragona, or any of the others, he was received with the usual exclamations: "Poor Zuli, what a hard
time you've had of it!"

"Never mind, never mind. It was not easy, but I tracked

them down. You needn't worry; the animals are stabled and well cared for. They are all right where they are. The cattle rustlers themselves aren't so well off. If their lives weren't so hard, you can be sure they'd never resort to this kind of thing. . . . Well, that's all there is to it. They're willing to return the cattle—but, as usual, you understand, in dealing with a gentleman like yourself through my good offices, without agreements or conditions, they leave it entirely up to your conscience. . . . Don't worry! Tonight, without fail, your animals will reappear on the hill, better-looking than ever."

He would have taken it as an affront to himself as well as to the landowners had he so much as suspected that the rustlers might be ambushed by the police that night. He knew only too well that if the gentry appealed to him, it was because they had no faith in the authorities. They would never get their cattle back that way. But working through Bombolo, any thought of treachery was ruled out.

Bombolo received the money—five hundred, a thousand, two thousand lire, according to the number of animals sequestered—and every week on Saturday night he brought the total sum to the peasants of the League, who assembled in a store near the top of San Gerlando. There he saw that "justice was done." That is, by computing each peasant's wages at three lire a day, those who had worked for only three tari that week received the difference. Those who, through no fault of their own, had "sat it out" without work were paid seven lire for the week or a lira a day. However, first of all, deductions were made for the small weekly pensions allotted the families of three members—Todesco, Principe and Barrera—who had been arrested one night by a scouting patrol and sentenced to three years in prison. They had not "sung." Another share was set aside as dues to the watchmen who co-operated by allowing themselves to be bound and gagged. If anything was left over, it was put aside as cash reserve.

Bombolo kept nothing for himself, not a cent. The

rumors going around Montelusa were malicious lies. He really had no need for the money. He had made a fortune in the East, where he had lived a long time. No one knew exactly where, nor how, but it was certain that he had money and was not interested in the relatively small sums that passed through his hands. They said you could see what he was by that fez, by his lazily watchful expression, his colorful speech, and the special odor given off by his whole person—spicy, exotic—thanks perhaps to the little leather pouches and small wooden boxes he always carried about him or from the Turkish tobacco he smoked. Because tobacco was a state monopoly, the foreign leaf had to be smuggled off boats in the nearby harbor. Some said he was engaged in shady business. They saw him, they said, sitting there hour after hour with that bright-red cylinder on his head, looking out to sea for all the world as if he were waiting for a sail to appear off Punta Bianca.

He had married into the Dimino family, rich land-owners, with holdings so vast you could walk all day and not come to the end of them. Even though their daughter had died four years after her marriage, old Dimino and his wife were so fond of Bombolo that, it was said, they would give him their last cent!

He was a kind of Robin Hood working for justice, happy in the respect, love and gratitude of the peasants, who looked on him as their king. He held them all in the palm of his hand. Experience had taught him that open meetings, in protest against the tyrannical avarice of the property owners, would only be broken up by the police and the ringleader carted off to jail. That was the way they had always administered justice in Sicily. Even the landowners took no stock in it. But in the store up there on San Gerlando, Bombolo meted out justice in his own way.

If those gentlemen-farmers insisted on paying no more than three tari a day—well, what they didn't give freely, they would have to give by force. Peacefully, without bloodshed or violence, and with all due regard for the welfare of the animals.

Bombolo had a notebook in which he listed all the proprietors of the district, their names, the extent and location of their lands, as well as their livestock, large and small. Each week he would call a secret meeting of his most trusted henchmen to decide, from the open notebook, who would "pay the tax" and which peasants were to make the raid. They would be chosen because of their familiarity with the place, their friendship with the watchmen or their daring.

"A small touch never hurt anyone" was one of his favorite sayings.

But he went wild when one of the members of the League was reported for leeching, or idling. He would go after him and shake him with both hands so violently that the culprit's beret would fly off and his shirt and pants would part company.

"Snake in the grass!" Bombolo would shout. "What do you take me for? A champion of thieves and vagrants? Down here you must sweat blood! Down here, on Saturday nights you must report with your back breaking with fatigue, or this will quickly become a den of thieves. If you don't work, I'll crush you underfoot. I'll tear you apart! *Work is the law!* Only by work do you win the right to lead a beast by the horns from the stable of its owner and proclaim, 'Until I am paid what I have rightfully earned by the sweat of my brow, I will keep this animal.' "

In those moments he was frightening. Everyone in the dark store would listen, silent as shadows, staring at the flame of the candle butt melting over the dirty table. After such violent outbursts, Bombolo would gasp for breath, his mighty chest heaving and croaking like an old frog. If one of them had dared look up, he would have seen real tears of rage glisten in Bombolo's eyes. At those moments, he saw his austere concept of justice abjectly compromised.

He felt the weight of responsibility and a certain scorn and bitterness for his undertaking. The peasants did not seem to appreciate the salary of three lire a day which he had managed to wring from the landowners by harassing them day after day.

It fed his pride to hear the farm gentry themselves say that they had never seen the peasants work harder or more willingly. This alone, in his eyes, purified and exalted the task he had set himself. For him, all those who heeded his constant preaching and granted a fair wage were sacred, and he wanted them to be just as sacred to every other member of the League. When money was needed and he could not turn up a name in his notebook to "pay the tax"—all those listed having already paid up—Bombolo would turn white with rage if a member timidly suggested one of the sacred few. They were untouchable.

Then what?

"Then," Bombolo would explode, tossing the notebook into the air, "*then* we bleed my father-in-law."

Two or three peasants would be assigned to go to the Luna domain, under cover of darkness, and to make off with six or seven big animals owned by Dimino—one of the first landowners to pay his men the equitable three lire a day.

By bleeding his father-in-law, Bombolo was robbing himself, because his son was Dimino's only heir. But he preferred to rob himself or his son rather than to go against what he knew was right. And what torment it was for him every time his father-in-law—dressed "old style" in knee breeches, black stocking cap with a pompon on the end, and little gold chains through his ears—sought him out and said, "What's the matter, Zuli? Is this the way they respect you? What's come over you? Have you lost your hold on them?"

"Spit in my face," replied Bombolo, eyes closed, drinking down the gall of Dimino's rebuke. "Spit in my face. What else can I say?"

He was only waiting until the three League members—Todesco, Principe and Barrera—were released from prison to dissolve the League itself. There were days when those three years seemed to him like a million.

When the day finally came, there was a big celebration in the store on top of San Gerlando. They drank and they danced. Bombolo beamed when he got up to make the final speech. He recalled their deeds and sang their praises. As a reward—the highest reward for those three who had suffered imprisonment—an honest wage had now been firmly established throughout the area. His task was accomplished, he said, and he could retire in peace and contentment. He brought down the house when he added that he had sent his red fez to his father-in-law, who had never been able to stomach the "crown." In giving up the fez he gave up his reign, and hereby declared the League dissolved.

Two weeks had not passed before the old Marchese, Don Nicolino Nigrelli, sauntered by the café as usual with the white ivory ball of his ebony cane held to his lips.

"Don Zuli, please do me a favor."

Bombolo went white as the marble table top and turned to look at the poor Marchese in such stupefaction that Don Nicolino backed away in fright and fell into a chair.

Bombolo stood over him, roaring between clenched teeth, "Again?"

Half fainting, although he was trying to smile, the Marchese lifted four fingers of his trembling hand and said, "Four, yes, as before. What's so new about that?"

Bombolo snatched the new hat off his head and tore it to shreds. Trembling, he moved between the tables, banging into them and upsetting the chairs. Then he turned on the Marchese, who still sat among the astonished customers, and cried, "Don't give them a single lira. By the Blessed Virgin! Don't give them anything. I'll have to think this thing over."

Couldn't those three—Todesco, Principe and Barrera—

be content with that "highest reward" of which Bombolo
had boasted at the last meeting of the League? If Bombolo
himself, toward the end, had allowed them to bleed his
own father-in-law, known to be among the first to concede
the higher wage, then why couldn't they, in all fairness,
continue to bleed the other landowners?

That evening, when Bombolo found them on San Gerlando after an all-day search, he attacked them like a wild
beast. They let him strike them and knock them about.
They even said he could kill them if he cared to: they
would not lift a finger to defend themselves, out of respect
and gratitude for all he had done. However, if he did this,
he would be killing them unjustly, for they knew nothing
at all about the theft. Their consciences were clear. League?
What League? There was no more League! Hadn't he dissolved it? Ah, so he threatened to denounce them? What
for? For their past? Then they were all in it, and he the ringleader. As to a raid on Marchese Nigrelli, they knew nothing about it. But they might well scout the countryside for
two or three days and question the brigands, as he had done
before them, riding all night in the rain and under the
stars.

Hearing them talk like this, Bombolo bit his hands in
rage and frustration. He said he would give them just three
days. If at the end of that time the four head of cattle had
not been returned without a lira of ransom—well, what
would he do? He didn't yet know.

What could Bombolo do? Even the landowners themselves—Nigrelli, Ragona, Tavella and all the others—tried
to convince him that there was nothing he could do. Where
did he come in? Hadn't he always acted as a disinterested
party? What was so different today? Why did he now refuse to help anyone? Go to the police? Where would that
get them? The police would not bring about the return of
their cattle, nor would they find the guilty party who made
off with them. The proprietors themselves said it was
simple-minded to expect the cattle to be returned without

compensation. They had to make a deal, they said—without agreements or conditions. Just so long as Bombolo would act as go-between!

And from the tone in which these things were said, Bombolo understood that they mistook his present indignation for play-acting, just as before they had misinterpreted his sympathy for the peasants.

In rage and despair he shouted that they should go back to paying the peasants three tari a day; they could at least do him that favor. Word of honor, they didn't deserve more than three tari! Shameless thieves! Dogs! Jailbirds! What then? Was he to burst his liver as well as his gall bladder because of these buzzards?

He sent his son to his grandparents up at the big Luna estate to ask them to return his red fez. Turk he was and Turk he would remain!

Two days later, bag and baggage, he went down to the harbor and boarded a Greek ship for the Levant.

The New Suit

THE SUIT POOR Crispucci had worn from time immemorial
reminded everyone of the bedraggled, discolored fur of a
stray dog. It could no longer be considered separate from
his body, or susceptible to change. That was why his employer, lawyer Boccanera, never dreamed of passing on to
him one of his own discarded but still wearable suits. From
the lawyer's point of view, Crispucci was perfectly satisfactory as he was, as Boccanera's clerk-messenger at a hundred and twenty lire a month.

Usually Signor Boccanera had only to say with a wink,
"Eh, Crispucci?" for Crispucci to grasp his meaning. But
today the clerk apparently understood little or nothing of
Signor Boccanera's long, friendly talk. He just stood there
in front of the lawyer's desk, his long arms dangling, his
body stooped and twisted into a letter S. From time to time
he opened his mouth, but no words were uttered. His
cheeks contracted, his yellow face puckered as he bared his
teeth in a grimace of scorn or pain, but perhaps it was only
a sign of concentration.

". . . And, my dear Crispucci, all things considered, I advise you to go. Your absence will mean serious difficulties for me, of course, but you should leave anyway. I will manage for a couple of weeks. It will take you at least that long to get through all the legal formalities and to clear things up. Then, too, I imagine you'll want to sell everything."

Crispucci raised his arms in a helpless gesture, his faded eyes staring fixedly into space.

"Yes," Boccanera went on, "everything should be sold—jewels, clothes, furniture. The jewels will fetch the most. At first glance, from the description in this inventory, you should get around a hundred fifty to two hundred thousand lire. Maybe more. There is also a pearl necklace. As for her clothes, of course, your daughter couldn't possibly wear them. Who knows what they're like! But don't count on getting much for them. Clothes never bring good prices, no matter how fine. If you're clever, you might get something for the furs—she seems to have had quite a collection. Now, mind what you do about the jewels. Better find out where they were bought. The boxes may be marked. I can tell you that the price of diamonds has gone way up and there are a number listed here! Brooch . . . another brooch . . . ring . . . earrings . . . a bracelet . . . another ring . . . ring . . . a brooch . . . bracelet . . . bracelet . . . quite a few, really."

At this point Crispucci raised his hand as a sign that he wished to be heard. On rare occasions he made this gesture and twisted his face in an effort to bring his voice up from the depths of silence into which his spirit seemed permanently sunk.

"Could I . . . might I," he faltered, "might I be so bold as to . . . one of . . . just one of those rings . . . for your wife?"

"What are you saying, my dear Crispucci?" exclaimed the lawyer. "For my *wife* . . . one of *those* rings? What could you be thinking of?"

"Excuse me," Crispucci said, dropping his hand and nodding several times in belated agreement. His eyes filled with
tears.

"No, on the contrary; I thank you very much for such a
generous thought. Come, come, dear Crispucci! I didn't
mean to offend you. I know. I understand; this is all very
sad for you. But remember you are not accepting this inheritance for yourself. You have a daughter, and it will not
be easy to find a husband for her without a dowry. Ah, yes,
I know. I know. It's hard. But money is money, dear Crispucci, and therefore one must close one's eyes to many
things. You have a mother, too! Besides, you are not in very
good health, and . . ."

Crispucci, who had nodded approval of everything else,
now opened his eyes with a look of annoyance when the
question of his health was raised. Bowing, he turned to
leave.

"Here, aren't you forgetting your papers?" the lawyer
asked, holding them out to him across the desk.

Crispucci turned, wiped his eyes with a soiled handkerchief, and took the papers.

"So you'll be leaving tomorrow?"

"Signor Lawyer," replied Crispucci as if he had made up
his mind to say something difficult, but then he stopped
short. He struggled a moment to hold back what was already on the tip of his tongue, then shrugged slightly, raised
his arms again and left.

He was about to say, "I'll go, if your honor will accept a
ring for your wife from my inheritance."

The other clerks in the office who had taken pleasure in
tormenting him these last three days, goading him cruelly
about his inheritance, had been promised, through clenched
teeth, one a silk dress for his wife, another a feathered hat
for his daughter, the third a muff for his fiancée.

"May she wear it in health," he muttered. "And what
about a couple of fine embroidered blouses, open down the
front, for your sister?"

"Would to God!"

Crispucci wanted all of them to be sullied as he felt he was in accepting the inheritance. He could probably dress all the women in town, he thought, after reading the long description in the inventory of the dead woman's elaborate wardrobe—closets and closets full of lingerie alone. If a remnant of good sense had not checked him, he would have collared passers-by with "My wife just died in Naples. She was thus and thus . . . but she left me this and that. Would you like something for your wife, your sister, your daughter? Half a dozen of the finest silk net stockings, for example?"

A balding, jaundiced young man with a longing to be stylish had been writhing these past days listening to all these fine offers in the office. He had been working there only a week, filling in as errand boy when he was not needed as a clerk. Mindful of his dignity, he scarcely spoke a word to anyone, but then no one ever spoke to him either. A slightly scornful smile played around the corners of his mouth as he listened to Crispucci. With a knowing gesture, he pulled on his yellow cuffs, or pushed them back under the too-short sleeves of his jacket.

That day, Crispucci had hardly come out of the lawyer's office and taken his hat and cane from the rack to go out when the new clerk, unable to resist, followed right behind him. The others, laughing, called from the top of the stairs:

"Crispucci, remember that blouse for my sister!"

"And the silk coat for my wife!"

"The muff for my fiancée!"

"An ostrich plume for my daughter!"

In the street, pale with rage, the young man accosted him.

"Why all this foolishness? Why scatter your inheritance like this? Has it any mark to show where it comes from? You've had this piece of good luck and you don't even know how to make the best of it! Are you crazy?"

Crispucci stopped short and eyed him.

"Good luck, yes!" the young man harped. "Good luck
before and good luck now! Years ago, to be freed when she
fled your house . . ."

"Ah, so you found out about that!"

"Yes, I found out! Well, what troubles, obstacles, anxiety
can you have now? Now she's dead, and you don't call that
luck? Not only is she dead and gone, but she left you
enough to begin a new life."

Crispucci stopped again to gaze at him.

"Perhaps you also found out that I have a daughter who
is not married?"

"That's why I'm talking to you."

"You certainly speak frankly."

"Very frankly!"

"And you believe that I should accept the inheritance?"

"You'd be a fool not to! Two hundred thousand lire!"

"And with two hundred thousand lire, you would like
me to give you my daughter?"

"Why not?"

"Because with two hundred thousand lire I could buy
something less shameful and odious than your proposal."

"You insult me!"

"No, I respect you. I respect you just as you respect me.
For a proposal like yours, I wouldn't pay more than three
thousand lire."

"Three?"

"Five, if you like, and a little linen thrown in. You have
a sister? Three silk blouses for her, open down the front.
I'll give them to you, if you like."

And he left him standing there in the middle of the
street.

At home, Crispucci said not a word to his mother or his
daughter. For that matter, in the sixteen years since his
tragedy, he had never allowed them to speak of anything
except matters strictly relating to their daily life. If either

of them so much as hinted at anything else, he turned such a look on her that her voice died on her lips.

He went to Naples the next day, leaving them not only in the most painful uncertainty about the inheritance but also in dread lest he do something rash.

Neighbors fanned their fears by repeating and commenting on all the queer things Crispucci had done during the past three days. One of them, wondering about the dead woman, asked idly, "How did she get to be so rich?"

"I heard her name was Marguerite," said another. "However, her linen, I understand, was marked 'R.B.' "

"Not 'B'—'R.C.' " corrected another. "Rose Clairon was what I heard."

"Ah . . . Clairon . . . Clairon . . . Wasn't that the name of a singer?"

"I don't believe so."

"Yes, of course it was, and what a singer! Not lately, of course, but she used to sing!"

"Rosa Clairon! Now I remember the name!"

The young girl, listening to all this, glanced at her grandmother with a feverish light in her deep-set eyes and a flush on her thin cheeks. The old woman, her heavy, yellow face deeply lined, adjusted thick-lensed spectacles on her nose. Since her operation for cataracts, her eyes looked enormous and vague between the long sparse lashes like insect antennae. She answered the women's idle gossip with low grunts.

There were some among them who hotly maintained that Crispucci was not as crazy as he was made out to be and that he should not be blamed if he did not want a stitch of that underwear to touch his daughter's pure young body. He would do better to give the clothes away if he did not want to sell them. Naturally, it was only right that they be distributed among the neighbors. In any case, a few presents at least! What a river of glistening silks, what a flow of foaming laces between banks of soft velvets and crests of

bright feathers would come into the squalor of that hovel!
Just the thought of it narrowed their eyes to slits. And Fina,
the young girl, listening to them and seeing their intoxication, wrung her hands under her apron and finally jumped
up and ran out of the room.

"Poor child," said one of them. "It's so hard for her."

"Do you think he'll make her wear mourning?" another
asked.

The old woman grunted, signifying that she knew nothing about it.

"Of course he will; it's only natural."

"After all, she was her mother."

"If he accepts the inheritance!"

"You'll see, he'll wear mourning too!"

"No . . . not him!"

"Not even if he accepts the inheritance?"

The old woman squirmed in her chair and Fina tossed on
her bed in the next room. That was the crux of the question: would he accept the inheritance?

The women had gone secretly to lawyer Boccanera at the
first news of Rosa Clairon's death, in alarm over Crispucci's
fury about the inheritance. They begged the lawyer, with
clasped hands, to prevent a silly refusal. What was to become of his daughter if Crispucci died? She had never had
anything since she was born, poor girl. He weighed the dis-
honor of the inheritance against his pride in honest poverty.
Why question such good fortune? This girl had not asked
to be brought into the world and had she not paid dearly
for her mother's shame?

Their doubts and torment lasted an eternity—eighteen
long days. Not a word did they hear in all that time. Finally,
one evening, the two women heard stumbling steps and
heavy breathing on the stairway. Porters were lugging up
eleven heavy trunks and boxes which they had brought
from the station.

Crispucci waited by the entrance door until the men
had carried everything up to his apartment on the fourth

floor. Then he paid them and, when all was quiet, he started up the stairs.

His mother and daughter, lamps in their hands, waited anxiously for him on the landing. At last they saw his bent head in a new green hat. He was wearing a new suit of rough brown wool, too, bought ready-made, no doubt, in a Naples department store. The pants covered the heels of his new shoes. The jacket gaped at the neck.

Neither one nor the other dared ask a question. The suit spoke for itself. Then, seeing her father go directly to his room, the young girl said just as his door was closing, "Have you had supper, Papa?"

Crispucci turned. With a new twist to his smile, and in a new voice, he replied, "*Wagon-restaurant.*"

Alberto Moravia (Pincherle)

[1907 —]

ONE OF THE world's leading novelists, Alberto Moravia has helped to rediscover the Italian short story which Boccaccio had exhausted in the fourteenth century with his *Decameron* (1348–1353). Of his several volumes of tales, only three collections have appeared in English: *Bitter Honeymoon* (1956), *Roman Tales* (1957), and *The Wayward Wife* (1960). Many others, still uncollected, have been published in periodicals and in the Italian dailies.

Born in Rome of an upper-middle-class family, Moravia was intended for a diplomat's career. But after several years of schooling he contracted tuberculosis of the bone and had to spend five years in bed, between the ages of 9 and 17, until 1924. Young Moravia turned this personal tragedy into an asset. He became an addict of boredom, "a frightful thing, yet a great creative force. A necessary poison. No one who is not bored can create anything." He wrote stories and poems; he became absorbed in his own private world of sensations, dreaming and reflecting on the psychological turmoils of childhood and adolescence; he read a book a day in one sanatorium, where he spent two years. Two of his most powerful stories—"A Sick Boy's Winter" (1930) and *Agostino* (1944)—reflect the pain, sadness, and indifference, the sensual urges, the terrors of his own adolescence, which became key moods of his fiction.

342

Before and during his life in the sanatoriums, Moravia was excited by literature, especially the dramas of Molière, Shakespeare, and Goldoni. Classical tragedies he considered "the greatest of all forms of artistic expression," and from them he learned the art of dialogue, taut structure, and the value of compressed time. He was intrigued by James Joyce's *Ulysses* mainly because it solved the problem of time like a drama. Dostoevsky and Gide taught him the art of dramatically presenting psychology and philosophy in fiction; their influence may have also led him to existentialism, as seen in his first novel *The Time of Indifference* (1929). Classical prose writers like Voltaire and Stendhal were his prose models; he rejected the realists Flaubert, Zola, and Pirandello. Paradoxically, though he was always drawn to somber writers, he admired the comic ones: "My great ambition is to write a comic book, but . . . it's the most difficult thing of all. . . . I would give all to have written a book like *Gargantua*." There is satirical comedy in *The Fancy Dress Party* (1940) and *Roman Tales*.

Moravia's own Italian heritage played a significant part in his life and art. Boccaccio's anecdotal plots with their diverse moods of ribaldry, irony, farce, skepticism, brutality, and romance helped to give a needed balance to Moravia's cynical outlook. The lurid, romantic qualities of Manzoni's prose, Goldoni's dramas of intrigue, and Pirandello's satires on the materialism and vanity of the bourgeoisie inspired further variety in Moravia's style and theme. The political evils of past and present Italy increased his attachment to human beings and their private destinies, rather than to history. He was critical of Machiavelli, whose political passions he linked with sexual frustration; and as a lifelong antifascist he fought Mussolini and censorship from 1929 to 1943, because the "use of man as a means and not as an end is the root of all evil." The impact of World War I, in which Italy engaged, destroyed traditional values, leaving Moravia "with the fact of sex . . . one of the most primitive and unchanging manifestations of the relationships with reality; and the same goes for the preoccupation with social and economic facts." These sexual, social, and economic tensions were distilled into his characteristic theme, the "relationship between man and reality." Even his prose was partly conditioned by life in the fascist world; it is a compact, cold, dissecting prose, almost machine-gun-like in delivery.

One cannot minimize Moravia's own innate talent. He says he was a born storyteller: "As a child, before I could even read or write, I used to tell stories out loud to myself, either in my room or in some lonely place, especially during the summer holidays by the sea." They were adventure stories, told in episodes. Later when he began his first disciplined writing he found his materials "totally unpunctuated," so he had "to read a sentence aloud to get its rhythm, cadence, and harmony." Though Freud's influence has been suggested, Moravia claims he captured the embittered psychology of his characters from his own experience and imagination.

The main body of Moravia's fiction is not far removed from the realists and naturalists who supposedly did not interest him. He deals with the values of the bourgeoisie and the proletariat, and though admittedly a moralist, he says: "In my view, the function of a writer is not to criticize anyway; only to create living characters." His men and women are sympathetically drawn; he has no "negative characters." They do not speak in dialect; rather Moravia captures the tone of their language. By combining narrative and dramatic techniques, Moravia unmasks with clinical penetration and unerring psychology the frustrating absurdities of individual existence and, in a larger sense, the moral decay of modern Italy.

The Treasure

AT THE TIME when I was working as a waiter at an inn
outside the Porta San Pancrazio, a certain market gardener
used to be a regular customer there; everyone called him
Marinese, either because he belonged to Marino, or, more
probably, because he was particularly fond of the Marino
wine. This man Marinese was extremely old; even he himself did not know how old he was. However, he used to
drink more than most young men, and when he was drinking he would chat with anyone who cared to listen—or
even, indeed, to himself. As everyone knows, we waiters in
inns, except when we are actually serving, spend our time
listening to the conversation of the customers. Marinese,
amongst a great many untrue stories, used often to tell one
particular one that had an appearance of truth—that the
Germans had stolen a chest of silver from the villa of a
prince near by, and had buried it in a spot which he,
Marinese, knew. Sometimes, if he was really drunk, he
would allow it to be understood that this spot was in his
own market garden. Anyhow, he used to say that, if he

From *Roman Tales* by Alberto Moravia, translated by Angus Davidson.
Copyright 1956, 1957 by Valentino Bompiani & Co. Used by permission
of the publishers, Farrar, Straus and Cudahy, Inc.

wanted to, he could become rich. And that some day he
would want to. When? "When I'm old and don't want to
go on working," he said, on one occasion, to somebody who
asked him. And this was a ridiculous answer because, if you
looked at him, you could see he must be at least eighty.

Well, I began thinking about this treasure, and I was
convinced that it existed because, some years back—during
the occupation, in fact—such a theft had really taken place
and the Prince had never got his silver back. When I
thought of it, it enraged me that it should be in the hands
of Marinese, who, some day or other, would be suddenly
struck dead in his hut, and then—good-bye to the treasure.
I tried to ingratiate myself with him, but the old man, like
a true swindler, made me stand him drinks and then would
not open his mouth. "Even if you were my son," he finally
said to me, with great solemnity, "I wouldn't tell you. . . .
You're young and you can work. . . . The ones who need
money are the old people who are tired and can't go on
any longer." In the end, in desperation, I took the other
waiter into my confidence—Remigio, who was pale and fair
and younger than me. He was immediately excited at the
idea—but in a foolish sort of way, like the fool that he was
—and began building castles in the air: we would get rich,
he would buy a motor-bicycle, we would open a bar together, and so on. I said to him: "The first thing to do is to
find this treasure . . . and don't get over-excited about it.
. . . We'll divide it into four—three shares for me and one
for you: is that all right?" He agreed to this, still in a state
of elation. And we made an appointment for that same
night; after midnight, at the beginning of the old Via
Aurelia.

It was the beginning of May, and, what with the starry
sky, and the brilliant moon that lit up everything like
daylight, and the soft air, I did not even feel that I was
doing anything wrong in assaulting an old man: I deluded
myself into thinking the whole thing was a joke. We started
off along the Via Aurelia, between its ancient walls, behind
which are market gardens and the gardens of convents. I

was carrying a spade, in case Marinese refused to let us have his, and I had given Remigio a small iron shovel, just so as to make him do something. I had bought a revolver and a charge of ammunition in the Piazza Vittorio, but I had put down the safety catch: you never know. To tell the truth, I too was feeling elated at the idea of the treasure and I regretted now having spoken of it to Remigio: it meant one share less which I might have had for myself. Besides, I knew he was a chatterbox, and that, if he talked, the game would end in prison. This thought worried me as we walked along between the walls. And so, all at once I stopped, and, pulling out the revolver, which so far I had not shown him, I said: "Now mind, if you talk I'll kill you." "But, Alessandro," he said, trembling all over, "what d'you take me for?" I went on: "We shall have to give some little thing to Marinese, so that he'll have his own interest in the affair and won't report us. . . . That means you'll have to give him something out of your share. . . . Is that understood?" He said yes, and I put the revolver back in its case and we walked on.

A little farther down the road, on the right, there was an ancient gateway, with pillars and a Latin inscription on the pediment. The gates themselves were painted green, and were all faded and broken; and I knew that behind those gates lay Marinese's market garden. I looked up and down the road, and, seeing that there was nobody about, pushed open the gate, which was unfastened, and went in, followed by Remigio.

When I looked at the garden—although I had not come to buy vegetables—I must admit that I almost let forth a cry of admiration. What a garden! In front of us, in the strong white moonlight, lay, in fact, the most beautiful vegetable garden I had ever seen. Glistening irrigation furrows stretched away in long straight lines, as though they had been traced out with a set-square; and between the furrows the vegetable plants, in rows, looked as if they were ascending in procession—playing the fool in the moonlight—towards Marinese's little hut, which could just be seen up at the top of the garden. There were gigantic lettuces, of the kind of which one is enough to fill the greengrocer's scales; splendid tomato-plants, supported on canes, and amongst the leaves tomatoes still green but big enough to burst; cabbages the size of a child's head; onions tall and straight as swords; artichokes, three or four to a plant; and there were endives, peas, beans, other kinds of lettuce—in short, all the vegetables of the season. Here and there, on the ground, as though left for anyone who wished to pick them up, I saw numbers of aubergines and cucumbers. There were also fruit trees, such as plums, peaches, apples, and pears, growing low and thick, full of still unripe fruit peeping out from amongst the leaves in the moonlight. You felt that every plant and tree had an intimate knowledge of the gardener's hand; and that it was not only profit by which that hand was guided. Remigio, who was thinking only of the treasure, asked impatiently: "Where's Marinese?" "Over there," I answered, pointing to the hut at the far end of the garden.

We walked along a little path between a row of garlic and a row of celery. Remigio put his foot on a lettuce, and I said to him: "You clumsy fool, look where you're going." I stooped down and picked a leaf from the lettuce he had trodden on, and put it in my mouth: it was sweet and fleshy and as fresh as though it had been washed in dew. And so we came to the hut; and Marinese's dog, which knew me, instead of barking came to meet me wagging its tail: it was a yellow dog, of the kind that market gardeners always have, but intelligent. I knocked at the closed door of the hut, gently at first, then louder, and finally, when nobody appeared, hammered at it with my fists and feet. His voice made us both jump, coming, as it did, not from inside the hut but from a clump of bushes near by. "Who is it? What d'you want?"

He had a spade in his hand; evidently he was busy in his garden even at night. He came towards us in the moonlight, his arms hanging loosely, his back bent, his face red and his chin bristling with white hairs—a typical gardener whose time, from dawn till sunset, is spent stooping·over his vegetables. I answered him at once: "Friends"; and he replied: "I haven't any friends." Then he came closer and added: "But you—I know you. . . . Aren't you Alessandro?" I told him I was indeed Alessandro; and, pulling the pistol out of my pocket, but without pointing it, I commanded him: "Marinese, tell us where the treasure is. . . . We'll share it between us. . . . But if you won't tell us, we're going to take it just the same." At the same time I raised the pistol, but he put his big hand upon it, as much as to say there was no need for that; then he bent his head and asked, in a thoughtful sort of way: "What treasure d'you mean?" "The silver; the silver that was stolen by the Germans." "But which Germans?" "The soldiers, during the occupation. . . . They stole it from that Prince. . . ." "What Prince?" "Prince—you know; and you said they'd buried it in the garden. . . ." "But what garden?" "Your garden, Marinese. . . . And don't play the fool. You know where it is . . . tell us and be done with it." Then, his head still bowed, he enunciated slowly: "Ah, you mean the treasure?" "Yes, of course, the treasure." "Come along then," he said eagerly: "we'll dig it up at once. Have you a spade? Take this one. . . . Come along and we'll give *him* a spade too. . . . Come on." I was somewhat astonished because I had not expected him to agree so quickly; but I followed him. He went round behind the hut, still muttering: "The treasure. . . . Now you'll see what a fine treasure it is"; and came back with a spade which he handed to Remigio. Then he started off, repeating: "Come along. . . . You want the treasure, and you shall have it."

The stretch of ground behind the hut was not cultivated, but was full of odds and ends and rubbish-heaps. Farther on, there was a row of trees and, behind them, a high wall, similar to the boundary wall of the garden on the side of the Via Aurelia. He took the path that ran along beside the trees, and went right to the farthest point of the garden, where the wall formed an angle. Here he turned suddenly, and, stamping his foot on the ground, said: "Dig here. . . . The treasure is here."

I took my spade and immediately began digging. Remigio, spade in hand, watched me. "You dig too," Marinese said to him; "don't you want any treasure?" Whereupon Remigio threw himself into the digging with such furious violence that Marinese added: "Steady on, take it quietly . . . there's plenty of time." At these words Remigio slackened speed and brought down the spade on his own foot. Marinese took hold of the spade, and turning it in his hands, said to him: "You must hold it like this . . . and each time it goes into the ground, you must press it down with your foot. . . . Otherwise you'll never learn to dig." Then he added: "Dig the same distance each way—about a couple of yards, not more. . . . The treasure's underneath there. . . . In the meantime I'm going to take a look round." "No, you don't," I said; "you stay here." "What are you afraid of?" he answered. "I've told you the treasure is yours."

So we went on digging, first, as best we could, breaking the surface, and then going deeper and deeper down, following the lines of a square which I had marked out with the point of my spade. The soil was hard and dry, and full of stones and roots; I threw the earth to one side, in a heap, and Marinese, who was doing nothing, thrust aside the stones with his foot or gave us advice. "Not so fast. . . . Tear away that root. . . . Take out that stone." Up came a long, black bone, and he took it and said: "It's a beef-bone. . . . You see, you're beginning to find things now." I could not make out whether he was speaking seriously or in jest. In spite of the coolness of the night I was damp with sweat; every now and then I looked at Remigio, and it made me angry to see that he too was panting and toiling zealously. We went on digging for quite a long time, and still nothing appeared: by this time we had made a square hole over three feet deep, and the soil at the bottom of it was moist and crumbling and brown, but there was no sign of any box or sack or other receptacle. All of a sudden I ordered Remigio to stop; and then I climbed out of the hole and said to Marinese: "Now tell me, where *is* this treasure? There's absolutely nothing here, and I believe you've been fooling us."

He took his pipe out of his mouth and answered at once: "You want to see the treasure? All right, I'll show it to you now." This time I did not prevent his going, for I was exhausted and, in my heart of hearts, I had almost ceased to mind about the treasure. I watched him as he went off in the direction of another small hut which I had not noticed before, which was behind the trees, against the boundary wall. "He's running away," said Remigio. "No," I answered, leaning on my spade and wiping the sweat from my brow, "no, he's not running away." And indeed, a moment later Marinese came out of the hut wheeling a barrow brim-full, so it appeared to me, of straw. He went to the hole, upset the straw into it, and then, putting one foot inside, began levelling it down with his hands. I asked hesitatingly: "Well, how about the treasure?" "This is the treasure," he replied; "look how beautiful it is!" And at the same time, taking up a handful of straw, he crumbled the watery, stinking stuff under my nose. "Look!" he said, "isn't it like gold? . . . It's the cow that made it. . . . You see what a treasure; where else will you find a treasure like that? . . . *That's* the treasure. . . ." He was talking to himself, indifferent to our presence; and then, still talking, he came up out of the hole, took the wheelbarrow, went and re-loaded it in the hut, brought it back to the hole and upset it there again. Once more he levelled it with his hands, still repeating: "Now you see the treasure. . . . This is the treasure." I looked at Remigio and Remigio looked at me, and then I plucked up courage and pulled out the revolver again. But Marinese at once brushed it aside as if it had been a mere piece of wood. "Stop it," he said; "none of that. . . . If you want silver, d'you know where you can find it?" "Where?" I asked innocently. "At a shop. . . . If you give them enough thousand-lire notes, you can have as much as you want." He had, in fact, been fooling us all the time. "What about this hole you made us dig?" asked Remigio in a subdued tone. "Why, that's my manure-pit . . . just what I was needing. . . . You've saved me the trouble."

My energy had all fizzled out. I reflected that I ought to threaten him, perhaps even to shoot him, but after all the digging and the disappointment, I felt quite incapable of it. So I said: "There isn't any treasure, then"; almost hoping that Marinese would confirm that it really didn't exist. But he, spiteful old devil that he was, answered: "There is and there isn't." "What d'you mean?" "I mean that, if you'd come in a friendly sort of way, in the day-time, there perhaps might have been . . . but as it is, there isn't." At the same time, taking no further notice of us, he started off towards the hut. I ran after him breathlessly and, taking him by the sleeve, said: "Marinese, for goodness' sake . . ." He half turned and asked: "Why don't you shoot me? Haven't you got a revolver?" "I don't want to shoot," I said. "Let's go halves." "Be honest, now," he said; "you haven't the courage to shoot. . . . You see, you're no good for anything. . . . Anyone else would shoot me. The Germans used to shoot." "But I'm not a German." "Well then, if you're not a German, good-night." With these words, he went into the hut and slammed the door in our faces.

So ended the story of the treasure. The following day, at the usual time, Marinese came into the inn, and, as I brought him his litre of wine, he cried: "Ah, you're the one who was after the treasure. . . . And what have you done with your pistol?" Luckily no one took any notice of this, because, as I said before, he chattered a great deal and most of what he said was nonsense. But, all the same, I did not feel safe; and also I did not like being made a fool of in front of Remigio, who knew all about it and laughed just as if he had not believed in the treasure himself. So I took advantage of an offer I had and went to work in a restaurant in Trastevere, in the Piazza San Cosimato. But Remigio stayed on at San Pancrazio.

The Secret

I

DON'T TALK TO me about secrets! I had one—and it was the kind that weighs on your conscience like a nightmare.

I am a truck driver. One beautiful spring morning, while hauling a load of lava rock from a quarry near Campagnano to Rome, I ran square into a man who was coming in the opposite direction on a motor bike. It was right at the 25 Kilometer marker on the old Cassia road. Through no fault of his, either. I had kept going on the wrong side of the road long after having passed a car, and I was speeding; he was on the right, where he belonged, and going slow. The truck hit him so hard that I barely had time to see something black fly through the blue air and then fall and lie still and black against the soft whiteness of a daisy field. The motor bike lay on the other side of the road, its wheels in the air, like a dead bug.

Lowering my head, I stepped down hard on the gas. I tore down the road to Rome and dropped my load at the yard.

The next day the papers carried the news: So-and-so,

forty-three years old, a jobber by trade, leaving a wife and several children, had been run down at Kilometer 25 of the Cassia road and instantly killed. Nobody knew who had struck him. The hit-and-run driver had fled the scene of the accident like a coward. That's exactly what the paper said: *like a coward*. Except for those three little words that burned a hole in my brain, it didn't take more than four lines to report on what was, after all, only the death of a man.

During the next couple of days, I could think of nothing else. I know that I am only a truck driver, but who can claim that truck drivers have no conscience? A truck driver has a lot of time to mull over his own private business, during the long hours behind the wheel or lying in the truck's sleeping berth. And when, as in my case, that private business is not all it ought to be, thinking can get to be really pretty tough.

One thing in particular kept nagging at me. I just couldn't understand why I hadn't stopped, why I hadn't tried to help the poor guy. I lived the scene over and over again. I would be gauging the distances again before passing that car; I would feel my foot pressing down hard on the accelerator. Then the man's body would come flying up in front of my windshield . . . and at this point I would deliberately block out the picture, as you do at the movies, and I would think, "Now, jam on your brakes, jump down, run into the field, pick him up, put him in the bed of the truck and rush him to Santo Spirito Hospital. . . ."

But, you poor fool, you're just dreaming again. I had *not* stopped, I had driven straight on, with head lowered like a bull after a goring. To make a long story short, the more I thought about that split second when I had stepped on the gas instead of jamming on the brakes, the less I could make it out. Cowardice—that was the word for it all right. But why does a man who has, or at least thinks he has guts, turn into a coward without a moment's warning? That stumped me. Yet the cold hard facts were there: the dead man was really dead; that split second when I might have stopped had passed and was now sinking farther and farther away and no one would ever be able to bring it back. I was no longer the Gino who had passed that car but another Gino who had killed a man and then had run away.

I lay awake nights over it. I grew gloomy and silent and after a while everybody shied away from me at the yard and after work: nobody wants to pass the time with a kill-joy. So I carried my secret around as if it were a hot diamond that you can't entrust to anyone or plant anywhere.

Then, after a while, I began thinking about it less and less and I can even say that there came a time when I didn't think about it at all. But the secret was still stowed away deep down inside me and it weighed on my conscience and kept me from enjoying life. I often thought that I would have felt better if I could have told somebody about it. I wasn't exactly looking for approval—I realized there was no pardon for what I had done—but if I could have told this secret of mine I would have thrown off part of its dead weight onto somebody else who would have helped me carry it. But who could I tell it to? To my friends at the yard? They had other things to worry about. To my family? I had none, being a foundling. My girl friend? She would have been the logical person because, as everybody knows, women are good at understanding you and giving you sympathy when you need it, but unfortunately, I had no girl friend.

II

One Sunday in May I went walking outside the Rome city gates with a girl I had met some time before when I had given her and one of her friends a lift in my truck. She had told me her name and address, and I had seen her again a couple of times. We had enjoyed each other's company, and she had made it clear that she liked me and would be willing to go out with me.

Her name was Iris. She was a lady's maid in the house of some wealthy woman who had lots of servants. I had fallen from the start for her serious little oval face and those great big sad gray eyes of hers. In short, here was just the girl for me in the present circumstances. After we had had a cup of coffee at the Exposition Grounds, with all those columns around us, she finally agreed in her shy, silent, and gentle way to go and sit with me in a meadow not far from St. Paul's Gate, where you get a good view of the Tiber and of the new apartment houses lined up on the opposite bank. She had spread out a handkerchief on the grass to keep her skirt from getting dirty and she sat quietly, her legs tucked under her, her hands in her lap, gazing across at the big white buildings on the other side of the river.

I noticed that there were lots of daisies in the grass around us; and like a flash I remembered the soft whiteness of those other daisies among which, just a month earlier, I had seen lying still and dead the man I had struck down. I don't know what got into me but suddenly I couldn't hold back the urge to tell her my secret. If I tell her, I thought, I'll get rid of the load on my chest. She wasn't one of those dizzy, empty-headed girls who, after you've told them a secret, make you feel so much worse than you did before, that you could kick yourself hard for having spilled all you know. She was a nice, understanding person who had doubtless had her share of knocks in life—and they must have been pretty rough knocks if the sad little look on her face meant anything. Just to break the ice, I said to her, in an offhand way:

"What are you thinking about, Iris?"

She was just raising her hand to choke back a yawn. Perhaps she was tired. She said: "Nothing."

I didn't let that answer get me down but quickly went on. "Iris, you know that I like you a lot, don't you? That's why I feel that I shouldn't hide anything from you. You've got to know everything about me. Iris, I've got a secret."

She kept on looking at the tall buildings on the other side of the river, all the while fingering a little red lump on her chin, a tiny spring pimple.

"What secret?" she asked.

With an effort I got it out: "I've killed a man."

She didn't move but kept on poking gently at her chin. Then she shivered all over, as though she had finally understood. "You've killed a man? And you tell me about it just like that?"

"And how else do you expect me to tell you?"

She said nothing. She seemed to be looking for something on the ground. I went on. "Let's get this thing straight. I didn't mean to kill him."

Suddenly she found what she wanted: picking a long blade of grass, she put it into her mouth and began chewing on it, thoughtfully. Then, hurriedly, but without hiding anything, I told her about the accident, bringing out the part about my cowardice. I got pretty wrought up in spite of myself, but already I was beginning to feel relieved. I concluded:

"Now tell me what you think about all this."

She kept munching on her blade of grass and didn't say a word.

I insisted. "I'll bet that now you can't stand the sight of me."

I saw her shrug her shoulders, lightly. "And why shouldn't I be able to stand the sight of you?"

"Well, I don't know. After all, it was my fault that poor guy got killed."

"And it bothers you?"

"Yes. Terribly." Suddenly, my throat closed tight as if over a hard knot of tears. "I feel as if I can't go on living. No man can go on living if he thinks he's a coward."

"Was it in the papers?"

"Yes. They gave it four lines. Just to say he had been killed and that nobody knew who had hit him."

Suddenly she asked, "What time is it?"

"Five-fifteen."

Another silence. "Listen, Iris, what does a man have to do to find out what's going on in that mind of yours?"

She shifted the blade of grass from one corner of her mouth to the other and said frankly, "Well, if you must know, there's nothing on my mind. I feel good and I'm not thinking about anything."

I couldn't believe my ears. I protested. "It can't be! You must have been thinking something about something. I'm sure of it."

I saw her smile, faintly. "Well, as a matter of fact, I was thinking about something. But if I tell you, you'll never believe it."

Hopefully, I asked, "Was it about me?"

"Good heavens, no! It had absolutely nothing to do with you!"

"What was it, then?"

She said slowly, "It was just one of those things that only women think about. I was looking at my shoes and seeing that they have holes in them. I was thinking that there is a big clearance sale on in Via Cola di Rienzo and that I've got to go there tomorrow and buy myself a pair of new shoes. There . . . are you satisfied?"

This time I shut up like a clam, my face dark and brooding. She noticed it and exclaimed: "Oh, dear! You're not mad, are you?"

I couldn't help blurting out: "Sure, I'm mad. Damn mad. Here I tell you the secret of my life, and it makes so little impression on you I wonder why I didn't keep it to myself!"

This bothered her a bit. "No," she said, "I'm glad you told me about it. It really did make an impression on me."

"Well, what kind of an impression?"

She thought it over and then said, scrupulously, "Well,

I'm sorry that such a thing had to happen to you. It must have been awful!"

"Is that all you've got to say?"

"I also think," she added, fingering the pimple on her chin, "that it's only right it should bother you."

"Why?"

"Well, you said so yourself. You ought to have stopped to help him but you didn't."

"Then you think I am a coward?"

"A coward? Well, yes . . . and then no. After all, a thing like that could happen to anybody."

"But you just said that I ought to have stopped!"

"You should have; but you didn't . . ."

At this point I saw her glance down at something in the daisies. "Oh, look! How pretty!"

It was an insect, a green and gold beetle, resting on the white petals of a daisy. Suddenly I felt as if I were emptied out—almost as if that secret over which I had agonized so long had vanished in the spring air, carried away, lightly, like the white butterflies that were flitting around in pairs in the sunlight.

Yet with one dogged last hope, I asked: "But tell me, Iris, in your opinion, was I right or wrong not to stop?"

"You were right and you were wrong. Of course, you ought to have stopped. After all, you had run into him. But, on the other hand, what good would it have done if you had? He was dead by that time anyway and you would probably have got into a terrible mess. You were both right and wrong."

After these words, a thought flashed through my mind. "This is the end of Iris. I'll never take her out again. I thought she was a bright, understanding girl. Instead, she is really nothing but a half-wit. Enough is enough." I jumped to my feet.

"Come on, let's go," I said. "Otherwise, we'll be late for the movies."

Once inside the theater, in the dark, she slipped her hand

into mine, forcing her fingers through mine. I didn't budge. The film was a love story, a real tear-jerker. When the lights went on at the end I saw that her big gray eyes were filled with tears and that her cheeks were wet. "I just can't help it," she said, patting her face dry with a handkerchief. "Pictures like this always make me want to cry."

Afterwards we went into a bar and ordered coffee. She pressed so close to me that our bodies touched. Just as the *espresso* machine let off a loud stream of steam, she said softly, "You know that I really like you, don't you?" staring at me with those great big beautiful eyes of hers.

I felt like answering: "Fine. You really like me, but you'll let me carry the whole weight of my secret alone!" Instead, I said nothing.

Now I understood that from her, as from everybody else, I could ask only for affection, nothing more than that.

I answered with a sigh, "I like you a lot, too."

But already she had stopped listening to me. She was peering at herself in the mirror behind the bar, absorbed and concerned as she fingered the little red lump on her chin.

Thomas Mann

[1875 — 1955]

THOMAS MANN'S ART flourished in spite of his lifelong conflict
with his bourgeois heritage. Hostile to the materialism, clan-
nishness, snobbery, and philistinism of his fellow burghers, he
still clung to his environment as a much needed balance to his
romantic intoxication with the realm of art. This double perspective he inherited from his father, a grain merchant and
senator of the medieval city of Lübeck; and his mother, of
mixed German-Portuguese stock from Rio de Janeiro, who loved
music and was a striking beauty. Johann Mann intended his son
for his business, which eventually collapsed; Thomas then
worked for a fire insurance company in Munich. But the at-
traction to art was too strong. His elder brother Heinrich was
already a novelist, and Thomas' hatred of his secondary school
education had turned him more ardently to humanistic studies
and to the lectures at the University of Munich. He was now
anxious to emulate other famous German burghers like Wagner
and Goethe. These key images of the artist and the burgher are
best represented in Buddenbrooks (1901) and "Tonio Kröger"
(1903).

The images of sickness and death are also highly significant.
When Thomas was 15, his father died. After one of his sisters
committed suicide, his mother became ill; years later, following
his mother's death, a second sister committed suicide. Mann
suffered another blow when his wife contracted a lung infec-

tion in 1912 and had to spend a good deal of time in sanatoriums. Even the literature and the philosophy of the age heightened Mann's melancholy. The romantic decadence of the 1890s, Schopenhauer's pessimism, Novalis' concept of genius as disease, Goethe's *Weltschmerz*—all these made him so conscious of decay and death that he saw his contemporary culture as a wasteland; at times, however, his understanding of death enhanced his faith in life and its meaning.

Mann's early attitude toward political issues in his country had a dual effect on his writing career. He took politics and Germany's involvement in World War I so seriously that he produced no important fiction between 1911 and 1924. Unproductive creatively, he still developed inwardly, expanding his knowledge of man and society. In the beginning Mann, influenced by Nietzsche, showed an intense nationalism by writing *Reflections of a Non-Political Man* (1918). When the Nazis dominated German politics, he moved away from nationalism, questioned his earlier fears of Europe's domination by England and France, and became sympathetic toward the democracies and an internationalist point of view. He went into exile in 1933, later denouncing Hitler in *Achtung, Europa!* (1938). He came to the United States in 1938 and returned to his homeland in 1952. Mann's political life links with his study of history, culture, psychology, and philosophy to make him one of the most profound writers of his time.

Before he wrote his famous novels and short stories, Mann wrote plays, poems, and critical essays. His first success in fiction came with a romantic-decadent story, "Fallen" (1894), while he was in the employ of the insurance company. He felt that he was really discovered by Oskar Bie, a music critic who, after reading "Little Herr Friedemann" (1897), wanted to see all of his work. Mann was right in claiming that his early fiction, collected as *Stories of Three Decades* (1936), all "wear the impress of much melancholy and ironic reflection on the subject of art and the artist; his isolation and equivocal position in the world of reality, considered socially and metaphysically and as a result of his double bond with nature and spirit." It was in "Tonio Kröger," however, that he "first learned to employ music as a shaping influence" on his art; a good portion of his fiction depends on poetic, musical motifs. Mann may have considered his short stories as relief from his major work—for most of them were written before, during, and after his novels —but they are impressive performances. Somehow he found time for essays (on artists like Tolstoy and Cervantes), which really served as critiques on his creative work.

Writing at a time when naturalism, symbolism, and expressionism were the literary fads, Mann is closely related to the traditional school of storytelling. His work often takes on an epic, biblical quality as he deals with an individual family or with an entire culture. A painstaking craftsman, his novels have a tendency to be too analytical and too intricate, while his short fiction is more direct and less verbose. His introspective intellectual heroes, spiritually sick and troubled by ever present ironies, represent man's doomed life of "sad elegance." Though his vision is essentially tragic, Thomas Mann is a master of parody, having written the greatest comic novel of the twentieth century, Confessions of Felix Krull (1954).

The Infant Prodigy

THE INFANT PRODIGY entered. The hall became quiet.

It became quiet and then the audience began to clap, because somewhere at the side a leader of mobs, a born organizer, clapped first. The audience had heard nothing yet, but they applauded; for a mighty publicity organization had heralded the prodigy and people were already hypnotized, whether they knew it or not.

The prodigy came from behind a splendid screen embroidered with Empire garlands and great conventionalized flowers, and climbed nimbly up the steps to the platform, diving into the applause as into a bath; a little chilly and shivering, but yet as though into a friendly element. He advanced to the edge of the platform and smiled as though he were about to be photographed; he made a shy, charming gesture of greeting, like a little girl.

He was dressed entirely in white silk, which the audience found enchanting. The little white jacket was fancifully cut, with a sash underneath it, and even his shoes were made of white silk. But against the white socks his bare little legs stood out quite brown; for he was a Greek boy.

Reprinted from *Stories of Three Decades* by Thomas Mann, translated by H. T. Lowe-Porter, by permission of Alfred A. Knopf, Inc. Also published by Vintage Books, Inc. Copyright 1931, 1936 by Alfred A. Knopf, Inc.

He was called Bibi Saccellaphylaccas. And such indeed
was his name. No one knew what Bibi was the pet name
for, nobody but the impresario, and he regarded it as a
trade secret. Bibi had smooth black hair reaching to his
shoulders; it was parted on the side and fastened back from
the narrow domed forehead by a little silk bow. His was the
most harmless childish countenance in the world, with an
unfinished nose and guileless mouth. The area beneath his
pitch-black mouselike eyes was already a little tired and
visibly lined. He looked as though he were nine years old
but was really eight and given out for seven. It was hard to
tell whether to believe this or not. Probably everybody knew
better and still believed it, as happens about so many
things. The average man thinks that a little falseness goes
with beauty. Where should we get any excitement out of
our daily life if we were not willing to pretend a bit? And
the average man is quite right, in his average brains!

The prodigy kept on bowing until the applause died
down, then he went up to the grand piano, and the audience cast a last look at its programmes. First came a *Marche
solonnelle*, then a *Rêverie*, and then *Le Hibou et les moineaux*—all by Bibi Saccellaphylaccas. The whole programme
was by him, they were all his compositions. He could not
score them, of course, but he had them all in his extraordinary little head and they possessed real artistic significance, or so it said, seriously and objectively, in the
programme. The programme sounded as though the impresario had wrested these concessions from his critical nature after a hard struggle.

The prodigy sat down upon the revolving stool and felt
with his feet for the pedals, which were raised by means of
a clever device so that Bibi could reach them. It was Bibi's
own piano, he took it everywhere with him. It rested upon
wooden trestles and its polish was somewhat marred by
the constant transportation—but all that only made things
more interesting.

Bibi put his silk-shod feet on the pedals; then he made

an artful little face, looked straight ahead of him, and lifted his right hand. It was a brown, childish little hand; but the wrist was strong and unlike a child's, with well-developed bones.

Bibi made his face for the audience because he was aware that he had to entertain them a little. But he had his own private enjoyment in the thing too, an enjoyment which he could never convey to anybody. It was that prickling delight, that secret shudder of bliss, which ran through him every time he sat at an open piano—it would always be with him. And here was the keyboard again, these seven black and white octaves, among which he had so often lost himself in abysmal and thrilling adventures—and yet it always looked as clean and untouched as a newly washed blackboard. This was the realm of music that lay before him. It lay spread out like an inviting ocean, where he might plunge in and blissfully swim, where he might let himself be borne and carried away, where he might go under in night and storm, yet keep the mastery: control, ordain—he held his right hand poised in the air.

A breathless stillness reigned in the room—the tense moment before the first note came. . . . How would it begin? It began so. And Bibi, with his index finger, fetched the first note out of the piano, a quite unexpectedly powerful first note in the middle register, like a trumpet blast. Others followed, an introduction developed—the audience relaxed.

The concert was held in the palatial hall of a fashionable first-class hotel. The walls were covered with mirrors framed in gilded arabesques, between frescoes of the rosy and fleshly school. Ornamental columns supported a ceiling that displayed a whole universe of electric bulbs, in clusters darting a brilliance far brighter than day and filling the whole space with thin, vibrating golden light. Not a seat was unoccupied, people were standing in the side aisles and at the back. The front seats cost twelve marks; for the impresario believed that anything worth having was worth paying for. And they were occupied by the best society, for it was in the upper classes, of course, that the greatest enthusiasm was felt. There were even some children, with their legs hanging down demurely from their chairs and their shining eyes staring at their gifted little white-clad contemporary.

Down in front on the left side sat the prodigy's mother, an extremely obese woman with a powdered double chin and a feather on her head. Beside her was the impresario, a man of oriental appearance with large gold buttons on his conspicuous cuffs. The princess was in the middle of the front row—a wrinkled, shrivelled little old princess but still a patron of the arts, especially everything full of sensibility. She sat in a deep, velvet-upholstered arm chair, and a Persian carpet was spread before her feet. She held her hands folded over her grey striped-silk breast, put her head on one side, and presented a picture of elegant composure as she sat looking up at the performing prodigy. Next her sat her lady-in-waiting, in a green striped-silk gown. Being only a lady-in-waiting she had to sit up very straight in her chair.

Bibi ended in a grand climax. With what power this wee manikin belaboured the keyboard! The audience could scarcely trust its ears. The march theme, an infectious, swinging tune, broke out once more, fully harmonized, bold and showy; with every note Bibi flung himself back from the waist as though he were marching in a triumphal procession. He ended *fortissimo*, bent over, slipped sideways off the stool, and stood with a smile awaiting the applause.

And the applause burst forth, unanimously, enthusiastically; the child made his demure little maidenly curtsy and people in the front seats thought: "Look what slim little hips he has! Clap, clap! Hurrah, bravo, little chap, Saccophylax or whatever your name is! Wait, let me take off my gloves—what a little devil of a chap he is!"

Bibi had to come out three times from behind the screen before they would stop. Some latecomers entered the hall and moved about looking for seats. Then the concert continued. Bibi's *Rêverie* murmured its numbers, consisting almost entirely of arpeggios, above which a bar of melody rose now and then, weak-winged. Then came *Le Hibou et les moineaux*. This piece was brilliantly successful, it made a strong impression; it was an effective childhood fantasy, remarkably well envisaged. The bass represented the owl, sitting morosely rolling his filmy eyes; while in the treble the impudent, half-frightened sparrows chirped. Bibi received an ovation when he finished, he was called out four times. A hotel page with shiny buttons carried up three great laurel wreaths onto the stage and proffered them from one side while Bibi nodded and expressed his thanks. Even the princess shared in the applause, daintily and noiselessly pressing her palms together.

Ah, the knowing little creature understood how to make people clap! He stopped behind the screen, they had to wait for him; lingered a little on the steps of the platform, admired the long streamers on the wreaths—although actually such things bored him stiff by now. He bowed with the utmost charm, he gave the audience plenty of time to rave itself out, because applause is valuable and must not be cut short. "*Le Hibou* is my drawing card," he thought —this expression he had learned from the impresario. "Now I will play the fantasy, it is a lot better than *Le Hibou*, of course, especially the C-sharp passage. But you idiots dote on the *Hibou*, though it is the first and the silliest thing I wrote." He continued to bow and smile.

Next came a *Méditation* and then an *Étude*—the programme was quite comprehensive. The *Méditation* was very like the *Rêverie*—which was nothing against it—and the *Étude* displayed all of Bibi's virtuosity, which naturally fell a little short of his inventiveness. And then the *Fantaisie*. This was his favourite; he varied it a little each time, giving himself free rein and sometimes surprising even himself, on good evenings, by his own inventiveness.

He sat and played, so little, so white and shining, against

the great black grand piano, elect and alone, above that confused sea of faces, above the heavy, insensitive mass soul,
upon which he was labouring to work with his individual,
differentiated soul. His lock of soft black hair with the
white silk bow had fallen over his forehead, his trained and
bony little wrists pounded away, the muscles stood out
visibly on his brown childish cheeks.

Sitting there he sometimes had moments of oblivion and
solitude, when the gaze of his strange little mouselike eyes
with the big rings beneath them would lose itself and stare
through the painted stage into space that was peopled with
strange vague life. Then out of the corner of his eye he
would give a quick look back into the hall and be once more
with his audience.

"Joy and pain, the heights and the depths—that is my
Fantaisie," he thought lovingly. "Listen, here is the C-sharp
passage." He lingered over the approach, wondering if they
would notice anything. But no, of course not, how should
they? And he cast his eyes up prettily at the ceiling so that
at least they might have something to look at.

All these people sat there in their regular rows, looking at
the prodigy and thinking all sorts of things in their regular
brains. An old gentleman with a white beard, a seal ring on
his finger and a bulbous swelling on his bald spot, a growth
if you like, was thinking to himself: "Really, one ought to
be ashamed." He had never got any further than "Ah, thou
dearest Augustin" on the piano, and here he sat now, a grey
old man, looking on while this little hop-o'-my-thumb performed miracles. Yes, yes, it is a gift of God, we must remember that. God grants His gifts, or He withholds them,
and there is no shame in being an ordinary man. Like with
the Christ Child.—Before a child one may kneel without
feeling ashamed. Strange that thoughts like these should
be so satisfying—he would even say so sweet, if it was not
too silly for a tough old man like him to use the word. That
was how he felt, anyhow.

Art . . . the business man with the parrot-nose was thinking. "Yes, it adds something cheerful to life, a little good white silk and a little tumty-ti-ti-tum. Really he does not play so badly. Fully fifty seats, twelve marks apiece, that makes six hundred marks—and everything else besides. Take off the rent of the hall, the lighting and the programmes, you must have fully a thousand marks profit. That is worth while."

That was Chopin he was just playing, thought the piano teacher, a lady with a pointed nose; she was of an age when the understanding sharpens as the hopes decay. "But not very original—I will say that afterwards, it sounds well. And his hand position is entirely amateur. One must be able to lay a coin on the back of the hand—I would use a ruler on him."

Then there was a young girl, at that self-conscious and chlorotic time of life when the most ineffable ideas come into the mind. She was thinking to herself: "What is it he is playing? It is expressive of passion, yet he is a child. If he kissed me it would be as though my little brother kissed me—no kiss at all. Is there such a thing as passion all by itself, without any earthly object, a sort of child's-play of passion? What nonsense! If I were to say such things aloud they would just be at me with some more cod-liver oil. Such is life."

An officer was leaning against a column. He looked on at Bibi's success and thought: "Yes, you are something and I am something, each in his own way." So he clapped his heels together and paid to the prodigy the respect which he felt to be due to all the powers that be.

Then there was a critic, an elderly man in a shiny black coat and turned-up trousers splashed with mud. He sat in his free seat and thought: "Look at him, this young beggar of a Bibi. As an individual he has still to develop, but as a type he is already quite complete, the artist *par excellence*. He has in himself all the artist's exaltation and his utter worthlessness, his charlatanry and his sacred fire, his burning contempt and his secret raptures. Of course I can't write all that, it is too good. Of course, I should have been an artist myself if I had not seen through the whole business so clearly."

Then the prodigy stopped playing and a perfect storm arose in the hall. He had to come out again and again from behind his screen. The man with the shiny buttons carried up more wreaths: four laurel wreaths, a lyre made of violets, a bouquet of roses. He had not arms enough to convey all these tributes, the impresario himself mounted the stage to help him. He hung a laurel wreath round Bibi's neck, he tenderly stroked the black hair—and suddenly as though overcome he bent down and gave the prodigy a kiss, a resounding kiss, square on the mouth. And then the storm became a hurricane. That kiss ran through the room like an electric shock, it went direct to peoples' marrow and made them shiver down their backs. They were carried away by a helpless compulsion of sheer noise. Loud shouts mingled with the hysterical clapping of hands. Some of Bibi's commonplace little friends down there waved their handkerchiefs. But the critic thought: "Of course that kiss had to come—it's a good old gag. Yes, good Lord, if only one did not see through everything quite so clearly—"

And so the concert drew to a close. It began at half past seven and finished at half past eight. The platform was laden with wreaths and two little pots of flowers stood on the lamp stands of the piano. Bibi played as his last number his *Rhapsodie grecque*, which turned into the Greek national hymn at the end. His fellow-countrymen in the audience would gladly have sung it with him if the company had not been so august. They made up for it with a powerful noise and hullabaloo, a hot-blooded national demonstration. And the aging critic was thinking: "Yes, the hymn had to come too. They have to exploit every vein—publicity cannot afford to neglect any means to its end. I think I'll criticize that as inartistic. But perhaps I am wrong, perhaps that is the most artistic thing of all. What is the artist? A jack-in-the-box. Criticism is on a higher plane. But I can't say that." And away he went in his muddy trousers.

After being called out nine or ten times the prodigy did not come any more from behind the screen but went to his mother and the impresario down in the hall. The audience stood about among the chairs and applauded and pressed forward to see Bibi close at hand. Some of them wanted to see the princess too. Two dense circles formed, one round the prodigy, the other round the princess, and you could actually not tell which of them was receiving more homage. But the court lady was commanded to go over to Bibi; she smoothed down his silk jacket a bit to make it look suitable for a court function, led him by the arm to the princess, and solemnly indicated to him that he was to kiss the royal hand. "How do you do it, child?" asked the princess. "Does it come into your head of itself when you sit down?" "*Oui, madame,*" answered Bibi. To himself he thought: "Oh, what a stupid old princess!" Then he turned round shyly and uncourtierlike and went back to his family.

Outside in the cloak room there was a crowd. People held up their numbers and received with open arms furs, shawls, and galoshes. Somewhere among her acquaintances the piano teacher stood making her critique. "He is not very original," she said audibly and looked about her.

In front of one of the great mirrors an elegant young lady was being arrayed in her evening cloak and fur shoes by her brothers, two lieutenants. She was exquisitely beautiful, with her steel-blue eyes and her clean-cut, well-bred face. A really noble dame. When she was ready she stood waiting for her brothers. "Don't stand so long in front of the glass, Adolf," she said softly to one of them, who could not tear himself away from the sight of his simple, good-looking young features. But Lieutenant Adolf thinks: What cheek! He would button his overcoat in front of the glass, just the same. Then they went out on the street where the arc lights gleamed cloudily through the white mist. Lieutenant Adolf struck up a little nigger dance on the frozen snow to keep warm, with his hands in his slanting overcoat pockets and his collar turned up.

A girl with untidy hair and swinging arms, accompanied by a gloomy-faced youth, came out just behind them. A child! she thought. A charming child. But in there he was an awe-inspiring . . . and aloud in a toneless voice she said: "We are all infant prodigies, we artists."

"Well, bless my soul!" thought the old gentleman who had never got further than Augustin on the piano, and whose boil was now concealed by a top hat. "What does all that mean? She sounds very oracular." But the gloomy youth understood. He nodded his head slowly.

Then they were silent and the untidy-haired girl gazed after the brothers and sister. She rather despised them, but she looked after them until they had turned the corner.

Disorder and Early Sorrow

THE PRINCIPAL DISH at dinner had been croquettes made of turnip greens. So there follows a trifle, concocted out of those dessert powders we use nowadays, that taste like almond soap. Xaver, the youthful manservant, in his outgrown striped jacket, white woollen gloves, and yellow sandals, hands it round, and the "big folk" take this opportunity to remind their father, tactfully, that company is coming today.

The "big folk" are two, Ingrid and Bert. Ingrid is brown-eyed, eighteen, and perfectly delightful. She is on the eve of her exams, and will probably pass them, if only because she knows how to wind masters, and even headmasters, round her finger. She does not, however, mean to use her certificate once she gets it; having leanings towards the stage, on the ground of her ingratiating smile, her equally ingratiating voice, and a marked and irresistible talent for burlesque. Bert is blond and seventeen. He intends to get done with school somehow, anyhow, and fling himself into the arms of life. He will be a dancer, or a cabaret actor, possibly even a waiter—but not a waiter anywhere else save at

Reprinted from *Stories of Three Decades* by Thomas Mann, translated by H. T. Lowe-Porter, by permission of Alfred A. Knopf, Inc. Also published by Vintage Books, Inc. Copyright 1931, 1936 by Alfred A. Knopf, Inc.

the Cairo, the night-club, whither he has once already taken
flight, at five in the morning, and been brought back crest-
fallen. Bert bears a strong resemblance to the youthful manservant, Xaver Kleinsgutl, of about the same age as himself;
not because he looks common—in features he is strikingly
like his father, Professor Cornelius—but by reason of an ap-
proximation of types, due in its turn to far-reaching com-
promises in matters of dress and bearing generally. Both
lads wear their heavy hair very long on top, with a cursory
parting in the middle, and give their heads the same characteristic toss to throw it off the forehead. When one of
them leaves the house, by the garden gate, bareheaded in
all weathers, in a blouse rakishly girt with a leather strap,
and sheers off bent well over with his head on one side; or
else mounts his push-bike—Xaver makes free with his employers', of both sexes, or even, in acutely irresponsible
mood, with the Professor's own—Dr. Cornelius from his
bedroom window cannot, for the life of him, tell whether
he is looking at his son or his servant. Both, he thinks, look
like young moujiks. And both are impassioned cigarette-
smokers, though Bert has not the means to compete with
Xaver, who smokes as many as thirty a day, of a brand
named after a popular cinema star. The big folk call their
father and mother the "old folk"—not behind their backs,
but as a form of address and in all affection: "Hullo, old
folks," they will say; though Cornelius is only forty-seven
years old and his wife eight years younger. And the Professor's parents, who lead in his household the humble and
hesitant life of the really old, are on the big folk's lips the
"ancients." As for the "little folk," Ellie and Snapper, who
take their meals upstairs with blue-faced Ann—so-called
because of her prevailing facial hue—Ellie and Snapper follow their mother's example and address their father by his
first name, Abel. Unutterably comic it sounds, in its pert,
confiding familiarity; particularly on the lips, in the sweet
accents, of five-year-old Eleanor, who is the image of Frau

Cornelius's baby pictures and whom the Professor loves above everything else in the world.

"Darling old thing," says Ingrid affably, laying her large but shapely hand on his, as he presides in proper middle-class style over the family table, with her on his left and the mother opposite: "Parent mine, may I ever so gently jog your memory, for you have probably forgotten: this is the afternoon we were to have our little jollification, our turkey-trot with eats to match. You haven't a thing to do but just bear up and not funk it; everything will be over by nine o'clock."

"Oh—ah!" says Cornelius, his face falling. "Good!" he goes on, and nods his head to show himself in harmony with the inevitable. "I only meant—is this really the day? Thursday, yes. How time flies! Well, what time are they coming?"

"Half past four they'll be dropping in, I should say," answers Ingrid, to whom her brother leaves the major rôle in all dealings with the father. Upstairs, while he is resting, he will hear scarcely anything, and from seven to eight he takes his walk. He can slip out by the terrace if he likes.

"Tut!" says Cornelius deprecatingly, as who should say: "You exaggerate." But Bert puts in: "It's the one evening in the week Wanja doesn't have to play. Any other night he'd have to leave by half past six, which would be painful for all concerned."

Wanja is Ivan Herzl, the celebrated young leading man at the Stadttheater. Bert and Ingrid are on intimate terms with him, they often visit him in his dressing-room and have tea. He is an artist of the modern school, who stands on the stage in strange and, to the Professor's mind, utterly affected dancing attitudes, and shrieks lamentably. To a professor of history, all highly repugnant; but Bert has en-tirely succumbed to Herzl's influence, blackens the lower rim of his eyelids—despite painful but fruitless scenes with the father—and with youthful carelessness of the ancestral anguish declares that not only will he take Herzl for his model if he becomes a dancer, but in case he turns out to be a waiter at the Cairo he means to walk precisely thus.

Cornelius slightly raises his brows and makes his son a little bow—indicative of the unassumingness and self-abnegation that befits his age. You could not call it a mocking bow or suggestive in any special sense. Bert may refer it to himself or equally to his so talented friend.

"Who else is coming?" next inquires the master of the house. They mention various people, names all more or less familiar, from the city, from the suburban colony, from Ingrid's school. They still have some telephoning to do, they say. They have to phone Max. This is Max Hergesell, an engineering student; Ingrid utters his name in the nasal drawl which according to her is the traditional intonation of all the Hergesells. She goes on to parody it in the most abandonedly funny and lifelike way, and the parents laugh until they nearly choke over the wretched trifle. For even in these times when something funny happens people have to laugh.

From time to time the telephone bell rings in the Professor's study, and the big folk run across, knowing it is their affair. Many people had to give up their telephones the last time the price rose, but so far the Corneliuses have been able to keep theirs, just as they have kept their villa, which was built before the war, by dint of the salary Cornelius draws as professor of history—a million marks, and more or less adequate to the chances and changes of postwar life. The house is comfortable, even elegant, though sadly in need of repairs that cannot be made for lack of materials, and at present disfigured by iron stoves with long pipes. Even so, it is still the proper setting of the upper middle class, though they themselves look odd enough in it, with their worn and turned clothing and altered way of life. The children, of course, know nothing else; to them it is normal and regular, they belong by birth to the "villa proletariat." The problem of clothing troubles them not at all. They and their like have evolved a costume to fit the time, by poverty out of taste for innovation: in summer it consists of scarcely more than a belted linen smock and sandals. The middle-class parents find things rather more difficult.

The big folk's table-napkins hang over their chair-backs, they talk with their friends over the telephone. These friends are the invited guests who have rung up to accept or decline or arrange; and the conversation is carried on in the jargon of the clan, full of slang and high spirits, of which the old folk understand hardly a word. These consult together meantime about the hospitality to be offered to the impending guests. The Professor displays a middle-class ambitiousness: he wants to serve a sweet—or something that looks like a sweet—after the Italian salad and brownbread sandwiches. But Frau Cornelius says that would be going too far. The guests would not expect it, she is sure—and the big folk, returning once more to their trifle, agree with her.

The mother of the family is of the same general type as Ingrid, though not so tall. She is languid; the fantastic difficulties of the housekeeping have broken and worn her. She really ought to go and take a cure, but feels incapable; the floor is always swaying under her feet, and everything seems upside down. She speaks of what is uppermost in her mind: the eggs, they simply must be bought today. Six thousand marks apiece they are, and just so many are to be had on this one day of the week at one single shop fifteen minutes' journey away. Whatever else they do, the big folk must go and fetch them immediately after luncheon, with Danny, their neighbour's son, who will soon be calling for them; and Xaver Kleinsgutl will don civilian garb and attend his young master and mistress. For no single household is allowed more than five eggs a week; therefore the young people will enter the shop singly, one after another, under assumed names, and thus wring twenty eggs from the shopkeeper for the Cornelius family. This enterprise is the sporting event of the week for all participants, not excepting the moujik Kleinsgutl, and most of all for Ingrid and Bert, who delight in misleading and mystifying their fellow-men and would revel in the performance even if it did not achieve one single egg. They adore impersonating fictitious characters; they love to sit in a bus and carry on long lifelike conversations in a dialect which they otherwise never speak, the most commonplace dialogue about politics and people and the price of food, while the whole bus listens open-mouthed to this incredibly ordinary prattle, though with a dark suspicion all the while that something is wrong somewhere. The conversation waxes ever more shameless, it enters into revolting detail about these people who do not exist. Ingrid can make her voice sound ever so common and twittering and shrill as she impersonates a shop-girl with an illegitimate child, said child being a son with sadistic tendencies, who lately out in the country treated a cow with such unnatural cruelty that no Christian could have borne to see it. Bert nearly explodes at her twittering, but restrains himself and displays a grisly sympathy; he and the unhappy shop-girl entering into a long, stupid, depraved, and shuddery conversation over the particular morbid cruelty involved; until an old gentleman opposite, sitting with his ticket folded between his index finger and his seal ring, can bear it no more and makes public protest against the nature of the themes these young folk are discussing with such particularity. He uses the Greek plural: "themata." Whereat Ingrid pretends to be dissolving in tears, and Bert behaves as though his wrath against the old gentleman was with difficulty being held in check and would probably burst out before long. He clenches his fists, he gnashes his teeth, he shakes from head to foot; and the unhappy old gentleman, whose intentions had been of the best, hastily leaves the bus at the next stop.

Such are the diversions of the big folk. The telephone plays a prominent part in them: they ring up any and everybody—members of government, opera singers, dignitaries of the Church—in the character of shop assistants, or perhaps as Lord or Lady Doolittle. They are only with difficulty persuaded that they have the wrong number. Once they emptied their parents' card-tray and distributed its contents among the neighbours' letter-boxes, wantonly, yet not without enough impish sense of the fitness of things to make it highly upsetting. God only knowing why certain people should have called where they did.

Xaver comes in to clear away, tossing the hair out of his eyes. Now that he has taken off his gloves you can see the yellow chain-ring on his left hand. And as the Professor finishes his watery eight-thousand-mark beer and lights a cigarette, the little folk can be heard scrambling down the stair, coming, by established custom, for their after-dinner call on Father and Mother. They storm the dining-room, after a struggle with the latch, clutched by both pairs of little hands at once; their clumsy small feet twinkle over the carpet, in red felt slippers with the socks falling down on them. With prattle and shoutings each makes for his own place: Snapper to Mother, to climb on her lap, boast of all he has eaten, and thump his fat little tum; Ellie to her Abel, so much hers because she is so very much his; because she consciously luxuriates in the deep tenderness— like all deep feeling, concealing a melancholy strain—with which he holds her small form embraced; in the love in his eyes as he kisses her little fairy hand or the sweet brow with its delicate tracery of tiny blue veins.

The little folk look like each other, with the strong undefined likeness of brother and sister. In clothing and haircut they are twins. Yet they are sharply distinguished after all, and quite on sex lines. It is a little Adam and a little Eve. Not only is Snapper the sturdier and more compact, he appears consciously to emphasize his four-year-old masculinity in speech, manner, and carriage, lifting his shoulders and letting the little arms hang down quite like a young American athlete, drawing down his mouth when he talks and seeking to give his voice a gruff and forthright ring. But all this masculinity is the result of effort rather than natively his. Born and brought up in these desolate, distracted times, he has been endowed by them with an unstable and hypersensitive nervous system and suffers greatly under life's disharmonies. He is prone to sudden anger and outbursts of bitter tears, stamping his feet at every trifle; for this reason he is his mother's special nursling and care. His round, round eyes are chestnut brown and already inclined to squint, so that he will need glasses in the near future. His little nose is long, the mouth small— the father's nose and mouth they are, more plainly than ever since the Professor shaved his pointed beard and goes smooth-faced. The pointed beard had become impossible— even professors must make some concession to the changing times.

But the little daughter sits on her father's knee, his Eleonorchen, his little Eve, so much more gracious a little being, so much sweeter-faced than her brother—and he holds his cigarette away from her while she fingers his glasses with her dainty wee hands. The lenses are divided for reading and distance, and each day they tease her curiosity afresh.

At bottom he suspects that his wife's partiality may have a firmer basis than his own: that Snapper's refractory masculinity perhaps is solider stuff than his own little girl's more explicit charm and grace. But the heart will not be commanded, that he knows; and once and for all his heart belongs to the little one, as it has since the day she came, since the first time he saw her. Almost always when he holds her in his arms he remembers that first time: remembers the sunny room in the Women's Hospital, where Ellie first saw the light, twelve years after Bert was born. He remembers how he drew near, the mother smiling the while, and cautiously put aside the canopy of the diminutive bed that stood beside the large one. There lay the little miracle among the pillows: so well formed, so encompassed, as it were, with the harmony of sweet proportions, with little hands that even then, though so much tinier, were beautiful as now; with wide-open eyes blue as the sky and brighter than the sunshine—and almost in that very second he felt himself captured and held fast. This was love at first sight, love everlasting: a feeling unknown, unhoped for, unexpected—in so far as it could be a matter of conscious awareness; it took entire possession of him, and he understood, with joyous amazement, that this was for life.

But he understood more. He knows, does Dr. Cornelius, that there is something not quite right about this feeling, so unaware, so undreamed of, so involuntary. He has a shrewd suspicion that it is not by accident it has so utterly mastered him and bound itself up with his existence; that he had—even subconsciously—been preparing for it, or, more precisely, been prepared for it. There is, in short, something in him which at a given moment was ready to issue in such a feeling; and this something, highly extraordinary to relate, is his essence and quality as a professor of history. Dr. Cornelius, however, does not actually say this, even to himself; he merely realizes it, at odd times, and smiles a private smile. He knows that history professors do not love history because it is something that comes to pass, but only because it is something that *has* come to pass; that they hate a revolution like the present one because they feel it is lawless, incoherent, irrelevant—in a word, unhistoric; that their hearts belong to the coherent, disciplined, historic past. For the temper of timelessness, the temper of eternity—thus the scholar communes with himself when he takes his walk by the river before supper —that temper broods over the past; and it is a temper much better suited to the nervous system of a history professor than are the excesses of the present. The past is immortalized; that is to say, it is dead; and death is the root of all godliness and all abiding significance. Dr. Cornelius, walking alone in the dark, has a profound insight into this truth. It is this conservative instinct of his, his

sense of the eternal, that has found in his love for his
little daughter a way to save itself from the wounding
inflicted by the times. For father love, and a little child
on its mother's breast—are not these timeless, and thus
very, very holy and beautiful? Yet Cornelius, pondering
there in the dark, descries something not perfectly right
and good in his love. Theoretically, in the interests of
science, he admits it to himself. There is something ulterior
about it, in the nature of it; that something is hostility,
hostility against the history of today, which is still in the
making and thus not history at all, in behalf of the genuine
history that has already happened—that is to say, death.
Yes, passing strange though all this is, yet it is true; true
in a sense, that is. His devotion to this priceless little morsel
of life and new growth has something to do with death, it
clings to death as against life; and that is neither right nor
beautiful—in a sense. Though only the most fanatical ascet-
icism could be capable, on no other ground than such
casual scientific perception, of tearing this purest and most
precious of feelings out of his heart.

He holds his darling on his lap and her slim rosy legs
hang down. He raises his brows as he talks to her, tenderly,
with a half-teasing note of respect, and listens enchanted
to her high sweet little voice calling him Abel. He exchanges a look with the mother, who is caressing her
Snapper and reading him a gentle lecture. He must be
more reasonable, he must learn self-control; today again,
under the manifold exasperations of life, he has given way
to rage and behaved like a howling dervish. Cornelius casts
a mistrustful glance at the big folk now and then, too; he
thinks it not unlikely they are not unaware of those scientific preoccupations of his evening walks. If such be the
case they do not show it. They stand there leaning their
arms on their chair-backs and with a benevolence not un-
tinctured with irony look on at the parental happiness.

The children's frocks are of a heavy, brick-red stuff, embroidered in modern "arty" style. They once belonged to

Ingrid and Bert and are precisely alike, save that little knickers come out beneath Snapper's smock. And both have their hair bobbed. Snapper's is a streaky blond, inclined to turn dark. It is bristly and sticky and looks for all the world like a droll, badly fitting wig. But Ellie's is chestnut brown, glossy and fine as silk, as pleasing as her whole little personality. It covers her ears—and these ears are not a pair, one of them being the right size, the other distinctly too large. Her father will sometimes uncover this little abnormality and exclaim over it as though he had never noticed it before, which both makes Ellie giggle and covers her with shame. Her eyes are now golden brown, set far apart and with sweet gleams in them—such a clear and lovely look! The brows above are blond; the nose still unformed, with thick nostrils and almost circular holes; the mouth large and expressive, with a beautifully arching and mobile upper lip. When she laughs, dimples come in her cheeks and she shows her teeth like loosely strung pearls. So far she has lost but one tooth, which her father gently twisted out with his handkerchief after it had grown very wobbling. During this small operation she had paled and trembled very much. Her cheeks have the softness proper to her years, but they are not chubby; indeed, they are rather concave, due to her facial structure, with its somewhat prominent jaw. On one, close to the soft fall of her hair, is a downy freckle.

Ellie is not too well pleased with her looks—a sign that already she troubles about such things. Sadly she thinks it is best to admit it once for all, her face is "homely"; though the rest of her, "on the other hand," is not bad at all. She loves expressions like "on the other hand"; they sound choice and grown-up to her, and she likes to string them together, one after the other: "very likely," "probably," "after all." Snapper is self-critical too, though more in the moral sphere: he suffers from remorse for his attacks of rage and considers himself a tremendous sinner. He is quite certain that heaven is not for such as he; he is sure to go to "the bad place" when he dies, and no persuasions will convince him to the contrary—as that God sees the heart and gladly makes allowances. Obstinately he shakes his head, with the comic, crooked little peruke, and vows there is no place for him in heaven. When he has a cold he is immediately quite choked with mucus; rattles and rumbles from top to toe if you even look at him; his temperature flies up at once and he simply puffs. Nursy is pessimistic on the score of his constitution: such fat-blooded children as he might get a stroke any minute. Once she even thought she saw the moment at hand: Snapper had been in one of his berserker rages, and in the ensuing fit of penitence stood himself in the corner with his back to the room. Suddenly Nursy noticed that his face had gone all blue, far bluer, even, than her own. She raised the alarm, crying out that the child's all too rich blood had at length brought him to his final hour; and Snapper, to his vast astonishment, found himself, so far from being rebuked for evil-doing, encompassed in tenderness and anxiety— until it turned out that his colour was not caused by apoplexy but by the distempering on the nursery wall, which had come off on his tear-wet face.

Nursy has come downstairs too, and stands by the door, sleek-haired, owl-eyed, with her hands folded over her white apron, and a severely dignified manner born of her limited intelligence. She is very proud of the care and training she gives her nurslings and declares that they are "enveloping wonderfully." She has had seventeen suppurated teeth lately removed from her jaws and been measured for a set of symmetrical yellow ones in dark rubber gums; these now embellish her peasant face. She is obsessed with the strange conviction that these teeth of hers are the subject of general conversation, that, as it were, the sparrows on the housetops chatter of them. "Everybody knows I've had a false set put in," she will say; "there has been a great deal of foolish talk about them." She is much given to dark hints and veiled innuendo:

speaks, for instance, of a certain Dr. Bleifuss, whom every child knows, and "there are even some in the house who pretend to be him." All one can do with talk like this is charitably to pass it over in silence. But she teaches the children nursery rhymes: gems like:

"Puff, puff, here comes the train!
Puff, puff, toot, toot,
Away it goes again."

Or that gastronomical jingle, so suited, in its sparseness, to the times, and yet seemingly with a blitheness of its own:

"Monday we begin the week,
Tuesday there's a bone to pick.
Wednesday we're half way through,
Thursday what a great to-do!
Friday we eat what fish we're able,
Saturday we dance round the table.
Sunday brings us pork and greens—
Here's a feast for kings and queens!"

Also a certain four-line stanza with a romantic appeal, unutterable and unuttered:

"Open the gate, open the gate
And let the carriage drive in.
Who is it in the carriage sits?
A lordly sir with golden hair."

Or, finally that ballad about golden-haired Marianne who sat on a, sat on a, sat on a stone, and combed out her, combed out her, combed out her hair; and about blood-thirsty Rudolph, who pulled out a, pulled out a, pulled out a knife—and his ensuing direful end. Ellie enunciates all these ballads charmingly, with her mobile little lips, and sings them in her sweet little voice—much better than Snapper. She does everything better than he does, and he pays her honest admiration and homage and obeys her in all things except when visited by one of his attacks. Some-

times she teaches him, instructs him upon the birds in the
picture-book and tells him their proper names: "This is a
chaffinch, Buddy, this is a bullfinch, this is a cowfinch."
He has to repeat them after her. She gives him medical
instruction too, teaches him the names of diseases, such as
infammation of the lungs, infammation of the blood, infammation of the air. If he does not pay attention and cannot say the words after her, she stands him in the corner.
Once she even boxed his ears, but was so ashamed that she
stood herself in the corner for a long time. Yes, they are
fast friends, two souls with but a single thought, and have
all their adventures in common. They come home from a
walk and relate as with one voice that they have seen two
moolies and a teenty-weenty baby calf. They are on familiar
terms with the kitchen, which consists of Xaver and the
ladies Hinterhofer, two sisters once of the lower middle
class who, in these evil days, are reduced to living "au pair"
as the phrase goes and officiating as cook and housemaid for
their board and keep. The little ones have a feeling that
Xaver and the Hinterhofers are on much the same footing
with their father and mother as they are themselves. At
least sometimes, when they have been scolded, they go
downstairs and announce that the master and mistress are
cross. But playing with the servants lacks charm compared
with the joys of playing upstairs. The kitchen could never
rise to the height of the games their father can invent. For
instance, there is "four gentlemen taking a walk." When
they play it Abel will crook his knees until he is the same
height with themselves and go walking with them, hand in
hand. They never get enough of this sport; they could walk
round and round the dining-room a whole day on end, five
gentlemen in all, counting the diminished Abel.

Then there is the thrilling cushion game. One of the
children, usually Ellie, seats herself, unbeknownst to Abel,
in his seat at table. Still as a mouse she awaits his coming.
He draws near with his head in the air, descanting in loud,
clear tones upon the surpassing comfort of his chair; and

sits down on top of Ellie. "What's this, what's this?" says
he. And bounces about, deaf to the smothered giggles ex-
ploding behind him. "Why have they put a cushion in my
chair? And what a queer, hard, awkward-shaped cushion it
is!" he goes on. "Frightfully uncomfortable to sit on!" And
keeps pushing and bouncing about more and more on the
astonishing cushion and clutching behind him into the
rapturous giggling and squeaking, until at last he turns
round, and the game ends with a magnificent climax of
discovery and recognition. They might go through all this
a hundred times without diminishing by an iota its power
to thrill.

Today is no time for such joys. The imminent festivity
disturbs the atmosphere, and besides there is work to be
done, and, above all, the eggs to be got. Ellie has just time
to recite "Puff, puff," and Cornelius to discover that her
ears are not mates, when they are interrupted by the arrival
of Danny, come to fetch Bert and Ingrid. Xaver, meantime,
has exchanged his striped livery for an ordinary coat, in
which he looks rather rough-and-ready, though as brisk
and attractive as ever. So then Nursy and the children
ascend to the upper regions, the Professor withdraws to
his study to read, as always after dinner, and his wife bends
her energies upon the sandwiches and salad that must be
prepared. And she has another errand as well. Before the
young people arrive she has to take her shopping-basket
and dash into town on her bicycle, to turn into provisions
a sum of money she has in hand, which she dares not keep
lest it lose all value.

Cornelius reads, leaning back in his chair, with his cigar
between his middle and index fingers. First he reads Ma-
caulay on the origin of the English public debt at the end
of the seventeenth century; then an article in a French
periodical on the rapid increase in the Spanish debt towards
the end of the sixteenth. Both these for his lecture on the
morrow. He intends to compare the astonishing prosperity
which accompanied the phenomenon in England with its

fatal effects a hundred years earlier in Spain, and to analyse
the ethical and psychological grounds of the difference in
results. For that will give him a chance to refer back from
the England of William III, which is the actual subject in
hand, to the time of Philip II and the Counter-Reformation, which is his own special field. He has already written
a valuable work on this period; it is much cited and got
him his professorship. While his cigar burns down and
gets strong, he excogitates a few pensive sentences in a
key of gentle melancholy, to be delivered before his class
next day: about the practically hopeless struggle carried on
by the belated Philip against the whole trend of history:
against the new, the kingdom-disrupting power of the
Germanic ideal of freedom and individual liberty. And
about the persistent, futile struggle of the aristocracy, condemned by God and rejected of man, against the forces of
progress and change. He savours his sentences; keeps on
polishing them while he puts back the books he has been
using; then goes upstairs for the usual pause in his day's
work, the hour with drawn blinds and closed eyes, which
he so imperatively needs. But today, he recalls, he will rest
under disturbed conditions, amid the bustle of preparations
for the feast. He smiles to find his heart giving a mild flutter
at the thought. Disjointed phrases on the theme of black-
clad Philip and his times mingle with a confused consciousness that they will soon be dancing down below. For five
minutes or so he falls asleep.

As he lies and rests he can hear the sound of the garden
gate and the repeated ringing at the bell. Each time a little
pang goes through him, of excitement and suspense, at the
thought that the young people have begun to fill the floor
below. And each time he smiles at himself again—though
even his smile is slightly nervous, is tinged with the pleasurable anticipations people always feel before a party. At half
past four—it is already dark—he gets up and washes at the
wash-stand. The basin has been out of repair for two years.
It is supposed to tip, but has broken away from its socket

on one side and cannot be mended because there is nobody to mend it; neither replaced because no shop can supply another. So it has to be hung up above the vent and emptied by lifting in both hands and pouring out the water. Cornelius shakes his head over this basin, as he does several times a day—whenever, in fact, he has occasion to use it. He finishes his toilet with care, standing under the ceiling light to polish his glasses till they shine. Then he goes downstairs.

On his way to the dining-room he hears the gramophone already going, and the sound of voices. He puts on a polite, society air; at his tongue's end is the phrase he means to utter: "Pray don't let me disturb you," as he passes directly into the dining-room for his tea. "Pray don't let me disturb you"—it seems to him precisely the *mot juste*; towards the guests cordial and considerate, for himself a very bulwark.

The lower floor is lighted up, all the bulbs in the chandelier are burning save one that has burned out. Cornelius pauses on a lower step and surveys the entrance hall. It looks pleasant and cosy in the bright light, with its copy of Marées over the brick chimney-piece, its wainscoted walls—wainscoted in soft wood—and red-carpeted floor, where the guests stand in groups, chatting, each with his tea-cup and slice of bread-and-butter spread with anchovy paste. There is a festal haze, faint scents of hair and clothing and human breath come to him across the room, it is all characteristic and familiar and highly evocative. The door into the dressing-room is open, guests are still arriving.

A large group of people is rather bewildering at first sight. The Professor takes in only the general scene. He does not see Ingrid, who is standing just at the foot of the steps, in a dark silk frock with a pleated collar falling softly over the shoulders, and bare arms. She smiles up at him, nodding and showing her lovely teeth.

"Rested?" she asks, for his private ear. With a quite unwarranted start he recognizes her, and she presents some of her friends.

"May I introduce Herr Zuber?" she says. "And this is Fräulein Plaichinger."

Herr Zuber is insignificant. But Fräulein Plaichinger is a perfect Germania, blond and voluptuous, arrayed in floating draperies. She has a snub nose, and answers the Professor's salutation in the high, shrill pipe so many stout women have.

"Delighted to meet you," he says. "How nice of you to come! A classmate of Ingrid's, I suppose?"

And Herr Zuber is a golfing partner of Ingrid's. He is in business; he works in his uncle's brewery. Cornelius makes a few jokes about the thinness of the beer and professes to believe that Herr Zuber could easily do something about the quality if he would. "But pray don't let me disturb you," he goes on, and turns towards the dining-room.

"There comes Max," says Ingrid. "Max, you sweep, what do you mean by rolling up at this time of day?" For such is the way they talk to each other, offensively to an older ear; of social forms, of hospitable warmth, there is no faintest trace. They all call each other by their first names.

A young man comes up to them out of the dressing-room and makes his bow; he has an expanse of white shirt-front and a little black string tie. He is as pretty as a picture, dark, with rosy cheeks, clean-shaven of course, but with just a sketch of side-whisker. Not a ridiculous or flashy beauty, not like a gypsy fiddler, but just charming to look at, in a winning, well-bred way, with kind dark eyes. He even wears his dinner-jacket a little awkwardly.

"Please don't scold me, Cornelia," he says; "it's the idiotic lectures." And Ingrid presents him to her father as Herr Hergesell.

Well, and so this is Herr Hergesell. He knows his manners, does Herr Hergesell, and thanks the master of the house quite ingratiatingly for his invitation as they shake hands. "I certainly seem to have missed the bus," says he jocosely. "Of course I have lectures today up to four o'clock;

I would have; and after that I had to go home to change."
Then he talks about his pumps, with which he has just
been struggling in the dressing-room.

"I brought them with me in a bag," he goes on. "Mustn't
tramp all over the carpet in our brogues—it's not done.
Well, I was ass enough not to fetch along a shoe-horn,
and I find I simply can't get in! What a sell! They are the
tightest I've ever had, the numbers don't tell you a thing,
and all the leather today is just cast iron. It's not leather at
all. My poor finger"—he confidingly displays a reddened
digit and once more characterizes the whole thing as a
"sell," and a putrid sell into the bargain. He really does
talk just as Ingrid said he did, with a peculiar nasal drawl,
not affectedly in the least, but merely because that is the
way of all the Hergesells.

Dr. Cornelius says it is very careless of them not to keep
a shoe-horn in the cloak-room and displays proper sympathy with the mangled finger. "But now you *really* must
not let me disturb you any longer," he goes on. "*Auf wie-
dersehen!*" And he crosses the hall into the dining-room.

There are guests there too, drinking tea; the family table
is pulled out. But the Professor goes at once to his own
little upholstered corner with the electric light bulb above
it—the nook where he usually drinks his tea. His wife is
sitting there talking with Bert and two other young men,
one of them Herzl, whom Cornelius knows and greets; the
other a typical "Wandervogel" named Möller, a youth who
obviously neither owns nor cares to own the correct evening dress of the middle classes (in fact, there is no such
thing any more), nor to ape the manners of a gentleman
(and, in fact, there is no such thing any more either). He
has a wilderness of hair, horn spectacles, and a long neck,
and wears golf stockings and a belted blouse. His regular
occupation, the Professor learns, is banking, but he is by
way of being an amateur folk-lorist and collects folk-songs
from all localities and in all languages. He sings them, too,
and at Ingrid's command has brought his guitar; it is hang-

ing in the dressing-room in an oilcloth case. Herzl, the actor, is small and slight, but he has a strong growth of black beard, as you can tell by the thick coat of powder on his cheeks. His eyes are larger than life, with a deep and melancholy glow. He has put on rouge besides the powder—those dull carmine high-lights on the cheeks can be nothing but a cosmetic. "Queer," thinks the Professor. "You would think a man would be one thing or the other—not melancholic and use face paint at the same time. It's a psychological contradiction. How can a melancholy man rouge? But here we have a perfect illustration of the abnormality of the artist soul-form. It can make possible a contradiction like this—perhaps it even consists in the contradiction. All very interesting—and no reason whatever for not being polite to him. Politeness is a primitive convention—and legitimate. . . . Do take some lemon, Herr Hofschauspieler!"

Court actors and court theatres—there are no such things any more, really. But Herzl relishes the sound of the title, notwithstanding he is a revolutionary artist. This must be another contradiction inherent in his soul-form; so, at least, the Professor assumes, and he is probably right. The flattery he is guilty of is a sort of atonement for his previous hard thoughts about the rouge.

"Thank you so much—it's really too good of you, sir," says Herzl, quite embarrassed. He is so overcome that he almost stammers; only his perfect enunciation saves him. His whole bearing towards his hostess and the master of the house is exaggeratedly polite. It is almost as though he had a bad conscience in respect of his rouge; as though an inward compulsion had driven him to put it on, but now, seeing it through the Professor's eyes, he disapproves of it himself, and thinks, by an air of humility towards the whole of unrouged society, to mitigate its effect.

They drink their tea and chat: about Möller's folk-songs, about Basque folk-songs and Spanish folk-songs; from which they pass to the new production of Don Carlos at the Stadttheater, in which Herzl plays the title-rôle. He talks, about his own rendering of the part and says he hopes his conception of the character has unity. They go on to criticize the rest of the cast, the setting, and the production as a whole; and Cornelius is struck, rather painfully, to find the conversation trending towards his own special province, back to Spain and the Counter-Reformation. He has done nothing at all to give it this turn, he is perfectly innocent, and hopes it does not look as though he had sought an occasion to play the professor. He wonders, and falls silent, feeling relieved when the little folk come up to the table. Ellie and Snapper have on their blue velvet Sunday frocks; they are permitted to partake in the festivities up to bed-time. They look shy and large-eyed as they say how-do-you-do to the strangers and, under pressure, repeat their names and ages. Herr Möller does nothing but gaze at them solemnly, but Herzl is simply ravished. He rolls his eyes up to heaven and puts his hands over his mouth; he positively blesses them. It all, no doubt, comes from his heart, but he is so addicted to theatrical methods of making an impression and getting an effect that both words and behaviour ring frightfully false. And even his enthusiasm for the little folk looks too much like part of his general craving to make up for the rouge on his cheeks.

The tea-table has meanwhile emptied of guests, and dancing is going on in the hall. The children run off, the Professor prepares to retire. "Go and enjoy yourselves," he says to Möller and Herzl, who have sprung from their chairs as he rises from his. They shake hands and he withdraws into his study, his peaceful kingdom, where he lets down the blinds, turns on the desk lamp, and sits down to his work.

It is work which can be done, if necessary, under disturbed conditions: nothing but a few letters and a few notes. Of course, Cornelius's mind wanders. Vague impressions float through it: Herr Hergesell's refractory pumps, the high pipe in that plump body of the Plaichinger female. As he writes, or leans back in his chair and stares into space, his thoughts go back to Herr Möller's collection of Basque folk-songs, to Herzl's posings and humility, to "his" Carlos and the court of Philip II. There is something strange, he thinks, about conversations. They are so ductile, they will flow of their own accord in the direction of one's dominating interest. Often and often he has seen this happen. And while he is thinking, he is listening to the sounds next door —rather subdued, he finds them. He hears only voices, no sound of footsteps. The dancers do not glide or circle round the room; they merely walk about over the carpet, which does not hamper their movements in the least. Their way of holding each other is quite different and strange, and they move to the strains of the gramophone, to the weird music of the new world. He concentrates on the music and makes out that it is a jazz-band record, with various percussion instruments and the clack and clatter of castanets, which, however, are not even faintly suggestive of Spain, but merely jazz like the rest. No, not Spain. . . . His thoughts are back at their old round.

Half an hour goes by. It occurs to him it would be no more than friendly to go and contribute a box of cigarettes to the festivities next door. Too bad to ask the young people to smoke their own—though they have probably never thought of it. He goes into the empty dining-room and takes a box from his supply in the cupboard: not the best ones, nor yet the brand he himself prefers, but a certain long, thin kind he is not averse to getting rid of— after all, they are nothing but youngsters. He takes the box into the hall, holds it up with a smile, and deposits it on the mantel-shelf. After which he gives a look round and returns to his own room.

There comes a lull in dance and music. The guests stand about the room in groups or round the table at the window or are seated in a circle by the fireplace. Even the built-in stairs, with their worn velvet carpet, are crowded with young folk as in an amphitheatre: Max Hergesell is there, leaning back with one elbow on the step above and gesticulating with his free hand as he talks to the shrill, voluptuous Plaichinger. The floor of the hall is nearly empty, save just in the centre: there, directly beneath the chandelier, the two little ones in their blue velvet frocks clutch each other in an awkward embrace and twirl silently round and round, oblivious of all else. Cornelius, as he passes, strokes their hair, with a friendly word; it does not distract them from their small solemn preoccupation. But at his own door he turns to glance round and sees young Hergesell push himself off the stair by his elbow—probably because he noticed the Professor. He comes down into the arena, takes Ellie out of her brother's arms, and dances with her himself. It looks very comic, without the music, and he crouches down just as Cornelius does when he goes walking with the four gentlemen, holding the fluttered Ellie as though she were grown up and taking little "shimmying" steps. Everybody watches with huge enjoyment, the gramophone is put on again, dancing becomes general. The Professor stands and looks, with his hand on the door-knob. He nods and laughs; when he finally shuts himself into his study the mechanical smile still lingers on his lips.

Again he turns over pages by his desk lamp, takes notes, attends to a few simple matters. After a while he notices that the guests have forsaken the entrance hall for his wife's drawing-room, into which there is a door from his own study as well. He hears their voices and the sounds of a guitar being tuned. Herr Möller, it seems, is to sing— and does so. He twangs the strings of his instrument and sings in a powerful bass a ballad in a strange tongue, possibly Swedish. The Professor does not succeed in identifying it, though he listens attentively to the end, after which there is great applause. The sound is deadened by the portière that hangs over the dividing door. The young bank-clerk begins another song. Cornelius goes softly in.

It is half-dark in the drawing-room; the only light is from the shaded standard lamp, beneath which Möller sits, on the divan, with his legs crossed, picking his strings. His audience is grouped easily about; as there are not enough seats, some stand, and more, among them many young ladies, are simply sitting on the floor with their hands clasped round their knees or even with their legs stretched out before them. Hergesell sits thus, in his dinner-jacket, next the piano, with Fräulein Plaichinger beside him. Frau Cornelius is holding both children on her lap as she sits in her easy-chair opposite the singer. Snapper, the Bœotian, begins to talk loud and clear in the middle of the song and has to be intimidated with hushings and finger-shakings. Never, never would Ellie allow herself to be guilty of such conduct. She sits there daintily erect and still on her mother's knee. The Professor tries to catch her eye and exchange a private signal with his little girl; but she does not see him. Neither does she seem to be looking at the singer. Her gaze is directed lower down.

Möller sings the "joli tambour":

> "Sire, mon roi, donnez-moi votre
> fille—"

They are all enchanted. "How good!" Hergesell is heard to say, in the odd, nasally condescending Hergesell tone. The next one is a beggar balled, to a tune composed by young Möller himself; it elicits a storm of applause:

> "Gypsy lassie a-goin' to the fair,
> Huzza!
> Gypsy laddie a-goin' to be
> there—
> Huzza, diddlety umpty dido!"

Laughter and high spirits, sheer reckless hilarity, reigns after this jovial ballad. "Frightfully good!" Hergesell comments again, as before. Follows another popular song, this time a Hungarian one; Möller sings it in its own outlandish tongue, and most effectively. The Professor applauds with ostentation. It warms his heart and does him good, this outcropping of artistic, historic, and cultural elements all amongst the shimmying. He goes up to young Möller and congratulates him, talks about the songs and their sources, and Möller promises to lend him a certain annotated book of folk-songs. Cornelius is the more cordial because all the time, as fathers do, he has been comparing the parts and achievements of this young stranger with those of his own son, and being gnawed by envy and chagrin. This young Möller, he is thinking, is a capable bank-clerk (though about Möller's capacity he knows nothing whatever) and has this special gift besides, which must have taken talent and energy to cultivate. "And here is my poor Bert, who knows nothing and can do nothing and thinks of nothing except playing the clown, without even talent for that!" He tries to be just; he tells himself that, after all, Bert has innate refinement; that probably there is a good deal more to him than there is to the successful Möller; that perhaps he has even something of the poet in him, and his dancing and table-waiting are due to mere boyish folly and the distraught times. But paternal envy and pessimism win the upper hand; when Möller begins another song, Dr. Cornelius goes back to his room.

He works as before, with divided attention, at this and that, while it gets on for seven o'clock. Then he remembers a letter he may just as well write, a short letter and not very important, but letter-writing is wonderful for the way it takes up the time, and it is almost half past when he has finished. At half past eight the Italian salad will be served; so now is the prescribed moment for the Professor to go out into the wintry darkness to post his letters and take his daily quantum of fresh air and exercise. They are dancing again, and he will have to pass through the hall to get his hat and coat; but they are used to him now, he need not stop and beg them not to be disturbed. He lays away his papers, takes up the letters he has written, and goes out. But he sees his wife sitting near the door of his room and pauses a little by her easy-chair.

She is watching the dancing. Now and then the big folk or some of their guests stop to speak to her; the party is at its height, and there are more onlookers than these two: blue-faced Ann is standing at the bottom of the stairs, in all the dignity of her limitations. She is waiting for the children, who simply cannot get their fill of these unwonted festivities, and watching over Snapper, lest his all too rich blood be churned to the danger-point by too much twirling round. And not only the nursery but the kitchen takes an interest: Xaver and the two ladies Hinterhofer are standing by the pantry door looking on with relish. Fräulein Walburga, the elder of the two sunken sisters (the culinary section—she objects to being called a cook), is a whimsical, good-natured sort, brown-eyed, wearing glasses with thick circular lenses; the nose-piece is wound with a bit of rag to keep it from pressing on her nose. Fräulein Cecilia is younger, though not so precisely young either. Her bearing is as self-assertive as usual, this being her way of sustaining her dignity as a former member of the middle class. For Fräulein Cecilia feels acutely her descent into the ranks of domestic service. She positively declines to wear a cap or other badge of servitude, and her hardest trial is on the Wednesday evening when she has to serve the dinner while Xaver has his afternoon out. She hands the dishes with averted face and elevated nose—a fallen queen; and so distressing is it to behold her degradation that one evening when the little folk happened to be at table and saw her they both with one accord burst into tears. Such anguish is unknown to young Xaver. He enjoys serving and does it with an ease born of practice as well as talent, for he was once a "piccolo." But otherwise he is a thorough-paced good-for-nothing and windbag—with quite distinct traits of character of his own, as his long-suffering employers are always ready to concede, but perfectly impossible and a bag of wind for all that. One must just take him as he is, they think, and not expect figs from thistles. He is the child and product of the disrupted times, a perfect specimen of his generation, follower of the revolution, Bolshevist sympathizer. The Professor's name for him is the "minuteman," because he is always to be counted on in any sudden crisis, if only it address his sense of humor or love of novelty, and will display therein amazing readiness and resource. But he utterly lacks a sense of duty and can as little be trained to the performance of the daily round and common task as some kinds of dog can be taught to jump over a stick. It goes so plainly against the grain that criticism is disarmed. One becomes resigned. On grounds that appealed to him as unusual and amusing he would be ready to turn out of his bed at any hour of the night. But he simply cannot get up before eight in the morning, he cannot do it, he will not jump over the stick. Yet all day long the evidence of this free and untrammelled existence, the sound of his mouth-organ, his joyous whistle, or his raucous but expressive voice lifted in song, rises to the hearing of the world above-stairs; and the smoke of his cigarettes fills the pantry. While the Hinterhofer ladies work he stands and looks on. Of a morning while the Professor is breakfasting, he tears the leaf off the study calendar—but does not lift a finger to dust the room. Dr. Cornelius has often told him to leave the calendar alone, for he tends to tear off two leaves at a time and thus to add to the general confusion. But young Xaver appears to find joy in this activity, and will not be deprived of it.

Again, he is fond of children, a winning trait. He will throw himself into games with the little folk in the garden, make and mend their toys with great ingenuity, even read aloud from their books—and very droll it sounds in his thick-lipped pronunciation. With his whole soul he loves the cinema; after an evening spent there he inclines to melancholy and yearning and talking to himself. Vague hopes stir in him that some day he may make his fortune in that gay world and belong to it by rights—hopes based on his shock of hair and his physical agility and daring. He likes to climb the ash tree in the front garden, mounting branch by branch to the very top and frightening everybody to death who sees him. Once there he lights a cigarette

and smokes it as he sways to and fro, keeping a look-out
for a cinema director who might chance to come along and
engage him.

If he changed his striped jacket for mufti, he might
easily dance with the others and no one would notice the
difference. For the big folk's friends are rather anomalous
in their clothing: evening dress is worn by a few, but it
is by no means the rule. There is quite a sprinkling of
guests, both male and female, in the same general style
as Möller the ballad-singer. The Professor is familiar with
the circumstances of most of this young generation he is
watching as he stands beside his wife's chair; he has heard
them spoken of by name. They are students at the high
school or at the School of Applied Art; they lead, at least
the masculine portion, that precarious and scrambling existence which is purely the product of the time. There is a
tall, pale, spindling youth, the son of a dentist, who lives
by speculation. From all the Professor hears, he is a perfect
Aladdin. He keeps a car, treats his friends to champagne
suppers, and showers presents upon them on every occasion, costly little trifles in mother-of-pearl and gold. So
today he has brought gifts to the young givers of the feast:
for Bert a gold lead-pencil, and for Ingrid a pair of earrings of barbaric size, great gold circlets that fortunately
do not have to go through the little ear-lobe, but are
fastened over it by means of a clip. The big folk come
laughing to their parents to display these trophies; and the
parents shake their heads even while they admire—Aladdin bowing over and over from afar.

The young people appear to be absorbed in their dancing
—if the performance they are carrying out with so much
still concentration can be called dancing. They stride across
the carpet, slowly, according to some unfathomable pre-
script, strangely embraced; in the newest attitude, tummy
advanced and shoulders high, waggling the hips. They do
not get tired, because nobody could. There is no such thing
as heightened colour or heaving bosoms. Two girls may

dance together or two young men—it is all the same. They move to the exotic strains of the gramophone, played with the loudest needles to procure the maximum of sound: shimmies, foxtrots, one-steps, double foxes, African shimmies, Java dances, and Creole polkas, the wild musky melodies follow one another, now furious, now languishing, a monotonous Negro programme in unfamiliar rhythm, to a clacking, clashing, and strumming orchestral accompaniment.

"What is that record?" Cornelius inquires of Ingrid, as she passes him by in the arms of the pale young speculator, with reference to the piece then playing, whose alternate languors and furies he finds comparatively pleasing and showing a certain resourcefulness in detail.

"*Prince of Pappenheim*: 'Console thee, dearest child,' " she answers, and smiles pleasantly back at him with her white teeth.

The cigarette smoke wreathes beneath the chandelier. The air is blue with a festal haze compact of sweet and thrilling ingredients that stir the blood with memories of green-sick pains and are particularly poignant to those whose youth—like the Professor's own—has been oversensitive. . . . The little folk are still on the floor. They are allowed to stop up until eight, so great is their delight in the party. The guests have got used to their presence; in their own way, they have their place in the doings of the evening. They have separated, anyhow: Snapper revolves all alone in the middle of the carpet, in his little blue velvet smock, while Ellie is running after one of the dancing couples, trying to hold the man fast by his coat. It is Max Hergesell and Fräulein Plaichinger. They dance well, it is a pleasure to watch them. One has to admit that these mad modern dances, when the right people dance them, are not so bad after all—they have something quite taking. Young Hergesell is a capital leader, dances according to rule, yet with individuality. So it looks. With what aplomb can he walk backwards—when space permits! And he knows

how to be graceful standing still in a crowd. And his partner supports him well, being unsuspectedly lithe and buoyant, as fat people often are. They look at each other, they
are talking, paying no heed to Ellie, though others are smiling to see the child's persistence. Dr. Cornelius tries to
catch up his little sweetheart as she passes and draw her to
him. But Ellie eludes him, almost peevishly; her dear Abel
is nothing to her now. She braces her little arms against his
chest and turns her face away with a persecuted look. Then
escapes to follow her fancy once more.

The Professor feels an involuntary twinge. Uppermost
in his heart is hatred for this party, with its power to in-
toxicate and estrange his darling child. His love for her—
that not quite disinterested, not quite unexceptionable love
of his—is easily wounded. He wears a mechanical smile,
but his eyes have clouded, and he stares fixedly at a point
in the carpet, between the dancers' feet.

"The children ought to go to bed," he tells his wife. But
she pleads for another quarter of an hour; she has promised
already, and they do love it so! He smiles again and shakes
his head, stands so a moment and then goes across to the
cloak-room, which is full of coats and hats and scarves and
overshoes. He has trouble in rummaging out his own coat,
and Max Hergesell comes out of the hall, wiping his brow.

"Going out, sir?" he asks, in Hergesellian accents, dutifully helping the older man on with his coat. "Silly business
this, with my pumps," he says. "They pinch like hell. The
brutes are simply too tight for me, quite apart from the
bad leather. They press just here on the ball of my great
toe"—he stands on one foot and holds the other in his
hand—"it's simply unbearable. There's nothing for it but
to take them off; my brogues will have to do the business.
. . . Oh, let me help you, sir."

"Thanks," says Cornelius. "Don't trouble. Get rid of
your own tormentors. . . . Oh, thanks very much!" For
Hergesell has gone on one knee to snap the fasteners of his
snow-boots.

Once more the Professor expresses his gratitude; he is pleased and touched by so much sincere respect and youthful readiness to serve. "Go and enjoy yourself," he counsels. "Change your shoes and make up for what you have been suffering. Nobody can dance in shoes that pinch. Good-bye, I must be off to get a breath of fresh air."

"I'm going to dance with Ellie now," calls Hergesell after him. "She'll be a first-rate dancer when she grows up, and that I'll swear to."

"Think so?" Cornelius answers, already half out. "Well, you are a connoisseur, I'm sure. Don't get curvature of the spine with stooping."

He nods again and goes. "Fine lad," he thinks as he shuts the door. "Student of engineering. Knows what he's bound for, got a good clear head, and so well set up and pleasant too." And again paternal envy rises as he compares his poor Bert's status with this young man's, which he puts in the rosiest light that his son's may look the darker. Thus he sets out on his evening walk.

He goes up the avenue, crosses the bridge, and walks along the bank on the other side as far as the next bridge but one. The air is wet and cold, with a little snow now and then. He turns up his coat-collar and slips the crook of his cane over the arm behind his back. Now and then he ventilates his lungs with a long deep breath of the night air. As usual when he walks, his mind reverts to his professional preoccupations, he thinks about his lectures and the things he means to say tomorrow about Philip's struggle against the Germanic revolution, things steeped in melancholy and penetratingly just. Above all just, he thinks. For in one's dealings with the young it behoves one to display the scientific spirit, to exhibit the principles of enlightenment—not only for purposes of mental discipline, but on the human and individual side, in order not to wound them or indirectly offend their political sensibilities; particularly in these days, when there is so much tinder in the air, opinions are so frightfully split up and chaotic, and you may so easily incur attacks from one party or the other, or even give rise to scandal, by taking sides on a point of history. "And taking sides is unhistoric anyhow," so he muses. "Only justice, only impartiality is historic." And could not, properly considered, be otherwise. . . . For justice can have nothing of youthful fire and blithe, fresh, loyal conviction. It is by nature melancholy. And, being so, has secret affinity with the lost cause and the forlorn hope rather than with the fresh and blithe and loyal—perhaps this affinity is its very essence and without it it would not exist at all! . . . "And is there then no such thing as justice?" the Professor asks himself, and ponders the question so deeply that he absently posts his letters in the next box and turns round to go home. This thought of his is unsettling and disturbing to the scientific mind—but is it not after all itself scientific, psychological, conscientious, and therefore to be accepted without prejudice, no matter how upsetting? In the midst of which musings Dr. Cornelius finds himself back at his own door.

On the outer threshold stands Xaver, and seems to be looking for him.

"Herr Professor," says Xaver, tossing back his hair, "go upstairs to Ellie straight off. She's in a bad way."

"What's the matter?" asks Cornelius in alarm. "Is she ill?"

"No-o, not to say ill," answers Xaver. "She's just in a bad way and crying fit to bust her little heart. It's along o' that chap with the shirt-front that danced with her—Herr Hergesell. She couldn't be got to go upstairs peaceably, not at no price at all, and she's b'en crying bucketfuls."

"Nonsense," says the Professor, who has entered and is tossing off his things in the cloak-room. He says no more; opens the glass door and without a glance at the guests turns swiftly to the stairs. Takes them two at a time, crosses the upper hall and the small room leading into the nursery. Xaver follows at his heels, but stops at the nursery door.

A bright light still burns within, showing the gay frieze

that runs all round the room, the large row of shelves heaped with a confusion of toys, the rocking-horse on his swaying platform, with red-varnished nostrils and raised hoofs. On the linoleum lie other toys—building blocks, railway trains, a little trumpet. The two white cribs stand not far apart, Ellie's in the window corner, Snapper's out in the room.

Snapper is asleep. He has said his prayers in loud, ringing tones, prompted by Nurse, and gone off at once into vehement, profound, and rosy slumber—from which a cannon-ball fired at close range could not rouse him. He lies with both fists flung back on the pillows on either side of the tousled head with its funny crooked little slumber-tossed wig.

A circle of females surrounds Ellie's bed: not only blue-faced Ann is there, but the Hinterhofer ladies too, talking to each other and to her. They make way as the Professor comes up and reveal the child sitting all pale among her pillows, sobbing and weeping more bitterly than he has ever seen her sob and weep in her life. Her lovely little hands lie on the coverlet in front of her, the nightgown with its narrow lace border has slipped down from her shoulder—such a thin, birdlike little shoulder—and the sweet head Cornelius loves so well, set on the neck like a flower on its stalk, her head is on one side, with the eyes rolled up to the corner between wall and ceiling above her head. For there she seems to envisage the anguish of her heart and even to nod to it—either on purpose or because her head wobbles as her body is shaken with the violence of her sobs. Her eyes rain down tears. The bow-shaped lips are parted, like a little *mater dolorosa's*, and from them issue long, low wails that in nothing resemble the unnecessary and exasperating shrieks of a naughty child, but rise from the deep extremity of her heart and wake in the Professor's own a sympathy that is well-nigh intolerable. He has never seen his darling so before. His feelings find immediate vent in an attack on the ladies Hinterhofer.

"What about the supper?" he asks sharply. "There must be a great deal to do. Is my wife being left to do it alone?"

For the acute sensibilities of the former middle class this is quite enough. The ladies withdraw in righteous indignation, and Xaver Kleingutl jeers at them as they pass out. Having been born to low life instead of achieving it, he never loses a chance to mock at their fallen state.

"Childie, childie," murmurs Cornelius, and sitting down by the crib enfolds the anguished Ellie in his arms. "What is the trouble with my darling?"

She bedews his face with her tears.

"Abel . . . Abel . . ." she stammers between sobs. "Why—isn't Max—my brother? Max ought to be—my brother!"

Alas, alas! What mischance is this? Is this what the party has wrought, with its fatal atmosphere? Cornelius glances helplessly up at blue-faced Ann standing there in all the dignity of her limitations with her hands before her on her apron. She purses up her mouth and makes a long face. "It's pretty young," she says, "for the female instincts to be showing up."

"Hold your tongue," snaps Cornelius, in his agony. He has this much to be thankful for, that Ellie does not turn from him now; she does not push him away as she did downstairs, but clings to him in her need, while she reiterates her absurd, bewildered prayer that Max might be her brother, or with a fresh burst of desire demands to be taken downstairs so that he can dance with her again. But Max, of course, is dancing with Fräulein Plaichinger, that behemoth who is his rightful partner and has every claim upon him; whereas Ellie—never, thinks the Professor, his heart torn with the violence of his pity, never has she looked so tiny and birdlike as now, when she nestles to him shaken with sobs and all unaware of what is happening in her little soul. No, she does not know. She does not comprehend that her suffering is on account of Fräulein Plaichinger, fat, overgrown, and utterly within her rights in dancing with Max Hergesell, whereas Ellie may only do it once, by way of a joke, although she is incomparably the more charming of the two. Yet it would be quite mad to reproach young Hergesell with the state of affairs or to make fantastic demands upon him. No, Ellie's suffering is without help or healing and must be covered up. Yet just as it is without understanding, so it is also without restraint—and that is what makes it so horribly painful. Xaver and blue-faced Ann do not feel this pain, it does not affect them—either because of native callousness or because they accept it as the way of nature. But the Professor's fatherly heart is quite torn by it, and by a distressful horror of this passion, so hopeless and so absurd.

Of no avail to hold forth to poor Ellie on the subject of the perfectly good little brother she already has. She only casts a distraught and scornful glance over at the other crib, where Snapper lies vehemently slumbering, and with fresh tears calls again for Max. Of no avail either the promise of a long, long walk tomorrow, all five gentlemen, round and round the dining-room table; or a dramatic description of the thrilling cushion games they will play. No, she will listen to none of all this, nor to lying down and going to sleep. She will not sleep, she will sit bolt upright and suffer. . . . But on a sudden they stop and listen, Abel and Ellie; listen to something miraculous that is coming to pass, that is approaching by strides, two strides, to the nursery door, that now overwhelmingly appears. . . .

It is Xaver's work, not a doubt of that. He has not remained by the door where he stood to gloat over the ejection of the Hinterhofers. No, he has bestirred himself, taken a notion; likewise steps to carry it out. Downstairs he has gone, twitched Herr Hergesell's sleeve, and made a thick-lipped request. So here they both are. Xaver, having done his part, remains by the door; but Max Hergesell comes up to Ellie's crib; in his dinner-jacket, with his

sketchy side-whisker and charming black eyes; obviously
quite pleased with his rôle of swan knight and fairy prince,
as one who should say: "See, here am I, now all losses are
restored and sorrows end!"

Cornelius is almost as much overcome as Ellie herself.
"Just look," he says feebly, "look who's here. This is un-
commonly good of you, Herr Hergesell."

"Not a bit of it," says Hergesell. "Why shouldn't I come
to say good-night to my fair partner?"

And he approaches the bars of the crib, behind which
Ellie sits struck mute. She smiles blissfully through her
tears. A funny, high little note that is half a sigh of relief
comes from her lips, then she looks dumbly up at her swan
knight with her golden-brown eyes—tear-swollen though
they are, so much more beautiful than the fat Plaichinger's.
She does not put up her arms. Her joy, like her grief, is
without understanding; but she does not do that. The
lovely little hands lie quiet on the coverlet, and Max Hergesell stands with his arms leaning over the rail as on a
balcony.

"And now," he says smartly, "she need not 'sit the live-
long night and weep upon her bed'!" He looks at the Professor to make sure he is receiving due credit for the
quotation. "Ha ha!" he laughs, "she's beginning young.
'Console thee, dearest child!' Never mind, you're all right!
Just as you are you'll be wonderful! You've only got to grow
up. . . . And you'll lie down and go to sleep like a good
girl, now I've come to say good-night? And not cry any
more, little Lorelei?"

Ellie looks up at him, transfigured. One birdlike shoulder
is bare; the Professor draws the lace-trimmed nighty over
it. There comes into his mind a sentimental story he once
read about a dying child who longs to see a clown he had
once, with unforgettable ecstasy, beheld in a circus. And
they bring the clown to the bedside marvellously arrayed,
embroidered before and behind with silver butterflies; and
the child dies happy. Max Hergesell is not embroidered,

and Ellie, thank God, is not going to die, she has only been "in a bad way." But, after all, the effect is the same. Young Hergesell leans over the bars of the crib and rattles on, more for the father's ear than the child's, but Ellie does not know that—and the father's feelings towards him are a most singular mixture of thankfulness, embarrassment, and hatred.

"Good night, little Lorelei," says Hergesell, and gives her his hand through the bars. Her pretty, soft, white little hand is swallowed up in the grasp of his big, strong, red one. "Sleep well," he says, "and sweet dreams! But don't dream about me—God forbid! Not at your age—ha ha!" And then the fairy clown's visit is at an end. Cornelius accompanies him to the door. "No, no, positively, no thanks called for, don't mention it," he large-heartedly protests; and Xaver goes downstairs with him, to help serve the Italian salad.

But Dr. Cornelius returns to Ellie, who is now lying down, with her cheek pressed into her flat little pillow. "Well, wasn't that lovely?" he says as he smooths the covers. She nods, with one last little sob. For a quarter of an hour he sits beside her and watches while she falls asleep in her turn, beside the little brother who found the right way so much earlier than she. Her silky brown hair takes the enchanting fall it always does when she sleeps; deep, deep lie the lashes over the eyes that late so abundantly poured forth their sorrow; the angelic mouth with its bowed upper lip is peacefully relaxed and a little open. Only now and then comes a belated catch in her slow breathing.

And her small hands, like pink and white flowers, lie so quietly, one on the coverlet, the other on the pillow by her face—Dr. Cornelius, gazing, feels his heart melt with tenderness as with strong wine.

"How good," he thinks, "that she breathes in oblivion with every breath she draws! That in childhood each night is a deep wide gulf between one day and the next. Tomorrow, beyond all doubt, young Hergesell will be a pale shadow, powerless to darken her little heart. Tomorrow, forgetful of all but present joy, she will walk with Abel and Snapper, all five gentlemen, round and round the table. will play the ever-thrilling cushion game."

Heaven be praised for that!

Franz Kafka

[1883–1924]

THE STORIES OF Franz Kafka walk that invisible tightrope which barely separates comedy and tragedy, man and his image of God. Only someone with the complex insight and indecisions of a Kafka could laugh, as he often did, while reading *The Trial* to his friends.

Kafka was an outsider for many reasons: he was born to a Jewish minority in Prague, years before Czechoslovakia gained national independence from the Austrian empire. He felt little attachment for his father's successful business firm (their dry-goods warehouse was just down the street from their home). Even his admiration for his father as a figure of family authority and awesome sufficiency, so great that a tender closeness or mutual understanding seemed unattainable, contributed to Franz' "earthweight." Love alternated with a rebelliousness which relieved him temporarily of that guilt and humiliation he suffered by comparison with his father. The recurring motif of man's failure to deserve any measure of recognition from the God he admires, as well as the preponderance of paradoxes and unexpected reversals which complicate a style deceptively transparent, seem more comprehensible in those terms with which Kafka himself described his writings. Thinking of the abyss between himself and his father, he called his work "a farewell deliberately drawn out."

In 1906, Kafka received his doctorate in jurisprudence at

413

the University of Prague. Two years later he was employed by
the Workers' Accident Insurance Institute, making claims for
mutilated laborers under the country's compensation laws. Once
he exclaimed to Max Brod, his close friend and, afterwards,
his biographer, "How modest these people are! Instead of storming the building and smashing everything to bits, they come to
us and plead!" Their ills added to his own, psychically and
physically; so that he sought relief in his paper work, which
often required long, detailed descriptions of the machinery involved in factory accidents—reminiscent of mechanical devices
for inscribing guilt on the human body in "The Penal Colony."
Such technical processes seem to have been as influential on
his style as the rich simplicity of Scriptures.

In the autumn of 1912, he became engaged in Berlin; but
although he had a sincere longing for family life, he wavered.
He drew up an account sheet of arguments for and against marriage (for example, he felt that, as a bachelor, some day he
would have sufficient savings to be able to stop work and become another Mann or Flaubert, whose writings he admired
as antidotes to romanticism). The engagement was broken after
a month. At once, and in one sitting, he wrote "The Judgment." As if to prove a kinship between himself and his servile
characters, he acknowledged that "Georg" and "Franz" have an
equal number of letters and that "Bende(mann)" and "Kafka"
have identical vowel arrangements. Such cryptic subtleties apparently were tokens, for him, that behind the mysterious dis-
order of the cosmos some cabalistic rationale existed. Within
the next two months he found further personal relief by starting Amerika and "The Metamorphosis."

His America is not a portrait of the country which he never
saw, but rather a fantasy of everything desirable which his self-
doubts had ever forbidden him. The divided self in "The Judgment" is far more typical of the author's torment, if Georg and
his friend in Russia are interpreted not as separate characters,
but as antagonistic inclinations within Kafka (or in Anyman):
his longing for love and acceptance; his imperative need for
loneliness as a condition of his art. The change from complaint to self-incrimination is as abrupt, but nevertheless as inevitable, as the reduction of Gregor to vermin in "The

Metamorphosis." The implied verdict in both resembles the confessional aspect of Kafka's book-length "Letter to My Father," which he wrote in 1919.

Nevertheless, whatever origins his inadequacies may have had in his relationship with his father, what his writings ultimately imply about man's place in the cosmos impersonalizes and universalizes Kafka's premonitions. Max Brod once said: "If the angels made jokes in heaven, it would have to be in Franz Kafka's language." Kafka knew intimately the early theories of Sigmund Freud who, for a time, lived in his neighborhood. But he rejected any suggestion that spiritual torment is a nervous disease. Perhaps his reading of the agonizing Danish philosopher Kierkegaard in 1913 was crucial, because within the following year he completed "The Penal Colony" and started *The Trial*. His submission to divine decree, however inscrutable or seemingly absurd, is clear in his fiction as surely as in his diaries. Although Kafka once complained wryly that God must have created man on a bad day, he also insisted that "writing is a form of prayer." *The Trial*, in which K. is executed for unknown crimes, has been compared with the Book of Job if nothing were ever restored to the victimized; *The Castle*, with *Pilgrim's Progress* if the pilgrim were outrageously degraded by those who had summoned him.

Regardless, the God-ache continues; and, far from despairing, the writer laughs tears of compassion, while suspending judgment of "what may remain permanently concealed. . . ." The artist, in "The Hunger Artist," is regarded by society as a semicomic performer only; but he does not presume to judge them in return. Max Brod held the opinion that Kafka "of all believers was the freest from illusions, and among all those who see the world as it is, without illusion, he was the most unshakable believer." His art of fiction accepts and uses to its own ends that suspension of rational laws—the dream as frightful, even casual reality—which he encountered everywhere.

In 1917, Kafka coughed blood; but began *The Castle* while resting on his brother-in-law's estate. Finally, during the desperate postwar months of 1924, he was taken to a Vienna clinic with his larynx so painfully riddled by disease that, during his last days, he could take only secondhand pleasure in food and drink, through others. His death left many stories still in fragmentary form.

Max Brod's refusal to honor Kafka's request that his writings be destroyed was the kind of contrary act that Kafka above all would have understood and, probably, commended.

The Judgment

IT WAS A Sunday morning in the very height of spring. Georg Bendemann, a young merchant, was sitting in his own room on the first floor of one of a long row of small, ramshackle houses stretching beside the river which were scarcely distinguishable from each other except in height and coloring. He had just finished a letter to an old friend of his who was now living abroad, had put it into its envelope in a slow and dreamy fashion, and with his elbows propped on the writing table was gazing out of the window at the river, the bridge and the hills on the farther bank with their tender green.

He was thinking about his friend, who had actually run away to Russia some years before, being dissatisfied with his prospects at home. Now he was carrying on a business in St. Petersburg, which had flourished to begin with but had long been going downhill, as he always complained on his increasingly rare visits. So he was wearing himself out to no purpose in a foreign country; the unfamiliar full beard he wore did not quite conceal the face Georg had known so well since childhood, and his skin was growing so yellow as to indicate some latent disease. By his own account he had no regular connection with the colony of his fellow countrymen out there and almost no social intercourse with Russian families, so that he was resigning himself to becoming a permanent bachelor.

What could one write to such a man, who had obviously run off the rails, a man one could be sorry for but could not help? Should one advise him to come home, to transplant himself and take up his old friendships again—there was nothing to hinder him—and in general to rely on the help of his friends? But that was as good as telling him, and the more kindly the more offensively, that all his efforts hitherto had miscarried, that he should finally give up, come back home, and be gaped at by everyone as a returned prodigal, that only his friends knew what was what and that he himself was just a big child who should do what his successful and home-keeping friends prescribed. And was it certain, besides, that all the pain one would have to inflict on him would achieve its object? Perhaps it would not even be possible to get him to come home at all—he said himself that he was now out of touch with commerce in his native country—and then he would still be left an alien in a foreign land embittered by his friends' advice and more than ever estranged from them. But if he did follow their advice and then didn't fit in at home—not out of malice, of course, but through force of circumstances —couldn't get on with his friends or without them, felt humiliated, couldn't be said to have either friends or a country of his own any longer, wouldn't it have been better for him to stay abroad just as he was? Taking all this into account, how could one be sure that he would make a success of life at home?

For such reasons, supposing one wanted to keep up correspondence with him, one could not send him any real news such as could frankly be told to the most distant acquaintance. It was more than three years since his last visit, and for this he offered the lame excuse that the political situation in Russia was too uncertain, which apparently would not permit even the briefest absence of a small business man while it allowed hundreds of thousands of Russians to travel peacefully abroad. But during these three years Georg's own position in life had changed a lot. Two years ago his mother had died, since when he and his father had shared the household together, and his friend had of course been informed of that and had expressed his sympathy in a letter phrased so dryly that the grief caused by such an event, one had to conclude, could not be realized in a distant country. Since that time, however, Georg had applied himself with greater determination to the business as well as to everything else.

Perhaps during his mother's lifetime his father's insistence on having everything his own way in the business had hindered him from developing any real activity of his own, perhaps since her death his father had become less aggressive, although he was still active in the business, perhaps it was mostly due to an accidental run of good fortune—which was very probable indeed—but at any rate during those two years the business had developed in a most unexpected way, the staff had had to be doubled, the turnover was five times as great, no doubt about it, further progress lay just ahead.

But Georg's friend had no inkling of this improvement. In earlier years, perhaps for the last time in that letter of condolence, he had tried to persuade Georg to emigrate to Russia and had enlarged upon the prospects of success for precisely Georg's branch of trade. The figures quoted were microscopic by comparison with the range of Georg's present operations. Yet he shrank from letting his friend know about his business success, and if he were to do it now retrospectively that certainly would look peculiar.

So Georg confined himself to giving his friend unimportant items of gossip such as rise at random in the memory when one is idly thinking things over on a quiet Sunday. All he desired was to leave undisturbed the idea of the home town which his friend must have built up to his own

content during the long interval. And so it happened to
Georg that three times in three fairly widely separated letters he had told his friend about the engagement of an unimportant man to an equally unimportant girl, until indeed,
quite contrary to his intentions, his friend began to show
some interest in this notable event.

Yet Georg preferred to write about things like these
rather than to confess that he himself had got engaged a
month ago to a Fräulein Frieda Brandenfeld, a girl from
a well-to-do family. He often discussed this friend of his
with his fiancée and the peculiar relationship that had developed between them in their correspondence. "So he
won't be coming to our wedding," said she, "and yet I have
a right to get to know all your friends." "I don't want to
trouble him," answered Georg. "Don't misunderstand me,
he would probably come, at least I think so, but he would
feel that his hand had been forced and he would be hurt,
perhaps he would envy me and certainly he'd be discon-
tented and without being able to do anything about his
discontent he'd have to go away again alone. Alone—do you
know what that means?" "Yes, but may he not hear about
our wedding in some other fashion?" "I can't prevent that,
of course, but it's unlikely, considering the way he lives."
"Since your friends are like that, Georg, you shouldn't ever
have got engaged at all." "Well, we're both to blame for
that; but I wouldn't have it any other way now." And when,
breathing quickly under his kisses, she still brought out:
"All the same, I do feel upset," he thought it could not
really involve him in trouble were he to send the news to
his friend. "That's the kind of man I am and he'll just
have to take me as I am," he said to himself, "I can't cut
myself to another pattern that might make a more suitable
friend for him."

And in fact he did inform his friend, in the long letter
he had been writing that Sunday morning, about his engagement, with these words: "I have saved my best news to
the end. I have got engaged to a Fräulein Frieda Branden-

feld, a girl from a well-to-do family, who only came to live here a long time after you went away, so that you're hardly likely to know her. There will be time to tell you more about her later, for today let me just say that I am very happy and as between you and me the only difference in our relationship is that instead of a quite ordinary kind of friend you will now have in me a happy friend. Besides that, you will acquire in my fiancée, who sends her warm greetings and will soon write you herself, a genuine friend of the opposite sex, which is not without importance to a bachelor. I know that there are many reasons why you can't come to see us, but would not my wedding be precisely the right occasion for giving all obstacles the go-by? Still, however that may be, do just as seems good to you without regarding any interests but your own."

With this letter in his hand, Georg had been sitting a long time at the writing table, his face turned towards the window. He had barely acknowledged, with an absent smile, a greeting waved to him from the street by a passing acquaintance.

At last he put the letter in his pocket and went out of his room across a small lobby into his father's room, which he had not entered for months. There was in fact no need for him to enter it, since he saw his father daily at business and they took their midday meal together at an eating house; in the evening, it was true, each did as he pleased, yet even then, unless Georg—as mostly happened—went out with friends or, more recently, visited his fiancée, they always sat for a while, each with his newspaper, in their common sitting room.

It surprised Georg how dark his father's room was even on this sunny morning. So it was overshadowed as much as that by the high wall on the other side of the narrow courtyard. His father was sitting by the window in a corner hung with various mementoes of Georg's dead mother, reading a newspaper which he held to one side before his eyes in an attempt to overcome a defect of vision. On the table stood

the remains of his breakfast, not much of which seemed
to have been eaten.

"Ah, Georg," said his father, rising at once to meet him.
His heavy dressing gown swung open as he walked and the
skirts of it fluttered round him.—"My father is still a giant
of a man," said Georg to himself.

"It's unbearably dark here," he said aloud.

"Yes, it's dark enough," answered his father.

"And you've shut the window, too?"

"I prefer it like that."

"Well, it's quite warm outside," said Georg, as if continuing his previous remark, and sat down.

His father cleared away the breakfast dishes and set them
on a chest.

"I really only wanted to tell you," went on Georg, who
had been vacantly following the old man's movements,
"that I am now sending the news of my engagement to St.
Petersburg." He drew the letter a little way from his pocket
and let it drop back again.

"To St. Petersburg?" asked his father.

"To my friend there," said Georg, trying to meet his
father's eye.—In business hours he's quite different, he was
thinking. How solidly he sits here with his arms crossed.

"Oh, yes. To your friend," said his father, with peculiar
emphasis.

"Well, you know, Father, that I wanted not to tell him
about my engagement at first. Out of consideration for him,
that was the only reason. You know yourself he's a difficult
man. I said to myself that some one else might tell him
about my engagement, although he's such a solitary creature
that that was hardly likely—I couldn't prevent that—but I
wasn't ever going to tell him myself."

"And now you've changed your mind?" asked his father,
laying his enormous newspaper on the window sill and on
top of it his spectacles, which he covered with one hand.

"Yes, I've been thinking it over. If he's a good friend of
mine, I said to myself, my being happily engaged should

make him happy too. And so I wouldn't put off telling him
any longer. But before I posted the letter I wanted to let
you know."

"Georg," said his father, lengthening his toothless
mouth, "listen to me! You've come to me about this business, to talk it over with me. No doubt that does you honor.
But it's nothing, it's worse than nothing, if you don't tell
me the whole truth. I don't want to stir up matters that
shouldn't be mentioned here. Since the death of our dear
mother certain things have been done that aren't right.
Maybe the time will come for mentioning them, and maybe
sooner than we think. There's many a thing in the business
I'm not aware of, maybe it's not done behind my back—
I'm not going to say that it's done behind my back—I'm
not equal to things any longer, my memory's failing, I
haven't an eye for so many things any longer. That's the
course of nature in the first place, and in the second place
the death of our dear mother hit me harder than it did
you.—But since we're talking about it, about this letter, I
beg you, Georg, don't deceive me. It's a trivial affair, it's
hardly worth mentioning, so don't deceive me. Do you
really have this friend in St. Petersburg?"

Georg rose in embarrassment. "Never mind my friends.
A thousand friends wouldn't make up to me for my father.
Do you know what I think? You're not taking enough care
of yourself. But old age must be taken care of. I can't do
without you in the business, you know that very well, but
if the business is going to undermine your health, I'm ready
to close it down tomorrow forever. And that won't do.
We'll have to make a change in your way of living. But a
radical change. You sit here in the dark, and in the sitting
room you would have plenty of light. You just take a bite
of breakfast instead of properly keeping up your strength.
You sit by a closed window, and the air would be so good
for you. No, Father! I'll get the doctor to come, and we'll
follow his orders. We'll change your room, you can move
into the front room and I'll move in here. You won't

notice the change, all your things will be moved with you. But there's time for all that later. I'll put you to bed now for a little; I'm sure you need to rest. Come, I'll help you to take off your things, you'll see I can do it. Or if you would rather go into the front room at once, you can lie down in my bed for the present. That would be the most sensible thing."

Georg stood close beside his father, who had let his head with its unkempt white hair sink on his chest.

"Georg," said his father in a low voice, without moving.

Georg knelt down at once beside his father. In the old man's weary face he saw the pupils, over-large, fixedly looking at him from the corners of the eyes.

"You have a friend in St. Petersburg. You've always been a leg-puller and you haven't even shrunk from pulling my leg. How could you have a friend out there! I can't believe it."

"Just think back a bit, Father," said Georg, lifting his father from the chair and slipping off his dressing gown as he stood feebly enough, "it'll soon be three years since my friend came to see us last. I remember that you used not to like him very much. At least twice I kept you from seeing him, although he was actually sitting with me in my room. I could quite well understand your dislike of him, my friend has his peculiarities. But then, later, you got on with him very well. I was proud because you listened to him and nodded and asked him questions. If you think back you're bound to remember. He used to tell us the most incredible stories of the Russian Revolution. For instance, when he was on a business trip to Kiev and ran into a riot, and saw a priest on a balcony who cut a broad cross in blood on the palm of his hand and held the hand up and appealed to the mob. You've told that story yourself once or twice since."

Meanwhile Georg had succeeded in lowering his father down again and carefully taking off the woolen drawers he wore over his linen underpants and his socks. The not particularly clean appearance of this underwear made him reproach himself for having been neglectful. It should have certainly been his duty to see that his father had clean changes of underwear. He had not yet explicitly discussed with his bride-to-be what arrangements should be made for his father in the future, for they had both of them silently taken it for granted that the old man would go on living alone in the old house. But now he made a quick, firm decision to take him into his own future establishment. It almost looked, on closer inspection, as if the care he meant to lavish there on his father might come too late.

He carried his father to bed in his arms. It gave him a dreadful feeling to notice that while he took the few steps towards the bed the old man on his breast was playing with his watch chain. He could not lay him down on the bed for a moment, so firmly did he hang on to the watch chain.

But as soon as he was laid in bed, all seemed well. He covered himself up and even drew the blankets farther than usual over his shoulders. He looked up at Georg with a not unfriendly eye.

"You begin to remember my friend, don't you?" asked Georg, giving him an encouraging nod.

"Am I well covered up now?" asked his father, as if he were not able to see whether his feet were properly tucked in or not.

"So you find it snug in bed already," said Georg, and tucked the blankets more closely round him.

"Am I well covered up?" asked the father once more, seeming to be strangely intent upon the answer.

"Don't worry, you're well covered up."

"No!" cried his father, cutting short the answer, threw the blankets off with a strength that sent them all flying in a moment and sprang erect in bed. Only one hand lightly touched the ceiling to steady him.

"You wanted to cover me up, I know, my young sprig, but I'm far from being covered up yet. And even if this is

the last strength I have, it's enough for you, too much for
you. Of course I know your friend. He would have been a
son after my own heart. That's why you've been playing
him false all these years. Why else? Do you think I haven't
been sorry for him? And that's why you had to lock yourself up in your office—the Chief is busy, mustn't be disturbed—just so that you could write your lying little letters
to Russia. But thank goodness a father doesn't need to be
taught how to see through his son. And now that you
thought you'd got him down, so far down that you could
set your bottom on him and sit on him and he wouldn't
move, then my fine son makes up his mind to get married!"

Georg stared at the bogey conjured up by his father. His
friend in St. Petersburg, whom his father suddenly knew
too well, touched his imagination as never before. Lost in
the vastness of Russia he saw him. At the door of an empty,
plundered warehouse he saw him. Among the wreckage of
his showcases, the slashed remnants of his wares, the falling gas brackets, he was just standing up. Why did he have
to go so far away!

"But attend to me!" cried his father, and Georg, almost
distracted, ran towards the bed to take everything in, yet
came to a stop halfway.

"Because she lifted up her skirts," his father began to
flute, "because she lifted her skirts like this, the nasty
creature," and mimicking her he lifted his shirt so high
that one could see the scar on his thigh from his war wound,
"because she lifted her skirts like this and this you made up
to her, and in order to make free with her undisturbed you
have disgraced your mother's memory, betrayed your friend
and stuck your father into bed so that he can't move. But
he can move, or can't he?"

And he stood up quite unsupported and kicked his legs
out. His insight made him radiant.

Georg shrank into a corner, as far away from his father
as possible. A long time ago he had firmly made up his mind
to watch closely every least movement so that he should

not be surprised by any indirect attack, a pounce from behind or above. At this moment he recalled this long-for-
gotten resolve and forgot it again, like a man drawing a
short thread through the eye of a needle.

"But your friend hasn't been betrayed after all!" cried his
father, emphasizing the point with stabs of his forefinger.
"I've been representing him here on the spot."

"You comedian!" Georg could not resist the retort,
realized at once the harm done and, his eyes starting in his
head, bit his tongue back, only too late, till the pain made
his knees give.

"Yes, of course I've been playing a comedy! A comedy!
That's a good expression! What other comfort was left to a
poor old widower? Tell me—and while you're answering
me be you still my living son—what else was left to me, in
my back room, plagued by a disloyal staff, old to the marrow of my bones? And my son strutting through the world,
finishing off deals that I had prepared for him, bursting
with triumphant glee and stalking away from his father
with the closed face of a respectable business man! Do you
think I didn't love you, I, from whom you are sprung?"

Now he'll lean forward, thought Georg. What if he top-
ples and smashes himself! These words went hissing
through his mind.

His father leaned forward but did not topple. Since
Georg did not come any nearer, as he had expected, he
straightened himself again.

"Stay where you are, I don't need you! You think you
have strength enough to come over here and that you're
only hanging back of your own accord. Don't be too sure!
I am still much the stronger of us two. All by myself I
might have had to give way, but your mother has given me
so much of her strength that I've established a fine connection with your friend and I have your customers here
in my pocket!"

"He has pockets even in his shirt!" said Georg to himself,
and believed that with this remark he could make him an

impossible figure for all the world. Only for a moment did he think so, since he kept on forgetting everything.

"Just take your bride on your arm and try getting in my way! I'll sweep her from your very side, you don't know how!"

Georg made a grimace of disbelief. His father only 'nodded, confirming the truth of his words, towards Georg's corner.

"How you amused me today, coming to ask me if you should tell your friend about your engagement. He knows it already, you stupid boy, he knows it all! I've been writing to him, for you forgot to take my writing things away from me. That's why he hasn't been here for years, he knows everything a hundred times better than you do yourself, in his left hand he crumples your letters unopened while in his right hand he holds up my letters to read through!"

In his enthusiasm he waved his arm over his head. "He knows everything a thousand times better!" he cried.

"Ten thousand times!" said Georg, to make fun of his father, but in his very mouth the words turned into deadly earnest.

"For years I've been waiting for you to come with some such question! Do you think I concern myself with anything else? Do you think I read my newspapers? Look!" and he threw Georg a newspaper sheet which he had somehow taken to bed with him. An old newspaper, with a name entirely unknown to Georg.

"How long a time you've taken to grow up! Your mother had to die, she couldn't see the happy day, your friend is going to pieces in Russia, even three years ago he was yellow enough to be thrown away, and as for me, you see what condition I'm in. You have eyes in your head for that!"

"So you've been lying in wait for me!" cried Georg.

His father said pityingly, in an offhand manner: "I suppose you wanted to say that sooner. But now it doesn't matter." And in a louder voice: "So now you know what else there was in the world besides yourself, till now you've known only about yourself! An innocent child, yes, that you were, truly, but still more truly have you been a devilish human being!—And therefore take note: I sentence you now to death by drowning!"

Georg felt himself urged from the room. The crash with which his father fell on the bed behind him was still in his ears as he fled. On the staircase, which he rushed down as if its steps were an inclined plane, he ran into his charwoman on her way up to do the morning cleaning of the room. "Jesus!" she cried, and covered her face with her apron, but he was already gone. Out of the front door he rushed, across the roadway, driven towards the water. Already he was grasping at the railings as a starving man clutches food. He swung himself over, like the distinguished gymnast he had once been in his youth, to his parents' pride. With weakening grip he was still holding on when he spied between the railings a motor-bus coming which would easily cover the noise of his fall, called in a low voice: "Dear parents, I have always loved you, all the same," and let himself drop.

At this moment an unending stream of traffic was just going over the bridge.

The Great Wall of China

THE GREAT WALL of China was finished off at its northern-most corner. From the south-east and the south-west it came up in two sections that finally converged there. This principle of piecemeal construction was also applied on a smaller scale by both of the two great armies of labor, the eastern and the western. It was done in this way: gangs of some twenty workers were formed who had to accomplish a length, say, of five hundred yards of wall, while a similar gang built another stretch of the same length to meet the first. But after the junction had been made the construction of the wall was not carried on from the point, let us say, where this thousand yards ended; instead the two groups of workers were transferred to begin building again in quite different neighborhoods. Naturally in this way many great gaps were left, which were only filled in gradually and bit by bit, some, indeed, not till after the official announcement that the wall was finished. In fact it is said that there are gaps which have never been filled in at all, an assertion, however, which is probably merely one of the many legends to which the building of the wall gave rise, and which cannot be verified, at least by any single man with his own

"The Great Wall of China" is reprinted by permission of Schocken Books Inc., New York, from *The Great Wall of China* by Franz Kafka, copyright 1946, 1948 by Schocken Books Inc., trans. by Willa and Edwin Muir.

eyes and judgment, on acount of the extent of the structure. Now on first thoughts one might conceive that it would have been more advantageous in every way to build the wall continuously, or at least continuously within the two main divisions. After all the wall was intended, as was universally proclaimed and known, to be a protection against the peoples of the north. But how can a wall protect if it is not a continuous structure? Not only cannot such a wall protect, but what there is of it is in perpetual danger. These blocks of wall left standing in deserted regions could be easily pulled down again and again by the nomads, especially as these tribes, rendered apprehensive by the building operations, kept changing their encampments with incredible rapidity, like locusts, and so perhaps had a better general view of the progress of the wall than we, the builders. Nevertheless the task of construction probably could not have been carried out in any other way. To understand this we must take into account the following: The wall was to be a protection for centuries: accordingly the most scrupulous care in the building, the application of the architectural wisdom of all known ages and peoples, an unremitting sense of personal responsibility in the builders, were indispensable prerequisites for the work. True, for the more purely manual tasks ignorant day laborers from the populace, men, women and children who offered their services for good money, could be employed; but for the supervision even of every four day laborers an expert versed in the art of building was required, a man who was capable of entering into and feeling with all his heart what was involved. And the higher the task, the greater the responsibility. And such men were actually to be had, if not indeed so abundantly as the work of construction could have absorbed, yet in great numbers.

For the work had not been undertaken without thought. Fifty years before the first stone was laid the art of architecture, and especially that of masonry, had been proclaimed as the most important branch of knowledge throughout the whole area of a China that was to be walled round, and all other arts gained recognition only in so far as they had reference to it. I can still remember quite well us standing as small children, scarcely sure on our feet, in our teacher's garden, and being ordered to build a sort of wall out of pebbles; and then the teacher, girding up his robe, ran full tilt against the wall, of course knocking it down, and scolded us so terribly for the shoddiness of our work that we ran weeping in all directions to our parents. A trivial incident, but significant of the spirit of the time.

I was lucky inasmuch as the building of the wall was just beginning when, at twenty, I had passed the last examination of the lowest grade school. I say lucky, for many who before my time had achieved the highest degree of culture available to them could find nothing year after year to do with their knowledge, and drifted uselessly about with the most splendid architectural plans in their heads, and sank by thousands into hopelessness. But those who finally came to be employed in the work as supervisors, even though it might be of the lowest rank, were truly worthy of their task. They were masons who had reflected much, and did not cease to reflect, on the building of the wall, men who with the first stone which they sank in the ground felt themselves a part of the wall. Masons of that kind, of course, had not only a desire to perform their work in the most thorough manner, but were also impatient to see the wall finished in its complete perfection. Day laborers have not this impatience, for they look only to their wages, and the higher supervisors, indeed even the supervisors of middle rank, could see enough of the manifold growth of the construction to keep their spirits confident and high. But to encourage the subordinate supervisors, intellectually so vastly superior to their apparently petty tasks, other measures must be taken. One could not, for instance, expect them to lay one stone on another for months or even years on end, in an uninhabited mountainous region, hundreds of miles from their homes; the hopelessness of such hard toil, which yet could not reach completion even in the longest lifetime, would have cast them into despair and above all made them less capable for the work. It was for this reason that the system of piecemeal building was decided on. Five hundred yards could be accomplished in about five years; by that time, however, the supervisors were as a rule quite exhausted and had lost all faith in themselves, in the wall, in the world. Accordingly, while they were still exalted by the jubilant celebrations marking the completion of the thousand yards of wall, they were sent far, far away, saw on their journey finished sections of the wall rising here and there, came past the quarters of the high command and were presented with badges of honor, heard the rejoicings of new armies of labor streaming past from the depths of the land, saw forests being cut down to become supports for the wall, saw mountains being hewn into stones for the wall, heard at the holy shrines hymns rising in which the pious prayed for the completion of the wall. All this assuaged their impatience. The quiet life of their homes, where they rested some time, strengthened them; the humble credulity with which their reports were listened to, the confidence with which the simple and peaceful burgher believed in the eventual completion of the wall, all this tightened up again the cords of the soul. Like eternally hopeful children they then said farewell to their homes; the desire once more to labor on the wall of the nation became irresistible. They set off earlier than they needed; half the village accompanied them for long distances. Groups of people with banners and scarfs waving were on all the roads; never before had they seen how great and rich and beautiful and worthy of love their country was. Every fellow-countryman was a brother for whom one was building a wall of protection, and who would return lifelong thanks for it with all he had and did. Unity! Unity! Shoulder to shoulder, a ring of brothers, a current of blood no longer confined within the narrow circulation of one body, but sweetly rolling and yet ever returning throughout the endless leagues of China.

Thus, then, the system of piecemeal construction becomes comprehensible; but there were still other reasons for it as well. Nor is there anything odd in my pausing over this question for so long; it is one of the crucial problems in the whole building of the wall, unimportant as it may appear at first glance. If I am to convey and make understandable the ideas and feelings of that time I cannot go deeply enough into this very question.

First, then, it must be said that in those days things were achieved scarcely inferior to the construction of the Tower of Babel, although as regards divine approval, at least according to human reckoning, strongly at variance with that work. I say this because during the early days of building a scholar wrote a book in which he drew the comparison in the most exhaustive way. In it he tried to prove that the Tower of Babel failed to reach its goal, not because of the reasons universally advanced, or at least that among those recognized reasons the most important of all was not to be found. His proofs were drawn not merely from written documents and reports; he also claimed to have made enquiries on the spot, and to have discovered that the tower failed and was bound to fail because of the weakness of the foundation. In this respect at any rate our age was vastly superior to that ancient one. Almost every educated man of our time was a mason by profession and infallible in the matter of laying foundations. That, however, was not what our scholar was concerned to prove; for he maintained that the Great Wall alone would provide for the first time in the history of mankind a secure foundation for a new Tower of Babel. First the wall, therefore, and then the tower. His book was in everybody's hands at that time, but I admit that even today I cannot quite make out how he conceived this tower. How could the wall, which did not form even a circle, but only a sort of quarter or half-circle, provide the foundation for a tower? That could obviously be meant only in a spiritual sense. But in that case why build the actual wall, which after all was something concrete, the results of the lifelong labor of multitudes of people? And why were there in the book plans, somewhat nebulous plans, it must be admitted, of the tower, and proposals worked out in detail for mobilizing the people's energies for the stupendous new work?

There were many wild ideas in people's heads at that time—this scholar's book is only one example—perhaps simply because so many were trying to join forces as far as they could for the achievement of a single aim. Human nature, essentially changeable, unstable as the dust, can endure no restraint; if it binds itself it soon begins to tear madly at its bonds, until it rends everything asunder, the wall, the bonds and its very self.

It is possible that these very considerations, which militated against the building of the wall at all, were not left out of account by the high command when the system of piecemeal construction was decided on. We—and here I speak in the name of many people—did not really know ourselves until we had carefully scrutinized the decrees of the high command, when we discovered that without the high command neither our book learning nor our human understanding would have sufficed for the humble tasks which we performed in the great whole. In the office of the command—where it was and who sat there no one whom I have asked knew then or knows now—in that office one may be certain that all human thoughts and desires were revolved, and counter to them all human aims and fulfilments. And through the window the reflected splendors of divine worlds fell on the hands of the leaders as they traced their plans.

And for that reason the incorruptible observer must hold that the command, if it had seriously desired it, could also have overcome those difficulties which prevented a system of continuous construction. There remains, therefore, nothing but the conclusion that the command deliberately chose the system of piecemeal construction. But the piecemeal construction was only a makeshift and therefore inexpedient. Remains the conclusion that the command willed something inexpedient.—Strange conclusion!—True, and yet in one respect it has much to be said for it. One can perhaps safely discuss it now. In those days many people, and among them the best, had a secret maxim which ran: Try with all your might to comprehend the decrees of the high command, but only up to a certain point; then avoid further meditation. A very wise maxim, which moreover was elaborated in a parable that was later often quoted: Avoid further meditation, but not because it might be harmful; it is not at all certain that it would be harmful. What is harmful or not harmful has nothing to do with the question. Consider rather the river in spring. It rises until it grows mightier and nourishes more richly the soil on the long stretch of its banks, still maintaining its own course until it reaches the sea, where it is all the more welcome because it is a worthier ally.—Thus far may you urge your meditations on the decrees of the high command.—But after that the river overflows its banks, loses outline and shape, slows down the speed of its current, tries to ignore its destiny by forming little seas in the interior of the land, damages the fields, and yet cannot maintain itself for long in its new expanse, but must run back between its banks again, must even dry up wretchedly in the hot season that presently follows.—Thus far may you not urge your meditations on the decrees of the high command.

Now though this parable may have had extraordinary point and force during the building of the wall, it has at most only a restricted relevance for my present essay. My enquiry is purely historical; no lightning flashes any longer from the long since vanished thunderclouds, and so I may venture to seek for an explanation of the system of piecemeal construction which goes farther than the one that contented people then. The limits which my capacity for thought imposes upon me are narrow enough, but the province to be traversed here is infinite. Against whom was the Great Wall to serve as a protection? Against the people of the north. Now, I come from the south-east of China. No northern people can menace us there. We read of them in the books of the ancients; the cruelties which they commit in accordance with their nature make us sigh beneath our peaceful trees. The faithful representations of the artist show us these faces of the damned, their gaping mouths, their jaws furnished with great pointed teeth, their half-shut eyes that already seem to be seeking out the victim which their jaws will rend and devour. When our children are unruly we show them these pictures, and at once they fly weeping into our arms. But nothing more than that do we know about these northerners. We have not seen them, and if we remain in our villages we shall never see them, even if on their wild horses they should ride as hard as they can straight towards us—the land is too vast and would not let them reach us, they would end their course in the empty air.

Why, then, since that is so, did we leave our homes, the stream with its bridges, our mothers and fathers, our weeping wives, our children who needed our care, and depart for the distant city to be trained there, while our thoughts journeyed still farther away to the wall in the north? Why? A question for the high command. Our leaders know us. They, absorbed in gigantic anxieties, know of us, know our petty pursuits, see us sitting together in our humble huts, and approve or disapprove the evening prayer which the father of the house recites in the midst of his family. And if I may be allowed to express such ideas about the high command, then I must say that in my opinion the high command has existed from old time, and was not assembled, say, like a gathering of mandarins summoned hastily to discuss somebody's fine dream in a conference as hastily terminated, so that that very evening the people are drummed out of their beds to carry out what has been decided, even if it should be nothing but an illumination in honor of a god who may have shown great favor to their masters the day before, only to drive them into some dark corner with cudgel blows tomorrow, almost before the illuminations have died down. Far rather do I believe that the high command has existed from all eternity, and the decision to build the wall likewise. Unwitting peoples of the north, who imagined they were the cause of it! Honest, unwitting Emperor, who imagined he decreed it! We builders of the wall know that it was not so and hold our tongues.

During the building of the wall and ever since to this very day I have occupied myself almost exclusively with the comparative history of races—there are certain questions which one can probe to the marrow, as it were, only by this method—and I have discovered that we Chinese possess certain folk and political institutions that are unique in their clarity, others again unique in their obscurity. The desire to trace the causes of these phenomena, especially the latter, has always teased me and teases me still, and the building of the wall is itself essentially involved with these problems.

Now one of the most obscure of our institutions is that of the empire itself. In Pekin, naturally, at the imperial court, there is some clarity to be found on this subject, though even that is more illusive than real. Also the teachers of political law and history in the high schools claim to be exactly informed on these matters, and to be capable of passing on their knowledge to their students. The further one descends among the lower schools the more, naturally enough, does one find teachers' and pupils' doubts of their own knowledge vanishing, and superficial culture mounting sky-high round a few precepts that have been drilled into people's minds for centuries, precepts which, though they have lost nothing of their eternal truth, remain eternally invisible in this fog of confusion.

But it is precisely this question of the empire which in my opinion the common people should be asked to answer, since after all they are the empire's final support. Here, I must confess, I can only speak once more for my native place. Except for the nature gods and their ritual, which fills the whole year in such beautiful and rich alternation, we think only about the Emperor. But not about the present one; or rather we would think about the present one if we knew who he was or knew anything definite about him. True—and it is the sole curiosity that fills us—we are always trying to get information on this subject, but, strange as it may sound, it is almost impossible to discover anything, either from pilgrims, though they have wandered through many lands, or from near or distant villages, or from sailors, though they have navigated not only our little stream, but also the sacred rivers. One hears a great many things, true, but can gather nothing definite.

So vast is our land that no fable could do justice to its vastness, the heavens can scarcely span it—and Pekin is only a dot in it, and the imperial palace less than a dot. The Emperor as such, on the other hand, is mighty throughout all the hierarchies of the world: admitted. But the existent Emperor, a man like us, lies much like us on a couch which is of generous proportions, perhaps, and yet very possibly may be quite narrow and short. Like us he sometimes stretches himself and when he is very tired yawns with his delicately cut mouth. But how should we know anything about that—thousands of miles away in the south—almost on the borders of the Tibetan Highlands? And besides, any tidings, even if they did reach us, would arrive far too late, would have become obsolete long before they reached us. The Emperor is always surrounded by a brilliant and yet ambiguous throng of nobles and courtiers —malice and enmity in the guise of servants and friends— who form a counter-weight to the Imperial power and perpetually labor to unseat the ruler from his place with poisoned arrows. The Empire is immortal, but the Emperor himself totters and falls from his throne, yes, whole dynasties sink in the end and breathe their last in one death-rattle. Of these struggles and sufferings the people will never know; like tardy arrivals, like strangers in a city, they stand at the end of some densely thronged side street peacefully munching the food they have brought with them, while far away in front, in the market square at the heart of the city, the execution of their ruler is proceeding.

There is a parable that describes this situation very well: The Emperor, so it runs, has sent a message to you, the humble subject, the insignificant shadow cowering in the remotest distance before the imperial sun; the Emperor from his death-bed has sent a message to you alone. He has commanded the messenger to kneel down by the bed, and has whispered the message to him; so much store did he lay on it that he ordered the messenger to whisper it back into his ear again. Then by a nod of the head he has confirmed that it is right. Yes, before the assembled spectators of his death—all the obstructing walls have been broken down, and on the spacious and loftily mounting open staircases stand in a ring the great princes of the Empire—before all these he has delivered his message. The messenger immediately sets out on his journey; a powerful, an indefatigable man, now pushing with his right arm, now with his left, he cleaves a way for himself through the throng; if he encounters resistance he points to his breast, where the symbol of the sun glitters; the way, too, is made easier for him than it would be for any other man. But the multitudes are so vast; their numbers have no end. If he could reach the open fields, how fast he would fly, and soon doubtless you would hear the welcome hammering of his fists on your door. But instead how vainly does he wear out his strength; still he is only making his way through the chambers of the innermost palace; never will he get to the end of them; and if he succeeded in that nothing would be gained; he must fight his way next down the stair; and if he succeeded in that nothing would be gained; the courts would still have to be crossed; and after the courts the second outer palace; and once more stairs and courts; and once more another palace; and so on for thousands of years; and if at last he should burst through the outermost gate—but never, never can that happen—the imperial capital would lie before him, the center of the world, crammed to bursting with its own refuse. Nobody could fight his way through here even with a message from a dead man.—But you sit at your window when evening falls and dream it to yourself.

Just so, as hopelessly and as hopefully, do our people regard the Emperor. They do not know what emperor is reigning, and there exist doubts regarding even the name of the dynasty. In school a great deal is taught about the dynasties with the dates of succession, but the universal uncertainty in this matter is so great that even the best scholars are drawn into it. Long-dead emperors are set on the throne in our villages, and one that only lives in song recently had a proclamation of his read out by the priest before the altar. Battles that are old history are new to us, and one's neighbor rushes in with a jubilant face to tell the news. The wives of the emperors, pampered and overweening, seduced from noble custom by wily courtiers, swelling with ambition, vehement in their greed, uncontrollable in their lust, practise their abominations ever anew. The more deeply they are buried in time the more glaring are the colors in which their deeds are painted, and with a loud cry of woe our village eventually hears how an Empress drank her husband's blood in long draughts thousands of years ago.

Thus, then, do our people deal with departed emperors, but the living ruler they confuse among the dead. If once, only once in a man's lifetime, an imperial official on his tour of the provinces should arrive by chance at our village, make certain announcements in the name of the government, scrutinize the tax lists, examine the school children, enquire of the priest regarding our doings and affairs, and then, before he steps into his litter, should sum up his impressions in verbose admonitions to the assembled commune—then a smile flits over every face, each man throws a stolen glance at his neighbor, and bends over his children so as not to be observed by the official. Why, they think to themselves, he's speaking of a dead man as if he were alive, this Emperor of his died long ago, the dynasty is blotted out, the good official is having his joke with us, but we will behave as if we did not notice it, so as not to offend him. But we shall obey in earnest no one but our present ruler, for not to do so would be a crime. And behind the departing litter of the official there rises in might as ruler of the village some figure fortuitously exalted from an urn already crumbled to dust.

Similarly our people are but little affected by revolutions in the state or contemporary wars. I recall an incident in my youth. A revolt had broken out in a neighboring, but yet quite distant, province. What caused it I can no longer remember, nor is it of any importance now; occasions for revolt can be found there any day; the people are an excitable people. Well, one day a leaflet published by the rebels was brought to my father's house by a beggar who had crossed that province. It happened to be a feast day, our rooms were filled with guests, the priest sat in the chief place and studied the sheet. Suddenly everybody started to laugh; in the confusion the sheet was torn; the beggar, who however had already received abundant alms, was driven out of the room with blows, the guests dispersed to enjoy the beautiful day. Why? The dialect of this neighboring province differs in some essential respects from ours, and this difference occurs also in certain turns of the written speech, which for us have an archaic character. Hardly had the priest read out two lines before we had already come to our decision. Ancient history told long ago, old sorrows long since healed. And though—so it seems to me in recollection—the gruesomeness of the living present was irrefutably conveyed by the beggar's words, we laughed and shook our heads and refused to listen any longer. So eager are our people to obliterate the present.

If from such appearances any one should draw the conclusion that in reality we have no Emperor, he would not be far from the truth. Over and over again it must be repeated: There is perhaps no people more faithful to the Emperor than ours in the south, but the Emperor derives no advantage from our fidelity. True, the sacred dragon stands on the little column at the end of our village, and ever since the beginning of human memory it has breathed out its fiery breath in the direction of Pekin in token of homage—but Pekin itself is far stranger to the people in our village than the next world. Can there really be a village where the houses stand side by side, covering all the fields for a greater distance than one can see from our hills, and can there be dense crowds of people packed between these houses day and night? We find it more difficult to picture such a city than to believe that Pekin and its Emperor are one, a cloud, say, peacefully voyaging beneath the sun in the course of the ages.

Now the result of holding such opinions is a life on the whole free and unconstrained. By no means immoral, however; hardly ever have I found in my travels such pure morals as in my native village. But yet a life that is subject to no contemporary law, and attends only to the exhortations and warnings which come to us from olden times.

I guard against large generalizations, and do not assert that in all the countless villages in my province it is so, far less in all the five hundred provinces of China. Yet perhaps I may venture to assert on the basis of the many writings on this subject which I have read, as well as from my own observation—the building of the wall in particular, with its abundance of human material, provided a man of sensibility with the opportunity of traversing the souls of almost all the provinces—on the basis of all this, then, perhaps I may venture to assert that the prevailing attitude to the Emperor shows persistently and universally something fundamentally in common with that of our village. Now I have no wish whatever to represent this attitude as a virtue; on the contrary. True, the essential responsibility for it lies with the government, which in the most ancient empire in the world has not yet succeeded in developing, or has neglected to develop, the institution of the empire to such precision that its workings extend directly and unceasingly to the farthest frontiers of the land. On the other hand, however, there is also involved a certain feebleness of faith and imaginative power on the part of the people that prevents them from raising the empire out of its stagnation in Pekin and clasping it in all its palpable living reality to their own breasts, which yet desire nothing better than but once to feel that touch and then to die.

This attitude then is certainly no virtue. All the more remarkable is it that this very weakness should seem to be one of the greatest unifying influences among our people; indeed, if one may dare to use the expression, the very ground on which we live. To set about establishing a fundamental defect here would mean undermining not only our consciences, but, what is far worse, our feet. And for that reason I shall not proceed any further at this stage with my enquiry into these questions.

Nadine Gordimer

[1923 —   ]

THE "IMPULSE OF CAIN" is the acknowledged constant theme
in Nadine Gordimer's stories, South African counterparts of
Albert Camus' Algerian fiction. Both writers are merciless ob-
servers of the same incongruities: how human need poisons
the very wells of its own gratifications; how even the more
kindly European *colon* or Afrikaaner may acquiesce in permanent "cauterization of the human heart" by allowing law and
custom to restrain fellow men from aspiring to a fully civilized
state.

To Nadine Gordimer *apartheid* is inhumane because it ag-
gravates the modern wound, already large, of alienation. Her
own childhood, in a small though wealthy gold-mining town,
was solitary. After an early education in convent schools she attended the University of the Witwatersrand in Johannesburg,
where she later settled. Whatever youthful ideals survived a
city culture where every other pillow concealed a gun and every
window was barred were tempered beyond need to be tested
further. Her personal ordeal has been authentically recovered in
such stories as "Another Part of the Sky" and in her first novel,
The Lying Days (1953).

Johannesburg has been called her Dublin: but unlike Joyce,
she has dared to be the critic within the walls. Since 1954, when
she married a local company director, her effort has been to
remain a conscience to herself and their children in the face

of the coarseness inevitably found in any divided city or divided self. Her Johannesburg is a white city surrounded by black "townships" where chipped brick and tin huts predominate and a pennywhistle life struggles to "make do." Between these two worlds is the precarious area of the "coloreds"—those of mixed ethnic origin. Johannesburg is a mile-high city; but, in the mid-twentieth century, it has hung suspended in its intemperate "emotional climate of privilege," its immigrant fathers mindless of their own past as wanderers and displaced persons.

Although her work has been compared with Virginia Woolf's and Katherine Mansfield's, Nadine Gordimer's own preferences are E. M. Forster and André Malraux, in whose *Passage to India* and *Man's Fate*, respectively, social consciousness combines with a high sense of art to create an "inner imprint." The infinite care of her craft seems particularly appropriate to short fiction. Her first volume of stories, *Face to Face* (Johannesburg, 1949), was expanded and became *The Soft Voice of the Serpent* when it appeared in America in 1952. Two other collections— *Six Feet of the Country* (1956) and *Friday's Footprint* (1960) —have extended her proposition that "men are not born brothers, they have to discover each other," without yet exhausting its possibilities for her. Each story has sought out the truth of nuance. None has met cocksure righteousness with even louder self-righteousness. Just when a character or a relationship seems indisputably fixed, circumstance jostles it into a new shape requiring reassessment.

This same dissatisfaction with easy judgments has made her novels difficult reading for those who require foreseeable outcomes for characters who, in turn, are mere fixtures in the formulas of event. "Continuity" is naturally less predictable in works which investigate the gradual breakdown of relations propped up by hypocrisy. After her semiautobiographical novel of disillusionment, *The Lying Days* (1953), Nadine Gordimer wrote *A World of Strangers* (1958) in which an uncommitted young Englishman, profoundly repelled in his childhood by a houseful of do-gooders, nevertheless becomes involved in African problems out of simple decency and out of a fundamental need. He cannot deny, although he does not welcome, the feeling he has of being a "stranger among people who were strangers to each other."

It is this need, this demand not to be loveless in spite of one's savagery, which makes Nadine Gordimer's stories compassionate in the midst of their accusations. If her fellow countrymen are sometimes appalling, that is precisely why she cannot ignore or desert them: because such an act of pride and hatred would surpass theirs. *Friday's Footprint*, because its stories contemplate the inhumanity of white African to white African exclusively, acknowledges best of all the shriveling personal loneliness which sometimes causes men, impatient to assume a final, fixed identity, to create one by violence and at the expense of other men.

The Defeated

MY MOTHER DID not want me to go near the Concession stores because they smelled, and were dirty, and the natives spat tuberculosis germs into the dust. She said it was no place for little girls.

But I used to go down there sometimes, in the afternoon, when static four o'clock held the houses of our Mine, and the sun washed over them like the waves of the sea over sand castles. I felt that life was going on down there at the Concession stores: noise, and movement and—yes, bad smells, even—and so I would wander down the naked road, with the hot sun uncomfortably drying the membrane inside my nose, seeing the irregular line of narrow white shops lying away ahead like a jumble of shoe boxes.

The signs of life that I craved were very soon evident: rich and careless of its vitality, it overflowed from the crowded pavement of the stores, and the surrounding veld was littered with sucked-out oranges and tatters of dirty paper, and worn into the shabby barrenness peculiar to earth much trampled upon by the feet of men. A fat, one-legged native, with the patient detachment of the business-

From *The Soft Voice of the Serpent* by Nadine Gordimer. Copyright 1950, 1951, 1952 by Nadine Gordimer. Reprinted by permission of Simon and Schuster, Inc.

man who knows himself indispensable, sat on the bald veld beside the path that led from the Compound, his stock of walking sticks standing up, handles tied together, points splayed out fanwise, his pyramids of bright, thin-skinned oranges waiting. Sometimes he had mealies as well—those big, hard, full-grown ears with rows of yellowish tombstones instead of little pearly teeth—and a brazier made from a paraffin tin to roast them by. Propped against the chipped pillars of the pavement, there were always other vendors, making their small way in lucky beans, herbs, bracelets beaten from copper wire, knitted caps in wonderful colors —blooming like great hairy petunias, or bursting suns, from the needles of old, old native women—and, of course, oranges. Everywhere there were oranges; the pushing, ambling crowds filling the pavement ate them as they stared at the windows, the gossips, sitting with their blankets drawn close and their feet in the gutter, sucked at them, the Concession store cats sniffed at the skins where they lay, hollow-cheeked, discarded in every doorway.

Quite often I had to flick the white pith from where it had landed, on my shoe or even my dress, spat negligently by some absorbed orange-eater contemplating a shirt through breath-smudged plate glass. The wild, wondering dirty men came up from the darkness of the mine and they lay themselves out to the sun on the veld, and to their mouths they put the round fruit of the sun; and it was the expression of their need.

I would saunter along the shopwindows amongst them, and for me there was a quickening of glamour about the place: the air was thicker with their incense-like body smell, and the sudden rank shock of their stronger sweat, as a bare armpit lifted over my head. The clamor of their voices—always shouting, but so merry, so angry!—and the size of their laughter, and the open-mouthed startle with which they greeted every fresh sight: I felt vaguely the spell of the books I had read, returning; markets in Persia, bazaars in Cairo. . . . Nevertheless, I was careful not to let them brush too closely past me, lest some unnamable *something* crawl from their dusty blankets or torn cotton trousers onto my clean self, and I did not like the way they spat, with that terrible gurgle in the throat, into the gutter, or, worse still, blew their noses loudly between finger and thumb, and flung the excrement horribly to the air.

And neither did I like the heavy, sickening, greasy carrion-breath that poured from the mouth of the Hotela la Bantu, where the natives hunched intent at zinc-topped forms, eating steaming no-color chunks of horror that bore no relation to meat as I knew it. The down on my arms prickled in revulsion from the pulpy entrails hanging in dreadful enticement at the window, and the blood-embroidered sawdust spilling out of the doorway.

I know that I wondered how the storekeepers' wives, who sat on soap boxes outside the doorways of the shops on either side of the eating house, could stand the breath of that maw. How they could sit, like lizards in the sun; and all the time they breathed in the breath of the eating house: took it deep into the recesses of their beings, whilst my throat closed against it in disgust.

It was down there one burning afternoon that I met Mrs. Saiyetovitz. She was one of the storekeepers' wives, and I had seen her many times before, sitting before the deep, blanket-hung cave of her husband's store, where a pile of tinsel-covered wooden trunks shimmered and flashed a pink or green eye out of the gloom into the outside—wearing her creased alpaca apron, her fat insteps leaning over her down-at-heel shoes. Sometimes she knitted, and sometimes she just sat. On this day there was a small girl hanging about her, drawing on the shopwindow with a sticky forefinger. When the child turned to look at me, I recognized her as one of the girls from "our school"; a girl from my class, as a matter of fact, called Miriam Saiyetovitz. Yes, that was her name: I remembered it because it was ugly —I was always sorry for girls with ugly names.

Miriam was a tousled, black-haired little girl, who wore a

red bow in her hair. Now she recognized me, and we stood looking at one another; all at once the spare line of the name "Miriam Saiyetovitz," that was like the scrolled pattern of an iron gate with only the sky behind it, shifted its perspective in my mind, so that now between the cold curly M's and the implacable A's of that gate's framework, I saw a house, a complication of buildings and flowers and figures walking, where before there was nothing but the sky. Miriam Saiyetovitz—and this: behind her name and her school self, the hot and buzzing world of the stores. And I smiled at her, very friendly.

So she knew we had decided to recognize one another and she sauntered over to talk to me. I stood with her in the doorway of her father's store, and I, too, wrote my name and drew cats composed of two capital O's and a sausage tail, with the point of my hot and sticky finger on the window. Of course, she did not exactly introduce me to her mother—children never do introduce their mothers; they merely let it be known, by referring to the woman in question offhand, in the course of play, or going up to speak to her in such a way that the relationship becomes obvious. Miriam went up to her mother and said diffidently: "Ma, I know this girl from school—she's in class with me, can we have some red lemonade?"

And the woman lifted her head from where she sat, wide-legged, so that you couldn't help seeing the knee-elastic of her striped pink silk bloomers holding over the cotton tops of her stockings, and said, peering, "Take it! Take it! Go, have it!"

Because I did not then know her, I thought that she was angry, she spoke with such impatience; but soon I knew that it was only her eager generosity that made her fling permission almost fiercely at Miriam whenever the child made some request. Mrs. Saiyetovitz's glance wavered over to me, but she did not seem to be seeing me very clearly: indeed, she could not, for her small, pale, pale eyes narrowed into her big, simple, heavy face were half-blind, and

she had always to peer at everything, and never quite see.
I saw that she was very ugly.

Ugly, with the blunt ugliness of a toad; the ugliness of
seeming not entirely at home in any element—as if the
earth were the wrong place, too heavy and magnetic for a
creature already so blunt; and the water would be no better:
too subtle and contour-swayed for a creature so graceless.
And yet her ugliness was without repellence. When I grew
older I often wondered why; she should have been repel-
lent, one should have turned from her, but one did not.
She was only ugly. She had the short, stunted yet heavy
bones of generations of oppression in the Ghettos of Europe; breasts, stomach, hips crowded sadly, no height, wide
strong shoulders and a round back. Her head settled right
down between her shoulders without even the grace of a
neck, and her dun flat hair was cut at the level of her ears.
Her features were not essentially Semitic; there was nothing
so *definite* as that about her: she had no distinction whatever.

Miriam reappeared from the shades of the store, carrying
two bottles of red lemonade. A Shangaan emerged at the
same time, clutching a newspaper parcel and puzzling over
his handful of change, not looking where he was going.
Miriam swept past him, the dusty African with his odd,
troglodyte unsureness, and his hair plastered into savage
whorls with red clay. With one swift movement she
knocked the tin caps off the bottles against the scratched
frame of the shopwindow, and handed my lemonade to
me. "Where did you get it so quickly?" I asked, surprised.
She jerked her head back towards the store: "In the
kitchen," she said—and applied herself to the bottle.

And so I knew that the Saiyetovitzes lived there, behind
the Concession store.

Saturday afternoons were the busiest. Mrs. Saiyetovitz's
box stood vacant outside and she helped her husband in the
shop. Saturday afternoon was usually my afternoon for

going down there, too; my mother and father went out to golf, and I was left with the tick of the clock, the purring monologue of our cat, and the doves gurgling in the empty garden.

On Saturdays every doorway was crowded; a continual shifting stream snaked up and down the pavements; flies tangled overhead, the air smelled hotter, and from the doorway of every store the high, wailing blare and repetition of native songs, played on the gramophone, swung out upon the air and met in discord with the tune of the record being played next door.

Miriam's mother's brother was the proprietor of the Hotela la Bantu, and another uncle had the bicycle shop two doors down. Sometimes she had a message to deliver at the bicycle shop, and I would go in with her. Spare wheels hung across the ceiling, there was a battered wooden counter with a pile of puncture repair outfits, a sewing machine or two for sale, and, in the window, bells and pumps and mascots cut out of tin, painted yellow and red for the adornment of handle bars. We were invariably offered a lemonade by the uncle, and we invariably accepted. At home I was not allowed to drink lemonades unlimited; they might "spoil my dinner"; but Miriam drank them whenever she pleased.

Wriggling in and out amongst the gray-dusty bodies of the natives—their silky brown skin dies in the damp fug underground: after a few months down the mine, it reflects only weariness—Miriam looked with her own calm, quick self-possession upon the setting in which she found herself. Like someone sitting in a swarm of ants; and letting them swarm, letting them crawl all over and about her. Not lifting a hand to flick them off. Not crying out against them in disgust; nor explaining, saying, well, I *like* ants. Just sitting there and letting them swarm, and looking out of herself as if to say: What ants? What ants are you talking about? I giggled and shuddered in excitement at the sight of the dried bats and cobwebby snakeskins rotting in the bleary little window of the medicine shop, but Miriam tugged at my dress and said, "Oh, come on—" I exclaimed at the purple and red shirts lying amongst the dead flies in the wonderful confusion of Saiyetovitz's store window, but Miriam was telling me about her music exam in September, and only frowned at the interruption. I was approaching the confusion of adolescence, and sometimes an uncomfortable, terrible, fascinating curiosity—like a headless worm which lay shamefully hidden in the earth of my soul—crawled out into my consciousness at the sight of the animal obviousness of the natives' male bodies in their scanty covering; but the flash of my guilt at these moments met no answer in Miriam, although she was the same age as I.

If the sight of a boy interrupting his conversation to step out a yard or two onto the veld to relieve himself filled me with embarrassment and real disgust, so that I wanted to go and look at flowers—it seemed that Miriam did not see.

It was quite a long time before she took me into her father's store.

For months it remained a vague, dark, dust-moted world beyond the blanket-hung doorway, into which she was swallowed up and appeared again, whilst I waited outside, with the boys who looked and looked and looked at the windows. Then one day, as she was entering, she paused, and said suddenly and calmly: "Aren't you coming . . . ?" Without a word, I followed her in.

It was cool in the store; and the coolness was a surprise. Out of the sun-naked pavement—and into the store that was cool, like a cellar! Light danced only furtively along the folds of the blankets that hung from the ceiling: crackling silent and secret little fires in the curly woolen furze. The blankets were dark somber hangings, in proud colors, bold and primal. They hung like dark stalactites in the cave, still and heavy, communing only their own colors back to themselves. They brooded over the shop; and over Mr. Saiyetovitz there beneath, treading the worn cement with his disgruntled, dispossessed air of doing his best, but . . .

I had glimpsed him before. He lurked within the depths of his store like a beast in its lair, and now and then I had seen the glimmer of his pale, pasty face with the wide upper lip under which the lower closed glumly and puffily.

John Saiyetovitz (his name wasn't John at all, really—it was Yanka, but when he arrived at Cape Town, long ago, the Immigration authorities were tired of attempting to understand and spell the unfamiliar names of the immigrants pouring off the boat, and by the time they'd got the "Saiyetovitz" spelt right, they couldn't be bothered puzzling over the "Yanka," so they scrawled "John" on his papers, and John he was)—John Saiyetovitz was a gentle man, with an almost hangdog gentleness, but when he was trading with the natives, strange blasts of power seemed to blow up in his soul. Africans are the slowest buyers in the world; to them, buying is a ritual, a slow and solemn undertaking. They must go carefully; they nervously scent pitfalls on every side. And confronted with a selection of different kinds of the one thing they want, they are as confused as a child before a plate of pastries; fingering, hesitating, this or that . . . ? On a busy Saturday they must be allowed to stand about the shop endlessly, looking up and about, pausing to shake their heads and give a profound "OW!"; sauntering off; going to press their noses against the window again; coming back. And Mr. Saiyetovitz—always the same, unshaven and collarless—lugging a blanket down from the shelves, flinging it upon the counter—and another, and then another, and standing, arms hanging, sullen and smoldering before the blank-faced purchaser. The boy with his helpless stance, and his eyes rolling up in the agony of decision, filling the shop with the sickly odor of his anxious sweat, and clutching his precious guitar.

Waiting, waiting.

And then Mr. Saiyetovitz swooping away in a gesture of rage and denial; don't care, sick-to-death. And the boy anxious, edging forward to feel the cloth again, and the whole business starting up all over again; more blankets, different colors, down from the shelf and hooked from the ceiling—stalactites crumpled to woolen heaps to wonder over. Mr. Saiyetovitz throwing them down, moving in jerks of rage now, and then roughly bullying the boy into a decision. Shouting at him, bundling his purchase into his arms, snatching the money, gesturing him cowed out of the store.

Mr. Saiyetovitz treated the natives honestly, but with bad grace. He forced them to feel their ignorance, their inadequacy, and their submission to the white man's world of money. He spiritually maltreated them, and bitterly drove his nail into the coffin of their confidence.

With me, he was shy, he smiled widely and his hand went to the stud swinging loose at the neck of his half-buttoned shirt, and drew as if in apology over the stubbled landscape of his jaw. He always called me "little girl" and he liked to talk to me in the way that he thought children like to be talked to, but I found it very difficult to make a show of reply, because his English was so broken and fragmentary. So I used to stand there, and say yes, Mr. Saiyetovitz, and smile back and say thank you! to anything that sounded like a question, because the question usually was did I want a lemonade?, and of course, I usually did.

The first time Miriam ever came to my home was the day of my birthday party.

Our relationship at school had continued unchanged, just as before; she had her friends and I had mine, but outside of school there was the curious plane of intimacy on which we had, as it were, surprised one another wandering, and so which was shared peculiarly by us.

I had put Miriam's name down on my guest list; she was invited; and she came. She wore a blue taffeta dress which Mrs. Saiyetovitz had made for her (on the old Singer on the counter in the shop, I guessed) and it was quite nice if a bit too frilly. My home was pretty and well-furnished and full of flowers and personal touches of my mother's hands; there was space, and everything shone. Miriam did not open her eyes at it; I saw her finger a bowl of baby-skinned pink roses in the passing, but all afternoon she looked out indifferently as she did at home.

The following Saturday at the store we were discussing the party. Miriam was telling Mrs. Saiyetovitz about my presents, and I was standing by in pleasurable embarrassment at my own importance.

"Well, please God, Miri," said Mrs. Saiyetovitz at the finish, "you'll also have a party for your birday in April. . . . Ve'll be in d'house, and everyting'll be nice, just like you want."—They were leaving the rooms behind the shop —the mournful green plush curtains glooming the archway between the bedroom and the living room; the tarnished samovar; the black beetles in the little kitchen; Miriam's old black piano with the candlesticks, wheezing in the drafty passage; the damp puddly yard piled with empty packing cases and eggshells and banana skins; the hovering smell of fish frying. They were going to live in a little house in the township nearby.

But when April came, Miriam took ten of her friends to the Saturday afternoon bioscope in celebration of her birthday. "And to Costas Café afterwards for ice cream," she stated to her mother, looking out over her head. I think Mrs. Saiyetovitz was disappointed about the party, but she reasoned then, as always, that as her daughter went to school and was educated and could speak English, whilst she herself knew nothing, wasn't clever at all, the little daughter must know best what was right and what was nice.

I know now what of course I did not know then: that Miriam Saiyetovitz and I were intelligent little girls into whose brains there never had, and never would, come the freak and wonderful flash that is brilliance. Ours were alabaster intellects: clear, perfect, light; no streaks of dark, unknown granite splitting to reveal secret veins of brightness, like thin gold, between stratum and stratum. We were fitted to be good schoolteachers, secretaries, organizers; we did everything well, nothing badly, and nothing remarkably. But to the Saiyetovitzes, Miriam's brain blazed like the sun, warming their humbleness.

In the year-by-year passage through school, our classmates thinned out one by one; the way seedlings come up in a bunch to a certain stage in their development, and then by some inexplicable process of natural selection, one or two continue to grow and branch up into the air, whilst the others wither or remain small and weedy. The other girls left to go and learn shorthand-and-typewriting: weeded out by the necessity of earning a living. Or moved, and went to other schools: transplanted to some ground of their own. Miriam and I remained, growing straight and steadily. . . .

During our matriculation year a sense of wonder and impending change came upon us both; the excitement of coming to an end that is also a beginning. We felt this in one another, and so were drawn together in new earnestness. Miriam came to study with me in the garden at my house, and oftener than ever, I slipped down to the Concession stores to exchange a book or discuss work with her. For although they now had a house, the Saiyetovitzes still lived, in the wider sense of the word, at the store. When Miriam and I discussed our schoolwork, the Saiyetovitzes crept about, very quiet, talking to one another only in hoarse, respectful whispers.

It was during this year, when the wonder of our own capacity to learn was reaching out and catching into light like a veld fire within us, that we began to talk of the University. And, all at once, we talked of nothing else. I spoke to my father of it, and he was agreeable, although my mother thought a girl could do better with her time. But so long as my father was willing to send me, I knew I should go. Ah yes, said Miriam. She liked my father very much; I knew that. In fact she said to me once—it was a strange thing to say, and almost emotionally, she said it, and at a strange time, because we were on the bus going into the town to buy a new winter coat which she had wanted very badly and talked about longingly for days, and her father had just given her the money to get it—she said to me: You know, I think your father's just right.—I mean, if you had to choose somebody, a certain kind of person for a father, well, your father'd be just the kind you'd want.

When she broached the subject of University to her parents, they were agreeable for her to go, too. Indeed, they wanted her to go almost more than she herself did. But they worried a great deal about the money side of it; every time I went down to the store there'd be a discussion of ways and means, Saiyetovitz slowly munching his bread and garlic polony lunch, and worrying. Miriam didn't worry about it; they'll find the money, she said. She was a tall girl, now, with beautiful breasts, and a large, dark-featured face that had a certain capable elegance, although her father's glum mouth was unmistakable and on her upper lip faint dark down foreshadowed a heavy middle-age. Her parents were peasants; but she was the powerful young Jewess. Beside her, I felt pale in my Scotch gingery-fairness: lightly drawn upon the mind's eye, whilst she was painted in oils.

We both matriculated; not so well as we thought we should, but well enough; and we went to the University. And there too, we did well enough. We had both decided upon the same course: teaching. In the end, it had seemed the only thing to do. Neither of us had any particular bent.

It must have been a hard struggle for the Saiyetovitzes to keep Miriam at the University, buy her clothes, and pay for her board and lodging in Johannesburg. There is a great deal of money to be made out of native trade concessions purchased from the government; and it doesn't require education or trained commercial astuteness to make it—in fact, trading of this sort seems to flourish in response to something very different: what is needed is instinctive peasant craftiness such as can only be found in the uneducated, in those who have scratched up their own resources. Storekeepers with this quality of peasant craft made money all about Mr. Saiyetovitz, bought houses and motorcars and banded their wives' retired hands with diamonds in mark of their new idleness. But Mr. Saiyetovitz was a peasant without the peasant's craft; without that flaw in his simplicity that might have given him checks and deeds of transfer to sign, even if he were unable to read the print on the documents. . . . Without this craft, the peasant has only one thing left to him: hard work, dirty work, with the sweet, sickly body-smell of the black men about him all day. Saiyetovitz made no money: only worked hard and long, standing in his damp shirt amidst the clamor of the stores and the death-smell from the eating house always in his nose.

Meanwhile, Miriam fined down into a lady. She developed a half-bored, half-intolerant shrug of the shoulders in place of the childish sharpness that had been filed jagged by the rub-rub of rough life and harsh contrasts. She became soft-voiced, where she had been loud and gay. She watched and conformed; and soon took on the attitude of liberal-mindedness that sets the doors of the mind slackly open, so that any idea may walk in and out again, leaving very little impression: she could appreciate Bach and Stravinsky, and spend a long evening listening to swing music in the dark of somebody's flat.

Race and creed had never meant very much to Miriam and me, but at the University she sifted naturally towards the young Jews who were passing easily and enthusiastically, with their people's extraordinary aptitude for creative and scientific work, through Medical School. They liked her; she was invited to their homes for tennis parties, swimming on Sundays, and dances, and she seemed as unimpressed by the luxury of their ten-thousand-pound houses as she had been by the contrast of our clean, pleasant little home, long ago, when she herself was living behind the Concession store.

She usually spent part of the vacations with friends in

Johannesburg; I missed her—wandering about the Mine on my own, out of touch, now, with the girls I had left behind in the backwater of the small town. During the second half of one July vacation—she had spent the first two weeks in Johannesburg—she asked me if she could come and spend Sunday at my home, and in the afternoon, one of the Medical students arrived at our house in his small car. He had come from Johannesburg; Miriam had evidently told him she would be with us. I gathered her parents did not know of the young man's visit, and I did not speak of it before them.

So the four years of our training passed. Miriam Saiyetovitz and I had dropped like two leaves, side by side into the same current, and been carried downstream together: now the current met a swirl of dead logs, reeds, and the force of other waters, and broke up, divided its drive and its one direction. The leaves floated clear; divergent from one another. Miriam got a teaching post in Johannesburg, but I was sent to a small school in the Northern Transvaal. We met seldom during the first six months of our adult life: Miriam went to Capetown during the vacation, and I flew to Rhodesia with the first profits of my independence. Then came the war, and I, glad to escape so soon the profession I had once anticipated with such enthusiasm, joined the nursing service and went away for the long, strange interlude of four years. Whilst I was with a field hospital in Italy, I heard that Miriam had married—a Doctor Somebody-or-other: my informant wasn't sure of the name. I guessed it must be one of the boys whom she had known as students. I sent a cable of congratulation, to the Saiyetovitzes' address.

And then, one day I came back to the small mining town and found it there, the same; like a face that has been waiting a long time. My Mother, and my Dad, the big wheels of the shaft turning, the trees folding their wings about the Mine houses; and our house, with the green,

square lawn and the cat watching the doves. For the first
few weeks I faltered about the old life, feeling my way in a
dream so like the old reality that it hurt.

There was a feel about an afternoon that made my limbs
tingle with familiarity. . . . What . . . ? And then, lying
on our lawn under the hot sky, I knew: just the sort of
glaring summer afternoon that used to send me down to
the Concession stores, feeling isolated in the heat. Instantly,
I thought of the Saiyetovitzes, and I wanted to go and see
them, see if they were still there; what Miriam was doing;
where she was, now.

Down at the stores it was the same as ever, only dirtier,
smaller, more chipped and smeared—the way reality often
is in contrast with the image carried long in the mind. As
I stepped so strangely on that old pocked pavement, with
the skeleton cats and the orange peel and the gobs of spit,
my heart tightened with the thought of the Saiyetovitzes.
I was in a kind of excitement to see the store again. And
there it was; and excitement sank out at the evidence of the
monotony of "things." Blankets swung a little in the doorway. Flies crawled amongst the shirts and shoes posed in
the window, the hot, wet, sickening fatty smell came over
from the eating house. I met it with the old revulsion: it
was like breathing inside someone's stomach. And in the
store, amongst the wicked glitter of the tin trunks, beneath
the secret whispering of the blankets, the old Saiyetovitzes
sat glumly, with patience, waiting. . . . As animals wait in
a cage; for nothing.

In their delight at seeing me again, I saw that they were
older, sadder; that they had somehow given themselves into
the weight of their own humbleness, they were without a
pinnacle on which to fix their eyes. Whatever place it was
that they looked upon now, it was flat.

Mr. Saiyetovitz's mouth had creased in further to the
dead folds of his chin; his hair straggled to the rims of his
ears. As he spoke to me, I noticed that his hands lay, with
a curious helpless indifference, curled on the counter. Mrs.

Saiyetovitz shuffled off at once to the back of the shop to make a cup of tea for me, and carried it in, slopping over into the saucer. She was uglier than ever, now, her back hunched up to meet her head, her old thick legs spiraled in crêpe bandages because of varicose veins. And blinder too, I could see: that enquiring look of the blind or deaf smiling unsure at you from her face.

The talk turned almost at once to Miriam, and as they answered my questions about her, I saw them go inert. Yes, she was married; had married a doctor—a flicker of pride in the old man at this. She lived in Johannesburg. Her husband was doing very well. There was a photograph of her home, in one of the more expensive suburbs; a large, white modern house, with flower borders and a fishpond. And there was Miri's little boy, sitting on his swing; and a studio portrait of him, taken with his mother.

There was the face of Miriam Saiyetovitz, confident, carefully made-up and framed in a good hairdresser's version of her dark hair, smiling queenly over the face of her child. One hand lay on the child's shoulder, a smooth hand, wearing large, plain, expensive diamond rings. Her bosom was proud and rounded now—a little too heavy, a little overripe in the climate of ease.

I could see in her face that she had forgotten a lot of things.

When his wife had gone into the back of the shop to refill my teacup, old Saiyetovitz went silent, looking at the hand that lay before him on the counter, the fingers twitching a little under the gaze.

It doesn't come out like you think, he said, it doesn't come out like you think.

He looked up at me with a comforting smile.

And then he told me that they had seen Miriam's little boy only three times since he was born. Miriam they saw hardly at all; her husband never. Once or twice a year she came out from Johannesburg to visit them, staying an hour on a Sunday afternoon, and then driving herself back to

Town again. She had not invited her parents to her home at any time; they had been there only once, on the occasion of the birth of their grandson.

Mrs. Saiyetovitz came back into the store: she seemed to know of what we had been speaking. She sat down on a shot-purple tin trunk and folded her arms over her breast. Ah yes, she breathed, ah yes. . . .

I stood there in Miriam's guilt before the Saiyetovitzes, and they were silent, in the accusation of the humble.

But in a little while a Swazi in a tobacco-colored blanket sauntered dreamily into the shop, and Mr. Saiyetovitz rose heavy with defeat.

Through the eddy of dust in the lonely interior and the wavering fear round the head of the native and the bright hot dance of the jazz blankets and the dreadful submission of Mrs. Saiyetovitz's conquered voice in my ear, I heard his voice strike like a snake at my faith: angry and browbeating, sullen and final, lashing weakness at the weak.

Mr. Saiyetovitz and the native.

Defeated, and without understanding in their defeat.

The Train from Rhodesia

THE TRAIN CAME out of the red horizon and bore down toward them over the single straight track.

The stationmaster came out of his little brick station with its pointed chalet roof, feeling the creases in his serge uniform in his legs as well. A stir of preparedness rippled through the squatting native vendors waiting in the dust; the face of a carved wooden animal, eternally surprised, stuck out of a sack. The stationmaster's barefoot children wandered over. From the gray mud huts with the untidy heads that stood within a decorated mud wall, chickens, and dogs with their skin stretched like parchment over their bones, followed the piccanins down to the track. The flushed and perspiring west cast a reflection, faint, without heat, upon the station, upon the tin shed marked "Goods," upon the walled kraal, upon the gray tin house of the stationmaster and upon the sand, that lapped all around, from sky to sky, cast little rhythmical cups of shadow, so that the sand became the sea, and closed over the children's black feet softly and without imprint.

The stationmaster's wife sat behind the mesh of her verandah. Above her head the hunk of a sheep's carcass moved slightly, dangling in a current of air.

They waited.

The train called out, along the sky; but there was no answer; and the cry hung on: I'm coming . . . I'm coming . . .

The engine flared out now, big, whisking a dwindling body behind it; the track flared out to let it in.

Creaking, jerking, jostling, gasping, the train filled the station.

Here, let me see that one—the young woman curved her body further out of the corridor window. Missus? smiled the old boy, looking at the creatures he held in his hand. From a piece of string on his gray finger hung a tiny woven basket; he lifted it, questioning. No, no, she urged, leaning down toward him, across the height of the train, toward the man in the piece of old rug; that one, that one, her hand commanded. It was a lion, carved out of soft dry wood that looked like spongecake; heraldic, black and white, with impressionistic detail burnt in. The old man held it up to her still smiling, not from the heart, but at the customer. Between its Vandyke teeth, in the mouth opened in an endless roar too terrible to be heard, it had a black tongue. Look, said the young husband, if you don't mind! And round the neck of the thing, a piece of fur (rat? rabbit? meerkat?); a real mane, majestic, telling you somehow that the artist had delight in the lion.

All up and down the length of the train in the dust the artists sprang, walking bent, like performing animals, the better to exhibit the fantasy held toward the faces on the train. Buck, startled and stiff, staring with round black and white eyes. More lions, standing erect, grappling with strange, thin, elongated warriors who clutched spears and showed no fear in their slits of eyes. How much, they asked from the train, how much?

Give me penny, said the little ones with nothing to sell. The dogs went and sat, quite still, under the dining car, where the train breathed out the smell of meat cooking with onion.

A man passed beneath the arch of reaching arms meeting gray-black and white in the exchange of money for the staring wooden eyes, the stiff wooden legs sticking up in the air; went along under the voices and the bargaining, interrogating the wheels. Past the dogs; glancing up at the dining car where he could stare at the faces, behind glass, drinking beer, two by two, on either side of a uniform railway vase with its pale dead flower. Right to the end, to the guard's van, where the stationmaster's children had just collected their mother's two loaves of bread; to the engine itself, where the stationmaster and the driver stood talking against the steaming complaint of the resting beast.

The man called out to them, something loud and joking. They turned to laugh, in a twirl of steam. The two children careered over the sand, clutching the bread, and burst through the iron gate and up the path through the garden in which nothing grew.

Passengers drew themselves in at the corridor windows and turned into compartments to fetch money, to call someone to look. Those sitting inside looked up: suddenly different, caged faces, boxed in, cut off, after the contact of outside. There was an orange a piccanin would like. . . . What about that chocolate? It wasn't very nice. . . .

A young girl had collected a handful of the hard kind, that no one liked, out of the chocolate box, and was throwing them to the dogs, over at the dining car. But the hens darted in, and swallowed the chocolates, incredibly quick and accurate, before they had even dropped in the dust, and the dogs, a little bewildered, looked up with their brown eyes, not expecting anything.

—No, leave it, said the girl, don't take it. . . .

Too expensive, too much, she shook her head and raised her voice to the old boy, giving up the lion. He held it up where she had handed it to him. No, she said, shaking her head. Three-and-six? insisted her husband, loudly. Yes baas! laughed the boy. *Three-and-six?*—the young man was incredulous. Oh leave it—she said. The young man stopped. Don't you want it? he said, keeping his face closed to the boy. No, never mind, she said, leave it. The old native kept his head on one side, looking at them sideways, holding the lion. Three-and-six, he murmured, as old people repeat things to themselves.

The young woman drew her head in. She went into the coupé and sat down. Out of the window, on the other side, there was nothing; sand and bush; a thorn tree. Back through the open doorway, past the figure of her husband in the corridor, there was the station, the voices, wooden animals waving, running feet. Her eye followed the funny little valance of scrolled wood that outlined the chalet roof of the station; she thought of the lion and smiled. That bit of fur round the neck. But the wooden buck, the hippos, the elephants, the baskets that already bulked out of their brown paper under the seat and on the luggage rack! How will they look at home? Where will you put them? What will they mean away from the places you found them? Away from the unreality of the last few weeks? The man outside. But he is not part of the unreality; he is for good now. Odd . . . somewhere there was an idea that he, that living with him, was part of the holiday, the strange places.

Outside, a bell rang. The stationmaster was leaning against the end of the train, green flag rolled in readiness. A few men who had got down to stretch their legs sprang on to the train, clinging to the observation platforms, or perhaps merely standing on the iron step, holding the rail; but on the train, safe from the one dusty platform, the one tin house, the empty sand.

There was a grunt. The train jerked. Through the glass the beer drinkers looked out, as if they could not see beyond it. Behind the fly-screen, the stationmaster's wife sat facing back at them beneath the darkening hunk of meat.

There was a shout. The flag drooped out. Joints not yet coordinated, the segmented body of the train heaved and bumped back against itself. It began to move; slowly the scrolled chalet moved past it, the yells of the natives, running alongside, jetted up into the air, fell back at different levels. Staring wooden faces waved drunkenly, there, then gone, questioning for the last time at the windows. Here, one-and-six baas!—As one automatically opens a hand to catch a thrown ball, a man fumbled wildly down his pocket, brought up the shilling and sixpence and threw them out; the old native, gasping, his skinny toes splaying the sand, flung the lion.

The piccanins were waving, the dogs stood, tails uncertain, watching the train go: past the mud huts, where a woman turned to look, up from the smoke of the fire, her hand pausing on her hip.

The stationmaster went slowly in under the chalet.

The old native stood, breath blowing out the skin between his ribs, feet tense, balanced in the sand, smiling and shaking his head. In his opened palm, held in the attitude of receiving, was the retrieved shilling and sixpence.

The blind end of the train was being pulled helplessly out of the station.

The young man swung in from the corridor, breathless. He was shaking his head with laughter and triumph. Here! he said. And waggled the lion at her. One-and-six!

What? she said.

He laughed. I was arguing with him for fun, bargaining —when the train had pulled out already, he came tearing after. . . . One-and-six baas! So there's your lion.

She was holding it away from her, the head with the open jaws, the pointed teeth, the black tongue, the wonderful ruff of fur facing her. She was looking at it with an expression of not seeing, of seeing something different. Her face was drawn up, wryly, like the face of a discomforted child. Her mouth lifted nervously at the corner. Very slowly, cautious, she lifted her finger and touched the mane, where it was joined to the wood.

But how could you, she said. He was shocked by the dismay of her face.

Good Lord, he said, what's the matter?

If you wanted the thing, she said, her voice rising and breaking with the shrill impotence of anger, why didn't you buy it in the first place? If you wanted it, why didn't you pay for 'it? Why didn't you take it decently, when he offered it? Why did you have to wait for him to run after the train with it, and give him one-and-six? One-and-six!

She was pushing it at him, trying to force him to take it. He stood astonished, his hands hanging at his sides.

But you wanted it! You liked it so much!

—It's a beautiful piece of work, she said fiercely, as if to protect it from him.

You liked it so much! You said yourself it was too expensive—

Oh you—she said, hopeless and furious. You. . . . She threw the lion on to the seat.

He stood looking at her.

She sat down again in the corner and, her face slumped in her hand, stared out of the window. Everything was turning round inside her. One-and-six. One-and-six. One-and-six for the wood and the carving and the sinews of the legs and the switch of the tail. The mouth open like that and the teeth. The black tongue, rolling, like a wave. The mane round the neck. To give one-and-six for that. The heat of shame mounted through her legs and body and sounded in her ears like the sound of sand pouring. Pouring, pouring. She sat there, sick. A weariness, a tastelessness, the discovery of a void made her hands slacken their grip, atrophy emptily, as if the hour was not worth their grasp. She was feeling like this again. She had thought it was something to do with singleness, with being alone and belonging too much to oneself.

She sat there not wanting to move or speak, or to look

at anything, even; so that the mood should be associated with nothing, no object, word or sight that might recur and so recall the feeling again. . . . Smuts blew in grittily, settled on her hands. Her back remained at exactly the same angle, turned against the young man sitting with his hands drooping between his sprawled legs, and the lion, fallen on its side in the corner.

The train had cast the station like a skin. It called out to the sky, I'm coming, I'm coming; and again, there was no answer.

Another Part of the Sky

COMING ACROSS THE dark grass from the main building to his dark house at eleven o'clock on a Sunday night he stumbled against the edging of half-bricks. End up, all sunk into the earth at the same level, they formed a serrated border along every pathway and round every flower bed in the place. The young boys had laid them with all their race's peasant pleasure in simple repetitive patterns, some memory beneath their experience of rotting corrugated iron and hessian recalling to their hands the clean daub of white zigzag round a clay hut. That would come, he supposed with a smile: they would want whitewash for the bricks.

There were roses growing behind the bricks, tattering the darkness with blacker spangles of reaching foliage. The boys had planted those too. "The man who pulled down prison walls and grew geraniums in their place"—of course the papers had got it wrong. Wrong, all wrong. Whenever things are written down they go wrong. Mistakes are the least of it; by the time they are stamped in print, words have spilt meaning and whatever of truth they have managed to scoop up. Geraniums for roses; that was nothing: but "the man who pulled down prison walls and grew geraniums in their place"—that was a glib summing up that left everything out. As a fact it was true; in the nine years that he had been principal of the reformatory, he had taken down the six-foot walls with the broken bottles encrusted on the top, he had set the boys gardening, he had helped them build playing-fields, begged musical instruments for them. The photograph of him sitting at his desk, dipping a pen. The photograph of the boys sitting cross-legged in the garden, numbers on their khaki backs, gleams of sun on their heads cropped of wool. . . . When did that moment, the moment of the article, of all the articles that had been written about him, all the lectures that had been given in his honor—when did it exist?

As his feet sounded suddenly on gravel, he made a little sighing noise, casting off the bland unreality of it. It left out everything. What had it to do with now, the sleeping darkness of the reformatory behind him, the burning starts of red and flashes of print jittering his inner sight, the quiet of the night veld darkness; the worry that filled all the spaces of his body as his breath did.

This morning he had stood amidst the voices of the boys at church service, this afternoon he had written the draft of a penal reform pamphlet, after supper he had sat with a table full of reports. His nostrils were wide with a pause of concentration, his eyes did not see. His wife sewed at some garment in her lap without looking; he was conscious now and then of the quiet wink of her glasses as she watched him.

All the day, half the night; the worry had been with him all the time. Now the surface of the day had been rolled away, and he was left with the worry, he took it with him as he went up the three steps, over her door mat made of old tire-strips, through the door that gave to his thumb as though the latch had been waiting for his touch. For a moment the night stood in the doorway: the great hard

polished winter sky that shone of itself—the nick of young
moon was a minor brilliant amongst white sharp stars—
without answer above the low heads of the kopjes; where
in that humming space was the young boy with the neat
head of a lizard? Then the door stood before night; and inside, the dry closed air of the house carried the unspoken
question (Have you heard? Any news yet?), the shape of
the telephone waited to ring. Here you could not escape
the answer coming. . . . The telephone was a nerve, ready
to jump.

Somewhere the boy who had lain in the clean discipline
of a dormitory and learned so quickly the ritual of the hands
and the bent head that made the day pass of itself in work,
lay crouched in a hovel of smoke and bright eyes and the
smell of breath and beer, and stared through hours at the
sluggish possibilities of idleness, rising and writhing in half-
discerned murk. Saw desire melt into violence . . . wanting
into having. Sat in the cave of hunched faces painted with
cosy fear by the light of a paraffin-tin fire, flickered with the
torn filth of old newspapers stuffed in corners (newspapers
that said stupidly, crime wave . . . robbery . . . old man
knifed in the street): and was free. That was the boy's
freedom; that was what he had run away to, a week ago.
—It was easy . . . there were geraniums, no walls.—It happened a few times every year, always with this same twinge
of peculiar pain to the principal: that was what they had
to run away to, these young boys; to that; that troubled
dreamlike existence of struggle and fear and horror which
was what they knew, which to them was freedom. The
governing board said consolingly: You mustn't get too
discouraged when your system has occasional failures—it
has justified itself magnificently in the long run, Collins.
And he smiled at them, being accustomed to having patience with people whose understanding is limited to their
own capabilities of feeling. Poor Collins, they said to each
other—he was a dreamer, an idealist, after all—he's just like

everyone else when he's proved wrong. Can't take the blow to his pride.

The boy had been gone now for a week and like others who had slipped from the cool bit of society tasting strange in their young hard mouths, he might have disappeared into the nameless faces of the native locations or he might have been brought back again to lower his head and watch himself watched. But yesterday the telephone had rung and the dutiful voice of the sergeant had said what he had been told to say: That boy that escaped from your place last week—there's been an old woman assaulted and robbed in Jeppe, and the description of the native that did it seems to fit the boy.—Yes, yes—The policeman read slowly through the description again.—Yes, that's right.—Well, that's all, we just wanted to tell you. There don't seem to be any fingerprints, unfortunately. But we should be able to get him. We just wanted to make sure we got the description right.—And the woman, is she badly hurt?— Fractured skull, ribs broken, the lot. He used an old dumb-bell that was lying around the kitchen.

The boy with the neat, small head of the lizard, the long small deft hands. As the principal felt quietly along the passage to the bathroom, he saw again, for the thousandth time, the momentary reassurance of a flash of the boy's face, lifted from his desk as you walked in. Like a pain let go, relief came: that boy could never have done it.

He closed the bathroom door with a muted creak so that he could turn on the light without its pale square opening on the wall in the bedroom where his wife lay. The warm after-scent of a bath met him. He turned on the hot tap gently and the water was drawn like a soft skein over his hand. In the little mirror that sweated runnels of con-densed steam from the bath, he saw his face with the non-recognition of weariness in his eyes. There was a moment of childish comfort, as if, having worried so much, the whole thing was accounted for, expiated. The boy could not have done the thing; not this boy, and he knew boys, had studied thousands of them, every hour of his day, for nine years. It was all right. He had not done it. The description could be anybody, was anybody. It was only that the police happened to have the description of the boy on hand because he had escaped, and so they turned to it first. Whenever they did not have anything to go upon, they fell back on something easy like this; it made it sound as if they had done something, were getting somewhere. "The police are investigating and have the situation well in hand." He knew the police, too, after nine years. Thousands and thousands of faces, all brown, all brown eyes, all thick mouths. That was how the white people of the town saw the black: they were all the same, how could you tell one from another unless he had a scar, or a limp? So if a young boy escapes from a reformatory, and a young boy assaults a woman, it must be the same boy.—He washed his face under the running tap, trying not to make a noise, gasping at the water. And then he found the towel and dried his face, dried the day off his face and left his eyes burning, almost enjoying the relief of their own weariness. A muscle twitched relaxation in one lower lid.

Then he saw her stockings, washed and hung side by side on the towel rail.

As he saw them, the symbol of her routine, the orderly living out of the day which she maintained always, no matter what troubled her, what exile of worry she experienced beside him and with him—for sometimes he told her his worry, and sometimes he did not and she knew it just the same and suffered it quietly and kept her knowledge of it from him—he knew that she was awake in the bedroom. She was awake and worrying. Her hands did the things they had always done in an unconscious effort to keep one sane and quiet reassurance, the safety of commonplace. But the very fact of the reassurance proved the existence of the worry. He could feel her eyes open in the darkness of the next room, staring at a ceiling she could not see, and at

once the comfort sucked away out of him and it seemed
he had to breathe hard short breaths to relieve the weighti-
ness of his chest. He stood there for a moment with his
head jerking and sagging with the intake and release of this
distressed breath, and it was all back again: Where was the
boy? Had he done it? He had done it. Could he have done
it? Was he the kind of boy to do it? With mechanical
repetition he enacted the talk with the police sergeant,
over and over again. Well, that's all, we just wanted to tell
you. We just wanted to make sure we got the description
right.—And the woman, is she badly hurt?—He used an
old dumbbell that was lying around. We just wanted to
tell you.—Yes, yes.—We just wanted to tell you. The cold
of the concrete floor was hardening up through his feet
as he stood dead still as though the worry were a pain that
might pass if he let it, submitted to its spasm and did not
give it the incentive of his own attempt to escape on which
to tighten its clutch.

His feet were cold as he turned off the bathroom light
before he opened the door (she would know from the very
meticulousness of his care that he knew there was no sleep
from which to awaken her) and felt across the passage into
the bedroom. The soft slump of his clothes as he undressed
moved like the darkness settling to itself; there was a pause
before the long creak of his bed as he let his body down.

Across the strip of rug that separated his bed from hers
he listened to her listening for him. She was so still, still
with consciousness; stiller than sleep, that deepens and
thins, floats and sinks, can ever be. Monday . . . Will it
be tomorrow? They've found him. He did it. How can you
fight against the time if it is coming, if it is to come; the
time of hearing: he did it.

And though she would not let him hear her breathing because she did not want to give it away, the answering conviction of her fear slipped silently out with her soundless
breath, and reached him. He did it. Oh did he do it?

But they did not speak. They would never speak. Somewhere below the face of the boy, a pang which had never yet found the right moment to claim attention lifted feebly like an eye of lightning that opens and shuts in another part of the sky. When would there be time to speak to her, to read the face of his wife as he struggled to read the suffering faces of the nameless, the dispossessed whom God made it incumbent upon him that he should spend his life reading?

The face lifted again from the desk. Brown eyes surrounded by a milky-blue rim, the flat flush ears, the sloping temples; the neat head of a lizard. . . . He studied the face, called it up again and again, searching.

The night was awake, listening to them.

They had both been asleep a short time when the knock came at the door. It dinned on sleep like thunder but at the instant of wakefulness it became a knock at the front door. The impact of dread, met at last! exploded his blood through his body like shot. His wife sat up for the light switch. The light blinded them both. His feet felt over the floor for his slippers and his arms went into his gown; the knocking was insistent but not loud, purposeful of the necessity to rouse, but considerate not to shock. His heart beat so slow and strong that every force of it seemed to swell his veins as if some painful object much too large for passage were being pushed through. He went through the house turning on light, acknowledged at last, behind him, and undid the latch of the door. It's all right, he was saying, Coming, coming. It was the voice that prisoners had heard in the condemned cell, the voice that came from somewhere, never failed him.

Ngubane, one of his assistants, stood there. With a thrill of recognition, he knew it, the lump in his blood ran fast and liquid and his heart torrented beats as drops of water fuse in the rush of a waterfall. He found his glasses in his hand and now he put them on and there was Ngubane in his neat overcoat for it had been his Sunday off and he was dressed for leisure. His own shoulders shielded the light from Ngubane's face, but he saw the man's mouth parted forward in a kind of gasp as he pressed in.

Something terrible has happened, burst Ngubane as if the opening of the door had released the words, and as the principal fell back to let the man in and the light slipped past and lifted the face out of the dark, he saw the astonishing twitch of lost control from Ngubane's nose to lip, blisters of sweat along his eyebrows. It seemed that their panic rose and met, equal. In a trance they went along the passage together, through a door; swallowed; sat down. Their eyes held one another.

I—sir, sir . . . , said Ngubane.

I know, I know, he said passionately. The nostrils of his short strong nose were arched back, two cuts of sorrow held his mouth firm down the sides of his cheeks. His head was lifted in an unconscious gesture to bear. Ngubane, who had seen it before in him, flared his nostrils in sudden tears of gratitude for strength, the strength of Collins. My brother —he was shaking, shaking his head as if to rid himself of what he saw—my brother was killed on the road now. I was riding beside him and it happened . . . he was killed.

Your brother?

My brother who was out with me in Johannesburg. My brother Peter the teacher from Germiston. The one you knew—who came . . . The bus didn't see and he was riding on the outside. He was killed, I didn't even see how it happened, he was riding there with me and then he was gone. . . .

Your brother? Collins was leaning forward with his face screwed up with the curious look of questioning closely, almost as if he were irritated with not understanding what the other was trying to say.

Two strings jerked in Ngubane's neck. He nodded till he could speak again. Peter, my brother.

He was killed on the road you say? Killed on the road. . . . Collins was repeating it to himself as if it were some marvel; the room, Ngubane, his own voice rising so oddly, seemed to be sliding rapidly away from him. . . . His head searched a little for air, his hand lying on its side on the table jumped, relaxed, faltered.

I'm sorry, he said, Ngubane, I'm sorry. He spoke quickly. His face was burning hot. He stood up quickly and had his hand on the man's shoulder. Tell me about it, Ngubane, he said. Speak of it.

As a child waits for permission to weep, the man put his head down on his arms and with his nose flattened against the tweed, let his eyes, showing yellow-white as they twisted up to Collins' face, slowly fill with a man's hard sorrow.

When the assistant had gone (they had given him something to make him sleep, words of comfort, and the comfort of promised action in the assurance that tomorrow he must take the day off to make arrangements for the funeral) the principal and his wife sat and had a cup of tea in the kitchen. The gulp of tea down their throats was easy between them. Come on, he said, and she tried the kitchen window to see if it was locked and flattened her hands against her dressing gown a moment in a pause before she went back to bed. He pottered about, locking up again, turning lights off, picking things up in vague question of why they should have been left where they were for the night. Then he came into the bedroom and got into bed. The two of them sighed as they moved about under their covers, settling for warmth and sleep.

Then they were still.

For a moment, you know, she said suddenly, I thought he'd come to tell us bad news about the boy.

Well so did I, he said.

She made a little sound that might have meant she was going to say something, or might have been a little sound of sleep.

He lay and the darkness came up to him, the darkness

spread out to the edges of his being, the darkness washed away the edges of his being as the sea melts the edges of the sand. But just as it was about to smooth out his head and wash down the pinnacles of his features like a sand-castle, a return of consciousness rose within him and swept it away.

So did I.

It came to him suddenly and it filled him with desolation as startling and wakeful as the thump at the door. It stiffened him from head to foot with failure more bitter and complete than he could ever have imagined. *I'm sorry. I'm sorry. Tell me about it.* The boy is alive so Ngubane is dead. The boy has not done it yet, so tea can be drunk. The boy has not done it so you may lie easy in the dark. A peace can take your mind while Ngubane goes home with his brother's death. If there is room for the boy, there is no room for Ngubane. This conscience like a hunger that made him want to answer for all the faces, all the imploring of the dispossessed—what could he do with it? What had he done with it? The man who pulled down prison walls and grew geraniums. He saw himself, standing up at a meeting, the flash of attention from his glasses as they looked up to him. The silence of his wife, going about her business whilst he worried, nine years he worried, turned from her to this problem or that. If you search one face, you turn your back on another.

He did not know how he would live through this moment of knowledge, and he closed his lids against the bitter juice that they seemed to crush out, burning, from his eyes.

Lusin (Lu Hsün)

[1881 – 1936]

CHINA, AT THE end of the nineteenth century, was still a feudal empire vulnerable to repeated military expeditions from European nations in violent search of trade concessions. Although the Revolution of 1911 ended the Manchu dynasty, the republic that emerged was only nominal. War lord rulers sold their sovereignty, as well as the hope for a vitalized nationalism, to Japanese demands. Having defeated the Russians in 1895, on Chinese soil, the Japanese could not be prevented from industrial expansion throughout Manchuria.

In such a climate of desperation, Chou Shu-jen (whose pen name became Lusin) spent his childhood. His scholar father sold their family land in Chekiang province in order to pay for the release of his grandfather, a Peking official imprisoned by the Manchus. Before Lusin's father died from the resultant impoverishment, the entire family came to know intimately both pawnshop and medicine shop. Lusin entered the imperial naval academy and, later, the engineering academy at Nanking, but decided in 1902 to study medicine in Japan. Gradually he became convinced that, because the importation of Western technology had not brought with it Western democracy, the appeal most urgently needed was to the mind of his people.

Returning to his home province in 1909, he taught physiology and chemistry at the Normal School; but when the 1911 Revolution ended in disillusionment, he secluded himself in literary scholarship at the Ministry of Education. The Allied decision, in 1918, to transfer German privileges at Shantung to Japan outraged Chinese students and precipitated the May Fourth Movement in 1919, against those ministers willing to sign the Versailles treaty. Lusin emerged as a reluctant leader of these new intellectuals.

In a 1918 issue of *New Youth* magazine, Lusin published the first Chinese story in *pai-hua* (the vernacular) and in modern form, shockingly different from traditional sketches. It was the "Diary of a Madman," whose title he borrowed from Gogol, whom Lusin had translated along with Chekhov, Tolstoy, John Stuart Mill, and others. In a cannibalistic culture (personifying the feudal society, still evident not only in political authoritarianism but also in the family's abusive chain of command) the protagonist expects daily to be devoured by his elder brother. His only hope is in the future (Lusin had been deeply influenced by T. H. Huxley's *Evolution and Ethics*): "Perhaps there are still some children who have not yet eaten a human being? Save, save the children. . . ."

"Diary" was reprinted in *Battle Cries* (1923), along with "The Real Story of Ah Q," a long satire mocking Confucianism's tendency to rationalize each subjection, each new corruption, as a "spiritual victory." Ah Q-ism came to represent national inertia in the face of famine, disease, and invasion. Reading this work, French novelist Romain Rolland is reported to have wept.

With a realism new to Chinese literature, Lusin's stories traced the victimization of underprivileged classes, often by customs which they all too readily embraced. Not in his translations, numerous though they were, but in his own unhappy experience he found his fiction's characters: the woman forced into a second marriage against her will and then scorned for her "immorality"; the man who, having failed civil service examinations, stoops to burglary and has his legs permanently crippled by his victim, the Provincial Scholar who was fortunate enough to have passed those same examinations. Lusin's stories often took on a symbolical cast, as in "Medicine," where the names Hua (Shuan) and Hsia were poetic synonyms for feudal and revolutionary China. In "Cloud over Luchen," there were political overtones; the "Emperor has mounted the Dragon Throne" referred to the brief restoration of the Manchu dynasty in 1917.

In 1921, Lusin received the leadership of the New Culture Movement from Hu Shih when the latter stubbornly advised a return to classical forms and virtues instead of exploration of the new. Lusin became a lecturer in the history of Chinese fiction at Peking, but in 1926 during violent student riots he was hunted out of the city by the government.

Because at no time in his life was he concerned with political doctrine, all wings of the Movement have claimed him. He was profoundly alarmed at the needless death of 47 students during the Peking incidents. The same humane feeling turned him, with equal horror, against Sun Yat-sen's admission of Communists into the nationalist Kuomintang party and, later, against Chiang Kai-shek's bloody purge of the Communists in 1927. These were "man-eaters" again, "slayers of the present moment." Lusin's students were on both sides, victims of one another. He no longer saw automatic relief in irresistible evolutionary processes. He found youth, whom he had glorified, committing its own atrocities.

Lusin had said: "Although all literature is propaganda, yet not all propaganda is literature." He could not suddenly write as if detached from the people about whom he cared; yet he did not welcome exploitation by either rebels or counterrevolutionaries who wanted him to advertise their "high-grade milk": "I am terribly lean and . . . I am a bull at that." He continued to criticize the new corruptions when he could, the perpetual error of thrusting foreign methods wholesale onto the Chinese without deliberation. But he wrote less and less. Shortly before his death, he said: "I feel I shall perhaps have nothing to say from now onwards. When the terror dies away, I do not know what will come: it may not be anything good."

Lusin died in extreme poverty, of tuberculosis, in 1936, still trying to unite his people, this time against the armed aggression of the Japanese. Besides two collections of short stories and one of ancient legends retold, he left China 32 volumes of translations, 2 volumes of letters, 14 volumes of notes and comments, and 7 studies of Chinese literature; as well as a heritage of indignation as savage as Swift's.

Cloud over Luchen

As THE SUN gradually gathered up its yellow rays along the mud banks of the river, the scorched leaves of the tallow trees seemed to recover their breath and a few striped mosquitoes began to buzz underneath the trees. The smoke died out in the chimneys of the peasants' homes facing the river. Women and children sprinkled water on the dusty ground in front of their own houses and set out low tables and benches. It was supper time.

The old folks and the men sat on the low benches and chatted, wielding huge palm fans. The children ran about or squatted under the tallow trees and played with pebbles. The womenfolk carried out *kan-ts'ai* and brown rice, hot and steaming. A pleasure boat went by, carrying a party of literary aesthetes, who, watching the scenes along the banks, were inspired to poetic sentiment about the villagers, uttering, "Unreflecting and without a worry in their heads—this is truly Rural Bliss."

But the sentiments of these literary lights did not exactly accord with the truth, for they could not hear what old Mrs. Nine Pounds was saying. She was at that moment greatly

From *Ah Q and Others* by Lusin, translated by Chi-Chen Wang for the Columbia University Press, 1941. Reprinted by permission of the translator.

put out by things in general: beating upon the leg of her stool with her frazzled palm fan for emphasis, she was saying,

"I have lived seventy-nine years and I have lived long enough. I do not want to see these signs of family decline. It is better that I died. In a moment we'll be eating supper, and yet she is eating toasted beans. She'll eat us poor!"

Her great-granddaughter Six Pounds, who was just then coming toward the supper table, thought better of it at the sight of the querulous woman. She ran to the river's edge and hid behind a tallow tree. Then she put out her little head adorned with two hornlike braids and said in a loud voice, "The old Would-Not-Die!"

Though old Mrs. Nine Pounds was of venerable age, she was not very deaf. However, she did not seem to have heard her granddaughter, and continued, "This proves that each generation is worse than the last!"

This village has a peculiar custom. When a baby is born, it is usually weighed and the weight in pounds becomes the milk name of the infant. After old Mrs. Nine Pounds had celebrated her fiftieth birthday she gradually became one of those who mourn for the good old times. When she was young, she said, the weather was not as hot as now, nor were the beans quite as hard. Her perpetual theme was that the world today is all wrong. Moreover, Six Pounds weighed three pounds less at birth than her great-grandfather, and one pound less than her father Seven Pounds. To the old lady these were indisputable proofs of her contention. Therefore she repeated with emphasis, "Truly, each generation is worse than the last!"

Her granddaughter-in-law Sister Seven Pounds came up with the rice basket as this sentiment was repeated and emphasized. She plumped down the basket on the table and said in a tone of vexation, "There you go again. When Six Pounds was born was she not actually six pounds and five ounces? Besides, your scales were specially made for you, with eighteen ounces to the pound. If a real sixteen-ounce scale had been used, our Six Pounds would have been over seven pounds. Come to think of it, grandfather and father might not have been actually nine or eight pounds. The scales used might have been only fourteen-ounce scales."

"Each generation worse than the last!"

Before Sister Seven Pounds answered, she suddenly espied her husband coming out of the lane. Thereupon she shifted the direction of her attack and shouted at him, "A fine time for you to be coming home, you dead corpse! Where did you hide off to die? You never care how long people hold up dinner for you, do you?"

Although Seven Pounds lived in the village, he was no ordinary peasant. Three generations, from his grandfather's time to his own, the men of his family had not touched the handle of a hoe. Like many other men of a more progressive nature, Seven Pounds made his living as a boatman. He made a round trip each day, in the morning from Luchen to the city and back to Luchen again by nightfall. Because of this he was well abreast of the times. For instance, he knew that at such and such a place the Thunder God struck dead a centipede monster, or that at such and such a place a maiden gave birth to a yaksha demon, and things of a like nature. He was, therefore, something of a personage in the village. However, in his family supper was still served without benefit of lamplight during the summer months, as was the custom of peasants, and he deserved a scolding for coming home so late.

Seven Pounds approached slowly, his head bowed, and sat down on a bench. In his hand he held a pipe with a brass bowl and an ivory mouthpiece and a stem of mottled bamboo more than six feet long. Six Pounds sneaked out from behind the tree and sat down beside him, greeting him, "dieh-dieh," but Seven Pounds paid no attention to her.

"Each generation worse than the last!" old Mrs. Nine Pounds said again.

Seven Pounds raised his head slowly and said with a sigh, "The Emperor has mounted the Dragon Throne."

For a moment Sister Seven Pounds was stupefied by the announcement, but then said with comprehension, "This is fine, for does it not mean that there will be general pardon by imperial grace?"

Seven Pounds sighed again and said, "I have no queue."

"Does the Emperor require queues?"

"The Emperor requires queues."

"How do you know?" Sister Seven Pounds asked, somewhat with alarm.

"Every one in the Hsien Heng wine shop says so."

Sister Seven Pounds began to feel that things looked black indeed for her husband, if they said so at the Hsien Heng wine shop, the chief source of news for the village. Glancing at her husband's shaven head, she could not suppress a mounting anger and resentment against him for having jeopardized his own safety. She almost hated him. In despair she filled a bowl with rice and thrust it in front of him and said, "You had better eat your rice. You will not grow a queue by pulling a long face!"

Imperceptibly the sun gathered up its last rays and the river recovered its coolness. The clatter of chopsticks and bowls echoed all over the open space and beads of sweat began to form on everyone's back. After finishing her third bowl of rice, Sister Seven Pounds glanced up and her heart began to beat violently when she saw fat, short Mr. Chao the Seventh coming toward them across the single-log bridge. What distressed her most was the fact that Mr. Chao was wearing his long gown of blue cotton cloth.

Mr. Chao was the proprietor of the Mao Yuan wine shop in the neighboring village and the most distinguished personage within a radius of thirty *li*. Because he was something of a scholar, he had about him the air of a man who had seen better days. He owned some ten-odd volumes of the *Romance of Three Kingdoms*, with commentaries by Chin Sheng-t'an, and used to sit over them and read aloud word by word. The extent of his erudition was such that he not only knew the names of the Five Tiger Generals but also their derived names. He knew, for instance, that Chao Yun's derived name was Tzu-lung, Chang Fei's was Yi-te and so on. After the Revolution he coiled up his queue on top of his head, like a Taoist priest. He used to say with many a sigh that if Chao Tzu-lung were alive to-day, the world would not have come to such grief. Sister Seven Pounds had good eyes; she immediately noticed that Mr. Chao had not coiled his hair on top of his head like a Taoist priest but wore it in a queue with the familiar, closely shaven circle around it. From this she concluded that the Emperor must certainly have mounted the Dragon Throne, that wearing the queue was obligatory, and that Seven Pounds' position was most surely of a very precarious character. For Mr. Chao never wore that long gown of his except on special occasions. In the last three years he had worn it only twice, once when pockmarked Ah Ssu, with whom he once had a quarrel, fell ill, and again when Mr. Lu, who once wrecked his tavern, died. This was the third time and it could only mean that he was celebrating something lucky to himself but unlucky to his enemies.

Sister Seven Pounds remembered that two years earlier her husband had, under the influence of liquor, insulted Mr. Chao by declaring that he was born of a "cheap womb." Therefore she immediately feared for Seven Pounds and she could not still her pounding heart.

As Mr. Chao approached, those who were sitting stood up and said, pointing to their bowls with their chopsticks, "Mr. Seven, please join us!" Mr. Chao nodded and said, "Please go ahead, please go ahead." He went straight to Seven Pounds' table, where he was greeted in the same fashion and returned the same answer. He looked at the fare of rice and steamed *kan-ts'ai.*

"How fragrant your *kan-ts'ai* is! Have you heard?" he asked, standing behind Seven Pounds and opposite Sister Seven Pounds.

"The Emperor has mounted the Dragon Throne," Seven Pounds said.

Sister Seven Pounds watched Mr. Chao's face and said with a placating smile, "Now that the Emperor has mounted the Dragon Throne, when are we going to have the general pardon by imperial grace?"

"General pardon by imperial grace? The general pardon will undoubtedly come in time," Mr. Chao said, and then continued with sudden severity, "But where's Seven Pounds' queue? Yes, the queue is an important matter. Do you know that during the Rebellion of the Longhairs it was a case of 'grow your hair and lose your head or shave your hair and save your head'?"

Seven Pounds and his wife had never had any book learning and so did not quite understand the allusion. But since the learned Mr. Chao said so, the situation must be very grave and unalterable. It was as if the death sentence had been pronounced. Seven Pounds was left speechless with a ringing in his ears.

"Each generation worse than the last," old Mrs. Nine Pounds took the opportunity to voice her grievance to Mr. Chao. "The rebels today only cut off people's queues, making them look like neither monk nor priest. But were the Longhair rebels like this? I have lived seventy-nine years and I have lived long enough. The Longhairs of the old days used whole bolts of red satin to wrap around their heads, with the loose ends hanging down as far as their feet. The Longhair kings used yellow satin, also dangling down to the feet. Yes, yellow satin and red satin, dangling down . . . I have lived long enough; I am seventy-nine years old."

Sister Seven Pounds stood up and murmured to herself, "What are we going to do? All of us, old and young, depend upon him for our living."

Mr. Chao shook his head and said, "That can't be helped. The punishment for not having queues is clearly written in the book. They don't take into account family circumstances."

When she heard that it was clearly written in the book, Sister Seven Pounds gave up all hope. She felt quite helpless and in her helplessness her resentment turned toward Seven Pounds. She pointed at the tip of his nose with her chopsticks and said, "He has brought all this upon himself, the dead corpse! When the rebellion started I told him that he should give up poling boats for the time being and should not go into the city. But he insisted on going into the city—on rolling into the city—and when he got there they got hold of him and cut off his queue. Formerly he had a nice, silky, black queue and now he looks like neither monk nor priest. It is all well and good for the jailbird to bring this upon himself, but what have we done? What are we going to do? You walking corpse of a jailbird!"

The villagers had by now hurried through their meal and were gathered around Seven Pounds' table. Conscious of the fact that he was something of a personage, Seven Pounds felt acutely the shame of being scolded by one's wife in public. He raised his head and gently remonstrated, "It is very well for you to say these things now, but, at the time, you . . ."

"You walking corpse of a jailbird!"

Among the onlookers Sister Eighteen was the most kindhearted. With her two-year-old son in her arms—he was born after the death of her husband—she was standing beside Sister Seven Pounds. She felt sorry for Seven Pounds and tried to put in a word for him, saying, "Sister Seven Pounds, let him be. People are not gods, so who is to foresee what is to come? And did you not say at the time, Sister Seven Pounds, that it was not so bad, after all, to be without a queue? Besides, there has been no official proclamation by his honor the magistrate."

Before she had heard it all, Sister Seven Pounds was already red around the ears. She pointed her chopsticks at

Sister Eighteen's nose and said, "What are you talking about, Sister Eighteen? As far as I can see I am the same person now as I was then, so how could I have said such a stupid thing? On the contrary, I cried for three days and three nights as everyone knows. Even Six Pounds, the little devil, cried."

Six Pounds had just finished her bowl of rice. She held out her empty bowl and asked for more. Whereupon, Sister Seven Pounds, who was looking for some object for her displeasure, brought down the points of her chopsticks on the child's head right between her hornlike queues and shouted, "Who told you to butt your snout into this, you men-keeping little widow!"

Crash, the empty bowl fell from Six Pounds' hand. It landed on the edge of a brick and a large piece broke off. Seven Pounds jumped to his feet, picked up the broken bowl, pieced it together, and examined it. "Your mother's——" he shouted and with one slap knocked down Six Pounds, who lay there crying. Old Mrs. Nine Pounds took her hand, helped her up, and led her away, saying "Each generation worse than the last."

Sister Eighteen was also aroused, and said in a loud voice, "Sister Seven Pounds, you are 'pointing at the chicken while really cursing the dog.'"

Mr. Chao had been an onlooker until Sister Eighteen said "Besides, there has been no official proclamation by his honor the magistrate." This angered him. Now he stepped forward and said, " 'To point at the chicken while really cursing the dog' is a small matter at a time like this. The imperial troops will soon be here. Now you must know that the protector of the imperial equipage this time is Marshal Chang, a descendant of Chang Yi-te of Yen. With his eighteen-foot snake spear, he has the strength of ten thousand warriors. Who can stand up against him?" He grasped his hands into fists, as if holding an invisible snake spear, and lunged forward toward Sister Eighteen saying, "Can you stand up against him?"

Sister Eighteen, child in arms, was trembling with passion but she was nevertheless frightened to see Mr. Chao, his face full of grease and sweat, his eyes bulging, lunge at her. She did not dare answer, but turned around and walked away. Mr. Chao also walked off. The onlookers blamed Sister Eighteen for bringing this upon herself. They made way for Mr. Chao; several men without queues, who had been trying to rectify the lack by growing one, dodged behind others so as not to be seen by him. Mr. Chao did not try to search them out. He walked through the crowd and, as he turned behind the tallow trees, he repeated, "Can you stand up against him?" He stepped upon the single-log bridge and sauntered off.

The stupefied villagers all admitted to themselves that indeed no one of them was able to stand up against Chang Yi-te and that consequently Seven Pounds must forfeit his life. Since Seven Pounds had committed a crime against His Majesty's laws, he had no business to be so proud and self-satisfied as he related the news he had gathered on his daily trips to the city. Consequently they felt pleased at the fix that Seven Pounds found himself in. They wanted to express themselves on the point, but found they really had nothing to say.

The buzzing grew louder as the mosquitoes flew past the naked backs to hold converse among themselves under the tallow trees. The crowd slowly broke up; one by one the villagers went home, shut their gates and went to bed. Sister Seven Pounds did likewise, grumbling all the while as she gathered up the supper things and took away the table and benches.

Seven Pounds took the broken bowl home and sat upon his doorsill, smoking. But in his worry he forgot to puff at his pipe, and it went out. He knew that the situation was very critical, and he wished to think of some way out, some remedy, but his ideas were vague and disjointed and there was no way to connect them up. "Queue, queue, how about the queue? . . . Eighteen-foot snake spear . . . Each generation worse than the last . . . The Emperor upon his Dragon Throne . . . The broken bowl must be taken to the city to be mended . . . Who can stand up against him? . . . It is clearly written in the book . . . His mother's——"

The next morning Seven Pounds poled the boat from Luchen to the city and returned in the evening as usual. At supper he told old Mrs. Nine Pounds that he had had the broken bowl mended in the city. The part broken off was very large and required sixteen brass clasps at three *cash* each, a total cost of forty-eight *cash*.

Old Mrs. Nine Pounds was dissatisfied as usual and said, "Each generation worse than the last. I have lived long enough. Three *cash* a clasp! But what sort of clasps are these? In the old days the clasps were different. I have lived seventy-nine years . . ."

From then on, although Seven Pounds went to the city as usual, a certain gloom hung over his household. The villagers avoided him, no longer caring to come to him for news of the city. Sister Seven Pounds had no civil words for him and frequently called him "jailbird."

One evening about ten days later, Seven Pounds returned from the city to find his wife in good spirits. "Did you hear anything in the city?" she asked him.

"I heard nothing."

"Has the Emperor mounted the Dragon Throne?"

"They did not say."

"Didn't anyone at the Hsien Heng tavern say anything about it?"

"No one said anything there either."

"I think the Emperor is not going to mount the Dragon Throne after all. I passed by Mr. Chao's shop today and saw that he was reading his books again. His queue is again coiled up on top of his head and he did not wear his long gown."

"Mm . . ."

"Don't you suppose that the Emperor is not going to mount the Dragon Throne after all?"

"I suppose, perhaps not."

Seven Pounds has long since recovered the respect of the villagers and of his wife and is treated by them with the consideration due to a person of his standing. Now as they are gathered in the open space before their respective gates for their summer meals, they again greet one another with good-natured laughter. Mrs. Nine Pounds celebrated her eightieth birthday long ago, and is as disgruntled and strong as ever. The two hornlike queues of Six Pounds have now grown into one braid. Although she has just begun to bind her feet, she is still able to help Sister Seven Pounds with the household chores. She is seen hobbling about the open space along the river bank now, the bowl with sixteen brass clasps in her hand.

Medicine

IT WAS LATE in an autumn night, after the moon had set but before the sun had risen; the sky was dark and blue, and all was asleep except habitual prowlers of the night. Hua Lao-shuan suddenly sat up, struck a match, and lit a grease-covered lamp, flooding the two rooms of the teahouse with a whitish-blue light.

"Are you going now, Little Shuan's father?" This was the voice of an old woman. From the inner room came a fit of coughing.

"Yes," Old Shuan answered, as he listened anxiously and buttoned up his coat. "Now give it to me," he said, holding out his hand.

Mother Hua fumbled under the pillow, produced a package of silver dollars and gave it to Old Shuan. He took it and put it in his pocket, feeling it from the outside to make certain that it was secure. He then lit his lantern and went into the inner room. A rustling sound could be heard, followed by another fit of coughing. Old Shuan waited until it subsided and said softly, "Little Shuan, don't get up. Your mother will take care of the shop."

As his son did not answer, Old Shuan concluded that he

By permission of the translator, Chi-Chen Wang.

had gone back to sleep. He stepped out into the street. It was still dark and only the gray road was clearly visible. The lantern lit up his feet, first one, then the other. He met an occasional dog, but none of them barked. It was much colder than indoors, and Old Shuan felt invigorated, as if transformed into a young man and endowed with the power to give life. He walked on with vigorous strides. The road became clearer and clearer and the sky brighter and brighter.

Suddenly the cross street which had taken on a sinister significance in Old Shuan's mind loomed before him and brought him to an abrupt halt. He walked back a few steps, found a shop that was still closed and stationed himself in the doorway. After a while he began to feel the chilliness in the air.

"*Heng!* the old bugger!"

"Seems pleased with himself . . ."

Old Shuan started. Glancing up, he saw several men go by. One of them even turned around and gave him an odd look. Old Shuan could not see his face but his eyes seemed to glint like those of a hungry man in sight of food. Old Shuan looked at his lantern and found that it had gone out. He pressed his pocket and was reassured by the hard lump. The street was filling up with people, loitering about in groups of twos and threes. At first there seemed to be something ghostly about them, but when Old Shuan looked sharply at them, there was nothing strange about them at all.

Presently some soldiers came marching up the street. At first, Old Shuan could only make out the white disks on the front of their jackets, but as they drew nearer, he was able to see the red trimmings on their uniforms. The sound of footsteps grew louder, and before he realized it, a large crowd had gone by. Those who had been loitering about closed in and surged forward like a tide. They halted suddenly just before they reached the cross street.

Old Shuan looked in that direction, but he could see only a wall of backs. All necks were stretched long, like ducks caught by unseen hands and drawn upwards. There was a silence, which seemed to be followed by some sound. The crowd stirred then and surged backward till they came upon Old Shuan, almost knocking him over.

"Hey, there! You hand over the money and I'll hand over the goods." A man dressed entirely in black stood before Old Shuan, his dagger-like eyes darting at him, making him shrink to half his size. The man held out one big hand toward him and in the other held a bright crimson roll, the crimson still dripping from it.

Old Shuan pulled out his money and held it in his trembling hand, but he did not dare take what was in the other man's hand. The man became impatient and shouted, "What is there to be afraid of? Why don't you take it?" As Old Shuan still hesitated, the man in black jerked the lantern out of his hand, tore off the paper shade, wrapped up the roll in it, and stuffed it into Old Shuan's hand; then he jerked the bag of money from Old Shuan, felt it, turned around and walked away, saying contemptuously, "The old bugger . . ."

"Who is it for?" Old Shuan seemed to hear someone ask. But he did not answer. His whole attention was centered upon the package; he felt like one carrying the only infant heir of ten generations; he banished everything else from his thoughts; he wanted to transplant the new life in that package into his family hoping to reap from it many blessings. The sun had risen, brightening the road leading straight to his shop and lighting up the partly obliterated legend on the arch over the cross street.

II

When Old Shuan reached home, the tea pavilion was already set in order, the tables all clean and bright. But there were no patrons as yet. Little Shuan was eating at a table in the back row, large drops of sweat running down his forehead. His lined coat stuck to his body, his shoulder blades showing through like a broad inverted V in relief. At this sight the father could not help frowning a little. His wife left the stove and joined him, looking at him inquiringly.

"Did you get it?" she asked with quivering lips.

"I got it."

They both went to the corner near the stove and held a conference. Mother Hua went out and returned shortly with a lotus leaf, which she flattened out on the table. Old Shuan opened up the lantern paper and rewrapped the crimson roll in the lotus leaf. Little Shuan had finished his rice, but his mother said to him hurriedly, "Stay where you are, Little Shuan; don't come here."

She fixed the fire, and Old Shuan stuffed the green package and the lantern paper spotted with crimson into the stove. As red flames and black smoke flared up and died out, a strange pungent odor filled the shop.

"How fragrant! What are you making?" This was Master Five, the hunchback. He spent all his day in the tea pavilion, the first to come and the last to go; he had just limped up to the table near the street and sat down. But no one answered him. "Roasted rice porridge?" Old Shuan hurried out and made his tea without answering the question.

"You can come in now, Little Shuan," Mother Hua called. As Little Shuan went into the room and sat down on a bench, his mother brought him something black and round in a dish, saying, "Eat this. It will make you well."

Little Shuan took it and regarded it for a while with a strange, indescribable feeling, as though holding his own life in his hands. Carefully he broke it in two. Some white vapor issued forth, and when the vapor had dissipated, he held the two halves of a white roll. In a short while it disappeared down his throat, but he could not tell how it tasted. The dish lay empty before him. On one side stood his father and on the other his mother, both regarding him intently with inquiring eyes. His heart palpitated and he had another fit of coughing.

"Sleep a little. You'll get well."

Little Shuan obeyed and went to bed, still coughing. Mother Hua waited until he stopped panting before she drew over him the patched sheet.

III

People began to gather in the pavilion. Old Shuan went around filling the covered tea cups from a large brass kettle. There were black circles around his eyes.

"Old Shuan, aren't you feeling well?" said a gray-bearded man. "Are you sick?"

"No."

"No? I didn't really think you were, you're all smiles," Graybeard retracted.

"Old Shuan is always so busy. If only his son . . ." Before the hunchback could finish speaking, a man with coarse features swaggered in, his black cotton gown unbuttoned but merely tied around his waist with a black sash, and said in a loud voice:

"Has he eaten it? Is he all right now? Old Shuan, you are a lucky one, I say. If I had not tipped you off . . ."

Old Shuan listened, smiling ingratiatingly, one hand holding the kettle, the other hanging respectfully at his side. The patrons, too, listened in respectful silence. Mother Hua, also smiling ingratiatingly, came out with cup and tea leaves, to which she added an olive. Old Shuan went to get more hot water.

"This will absolutely cure him. It is different from what you usually get. Just think, it was still warm when you got it!" the man continued.

"It is quite true, if not for Uncle Kang, how could we have known . . ." Mother Hua said gratefully.

"I guarantee that he will get well, I guarantee it! I

guarantee that this fresh human blood will cure any kind of consumption!"

At the word *consumption*, Mother Hua frowned with displeasure, but immediately forced a smile as she walked away. Uncle Kang did not notice this, but continued to talk noisily. Little Shuan woke up and joined in with his coughing.

"So it was your Little Shuan that met with such good luck. Of course, he will get well. No wonder Old Shuan has been all smiles this morning," Graybeard said. Then he walked up to Uncle Kang and asked humbly, "I heard, Uncle Kang, that the prisoner was a Hsia boy. Whose son was he? Just what was the charge?"

"Who else but the son of Mother Hsia the Fourth? The little beggar!" Pleased with the attention that he was getting, Uncle Kang talked louder than ever, his meaty face distorted. "The little beggar did not care about his life. That's all. But I did not get anything out of it this time, even the clothing that was stripped from him went to Redeye Ah-yi, the jailer. The luckiest man is our Uncle Shuan here; next comes Master Hsia the Third, who got twenty-five ounces of snow-white silver as a reward. He pocketed it all and did not have to spend a *cash*."

Little Shuan emerged from the small room, his hands pressed to his chest to quiet his coughing. He went to the stove, dished out a bowl of cold rice, poured some hot water over it, sat down and began to eat. Mother Hua followed him and asked solicitously, "Little Shuan, do you feel better? Are you still hungry?"

"I guarantee it, I guarantee it," Uncle Kang said after a brief glance at Little Shuan but turned to his audience, and continued, "Master Hsia the Third was a clever one. If he had not informed the authorities, he and all his family would have been executed. But now? Silver! The little beggar was a rare one. Even in prison he tried to incite the jailer to rebellion!"

"Ai-ya! Is that possible?" a young man about twenty years old said indignantly from a back row.

"You must know that Redeye Ah-yi went to spy on him, and so they talked. 'This land of the Great Ch'ing dynasty belongs to all of us,' he said. Why, it's treason to talk like that. Redeye knew that he had only an aged mother, but did not suspect that he would be as poor as he was. He could not press the least bit of oil out of him. He was angry enough to explode as it was without the little beggar trying to tickle the tiger's head. So he gave him two blows in the face!"

"Brother Yi is a good boxer; those must have been good, hearty blows," the hunchback in the corner said with relish.

"The lowly beggar did not seem to mind. He only said, 'How pitiable! how pitiable!' "

"Why should a traitor like him deserve any pity?" Graybeard asked.

Uncle Kang looked at the speaker contemptuously and said, "You did not hear me right. He seemed to mean that Ah-yi was to be pitied."

The listeners were puzzled and the conversation stopped. Little Shuan had finished his rice and was sweating all over, steam arising from his forehead.

"Ah-yi was to be pitied! That's raving mad. He must have gone mad," it suddenly dawned upon Graybeard.

"He must have gone mad," agreed the young man of about twenty. This great discovery restored life to the people in the tea pavilion. Taking advantage of the noisy chatter, Little Shuan coughed violently. Uncle Kang went to him, slapped him on the shoulder, saying:

"I guarantee it, Little Shuan. Don't cough like that. I guarantee it."

"Yes, gone mad!" said the hunchback, nodding his head.

IV

There was a piece of public land by the city wall outside

of the Western Gate; through the middle of this field was a path made by men seeking a short cut. It formed a natural division: to the left of the path were buried those who perished in prison or died by the executioner's sword; to the right were the tombs of the destitute. On either side the mounds had risen in great numbers, like huge round rolls that the rich use at birthday celebrations.

It was unusually cold at the Clear Bright festival of the following year; the willows had just sprouted tiny buds half the size of grains of rice. Mother Hua was at a new tomb on the right shortly after dawn. She set out four dishes and a bowl of rice, burned the spirit paper, and cried. She sat abstractedly on the ground as if waiting for something, though she herself did not know what. A breeze stirred her hair, which was without doubt whiter than the year before.

Another woman approached on the path, her hair also streaked with white, and her clothes worn. She held an old lacquered basket from which a string of paper ingots was suspended, and walked with difficulty. When she saw Mother Hua, she seemed to hesitate and her pale face seemed to reflect shame and humiliation, but finally she went resolutely to a tomb on the left and set down her basket.

The tomb was directly across from Little Shuan's, separated from it only by the path. Mother Hua watched as she set out four dishes and a bowl of rice, burned the paper ingots, and cried, and she said to herself that it must be her son's tomb. The old woman lingered and looked around a while, when she seemed to be startled by something. Her hands trembled, she walked back a few steps, and stood there staring.

Fearing that she might go insane with grief, Mother Hua stood up, crossed the path, and said to her softly, "Do not cry any more; we had better go home."

The other woman nodded, her eyes still staring upward, and said in a hushed voice, "Look, what could that be?"

Following her finger, Mother Hua's eyes were directed to

the tomb before her. The grass had not yet grown over it, and there were left ghastly patches of yellow earth. When she looked more carefully, she too was startled, for there was clearly a circle of red and white flowers around the top of the tomb.

Though their eyesight was not good, they could distinguish clearly the red and white flowers. There were not many of them and they did not seem very fresh, but they were neatly arranged in a circle around the summit of the mound. Looking around, Mother Hua could see only a few scattered white flowers such as are found in the fields in the early spring; she experienced suddenly a feeling of discontent and emptiness. The other woman stepped up to the tomb and looked more intently, saying to herself, "They are not rooted. They could not have gotten there by themselves. But who could have come to a place like this? The children would not come here to play, and our relatives have long ceased to come. What does this mean?" She reflected for a while and her tears began to flow again. She said in a loud voice:

"Yu-erh. Is it because they have wronged you, and you cannot forget, that you have shown your presence today? I know now, Yu-erh. They must have framed you. But they will be punished, for heaven knows all. You can now close your eyes and rest in peace." She looked around and saw a crow perched on a barren tree. "If you are really here and can hear my words, make the crow fly to the top of your tomb. Let me know that you are here!"

The breeze had ceased; the dry grass stood straight and still like wires of brass. A dead silence fell. The two women stood in the grass, looking up at the crow, but the crow remained on its perch, as still as if cast of iron, its head tucked in because of the chill of the morning.

A long time passed by; more people came with offerings for the dead, appearing and disappearing among the tombs.

Mother Hua felt a little relieved though she knew not why. Again she said, "Let us go home."

The other woman sighed, listlessly gathered up the rice and dishes, lingered a moment longer, and finally went away, murmuring to herself, "What does such a thing mean? . . ."

After they had walked about twenty or thirty paces, they suddenly heard a loud "Wah . . ." They both shuddered and looked around, just in time to see the crow open its wings, leap off and fly away, straight as an arrow into the distant sky.

The Widow

THE YEAR-END according to the old calendar is, after all, more like what a year-end should be, for the holiday spirit is not only reflected in the life of the people, but seems to pervade the atmosphere itself. Frequent flashes light up the heavy, gray evening clouds, followed by the crisp report of firecrackers set off in honor of the Kitchen God. Those fired in the immediate neighborhood explode, of course, with a louder noise, and before the deafening sound has ceased ringing in one's ears, the air is filled with the acrid aroma of sulphuric smoke. On such an evening I returned for a visit to my native village, Luchen. As we no longer had a house there, I stayed with His Honor Lu the Fourth. He was my kin—my Uncle Four, as he was one generation above me—and a very moral and righteous old graduate. He had not changed much since my previous visit; he had grown a little older, but he did not yet have a beard. After we had exchanged greetings, he remarked that I was stouter, and immediately thereafter launched into a tirade against the reform movement. I knew, however, that his tirade was not directed against me but against the ancient reformers of the nineties, such as K'ang Yu-wei. In any case we could

From *Ah Q and Others* by Lusin, translated by Chi-Chen Wang for the Columbia University Press, 1941. Reprinted by permission of the translator.

not be said to understand each other, and I was left alone in the study shortly afterwards.

I got up very late the next day. After the midday meal I went out to call on friends and relatives. On the third day I did the same thing. None of them had changed much, they were merely a little older. All were busy with preparations for the Invocation of Blessings, the most solemn and elaborate ceremony of the year, at which they offered the most generous sacrifices to the God of Blessings and prayed for good luck for the coming year. Chickens and ducks were killed and pork was bought at the butcher's. Carefully washed by women (whose hands and arms—some adorned with silver bracelets—became red from long immersions in the water), and then boiled and studded with chopsticks, they were offered with candles and incense in the early hour of the fifth watch. Only the male members of the family participated in the ceremony, which was always concluded with firecrackers. Every year it was like this in families that could afford it, and so it was this year.

The overcast sky grew darker and darker, and in the afternoon it began to snow. The dancing snowflakes, as large as plum flowers, the smoke from burning incense and from the chimneys, and the bustle of the people all gave Luchen a festive air. When I returned to Uncle Four's study, the roof tops were white, making the room lighter than usual at that hour. I could make out very clearly the large *shou* (longevity) character on a scroll hung on the wall, a rubbing based on what was supposed to be the actual handwriting of the Taoist immortal Ch'en T'uan. One of the side scrolls had come off and lay loosely rolled up on the long table against the wall; the one still hanging on the wall expressed the sentiment "Peace comes with understanding." I strolled over to the desk by the window and looked over the books. There were only a few odd volumes of the K'ang Hsi Dictionary and an annotated edition of the *Analects*.

I decided that I must leave the next day, whatever happened. What had depressed me most was a meeting with

Sister Hsiang-lin the day before. I encountered her in the afternoon as I was returning home along the river bank after visiting some friends in the eastern part of the village, and by the direction of her vacant stare I knew that she was heading for me. Of the people that I had seen at Luchen on this visit no one had changed as much as she. Her gray hair of five years ago had turned entirely white; she was not at all like a woman of only forty. Her face was intolerably drawn and thin; it had lost its sad and sorrowful aspect and was now as expressionless as if carved of wood. Only an occasional movement of her eyes indicated that she was still a living creature. She held in one hand a bamboo basket containing a chipped and empty bowl; with the other hand, she supported herself with a bamboo stick, a little split at the lower end. She had evidently become a beggar.

I stopped, expecting her to ask for money.

"Have you come back?" she asked.

"Yes."

"I am very glad. You are a scholar, and you have been to the outside world and learned of many things. I want to ask you about something." Her lusterless eyes suddenly lighted up, as she advanced a few steps towards me, lowered her voice, and said in a very earnest and confidential manner, "It is this: is there another life after this one?"

I was taken aback by the unexpectedness of the question; the wild look in her eyes, which were fixed on mine, gave me a creepy sensation on my back and made me feel more uncomfortable than I used to at school when an examination was sprung upon us, with the teacher watching vigilantly by our side. I had never concerned myself with the after life. How was I to answer her now? Most people here believe in the survival of the soul, I thought rapidly as I considered an answer, but this woman seemed to have her doubts. Perhaps it was a matter of hope with her, the hope that there was an after life and that the after life would be a better one than this. Why should I add to the unhappiness of this miserable woman? For her sake I had better say that there was another life after this one.

"Maybe there is . . . I think," I said haltingly and without conviction.

"Then there would also be a hell?"

"Oh! Hell?" I was again taken unawares and so I temporized, "Hell?—It would seem logical . . . though it may not necessarily exist . . . but who cares about such things?"

"Then we will meet members of our family after death?"

"Er, er, do we meet them?" I then realized that I was still a very ignorant man and that no amount of temporizing and cogitation would enable me to stand the test of three questions. I became less and less sure of myself and wished to recant all that I had said. "That . . . but really, I cannot say. I cannot really say whether souls survive or not."

Before she could ask any more questions, I fled back to Uncle Four's house, very much agitated in spirit. I told myself that my answer to her questions might lead to something unfortunate and that I should be held responsible for what might happen. She probably felt lonely and unhappy at a time when others were celebrating; but was that all, or had she formed a definite plan of action? Then I laughed at myself for taking such a trivial incident so seriously, for pondering upon it and analyzing it. The psychologists would undoubtedly call such a morbid interest or fear pathological. Besides, had I not explicitly said "I cannot really say," thus annulling all my answers and relieving myself of all responsibility?

"I cannot really say" is a very useful sentence. Inexperienced youths are often rash enough to give answers to the difficult problems of life and prescribe remedies for others, and thus lay themselves open to blame when things go wrong. If, however, they qualify their statements by concluding them with "I cannot really say," they will assure themselves of a safe and happy life. I then realized the indispensability of this sentence, indispensable even when one is talking with a beggarwoman.

But my uneasiness persisted; I kept recalling the meeting with a presentiment of evil. On this dark, heavy, snowy afternoon in that dreary study my uneasiness became stronger. I felt I had better go away and spend a day at the county seat. I recalled Fu-hsing-lou's excellent shark's fin cooked in clear broth at only a dollar a plate, and wondered if the price had gone up. Although my friends of former days had scattered hither and yon, I must not fail to feast upon this delicacy, even if I had to eat by myself. Whatever happens, I must leave this place tomorrow, I repeated to myself.

Because I have often seen things happen which I had hoped would not happen, which I had told myself might not necessarily happen, but which had a way of happening just the same, I was very much afraid that it would be so on this occasion. And surely something did happen, for towards evening I overheard a discussion going on in the inner courtyard. Presently it stopped, and after a silence I distinguished the voice of Uncle Four.

"Of course a *thing like that* would choose of all times a time like this."

I was first puzzled and then felt uncomfortable, for the remark sounded as if it might have something to do with me. I looked out the door but did not see anyone that I could ask. Not until the hired man came in to replenish my tea toward suppertime did I have an opportunity to make inquiries.

"With whom was His Honor Four angry a little while ago?" I asked.

"Who else but Sister Hsiang-lin?" he answered very simply.

"Sister Hsiang-lin? What did she do?" I hurriedly pursued.

"She died."

"Died?" My heart sank and I almost jumped. My face must have changed color. But the man did not raise his head and so did not notice it. I calmed myself and continued:

"When did she die?"

"When? Last night or early this morning. I can't really say."

"What did she die of?"

"What did she die of? Why, what else would it be if not poverty?" the man answered in a matter of course way and went out without ever raising his head to look at me.

My terror was transient, for I realized that, since that which was to come to pass had come to pass, there was no longer need for me to worry about my responsibility. Gradually I regained my composure; a sense of regret and disquiet only occasionally intruded. Supper was served, with Uncle Four keeping me company. I wanted to find out more about Sister Hsiang-lin, but I knew that though he had read that "Ghosts and spirits are only the manifestations of the two cardinal principles of nature," he was still subject to many taboos; that such topics as sickness and death should be carefully avoided at a time when New Year blessings were about to be asked; and that if I must satisfy my curiosity, I should resort to some well-considered euphemism. As I unfortunately knew no such euphemisms, I withheld the question I was several times on the point of asking. From the look of displeasure on his face I began to imagine it quite possible that he considered me a "thing like that" for coming to bother him at such a time; thereupon I hastened to set him at ease and told him that I was going to leave Luchen the following day. He did not show much warmth in urging me to stay. Thus we dragged through supper.

Winter days are short at best, and, with snow falling, night soon enveloped the village. Everyone was busy by the lamplight, but outdoors it was quiet and still. Falling upon a thick mattress of snow, the flakes seemed to swish-

swish, making one feel all the more lonely and depressed. Sitting alone under the yellow light of the vegetable oil lamp, I thought of the fate of the poor, forlorn woman who had been cast into the garbage dump like a discarded toy. Hitherto she had continued to remind people of her miserable existence in the garbage dump, much to the surprise and wonder of those who have reason to find life worth living. Now she had at last been swept away clean by the Unpredictable. Whether souls continue to exist or not I do not know, but I did know that at least one who had no reason to find life worth living was at last no longer living and that those who looked upon her as an eyesore no longer had to look at her. It was a good thing, whether looked at from her point of view or from that of others. As I listened to the swish-swishing of the snowflakes outside and pondered along this line of thought I began to take comfort and to feel better.

And I began to put together the fragments that I had heard about her until her story became a fairly coherent whole.

Sister Hsiang-lin was not a native of Luchen. One year in the early part of winter they needed a new maid at Uncle Four's and the middlewoman, old Mrs. Wei, had brought her. She wore a black skirt, a blue, lined coat and light blue vest, and her hair was tied with white strings as a sign of mourning. She was about twenty-six years old, of a dark yellow complexion, with a faint suggestion of color in her cheeks. Old Mrs. Wei called her Sister Hsiang-lin, said that she was a neighbor of her mother's and that as her husband had recently died she had come out to seek employment. Uncle Four frowned and Aunt Four guessed the cause; he did not like the idea of widows. But the woman had regular features and large, strong hands and feet. She was quiet and docile and it appeared that she would make an industrious and faithful servant. Aunt Four kept her in spite of Uncle Four's frown. During the trial period she worked all day as though unhappy without employment. She was strong and could do everything that a man could do. On the third day they decided to keep her, at a monthly wage of 500 cash.

Everyone called her Sister Hsiang-lin; no one asked her surname, but since the middlewoman was from Weichiashan and said that she was a neighbor of her mother's, her name was probably Wei. She was not talkative and spoke only in answer to questions, and that rather briefly. Not until after some ten days did it gradually become known that she had at home a stern mother-in-law, a brother-in-law about ten years old and able to go out to gather fuel, and that her husband who had died in the spring was ten years younger than she and also made his living by cutting firewood. This was all that was known about her.

The days went by quickly and she showed no signs of losing her initial industry; she never complained about her fare or spared her strength. People all talked about the woman help in the house of His Honor Lu who was more capable and industrious than a man. At the year-end she did all the cleaning, sweeping, and killed the chickens and ducks and cooked them; it was actually not necessary to hire temporary help. She seemed happy too; her face grew fuller and traces of smiles appeared around the corners of her mouth.

But shortly after the New Year she returned one day, pale and agitated, from washing rice at the river; she said she had seen a man who looked like an elder cousin-in-law loitering in the distance on the opposite bank, and she feared he was watching her. Aunt Four questioned her but could get no more out of her. When he heard of this incident, Uncle Four knitted his brows and said, "I do not like it. I am afraid that she ran away from home."

As a matter of fact, she had come away without her mother-in-law's permission, and it was not long before this supposition proved to be true.

About ten days later, when the incident had been almost forgotten, old Mrs. Wei suddenly appeared with a woman about thirty years old, whom she introduced as Sister Hsiang-lin's mother-in-law. Though dressed like a woman from the hill villages, she was self-composed and capable of speech. She apologized for her intrusion and said that she had come to take her daughter-in-law home to help with the spring chores, as only she and her young son were at home.

"What else can we do since her mother-in-law wants her back?" Uncle Four said.

Therefore, her wages, which amounted to 1,750 *cash* and of which she had not spent a penny, were handed over to the mother-in-law. The woman took Sister Hsiang-lin's clothes, expressed her thanks, and went away.

Sister Hsiang-lin was not present during this transaction and it did not occur to Aunt and Uncle Four to summon her. It was not until toward noon when she began to feel hungry that Aunt Four suddenly remembered that Sister Hsiang-lin had gone out to wash rice and wondered what had happened to her.

"Aiya! Where is the rice?" she exclaimed. "Did not Sister Hsiang-lin go out to wash the rice?"

She began searching for the washing basket, first in the kitchen, then in the courtyard, then in the bedroom, but there was no trace of it. Uncle Four looked outside the gate but did not see it either, and it was not until he went to the river that he saw the basket resting peacefully on the bank, a head of green vegetable beside it.

Then he learned from eyewitnesses what had happened. A covered boat had been moored in the river all morning, but no one paid any attention to it at the time. When Sister Hsiang-lin came out to wash rice, two men that looked like people from the hills jumped out, seized her as she bent over her task and dragged her into the boat. Sister Hsiang-lin uttered a few cries but was soon silent, probably because she was gagged. Then two women embarked, one a stranger and the other old Mrs. Wei. Some thought that they did see Sister Hsiang-lin lying bound on the bottom of the boat.

"The rascals! But . . . ," Uncle Four said.

That day Aunt Four cooked the midday dinner herself, while her son Niu-erh tended the fire.

Old Mrs. Wei returned after the midday dinner.

"What do you mean by your outrageous behavior? And you have the audacity to come back to see us!" Aunt Four said vehemently over the dishwashing. "You brought her here yourself, and then you conspire with them to kidnap her, causing such a scandal. What will people say? Do you want to make a laughingstock of us?"

"Aiya, aiya! I was duped, really, and I have come back to explain. She came to me and asked me to find a place for her. How was I to know that her mother-in-law knew nothing of it? I beg your forgiveness. It was all my fault, old and weak woman that I am. I should have been more careful. Fortunately, your house has been noted for its generosity and I know you would not return measure for measure with people like us. I shall most certainly find you a good maid to atone for myself."

Thus the episode was closed and shortly afterwards forgotten.

Only Aunt Four, who had difficulty in finding a satisfactory servant, sometimes mentioned Sister Hsiang-lin, whose successors either were lazy or complained of their food, or both. "I wonder what has become of her," Aunt Four would say, hoping that she might come back again. By the beginning of the following year she gave up this hope.

Toward the end of the first month, however, old Mrs. Wei came to offer her New Year's greetings. She was slightly intoxicated with wine and said that she had been

observed around her eyes, which were not as alive as before. Old Mrs. Wei again accompanied her and made this recital to Aunt Four:

"This is truly what is called 'Heaven has unpredictable storms.' Her man was a strong and sturdy one. Who would ever have thought that he would die of influenza? He had gotten well, but he ate a bowl of cold rice and it came back again. Fortunately she had her son and she was capable, could cut firewood, pick tea, or raise silkworms. She was managing all right. Who would ever have thought that her child would be carried off by a wolf? Spring was nearing its end and yet a wolf appeared in the village. Who would have thought of such a thing? Now she is alone. Her elder brother-in-law took possession of her house and put her out. She is now at the end of her road and has no other way except to appeal to her old mistress. Now she has no entanglements and as *tai-tai* happens to be in need of a new maid I have brought her. I think as she is familiar with things here she would be much better than a strange hand."

"I was a fool, really," Sister Hsiang-lin raised her lusterless eyes and said. "I knew that the wild beasts came down to the village to seek food when they couldn't find anything in the hills during the snow season, but I did not know they would come down in the spring. I got up early and opened the door. I gave a basket of beans to our Ah Mao and told him to sit on the gate sill and peel them. He was an obedient child and did everything I told him. He went out and I went behind the house to cut wood and wash rice. After putting the rice in the pot, I wanted to put the beans over it to steam. I called Ah Mao but he did not answer. I went out and looked. I saw beans spilled all over the ground but could not see our Ah Mao. He never went out to play at the neighbors' but I went and looked for him. I did not find him. I was frightened and asked people to go out and search for him. In the afternoon they found one of his shoes in the bramble. They all said that there was no hope, that the wolf must have got him. They went into the bush and sure enough they found him lying in the grass, all his insides gone, his hand still holding on tightly to the handle of the basket . . ." She broke off sobbing.

Aunt Four hesitated at first, but her eyes reddened after hearing the story. Then she told Sister Hsiang-lin to take the basket and bundle to the maid's room. Old Mrs. Wei sighed with relief, and Sister Hsiang-lin seemed to feel better than when she arrived. As she was familiar with the house, she went and set her things in order without being directed, and thenceforward she again became a maid-servant at Luchen.

And everybody called her Sister Hsiang-lin as before.

But this time her fortune had changed considerably. Two or three days later her employers realized that her hands were not as clever and efficient as formerly, her memory failed, her deathlike face never showed the shadow of a smile. Aunt Four could not conceal her displeasure. Uncle Four had frowned as usual when she came, but made no protest as he knew how difficult it was to find a satisfactory servant; he only cautioned Aunt Four, saying that though such people were a pitiable lot, yet she was after all a bane against morality, and that it was all right for her to help in ordinary tasks but she must not touch anything in connection with the ancestral sacrifices. These Aunt Four must prepare herself, else they would be unclean and the ancestors would not touch them.

Preparation of the ancestral sacrifices was the most important event in Uncle Four's house and Sister Hsiang-lin used to be busiest at such a time. Now she had nothing to do. When the table was placed in the center of the hall with a curtain in front of it, she started to arrange the wine cups and chopsticks as she used to do.

"Sister Hsiang-lin, please leave those things alone. I will arrange them," Aunt Four hastened to say.

She drew back her hands in embarrassment and then went to get the candlesticks.

"Sister Hsiang-lin, leave that alone. I'll get it," Aunt Four again said hastily. After hovering around for a little while, Sister Hsiang-lin withdrew in bewilderment. The only thing she was permitted to do that day was to tend the fire in the kitchen.

People in the village still called her Sister Hsiang-lin, but the tone of their voices was different; they still talked with her, but they were scornful of her. She did not seem to notice the change; she only stared vacantly and recited the story that she could not forget, night or day—

"I was a fool, really . . ." Her tears would flow and her voice grow tremulous.

It was a very effective story; men would stop smiling and walk away in confusion; women not only seemed to forgive her and to banish the look of scorn on their faces, but shed tears with her. Some older women, not having heard her own recital, would come to her and listen to her until her voice broke, when they would let fall the tears that had been gradually accumulating in their eyes, heave some sighs and go away satisfied. She was their chief topic of conversation.

Sister Hsiang-lin continued to repeat her story and often attracted three or five listeners. But the story soon became familiar to everyone, and after a while even the kindest and most patient of old ladies ceased to shed any tears. Still later almost everyone in the village could recite her story, and was bored by it.

"I was really a fool, really," she would begin.

"Yes, you knew that wild beasts came down to the village to seek food only when they cannot find anything in the hills," people would thus stop her and walk away.

She would stand gaping and staring for a while and then walk away, a little embarrassed. Still, she tried to bring up the story of Ah Mao by some ruse—a basket, beans, or some other children. For instance, if she saw a child two or three years old, she would say, "Ai-ai, if our Ah Mao were alive he would be as big as that . . ."

The children were afraid of her and of the look in her eyes, and they would tug at their mothers' coats and urge them to go away. And thus Sister Hsiang-lin would be left alone to wander off by herself. Soon people caught on to her new trick; they would forestall her when there were children around by saying, "Sister Hsiang-lin, if your Ah Mao were alive, would he not be as big as that?"

She might not have realized that her sorrow, after having been carefully chewed and relished for so long, had now become insipid dregs, only fit to spit out; but she was able to sense the indifference and the sarcasm in the question and to realize that there was no need of her answering it.

The New Year festivities last a long time in Luchen and begin to occupy people after the twentieth of the last month of the year. At Uncle Four's house they had to hire a temporary man helper, but the work was too much for him and another woman was hired. But she, Liu-ma, was a devout vegetarian and would not kill the chickens and ducks; she only washed dishes. Sister Hsiang-lin had nothing to do but tend the fire. She sat and watched Liu-ma wash the dishes. A light snow was falling outside.

"Ai-ai, I was really a fool," Sister Hsiang-lin soliloquized after looking at the sky, sighing.

"Sister Hsiang-lin, there you go again," Liu-ma looked at her impatiently. "Let me ask you, did you not get your scar when you dashed your head against the table that time?"

"Mmm," she answered evasively.

"Let me ask you, why did you finally give in?"

"I?"

"Yes, you. I think you must have been willing. Otherwise . . ."

"Ah-ah, but you do not know how strong he was."

"I do not believe it. I do not believe that a strong woman like you could not resist him. You must have finally become willing though you now blame it on his strength."

"Ah-ah you . . . you should have tried to resist him yourself," she said with a smile.

Liu-ma laughed, her wrinkled face shriveling up like a peach stone; her tiny dry eyes shifted from the scar on Sister Hsiang-lin's forehead to the latter's eyes, discomforting her and causing her to gather up her smile and turn her eyes to look at the snowflakes.

"Sister Hsiang-lin, you have miscalculated badly," Liu-ma said mysteriously. "You should have resisted to the end, or dashed your head until you were dead. That would have been the thing to do. But now? You lived with your second man only two years and got for it a monstrous evil name. Just think, when you get to the lower world, those two ghost husbands will fight over you. Whom would they give you to? The Great King Yenlo could only have you sawed in two and divided between them . . ."

Sister Hsiang-lin was terrified: this was something that she had not heard about in the hills.

"I think you should atone for your crime while there is still time. Donate a doorsill to the T'u-ti temple as your effigy, so that you might be trampled upon by a thousand men's feet and straddled over by ten thousand men's legs as atonement for your great sin. Then you may escape the tortures in store for you."

Sister Hsiang-lin did not say anything then, but she must have been deeply affected. The next day she got up with black rings around her eyes. After breakfast she went to the T'u-ti temple on the western edge of the village to donate the doorsill. At first the keeper would not accept the gift, but her tears and entreaties finally prevailed and he accepted the offer at the price of 12,000 cash.

She had not spoken with anyone for a long time, for she had become an avoided object because of the tiresome story about her Ah Mao; nevertheless, after her conversation with Liu-ma—which seemed to have been broadcast immediately—people began to take a new interest in her and would try to coax her to talk. As to the subject, it was naturally a new one, centering upon the scar on her forehead.

"Sister Hsiang-lin, let me ask you, why did you finally give in?" one would say.

"Ai, too bad you broke your head for nothing," another would echo, looking at her scar.

From their faces and voices she gathered that they were making fun of her; she only stared vacantly and said nothing, later she did not even turn her head. She tightened her mouth and went about her duties—sweeping, washing vegetables and rice, running errands, bearing the scar of her shame. In about a year, she got all the wages that Aunt Four had kept for her, changed them into twelve Mexican dollars, asked for leave to go to the western edge of the village. She soon returned and told Aunt Four that she had donated her doorsill at the T'u-ti temple. She appeared to be in better spirits than she had been for a long time and her eyes showed signs of life.

She worked unusually hard at the ancestral sacrifices at the winter solstice. After watching Aunt Four fill the dishes with the sacrificial things and Ah Niu place the table in the center of the hall, she went confidently to get the wine cups and chopsticks.

"Don't you bother, Sister Hsiang-lin!" Aunt Four said in a panicky voice.

She withdrew her hands as if from a hot iron, her face black and pale like burnt coal. She did not try to get the candlesticks. She only stood as if lost, and did not go away until Uncle Four came in to light the incense sticks and dismissed her. This time the change in her was extraordinary. Not only were her eyes sunken the next day, but her wits seemed to have left her entirely. She became terribly afraid, not only of the night and dark corners, but also of people, including her own employers. She would sneak about, trembling like a mouse that had ventured out of its hole in daylight; or she would sit abstractedly like a wooden idol. In less than half a year, her hair became gray, her memory grew worse and worse, until she sometimes forgot to go out to wash rice in the river.

"What is the matter with Sister Hsiang-lin? We should not have kept her in the first place," Aunt Four would say sometimes, in her hearing, as a warning to her.

But she continued in the same condition, and showed no signs of recovering her wits. They began to think of sending her away, to tell her to go back to old Mrs. Wei. When I was still living at Luchen they used to talk of sending her away, but they only talked about it; from what I saw on this visit, it was evident that they did finally carry out their threat. But whether she became a beggar immediately after leaving Uncle Four's house, or whether she first went to old Mrs. Wei and then became a beggar, I could not say.

I was awakened by loud explosions of firecrackers close by. As I blinked at the yellow lamp flame about the size of a bean I heard the crackling of a string of firecrackers—the New Year's ceremony was on at Uncle Four's and I knew that it must be about the fifth watch. With half-shut eyes I heard dreamily the continued crackling in the distance; it seemed to form a thick cloud of festive sounds in the sky, mingling with the snowflakes and enveloping the entire village. In the arms of this festive sound, I felt carefree and comfortable, and the fears and melancholy I had felt all the previous day and the first part of the night were swept away by this atmosphere of joy and blessedness. I fancied that the gods and sages of heaven above and earth below, drunk and satiated with incense and sacrifices of wine and meat, were reeling unsteadily in the sky, ready to confer unlimited blessings upon the inhabitants of Luchen.

II

DIALOGUES
ON
SHORT FICTION

Virginia Woolf on Anton Chekhov

... Our first impressions of Tchekov are not of simplicity but of bewilderment. What is the point of it, and why does he make a story out of this? we ask as we read story after story. A man falls in love with a married woman, and they part and meet, and in the end are left talking about their position and by what means they can be free from "this intolerable bondage."

. . . .

But is it the end we ask? We have rather the feeling that we have overrun our signals; or it is as if a tune had stopped short without the expected chords to close it. These stories are inconclusive, we say, and proceed to frame a criticism based upon the assumption that stories ought to conclude in a way that we recognize. In so doing we raise the question of our fitness as readers. Where the tune is familiar and the end emphatic—lovers united, villains discomfited, intrigues exposed—as it is in most Victorian fiction, we can scarcely go wrong, but where the tune is unfamiliar and the end a note of interrogation or merely the information that they went on talking, as it is in Tchekov, we need a very daring and alert sense of literature to make us hear the tune, and in particular those last notes

From "The Russian Point of View," *The Common Reader, First and Second Series*, Harcourt, Brace and Company, 1948, pp. 246–248.

which complete the harmony. Probably we have to read a great
many stories before we feel, and the feeling is essential to our
satisfaction, that we hold the parts together, and that Tchekov
was not merely rambling disconnectedly, but struck now this
note, now that with intention, in order to complete his meaning.

We have to cast about in order to discover where the emphasis in these strange stories rightly comes. Tchekov's own
words give us a lead in the right direction. ". . . Such a conversation as this between us," he says, "would have been un-
thinkable for our parents. At night they did not talk, but slept
sound; we, our generation, sleep badly, are restless, but talk a
great deal, and are always trying to settle whether we are right
or not. . . ." Tchekov, too, is aware of the evils and injustices
of the social state; the condition of the peasants appalls him,
but the reformer's zeal is not his—that is not the signal for us
to stop. The mind interests him enormously; he is a most subtle
and delicate analyst of human relations. But again, no; the end
is not there. Is it that he is primarily interested not in the
soul's relation with other souls, but with the soul's relation to
health—with the soul's relation to goodness? These stories are
always showing us some affectation, pose, insincerity. Some
woman has got into a false relation; some man has been per-
verted by the inhumanity of his circumstances. The soul is ill;
the soul is cured; the soul is not cured. Those are the emphatic
points in his stories.

Thomas Mann on Fyodor Dostoevsky

THERE IS NO doubt that the subconscious and even the consciousness of this gigantic creative mind was always burdened by a heavy sense of guilt, the true criminal feeling. It was not, this feeling, all hypochondriac. It belonged with his disease, it was the religious sickness, the mystical *kat exochen*, epilepsy.

. . . .

"It is the exceptional circumstances," Nietzsche said, "that condition the artist: all those who are deeply ingrown and involved with morbid phenomena; so that it seems impossible to be an artist and not to be morbid." The German philosopher probably did not know the nature of his illness, but he did precisely know what he owed to it; and his writings, the letters as well as his books, pay homage in the heroic key to the value of disease as understanding.

. . . .

Disease; but after all and above all it depends on who is diseased, who mad, who epileptic or paralytic: an average dull-witted man, in whose illness any intellectual or cultural aspect is non-existent; or a Nietzsche, a Dostoyevsky. In their case something comes out in illness that is more important and conducive to life and growth than any medically guaranteed health

Joseph Warner Angell (ed.), *The Thomas Mann Reader*, Alfred A. Knopf, 1950, pp. 438, 441, 443.

or sanity. The truth is that life could never in all its life get on without the morbid; and anything more stupid would be hard to find than the saying that from disease only disease can come. Life is not fastidious: one may truthfully say that creative genius, genius-purveying disease, taking its obstacles on high horse, leaping exultant from crag to crag, is a thousand times dearer to it than healthiness trudging afoot. Life is not nice: remote from its thought is any distinction between sickness and health. It clutches the daring products of disease, consumes and digests them, and what it does with them makes them health. A whole host, a generation of sound, healthy, receptive youth flings itself on the work of morbid genius, genius sprung from disease; wonders, admires, extols; carries it away and changes it within itself, finally bequeathing it to culture, which does not thrive on home-made bread alone. And all of them will swear by the name of the great morbid genius, thanks to whose madness they need not be mad. Upon his madness will they feed in health, and in them he will become sane.

In other words: certain conquests made by the soul and the mind are impossible without disease, madness, crime of the spirit; the great morbid ones are the crucified, sacrifices on the altar of humanity, to the end that it shall be uplifted, its understanding and feeling enlarged, its health lifted to a higher plane. Hence the religious aura so visible about the lives of such men, hence the profound influence upon their consciousness. But hence too the sense, as it were the foreknowledge of power and triumph, of life being in all its anguish vastly heightened.

Joseph Conrad on Guy de Maupassant

THE INTEREST OF a reader in a work of imagination is either ethical or that of simple curiosity. Both are perfectly legitimate, since there is both a moral and an excitement to be found in a faithful rendering of life. And in Maupassant's work there is the interest of curiosity and the moral of a point of view consistently preserved and never obtruded for the end of personal gratification. The spectacle of this immense talent served by exceptional faculties and triumphing over the most thankless subjects by an unswerving singleness of purpose is in itself an admirable lesson in the power of artistic honesty, one may say of artistic virtue. The inherent greatness of the man consists in this, that he will let none of the fascinations that beset a writer working in loneliness turn him away from the straight path, from the vouchsafed vision of excellence. He will not be led into perdition by the seductions of sentiment, of eloquence, of humour, of pathos; of all that splendid pageant of faults that pass between the writer and his probity on the blank sheet of paper, like the glittering cortege of deadly sins before the austere anchorite in the desert air of Thebaide. This is not to say that Maupassant's austerity has never faltered; but the fact remains that no tempting demon has ever succeeded in hurling him down from his high, if narrow, pedestal.

. . . He refrains from setting his cleverness against the elo-

"Guy De Maupassant," *Notes On Life And Letters*, Doubleday, Page and Company, 1924, pp. 26–27, 29.

quence of the facts. There is humour and pathos in these stories; but such is the greatness of his talent, the refinement of his artistic conscience, that all his high qualities appear inherent in the very things of which he speaks, as if they had been altogether independent of his presentation. Facts, and again facts are his unique concern. That is why he is not always properly understood. His facts are so perfectly rendered that, like the actualities of life itself, they demand from the reader the faculty of observation which is rare. . . .

. . . .

Maupassant's renown is universal, but his popularity is restricted. It is not difficult to perceive why. Maupassant is an intensely national writer. He is so intensely national in his logic, in his clearness, in his aesthetic and moral conceptions, that he has been accepted by his countrymen without having had to pay the tribute of flattery either to the nation as a whole, or to any class, sphere or division of the nation. . . . What is wanting to his universal success is the mediocrity of an obvious and appealing tenderness. He neglects to qualify his truth with the drop of facile sweetness; he forgets to strew paper roses over the tombs. The disregard of these common decencies lays him open to the charges of cruelty, cynicism, hardness. And yet it can be safely affirmed that this man wrote from the fulness of a compassionate heart.

Henry James on Guy de Maupassant

THE AUTHOR FIXES a hard eye on some small spot of human life, usually some ugly, dreary, shabby, sordid one, takes up the particle, and squeezes it either till it grimaces or till it bleeds. Sometimes the grimace is very droll, sometimes the wound is very horrible; but in either case the whole thing is real, observed, noted, and represented, not an invention or a castle in the air. M. de Maupassant sees human life as a terribly ugly business relieved by the comical, but even the comedy is for the most part the comedy of misery, of avidity, of ignorance, helplessness, and grossness.

. . . .

It is surely by his Norman peasant that his tales will live; he knows this worthy as if he had made him, understands him down to the ground, puts him on his feet with a few of the freest, most plastic touches. M. de Maupassant does not admire him, and he is such a master of the subject that it would ill become an outsider to suggest a revision of judgment. He is part of the contemptible furniture of the world, but on the whole, it would appear, the most grotesque part of it. His caution, his canniness, his natural astuteness, his stinginess, his general grinding sordidness, are as unmistakable as that quaint and brutish dialect in which he expresses himself, and on which

"Guy De Maupassant," *Partial Portraits*, Macmillan and Company, 1888, pp. 266, 268–269, 284–285.

our author plays like a virtuoso. . . . If it is most convenient to place *La Maison Tellier* among the tales of the peasantry, there is no doubt that it stands at the head of the list. . . . Every good story is of course both a picture and an idea, and the more they are interfused the better the problem is solved. In *La Maison Tellier* they fit each other to perfection; the capacity for sudden innocent delights latent in natures which have lost their innocence is vividly illustrated by the singular scenes to which our acquaintance with Madame and her staff (little as it may be a thing to boast of), successively introduces us. The breadth, the freedom, and brightness of all this give the measure of the author's talent, and of that large, keen way of looking at life which sees the pathetic and the droll, the stuff of which the whole piece is made, in the queerest and humblest patterns.

. . . .

. . . If he is master of his art and it is discouraging to find what low views are compatible with mastery, there is satisfaction, on the other hand, in learning on what particular condition he holds his strange success. This condition, it seems to me, is that of having totally omitted one of the items of the problem, an omission which has made the problem so much easier that it may almost be described as a short cut to a solution. The question is whether it be a fair cut. M. de Maupassant has simply skipped the whole reflective part of his men and women—that reflective part which governs conduct and produces character.

Aldous Huxley on D. H. Lawrence

LAWRENCE'S SPECIAL AND CHARACTERISTIC gift was an extraordinary sensitiveness to what Wordsworth called "unknown modes of being." He was always intensely aware of the mystery of the world, and the mystery was always for him a *numen*, divine. Lawrence could never forget, as most of us almost continuously forget, the dark presence of the otherness that lies beyond the boundaries of man's conscious mind. This special sensibility was accompanied by a prodigious power of rendering the immediately experienced otherness in terms of literary art.

Such was Lawrence's peculiar gift. His possession of it accounts for many things. It accounts, to begin with, for his attitude towards sex. His particular experiences as a son and as a lover may have intensified his preoccupation with the subject; but they certainly did not make it. Whatever his experiences, Lawrence must have been preoccupied with sex; his gift made it inevitable. For Lawrence, the significance of the sexual experience was this: that, in it, the immediate, non-mental knowledge of divine otherness is brought . . . to a focus—a focus of darkness.

. . . .

. . . Art, he thought, should flower from an immediate impulse towards self-expression or communication, and should

"D. H. Lawrence," *Collected Essays*, Harper & Brothers, 1959, pp. 117–118, 120–121.

wither with the passing of the impulse. Of all building materials
Lawrence liked adobe the best; its extreme plasticity and extreme impermanence endeared it to him. There could be no
everlasting pyramids in adobe, no mathematically accurate Par-
thenons. Nor, thank heaven, in wood. Lawrence loved the
Etruscans, among other reasons, because they built wooden
temples, which have not survived. Stone oppressed him with its
indestructible solidity, its capacity to take and indefinitely keep
the hard uncompromising forms of pure geometry. Great buildings made him feel uncomfortable, even when they were beautiful. He felt something of the same discomfort in the presence
of any highly finished work of art. In music, for example, he
liked the folk song, because it was a slight thing, born of immediate impulse. The symphony oppressed him; it was too big,
too elaborate, too carefully and consciously worked out, too
"would-be"—to use a characteristic Lawrencean expression. He
was quite determined that none of his writings should be
"would-be." He allowed them to flower as they liked from the
depths of his being and would never use his conscious intellect
to force them into a semblance of more than human perfection,
or more than human universality. It was characteristic of him
that he hardly ever corrected or patched what he had written.
I have often heard him say, indeed, that he was incapable of
correcting. If he was dissatisfied with what he had written, he
did not, as most authors do, file, clip, insert, transpose; he re-
wrote. In other words, he gave the *daimon* another chance to
say what it wanted to say. . . . He was determined that all he
produced should spring direct from the mysterious, irrational
source of power within him. The conscious intellect should
never be allowed to come and impose, after the event, its abstract pattern of perfection.

Joseph Conrad on Stephen Crane

"YOU ARE AN everlasting surprise to one. You shock—and the next moment you give the perfect artistic satisfaction. Your method is fascinating. You are a complete impressionist. The illusions of life come out of your hand without a flaw. It is not life—which nobody wants—it is art—art for which everyone— the abject and the great—hanker—mostly without knowing."

. . . .

"I am very curious to know your idea [for a play, *The Predecessor*]; but I feel somehow that collaborating with you would be either cheating or deceiving you. In any case disappointing you. I have no dramatic gift. You have the terseness, the clear eye, the easy imagination. You have all—and I have only the accursed faculty of dreaming. My ideas fade—yours come out sharp cut as cameos—they come all living out of your brain and bring images—and bring light. Mine bring only mist in which they are born, and die."

. . . .

"His eye is very individual and his expression satisfies me artistically. He certainly is *the* impressionist and his temperament is curiously unique. His thought is concise, connected, never very deep—yet often startling. He is *the only* impressionist and

R. W. Stallman and Lillian Gilkes (eds.), *Stephen Crane: Letters*, New York University Press, 1960, pp. 154, 155–156, 167.

only an impressionist. Why is he not immensely popular? With his strength, with his rapidity of action, with that amazing faculty of vision—why is he not? He has outline, he has color, he has movement, with that he ought to go very far. But— will he? I sometimes think he won't. It is not an opinion—it is a feeling. I could not explain why he disappoints me—why my enthusiasm withers as soon as I close the book. While one reads, of course he is not to be questioned. He is the master of his reader to the very last line—then—apparently for no reason at all—he seems to let go his hold. It is as if he had gripped you with greased fingers. His grip is strong but while you feel the pressure on your flesh you slip out from his hand —much to your own surprise."

Ezra Pound on James Joyce

. . . MR. JOYCE'S MERIT, I will not say his chief merit but his most engaging merit, is that he carefully avoids telling you a lot that you don't want to know. He presents his people swiftly and vividly, he does not sentimentalize over them, he does not weave convolutions. He is a realist. He does not believe "life" would be all right if we stopped vivisection or if we instituted a new sort of "economics." He gives the thing as it is. He is not bound by the tiresome convention that any part of life, to be interesting, must be shaped into the conventional form of a "story." Since de Maupassant we have had so many people trying to write "stories" and so few people presenting life. Life for the most part does not happen in neat little diagrams and nothing is more tiresome than the continual pretence that it does.

Mr. Joyce's *Araby*, for instance, is much better than a "story," it is a vivid waiting.

It is surprising that Mr. Joyce is Irish. One is so tired of the Irish or "Celtic" imagination (or "phantasy" as I think they now call it) flopping about. Mr. Joyce does not flop about. He defines. He is not an institution for the promotion of Irish peasant industries. He accepts an international standard of prose writing and lives up to it.

He gives us Dublin as it presumably is. He does not descend

T. S. Eliot (ed.), "Dubliners and Mr. James Joyce," *Literary Essays of Ezra Pound*, New Directions, 1954, pp. 400–401.

to farce. He does not rely upon Dickensian caricature. He gives us things as they are, not only for Dublin, but for every city. Erase the local names and a few specifically local allusions, and a few historic events of the past, and substitute a few different local names, allusions and events, and these stories could be retold of any town.

. . . Good writing, good presentation can be specifically local, but it must not depend on locality. Mr. Joyce does not present "types" but individuals. I mean he deals with common emotions which run through all races. . . . He writes as a contemporary of continental writers. I do not mean that he writes as a faddist, mad for the last note, he does not imitate Strindberg, for instance, or Bang. He is not ploughing the underworld for horror. He is not presenting a macabre subjectivity. He is classic in that he deals with normal things and with normal people. A committee room, Little Chandler, a nonentity, a boarding house full of clerks—these are his subjects and he treats them all in such a manner that they are worthy subjects of art.

D. H. Lawrence on Thomas Mann

THOMAS MANN . . . is personal, almost painfully so, in his subject-matter. In "Tonio Kröger," the long *Novelle* at the end of the *Tristan* volume, he paints a detailed portrait of himself as a youth and younger man, a careful analysis. And he expresses at some length the misery of being an artist. . . . It is because the stress of life in a young man, but particularly in an artist, is very strong, and has as yet found no outlet, so that it rages inside him in *Sturm und Drang*. . . . He [Mann] has never found any outlet for himself, save his art. He has never given himself to anything but his art. This is all well and good, if his art absorbs and satisfies him. . . . But then there are the other artists, the more human, like Shakespeare and Goethe, who must give themselves to life as well as to art. And if these were afraid, or despised life, then with their surplus they would ferment and become rotten. Which is what ails Thomas Mann. He is physically ailing, no doubt. But his complaint is deeper: it is of the soul.

. . . .

Thomas Mann seems to me the last sick sufferer from the complaint of Flaubert. The latter stood away from life as from a leprosy. And Thomas Mann, like Flaubert, feels vaguely that he has in him something finer than ever physical life revealed. Physical life is a disordered corruption, against which he can

Anthony Beal (ed.), *D. H. Lawrence, Selected Literary Criticism*, The Viking Press, 1956, pp. 260–261, 265.

fight with only one weapon, his fine aesthetic sense, his feeling for beauty, for perfection, for a certain fitness which soothes him, and gives him an inner pleasure, however corrupt the stuff of life may be. There he is, after all these years, full of disgusts and loathing of himself as Flaubert was, and Germany is being voiced, or partly so, by him. And so, with real suicidal intention, like Flaubert's, he sits, a last too-sick disciple, reducing himself grain by grain to the statement of his own disgust, patiently, self-destructively, so that his statement at least may be perfect in a world of corruption. But he is so late.

Already I find Thomas Mann, who, as he says, fights so hard against the banal in his work, somewhat banal. His expression may be very fine. But by now what he expresses is stale. I think we have learned our lesson, to be sufficiently aware of the fulsomeness of life. And even while he has a rhythm in style, yet his work has none of the rhythm of a living thing, the rise of a poppy, then the after uplift of the bud, the shedding of the calyx and the spreading wide of the petals, the falling of the flower and the pride of the seed-head.

Thomas Mann on Franz Kafka

BUT THOUGH HIS gaze make us conceive of him as a Novalis from the east of Europe, yet I should not care to dub Kafka either a romantic, an ecstatic, or a mystic. For a romantic he is too clear-cut, too realistic, too well attached to life and to a simple, native effectiveness in living. His sense of humor—of an involved kind peculiar to himself—is too pronounced for an ecstatic. And as for mysticism: he did indeed once say, in a conversation with Rudolph Steiner, that his own work had given him understanding of certain "clairvoyant states" described by the latter. . . . He was a dreamer, and his compositions are often dreamlike in conception and form; they are as oppressive, illogical, and absurd as dreams, those strange shadow-pictures of actual life. But they are full of a reasoned morality, an ironic, satiric, desperately reasoned morality, struggling with all its might toward justice, goodness, and the will of God. All that mirrors itself in his style: a conscientious, curiously explicit, objective, clear, and correct style, which in its precise, almost official conservatism is reminiscent of Adalbert Stifter's.

. . . .

. . . Franz Kafka, late and doubting and almost desperately complicated representative of German letters, certainly felt the purest respect and reverence for Goethe; and from Goethe we

Willa and Edwin Muir (trans.), "Homage," *The Castle*, Alfred A. Knopf, 1954, pp. ix, x, xiii.

543

have the saying: "Man can find no better retreat from the world than art, and man can find no stronger link with the world than art." A wonderful saying. Solitude and companionship—the two are here reconciled in a way that Kafka may well have admired, without being quite willing or able to admit it, because his productivity depended on the strife within him, and on his feeling of being "remote from God," his insecurity. His joy and gratitude when he was able to write might have taught him that art "links" us not only with the world, but also with the moral sphere, with the right and the divine. And this in a double sense, by the profound symbolism inherent in the idea of the "good." What the artist calls good, the object of all his playful pains, his life-and-death jesting, is nothing less than a parable of the right and the good, a representation of all human striving after perfection. In this sense Kafka's work, born of his dreams, is very good indeed. It is composed with a fidelity and patience, a native exactitude, a conscientiousness—ironic, even parodistic in kind, yet charming to laughter—with a painstaking love, all proof that he was no unbeliever, but in some involved fashion of his own had faith in the good and the right. And the discrepancy between God and man, the incapacity of man to recognize the good, to unite himself with it and "live in the right," Kafka took this for the theme of his works, works that in every sentence bear witness to a humorously, fantastically despairing good will.

Albert Camus on Franz Kafka

THE WHOLE ART of Kafka consists in forcing the reader to re-read. His endings, or his absence of endings, suggest explanations which, however, are not revealed in clear language but, before they seem justified, require that the story be reread from another point of view. Sometimes there is a double possibility of interpretation, whence appears the necessity for two readings. This is what the author wanted. But it would be wrong to try to interpret everything in Kafka in detail. A symbol is always in general and, however precise its translation, an artist can restore to it only its movement: there is no word-for-word rendering. Moreover, nothing is harder to understand than a symbolic work. A symbol always transcends the one who makes use of it and makes him say in reality more than he is aware of expressing. In this regard, the surest means of getting hold of it is not to provoke it, to begin the work without a preconceived attitude and not to look for its hidden currents. For Kafka in particular it is fair to agree to his rules, to approach the drama through its externals and the novel through its form.

. . . .

You see that it is hard to speak of a symbol in a tale whose most obvious quality just happens to be naturalness. But naturalness is a hard category to understand. There are works in which

"Hope and the Absurd in the Work of Franz Kafka" *The Myth of Sisyphus and Other Essays*, Alfred A. Knopf, 1955, pp. 124, 126–127.

the event seems natural to the reader. But there are others (rarer, to be sure) in which the character considers natural what happens to him. By an odd but obvious paradox, the more extraordinary the character's adventures are, the more noticeable will be the naturalness of the story: it is in proportion to the divergence we feel between the strangeness of a man's life and the simplicity with which that man accepts it. It seems that this naturalness is Kafka's. . . .

Likewise, *The Castle* is perhaps a theology in action, but it is first of all the individual adventure of a soul in quest of its grace, of a man who asks of this world's objects their royal secret and of women the signs of the god that sleeps in them. *Metamorphosis*, in turn, certainly represents the horrible imagery of an ethic of lucidity. But it is also the product of that incalculable amazement man feels at being conscious of the beast he becomes effortlessly. In this fundamental ambiguity lies Kafka's secret. These perpetual oscillations, between the natural and the extraordinary, the individual and the universal, the tragic and the everyday, the absurd and the logical, are found throughout his work and give it both its resonance and its meaning. These are the paradoxes that must be enumerated, the contradictions that must be strengthened, in order to understand the absurd work.

A symbol, indeed, assumes two planes, two worlds of ideas and sensations, and a dictionary of correspondences between them. This lexicon is the hardest thing to draw up. But awaking to the two worlds brought face to face is tantamount to getting on the trail of their secret relationships. In Kafka these two worlds are that of everyday life on the one hand and, on the other, that of supernatural anxiety. It seems that we are witnessing here an interminable exploitation of Nietzsche's remark: "Great problems are in the street."

Index of Authors and Titles

"All righty, then why don't you hook up with Moose when you get down there next month and the both of you work together on getting this operation off the ground. You'll be in charge of getting Fuskie Krew up to speed on the details of the big day, while Moose will stay in contact with the moles we've got paid off within the Daufuskie police department on the arrival and day-to-day movements of the visiting chief of police. Doctor Buzzard is going to ship thirty-three-thousand-dollars worth of assault weapons, clips, an' ammo to equip the Krew for the job at hand. I know that seems like a waste of money and way overdoing it, but you can never be too careful. Plus, this is a job that absolutely, positively cannot fail, because there's just too much at stake for failure of any kind. You do understand that, don't you?" Tolliver asked.

Whiskey nodded slowly while crushing his cigar butt into an empty soda can. "I feel you, but y'all gon' have ta work overtime ta keep this shit from gettin' back ta Mickey's baby girl, 'cause I know damn well y'all got mo' dan a li'l bit o' cops who consida deyself loyal to da department, feel me? And dat's all we need to blow da lid off da whole goddamed operation. So y'all dudes gotta make sho' dat everybody down wit' da program keep dey fuckin' mouths shut," Whiskey emphasized sternly.

Everyone gathered together in the interior of the barbershop nodded together in silent agreement to the young enforcer's statements, realizing the truthfulness of his words.

Chapter 13

"Sea Island Thugs"

"Shawty, gimme a hit o' dat dank, son," a young, bright-eyed ruffian said, reaching out with an outstretched hand to receive a thick blunt from a homie seated nearby, puffing away, as a heavy cloud of reefer smoke ascended above he and his fellows playing poker within the crowded living room of a Daufuskie Island mobile home.

As the heavy bass-laced tracks of Trick Daddy filled the smoky, gangsta-crowded living room, Whiskey stood near the refrigerator looking at an assortment of glossy assault weapons that Hilton Head's lovely sister assassins, Candice and Naomi Forrester, were showing him. He smiled broadly, stroking the silvery, metallic muzzle of a polished AR-15 rifle and fondly admiring its lethal beauty.

"She's quite a looker, ain't she?" Naomi unloaded a handful of ammo boxes from an opened suitcase sitting atop the kitchen table.

Looking up from his inspection of the weapon, Whiskey

winked an eye at the attractive sisters smiling back at him as he checked out their hardware with growing satisfaction. "Oh yeah, y'all got some serious firepower right here. My mans an' dem gon' buy up all o' dis work up off you." He gently placed the AR-15 back down alongside the other smuggled guns on the table.

Candice unloaded another suitcase of smuggled items, this one being three dozen clips of different sizes to fit both handguns as well as rifles.

Naomi tallied up the total cost of the weapons on a small calculator as her sibling removed the empty gun magazines from their container. She tapped off a final price tally on the instrument's keypad then turned to Whiskey. "I'll say we'll let this stash go for, what, two thousand two hundred. Now that's really cheap for what you're getting, and of course it's only 'cause we know you and you're our peeps an' shit. Nobody else would walk away with all of these guns for that kinda chicken change. Plus, we wanna get rid of Mickey O'Malley just as bad as anybody else down here, ya know? Shit, we're losing money and clientele as a result of this dumb-ass cop's so-called war on drugs. Fuck that. My sister an' I want this punk bitch dead now. And we're now ready and willing to help you cats take care of that too."

"Gimme my moneeee!" yelled one of the boys sitting around the card-cluttered poker table. He gleefully pumped his fist in the air, before slapping high-fives all around with his malt liquor-guzzling partners.

Candice asked, "Why y'all need so many guns though? I mean, I ain't mad at cha, though, but it's like y'all tryin' to kill a whole gang o' cops, rather than just this one dude."

"Don't start me to lyin', baby girl. Shit, I just do what da powers dat be tell me ta do, ya know? And dem powers tell me ta buy da very best state-o'-da-art weaponry fa dese li'l thug niggas down here, 'cause dem peoples I fucks wit' want hitmen set up all over Fuskie on da day o' da murda. So no matter where he turns or where he goes, he's gonna run into a hired gun, feel me?"

"I see. Yeah, Beaufort County ballers have lost well over a million dollars ever since ya man Mickey O'Malley brought his doughnut-eatin' Irish ass down here." Naomi dropped her calculator back down into her Dooney & Bourke leather handbag.

As the youngsters yelled and carried on boisterously at and around the smoke-surrounded poker table, Whiskey slowly began peeling off one "Benjamin Franklin" after another from a huge rubber band-wrapped roll of cash to pay for the deadly cargo that would be used to off the South's most hated lawman.

On December 8, 2005 David Ambrosia hosted a release party for Godiva's newly released album, *Party Favors*. Starting at ten PM, a steady stream of well-wishers and fans entered through the mahogany front doors of West Peola's posh 95 South nightclub.

By the time the lady of honor herself arrived an hour later, the place was packed with over a thousand fans, not counting the four thousand more huddling impatiently near the entrance in the night chill of the parking lot.

The famous VIP upper room was alive with the thumping music and beautiful people who all pushed and pressed their way through and around each other to get a few seconds to schmooze with Godiva. Cameras flashed, and champagne corks popped all around the room, as the incessant din of the chattering groupies raged in the background along with the booming sound systems.

Office Columbus, dressed down in Southwestern denim-style outfit, came over to the bar where Whiskey stood and took a seat on one of the few empty stools available. He ordered a shot of Jack Daniel's on the rocks, and attempted to score with a slender, hippy dark-brown cutie with a weak pickup line, causing her to quickly turn her bare back to him in a blatant show of disinterest.

"Dat's all right, darlin'. After a coupla shots of Jack, you'll be ridin' home wit' me tonight. You just don't know it yet, is all. Hey, Whiskey, my man, how da hell are ya? Dem Gullah folks been treatin' you okay or what?"

Due to his preoccupation with the wide variety of sexy women clustering around Godiva, giggling like school-girls as they took snapshots of the smiling recording artist signing autographs in the middle of the crowd, Whiskey barely acknowledged the redneck policeman with a nod as he took a sharp swallow of gin and grape-fruit juice.

Columbus took the shot of liquor slowly to his thirsty lips. "Maurice told me dat you done gone an' got dem fine-ass Forrester sistas to help wit' da O'Malley thing, huh. Sweet."

Whiskey glanced at the off-duty cop with irritation and put up a thick finger to his lips. "C'mon, son, watch ya mouf up in here. You don't know who listenin' ta dis conversation. I know you know betta dan dat, pimp."

"My bad, my bad. I didn't feel anybody could hear us over these goddamned loud speakers in here. Besides, everybody's so caught up wit' Godiva over there dat I seriously doubt dat anyone's payin' da slightest bit o' attention ta us."

Whiskey wrinkled his brow in dismay. "You just can't be too careful out here nowadays, Hank. You of all people oughta know dat."

"A'ight, a'ight, you've made your fuckin' point, okay? Calm down, dude. Anyway, it seems like li'l miss superstar over there is so stuck on herself dat she ain't even bothered ta tell her bosom buddy Courtney O'Malley to lay off da boys in da hood even a li'l bit. Not to mention da fact o' her an' ya boy David Ambrosia refusin' ta return our phone calls an' whatnot, which is pissin' off just about everybody dat had anything ta do wit' dis bitch gettin' on da map."

Whiskey took another sip of gin and juice. "I spoke ta David twice down in Fuskie and he told me dat he already talked to Courtney 'bout da fava her girl Godiva owe us fa helpin' her win da *Pop Star* competition and he said to me outta his very own mouf dat da bitch was callin' off da dawgs from sweatin' our dope spots out in South Peola. An' peep dis, David even wired a li'l bit o' change, fifteen hundred to be exact, to help wit' payin' da young bucks who gonna be down wit' dat thing, feel me? So I dunno why he ain't hittin' y'all back on da phone."

Suddenly a recognizable figure emerged from the dense crowd to take a seat at the bar among them. It was Maurice Tolliver dressed to the nines in a finely tailored rust-colored Emporio Armani suit. "What's up, what's up, people?"

Columbus chuckled. "Ain't shit. Just kickin' it up in

here wit' our buddy Whiskey, an' a whole lotta pretty li'l bitches."

"I see. I just got back from LA, Compton to be exact. I've got family, but in Inglewood. But that wasn't really why I went out West. David Ambrosia hipped me to the job that you pulled off for his guy, DiVante Lovett, a while back. Well, to make a long story short, this cat was so impressed by the thoroughness of the hit on your part that he pretty much promised to help David or you out anytime you may need him in the future. So that was an opportunity that I felt we would benefit from, especially right now. As you already know, DiVante's the leader of one of South Central's largest gangs, the Reapers, second in size only to the Crips, but even more violent, from what I'm told.

"Anyway he's more than willing to contact a few of his business associates down in Charlestown to take advantage of a suddenly booming crystal meth trade taking shape down here in the Atlantic coastal states. Both he and I believe that by investing in this crystal meth craze we can recoup some of the millions that fat fuck O'Malley cost us over the past few months. What do you guys think about that idea?"

Columbus raised a glass of Jack Daniel's on ice in a toast to his partner's entrepreneurial skills.

"Maurice, do you care dat we here in public? I just got through warnin' Hank 'bout dat dumb shit. C'mon, dawg, y'all makin' us hot, don't ya think? Besides, I ain't worried 'bout doin' no bidness right about now, 'cause we kin do dat whenever. Shit, Charlestown ain't nothin' but a stone's throw away from Fuskie, but ain't nobody gon' be able to do a goddamned thing as long as Chief O'Mal-

ley has anything to do with it. I think we gotta stay fo-
cused on gettin' rid o' da Irishman befo' we kin even
think 'bout makin' money or slangin' any kinda new
product out on da streets."

On December 19, interim police chief Courtney O'Malley called an emergency meeting with twenty-two of her
most decorated officers. One by one, the top brass of
Peola's tightly run police department came marching
through the training academy doors to take a seat at one
of the simple sawdust desks lining the clean, waxed tile
floor. Corporals, sergeants, lieutenants, captains, and three
majors shuffled over to their desks and sat silently.

Officer Maurice Tolliver had received his corporal bars
on December 3 after several months of recommendations
by his peers on the force, including Hank Columbus.
Though he felt no desire whatsoever to attend this early-
morning supervisor meeting, he had no choice, since it
was mandatory for every officer with stripes. He made
sure that he sat near the rear of the large gymnasium-size
room. He fiddled briefly with his BlackBerry before
putting it away upon the chief's arrival.

Courtney O'Malley was a busty, freckled-faced red-
head with bright green eyes, which stared out fiercely at
the assembled police officers seated before her as she
stood at the podium. "Good morning, ladies and gentlemen. I'm so very glad that each and every one of you
could make it here this morning. There is coffee and
doughnuts out in the hall for you guys after we get finished up here this morning, okay? And for you healthy
types, there's green tea and trail mix.

"Well, now that all that's out the way, I want to let you

all know why I brought you here. It has come to my attention that certain members of this department are taking drug money and narcotics from raids on known stash houses, as well as taking bribes from area traffickers. Can you men and women of this esteemed department fathom, if even for a nanosecond, betrayal of this magnitude?"

A few cops shifted about uncomfortably in their seats, while others mumbled softly among themselves.

"Oh yeah, it's disgusting, I know. But don't worry, people, I will not sit back idly while a few pathetic renegade officers bring disgrace to this proud department and this town. My father has devoted his life to the development of the Peola Police Department and providing the citizens of our community with a safe haven from the ills, which unfortunately affect many of our nation's largest cities. That was his number one priority, as it is now mine in his absence.

Several high-ranking majors and captains seated in the front row nodded their heads in agreement with the young chief.

"I say we lock every last one of 'em up whenever and wherever we find 'em and throw away the goddamned keys," one brash young sergeant announced.

Scattered handclaps broke out throughout the room.

Courtney O'Malley smiled as she brushed away a frock of fiery red locks from her face. "You, sir, are absolutely correct. I feel the same way, as do most of us here." She noticed Tolliver dozing off at the rear of the room. "Isn't that right, Corporal Tolliver?"

Stirring himself abruptly, the newly decorated sergeant said, "Uh, yes, yes, ma'am, that's right. We're going to do everything possible to bring any criminal in this town to justice. Including any police officer who breaks the law, ma'am."

Mild laughter escaped the lips of a few cops in the audience, and the chief of police grinned at the sergeant's mild embarrassment.

"Well, Corporal Tolliver has been on an extended vacation on the West Coast, so I'm sure his drowsiness stems from jetlag and hopefully not boredom," she said, bringing some amusement to the otherwise serious-minded meeting.

"However, ladies and gentlemen, we are dealing with a grave situation here, one which our fine detective branch has been investigating since early October of this year. We brought in several persons of interest over the past few weeks to answer some pertinent questions and to provide us with some possible leads in this ongoing case we're building. Among the perps who were interviewed were some this town's top drug traffickers, largely from the projects of South Peola, such as Paul and Marion Ballard of the Bad Boyz II Syndicate, Edward Anderson, also known as Bonecrusher down in that part of town, as well as a handful of lesser-known hoodlums.

"As is the norm among these criminal scumbags, even after hours of intense interrogation here at the precinct, we ended up having to let each one of them go with even less info than when we had when we first brought them in for questioning. So I've arranged to have extra officers monitor the open-air drug markets throughout South Peola, as well as place hidden cameras and listening devices in strategic areas around these drug hot spots.

"I intend to bring these rogue cops and their drug-dealing allies to justice no later than the end of January, people. That's next month. So let's get our shit together and catch these assholes ASAP."

As the final few handclaps died down, a distinguished-looking lieutenant, tall and straight, with impeccably pressed uniform and highly shined brass, stood. "Chief O'Malley, it is my understanding that there might even be reason to believe that certain prison gangs here in Peola's penal system and abroad who have considerable influence outside as well as behind bars often bankroll criminals to execute a variety of illegal acts, from drug trafficking, weapons smuggling, money laundering, and even murder. One of the names that draws an immediate red flag is that of Marion Lake, now residing in a South Carolina prison down in Beaufort County's low country. Even though he's now imprisoned, he is still a force to be reckoned with."

The chief of police gritted her teeth at the very mention of her father's long-time nemesis. She cleared her throat and steadied herself by grabbing a firm hold of the podium. Then she adjusted the microphone to her liking. "Thank you, lieutenant. This is indeed a crucial observation on your part, and one that will not go without a thorough investigation in the very near future. I assure you, Mr. Lake has been a menace to society ever since he began his criminal career in pre-Hurricane Katrina New Orleans. I know, because my father has collected a virtual library of criminal files on him alone, much of which he himself inherited from his boss, the honorable Leon Rossum.

"Don't worry, Marion Lake is going to remain a locked-up loser for a long, long time, if not for the rest of his pathetic life. I'll personally see to that, and I'll also make sure that any prison-run crime rings either here in Akron Corrections or elsewhere will be eliminated completely. You can take that to the bank."

The officers stood and gave her a rousing round of applause that lasted for several minutes.

"If I have my way—which I almost always do, just ask my dad—I'll see to it that Marion Lake is transferred back to the Leavenworth Federal Pen where he resided before he was allowed to move back down to the South. Give me a few weeks and I'll make some phone calls to a few friends of mine down in the South Carolina Governor's Mansion, and Mr. Lake will be Kansas-bound and well out of our hair."

Courtney O'Malley spoke for another ten minutes then thanked her top brass for attending the meeting and formally dismissed them from the gymnasium.

As the officers all arose simultaneously from their seats, Officer Tolliver slipped through the crowd and out the door as his co-workers gathered in the adjourning hall to chit-chat while having coffee and such. He had an important phone call to make.

Christmas morning in the Battle household was a laughter-filled, festive affair, with Tasha's three young sons gleefully ripping open present after present under the snow-white, ornament-adorned Christmas tree standing in the middle of her living room. While the boys compared notes on who received the best gifts, their mother and older sister Peaches began adding the finishing touches to a holiday meal, its delicious, mouth-watering aroma filling the entire room.

Whiskey, Alonzo, and their cousin, Lil' Shane, proceeded downstairs to the basement apartment to get high and converse.

"Dawg, y'all niggas wouldn't believe da kinda paper we pullin' out in Hemlock Hills off o' da crystal meth shit. Dem rich white kids been buyin' da shit up like hot cakes up in West Peola. I been buyin' da meth in bulk from some cats down in Beaufort who work for ol' Doctor Buzzard. From what I hear, he gettin' it from a bunch o' MS-13 eses from DC. But, hey, who knows, and who gives a fuck? As long as me and my niggas stay gettin' dat money, know what I'm sayin'? I say we makin' over fifty thousand or mo' a week movin' meth. Just last week I musta got my dick slobbed on by mo' den seven white hoes at da same mufuckin' time, just fa givin' dem bitches ten grams o' meth, pimp. Since then, I stay wit' no less than ten grams o' meth 'cause I know I'm gon' get coochie from da fly snow bunnies up on da West Side, feel me?"

Tasha and Peaches yelled for the three men to come for dinner.

Alonzo took one last deep drag from the strong-smelling blunt and exhaled a thick cloud of smoke.

"A'ight, tell ya what, lemme get five hunit grams o' dat crystal up off you tonight 'cause I wanna have first dibs on introducing dat shit to dem caked-up crackas down in South Cack befo' anybody else beat me to it. 'Cause once we get rid o' Chief Mickey O'Malley's bitch ass, it's on. Da way dat bitch Courtney goin', dat hit might never happen. My man Maurice told me dat Courtney O'Malley is crackin' down on all o' dat crooked-cop shit, so now da police dem who used to do bidness wit' us is runnin' scared. So I dunno 'bout all dat kill-O'Malley shit dat's s'posed to take place."

Lil' Shane choked, hacking hard from the overwhelming potency of the purple haze that had just entered his lungs.

"Ain't nobody worried 'bout dat broad. She know what's up. David gon' get her mind right." Whiskey winked at his brother and cousin as they ascended the old wooden staircase, which creaked and groaned under their combined weight. "C'mon, let's eat, y'all. Ya don't wanna get Tasha pissed."

Later that night, the trio drove down to the Hemlock Hills projects. Within the trunk of Lil' Shane's black Bentley Continental GT was a cache of fifty grams of crack, five kilos of powder, fifty kilos of heroin, three pounds of marijuana, and several machine guns.

During the drive out to South Peola, Lil' Shane and Alonzo discussed Godiva's well-known promiscuity. According to the dealers, Peola's infamous detective Tyrone Warner was none too happy that Mickey O'Malley had snubbed him in favor of his daughter for interim police chief.

As a result, the fourteen-year veteran of the Peola Police Department despised his boss's feisty young daughter, Courtney, who felt similar hatred for him. He knew of the tight-knit friendship his new chief had with superstar songstress Godiva and had knowledge of David Ambrosia's criminal activities as well. He then had the offices and recording studio of David Ambrosia wiretapped to record anything that might incriminate Ambrosia or his artists.

Within minutes the familiar sight of Hemlock Hills'

rusted wrought iron gates came into view. Alonzo reached into the breast pocket of his North Face jacket and retrieved a neatly rolled blunt. As the sleek black automobile pulled up against the curb in front of Eddie's Barbershop, Alonzo lit the end of the blunt and inhaled deeply as he exited the vehicle.

Dozens of drug-dealing youths raced to the car, opening the trunk and removing the illicit contents.

One cornrow-wearing thug stepped over to Alonzo and placed a briefcase filled with neatly lined rows of cash onto the hood of the Bentley. "Bonecrusher told me to give you da money for da products. He said he'll be here in a few minutes after he get back from da bank," the thug said, stepping back slightly.

"I ain't goin' no place, pimpin'. I just got here." Alonzo passed the blunt to his brother Whiskey.

Whiskey puffed on the *L*. "Y'all hear anything from David an' dem?"

"Naw, dawg, he been too busy settin' up Godiva with TV interviews and late-night performance spots to fuck wit' us li'l folks out here," the thug answered.

"I think I know David a li'l bit betta than you, pimp, an' I know fa sho dat he got our back, believe dat," Whiskey commented.

Alonzo and Lil' Shane smiled as they leaned up against the Bentley and saw the buzz of activity on the corners near the barbershop. A steady stream of cars, expensive models from the upper-crust communities of West and North Peola, pulled up one, no more than fifteen or twenty minutes apart, to buy their narcotics of choice from the ghetto youths, who approached the curbside window.

Lil' Shane and Derek Myers oversaw a group of unemployed high-school dropouts and newly released ex-cons that numbered around sixty strong. The men of various ages wore different color jackets to identify what type of drug they peddled—green for marijuana, white for cocaine, yellow for crack, and so forth. This ingenious method netted the two ballers ninety-one grand a day. Two Peola police squad cars always remained along the outskirts of the projects, acting more as sentries for the dope boys than monitoring them for the chief of police.

Whiskey took the blunt from his little brother's hand and put it to his lips. Dope boys raced back and forth along the street across from the barbershop slangin' their wares to one eager customer after one another.

"Ain't it a thing o' beauty, big brotha?"

"Fa sho. We taught dem two li'l knuckleheads well. Almost too well. Hell, dem li'l mufuckas makin' mo' money dan we did at their age. You realize dat?"

Alonzo grunted. "Shit, yeah, 'specially wit' dat crystal meth shit. I musta counted ten cars already dat pulled up to da curb just to buy meth alone. Dem boys on da come-up, no doubt."

"I'm gonna get Derek to go wit' me when I head back ta Fuskie. I might git him ta peel ol' Mickey O'Malley's cap back. Whatcha think 'bout dat?"

Alonzo took back his blunt and dragged on it deep and long before finally exhaling. "Da li'l nigga is a Bad Boy II Syndicate member, ain't he? Right, so you already know he ain't no stranger to pullin' a trigga. It sho as hell wouldn't be da first time."

"Ya think so?"

"C'mon, son, stop playin' wit' me. You know dat you gotta murk somebody just ta join up wit' da Syndicate niggas." Alonzo dropped the smoldering roach down on the pavement, crushing it underfoot. "Godiva and David need ta send money or whatever they need to provide us wit' to get rid o' Mickey O'Malley. I don't give a fuck if he's her best friend's pops. If it wasn't for niggas out here an' in dem jail cells all across da nation gettin' their peeps to vote for Godiva on dat cheesy-ass karaoke show which, for real, niggas in da hood didn't give a fuck about, she wouldn't be all high an' mighty right now. She betta not ever get it twisted, neither her man. Dat li'l favor came wit' a price tag attached. Dem two mufuckas owe us, son, big time."

Whiskey shook his head slowly. "C'mon, calm down, man. You know David as well I do, don't you? You know yourself David always been a man o' his word, right? Shit, he da one founded da Bad Boyz II Syndicate. Dese li'l nappyhead dope boys runnin' 'round out here gettin' paper 'cause o' David Ambrosia, nigga. An' dat's real talk. So I'm gon' say it again regardless o' what y'all cats say or think 'bout my man David. I know David. I know dat his word is his bond, an' dat's it an' dat's all."

Alonzo watched as Lil' Shane and Derek Myers directed their drug runners from the sidelines like two winning football coaches, to secure sales from the procession of vehicles pulling up nonstop.

"A'ight then. If you so sure dat David is 'bout it-'bout it, then so be it. Keep talking to 'im. From now on you'll be da middleman between Hollywood and da hood. How 'bout dat?"

Whiskey grinned lightly. "Oh, so now I'm an errand boy, or better yet a secretary, huh?"

"Hey, you da one sayin' how close you are to David. An' didn't you fuck Godiva befo'? So you would be da perfect bridge between us and dem."

"Look, I ain't tryin' ta be nobody's official messenger or nothin'. I've been doin' too much already."

Alonzo quickly checked messages on his cell phone before flipping it shut. "Just make sure your friends do what's right, that's all, a'ight?"

"You trippin', son. I dunno what's gotten into you, thinkin' David is somehow untrustworthy, but you need ta let it go."

"Naw, Whiskey, you da one who's trippin', pimp. You might o' spoken to David and Godiva lately, but da rest o' us ain't seen hide nor hair o' dem people since she won it all on dat TV show two months ago. Dem two mufuckas ain't thinkin' 'bout us niggas out here. They used us to get what they want, an' now they gone. Dat's what I think."

Whiskey hopped up onto the wide hood of his cousin's Bentley. "Who you really need to be worried 'bout an' suspicious of is Chief Courtney O'Malley, not David or Godiva. It's dat bitch who ain't followin' orders an' shit. Godiva done told da bitch how key ballas on da outside an' in da pen helped her get on da map an' how she needed for her to back off all da hustlas here in da city, an' she gave Godiva her word dat she'd lay off wit' all o' dat Robocop bullshit. But so far she's been nothin' but a lyin', fake-ass bitch. Ya boy Maurice called me, lettin' me know how dis bitch is gettin' ready to go after her very own officers who been workin' with da hustlas down here in South Peola. Plus, she somehow got word dat our pops been runnin' things outside from inside da pen, and now she fixin' ta ship him back out to Kansas. Leavenworth, to be exact."

"Whaaaat!!? Nigga, you gotta be bullshittin' me."

"I wish I was, but I ain't. I'm gonna tell Snookey 'bout it when I get back down dere later on this week. 'Cause we gotta beat dis ho to da punch befo' it's too late."

Alonzo clenched his brother's hand in a brotherly embrace. "Fa sho. But I tell you what—Ain't nobody gon' fuck with our father without gettin' touched, son. I mean dat shit."

Whiskey playfully threw a few short jabs at his younger sibling's taut midsection. "I know what you're thinkin', Alonzo, and I'm tellin' you, don't do it."

"Don't do what?"

"You know what da fuck I'm talkin' 'bout, nigga."

"So I guess we gon' just sit back an' let some dumb bitch send our father back out to Leavenworth, an' it's cool, right?"

Whiskey placed his muscular arm around Alonzo's shoulder. "Wrong. Trust me, li'l brotha, we ain't gotta kill Courtney, 'cause she's already dead. She just don't know it yet. An' you can kill a person in more ways than one, always remember dat."

Chapter 14

"Peola's Finest"

At approximately 8 AM on December 28, 2005, Peola Police Chief Courtney O'Malley sat behind the huge mahogany and granite desk in her father's office, slowly sipping on a hot mocha latte as she awaited the arrival of Detective Tyrone Warner.

At 8:07, he entered her office and approached her desk, reaching across and shaking hands with his boss. She offered him coffee and doughnuts from on a small wooden table beside her, but he politely refused and sat down on the leather chair in front of the desk.

"Good morning, Detective Warner. I'm so glad that you could take some time out of your busy schedule to meet with me this morning. It won't take long, I assure you."

"It's not a problem," the lean detective said. "I've been wanting to speak to you as well."

"Oh really? Well, that's just swell. By the way, remember the report I placed on your desk concerning the placement of monitoring devices in the South Peola drug spots?"

"Oh yeah, what about it?" he asked calmly.

"You haven't done anything at all about it, that's what, and I want to know why."

"I'll get around to it in time. I've got a shitload of cases that I've got coming up, so there you have it."

The police chief rose up from her desk and walked around it to the front. "You know what, Detective? There's three things that really irritate me. One, I hate balding guys who insist on going with a comb-over, when it's clearly obvious that it fools no one and just looks plain ridiculous. Second, I hate really fat people who try to squeeze in spandex, because that's just wrong. And, finally, I hate it when people don't follow orders—especially those who work for me, *capisce*?"

The detective leaned forward, a mild smirk creasing the corners of his lips. "Miss O'Malley, no disrespect to you, ma'am, but as I said to you just a minute ago, I have been swamped with paperwork that's been stacked up on my desk since early September. I've got narcotic, homicide, and rape cases, so it's not that I disregarded your request. I just simply lost track of it in lieu of everything else that I've had to deal with. I'm telling you, chief, I've got a fuckin' full plate."

The police chief hopped up onto her desk. "All right then, I'll accept that as fair enough, but I need for you to put the rest of your work on the back burner for now and focus on placing those closed-circuit cameras in the hot spots we spoke of earlier."

"I'm all ears. What exactly do you want me to do with these monitoring devices, chief?"

"I'd like for you to place cameras all over the projects of South Peola, namely Hemlock Hills, Badlands Manor, and the Geneva neighborhood drug spots, and believe you me, there's quite a few of them scattered all over the place."

"All right, that's not a problem, but an operation such as that would take weeks, if not months, to complete, considering the sheer size of the area itself we have to cover."

Courtney O'Malley raised her coffee mug up to her lips to savor another sip of her latte. "Oh, don't worry about that, Detective. I've already been in contact with several area contractors, as well as Bell South, who've both expressed interest in working with us to cover those areas with cameras."

"Chief, if I may interject, I believe that this counter-surveillance project of yours may be easier said than done. First of all, even with police escorts, these areas could prove dangerous to any contractor working within them, especially when the local dealers catch on to what they're really up to."

Courtney O'Malley ran her pale, slender fingers through her curly red hair and sighed softly as she stared up at the ceiling for a few seconds.

"Detective, I may not have the amount of years as you in law enforcement in general and in this department in particular, but I will say this—I've learned this business from the best goddamned police officer in the world, and that would be none other than Mr. Mickey O'Malley, who just also happens to be my dad. He always said to me, 'Honey, in this line of work you can never let the bad guys feel as though they can intimidate you, because then they've won.' And then he'd say to me, 'So never let them win.' So, with that said, do you even think for one minute that the threats or street machismo of a few idiot kids are going to weaken my resolve? If so, think again.

"As a matter of fact, Detective, I've been hearing some rumors from my sources close to the streets who inform me that there's been some buzz recently concerning my father's work with the authorities down in Daufuskie Island. Obviously, the local drug traffickers are none too pleased with his presence there or his training of their police force. I want you to pull the files on every last drug dealer, gang member, pimp, etcetera down in Beaufort County, South Carolina. I've already contacted the sheriff's department down there, and they've okayed our investigation. I want answers, facts, and leads on this ASAP, because my father could be in danger, and I'm not having it."

"You got it, kid. I'm on it as of today." The detective rose from his seat to shake the chief's hand.

"Good. You have a great day now, Detective. I'll be speaking with you later in the week."

"Not a problem, Chief. Take it easy."

Chapter 15

"Daufuskie Day"

The Forrester sisters, Candice and Naomi, had helped load the magazines with ammo before handing the firearms over to the island youth as they headed toward the parked cars along the side of the darkened county road.

A call on Corporal Tolliver's cell phone from Candice informed of the impending murder about to take place miles away from him, far across the state line that divided Georgia and South Carolina.

Tolliver felt a surge of adrenaline rush through the bloodstream as he ended the brief phone call. He then contacted his police partner in crime, Hank Columbus, who yelled out in excitement, nearly toppling the naked honky-tonk floozy from the cheap hotel bed they'd been sharing for the night.

"C'mon, niggas! Let's ride!" Eight ski mask-wearing gunmen yelled as they boarded two hoopties, an old slate-gray '81 Buick Skylark, and an off-white Ford El Camino that coughed and sputtered with noisy resistance before finally turning over to a humming start. Three 6 Mafia's smash hit, "Stay Fly," blasted out from the Pioneer speakers in the Skylark with enough bass to vibrate the very dirt road on which it stood, while the thugs riding in the El Camino pumped out Bun B and Ying Yang Twins's "Git It" as their choice of mood music.

As the two vehicles proceeded along Daufuskie Island's moon-dappled, forest-lined dirt road toward Mickey O'Malley's Haig Point bungalow, cellular phone calls between underworld conspirators in both the Peach and Palmetto states buzzed for over thirty minutes, briefing everyone involved about the events unfolding on the tiny sea island sandwiched in between Savannah and Hilton Head.

"Operation Cop Killer," as it was informally known among the crooked cops of the two regions in on the murderous plot, was now officially underway at last.

It was 11:18 PM when Tolliver first received word of the hit from Candice Forrester. Now at 1:37 AM, he would again receive word again.

Only two hours and some change later, the Mickey O'Malley hit, supposedly bought and paid for by David Ambrosia along with incarcerated crime boss Snookey Lake, had gone terribly wrong.

The hoodlums attempted a late-night home invasion of the Irishman's residence instead of staking out the house over the course of the night and waiting for him to emerge during the pre-dawn hours in sweats to run a few miles with Lucky, his Golden Retriever.

They would then kidnap him as he jogged along the narrow hunting trail beside Bennett's Road, bounding and gagging him, then dispatching him with several gunshot blasts to the upper body. He of course would then end up buried in one of the sea island's many saw grass-covered quicksand spots.

But unfortunately for the low-country big ballers, none of that ever materialized, as had been discussed for weeks in advance. The ghetto youth, stoned out their minds from heavy consumption of cheap malt liquor and marijuana, underestimated the wily old police chief, whose many years of experience on the force had equipped him with the self-defense skills to survive just such an ordeal.

Though O'Malley lived alone at the end of a scenic but lonely country surrounded by a dense wooded area, the small cottage was fully equipped with expensive state-of-the-art surveillance cameras and security alarms, which instantaneously alerted him to the immediate threat looming on his property. Not to mention Lucky's persistent and frenzied barking in the dimly lit living room.

The first three armed toughs fired upon the front door with a furious volley before recklessly storming the bullet-riddled doors, only to be quickly mowed down one by one by the spewing barrels of flame from the police chief's service revolver.

Keeping the handgun in front of him, O'Malley cautiously slid out the darkened interior of the hall closet and against the smooth walls of his living room. He noticed the still, bloodied forms crumpled along his living room floor.

Three of the boys lost their nerve and opted to flee instead of face a similar fate.

Two of their hardier partners squeezed off a few rounds at the open door, which brought no return fire.

Until they attempted to approach within five feet of the wooden steps leading up toward the entrance.

A gruesome headshot immediately felled the nearest ski mask-clad invader, who died before he dropped lifelessly onto the Irishman's pumpkin patch, his skull shattered. The other tried to crouch down behind an outside tool shed but was taken out with two shots to the chest. He fell up against the front of the shed, his fingers squeezing the trigger of the Uzi and rattling off a series of shots that zipped harmlessly into the chilly night sky. Then his hand dropped limp onto the damp ground and released its hold on the weapon.

Three of the young men made their way to the El Camino, only to be apprehended by over a dozen Dausfuskie Island police officers hopping out of numerous siren-wailing squad cars that surrounded the nearby intersection.

It was over. The plot to kill Mickey O'Malley had come to an unexpected and disappointing end. This major setback would indeed bring more than just a little unwanted attention to everyone involved with the conspiracy to off the visiting police chief. More than likely, they'd face the stiffest of legal penalties. Which would mean that heads would have to roll gangland-style for the mistake.

Chapter 16

"When the Shit Hits the Fan"

The local newspapers ran bold headlines of the attempted murder of Peola police chief Mickey O'Malley. By the end of the week following New Year's Day 2006, the sensational news story had spread like wildfire all across the Deep South. Television, radio, and newspapers ran updates around the clock on the incident.

There was more than a little evidence of involvement from rogue officers within the Daufuskie department as well as those departments on the outside, and as a co-conspirator in the botched attempt David Ambrosia's name would come up several times during the week that followed.

David Ambrosia would soon prepare a live response via satellite in a passionate press conference in which he would deny any involvement in the bloody home invasion and reiterate his close friendship with the police chief and his daughter.

Meanwhile, the local chapter of the FBI, led by Agent

Mohammed—he had brought Snookey Lake to justice many years earlier—uncovered damaging evidence that David Ambrosia had indeed dealt with known drug dealers throughout the South as well as various street gangs from Los Angeles. The unsavory media attention formed a dark cloud over what had been America's premier feel-good story.

Godiva was enraged by news of the attempted murder of her best friend's father and immediately broke off the June '06 wedding.

Whiskey himself received a late-night e-mail from Godiva. It read:

> Hey Whiskey, it's me, Godiva. Look, I just gotta let ya know that I'm no longer engaged to David, nor am I going to remain a part of the Spanish Moss Records Incorporated family. I no longer want any affiliation with them at this time. It is not in the best interest of my music career to continue on with the partnerships that had been forged previously, including those with your dad Snookey and his affiliates.
>
> I do understand fully what you guys did for me during my time as a contestant on the *Pop Star* competition, and though I have been really, really busy performing all over the country, I have spoken to Courtney as you well know about keeping five-O off your back and out of sight.
>
> But I don't agree to killing anybody. Certainly not Chief O'Malley, who is not only my best friend's dad, but also is like my own dad. I still love David,

but I can't allow him to ruin my career like he's ruined himself.

Courtney has promised me that she will be my manager and agent from this point on, as she has a master's degree in business management and an accounting degree from the University of Georgia. She will handle everything concerning my career, including security. So at this time I'm separating myself from everyone. I'll contact you soon, my dear, all right?

Luv ya!

Godiva

Chapter 17

"Is This the Thanks I Get?"

Over two dozen Gullah hoodlums and their homies were rapidly arrested, tried, and convicted of masterminding the plot along with the famous Marion "Snookey" Lake to kill Police Chief O'Malley. By mid-January a majority of the drug dealers and gangstas of South Carolina and Georgia's low country regions were either already behind bars or on trial.

Chief Mickey O'Malley and his daughter launched their very own witch-hunts, which in tandem with the investigation already being handled by the feds, turned up several more conspirators to the attempted murder case that came to be known in the media as "The Daufuskie Cop-Killer Trials."

Few from the hood managed to avoid police scrutiny. Not even Peola's elite.

On the morning of January 18, 2006, thirteen Peola police officers stormed David Ambrosia's swank, Italian-style villa out in Pemmican, West Peola. Corporal Tolliver and Officer Columbus were among the policemen on the scene as their fellow officers escorted an angry and disheveled Ambrosia in handcuffs toward an awaiting squad car sitting along the curb just outside of the fourteen-foot-tall brass gates surrounding the twenty acres of lush, rolling hills, pine forests and meandering streams that was the music mogul's property.

As his uniformed captors escorted him to the open back door of the Crown Victoria, Ambrosia, dressed in a heavy London Fog coat over his silk Emporio Armani pajamas and leather house slippers grumbled something incoherent to his handlers as they eased into the backseat and closed the door behind him.

The feds had reason to believe that David Ambrosia had funded his studio and recording label with seed money he'd borrowed from key street gangs such as his very own Bad Boyz II Syndicate and underworld heavyweights like Snookey Lake, DiVante Lovett, and Joi Stevens, to name a few. In return, he would allow these criminals to launder money through his business, conduct drug trafficking operations to high-end celebrity clients, and even contract out murder-for-hire at times.

Thirty minutes later the police convoy ended up in front of the Peola police precinct, where several cops emerged from their vehicles with their famous suspect in tow.

Ambrosia walked along between two solemn-looking officers, saying little besides a nasty comment or two about Courtney O'Malley. He was quickly processed and led downstairs to a small private jail cell, where they removed his cuffs before slamming the shiny metal bars shut.

Ambrosia walked over and grasped two of the bars in front of him, squeezing angrily with clenched fists. He pressed his handsome face against the cold bars and watched the guard walk away down the hallway, jingling a heavy ring of keys.

Less than an hour later, Whiskey and Alonzo showed up at the front desk of the precinct. The pretty, young fair-skinned girl behind the desk with the light gray eyes showed pleasant surprise as the brothers approached.

Fresh out of the academy, she'd once dated Alonzo back in high school, and tried to catch up on events before signing them in on the register.

"All right, boys, I'm sorry to inform you, but Mr. Ambrosia is currently being held without bond. I'm sorry, but I can have an officer lead you downstairs to the holding cells to visit with him if you'd like."

Within minutes the brothers were standing outside David Ambrosia's jail cell. David was chatting away on his Blackjack before noticing his childhood friends standing in the hall. He ended the call and stuck his hand through the narrow bars and grasped the palms of both men in the strong handshake.

"Dawg! I'm soo fuckin' ticked-off right now! You have no idea how pissed-off I am behind all of this bullshit!" Ambrosia snarled.

Alonzo leaned in closer to the cell door. "I kin imagine how you gotta feel, my dude. But you already know how we do shit, right? We gonna get you outta dis mufucka in no time. We brought bail money down here, but dat li'l bitch done gone an' held you wit'out bail. Did you know dat shit?"

"Nope. Didn't know anything about that. But it's all good though, because I've already hired Mark J. Burton the third and Carolyn Myers-Pierce, so I'll be outta here soon enough."

Alonzo asked, "Who the fuck are they?"

"Dude, you gotta be kiddin' me. You don't know? Those two are only the best lawyers money can buy, that's all. Who do you think got Katrina Ricks off scot-free back in ninety-one? Everybody in the country remembers that trial that was held up in Washington, DC back then, because the feds had been trying to nail Katrina for a while. She was a fuckin' street legend in DC for years before her trials. Anyway, she was facing life for murder, and guess what? She livin' overseas now with her daughter, or so I've heard."

Whiskey said, "Oh yeah, you talkin' 'bout dat ballin'-ass broad, Southeast Trina, right? Yeah, I remember dat shit like it was yesterday. Dat trial was all over da news every fuckin' day."

Alonzo placed his hands into the pockets of his baggy jeans, hanging his head reflectively. "Look here, David, Godiva done used us and used you too. Da bitch ain't nothin' but a strip club ho, for real. You betta off without her dumb ass, but like ya said, it's all good though, 'cause she gonna get hers befo' too long. You betta believe dat. And as for you know who, we got dat fa ya, my man. Don't worry, a'ight?"

David Ambrosia noticed Alonzo looking over at a nearby guard standing silently across the hall. "Don't worry about that guard, dude. I've already slipped him a little something that will keep him quiet as we kick it down here for a minute.

"Whiskey, I gave that woman all of my energy and helped get her to the top of the *Billboard* charts. Did you know that? Well, that's a fact. Also, I've booked a year's worth of television performances, radio interviews, and a ten-city tour for her, and this is how she repays me? Her and that bitch, Courtney O'Malley. Well, check it, before I got into the music industry, I was a hustler, and the code of the streets prompts me to take care of a situation once and for all after I get up outta here. I promise, my sweet, sweet Godiva is going to have the shortest career of any singer in history. You guys heard of Janis Joplin before, right? Or maybe Kurt Cobain?"

The brothers nodded their heads simultaneously.

"Yeah, well, once I get myself together and get out from behind this jail cell, which won't take long, my former artist and fiancée is going to join them in the great studio in the sky."

Whiskey and Alonzo drew even closer to hear Ambrosia.

"It's one thing to cheat on me with other guys—Didn't think I knew that, did ya?—break off our wedding engagement, fire me as her manager, jump ship from my record label. I even forgave her for taking on a spiteful bitch like Courtney as her new manager. But one thing I can't forgive is setting me up to be arrested and sent to prison. She knew all about the events; now she's playing the innocent role. She knows that there was a cost. She owed certain individuals in the game when me and Snookey pulled strings to get her to win votes. We had people all over the United States to tune in to that program and vote for her. That took the influence of some of the nation's top shot-callers, both in prison and on the street, to make that happen. Yet she thought nothing of even sending a thank-you card to those who helped her get to where she's at currently, largely because of her association with Courtney, who obviously had much more influence on her than I even realized.

"When you guys came in to see me, I was speaking with your dad. He was pissed. He caught wind of Courtney's plan to transfer him back to Leavenworth Penitentiary, and do you know what he said to me? He said that Joi Stevens said to him that it's a Gullah saying, 'If you kill da head, da ass gotta dead,' which means now that Courtney is riding the crest of Godiva's major success. We gotta do it, y'all. We gotta hit Godiva."

The three men agreed silently as to the necessity of job at hand, and as the brothers left Ambrosia behind, they both seemed ready to begin the orchestration of an urgent call to duty for the boys in the hood.

TO BE CONTINUED . . .